DHRUVAPUTRA

[The Son of Dhruva]

DHRUVAPUTRA
[The Son of Dhruva]

by

Amar Mitra

Translated by

Ketaki Datta

BLACK EAGLE BOOKS
Dublin, USA | Bhubaneswar, India

Black Eagle Books
USA address:
7464 Wisdom Lane
Dublin, OH 43016

India address:
E/312, Trident Galaxy, Kalinga Nagar,
Bhubaneswar-751003, Odisha, India

E-mail: info@blackeaglebooks.org
Website: www.blackeaglebooks.org

First International Edition Published by
Black Eagle Books, 2023

DHRUVAPUTRA
by **Amar Mitra**

Translated by **Ketaki Datta**

Original Copyright © Amar Mitra
Translation Copyright © Ketaki Datta

Cover & Interior Design: Ezy's Publication

ISBN- 978-1-64560-491-4 (Paperback)
Library of Congress Control Number: 2023952667

Printed in the United States of America

Dedicated
to
such readers
of
this subcontinent
who are fond
of
folklores and narratives

Translator's Note

Translating this Sahitya Akademi award-winning novel was not a cakewalk for me. The archaic, Sanskritised expressions, turns of phrases demanded faithfulness as well as authenticity. Harnessing beauty to appropriateness was a real gauntlet thrown down on me. I tried to keep intact the pristine appeal of the original Bengali novel, again deviating a bit to add a charm of modern times was an undeniable requirement.

As a translator, I had to negotiate with the parameters of diction as well as punctuation. If I come to the point of 'diction', the classification of 'you' in Bengali had to be taken care of. For example, in the Bengali novel, Amar Mitra, the novelist, has put 'you' as an address of 'affection' in the mother's lips. This 'you' can be 'thou', or 'you' can be kept for better comprehension of the readers, by and large. But, usually, 'thou' as an archaic word is followed by befitting verbs like 'dost not', 'canst not'. But I have taken a liberty and with 'thou', 'thee', 'thy', I have put the modern usage of similar verbs, like 'do not', 'cannot', so on. It may raise an objection, but, the present-day readers had to be kept in view as well. They may accept the replacement of 'you' by 'thou', considering the 'affection' factor, but the archaic usage throughout would simply come in the way of literary exquisiteness and a wider acceptance. I have tried to make the diction a bit modern, which is quite archaic in the original novel, to make it reach wider audience.

The 'Glossary', at the end, would be of great help to the non-Indian as well as non-Bengali readers. Thus, appreciating the literary charm of this novel will not be difficult at all.

Hope the readers will find this book an enjoyable and absorbing read too. And that will be the highest reward, I can just dream of.

Dr. Ketaki Datta
Kolkata
December, 2023

Acknowledgements

This translation was not an easy work to accomplish. This novel has an extensive canvas with "God's plenty" and historical plenitude in its matrix. The language is mostly steeped in Sanskrit idioms and phrases, most of which have gone obsolete by now. Hence, Haricharan Bandyopadhyay's and Nagendranath Basu's Bengali lexicons were of immense help to me. In translating this text, the kind souls who proffered their help readily, are:

Dr. Gitanjali Chatterjee: A constant support, whose words of encouragement transformed an indolent me into a diligent one! Words can work wonder sometimes which umpteen cups of energy-drinks fail to do, no doubt!

Dr. Bharat Chandra Saha: A Professor and Dean of Farm-Science, a messiah to me, who offered every kind of succour I needed, from encouraging words to the printing and binding assistance, which are the essentials one cannot turn a blind eye to. His regular concern for my work will keep me indebted to him, all my life!

Prof. Nrisingha Prasad Bhaduri: A doyen of Sanskrit literature, who needs no introduction! His generous help with the Sanskrit coinages and shlokas made this translation possible. My gratitude to him knows no bounds.

Mr. Bijoy Dey: Not just a Librarian of Bidhannagar College, Kolkata, but a driving force behind this tome. It was he, who helped me find difficult words in the relevant lexicons, it was he, who goaded me to finish it on time, creating a congenial atmosphere in the library, enthusing me to work for hours together almost every day after the classes.

Partha Pratim Das: A former student of mine at Bidhannagar College, now an academic, pushed me hard to find a publisher for this tome. I owe him a lot.

Mr. Amar Mitra: The writer of the original novel helped me with difficult words which I failed to comprehend on my first reading of the book. His constant support meant a lot to me.

Last but not least, my brother, Kalyan Kumar Dutta, his wife, Gopa Dutta, and my only nephew, Arkaprava Dutta, kept me in good humour always, so that, I could finish this translation with perfect elan. And of course, I am thankful to Satya Pattanaik of Black Eagle Books for taking up this momentous volume for making it see the light of day.

Now the readers I look up to, with much hope and expectation. Their word will be the final one. Hope they will like my translation, which I tried to make as lucid as possible in diction, in expression as well. Their appreciation will be my ultimate reward.

1st December, 2023   **Ketaki Datta**
Kolkata

ONE

It was Deepavali. In each house of Vishala, Goddess Lakshmi, the deity of wealth and prosperity would be worshipped. And all negatives would be done away with. Cities like Vishala, Ujjwain, the capital of Avanti, the temple of Lord Mahakaaleswar with a golden spire and the two water-bodies: Shipra and Gandhavati, would dazzle with the bright lamps. Lamps would light up the thresholds and the window-ledges of each house of the city of Avanti. The wide roads would remain chock-a-block with people, all night. Music soirees would be there in each dwelling, the tinkle of anklets, the lilt of Veena, the melodious tunes of Vallaki, Mridanga would resonate across the chilly air of the city. The air would be laden with the fragrance of flowers, aguru, sandalwood, joss-sticks and wine.

Open markets were on because of Deepavali. As the sellers and buyers jostled in droves, the market had gradually expanded till the eastern bank of the river Shipra. The fair in Ujjwain was crammed with people from all walks of life, the traders and businessmen were from inland and abroad, from the twin ports on the Arabian Sea, lying in the west of Avanti, and even from far-off lands like Barugaza, Shurparak, so on.

They had come from distant lands of grapevines. The businessmen hailed from far north-west, Balkh, Gandhaar, Purushpur, Cambodia and from the riverine borderlands of the Indus. Armed with the famous yellow silk from Balkh, the sprightly horses from Cambodia. Along with them had come the mountain ponies, blankets, yellow turmeric, pure gold ornaments and stones of various hues and sheen. Several tradesmen from Magadh, Kosala, Bengal and Arab had assembled there with various wares to sell. They would take along various gems and treasures, valuable stones and stone-made objets d' art, sandalwood, colourful cotton apparels, superfine muslin, pigeons, peacocks, and sundry such items. Since quite a few days, the buying-selling spree had reached a considerable high. The whole market-place stood abuzz in the morning of Deepavali, with the busy buyers and sellers amidst the hullabaloo of the onlookers. Strange noises came from the stalls of the ironsmith, the brass-dealers, the conch-shell sellers: metallic twang-twang, grating ghrrrr…ghrrrr, and an aerial swoosh-swoosh! All sounds commingled with voices of the people.

Old Shivnath who came to join this Deepavali fair traversing twenty miles, was looking for the trader from Shurparak Port, who came here last Bhadra. The trader ran into a young boy in his callow youth on this Shurparak port, to be precise. A blue-eyed boy, fair-complexioned like the Greeks, not so tall, with black, dishevelled tufts of thick, unkempt mane, cascading down his shoulders, with his beard all over his cheeks. A white shawl covered Shivnath's torso, he was dressed in a cotton cloth, dipped in the colour of Seuli flowers. He came to Ujjwain by the end of Bhadra to cull coloured linen. The ships were about to set sail in the middle of the month of Ashwin. Even this year saw no monsoon. The favourable south-westerly winds too were weak in momentum. Yet the ships from the west were sailing in, propelled by the slow wind. The north-easterly winds had begun to set in. The fleets of ship were adrift to their native lands. Shivnath was searching for that trader. Though he hailed from Kosala, he used to stay mostly at Shurparak port for his business. He said he would come with the businessmen from far-off lands for the Deepavali fair. He would come with some tidings to share too. If possible, he would come along with him. Particularly with that youth. How would Manibhadra, a trader from Sopara, know that the youth hailed from Ujjwain?

The businessmen from Arabian lands who used to come very often to Ujjwain, wearing long robes, from neck to feet, were well conversant with the Malaviya tongue. Any greenhorn trader, who came for the first time to this Lord Mahakaaleswar-blessed El Dorado, was assisted by his fellow-travellers. Shivnath was on the look-out for Manibhadra. None could highlight his whereabouts. The traders from foreign lands looked at each other's face curiously. Shivnath was approaching sixty, nearly the whole of his pate had turned hoary, white beard grew on his cheeks, the eyes had gone hazy and their sheen kept fading behind the gloom on his face. Shivnath, a man of medium height and dusky complexion, had his body covered by a deerskin wrapper and he had come bare-feet. He was out at dawn, when the hint of light on the eastern horizon was seen. The universe was cold, bluish and pearly, all around. While walking, he stood still to enjoy the sunrise from a long-stretched cornfield. This year the harvest of millet was quite poor. The month of monsoon sped by, almost cloudless. Standing in the moribund millet-field, he had seen how the Sun-God, lost in sleep amidst the foliage kept bobbing up and above. The memories of his friend's son flashed past his mind. Many a day, Shivnath enjoyed a glimpse of the city of Ujjwain, straight from the bank of the river Gambhira. Joining his palms in reverence, he cast a gaze at the Mahakaaleswar temple, the abode of Lord Shiva and prayed to the Sun-God:

Om Jabakusuma Sangkasham Kashyapeyan Mahadyutim
Dhwantarin Sarvapaapaghnam Pranotohosmi Divakaram.

[Oh the radiant Son of the sage Kashyapa, crimson like china-rose buds, Oh Lord, dispelling all shades of darkness, subduing all sins of all sorts, You manifest Yourself, and, I reverently bow down to you, oh Lord of the Day!]

Shivnath was a Vaishya by caste. His friend, who died untimely, was a Kshatriya, caste-wise. Though Dhruva hailed from Kshatriya background, shunning royal courts and retinue of army, he entered into business with Subhag Dutta, a businessman of Ujjwain. His son was never into business, though he was curious to know its nitty-gritty. He was a scholar, and, he was about to stake his gradual claim to almost all scriptures in terms of knowledge. It was, as it were, the descendant of Kshatriya clan was getting back his lost claim. Yet he wondered, how could the son of such a tramp, nitwit fellow like Dhruva excel to such an extent?! He used to roam around the countries like Bengal, Kalinga, Shurparak, Barugaza and ports of different lands. From the Arabian Sea, the Eastern Sea, the Southern Ocean, to the Reba and Tapti rivers, to the mountains like Malay Chandan he trotted along. A madcap, an absolute lunatic was his friend, Dhruva!

Someone had spoken of Manibhadra. He brought brihidhanya to Ujjwain, from Pataliputra. He claimed to have run into that trader from Kosala, who was on his way to Bengal, a trader was to wait for him, culling Guvak from the banks of the Red river. He would return to Shurparak with Guvak. He failed to come to Ujjwain, this Deepavali.

The trader from Pataliputra was Brikodar. In appearance, he took after the second Pandava. A strapping, copper-complexioned fellow, and, by this young age, he lost much of his mane, quite alarmingly.The man was wondering why he had been summoned, why at all , didn't he pay his debt or what?

The old man shook his head, "Nay, not at all, look, you hang about different places, have you ever seen such a youth?" Shivnath described the stature and appearance of the son of Dhruva. The man stood agape in wonder and said, "I come across a lot of people. Even, someone from among them might even look like him, but, who, exactly was he? Again, who are you talking about?"

Shivnath retorted, "I mean, Manibhadra. If you ever meet him, tell him that I kept waiting for him. He promised to bring news of the youth, of whom I have just talked".

Brikodar seemed to be quite a nice fellow, he said, "I shall also be on the look-out for him. But why, what's wrong, is he your son?"

"He was like my son, may be even more, he left Avanti with a heavy heart."

"Why?"

Shivnath kept quiet. Would it be right to disclose the truth amidst this jostling crowd? People from all walks of life roamed about, which ear would catch his words, who could tell? Again, it was the time for brisk transactions, though Brikodar had quite a few helps to manage everything, even though almost a big chunk of his wares was sold out, which he had brought in, on three horse-drawn carriages! Yet, he was busy. But, Brikodar was all agog to know. He demanded to know again. A thin, wan smile toyed on the lips of Shivnath, he gibbered about his friend, Dhruva, he gave a sketchy introduction of his son too.

Brikodar's curiosity mounted. No, it was not regarding the son of Dhruva, but Dhruva himself. It was even natural, as his interest shifted to commerce from martial art, which he gave up, being a son of the Kshatriyas. He was curious to know which commercial interests he had, which items he used to trade in, at what prices they came for, so on. This man [Brikodar] must have been a block-head. Dhruva breathed his last almost twenty-five years ago. Then, Avanti was ruled by Gandharvasen, the father of King Bhartrihari. It was not a tale of the present day. What would he do by knowing the price of things of those times?

Brikodar said, "Do you know how familiar are the foreign traders with Guvak ? To them, Guvak seems to be a kind of fruit that grows in the Shurparak port."

A smile curled up the corner of Shivnath's lips, it was Dhruva who told him that since ages Guvak was known as betel nut in the foreign lands. Nearing the Arabian Sea, this fruit of the East immediately changed its name. Brikodar had come to know about it lately from Manibhadra, the trader of Shurparak wharf. Where did he meet him? Ah, in the city of Bidisha! Both the traders spent a night together at an inn. Brikodar blabbed, "How will it be if we again meet on our way of return at Bidisha?"

Shivnath's face again beamed with smile. So, Brikodar would have to wait for long at Bidisha. If Manibhadra were that trader by any chance, he would take much time to return from the Eastern country. Wasn't it quite far? Again, if he took a detour on his way back, descending down the path, running parallel to the sea-coast? No, it would perhaps be not so, coming straight by this way from Pataliputra would be the safest route perhaps. However, Shivanath had no clear-cut idea about it. He had never gone out of Avanti. And again, had he ever seen this city of Avanti, inside out? And, he had never been to the town of Bidisha. His life got spent in tilling the lands. His world centred round the villages that dotted the roads crisscrossing Gambhira, Ujjwain; the rivers like Shipra, Gandhavati and the Sapta Sarovar. He heard that Bidisha lay to the south-east, a Cambodian horse might reach him there in five days or six while this horse-drawn carriage would fail to take him there not even in a couple of weeks. Brikodar added again, "Sir, as I am into business, we must surely meet some day, in fact, I am planning to pay a visit to the port with millet from here, but no, not this time, as I am going to be a father soon."

"Splendid! No doubt, it's a great news! Is it the first time?"

"Yes, Sir, I shall have to return to Pataliputra, my village being closer to that place. Hence you understand, I am not going to meet Manibhadra this time, got me?"

Brikodar was speaking in such a way as if this man was known to him since ages. This man had been disconsolate to know that he was not going to see Manibhadra in Bidisha. He was saying, "It would have been fantastic if we saw each other. As the popular belief goes, business with the traders of foreign lands brings huge profit." But he was really afraid of them. He hardly hesitated to come to Bidisha or Ujjwain from Pataliputra, but it called for grit to trade with the foreign businessmen at the port. While returning from Bidisha, he had already thought of seeking help from Manibhadra. Did he know that Manibhadra used to speak the language of the people of the other religions too?

Shivanth fell silent again. How would he know? Only for a day he had talked to Manibhadra. If met by chance, he would even fail to recognize him. Yet yes, perhaps he would suddenly remember him, as he had committed his name to memory in connection with tracing the son of Dhruva. Brikodar made a foray into commerce lately and it was his first time. Hence, he was over-zealous. He had even made good profit by selling the Brihi rice. In Bidisha, he had emptied two horse-carriages too. Here, many more traders from Pataliputra had come. They would set off together, precisely by tomorrow.

Shivnath felt like buying something for Gandhavati. What would he take home? Since the son of Dhruva had left Avanti, this fatherless granddaughter of Shivnath lost all her mirth. Reba, his daughter-in-law, whose husband used to stay abroad and her daughter, Gandhavati… the old man heaved a long sigh. Five years had sped by since the war of Dashpura. Since then, Kartikkumar, who went to war, had not come back, though the troops of Avanti returned after conquest of the Huns. Vacuity hung heavy on his heart, especially in these days of festivity; it seemed to be all-pervasive, or even more.

Brikodar looked closer at Shivnath and asked," What's wrong with you, Sir?"

"Nothing at all. I have to go back and it will take long, the sun will be up above while walking, and again I have some shopping to do."

"But you have not mentioned clearly, what I am to convey to Manibhadra".

Strange! It seemed, as if he was sure of running into Manibhadra and even at that inn in Bidisha! And being informed by him, Manibhadra would rush to Ujjwain from Bidisha! When he would meet Manibhadra was uncertain, and, whether they would ever meet was even more! Shivnath said to Brikodar, "Tell him that someone was waiting for him in Ujjwain".

"You mean, the youth you had been talking about?"

"Yes, I need to know his whereabouts, as Manibhadra said that he had met him at Shurparak port".

"Are you sure that he hasn't set sails on the sea?"

Shivnath got frightened. He fixed a puzzled stare on Brikodar's face. It was not that such fear had not assailed his soul before, but he steered clear of it, with much care. But a man who had been to the port, might even bid adieux to this land for good. Manibhadra had not come up with any news. Who could tell where Dhruvaputra had been?

Brikodar said, "I too feel like paying a visit to the land of the Yavanas, look there Sir, I heard of him to come all the way from Balkh - a Yavan merchant, the colour of his skin though scorched and sallow, he sports a magnificent physique, look at his hair, it looks like real silk, rather than just silky, begotten of the silk made in Balkh - it is learnt that they hail from a land by the seas. Is it true?"

Shivnath kept listening. Dhruvaputra could have resonated with such observations. He was not at all interested in these matters. He was overcome with sadness. Dhruvaputra was so well-informed! He could detect whether this man, Brikodar, was telling the truth or half-truth, or stating a strange, unknown fact.

Brikodar said, "As he has not returned yet till Bhadra, Ashwin, Kartik—he might have set sails on the sea. I heard of a youth from Bidisha had gone out to make it big to the land of the Yavanas."

Shivnath felt jeopardized, deeper within. It would, perhaps, have been better if he had not come to know that person. He was leaving him scared now. Dhruvaputrahad not gone away in Bhadra, he had left this land during late Spring before the last, on a full moon night in Chaitra, on the day of worshipping Kamadeva, the festival of colours. Preceding that, he had come here leaving Ujjwain, on an insult. Subhag Dutta, the merchant, who provided him with shelter, asked him to leave this city as he learnt about his keen desire for the harlot, Devadutta, his keep, the woman of his lust. Now, Shivnath would push off.

"I am here today, all day long", said Brikodar, and suddenly his memory was jogged, "Oh yes, but you didn't mention the reason of his leaving Avanti"!

Shivnath rejoined, "Let it wait as of now. Please find out from Manibhadra".

Brikodar stopped him short, "Please stand here for a bit longer".

Shivnath nodded. What would he buy for Gandhavati? Pearl string. It would cost him much. Ujjwain was a land where almost ten varieties of pearl were dealt in. Varieties of pearls ranged from the Tamraparni river, Malaykoti ranges , Pashikya river, Kula river of Ceylon to the Haimavat variety of the Himalayas. He would have to walk up towards the pearl-stall then. He came determined to buy a pearl-string to win back the lost smile on the lips of his grand-daughter. He had to come to a sudden halt and turn back as he was threading his way in the crowd. Ignoring the throng, the courtier, Uddhavnarayan, had made way into the fair, riding a pony! Clutching the shoulder of Shivnath, he reined his horse and jumped off its back and said," So you are here, Uncle, I was just looking for you."

Shivnath's face grew radiant in hope. So, was Uddhavnarayan here with the news of Dhruvaputra? Or after a long wait, Kartikkumar's whereabouts came to be known, who was yet to return after the Hun Victory? Drawing the reins of the horse, Uddhav asked, "Where are you going? I need to see you badly."

"Anything about Dhruvaputra?"...in a feeble voice inquired Shivnath.

"That lecher's news, that ungrateful chap you mean?!"

"But why are you saying so?"

"The inhabitants of Ujjwain are still in umbrage with him, you have no idea how deeply Subhag Dutta, the merchant, is hurt! The royal court is still ignorant of this news, otherwise, you would have been called, Sir! Anyway, do not be afraid, I know everything, come on, let us talk after I tether the horse to the Ashok tree."

TWO

Uddhavnarayan was loud in demand as he was a man of the King's court. It was yet to be tested whether he had more power than actually he was entitled to exercise. However, he used to claim thus. He was a man of short stature, his body was wrapped in a yellow silk shawl, with a vest made of wool on it. A blue silken turban adorned his head, while greenish silken cloth encircling his waist from the land of Pundra added to his charm. A mere glance at Uddhavnarayan's eyes would point to his slyness and nothing else.

Shivnath had no idea of what Uddhav did. Yet, he doubted him to be the Sessions-Judge of the King's court, the King's spy. Uddhavnarayan hailed from a village situated on the other side of the river, Gambhira. The path ran by the house of Shivnath. Even a few years back, Shivnath had seen Uddhav walking up the road leading to the city, in soiled attire. He was also seen to return, dejected. All of a sudden, opportunity bobbed on his way. He used to talk excellently, indeed. But why would Uddhav come here for that? In what way was he related to Shivnath at all? He saw Uddhavnarayan to cross the river, with his own eyes. Way back in years, when he used to go to Ujjwain, he used to stand for a while, by the edge of a cornfield. These days, Shivnath could not get down into the land, felt giddy, the land stood tilled by other farmers who took half of the harvest, leaving the rest for him. Uddhav stood there, keeping an eye on the distribution of shares.

Uddhav did not tether his horse to the Ashok tree. Taking the rein in his hand, he was trying to pacify the horse but the patience of the Tibetan horse stood tested by the din and bustle of brisk business there.

Controlling the sprightliness of the horse quite often, Uddhav grew keen on glorifying his individuality before the old man. He asked, "Time is running out. Where were you up to"?

"Just heading on to the shop".

"Who were you talking to, if I may know?"

"To a tradesman from Patuliputra. He is here with the Brihi variety of rice."

"Will you buy it?"

Shivnath nodded in the negative. "No, I was just trying to find out."

"What were you keen on figuring out, in particular?" Saying so and failing to tame the horse, Uddhav went on tethering the horse to the Ashok tree. And went on, "This is an overly spirited horse from Tibet, you know, though the Cambodian horses are even more spirited than this and I would be provided with one such by the King's court. The Army-Commander is truly fond of me, you know, a spy had been caught in the net just a few days back, he was looking for God's Way are you cognizant of all this?"

Shivnath nodded in the negative. He knew next to nothing. Life ran at ease even without knowing anything. But, as ill luck would have it, he was in jeopardy now. His son was no more, and the one who could make him forget the shock of losing his son, too, was absent.

Uddhav asked, "Could you please tell me the name of the man?"

"Brikodar, hailing from Pataliputra."

"Why do you talk to strangers from other states?"

Shivnath kept looking at Uddhav with fear in his eyes. Is it that youth who used to stand looking at the distribution of crops for long? He sought his advice on how to win land from the King, free of tax. Getting the land, he would grow crops there, hiring other peasants. Uddhav seemed to have taken another birth on this earth! Everything was possible in this world! Uddhav was interrogating him minutely!

"What were you discussing with Brikodar?"

"Manibhadra is a trader of Shurparak wharf", saying so Shivnath grew wary of his own words. Why was Uddhav so curious? Even the way of his inquiry was suspicious. Why would he have to answer all his queries? He was in no way indebted to Uddhav. Did he seek any help from Uddhav? Oh yes, last Sravan he had told him, indeed, that he would have to go to the King's court in order to make an appeal to the chief accountant, regarding some issues. The matter, however, he held from Uddhav. Even Uddhav had no time to lend his ears to it. Thereafter,it did not make much progress.

"Who is Manibhadra?"

"A merchant from Kosala."

It was not possible to know what one was up to and where. Uddhav muttered, "But scraping an acquaintance with just anyone is not good too. Can you tell apart the bad man from the good one?"

Uddhav's voice was a bit sharp, insinuating, somewhat like a spear, Shivnath was feeling humiliated, he rejoined, "But I am honest and candid, for sure."

"Therein lurks peril! Lots of foreigners from alien lands throng to Ujjwain market that you would not even make out which collusion you are being entangled in or whether the trader you scrape an acquaintance with is a spy in disguise or not! Check all these things before being friends with a stranger from a different land."

Shivnath was visibly frightened as Brikodar was from Pataliputra.

"You will never know from where the person hails or what his intention is, but I can easily ascertain the inner desires of anyone by watching his overall appearance keenly as I have mastered the art of body-language".

Shivnath smiled, "That is quite expected."

Well, remember what I have said, stay alert, I have noticed you speaking with the man very often! I am your well-wisher, if someone would have been there instead, I would have dragged him to the King's court. Just a few days ago a person had been nabbed, you know the Huns, a barbaric race, who are not yet wholly subjugated, and are still on the look-out for an opportunity."

Shivnath nodded. He had no clue. Presently, he was panic-stricken. Was then Brikodar a man in disguise, no merchant at all? But how was it possible? Couldn't a man be read by his looks? Brikodar was a good and simple-hearted man. But it could never be shared with Uddhavnarayan. If he did, another round of discourse would follow. Just now he said that the man, who was caught, came from the bank of the Indus with loads of gems and jewels. On the northwest shoreline of the Indus, the Huns had set up a colony since the last few years. Losing the Dashpura battle, they had receded from this locale, no doubt, but their efforts were still on, they kept gleaning information, stealthily. Again, who hadn't an eye on Avanti and Ujjwain, after all?

Shivnath said,"I know next to nothing about all these things."

"It's not for you to know, again how will you? Just abide by my warning, stay alert! Your son has lost his life in the Battle of the Huns. I do not want you to be in any peril".

Shivnath looked dejected,"I am yet to get any news of my son, who has gone missing only, and I am sure, he has not been killed in the war!"

Uddhavnarayan smirked, "If he would have been alive, he would definitely come back with the troop of soldiers, you can easily be sure of it — you are in pain, but it is the truth indeed. Please observe his obsequies, otherwise his soul will never be free and that again for no reason whatsoever."

Shivnath got slightly agitated, "Please keep quiet, I do not want to hear such nonsense!"

Uddhavnarayan smiled to say, "I understand, you feel sad. Even I empathize with your feelings, he was a patriot and loyal to the King, after all!"

In an agitated tone, Shivnath said,"His wife and daughter are waiting anxiously for him since the last five years. I am also looking forward to getting my son back, and, you are negating our avid wait, our keen desire outright - he must come, something has definitely transpired to delay his return, many of them even come back after an interregnum of ten-twelve years, so what? May be, Kartikkumar has lost his way!"

Shivnath was failing to drive his logic home, rather appropriately. How was it that he was not finding his way for five long years? Ujjwain was known to people, far and wide, it was not so difficult to come back here. He might have gone elsewhere with a caravan of merchants for trading. But again, how was it possible? He was blindly in love with his wife and daughter. Victory in war was theirs and yet he did not return home. What did it signify? Shivnath felt utterly insecure within. The list of the dead soldiers in the war did not show Kartikkumar's name. It might be a mistake. He was not killed as his name did not figure in the list — it might be a notion that would hardly find a buyer. Or, there might be a distant possibility that the alien Huns, vanquished in war, had abducted him to slay elsewhere. It was not that, such nightmares did not haunt his mind, but he cringed in fear at the very thought.

Uddhavnarayan iterated, "Let such things be kept at bay, I shall not cause you pain, in such a morning of Deepavali, and I have not even come to see you for that matter . Now, the person you are looking for is not your son, none of your blood-relation but your friend's son, the depraved one. Where has he gone?"

Shivnath threw a confused glance at Uddhav. He was putting his blue headgear firmly on his head, and while doing so, he inquired, once again, "Where has he disappeared?"

"No clue".

"But he has certainly gone somewhere."

"I am keen on finding it out".

"No need of any search, it can be surmised that, he has gathered all information of Ujjwain and has gone to the right place. And who can even prove that he hasn't joined the enemy camp?"

Shivnath had fallen silent. Had Uddhavnarayan gone out of his mind? Which enemy did he mean? Avanti was quite calm. No battle had broken out, at all, following that of the Huns. The son of Dhruva would take up espionage! A little later, Shivnath asked, "What have you called me for?"

Uddhav said, "Where were you going? Come let us go riding a horse!"

"Nowhere as such. Will return to my hamlet itself, just had been toying with the idea of dropping by a pearl-shop."

"Why? Why a pearl-stall"?

Shivnath turned a bit stiff, rejoining, "It's a personal need".

Uddhavnarayan smiled, "Nothing should be held back as a secret if a royal servant, especially the King's man asked. It was not even feasible to hide."

"Familial matter."

"How is it familial? Will you buy a pearl-string?"

"Oh yes", Shivnath looked at the other direction and answered.

Uddhavnarayan kept smiling as he said, "Can't you say this to me? Look uncle, you can feel easily that time is out of joint. You are going to the pearl-shop, to the paddy-seller and all other places, - it may seem suspicious to some eyes. We have to keep a vigil on everything, have to know what each citizen is thinking, the duties and responsibilities of a man of the royal court is not that easy, our work is to doubt always, to sniff out for something suspicious."

"Might be so... no idea".

"Come let us go to the pearl-counter. Who will wear a pearl-necklace? Your grand-daughter?"

Shivnath smiled and nodded in the affirmative. Now he felt at home, a bit though. Now it seemed to him that Uddhavnarayan excelled in the art of eloquence, he was just a person of mere words. He was garrulous so long, just to make him feel the significance of his position. But why would he accompany him to the pearl-shop? Were his misgivings then real?

Shivnath was annoyed, he asked, "Do you take me to be a suspect"?

"No, no, I know you well, I like your family too, your granddaughter is so charming, how old is she now?"

Shivnath hated redundant curiosity and he expressed it, "If you know me, why are you stalking me?"

"No, no, no stalking at all, you are going to buy a pearl-string, I am coming along to ensure that you are not cheated. You are buying for your grand-daughter, I presume. Gandhavati is a paragon of beauty, to be precise."

Oh God, what did he say? Shivnath came to an abrupt halt.

What nonsense did Uddhavnarayan utter? This wasn't good at all. Voicing enchantment for the beauty of a woman of no relation would be nothing but a discourteous gesture of a man.

Again, Uddhav was re-adjusting his headgear and while tying it, he asked, "Hasn't she come of a marriageable age"?

Long after, Shivnath could make out the concealed import of Uddhavnarayan's conversation. Uddhav went up and stood beside him to say, "Enough perks are provided by the Royal Court apart from the monthly allowance. Why will you buy a pearl necklace, paying money? Come, they will give you in gratis, if I ask them for it. The traders always curry favour with us, will they be able to carry on their business without our gratification?"

"No, no, I shall buy paying the exact price. I have come prepared".

Uddhavnarayan broke into a laughter, "Keep your coins aside, it will come handy later on many occasions, I shall buy you the necklace which looks nice on Gandhavati, please hand it to her. The day of Deepavali is auspicious, one should take jewellery home".

Shivnath's reply came pat, "That is on the day of Dhanteras".

"Let it be so, no doubt today is a new-moon day, but the occasion of Deepavali is chosen to observe Dhanteras. Let me buy a pearl-necklace for Gandhavati with hundred beads in a row, it is called Devchhanda, do you have any idea?"

"No idea. But why will you give her?"

"It is my pleasure to gift her, that's it", retorted Uddhavnarayan.

"Is such the desire of a man of the Royal Court?"

Uddhavnarayan smiled, "You can think that way if you like. Perhaps you understand that my gift is for your granddaughter, and please give this matter a little thought."

Shivnath walked speedily in the opposite direction. Almost running and gasping for breath, he disappeared in the milling throng of the buyers and sellers. His heart was pounding hard. He could make out the intention of the King's courtier. Gandhavati had no luck to have a pearl-necklace. The old man did not stop anymore. He kept walking towards the west, towards Gambhira. He was assailed with fear. He was afraid if Uddhavnarayan rushed to this end, riding his Tibetan horse!

Uddhavnarayan was in for despair as Shivnath left abruptly. He thought of compelling Shivnath to buy the pearl-wreath, walking close to his heels. But he was intelligent. He did not proceed further. What had befallen him all of a sudden! On seeing Shivnath, he was immediately reminded of his granddaughter. That budding damsel was just a mesmerizing beauty! He had chanced upon her a few days back, by the road, lifting water from a well. He convulsed in desire, ogling at her. This was Deepavali, a day of joy and delight! He had already made up her mind to spend the whole day at Chaturika's, the harlot's place. He was looking for something from the Deepavali fair, if possible, before paying her a visit. Uddhavnarayan moved forward with tardy steps. Not towards the Ashok tree, but to the pearl-shop. He was a bit tired. As a man drooped into a short-lived spell of ennui following a sexual union, Uddhavnarayan was in such a languor. He was feeling desperate now. As a man stood utterly frustrated following masturbation, Uddhavnarayan seemed to be in such a bout of despondency. The way he was soaring high on wide-spread wings of imagination proved absolutely vain. He could have retired to the bawdy-house, shorn of all worries, if he could only hand the pearl-necklace to Shivnath! He could have been truly delighted. It would have been a step forward towards winning Gandhavati.

Now Uddhav would ride straightaway to the brothel. Thoughts on Gandhavati might be pushed to a later occasion. Uddhav had taken a pledge within, he would definitely make Gandhavati his own. That, however, would come next. For fun and enjoyment, no maid would dare emulate a whore! This was Deepavali. All the brothels were being decked up with flowers. They were to look spick and span. Though the fallen women were still fast asleep, Uddhavnarayan and the ilk had made up their mind to set off. Besides the time spent in the fair, they would keep aside rest of the hours for the whorehouse.

The pearl necklace for Gandhavati could not be procured, it could be done for Chaturika though, thought Uddhavnarayan. This day being Deepavali, he could fain get his beautiful woman he was so fond of, her own pussy-cat, a hundred-bead- pearl necklace to wear round her neck. Uddhavnarayan imagined Chaturika inwardly. She was a damsel with ravishing youth. She was certainly more adroit in displaying charms of youth and feminine wiles than Gandhavati, the daughter of Gambhira. Yet, Gandhavati was driving him even more romantic. Uddhavnarayan thought that Gandhavati was no match for Chaturika. Feminine beauty differed from one woman to the other. Who could possess the voluptuous youth like Chaturika? Could Uddhavnarayan ever think of spending all day and night of Deepavali with this nineteen-year-old damsel if she had a golden-champak-flower complexion? Would she ever be gratified by Uddhavnarayan, if her eyes were not feline or if she had a graceful face like Devadutta, the queen of whores? Dull-complexioned Chaturika had mastered neither the art of veena-playing nor dancing, whatever little she knew was just futile. If she would, at all, have been like Devadutta! Standing straight, Uddhav closed his eyes. Devadutta was the numero uno beauty of this city, fit to be enjoyed by the gods, the ardent admirer of her beauty was Subhag Dutta, the merchant, the richest and the most influential person around. In Uddhav's thoughts on women, Devadutta must not figure, no matter what. He was scared of drooling on Devadutta. Rather, Gandhavati could be won quite effortlessly.

Uddhav opened his eyes. He could banish Devadutta from his mind. Uddhav ran into Mahaparshwa, the patrolling cop, at the red-light vicinity. Sickly, lanky Mahaparshwa stood aslant like a long stick and asked, "Hello Uddhavnarayan, are you here with any news? Or am I to pass on any tidings to anyone? Would you like to consider a new entrant or go straight to Chaturika?"

Uddhav slapped on the loosely hung head of Mahaparshwa and said, "If I go somewhere to see someone, that is purely my own will, but where are you heading on to, so early this morning?"

"To look for a client as today is the most fruitful day for brisk transaction", Mahaparshwa smirked, "I had to stay awake much late into last night, hours of sleep had to be compromised. But the fair would not last long, Sir. New people have arrived at this city, buying-selling has poured money, jingling in the pockets of the traders. Don't you understand?" Mahaparshwa screwed his eyes up and then kept walking at a brisk pace. He melted into the milling crowd of the market-place.

THREE

Shipra river flew by on the western end of Ujjwain, taking its course northward, issuing from the south. Walking along the bank of the Shipra, for quite long, Shivnath would have to leave the river behind to take the road in the west, leading to Gambhira. Both the river and the hamlet were known by the same name: Gambhira.

Reaching near the Mangalnath Temple, the trepidations in the heart of the old man subsided. While traversing the long way, he had to halt many a time behind the trees, like, Banyan, Sacred fig, Peepul, so forth. He had to stay wary whether any King's man was approaching. Peril seemed to pop up from nowhere. And that Uddhavnarayan! How dour his countenance was, how modest his gestures! It was even learnt that he used to consult Dhruvaputra on how to scrounge favour from the Royal Court. Dhruvaputra was the best student of Sandipani Ashram, he used to live in Ujjwain itself. Subhag Dutta, the merchant, used to shoulder all expenses of his scripture-learning. Being a part of the royal force, savouring the royal power a bit, how altered was Uddhavnarayan!

The old man inhaled as he kept standing. He was perspiring profusely. With a nubile daughter at home, fear of such troubles could not be ruled out. If Gandhavati's father, Kartikkumar, would have been present, Uddhavnarayan would coil up like a worm in front of him. Uddhav of such a short height would invariably be trampled under the feet of Kartikkumar! Kartik would have killed him by pressing him in between two fingers! How strong and valiant his appearance was, how towering his stature had been and how magnificently wide was his chest! He would have certainly won a post in the Royal Court if he would return from the battlefield! He could even have been employed in the infantry as a superintendent of a certain department! He, sources averred, had fought, courageously, tooth and nail. The Hun soldiers were dispersing before his prowess. He kept wounding and slaying the enemy soldiers with the lash of his lance, incessantly. According to hearsay, the army was beating a retreat, on seeing Kartikkumar. Kartikkumar was chasing them from behind, along with his brothers-in-arms. Bhairab had narrated everything. A milkman by profession, of the same age as Kartikkumar, Bhairab too had gone for war. Even he had come back. He came to relate the tale of Kartikkumar's heroic feat to Gandhavati, Dhruvaputra and Gandhavati's mother. The battle being over, the troops of Avanti got stranded at Dashpura for ten days more. The dead soldiers had been cremated in the war-field itself. A platoon of the army stayed back in that place. Nay, Kartikkumar was not present there in that section. Why no search-operation had been ordered for him, was still an astounding mystery. A petty soldier had been forgotten somehow by all, in the joyful celebration of victory on the Huns . Stepping into Ujjwain, all were reminded of him. It was said that he had gone missing. Now Uddhavnarayan was saying that he was no more. How could it be proved that he was dead, after such a length of time? Five years had sped by. The wait might be extended to twelve years, quite easily. Reba, the daughter-in-law, said that she would wait for life for her husband, if her father-in-law permitted so. Eight years for the nonce and later the daughter-in-law could wait for four years more. If alive, would he not come back by then? The words of Uddhavnarayan kept smarting within. Why was he keen on announcing Kartikkumar's demise? What was his intention? And again, whatever he said with regard to Dhruvaputra was alarming too. He was sheltered by the Huns, he stayed as a friend of the foes of this nation! Words could never be more harsh and devilish than this. Uddhavnarayan was trying to keep his[Shivnath's] mind in chains with such words. Shivnath paced a little forward. Beside Mangalnath Temple stood the ashram of Brishavanu. He was a renowned astronomer, he had considerable fame for his knowledge in celestial sphere too. He could amazingly watch sundry stars, bare-eyed, even at this age. He was well over fifty, to be precise. Youths from all corners came to learn the art of astronomy from him, even Dhruvaputra mastered the art of identifying the stars of the firmament under his tutelage. He used to help Gandhavati master the art of locating the stars in the evening. Gandhavati owed her ability to recognize the celestial bodies like Swati, Chitra, Avijit, the Orion or the Ursa Major to the guidance of her friend, Dhruvaputra. Sky-watching was his joy, his passion. Such thrill,such passion had been instilled into the heart of Gandhavati. It seemed that the ways of entrance of Gandhavati's mind stood blocked. No, she did not point to her mother, Reba, by throwing a glance at the sky anymore, "See yonder, Maa, our mother Arundhati can be seen, beside Bashistha, the sage".

"Who made you recognize it?" Asked Reba in a singsong voice.

"Why, my friend?" answered Gandhavati in a soft tone. Yet, her voice made way to Shivnath's ears. He used to be all ears at this time of the day. How often he laughed within. Gradually, a desire secretly took birth in his mind. Who would make someone acquainted with the star, Arundhati? In the heyday of his youth, Shivnath himself had made his newly-wed wife recognize the star, standing in his courtyard. Reba got to know the star because of Kartikkumar, her husband.

Shivnath stood still, kept thinking, should he drop in at the ashram? Should he see Brishavanu, sharing his anxiety with him? Where was Dhruvaputra, where again was Kartikkumar? Was Uddhavnarayan's statement true at all? Or, were all these just futile figments of his imagination? Was the whole of it begotten of some deceit? Was it true, that, Dhruvaputra, being humiliated, left Avanti for the Kingdom of the Huns, by the river Indus? Was it ever plausible? Would a man annihilate himself thus, on betrayal in love? And was it true that Kartikkumar had been slain? What did he come to know in the dawn of Deepavali? A death-news! How, so glibly, could Uddhavnarayan say that Kartikkumar was no more? He would have to break this news to his daughter-in-law and granddaughter, reaching Gambhira all the way from Ujjwain. Shivnath came and sat on the bank of the Shipra river, all alone. A fresh Chchatim tree sheltered his head with an expansive shade. Taking off the shawl from his body, Shivnath kept whiffing on his chest and calming down.

On the other end of the river, the farmers got busy in the millet fields. But where was good harvest this time? The rains were so scanty. How much crops by way of tax would be levied by the taxmen of the Chief Accountant? The crops died a premature death owing to lack of rains. For long it had gone without rains. Dew kept falling, even when the thirst for rains stayed unquenched. Dews kept drenching grounds, since more than a month. The sky stayed ashen. The whole expanse of the firmament stood singed, it seemed.

Here the Shipra river had assumed a crescent shape. Meandering from the south, making a foray into the east, it had taken a southward bend again. Down the right bank, a young lad was descending into the water of the river. Looked the same age as Dhruvaputra. Did he know Dhruvaputra? The water level of the river had gone such low as to touch the bottom. The rush of the current was quite feeble. Nature wore a wasted look. Shivnath kept looking at the brat. The young man of medium height was coming up, having a rinse and wash. Copper-complexioned, close-cropped, curly-haired. Such hair-style could be found among the wild, ancient people of this land who used to live on hunting. On the head, they used to tie a green bandanna coloured with the extract from green leaves, in which the peacock feathers stayed tucked, on the shoulder they toted a bow, and in the hollow of a holder made of bamboo-slats, the arrows. What robust physique they possessed! Anyone would stand glancing at their dark-skinned, bare torso. The youth reminded him of a hunter. Though, it appeared, that, this lean-bodied youth would not be able to bear the weight of either a bow or a spear. Shivnath rose and moved forward. The young man stopped. His eyes had a curious glance. Shivnath inquired of him, "Hello Sir, are you a pupil at Brishavanu's, the Acharya's, ashram?"

Nodding 'yes', the young man asked, "And you?"

"I am coming from Gambhira, is the Acharya in?"

Shivnath kept walking beside the youth. From Sonagaon,a hamlet situated at the foothills of Nichoih range of Dasharno, Tamradhvaj had come to Brishavanu. He wished to master both astronomy and astrology before returning to Bidishanagar, he hailed from. The young man went on talking as they moved together, he belonged to the Vaishya caste, his father was into sales.

Shivnath asked, "Do you know Astrology?"

"Why do you ask this?"

Shivnath replied," No, nothing as such. Let me see the Acharya, Dhruvaputra is his disciple, after all."

Tamradhvaj said, "The Acharya is quite tense."

"Why?"

Tamradhvaj threw a glance at the sky, "Since more than a couple of years, Avanti has gone without rain!"

Shivnath swung his head, "Exactly! Neither millet nor maize could be reaped."

Tamradhvaj said, "This had never transpired during King Bhartrihari's reign."

Shivnath expressed his unanimity with him saying, "During King Bhartrihari's rule, there had been enough rain and plenty of food."

Tamradhvaj informed, "The Acharya is busy in calculations".

"Which calculations"?

"To ascertain the reason behind this drought".

"Then can't I see him?"

"I don't know. Are you here for some astrological calculations?"

"Yes", said Shivnath. So heated is the sun! Never had it happened during such a dewy season. The old man gibbered, "I am in a tizzy, quite confused".

Tamradhvaj said, "The Acharya is sitting with stars and planets, well-arranged. He is engrossed in it, please come in, be silent."

Both of them stepped into the ashram. Then, going round the ashram-hut with gingerly steps, they came to the rear to find Acharya Brishavanu, sitting in front of a birch-leaf, on which he etched a chequered pattern to ascertain the positions of the stars and planets. A solemn face, covered with beard. Though he was old in years, not a single tress turned gray yet. His hair and beard were remarkably pitch-black. A wide courtyard, cleanly mopped.

In a muffled tone, Tamradhvaj quipped, "Now there is least possibility of segueing on to some other calculation for the Acharya. The way he is observing the celestial bodies shows that he will first reach a decision on the fate of Avanti and then would concentrate on something else. His calculations are meant for delving into the fate of Avanti!"

Shivnath glanced at the sky. A little hazy, blue sky. Was it at all true that the god-like heavenly bodies would decide the fate of Avanti from the firmament? Definitely they did, otherwise why would the sky of Avanti remain cloudless since ages? Both the Sravana and the Bhadra slipped by without a drop of rain. Wasn't there any reason for it? Tamradhvaj said, Acharya Brishavanu had to explain to the Royal Court why it went arid, without rain and why again the crops were devastated".

Both of them had moved to the border of the courtyard. From here they could see the Acharya but there was least chance for their voices to reach his ears. Shivnath expressed to Tamradhvaj, "If the constellation of stars and planets creates opposition on the sky of Avanti, will it cast an adverse shadow on the inhabitants of Avanti too"?

Tamradhvaj smirked, "Crops have been ruined indeed, how can it make the people of Avanti happy?"

Someone might disappear, or go missing from Avanti... would it also owe to the juxtaposition of stars and planets on the sky of Avanti, gone awry?"

Tamradhvaj shook his head, "How shall I say? I cannot assume anything without proper knowledge, I cannot utter a single word even!"

"You learn astronomy under the tutelage of the Acharya, don't you?"

"This is an unfathomable mystery! Casting glance at the night sky I feel so small!" Tamradhvaj was again retracing his steps towards the Shipra river, muttering under his breath. Shivnath was close at his heels. Tamradhvaj doubted whether he had learnt anything at all. He would never be able to recognize all the stars and planets even in the next ten births. Hundreds and millions of droplets of light! Again, it could not be gainsaid that, Achryadeva himself even did not know the names of all the stars, let alone recognize them. In fact, no one perhaps knew for that matter. Numerous stars adorned the Milky Way. Tamradhvaj turned around while saying so, then lowering his voice, he resumed, "Rainfall depends on the ascent and descent of the planet, Venus, crops grow after the rains, the Venus only sends the seeds of birth to this earth."

"Wonderful, you spoke so well"!

"These are not my words, but the Acharya's! He is now keen on exploring the mode of transit of the Venus on fifth day of the lunar fortnight in Asad for over a couple of years, in the sky of Avanti. But at this time of the evening, the Venus is not visible. After seven days more, the Lord of Venus will appear in the sky of dawn - everything is going disorderly, though the order of the sky never gets disrupted, even by a whit. Sunrise, sundown, full moon, new moon, the rise and fall of the stars are governed by a strict and definite order. Sir, my mind is going scattered now, I do not know why I am being shaken by this ruthless look of nature.

In an inaudible voice, Shivnath said, "The Acharya would be able to explain this". Tamradhvaj swung his head and said, "Yes he can do that, but the mindscape is much more expansive than the sky that runs overhead. Who else but the Eternity will glance around the firmament in its wholeness? My mind again holds the vast universe in its cocoon!"

Shivnath got startled. There was a hint of deep involvement in the words of the young learner. He went on iterating, "In fact, I sit here fixing my gaze on the sky, I am trying hard to locate the star, Arundhati, but it is slipping off, eluding my vision again and again. So minuscule it is in size that, when it hides from sight, my heart goes pit-a-pat. Any idea…?"

"What"? Shivnath seemed to be a-stir by the profound curiosity of Tamradhvaj!

"No, but why, why will Arundhati fade out from his eyes?"

"From whose eyes?"

"No, let it be left at that, look Sir, the King of Avanti is quite solicitous to know the reason of this lack of rain, and even if it is detected, can rainclouds be welcomed on the canvas of the sky thereafter?"

"That calls for the sweet will of Eternity!"

"Who can tell?"

Shivnath heaved a long sigh and said, "Who knows when it will rain"!

"What will rainfall do now?"

That is true, Shivnath smiled, "It will shower again in another Sravan, which is ages away. A fair will be held vicinity of the Mahakaal temple on the occasion of new moon in Sravan." Tamradhvaj said, "In Avanti, twenty-three bucketful of rains make a normal harvest. But in the last couple of years, an overall dip by ten bucketful of shower played havoc with the harvest of crops".

"And in your Dasharno?"

"Rainfall is sparse, the cane woods and the rivers have all gone dry. Have gone emaciated. However, I may not be correct, I just learnt from the merchants from Dasharno, who dropped by Ujjwain."

"How long are you here?"

"Since the month of Asad of the year preceding the last one, since then I am a witness to this relentless mien of Nature."

They were pacing up together. Shivnath began to take a fancy to the youth. He was a bit talkative, again, who was there to talk to, in this ashram? Where were the other followers of Brishavanu? Did Tamradhvaj stay alone?

Tamradhvaj could surmise his doubt and answered, "All the disciples have gone home, now is the time of reaping harvest, you know. I am here alone".

"Haven't you gone too"?

Tamradhvaj swayed his head, "Dasharno is far off. I could not leave. Once I go back home, I may not come here again. What exactly do you want to learn from the Acharya?"

Would he disclose everything to Tamradhvaj? Could Scriptures and Astronomy trace a missing person? Could it locate the man infallibly, if at all?

Tamradhvaj inquired, "Of whom are you talking?"

Shivnath was taken aback. Could this knowledgeable youth read one's mind? It is, no doubt, amazing! What does he mean by 'of whom'? Does he know about Dhruvaputra? Or of Gandhavati's father Kartikkumar's failure to return home from the war that he had gone for?

Tamradhvaj retorted,"How can I calculate unless you enlighten me yourself?"

Shivnath asked, "Will you be able to pinpoint the exact location of the person, gone untraced?"

Tamradhvaj stood facing the river, Shipra. On the other bank, across the river, the field with unyielding millet crops lay stretched. Unclear, ashen sky. How would the sky be clear without downpour? Tamradhvaj turned towards him and said,"Your concern is acute, how can I tell you anything if you do not open up at all regarding the month, the lunar day, the exact time?"

Then Shivnath spoke out," Do you know everything that matters"?

Tamradhvaj kept mum. Shivnath said, "Dhruvaputra was a bonafide learner of this ashram of the Acharya. He was the son of a friend of mine and following a painful incident..."

Tamradhvaj rejoined, "I can read your words. I know a bit, heard even, yet you tell me yourself. Unless you speak out, you will not be free of the burden".

Staring amazed at Tamradhvaj, Shivnath was overwhelmed. How could he know everything by this time? Who, exactly, was this youth from Dasharno? Shivnath clasped both the hands of Tamradhvaj. He went on narrating the tale of Dhruvaputra with uninterrupted ease. Tale of Kartikkumar. That of Uddhavnarayan. Where were they? Would Tamradhvaj be able to enlighten him of Kartikkumar's existence somewhere on this earth or otherwise?

While listening, Tamradhvaj extricated his hand. Alighting the steps on the bank of the river, Shipra, in gingerly pace, he inched towards the water, flowing by. Shivnath too kept walking close behind him. The shadow of the sky fell on the water-surface. Tamradhvaj stood stock-still, gazing steadfast at the water. Shivnath eyed the reflection of his face. The birds were flying above his head. A flock of parrots. The sunrays being reflected by the water hit Shivnath's face straight. Time was fleeting by. Shivnath kept going down into the water, step by step. Crouching on the last step, placing his hand on the water of the river,Shipra, in an inarticulate voice, Shivnath blabbed out, " We are your children, won't you be kind enough to uphold the shadow of your lost child on the water again, oh mother?"

FOUR

The Seven Sages usually cannot be seen in the sky at this hour!

"Yes Maharaj, you know the sky indeed," In a mild voice, said Acharya Brishavanu, "The Seven Sages will make themselves visible in the Northern sky, once again in Magh along with Arundhati, the wife of Vashistha, the sage of much repute".

It could not be made out whether King Bhartrihari could hear or not. His face was upturned, his gaze was fixed on the sky above. His sight seemed to transcend this universe, the expanse of the heavens, the trajectory of the celestial bodies, the whole of the creation, as it aimed at the boundless. In the evening, King Bhartrihari had come all alone to the ashram of Acharya Brishavanu, which stood on the lap of Mangalnath Temple by the river, Shipra, from the palace through the God's Way. It was the day of Kartik Purnima. The full moon adorned the mid-sky. The chilly night was enveloped in moonshine. In the moonshine, the Shipra river seemed like a milky white stream, issuing out of the heavens. King Bhartrihari kept gibbering," Yonder in the north-east stands the Taurus, Aries lies a little west of Taurus and above it perches the galaxy of the Pisces.

Brishavanu suggested, "Look at the mid-sky, you can also espy Capricorn and Aquarius, side-on, wee-bit towards the south. Yonder there, look Maharaj"!

King Bhartrihari saw the sparkling Sravana just on the top of his head, relegated a bit to the west. Avijit stood at the north. He was getting to know the stars on the firmament. He learnt to read the stars sitting beside Brishavanu, for good many evenings.

Brishavanu said,"On the full-moon night during Kartik, the moon hovers over the Krittika star, can you spot Krittika, Maharaj"?

The King did not rejoin. Jerking his head, he heaved a sigh. And held his woolen shawl a bit loose around his torso. By Kartik, winter usually hits the city of Avanti, this year it might slack up. But why, there was hardly any chill this time! No rain, no drenched earth, how would winter make its presence felt? The northerly was yet to hit Avanti! The King blabbed," The Venus cannot be seen at this time, right?"

"No, may be after a few days by the close of this month, during dawn, the Venus would pop up, preceding the sunrise in the sky. The educator of the Gods, Jupiter, had been there in the western sky even on the first evening of the month, but now it is there no more. Maharaj, please come in, now is the time of dewfall, your body may not adjust to it."

The King of Avanti entered the Ashram through the courtyard. His seat had been properly arranged by Tamradhvaj. He showed the way to King Bhartrihari with a lamp in his hand. In the soft glow of the light, King Bhartrihari and Acharya Brishavanu sat face-to-face. The casement stood open. The moonshine fell straight on the King. He snuffed out the lamp, waving his hand. The moonshine was quite luminous.

"Yes, the fog is yet to intensify, and you have seen already how clear the sky is".

The King remained silent. Tamradhvaj sat slouching at the corner of the room, plunged in darkness. This was the third time King Bhartrihari had come on a visit, since his joining in here. This time he was looking somewhat pensive. It was the full moon day of Kartik, Deepavali passed by just early this month. Within another fifteen days, the city of Ujjwain would again host a fair. This would be a livestock one. But this fair held out an ample charm of diversity. In fact, this morning the Acharya kept saying that too many animals had not herded in, this year. The camels from the desert, the elephants from the East, Tibetan horses used for drawing gigs, even the speedy horses from Cambodia too used to make a beeline to this fair of Ujjwain. Besides, peacocks, pigeons and birds of various kinds were sold here in profusion. Lambs, cattle and he-asses used to throng the fair in droves. In the morning of a full moon day in the month of Kartik, the bank of the Shipra river remained replete with the calls of numerous wild animals. The night preceding that of a full moon was the penultimate one of a lunar fortnight in which the traders used to enter the city with their animals, all through the night. The Acharya sat till late into the night to take a look at the herd of beasts, traversing their way across the other end of the road, in moonshine. The silence of the fourteenth night of a fortnight stood intervened by the call of the wild animals. Those who accompanied them, especially the rustic ones who entered with the he-asses belted out songs with strange tunes. Those songs were typical of their voices only. The Acharya stood mesmerized by it. Last night was a still one. The herds of beasts had queued in, no doubt, but they were quite limited in number.

The King inquired, "Can you discern the reason behind the drought"?

Brishavanu blurted forth, "The Venus..." He stopped and said, a while later, "No, Maharaj".

The King said, "The season for sowing wheat iss about to be over, the soil lacks in moisture and it is just unprecedented; those who had sown wheat complain of the seeds failing to germinate".

Brishavanu opined, "Sometimes it may so happen — drought, damage of crops, all these are caprices of Nature".

"Only a whim? And nothing else?"

Brishavanu rejoined, "May not even be so, rather it may be the law of Nature on the contrary haven't we witnessed drought before"?

Two rainy seasons had gone cloudless in tandem, had ever such things ensued since his ascension of the throne?

"Please Maharaj, do not be stressed. Just as the physical state of man varies from day to day, often being affected by indolence, sometimes by temperatures running high, Nature, too, is pliant alike", Brishavanu consoled.

Bhartrihari kept swaying his head and refuted, "But escalating body temperatures, dipping coldness or lethargy have enough reason behind them and the medics are aware of these causes, and, prescribe measures accordingly so that the body is brought back to its previous healthy state. I am keen on knowing the reason, are you getting anything by your calculations"?

Brishavanu got next to nothing at all. Calculating or watching the position of stars and planets in the sky, he found no such remarkable sign that could lead him to ascertain the reason for such a drought! No exception could be found in the movement of the planets.

King Bhartrihari said, "This year too dewfall has commenced at the advent of Ashwin".

Pat came Brishavanu's reply, "Yes, I know. I am not taken in for any surprise".

"Dewfall draws curtain on the monsoon, declaring its end - rain eludes us this year just as the last year, yet..." Brishavanu said, "There's dewfall in early autumn because of drought and this is no wonder! Let me see whether I can find out any reason for the lack of rainfall."

"Did you watch the star, Jyestha of Vrischik orbit last Sravan"?

Brihvanu was astonished and asked, "Why?"

"Did you notice any exception?"

Brishavanu moved his head from one end to the other and said, "No, you know well that the position and transition of stars and planets abide by a cosmic order, which can hardly be disrupted. No exception met my eye".

The King of Avanti bit his lower lip. Suddenly he sprang up to ask,"Can Vrischik, the zodiac, be observed at this moment"?

"I had watched it on the south-western horizon last month, even early this month it was within my ken, but now it has gone down along with the sun".

The King said,"In Sravan, I had espied the stars of Vrischik constellation on the southern sky, it was possible because the sky was cloudless . I had no idea, but someone opined that at that time, the yellow colour of the brightest star of Vrischik galaxy, Jyestha, had undergone a change, it had turned bluish white, and it connotes that this star heated up and hence rainfall eluded the city of Avanti."

Brishavanu stopped. He was listening to Bhartrihari, the King of Avanti. This was something astounding. Jyestha star had suffered a change in colour! Who had uttered it? Was it ever possible? Was any new astronomer there in the city? And wouldn't he know anything? ...

The King asked, "Did you locate any new star"?

"Who told you about the change in colour of the Jyestha or of any new star for that matter"?

Bhartrihari fell silent. He walked out of the room to the courtyard in slow pace. The King was heading towards the Shipra river, in the soft chill. Brishavanu was following close at his heels. Tamradhvaj was behind Brishavanu by a few strides. How many stars from among the thousands were known to man?! And again, someone had again spotted a new star! The planets and stars were thousands of millions of years old! How would they be born again, anew?

Brishavanu questioned, "Where is that star"?

"In the two months, Asad and Sravan, while the Venus drooped down the western horizon, it bobbed up on the eastern sky, and then traversed to the west all night and set down way before dawn, by the midnight, to be precise", maintained the King.

"Did it transit briskly"?

"Yes".

"Who said so? I wish to talk to that astronomer. Have you seen yourself,

Maharaj? By no law can such a star be descried, sunrise and sundown follow certain limits of time, both the day and night abide by the laws of time, and I have marked that, the rise, set, transit of the astral bodies of the sky are all shackled to Eternity. If a star rises as the Venus goes down, how again can it glide down at the dead of night? In the traversal from the east to the west, it surely needs to maintain a certain space, in between"!

Bhartrihari turned back and shot a glance. Acharya stopped short. Bhartrihari's eyes glowed and calmed simultaneously, it seemed. Stooping a bit, said he, "Now I must make a move. I told you whatever I learnt. Please keep the words to yourself".

"But I want to interrogate that astronomer in front of you!"

Bhartrihari smiled and said,"Let it be left at that. I wanted to verify the truth of the statement, your words confirm my faith and I am assured".

The King walked away through the moonshine. Traipsing along the river bank of Shipra to a scheduled place, he would enter the God's way through a latent detour. He had left a ghee-lamp there, behind the rocks. The tunnel was too dark. He was aware of this way. Even Bhanumati, the queen, knew of it. This way was earmarked for the Kings and the queens. The King would reveal the secret of this path to his heir. However, the Army-Chief was supposed to know the mark and direction of this path. But the Chieftain of the Army of Avanti, the younger half-brother of King Bhartrihari, Bikram knew nothing about this path. He did not even reveal his curiosity to him [the King].

As King Bhartrihari left, Tamradhvaj came and stood before Brishavanu and demanded, "Hasn't your numerical judgments revealed anything at all, Acharya"?

Brishavanu shook his head, "No, nothing untoward has caught my attention".

Tamradhvaj iterated, "But he is talking about a new star!"

"I do not know".

"The rain-clouds have disappeared from the canopy stretching over Avanti. And how again was the constellation of planets and the zodiac in the months of Asad and Sravan"?

"That I had already pointed out in the months of Asad and Sravan".

"But you were into a fresh calculation spree again, weren't you"?

Brishavanu chose not to rejoin. He stretched his gaze on the universe and the sky, awash with moonshine. Tamradhvaj went reticent. Long after, Tamradhvaj asked, "If a person goes missing, which numerical analysis can help trace him"?

Brishavanu turned towards Tamradhvaj and inquired, "Who has gone missing"?

Tamradhvaj answered, "You know him, he mastered the art of recognizing stars under your guidance. A man had come here from Gambhira, in the morning of Deepavali. Along with his son and his friend's son…"

Brishavanu understood. He did not even know this. He had never disclosed that he knew this art! He heard that, the Buddhist Tantriks of Mahayana order mastered such calculations. Tamradhvaj was close at the heels of Brishavanu. Brishavanu began to consider himself an ignoramus. He could not proffer any befitting reply to the King's queries. And now, he failed to answer Tamradhvaj even. He looked up to the sky once again. He had no efficiency to read the etchings on the firmament.

Tamradhvaj informed, "On the day of Deepavali, a merchant had arrived at Avanti, I mean, Ujjwain, from Dasharno, all his food-grains had been plundered on the way."

"Oh God!" Brishavanu turned to look at him.

"Again, another trader was returning home after brisk sales, he too had lost all his belongings".

"How do you know"?

"This morning, I gathered this from the beast-fair, all were talking about it."

"Such incidents never usually happen in Avanti"!

"But it has transpired! Haven't you marked the King, feeling a bit insecure?"

Yes, it had struck Brishavanu. If Tamradhvaj was correct, there was every reason for the King to feel imperiled. Both of them stood in the courtyard at that time.

Tamradhvaj added, "In each month, in every season, lots of stars go on hibernation, as the Seven Sages are invisible lately, you certainly know when they will re-surface".

"Yes, I know", Brishavanu dittoed, "You know too".

"I know, from the month of Magh the Seven Sages will again begin to reveal themselves, in Phalgun the Seven Wise hermits would be seen on the north east horizon, the Milky Way will then change its course, it will stream down from the north to the south. But if it can be predicted when the planets and stars on the sky would be visible, when again they will disappear, in which season the missing star will make a comeback on the celestial sphere, then why can't a missing person's return be predicted?"

Brishavanu looked on at his disciple, with amazement writ large on his face. He sat under the sewli tree in the lawn on the dew-drenched ground. Tamradhvaj sat in front of him. Brishavanu told him, His son has gone missing in the Battle of Hun, his friend, Dhruva's son has left the city of Avanti, are you cognizant of these facts? Do you know the reason of his leaving"?

"Yes, I have heard".

Brishavanu said, "The astral bodies of the sky are bound by a systemic order, I have never seen any contravention in this regard in my life but a man's life is way different from that".

"Man is subject to the influence of the stars and the planets indeed".

"I know that exactly". Brishavanu looked up at the sky. He could feel his knowledge to be somewhat circumscribed. As Tamradhvaj kept saying, was it really possible to know all this? Did the planet or the concurrence of a zodiac sign during the moment of a person's birth really control his life? Could this branch of knowledge help reveal the truth of a person's life or all the facts regarding his birth? He tried to elicit the truth from Tamradhvaj, "What have you told Shivnath"?

"I went to Gambhira just a couple of days back".

"Why?"

"Just as such, I longed to see the river, Gambhira, and other curiosities too fortified my wish."

"How did you find it?"

Tamradhvaj kept silent. He had gone there and got to know two women like Tapasi and Uma ... a mother and a daughter— Reba, a mother; Gandhavati, a daughter. Both were like the two rivers. Tamradhvaj had come back with the horoscopes of both of them along with Dhruvaputra and Kartikkumar. He had also noted down the time and date of leaving their home. But it was left at that. He could not make out what he would do now with all such information. How beautiful the mother and the daughter had been! They sat on the verandah, next to each other. He sat in the courtyard. Old and wizened Shivnath sat facing him. When he was about to leave the place, both the ladies came down to the open yard. Their faces held out an avid appeal. Gandhavati sought from him, whether he mastered any art with the help of which he could visualize a lost person!

"From where did Gandhavati get to learn of this skill?" Tamradhvaj demanded to know.

She heard that the Buddhist Tantriks could visualize both the past and the future. Across Gambhira, in a far-off secluded forest, on the lap of a mountain, a profoundly wise man was heard of making his presence felt. The daughter and the mother were planning to visit him.

Brishavanu opined, "None would be more of a dunce than those Mahayana Tantriks".

Tamradhvaj said, "Though I brought along the birth-charts and the other dates and time, they would be of no help at all. I feel extremely embarrassed, I have promised them to pay a visit just after the Kartik Purnima and I know they will wait for me."

Brishavanu did not say anything. He got to his feet to go inside the dwelling. While leaving, he asked, "How old is Kartikkumar's daughter"?

"Thirteen-year-old, may be."

Brishavanu threw his glance at the sky. How can the full moon and the thirteen-year-old be told apart? Rather, the thirteen-year-old would mellow gradually like a full-moon. He looked into the eyes of Tamradhvaj. The youth lowered his eyes. His eyeballs were glistening with tears, he noticed.

"Has her marriage been fixed?" Brishavanu inquired.

Tamradhvaj shook his head. Brishavanu went in. Tamradhvaj kept standing in the inner courtyard. He swept his gaze on the stars, Avijit and Srabana, above his head, one after another. He turned around again and again to espy the stars and the planets. He fixed his mesmerized gaze on the sky, inundated with moonshine. Gradually, the sky drifted out of his range of vision. A calm, peaceful face popped up in front of his eyes instead. It was looking at Tamradhvaj with an unblinking gaze from the sky. She was waiting for the son of Dhruva. Which Dhruvaputra? The one who had fallen head over heels in love with the chief harlot of the city and had left this land of Avanti, being utterly humiliated. How beautiful that damsel was! The very thought of her made Tamradhvaj shiver all over. As many times he thought of the Gambhira river, the Gandhavati river bobbed up, instead. As many times he was looking east at the golden spire of the Mahakaaleswar Temple by the Gandhavati river, from across the river-bed of the Shipra, he was being reminded of the country girl. She came forward on her own and asked, "Please tell me where he is now, has he been sheltered in the Hun Kingdom or hasn't?"

Wouldn't it be nice if he could tell her something pleasant? The young maiden could have laughed then, carefree! While retracing his steps home, Tamradhvaj turned around abruptly to find Gandhavati fixing him, just him, with a steadfast gaze, holding a neem tree in her embrace, by the roadside.

FIVE

Reba inquired, "How many days have slipped by"?

In an inaudible voice answered Gandhavati, The month of Aghran is on the move, three months more to go. And the Chaiti Purnima is just six fortnights away… That Spring was at its peak, leaves fell from the trees incessantly, the cotton kept flying in the air, the bumble-bees kept circling round, the air was so redolent with the fragrance of the mango-buds, don't you remember, Maa, it was the auspicious day of Madanotsav?"

Reba raised a frightened hand to stop her short, "Stop, Sugandha, please do hold your tongue, in the month of Ashwin, where do we find mango-shoots and where again the Madan Festival at such time of the year?"

The words seemed to elude Gandhavati, she kept whispering, "We went to the Temple of Lord Kamadeva, for worshipping, all had thronged there. The queen had come along with a bevy of paragons of beauty from all over Ujjwain, whose lovers were handsome like Kandarpa, they were chasing each other, throwing flowers and colour-pigments at one another in a festive spree … the temple yard was strewn over with Ashok blossoms!"

Reba went on gibbering, "It was the Krishna Saptami of Ashwin, the sky was star-studded, I sat in the courtyard all night, the dews began to fall… The day remains etched on my mind's canvas till date."

Then too, Gandhavati failed to catch the words. She was lost in the memories of the day of Chaiti Purnima. It was her maiden visit to the Kamadeva Temple, on the day of Madanotsav. Mother had sent her. Parvati, the old crone, accompanied her. The old woman was a crook, to the bottom. She came back with her cloth loaded with Ashok and Bakul flowers. Dhruvaputra, her companion, stayed indoors. Her eyes were still charmed by the winsome appearance of Kamadeva and Kandarpa! The lovers, passion-stricken, smeared with colour-grains, kumkum, adorned with

Ashok blossoms all swam before her eyes. All the men were just the replica of Lord Kamadeva! All the lovers too were. How brilliant Lord looked! Well-formed nose, thighs, waist, shanks — all were well-shaped and round! The yolk-hued cloth lay around his waist. Wide, expansive chest! On seeing Him, she had been reminded of the face of the Son of Dhruva. She was quaking in romance, all alone. How elegant His appearance was! Both His eyes, face, lips, feet, nails — all were blood-red. He sat on the heap of Bakul flowers, on the back of a mythological aquatic animal, Makar. The ambience in the temple was teeming with the fragrance of newly-bloomed Bakul flowers on all four corners of the idol, the flower-bow, the flower-arrow stood clasped in his hands. If a flower-arrow had been charged, the lovers would turn mad for lovemaking. Gandhavati came back blessed with the divine heat of the lamp, lit with clarified butter.

Reba, her mother, said, "Five years seem so long! Much time flew by."

As the sigh wafted into her ears, Gandhavati lowered her face, abashedly. Melancholy hung heavy on her eyelids. Her mother was mixing up one lunar day with the other. Mother was speaking of the seventh lunar day of the new moon fortnight in the month of Ashwin. A journey had started off that day. That was yet to come to an end. The man of this house was yet to return. Her father's face was getting blurred before her eyes gradually. Yes, it was getting blurred. That face was superseded by that of Dhruvaputra, which was growing distinct, prominent instead. Gandhavati remembered the face of her father, Kartikkumar, turned sepia. She seemed to hear a call. Who would call her aloud, Sugandha, Sugandha? When, on which day, at what time, from inside the effulgence of which star? The Milky Way was alive overhead, and Sravana, the star, in its bosom. Beyond the galaxy, the stars - Avijit and Swati — were blazing. Dhruva, Saptarshi and Satabhisha, all these stars had been there too. The man was bowing down in reverence to all those astral bodies, standing straight in the courtyard. All the memories came alive in her mind. She failed to remember how frequently Kartikkumar tied his turban and again unfastened it in the afternoon. In the darkness, he stood and called her, Sugandha, my mother, oh mother, Sugandha, oh my Sugandha! She remembered all, but could not say why the face kept fading out! His father had gone away for a war. To quell the uprising Huns.

Reba came back to consciousness by this time. She was so unfortunate that her sighs mingled with that of her daughter. How long would she stay young? As earth turned into rock because of the lack of rains, same fate would befall her. Would that man ever come back? Even then, she kept looking down the way for him. She was sure of his return and hence waiting was obvious.

Reba called her daughter, "What were you saying? Chaiti Purnima, Madanotsav?"

Gandhavati's large eyes went green at their rims. She turned towards her mother. Her mother observed, her daughter had attained the looks of an ascetic. Her daughter skipped her night's sleep. She wove beads into a wreath, she even gave up tying her hair up. She was so fond of these kunda flowers of the autumn that she used to deck herself with it. She had given up everything now.

Gandhavati sought her mother's attention, she said, "This year winter seems to come quite early, Maa"!

Reba fell quiet. She understood, her daughter was not in a mood to reminisce the days of Madanotsav. She was talking about winter instead. Where was winter? In other Aghrans of yesteryear, chill seemed to freeze her even more. Nature was not showing any sign of winter at all, this year. Dewfall had set in after the drought. Such dewdrops would never usher in winter. Her daughter sat utterly dejected! Less agile, as a woman past her prime, or one who had been claimed by senility, bit by bit. Gandhavati was mumbling, "So many full moon days have slipped by even after, from Baishakhi Purnima to the forthcoming Aghran Purnima, seven full moon days have gone by even after a year, another one is awaited, Maa! That night, the star, Agastya, was twinkling in the southern sky, he walked down south-east eyeing the star, he moved on, brushing past the city of Ujjwain, it seemed".

Reba grew listless to say, "At the appearance of Agastya, clouds begin to pile up on the sky gradually, the gods in the heavens get gratified, rains fall. Even that year with seven full moon days and so many fortnights passing by, the desired amount of downpour stood elusive, where was it? Thy grandpa had strewn wheat seeds in the fields, they neither sprouted nor those which germinated had any promise of life, earth solidified into rocks. Was it true then that saint Agastya surfaced in the sky? Or this year did the star appear in the sky at all?"

"Yes Maa, I was taught to read the sky by Dhruvaputra, my friend, and after that I never fail to recognize a star, I know the star, Arundhati, I can locate her in the sky, she stays beside Vashistha, the hermit. At that time, the Seven Sages stood on the northern firmament and maintained status quo, even till the next Chaiti Purnima."

Mother kept looking at her daughter in amazement. That heartless bloke had taught her to locate Arundhati too! If he did so, it was unfair of him to leave Gandhavati. Reba lowered her face. She tried to think out the reason behind her daughter's present statement. She was reminded of recognizing the Arundhati, standing here in this courtyard, following her wedding. Kartikkumar had pointed it out to her. It seemed, Kartikkumar had learned to locate such a little star only for her. He only let her recognize the Arundhati, setting aside all the bright, sparkling he- and she- stars of the heavens! It was mandatory for him to let his wife recognize the star and he did accordingly. And, Kartikkumar was a soldier. He had to find a place in the King's army, getting familiar with the star, Arundhati! Each evening, he used to ask her, "Reba, can you see Arundhati, the goddess"?

Reba whispered, "Did Dhruvaputra help you recognize the star? Did he really? Himself?"

"Yes, Maa!"

Gandhavati sat, lowering her head. Both her eyes were getting moist. She knew well that it was a part of wedding rituals. During the act of Kushandika, the newly-wed wife was shown the Arundhati. Mother had definitely espied it. And after that, while she stepped in this house, father had shown her, in the evening…

Gandhavati uttered in a sibilant voice, "Maa, tell me about my father, how he had gone to the war"!

Reba answered, "Surprising, no doubt! That day had a great promise for setting out for any travel. As the Satabhisha bobbed up in the sky in the gloaming, he began his journey, hope thou haven't forgotten it, he would have to go to the north-east nook of Ujjwain and from there the troop of soldiers would leave for Dashapura the following morning. He took the bank of the river to the north and then walked to the east. The very next day, the army from Avanti filed up to the west by this way only, I sat up all night in the inner yard."

"The evening of Krishna Saptami must have been pitch-dark."

"Yes, it was so. The month was Ashwin, the sky was clear after a spell of downpour, just after sundown numerous stars lit up the sky, Sravana, Avijit, Galaxy of Seven Sages, constellation of Hansa, Dhruva, Satabhisha, he had traced his trajectory with the help of starlight, he was valorous, why would he be afraid of the dark?"

"But that man hasn't come again, Maa"!

Reba startled and said, "Who, who hasn't come? You mean Tamradhvaj, that disciple of Acharya Brishavanu of Dasharno, who came here before Kartikpurnima?

He hasn't come as he hasn't found anything by his calculations"!

"He came along with grandpa, but grandpa hasn't gone there anymore!"

"I do not know". Reba fell silent. She was spending her days in silent fear! What revelations would be there on Tamradhvaj through his reading? Who could tell? Tamradhvaj had not turned up. It would be fine if he did not come again. Reba was encouraged by his presence on the first day as he came to pay a visit. Later, she surmised him to give up reading the horoscope. What if he came with a piece of heartbreaking news? What if the hope she had woven around the man who went missing after the Battle of the Huns, got a violent jolt? If the hope got belied altogether?

"Shall I ask grandpa"?

"No", came Reba's faint rejoinder, "No amount of calculations can bring him back, he must return once he is cured of illusion. Dhruvaputra shall definitely come back."

"And father"?

Reba hung her head low. The daughter should have understood her! Wasn't her daughter tense too? Her peace of mind was blown off since the day Tamradhvaj had come to collect Kartikkumar's birth-chart and date and time of his setting out for war. One evening after Deepavali, her father-in-law had talked about Uddhavnarayan to her, following which her fear shot up manifold. Apprehension would increase invariably. She, too, had nightmares for a few days. In her sleep, she even heard Kartikkumar calling her. How handsome a husband she had! How well-built his physique had been! She had adorned him before he went to war. She had taken off her necklace to stash it away, as her husband was out on war. Before he left, she could not put on the yellow sari which Kartikkumar had brought for her though she was planning to wear it often. She had kept it aside in her trunk with much care. She thought, the soldiers might, perhaps, be back before Deepavali or in four fortnights they definitely would. Then drawing a mark of victory on her husband's forehead … how keenly she longed for his return! The army however returned before Maghi Purnima. It took too long for winning the battle. The Huns were almost impossible to vanquish! They were a race of warriors to the core. Plunderers, to be precise. The army of Avanti aimed at putting an end to the Hun race by hounding them out from the northern border of Saurashtra. They had almost gone extinct. Grapevine has it, that they had settled on the bank of the river Indus, more towards the north-west. The troops of soldiers of Avanti did a commendable job in that battle. They had saved the peasants and the subjects from the attack of the pillagers. Everything went well, only Kartikkumar did not come back with the victorious army. Reba remembered each bit of it. Nothing stood obliterated from her memory. That year, since the morning of Krishna Saptami her husband kept cleaning the sword, that lay unused since ages. He rubbed his headgear a-sparkle with a piece of lemon. He shaved his mane and pared his nails, calling in a barber. The man seemed to effervesce in excitement of going for a battle. He rushed to the bush behind their hut with the dazzling sword in his hand. He kept on brandishing the metal blade, cutting the air with a swishing noise. Don't thou remember, Sugandha?

Gandhavati remembered sketchily. Mother had beaded a garland with Kurantak blossoms. She made sandal paste. Mother had adorned her husband with a garland

and sandal-paste. While leaving home, father had cast his eyes on a pitcher filled to the brim, a lamp lit with clarified butter and all such things. Blowing the conch-shell, her mother had spread the news of her husband, Kartikkumar's setting out for war, far and wide. Just after her father had gone, her mother became an ascetic. She gave up doing her hair, wearing ornaments, putting on colourful clothes. Gandhavati looked at herself. She shuddered doing so. Whatever her mother did after her father left for war, she was going to step into her shoes, by repeating such actions. Did she wear any colour? Where had gone colour, whither were her jewellery, where again her hair-do? She used to forbid her mother, even though she wanted to do her hair. Gandhavati bit her lips. For whom was she waiting? Her companion, Dhruvaputra? He was enamoured of Devadutta, the chief harlot of Ujjwain, he had gone missing, being spurned by her. She had given up everything for her friend, but had he ever nurtured a wee-bit of concern at some nook of his heart for her?

Gandhavati muttered under her breath, "He will not come back, Maa, I think".

Mother lifted her face up and asked, "Are thou talking of Dhruvaputra"?

"Yes, Maa".

Reba fell silent. The daughter was seeking solace from her. What assurance to her daughter would she proffer? Let her daughter be strong at heart. Let her go on waiting. Let her burn in love for her lover, who was absent, let her bear the pangs of rejection! How deep was her pang of estrangement from her lover? Wasn't she watching her mother? She was still waiting for her husband who went missing after war! Full moon days, Krishna Saptami—all passed by in numbers, the pathway looked desolate, secluded! She, herself, was feeling desolate too. Reba suggested, "Thou love him and keep waiting for him, but for how long"?

Gandhavati rejoined, "Let us give up on Tamradhvaj, a female hermit has come to yonder west, she has put up in the foothills, we can approach her for knowing about the future that awaits him, can't we?"

"No, don't thou feel scared"?

Gandhavati said, "How much fear, how much sadness am I to come to terms with, for continuing to live"?

"He had fallen for a whore. Don't thou despise him"?

"Despise! What for?" Gandhavati was taken aback.

Reba felt like striking her daughter. She came of a marriageable age. The moment would slip off in a few days. For whom had her daughter turned into an ascetic? Who was he? A heartless, ungrateful chap who had gone to sacrifice all that belonged to him for a fallen woman! And her daughter kept observing the absence of that man so strictly! Her old father-in-law had talked to her about Uddhavnarayan. Uddhavnarayan was trying to intimidate them by referring to that incident, it was crystal-clear. Uddhav was keen on marrying Gandhavati. Reba got to her feet to say, "I am simply confused, why aren't thou nursing hatred for him, Sugandha, he doesn't love thee, and thou have given up sleep for him, don't thou know that he has gone to the Kingdom of the Huns, by the bank of Indus?"

"Who said"? Gandhavati screamed in affliction.

"News has reached, thy grandpa knows".

"No, it just can't happen".

"It can, he has grown up with you, yet he hasn't looked lovingly at you at all, and stepping into Ujjwain, he has" … Reba's voice betrayed her agitation, "He has been rejected. Well, he got a befitting punishment, I do not want him to come back here."

"What's wrong with you today, Maa"?

"Nothing at all, I am just voicing the truth".

"It's not the truth, Maa".

Reba smiled, tied up her open tresses in a knot, Thou keep thy eyes shut, it will hardly snuff out all the stars in the sky, nor the sun will go down untimely. Listen Sugandha, give up the hope of getting him back, we have to live, waiting for such a lunatic will bear no fruit at all, once he enters this city, he will be held captive, he has taken refuge to the Huns, after all".

"A blatant lie, out-and-out"!

"The King's words are true".

"The King hasn't said anything, the King doesn't know him".

"He knows, the King does not have to know him personally, if his men recognize him, that will suffice! Uddhavnarayan is the King's man, his words need no confirmation and again when the King's woman matters" – Reba goes silent.

"Uddhavnarayan is telling a lie".

"He is a man of the royal court, his words will never be taken as a lie, the King has definitely learnt everything, whatever the King comes to know from his employee, he believes every word of it. Look Sugandha, thou too have been deceived by that Dhruvaputra, never utter his name again".

Gandhavati was convulsing noticeably. She had never dreamt of hearing such words from her mother. Rather, her mother had advised her to keep herself strong. Gandhavati's eyes were getting moist and her vision, blurred. Striving hard to stall the tears that welled up, she covered her face with both her hands. Reba said, "No amount of crying will bear any result, why do thou keep waiting for a mirage, a man of the King's court seeks thy hands in marriage" …

"No", Gandhavati stood up with an expanded hood, like an injured serpent! She kept shaking her head, muttering, "He is dishonest"!

"Who is honest? That Dhruvaputra? How can we disregard the overture as it comes from Uddhavnarayan?"

"How can he come up with a proposal while I awaiting someone else?"

"Enough is enough! Let thy words be swallowed in, we have to live on, after all, Sugandha!"

Gandhavati did not wait there for an instant. She kept retracing her steps. She was being overcome with fear. She could not reason for such a bizarre attitude of her mother. Covering her face with two hands, she began to take to the street, leaving the courtyard behind. She was tracing her steps to Gambhira. Reba was walking behind her. She was staggering as she followed Sugandha. What exactly had befallen her! Nothing at all. She had to accept this truth now. She had to. If her daughter's youth would fade out somehow after this, would that Uddhavnarayan look at her at all? How beautiful her daughter was! Let her daughter retaliate the deception by marrying Uddhavnarayan! Dhruvaputra fell head over heels in love with the leading paragon of beauty of Ujjwain. Why would Gandhavati wait for him? Uddhavnarayan had expressed his interest to her father-in-law even a few days back. Shivnath had related the incident of the pearl necklace to his daughter-in-law. Reba shot glances of amazement at her daughter! Who would not be attracted to this winsome youth? Only Dhruvaputra proved otherwise…! How would Devadutta, supersede her daughter in beauty? Would she surpass this tender beauty ever? Reba noticed, how the dust-laden path of autumn began to bear the footprints of Gandhavati! Each footprint seemed to resemble a flower! Reba could spot the semblance of a land-lily on the surface of this ruthless earth. Reba could hear the jingle of her anklet. She had gone out of mind. If not so, how could she hurt Gandhavati so heartlessly?

Reba called out, "Sugandha, please wait, listen to me!"

"Do not fear, Maa, I shall not die, I shall not get lost, I shall keep waiting for him, I will, Maa! Please go back, I am going to the bank of Gambhira, please do not think of me, even you know that none of your words is true!"

SIX

Saurashtra lay in the west of Avanti. And in the north of Saurashtra ran a desert. That land bordering the Arabian Sea was the habitation of the Gurjars. In Devadutta's veins ran the blood of the Gurjars. The blood of the Ionian Greeks mingled in it. Her mother, Rasamanjari, was a famous courtesan of Saurashtra, adept in the sixty-four ways of lovemaking and scriptures, a dancer of repute and a qualified woman in every sense of the term. She had to come absconding to the city of Avanti after a quarrel with a landlord at Saurashtra. Devadutta was aware of that incident. The senior citizens of Avanti too were. Even Chaturika heard it from Devadutta. It dated back many years. It transpired during the reign of Gandharvasen, the father of Bhartrihari.

Gandharvasen had offered refuge to Rasamanjari—the leading beauty, the woman of ample virtues. Rasamanjari had a four-month-old daughter on her lap, Devadutta, whose father was a Greek merchant, slain by the landlord of Saurashtra. If all had gone on well, Rasamanjari would have set sail to Balkh, with that merchant, in the vicinity of the Caucasus range, by the river, Oxus. The merchant hailed from that place itself. Devadutta heard of the sacred Oxus river [Rasamanjari used to call it Aksu] of Balkh, verdant with crops, from none but her mother, Rasamanjari, who in turn, heard from her lover, hailing from the land of the Greeks. In her mind, Devadutta had a vain fancy on the river, Oxus, she wove dreams around it. She would pay a visit to the land of her father, even though for once. She would purify herself by having an ablution in the waters of the Oxus. The land, Balkh, the Caucasus range — was her fatherland. Her dreams made room for it.

Rasamanjari had to wait for the birth of the child as conceived already. Balkh, Oxus river — they were far-off, after all. Crossing the river, Indus, traversing through Purushpur, Taxila, Gandhar and sundry other lands, one had to reach there. Three seasons might have been taken to reach that place. The way was almost inaccessible. Rivers, mountains, forests were to be crossed to reach such distant lands. The anxious wait of Rasamanjari only threw her in jeopardy. Her lover died, and, to evade the lustful grip of the landowner, she had to set out for Ujjwain, braving such monsoon. They were decided to start for the land of Balkh in the month of Ashwin itself. Devadutta culled all such details of the trouble-torn days from her mother.

No doubt, Rasamanjari came to Ujjwain, as she was supposed to go to the land of Oxus, after a visit to Ujjwain with the Greek merchant, Antiochus. She had hoped against hope that Antiochus would survive all odds till the last. And if he lived, he would definitely come to Ujjwain. He heard of the rivers, Shipra, Gandhavati and the Mahakaaleswar temple from Rasamanjari. He even learnt that Rasamanjari would pay a visit to Lord Mahakaal before setting out on a journey to the far-off land. The Shipra and Gandhavati were equally sacred like their river, Oxus.

Her mother waited avidly for her paramour. Her life was a long wait. King Gandharvasen had fallen in love with Rasamanjari, in the meantime. Devadutta's mother was caught between double concerns. Out of deep gratitude, she had never disowned the King Gandharvasen. Being a courtesan, she was not even entitled to do so. Yet, her demeanours could have betrayed otherwise. Her second love was King Gandharvasen.

King Gandharvasen used to appreciate the talents of the damsel from Saurashtra. She was adept in dance. Devadutta had even inherited her mother's talent. Saurashtra-blood also ran in her veins. No courtesan from any other place could emulate their expertise in dance. In some distant days of yore, the women of Saurashtra took lessons in the art of dancing from the milkmaids of Dwarka. The milkmaids, in turn, had mastered the art of dancing under the tutelage of Usha, the Princess of Sonitpur, the daughter of King Bana, in order to entertain Lord Krishna. Usha was the companion of Parvati, daughter of the Himalayas. Usha had been born at Sonitpur, on a curse. Usha had taken lessons in amorous dance-postures from Parvati. Parvati had invented this form of dancing in order to impress her consort, Mahadeva. The amorous mode of dancing which Devadutta inherited from Rasamanjari actually belonged to none but Parvati. Parvati is remembered through dance, as an art of expressing love.

Chaturika had come to Devadutta for learning the art of dancing. None in Avanti could emulate Devadutta, the daughter of Rasamanjari, in dance. Chaturika was a maidservant's daughter. Her mother was the confidante of Rasamanjari but had not learnt the art of dancing.Her days were spent in serving Rasamanjari. Chaturika knew well that if the pinnacle of success in the courtesan's calling had to be attained, the art of dancing was to be mastered. She had to master the sixty-four ways of copulation for ultimate pleasure. Why would the men visit the whore if she lacked in competence in these two forms of art? In order to add zest to youth, to make it blossom, these two forms of art were the most essential. A harlot ignorant of all such competence, could only be an inamorata. And that man would be an ordinary one, no King's officer would even spare a glance at her. And if she had no worth, she would not even be in a position to reject anyone. Dancing as an art is nonpareil in winning the heart of a man. Devadutta however maintained a different view, she used to say, why only man, in order to awaken one's own self, to purify one's body and mind, dance-rhythm was the best art. Devadutta used to put it amazingly, "This body is governed by rhythm and to manifest such synchronized movements of the body distinctly, dance is the only medium. Dance is that art-form through which quest for God can be initiated by offering oneself".

Conjoining the two feet together, placing the nails in a straight line and stretching out the two hands on both sides like two long creepers and bringing the knees and the shanks in close contact, Devadutta instructed," This is 'samanakham', the body will be sans weight and now with a 'patakanjali' mudra held firm on the chest, protrude the lower end of your face forward, like this"…

Chaturika was imitating the posture. Holding the folded palms near the breast, she was trying to look exactly like Devadutta and she could hear the dulcet utterance of the accompanying shloka for the dance, by Devadutta:

Patakanjali bakshahstham prasarito shirodharam
Nikunchitam sakutam cha tallinam karanam smritam…

[The two palms being pressed together in an 'anjali' pose near the breast, with the neck held high and the shoulder bent: this dance-posture is named 'Leena'] "Now you recite, Chaturika!"

Chaturika smiled, "I can't do that".

Devadutta exhorted, "This is the time of prayer for taking a deep plunge in one's own self, time for remembering Shankar, Parvati, the ancient maestros of dance as they are. The tales which I narrated, hope you remember, pray inwardly to Usha-the Princess of Sonitpur, the milkmaids of Dwarka, the damsels of Saurashtra. I remember my mother Rasamanjari as I have inherited this art from her, and now this is thy turn to master this art. Who could emulate my mother in dance, in this city of Avanti? Now, look at me."

Putting an end to 'Patakanjali', Devadutta kept shaking her two hands like the wings of a duck. And then both her hands began to rotate. In a trice, moving the tips of arms, shoulder and elbows rhythmically, along with both her hands, Devadutta stood stock-still by holding the back of her two palms, like wings of a duck, upside down. Chaturika's eyes wore an amazed look. She seemed to be blessed to see the beauty of Devadutta, which unfolded before her eyes in just a few moments.

Chaturika asked, "How do you accomplish it"?

The legs of Devadutta parted from each other to attain a triangular mudra. The two hands came to rest on the waist and the corner of her lips curled up into a joyful smile, both her eyes sparkled like a fresh blossom, with loads of cheer and gratification.

Chaturika asked, "Which dance have you choreographed for Lord Mahakaaleswar on the day of Aghran Purnima"?

Devadutta rejoined, "That is for Lord Mahakaal to enjoy first".

"Will Lord Mahakaal truly enjoy"?

With her feet akimbo, shanks bent, Devadutta made a Swastika symbol with elan. Moving her hands downward and then holding them up near the breast, lowering her face, she uttered in an inaudible voice, "The King of Avanti will surely come."

"If he does not turn up"!

The gratification, the grace that adorned Devadutta's body, from head to toe, began to fade out gradually. Her eyelids lost movement, both the eyeballs drooped down, came to a standstill, lacking in lustre. The light in her eyes snuffed out. Devadutta lifted her pale face up, slowly, her eyes were half-closed, in an indistinct voice she asked, "Would thou go away for once?"

Chaturika was striving hard to appropriate the dance mudras which had just been demonstrated, by joining her hands in 'Patakanjali' mudra, on her breast. The union of her palms was getting disrupted as she was about to extend the lower end of her face forward. She was praying in her mind to Shankar, Parvati and the milkmaids as she was failing to synchronize one limb with the other. She was not succeeding to create an ambience of deep involvement, as the morose face of Devadutta stood before her eyes. She said, "My friend, the King of Avanti will perhaps go to Mahakaal, also the queen accompanying him".

"Who said so?" Devadutta looked up, melancholy seemed to give way to calm on her mien, she whispered, "Let the queen come, she too will watch the performance of Devadutta, which she would never get to witness in this city of Avanti, I am sure!"

While finishing her statement, Devadutta seemed to float her expanded arms on her head like a canopy, folding them right from her elbow. She contorted her five fingers to create Mrigashirsha mudra. Bending her right hand near her breast, her five fingers twisted to give rise to the same mudra. The right leg was timorous, the left curve of the waist lay bare a little. Devadutta began to convulse in keeping with the rhythm of the dance and kept muttering, "If the King of Avanti would come here!

King Gandharvasen used to frequent my mother's place and King Bhartrihari learnt a lot from my mother!"

Chaturika undid Patakanjali, and grew busy in forming Mrigashirsha with both her hands, in imitation of Devadutta, and sat down on the floor, all of a sudden and said, "Let me watch you,my friend"!

"Who has told thee that the queen will come too"?

"Who said"? Chaturika's face hung low. Would she inform her the name of the person who told her? Uddhavnarayan was her source of information! But how he had oame to know the news of the inner court of the King of Avanti still remained a mystery to Chaturika. She did not demand to know even. Uddhav once said that curiosity of a whore would not help her in her calling. Rather it would prove detrimental. All curiosity would be Uddhav's only. He would be curious about who came to pay a visit to Devadutta's residence, Devadutta, the paragon of beauty, the leading whore of Ujjwain! When did the person see her? Chaturika stopped as Devadutta motioned to her. She came up to Devadutta. Devadutta's mudra had altered by then. She posed with a 'Mayuram' mudra. The ring finger and the thumb stood locked in each other. The other fingers lay expanded. Stretching her gaze beside the upturned right hand of Devadutta, far beyond the open window, Chaturika could eye the golden spire of the Mahakaal Temple. Among the courtesans of Ujjwain, Devadutta's house was the most attractive one. Gandharvasen got this abode built for Rasamanjari, her mother. From each room, the pinnacle of the temple could be seen. And standing by the window, one could gaze at the sandy bank of the river, Gandhavati, the narrow stream.

Devadutta asked, "Will the King of Avanti come at the advent of evening? With the rise of the moon, I mean"?

Chaturika swung her head to say, "I don't know".

Relaxing her body, Devadutta kept creating various dance-mudras with both her hands. Holding the two thumbs of the clenched fist up and erect, she created 'Shikhara' mudra. Setting the forefinger and the middle finger on the right thumb, she stood in a delicate, graceful posture. Her fleshy breasts began to heave as she kept inhaling and exhaling. Bending a little, bringing her lips to the ears of Chaturika, she asked, "Would thou like to go to the King of Avanti"?

"Again??" Astonished, Chaturika stood apart. She remembered the day when she went to the King of Avanti with the invitation of Kartik Purnima. Devadutta, the public woman, would be performing her dance in her courtyard and she was keen on having the gracious presence of the King of Avanti. She had reached the invite etched on the bark of the birch, to King Bhartrihari, through a sentry of the Royal Palace.

She waited. The sentry returned to hand her fourteen gold coins. He gave back the invitation letter, stating that the King had thanked for the welcome but he would not be able to attend as some other engagement would keep him busy that day.

Distributing those coins among many, Chaturika had come back with seven gold coins in her hand. She gave the maidservant just two coins, who took her to the security man. How would five coins look paltry? But she felt empty-handed. Certainly, she had nothing in her hand. Devadutta's face looked bloodless, pale, as her invite went unaccepted. Nothing in it was to prove that the King of Avanti had taken a look at it. He had definitely taken a look at it, otherwise how would the sentry fetch gold coins? The Kartik Purnima was spent in dejection. That day she skipped her hair-do, she did not adorn herself with flowers.

Devadutta said, "Young Bhartrihari used to see Rasamanjari, how could his poetry flourish if my mother did not contribute to it? Mother herself remarked, Kumar Bhartrihari's heart was really impeccable, Goddess Saraswati inhabited there. Tell me Chaturika, can anyone in Avanti match his knowledge in Rasasatra? His poetic creation on sexual union owed primarily to the lessons imparted to him by my mother, Rasamanjari, some find eroticism in it, some again look for the unalloyed joy of life in itself, many of the shlokas of that Book of Verses on Intimate Union, are still treasured in my memory".

Chaturika kept silent. She failed to comprehend the inner meaning of each and every utterance of Devadutta. She had no idea even how the King Bhartrihari had interpreted Sringara rasa. For her, the word Sringara was synonymous with the lust-torn face of Uddhavnarayan, the man of the Royal Court. What would he understand beyond the bodily pleasures? Nothing at all. She had to master the art of dancing, veena-playing only for Udhavnarayan, hoping that he would oppress her less in his intoxicated frenzy! He would then let go of her body. He would then at least feel that she had a mind too, apart from her body.

Devadutta said, "The King of Avanti will surely come in the evening. Now get lost"

Chaturika was engulfed in the darkness of her mind. She however perceived that in King of Avanti's heart, Devadutta had not even a whit of existence. Grapevine sources averred that, the King of Avanti never would cast a glance straight at any other woman save the queen, Bhanumati, the maid from Kankhal. The immaculateness of which Devadutta spoke was so true, that his thoughts and imaginings of Sringara rasa pivoted round his better half only. Despite all this, she thought that the King of Avanti had not done justice to her good reputation, on the day of Kartika Purnima. He had no right to hurt anyone's feelings. Being the King of Avanti, he would respect the people who used to revere him in turn. The subjects' hopes and aspirations pinned on him. He had to read the inner mind of the people if he wished to run the administration well. Why would he insult the chief courtesan of the city? Who else would match Devadutta in talents in the whole of Avanti? The queen would stand nowhere if compared to Devadutta in any possible way. Perhaps, the King of Avanti had not gone through the missive that day. He had not accepted it even. If he had, he would be readily impressed by the pearl-drop-like handwriting. How amazingly picturesque was her calligraphy! Her narration and elaboration too were wonderful! Her expressions were so exquisite! In her letter, the shlokas of Sringara rasa had been excerpted too. What had she been made to learn by heart by Devadutta? Chaturika could remember nothing. She forgot all that she learnt. She had no idea for how long would her memory be able to retain this art of dancing, various mudras and the varying amorous postures and gestures! Going home straight from here, if she saw Uddhav, even her own face would appear like a stranger's!

Devadutta was doing and undoing different mudras in her hand. She moved to sit with her back on the wall by making and breaking the mudras. Before her, folding her knees, expanding her thighs sat Chaturika. Devadutta placed her hand on Chaturika's thighs and in a deep, intense voice asked, "Did that King's man relate the news of the King of Avanti"?

"Let go of that matter", Chaturika rejoined.

"I shall carve such a brilliant dancer out of you, that, the richest man of Avanti will be only your guest and that Uddhavnarayan will be relegated to the post of a sentry, I bet"!

"Let it be left at that! Subhag Dutta, the business magnate, has been enamoured of your beauty and talents as well", said Chaturika in a low voice.

"And that enchantment would take only thee into its folds, thou have to learn all such finesse from me and again who else is such feline-eyed like thee, in this city"?

"That is why I am ugly".

"Who says"? Devadutta touched the eyelids of Chaturika and in a muffled voice she said, "My mother was just a little dull-complexioned like thee, I have the blood of my father Antiochus in my veins; the Greeks are usually fair-complexioned, though they are attracted to the lissome, dark-complexioned women!"

Chaturika was beside herself in amazement! Lowering her face, she looked at herself. Fulsome, well-shaped breasts, banana-stalk-like thighs, silk-smooth skin! Tears welled up in her eyes. Whenever the King's man grew beastly in sexual hunger, he seemed to gobble her up. Her body stayed draped with an apparel. Could

Devadutta ever know that she bore innumerable scratches of nails and bites of teeth on her pair of breasts and her thighs? In order to ward these off, she needed some other inebriation. Sometimes she thought of screaming aloud in distress to let the citizens of the city, the passers-by and all others know of the oppressive behaviour of Uddhavnarayan. To get into sexual union with a whore against her will and inflicting tortures on her was nothing but a culpable offence. The King of Avanti would surely take measures against it, if duly informed.

Devadutta declared, "Listen Chaturika, I shall not perform this dance before anyone save King Bhartrihari, no, not even Lord Mahakaaleswar!"

Chaturika stuck out her hand to place it on the lips of Devadutta, thus stopping her short, and said,"Fie on you, what sinful words are you uttering?"

"Where do you find sin in it?"

"Mahakaal is the source of your inspiration, He is your foremost Guru!"

"I think of Kumar Bhartrihari inwardly, since when he used to frequent this place. At that time, nature began to speak through my body, my cells were aflutter with the onrush of blood, my physique kept blooming like a flower gradually, my mother used to exhort, only by grace of the King, a courtesan would be able to flourish her genius in every possible way. The pair of eyes of Kumar Bhartrihari still hogs my memory. With such rapt attention, he used to listen to my mother's words, give patient hearing to mother's views on the elucidation of dance, the rhythm of the bodies of man and woman, he had even seen me dancing, when Maa imparted lessons to me, teaching me which arrangement of feet, which mudras of hand or which movements of eyes would reveal which particular emotional state. At the back of my mind, the King only reigns supreme, King Bhartrihari is my sole inspiration."

"Let these words be locked in the recesses of your mind, dear friend!"

Devadutta iterated, "Whoever thou name, Mahakaal, Parvati or the milk-women, of whomsoever I narrated to you, are all formless, thou may always name them, but thou must have someone adorable, fit to be worshipped, who must be of flesh and blood and all thy education would be complete if thou remember him."

"Who is he? I cannot think of anyone save that Uddhav, the thought of whom sometimes leaves me romantic and sometimes scared"!

"I have already predicted that the richest person in this city will be won over by your qualities, even Army Chieftain Kumar Bikram would be impressed by you, Uddhavnarayan will then keep the door, I tell you".

Chaturika got startled, "No! No, my friend, if these words reach any ears somehow, I shall stand threatened, Uddhav will kill me, he is ruthless to the bottom, he is fond of oppressing others, let it be left at that, friend, let go of such words!" Chaturika kept panting while saying so. Her whole body kept trembling in excitement. She had seen Kumar Bikram. How valiant he was! What great a soldier he had been! He himself had subjugated the Huns! She had heard about the Army Chieftain from Uddhav. Very often, Uddhav used to talk about his being close to the Army Commander. In order to prove the extent of his might and influence, he used to talk about Kumar Bikram, Subhag Dutta, the merchant, while molesting her, while leaving her body sore with marks of scratch. Even engaging in varying postures of union, in reaching the acme of passionate frenzy, he used to narrate about Kumar Bikram. How strange! How could Devadutta talk about Kumar Bikram? On which assumption? She never wished to think of him. She felt small, she was struck with apprehension. How could she again name the merchant riding the golden chariot? Let these matters rest for now. Let this moment be obliterated,let this time be forgotten. Just like a lunar day, let it pass by. Chaturika drifted to another topic. In a muffled voice she said, "Do you have any idea, where is that poet now, the young gentleman from Gambhira, who sought your love"?

Devadutta went a little absent-minded, both her eyes turned above, the daughter of Rasamanjari grew indifferent, she kept muttering," You mean, that son of Dhruva, who used to narrate to me about Balkh, the river Oxus and the Greek hero, Alexander?"

"On your rejection, he has left for elsewhere bidding adieux to Avanti for good!"

"Yes, he has gone indeed, it is going to be a couple of years now, he had a profound knowledge of the Greeks, he promised to take me to Bidisha, a tomb has been erected there in the honour of Heliodorus, a Greek prince of Purushpur."

"You had given him much indulgence,hence he had fallen in love with you!"

"He was a man of virtues and he deserved respect for that, but if he took it to be", stopping in the middle of her words, Devadutta went listless, she was feeling sad for him.

"Grapevine has it that he has gone to the Kingdom of the Huns to seek refuge, by the north-west bank of the river Indus".

"Who told you"?

Chaturika maintained a studied silence. Devadutta would easily guess the name of the person who told her. For her, the source of information was just one. The young bloke had promised her to take her to the land of Balkh. Tender age! Both of them were of the same age. He used to behave like a child. He was strikingly handsome! Quite wise too! He was all praise for her talents. But how everything went haywire at last! Devadutta turned around to stretch her gaze to the sky! The light of the firmament was about to fade. It was afternoon. She closed her eyes. Devadutta was all ears to listen to the murmur of the river, Oxus, in her imagination. She went motionless, all alone. The richest merchant of this city, Subhag Dutta, had insulted the youth. The youth's father and he had become partners in a trade, years ago. His insult was much more brutal than hers. The trader, Subhag Dutta, had arranged for the youth's education and sent him in here. Again, he was the man who hounded him out of this city, humiliating him utterly.

Devadutta heaved a sigh. He was not a man to seek shelter at the Huns, no, not by any means. Yes, she was reminded of his face. He seemed to take after a Greek, doubtlessly. Or, did he look like a God? How solemn his blue eyes had been! How strange the youth was! He used to glean information on travelling to the lands of the merchants, who used to come on trade to Ujjwain. Those locales- the land of Balkh, river Oxus, Kandahar, Purushpur, the ravines in the mountains, all swam before his eyes! The Greek traders were taken by surprise! When had the brat gone to those lands? She could not ward off the humiliation, Dhruvaputra had to undergo. Rather, it spread like wildfire that she had chased him out of the city by insulting him severely. At her insistence, the merchant Subhag Dutta had beaten Dhruvaputra, black and blue, the man who had offered him shelter turned rude enough to oust him from the city! How was the nature of the youth? How was it so, that the young bloke who had profound knowledge at his command, unquenchable curiosity for knowing more at his disposal, illimitable imagination to bank upon, had not the least assumption of the affinity of his father's friend? How could he relate his inner desire to Subhag Dutta?! Again, how could Devadutta, who was adept in reading the mind of a man fail to comprehend Dhruvaputra's mind? Only Chaturika could read the matter well. She threw a hint at her, "My friend, have you noticed the eyes of Dhruvaputra, whom the merchant has sent in"?

"Blue, just like the blue ocean, I heard an ocean to be like that".

"I know the colour 'blue', and when that blue turns bluer, have you marked how desirous of you he becomes, my friend"?

Devadutta had laughed away the words of Chaturika. But was it true? Didn't she quiver in desire, eyeing Dhruvaputra?

Seven

Queen Bhanumati's toilette was about to finish. The old maid Nipunika kept observing her minutely. If, by any chance, a little remiss somewhere went undetected! The queen stood in front of the mirror. The day was Shukla Chaturdashi. Why she had dressed up as a lady, keen on an assignation, was beyond the comprehension of Nipunika. Tomorrow would be the Aghran Purnima. A hearsay did round that King Bhartrihari would be going to Mahakaal. However, that which was doing rounds in the inner court of the palace might not be true. Again, on the contrary, something true might not reach their ears. Uttering the truth might cause umpteen problems. The maid Nipunika knew well that turning blind eye to everything would be the best.

The mirror was watching Bhanumati, the queen. The mirror reflected her wide eyes. The eyes wore a strange look. Nipunika had learnt about this glare from Rasamanjari. The eyelids were a bit a-flutter, the vision, blurred, though a profound excitement of passion stood pervasive. An engrossment in pleasure was exactly what stood distinct in Bhanumati, at that moment. Nipunika, however, kept watching her eyes only! Those eyes sometimes reflected elegant charm, sometimes pleasant gratification, again at moments it displayed perplexity and sometimes again just a long gaze! Sometimes in a half-trance, when her eyeballs made slight movements, the fragrance of sandalwood pervaded the room, and the imagination kept igniting pleasure from within, leaving her nonplussed. A moment ago, when the queen was busy sprinkling sandal-dust on her breasts, her eyes exhibited a look, which could only be found in someone, if inebriated! Two eyelids grew so heavy that the eyeballs seemed to have been concealed. In wide-eyed wonder, Nipunika had marked the queen's breasts tighten in intense desire! She was even overcome by fear. Was then the queen indulging in self-love in her mind? Alack, what a pity, oh queen of Avanti!

Nipunika was a resident of this inner house since long. She had been here since the reign of King Gandharvasen. She was adept in dealing with cosmetics and nitty-gritty of adornment. She had all tricks of toiletry at her fingertips. She was proficient in making the ugly look beautiful. She also knew that it was even more an uphill task to make the beautiful look a shade more graceful than upgrading the ordinary to the status of a beauty! She had observed that a paragon of beauty turned shorn of her grace if she was subject to much embellishments and toiletries. All cosmetics and jewellery stood futile in front of the beauty of queen Bhanumati. Nipunika had mastered this art under the tutelage of Rasamanjari. Rasamanjari used to say that if anyone adorning herself thought that all her beauty was for God only, her looks would be graciously manifested. While reminding queen of Avanti of this truth, Bhanumati had burst into a peal of laughter, expressing, "Oh, how silly such things sound! Will God ever certify how beautiful I am! Only he will appreciate my looks for whom I am dressing up so meticulously"!

"Never say so, Lord Mahakaal is there"!

Folding her palms in reverence, praying to Lord Mahakaal inwardly, Bhanumati said, "Let Lord Mahakaaleswar be there, I pay my respects to Him, but my grace is only for him, of whom I think always".

Who knew what had befallen the queen of Avanti! She, who had given up dressing primly, had got down to dolling herself up today! Since the noon, Nipunika seemed to construct the goddess of beauty, bit by bit. Decking her with Karabi blossoms, she made the queen of Avanti wear a long necklace, golden bangles, ear-danglers, moon-wreath, and armlets. She had dyed her feet with lacquer. And, she had added a bright golden sparkle to the skin of the queen by daubing it with sandal-granules. The queen had matured in years. The dame of fourteen of yesteryears would be completing another fourteen years in this city of Avanti. That tender, full-moon-beauty grew mesmerizing now. The old maid Nipunika had felt the warmth of Bhanumati's body for quite sometime. But at this age, the body would better have turned cool. And the body would gradually turn cooler too. The queen of Avanti was just like the Goddess Lakshmi of the Avanti household. How would she survive with such heat on her body?

Nipunika had sensed that the queen's charming body had not lost an iota of heat even after smearing sandal paste all over, at such cold wintry Aghran. The maid had marked how her breasts were about to explode, tearing through her brassieres. After all, the mind's reflection is borne by the body! At each moment, the endearing, beauteous gaze of the Lakshmi of the city of Avanti was changing! The mildness was fading out from the eyelashes and the eyeballs. All of a sudden, the eyeballs began to rotate, marked with brisk movements and the eyelashes upturned! The old maid was, however, not unfamiliar with such emotional crests and troughs. Who could tell what was surfacing in the mind of the queen, in quick succession? She, herself, only knew what she was imagining. The wizened handmaid even scared to fancy that. Closing the eyes would mean an utter relief.

Bhanumati turned around to face the maid, the momentary bewilderment was no more there on her face, flashing a smile of gratification she asked, "Is everything all right"?

Nipunika kept looking at the queen. Her gaze lowered to the part of the Mekhala wound round her waist, down to the navel. In an indistinct voice she asked, "Aren't you feeling the chill, my dear queen"?

Whither is winter, no rains had been here this time, naturally winter too would not appear.

The northerly winds have begun to make their presence felt, if you go to Mahakaal, go by covering your head and putting on woollens.

"Winter too is absent", Bhanumati spoke under her breath.

The old maid kept fixing her with an overwhelmed gaze. So beautiful was the queen of Avanti, and the charm intensified with each passing day! Nipunika said, smilingly, "You look far more beautiful, Maa".

This statement shot up a look of intense obsession in the eyes of Bhanumati. Her glance grew askance. A crooked smile flashed across her lips, she inquired, "Does it owe to the magic of your fingers or mine"?

Nipunika, the maid gathered courage to reply, "It owes to your husband, it's the trick of his fingers, Maa".

"Keep quiet, you maid, shut up, thou transgress all limits"!

Nipunika's face turned pale. She could not have her grip on anything in the inner house, something had gone amiss in here! Whatever she said was apt and necessary. At least, Rasamanjari had taught her thus. Was there any wife who would turn deaf ears to the eulogy of her husband?

The queen seemed to discover herself anew from different angles in front of the mirror! She was holding herself a-blossom before the looking-glass, again and again. And pirouetting round, what flashed across her mind God knew, she asked, "What would one do if the mirrors had not been there"?

The old maid did not answer. It was better to keep quiet as an intelligent human. With each day, Bhanumati was growing whimsical, nonchalant! It was difficult to make out what exactly made the queen wrathful!

Bhanumati kept wiggling the fingers of both her hands to form mudras, and said, "The very mirror is the man to me, don't you take a mirror as the male? See how it sucks us in"!

All seemed to be beyond the comprehension of Nipunika, the maid. She was enjoying the graceful, playful movements as reflected in the looking-glass. She was swaying her body and the neck before the mirror, graceful postures of the body owed much to the various ways of shuffling of feet. The queen muttered, "Dressing up for me is for the mirror, I enjoy looking at myself".

Nipunika sought her permission, "May I take your leave now?"

"No, why should thou go away"? Bhanumati turned around, she plunged in the seat by then. She seemed to get lost in a thought and abruptly she ordered, "Now take off all that adorns me".

"Why?" The maid was visibly startled.

"Please take off this Swarnatilak"! Bhanumati touched her head.

The maid kept looked, amazed, at the queen of Avanti. The queen was saying, "Yes, I have dolled myself up, the reason no more exists. But why have I dressed up, it would be better if... hello Nipunika, why have I adorned myself?"

Nipunika did not have the slightest idea. The queen was supposed to stay beautifully dressed up. The King would pay a visit to this inner house in the evening. Would he like to see his queen, without proper embellishments? The queen was swaying as she sat. She was knitting her fingers into different mudras to hold them up before her eyes. Some of them, the maid was familiar with. The queen was arranging her ten fingers of both hands to form the mudras denoting lust and desire. Desire was appearing distinct in her eyes, eyebrows, nose and lips. The old maid knew the queen, in and out. Yet these days she failed to fathom her mind as she did it before. How strange! She did not have to help her dress up ever since she came along as a close companion of the newly-wed young damsel to Avanti from Kankhal. She did not have to touch the body of that pleasure-loving wife of the King. The Princess of Kankhal used to dress up herself, keeping her standing there to watch. Sometimes again, she used to get her husband dress her up. How fervent she was at that time! The whole day got devoted to dolling her up. This inner palace stayed redolent with the fragrance of sandalwood. All had undergone change over so many years! Indolence became the sole companion of the childless queen. The maid stood doubting the whims of the capricious queen, her eagerness of doing or not doing a thing!

Bhanumati inquired, "Oh Maid, what for am I dressing up today?"

Maid Nipunika stayed silent awhile, and a little later she mumbled, "Tomorrow is slated for a visit to Mahakaal".

Bhanumati replied, "Mahakaal has deceived me always".

The old maid lifted her folded palms to her forehead, saying, "Why Maa, you are a Princess as well as a 'Queen' all because of the will of Lord Mahakaal, you are enjoying the company of your husband, you are the apple of his eye! Lord Mahakaal has showered precious gifts on you!"

Bhanumati raised both her hands to free her forehead from Swarnatilak. She spun round to look into the mirror and kept muttering, "Lord Mahakaal has blessed me with everything and again with nothing, I am just a destitute, Nipunika"!

The old woman's eyes got moistened. The queen was ruing for the unborn offspring. Though childless, there was no dearth in the King's love for her. If the King of Avanti willed, he could marry once again. But he had not done that. It proved how profound was his love for the queen.Bhanumati wailed, "Can't it happen to me now, Nipunika"?

Maid Nipunika consoled her, "Why not Maa"?

"The royal physician failed, no sacrificial offerings to God bore any fruit, benediction of a hundred Brahmins too went in vain, even feeding rice to the hungry fell through ... what will happen to me, Nipunika"?

Nipunika stood silent. What would she say? She was no less astonished herself! A child was not born even after observing all such rituals! Was she then a fruitless tree? She even whispered sundry mantras to her ears, and consulting the ancient seers of Avanti she informed her the perfect day and time of intercourse, and tallying the position of the moon and other stars accordingly, the King and the queen went to bed. The union proved to be in vain. Nipunika even visited the bawdyhouse to cull tips on lovemaking but that too did not work. King Bhartrihari was a veteran in lovemaking, adept in sexual union, as she learnt from the queen, but all proved to be fruitless.

Bhanumati demanded of her, "Have you learnt anything new"?

Nipunika replied, "About a couple of miles to the West of Avanti, even beyond Gambhira, in the lap of a far-off hilly range, a spiritually-enlightened female-hermit has come—would you like to consult her, Maa"?

Bhanumati was untying her necklace quite gingerly, she unhooked her brassiere too. Her eyes were closed. She seemed to doze off.

The maid continued, "She is from Vaishali, she mastered the art of Tantra and chanting mantras from the distant land of Praagjyotishpur, situated beyond the Lohitya river to the distant north-east. She stands a fair chance of solving this problem".

Opening her eyes wide, Bhanumati asked, "Who had passed on such an information to you"?

The maid looked hither and thither. Today the inner court was safe, though the walls too had ears. In a lowered voice, she said, "I went to her, Maa, how sweet was her speech, she is quite old, she might be a hundred-year-old woman or even a two-hundred-year-old one. I heard that there is a seat of Kamadeva in Praagjyotishpur. Making a woman pregnant is just an easy task for that hermit-lady to accomplish. Would you like to see her, Maa"?

"When did you go"?

"Day before yesterday, on the day of Ekadashi".

"But you never told me"?

"What to tell, Maa, I feel very sad, the queen of Avanti is childless, I went to see her on an information, but she is keen on seeing you, she cannot decide anything without meeting you up".

"Can't she come here, herself"? An ardour showed up on the queen's face.

"How will she come, Maa, the Brahmin savants despise her, she is Vajrayani, she practises brutal pagan ways of life. She never pays a visit to anybody's residence".

The queen had gone silent. The old maid's words were not a fib. The doorkeeper would never allow the lady ascetic to enter. If she had to enter the city, she would do it stealthily, in the dark. The female ascetics of the heretic faith never would come down among the people of any hamlet. They would have to approach her instead.

Bhanumati asked, "What if I go to her"?

The old maid servant was visibly scared, "How will you go there, Maa? If you can, it will be fantastic, just bowing down to her with an offering of five betel-leaves, five guvak nuts, a handful of mustard seeds, and five gold coins would do".

"When shall I go, tell me, on which tithi"?

The old woman whispered, "You will go, fine… but will it be a secret, Maa"?

"Can't she be invisible? I heard that female sages may nullify their physical presence and be invisible with the aid of 'yogic' forces, doesn't she know the art of being invisible"?

"What sort of art is that, Maa"?

"To remain invisible".

"Won't she know, she knows everything, and these are just futile things to her".

"Then let her come being invisible to mortal eyes".

Nipunika, her maid was in for trouble. Then she had to approach that ascetic with such words of request. But even if she kept herself imperceptible to ordinary eyes with the aid of 'yoga', will her presence be unperceived? People say that even the Brahmins and the priests can practice such art. They can look into the Heavens, cosmos and the earth and they claim that no knowledge regarding the heaven and the earth elude them. If Nipunika were held responsible for everything in the long last, then? She might run the risk of being decapitated too. The doorkeeper would not know, the King, the minister, the Army chieftain, none will have any knowledge of it and a stranger would make a foray into the inner recess of the palace! It would be better if the queen herself went to see her. Let her apprise the King of this matter and others too. She would then set out on her mission to see the lady hermit. The maid, Nipunika, would accompany her, serving obediently at her feet.

The queen opined, "And again the lady charmers know a lot of things, they know the art of mesmerizing others, Tantra and chanting mantras. If I covet someone and fail to get him, they would even come to my aid by making me get the person I long for. Aren't all this true"?

Nipunika replied, "Perhaps…"

"I heard it to be true". Saying so, the queen began to untie the flower-wreath from her hair. The petals of Kunda blossoms got strewn on the stone floor. As she was about to undo her bun, Nipunika came shouting in protest. "What are you up to, Maa? After such elaborate dress-up, the chignon was tied for long. Why are you dismantling all, let me call Kanchuki, let him see the King and let the King come in".

Bhanumati raised her hand to intervene, "Stop it! Hasn't the King seen me in haute couture"?

"Is there any other man in Avanti like him? He is the King of Avanti in the real sense of the term. He annuls the invitation of Devadutta, the harlot repeatedly, never sets his gaze on any other woman, though everything here belongs to him, who else is more fortunate than you? You have no other woman to share your husband with, even though the Brahmin priests suggested a second marriage, he hasn't yet gone for it" —

"Stop, Nipunika, stop all that nonsense, I cannot put up with that golden fortune"!

To her utter dismay Nipunika observed, the queen was about to give up her apparels and ornaments, she was decked with. Bhanumati was muttering, "I wish he would see Devadutta, the whore, if he marries her, I stand saved, I would no longer be held guilty".

The old maid said, "The fallen woman knows the wiles and even a lot more things, but you are matchless in your beauty, compared to you, she is uncouth, ugly indeed".

Suddenly, Bhanumati burst out in anger! She went in a tizzy. Her head sprung upward and downward, her eyeballs grew restless, the eyelashes fluttered, her voice rasped, turned harsh as she said, "Just hold your tongue, will you? How dare you compare me with a whore? I was the Princess of Kankhal, a prostitute is a prostitute, after all"!

The maid, elderly and wizened, was overcome with fear. She began to tremble. Joining her two palms she lowered her head on the feet of the queen and wailed, "You are doubtlessly a goddess, the Lakshmi of Avanti, let me be forgiven, Maa, I did not have any ulterior motive in saying so".

Bhanumati was back in joy again, gently, by degrees. The intimidated maid had moved quite a few steps back. She stood with her head, hung low. Bending both her hands backwards, Bhanumati was trying to weave a chignon. Her swollen breasts heaved in inhalation and exhalation. While tying the bun, she looked at the old maid, twitching her neck aside. In a muffled voice, she issued an order to her, "Go then, to the Army Chieftain, Bikram, to inform that I shall be coming to play dice with him, this evening".

Nipunika, the maid, was really fearing this. She was even apprehending that this might happen. Why she had dolled herself up was now clear to her. Her conjecture did not prove false. She found the queen to dress up once again as a beloved, keen on meeting her lover.

Bhanumati said, "What if I go to his place? Go now, deliver the message".

Retracing her steps, one behind the other, the maid reached the door and stood there. She was familiar with this inner court, since ages. Who else would know the inner house better than her? Leaving the queen in inner recess of the palace, King Gandharvasen used to send invites to the harlot, Rasamanjari, into the room overlooking the sea, at the end of the arbour. She had seen the sad face of the two wives of Gandharvasen. Gandharvasen thrust the swing forward on which his younger queen sat, and his wife, the mother of Bhartrihari, shed tears, indoors. King Gandharvasen of Avanti was absorbed in aquatic sports with the queen, with the newly-bloomed damsel, while the older queen stayed bowing down to Lord Shiva, the guardian deity of the family, all the time. She had witnessed the wrath of the queens as well as that of the humiliated wives of the King! Both the queens were on the way to the brothel, and Nipunika, the maid, kept leading them there. Both of them hid their faces behind the veil. They went to Rasamanjari to beg their husband of her. They were captivated, they stood enchanted by the grace and talents of Rasamanjari! They learnt several tricks of winning a man's heart, of novel postures of sexual intimacy from Rasamanjari. The women who kept indoors did not know what the whores did. They would never know. No way had been there to know.

All of a sudden, the queen demanded, "Devadutta, I mean, the whore, how beautiful is she, in reality"?

"I do not know, Maa, I know next to nothing".

"Go there, reach Kumar Bikram the message, go with this flower-wreath, tell him that I have bitten the petals of this flower, hence one or two have dropped off, tell him that this is the garland I wore, it bears the warmth of my breasts, go Nipunika, make haste, you old lady, make sure that none hears you, tell him that if he fails to turn up, the lines of kajal on my eyes would disappear"…

What would the old maid do now? She kept walking out of indoors, with ginger steps, concealing the flower-wreath under her shawl. How sprawling the inner wing of the palace was! So many rooms! Where would the queen and her brother-in-law sit together, who could tell! The old maid's face bore no mark of any reaction now. How could these things be new to her? Just a few days back, it was she who sent Devadutta's missive to the King!

EIGHT

Uddhavnarayan had come to pay a visit to the feline Chaturika. Uddhav had promised to come to her place on the full-moon night of Aghran, hence she did not allow any visitor that evening. She even asked many to leave from her door. Among them,there was a trader from Magadh too. He was ready to pay loads of gold coins. But Chaturika dared not welcome him to her room. She would not be able to stay back in this city antagonizing Uddhavnarayan, which would result in her being chucked out to build a shack in the red-light zone, outside the precincts of Ujjwain. But the pimp, Mahaparshwa, had allured the merchant of Magadh from the inn to this place, with much guiles. The merchant was known to be an honest man. He came to halt at Ujjwain on his way to Mathura. He possessed immense wealth. He was of refined taste. Showing him around many rooms, he could make him decide upon Chaturika and winked at her to make her understand that he was rich enough to extract money.

Uddhav did not come on that full moon night. He turned up on the day of Pratipad. Uddhav said that he had been employed for keeping a vigil on the Mahakaal Temple and it fell on his lap so suddenly.

Pious, virtue-seeking souls used to throng up to Mahakaal temple, in droves. Numerous bad elements might have been there among them. Hence, Army Chief Kumar Bikram had trusted him with the responsibility of inspecting the Mahakaal temple. The King and the queen decided to set out to Mahakaal, the peacock-boat on the Gandhavati river stood decked up accordingly, the players were ready with the Veena in their hands, the hoi polloi were debarred from entering the temple-yard right from the afternoon, the devadasis got ready for their dance recitals, and the fallen woman, Devadutta, too had gone there in the evening.

Chaturika grew curious, "When did the King come, where did the queen stand, on his left or on the right"?

Uddhav ordered, "Come, arrange the goblets".

Chaturika grumbled, "You have to make good for yesterday's absence and today's visit as usual, a couple of days I mean, My Lord!"

Uddhav, in his mind, kept musing, Hey you, harlot, you could have enjoyed to your heart's content with the merchant from Magadh! I am back just within three hours from Mahakaal, I could have returned even earlier. But I chose not to, as I got a new wench at the priest's and in the outhouse of the priest, we had a whale of time together, but a too-young damsel had a lot of trouble to give, she kept on weeping so bitterly that my desire died young. However, if I came to know about the Magadh merchant's presence in your room, I would have caused you severe pain. Chaturika said, "Subhag Dutta, the merchant, came to Devadutta's room in the late hours of night, after her return from Mahakaal".

Uddhav went on mentally, I am not in the same plight as his, having immense wealth at my disposal, I could have easily brought in a pure foreigner woman from the land of the Greeks! The merchant had fallen for Devadutta, and the whore was just a nitwit! She could have made fortune if she desired but she failed.

Chaturika blabbed, "But you haven't spoken of the King and his queen".

Uddhav noticed that the whore was overcome with desire that evening. She had stretched her two painted feet forward, in front of Uddhav. Uddhav grew a little restless. He jabbed his forefinger into Chaturika's feet and kept mumbling, "But neither the King nor the queen had turned up".

"Oh Lord! But why"? Chaturika feigned ignorance.

Uddhav did not answer. It was unlawful to talk about the King and the queen in this red-light ghetto. Being the King's man, he had no inkling of any motive of anyone here. Who could tell, where and how someone was eavesdropping the secret. He had fished out a small, silk reticule from his waist. He kept it near the feet of Chaturika. Chaturika pretended ignorance of its presence and inquired again, "Didn't the King and the queen go there"?

Uddhav was irked. Such curiosity was simply unbecoming of a whore. He grew somewhat suspicious and kept observing Chaturika minutely, rather all of a sudden. He began employing her knowledge of body-language. He kept watching the pair of eyes of the prostitute keenly. What did Chaturika want to say? Disallowing the trader of Magadh in her room was hardly a proof of any kind at all. It might be a ruse. Who would emulate a woman in storing diplomatic wits in her brains? Who would be more sly than a woman and a fallen one at that? Women are too devilish, and their weapon, their strength lies inside the brain. The sages, no doubt, had opined that the women are the source of all evil. A woman can make or break anything, she could even implicate him quite easily! Uddhavnarayan grew more wary as he kept on thinking deeply. Which other way would be the best for a woman to render service save entertainment? Uddhav kept measuring Chaturika with suspicion in his eyes. What did the sages predict about the dark-complexioned young women? Uddhav failed to recall, yet he was certain that they had nothing to speak in favour of them! A woman with well-shaped breasts and hips was a trigger to lust, even though she was dusky-complexioned like clouds. Lust is nothing but the forerunner of all disasters. Uddhav could not reach any decision on vetting Chaturika with his keen gaze. This prostitute was of 'Hastini' character, that is, inordinately lustful, yet that could not prove anything concretely though. Uddhav was thinking, it would have been wonderful if something could be proved, if the doubts would be authenticated! If he could catch Chaturika as an accomplice in any collusion, then he could transfer her straight from the whorehouse to the prison, and from there just out of the city, chopping her two hands off!He could stand a chance of promotion in that case, a better position in the Royal Court, at least! Did he have that fortune coming his way? If a woman was lost, ten such women would come to replace her but was it so easy to trace any conspiracy? He had been in the Royal Court since ages, he was even employed as a sessions-judge, but had he ever been successful in putting any conspirator behind the bars? It would have been fantastic if he could do so. Then Gandhavati, that girl of Gambhira, would come to grovel at his feet. Which object could not be bought by power ever? Is there any power greater than the Royal one in this world?

Uddhav asked, "Was the trader really from Magadh or a Greek from the West"?

Chaturika was tickled to peals of noisy laughter, "Go search for him, go along with Mahaparshwa to find out the inn where he has put up, he took a fancy on me, but I declined his offer only for you, hey dear, you did not tell me why the King and the queen had not attended".

Flicker of misgivings made Uddhav wary, he answered, "The queen had been down with headache".

"Who told you"?

"It is from the inner house. Why haven't you opened the reticule as yet?"

Moving the bag aside, Chaturika stuck out her naked shanks and lacquered feet towards Uddhav, and giggled, saying, "I, too, told the merchant from Magadh that I had a bad headache, I was out of sorts, I feigned all that, so how could he approach me?"

Uddhav was looking at Chaturika with wide-eyed wonder. He seemed not to get the words of Chaturika, though he thought he could. Bending down on Chaturika, he rested his hand on her well-fleshed thigh, over the attire she wore. He kept muttering, "How can I say what has gone wrong in the inner house of the palace? Who can say? The city of Avanti is going to dogs because of the childless King, he is not even marrying for the second time, has he done it right"?

Suddenly Chaturika was caught by the words of Uddhavnarayan and fixed him with an astonished look. Why was he saying it all, such off-hand? Her case had nothing to do at all with that of the King and the queen!

Uddhav went on, "This is just ominous. Can a childless King bring happiness and prosperity to this Kingdom? These words are doing rounds everywhere. Can't you see how drought is raging across the land? The King has no right to occupy the throne anymore"!

Chaturika's eyeballs glowed. A flash of smile could be seen at the corner of her lips, she said, "Right, the King has much responsibilities, there is no rain, but why are there no sacrificial rites to make it happen"?

Uddhav rejoined, "The King does not run the administration well".

Chaturika said, "Exactly so. But I think, that is only in the inner wing of his palace".

"The people of Avanti are deprived of happiness as well as sleep".

Chaturika swung her head saying, "But I enjoy good sleep indeed".

"Now, the throne of Avanti would change hands, would you tell me who could be the rightful claimant to it, the Army-Commander or the richest man of the city: Subhag Dutta? If a merchant ascends the throne, business and trade would get a fillip and the city, too, would catapult to a better state and even the rich would shoot up in number".

Chaturika's face showed visible signs of change in expression. She was astonished. It was followed by a loud laughter and her words of protest, "What are you saying? You are very clever, my name is Chaturika, and you are the slyest of all Sessions Judges, you have come to test me in the guise of a pleasure-seeker, no King on this earth would emulate the virtues of the King of Avanti, he is a man with a poet's mind!"

Uddhav's face changed colours. Oh God! How blatantly he committed a mistake! On the one hand, his trick was revealed to Chaturika, and on the other, he let her know the words which were rife in the city at present! He had been here for joy. Last night was the worst for him. Raping had accorded him a kind of pleasure no doubt, but the wails of the woman drained out that comfort absolutely! It would have been better if he dropped in at Chaturika's, instead. How strange! Why did he grow keen on testing the harlot? Was the whore a claimant to the throne? Or, did she nurse the thought of ascending the throne at the back of her mind, that too stealthily?Yonder, Chaturika had draped her uncovered body, limbs and feet with a mekhala. She had concealed her body behind a soft stole. Uddhav construed that he had played his dice wrong. It was the fallen woman who kept gauging him, instead, for so long.

Uddhav tried to smile, "Why shall I test you? Please pour drink in the goblet, please open the reticule to see what I have come with for my Chaturika! Not even the trader from Magadh would have given you such ornaments!"

"What have you brought along? This Chandrahaar?"

"Please see on your own by opening it".

"A necklace, an armlet"?

"Why don't you open it"?

"Swarnatilak, anklet, coronet, golden bangles"?

"Ah, why don't you see yourself"?

Chaturika unfastened the reticule, negligently. A pearl necklace slipped out from within, she kept eyeing the pearl-beads with utter nonchalance.

"Do you like it, my pussy?" Uddhav flicked at the cheeks of Chaturika.

Chaturika waved her head slowly, she said, "I do not have any need of such things".

Uddhavnarayan was visibly startled. What was the harlot saying? Was she planning to press him for more? If pearl necklace was not her choice, which one would she go for? Did the trader from Magadh visit her then? Did he enter the room? Chaturika was holding back everything from him, perhaps.

Again doubts went assailing Uddhav's mind. His calling demanded such suspicion. He loved to suspect. If he could find out that this whore was involved in collusion with the merchant from Magadh against the King, his promotion was certain. Such sex-workers would line up in droves if he looked out for. Animals and birds used to jostle in the Kartikpurnima fair; women, too, were available in plenty - sold in the fair as well as outside.

Chaturika kept mumbling, " Mahalata, Chandrahaar, Swarnatilak, armlets, bangles, anklets, and again necklace of so many varieties! Even I do not know the names of all these ornaments, would you like to take a look, Mr. Sessions Judge"?

Doubt intensified. Uddhav kept measuring Chaturika with misgivings writ large on his eyes. He would love to be suspicious of her. If doubt got intense, he would be smitten badly with lust! His body would thrill with romance all over. Both the lips would dry up. Uddhavnarayan moistened his lips with the fluid of his tongue. He prayed in his mind, Oh Lord Mahakaal,let the suspicion be true. Women are mute weaklings,no pleasure could be better than doubting them. Uddhav imagined, Chaturika, the harlot, had been thrown behind the bars on the charge of colluding against the King. He would ensure that she be terribly oppressed in the prison by predators, and would get her raped by the sentries. A conspiracy against the King?! Which sin could be more heinous than this? How easy it was to punish a woman, a harlot at that! The savants and the sages have already opined that, a whore cannot be trusted! Uddhav's inhaling and exhaling got deeper in excitement. If his suspicion would prove to be true, both the ears of the whore, Chaturika, could be peeled off. If he could succeed in doing this, his respect in the Royal Court would be double-fold, in the bawdy-houses he would be attended by many more comfort-women. His suspicion must come true, otherwise Chaturika, who used to satisfy his bodily needs for free, who could be won over by one or two gold coins, would not dare turn blind eye to the wreath made of hundred wavy pearl beads! How exquisitely carved was this pearl necklace, Uddhav was keen on gifting her, since Deepavali! He failed to collect it. He had to get it in gratis, for sure! This necklace, this divine, wavy-beaded necklace he would have to get one more, for Gandhavati! Uddhav was overcome by utter distrust! Now he had to know the name of the new paramour of Chaturika, by hook or by crook. Which man from a foreign land? Was he still there in this city? Lady-luck would smile on him, if he could succeed in imprisoning both the accomplices together. Where were the jewelleries, Chaturika was naming? Where exactly? What was the whore saying? On the full moon night, she got such jewellery that they were enough to cover her body! No drapery was needed for the body let alone the floral ornaments! She broke into giggles as she had varieties of necklace to wrap her breasts up, no need of any brassiere was there! She seemed to have got all the gems of the King's treasure-trove last night! Her body would be swathed in gold. She was waiting for Uddhav, she would bedeck herself with that jewellery, just under his gaze!

Oh God, what a mess! Uddhav's eyes opened wide in astonishment. His body temperature shot up. Was Chaturika a prostitute, in its truest sense? Dance-steps that she learnt were of no use at all. If she met a proper connoisseur, she would have to go to the outskirts of the city to earn her bread by prostitution. She was here for the kindness of Devadutta and the mercy of Uddhavnarayan. Did ever Uddhav forget to remind her so? Didn't he ever remind her repeatedly that she was here by the grace of the Army-Chief? Yes, the charm of this whore's youth was simply stunning! This youth was definitely fabulous for enjoyment! But whoever is not blessed with youth, who doesn't look her best in youth- all do, even a bitch does! A young damsel is nothing but an object of desire! Did he have any dearth of youthful women? He was a part of the Royal Force. All these came his way unencumbered, as it happened last night! Even the old Brahmin, the main assistant of the Chief Priest, was entitled to feast on her flesh at his will, let alone the Chief priest himself! Who had presented Chaturika with such loads of jewellery? Was she worthy of all that? Could anyone ever receive such treasures just for sexual intercourse or adeptness in the art of lovemaking?

Chaturika got to her feet. Toting a big silk portmanteau from the room inside, she left it on the floor. A strange noise from a blended collision of metal and stones could be heard. Uddhav started. He turned to see. The door was bolted as ever. This silk bag was quite precious! This could not be used by all and sundry. Could an ordinary citizen give away all her ornaments, such bagful? Then the sun would definitely rise in the west.

Uddhav asked in a dry voice, "All the ornaments"?

"Yes, open it to check".

"A—ll"! Uddhav kept looking at the whore with his eyes wide in wonder! Now, she took off all the jewelleries, save the floral trinkets with which she adorned herself. He did not look at the bag. He seized Chaturika with both hands and demanded, "Are these all gold, these gems and jewels"?

"Just see on your own"! Chaturika burst into a ringing laughter, "I would never be able to cull such treasures in all my life, neither you nor I had seen such plenty"!

Uddhav kept musing to himself, "You may not see, but who says that I shall not get to see in future, you floozy?" While muttering, Uddhav stole a look at the uncovered mouth of the portmanteau. Inside the room, a lamp was lit and it was not reaching the bag, though, the sparkling glitter from the bag seemed enough to light up the whole of the room. The night was in its wee hours. Chaturika had accrued such an amount of jewellery, for which she must have committed some sin. No crime, no reward! Uddhavnarayan got much more excited to tear off the brassiere, that Chaturika wore. Chaturika screamed, "What are you doing, eh? Why are you so keen today? Let me arrange the flagon and the goblet and drink wine." Freeing herself from the clutch of Uddhav mightily, Chaturika began to fill the goblet with wine. Then, Uddhav warily touched the portmanteau. His hands seemed to be scorched by its heat. He kept putting the ornaments on the floor, taking each from the bag, both his hands being loaded with the jewellery. It was even more than what Chaturika had said. Who could gift her such jewel-sets? Abruptly, Uddhav's body temperature slumped. His doubt might prove wrong or just to the contrary. Perhaps the King, the King himself had been charmed by this whore! Last night, the King had not gone to the Mahakaal. Did he come here instead? What an utter ruin! Then he would be thrown into the prison! What an audacity of a petty servant of the royal court to enter the room of a whore, chosen by the King for himself? Or was it Kumar Bikram who came here? Or Subhag Dutta, the merchant? A woman who could cater to the sexual desire of such men would definitely be a gem herself! She was much more valuable than all those chunks of jewellery! Uddhav recoiled in the dazzle of the ornaments. He cast a frightened glance at the fallen woman. He failed to assess the worth of this whore himself. Was she fit for getting so much? He was just a dolt! Would Chaturika ever fetch this portmanteau to him displaying all the jewelleries inside, if there had been any reason for suspicion in the least? Uddhavnarayan sat with his head bent low. He should have perceived it earlier. Now he would have to seek mercy of this whore, bowing down his head to her feet and escaping thereafter. If she got a call from either the King or the Army-Chieftain or the merchant, then? He had torn off her bra. What a daring crime! He could even have to undergo a serious punishment like getting his left hand chopped off, by the order of His Highness!

Chaturika had offered the goblet to him, covering her naked breasts with a fine piece of cloth. She bent in front of him, asking in a cajoling, unctuous tone, "Hey my love, hey dear Sessions Judge, have you fallen asleep"?

NINE

Uddhav had gone tipsy after swigging two sips of wine. He was feeling dizzy. The light inside the room appeared brighter to his eyes. Chaturika had disembowelled the jewel-box on her well-made bed. The gems were sparkling. After boozing, Uddhav could not sit straight. His dizziness was leaving him more debilitated. Chaturika had grabbed a gem-studded necklace in her hand from the pile of ornaments and asked, "Do you know the name of this necklace?"

Uddhav swayed his head in the negative. Tears were clouding his vision. Alas, who knew Chaturika to be so talented? Uddhavnarayan gawked at Chaturika's face in amazement. He was now ready to push off. He would have to know the fact from Mahaparshwa, the pimp. Suddenly the inebriated Uddhav was overcome with lust. He began to pine for the absence of his beloved. Chaturika would now rise far higher, he would have to keep her door, it seemed. He would have to carry out the order of the Army-Commander. He was quite scared of Kumar Bikram, the Army-Chieftain! His very presence in front of him made him go weak in the knees, trembling! To face the King was even more difficult — it left him jittery. However, it never had happened before he became a servant of the King! As an ordinary citizen he had gone to the Royal Court, many a time. He had even gone to Subhag Dutta, the merchant, a number of times. Now, he had to stand before the merchant with a lowered countenance. The merchant had a profound influence on the Royal Court. Uddhav feared if Subhag Dutta, the merchant, came to stand in front of him at the door! Uddhav's future would turn bleak!

Uddhav's eyes seemed to be dazzled as he looked at the necklace which Chaturika had lifted up. It seemed to be like the glow of the afternoon sun! Diamond seemed to be engraved on the golden plates. Chaturika was turning voluptuous gradually, she was beckoning at Uddhav, asking, "Is this necklace made of costly pearls obtained from an elephant's head"?

Uddhav shook his head to admit his ignorance. He was listening to Chaturika in utter amazement—Saptalahari necklace, Pearl neckpiece, Sita wreath! Holding the Chandrahaar up, Chaturika called, "Would you please help me in wearing this?" Loosening the grip of her mekhala, the whore exposed her waist. Uddhav grew more nervous. Was Chaturika keen on laying a snare for him? He felt drunk, sitting in front of the woman who had won the attention of the most influential and the richest man of Avanti! He was casting his glance at the precious waist! Uddhav retraced his steps to declare, "I shall leave for now".

Chaturika fell giggling, "Oh my man! What's wrong with you? Come near, please help me wear all these, let me see how I look if I deck myself with all these ornaments!" Chaturika stuck out her feet to him and implored, "Please help me wear the anklet, I shall dance like Devadutta, adorned with all the jewelleries! See, how I have mastered the art"!

Uddhav kept trembling now! Alas, oh Mahakaal! In which snare had he stepped in? He had never seen such ornaments before! Doubt surfaced in his mind instantly. Who could say whether all these ornaments were pilfered? He tried to jog his memory regarding the cases of theft in the city lately! A gang of dacoits had snatched off all the possessions of a man who was on his way to Bidisha from Ujjwain. Weren't all these the plundered booties? Uddhav saw Chaturika laughing, placing her feet near his lap! Even the whore got drunk! Uncovering herself till her thighs, Chaturika was welcoming him. Restraining his lust, Uddhav inquired in a voice steeped in doubt, "Who has given you such large chunks of ornaments?"

Laughing noisily, Chaturika sprawled on her bed, "Is my man getting envious?"

"This is an invaluable treasure, do you know its worth"?

The harlot twirled her neck a little to throw a look back and answer, "No, I know next to nothing, since last night I am just turning the jewellery-bag upside down on the bed, toying with them, listening to the sonorous twang of the collision of the gold ornaments. All night I stayed up awake, without dozing off a bit. I kept thinking, when my man would come, when would I be adorned by him with these ornaments? What would it be like if I wear so many jewelleries on my own, without you looking on"?

The whore sat up. Her upper torso stood bare, the mekhala was somehow veiling the lower region of the body, loosened from the loins. Uddhav saw the onslaught of lust in the young damsel. It was writ large on her lips, breasts! Uddhav was growing daring, bit by bit. This whore was not a nincompoop that she would dare indulge in sexual union with him displaying the presents she had won from either the King, the Army Chief or the Merchant! This must have been pilfered items. And that was why, she was so wily today! He had to put much effort to budge a thread from her body at other times! It was next to impossible to derive the maximum pleasure from sexual intercourse without the perfect cooperation of the harlot! One aspect of coition was arduous endeavour! Again, today Chaturika had a different appearance! Uddhav sat straight. If these ornaments were stolen objects belonging to the merchant from a foreign land, they had to be surrendered to the Royal Court. If he had done that, it would facilitate the probability of his professional uplift. He would be more empowered. Again, if he would enjoy the fabulous chunk of ornaments himself by grabbing them selfishly, it would be no less gainful even. The harlot would have to face the music for these valuables.

Uddhav inquired, "How did you get such ornaments"?

"Got it", Chaturika chose not to divulge anything.

"But I should know, who has given this to you. I am entitled to keep all information at my fingertip".

Chaturika said, "Do you have to know everything and all"?

Uddhav's suspicion intensified, "I must have to know, who is capable of giving you such ornaments"?

Chaturika rejoined, "What if you don't know"?

Uddhav could sense that Chaturika was keen on concealing the fact. He would not allow her to hold it back. He must interrogate her and force the truth from her. He must know. Uddav asked blatantly, "Are these pilfered treasures"?

"What do you mean to say"?

"The band of plunderers looted all that the alien merchant had possessed, it had just happened the day following Deepavali. And sources aver that he had exactly this amount of jewellery with him".

Without adding least importance to the information, Chaturika said, "Have I plundered or are you the real robber — don't I know you, my love?"

The sexual appeal of the words of Chaturika failed to move Uddhav, he could make out easily that the whore was trying to win his heart with her beauty and lovemaking. Why would he be duped? He was a servant of the King! He dreamt of grabbing more power from the royal force. This was his secret desire. He said, "I am being assailed by doubt"!

Chaturika got visibly irritated now, "Which doubt"?

"You cannot understand that, just tell me now who has presented you with such amount of jewellery"!

Turning her face aside, placing the Chandrahaar on her waist, she muttered under her breath, 'I could have bedecked myself with all the ornaments alone if I could sense things to come to such a pass! How come you are devoid of all sense of humour being a person of the Royal Court? Would you like to know who has gifted? You would be taken by surprise on hearing the name, I tell you'.

Puckering both his eyebrows, Uddhavnarayan stayed gazing at the slut. Again, he was being overcome by hesitation within. Who had given, who could give? The idea of pilfering stood negated. Again, he was taken by fear. Was Chaturika testing him? Then, what he thought to be true before came proven. Chaturika would have concealed it, if it was a pilfered object.

Chaturika answered, "All these were presented by a rich person".

Uddhav grew cold within. He lost all courage again to ask who that rich man could be! Chaturika drew closer to him. She drew in Uddhavnarayan stretching her two arms. Uddhav seemed to be like a reticent, stock-still stone.Nothing stirred in Uddhav even at the touch of Chaturika. Chaturika's mouth rested on his ear. Uddhav could feel the touch of the lips, the flick of Chaturika's tongue could be felt on the tip of his ear. The whore held him in a tight embrace and in a muffled voice said, "You would be in for astonishment on hearing the name".

"Whose name?" Nonplussed Uddhavnarayan could not think of any line of action.

As Chaturika whispered the name, Uddhavnarayan extricated himself from Chaturika's bear-hug and jumped off. Alighting from the bed, moving to the dark corner of the room he stood panting for breath. Chaturika was dazzling under the illumination of the lamp! She wore a gem-studded golden string around her neck and Swarnatilak on her forehead. Chaturika was dressing up. How strange! How could his fear come to be true? Where had he come then? Lowering his face, he stood hiding in the darkness. Oh, what miracle had been made possible by this wisp of a young lady! Was youth so powerful? No art had been mastered by this prostitute, yet the man she had been able to impress would have driven Uddhav to shivers. After such long efforts, the name came into the open. Uddhav threw a bewildered glance at the harlot. Was this that Chaturika who had to bear her allegiance to Uddhav even after he struck her? Was this that Chaturika who had yielded to all the pervert demands of Uddhav, for days on end? In the amorous journey, whatever mindless action Uddhav demanded of her, she acquiesced in, like a faithful maidservant. It seemed, as though Uddhav had entered the room of the Chief Prostitute of the city by mistake. As per his ability, he would have to go to the red-light locale burgeoning on the border of the city to satisfy his sexual needs. How could he make a foray in here?

Chaturika came forward, sparkling. She had bedecked herself with more jewels. All her limbs were aglow with the illumination from the lamp. Uddhav stood all quiet. He was afraid of glancing at Chaturika. This harlot was not meant for his pleasure. The man, who was fond of this woman, had allowed Uddhav to taste the royal power as he begged. If that man came to know, Uddhav would have to face the same fate as the youth from Gambhira, who had left the city of Avanti for good. No sooner the youth entered Avanti than Uddhav would make sure to throw him into the prison, by any means. And before that, he would have to marry Gandhavati and confine her to the precincts of home. Uddhav experienced a sudden brainwave! Even three days back, he was the 'paramour' to this harlot! He could finalize his union with Gandhavati with the aid of Chaturika herself. If Chaturika made such an overture to her new 'lover', Shivnath would never be able to turn down the latter's entreaty.

Chaturika was exhaling hot breath standing at an arm's length. She was growing desirous. Did that ever happen? Would it ever occur? As many times Uddhav made love to her, he had to take the initiative each time. He had to arouse this whore. Many a time, she even had a sexual intercourse against her will. But now what was he being witness to? The contraction of Chaturika's eyeball, the juicy pout forming on her lips, the heaving of her breasts with inhalation-exhalation confirmed the desire of her body just for coitus. Extricating herself from his grip, severing all ties with him, why she kept throwing him lovelorn looks again, he wondered. Uddhav lowered his head. He closed his eyes. Now it was a sin to look lustfully at Chaturika. Chaturika had become a part of the royal force on winning her new lover, which Uddhav could hardly dream even. Uddhav did not want to remember anything related to her now. The harlot who had been the woman of his pleasure, now seemed to be someone else. The woman before whom Uddhav was standing, was the apple of someone's eye, who was counted as one of the best gentlemen of this city. Rather, Uddhav would seek the favour of Chaturika from now on. Winning her trust, he would be favoured by the man of highest honour of this city in turn. His life would thus be blessed!

Chaturika giggled, "Are you frightened, my love"?

With a failing voice, Uddhav could not utter a single word. He could sense with his head hanging low, that even the little distance they had between them, stood obliterated. The whore took him in a deep embrace with both her arms. This touch was different. Uddhav, usually accustomed to the flower-decked touch of a floozy, felt as though his skin would be frazzled if he abraded against the jewellery, Chaturika decked herself with! Uddhav felt as though a golden idol would smother him to death than any woman of flesh and blood. The woman was made of metal it appeared, right from her breasts and thighs to the whole body. An awful noise issued out of the friction of jewelleries. Uddhav was not familiar with such clank. Uddhav's blood in the body seemed to get frozen by the chilly current coming up from the stony floor of the room. What an utter ruin! It seemed as though Chaturika was keen on avenging all humiliations she suffered so far! Why should she seek Uddhavnarayan's company, after winning presents from Subhag Dutta, the affluent merchant? Uddhav seemed to bow down to the feet of Chaturika, extricating himself from her embrace. He seemed to apologize to her! The merchant would be happy to know that. Even the comfort-woman of the merchant was to be worshipped by Uddhav! Before leaving with a bow-down to Chaturika's feet, it would be wiser to get hold of the pearl necklace. The pearl necklace fell in wrong hands. It would simply pale into insignificance beside such sparkling ornaments! Uddhav lifted his face up to find that the pearl-string which he had presented, stood encircling the breasts of Chaturika. She had even put that on. She wouldn't let go of anything, it seemed!

Chaturika implored, "Hey my love, won't you help me wear an anklet"?

In a weary voice, Uddhav said, "Please let me have it, where is the pair of anklets"?

Chaturika kept giggling, jerking him with both hands. She whispered near his ears, "I am yours still, Oh Mr. Sessions Judge! Tell me, do the gold ornaments leave the body warm? Since last night, as many times I kept tinkering with these jewelleries, my body heated up each time. But why are you upset? Listen dear, no doubt these gems and jewels are gifts from Subhag Dutta, the merchant, but not for me, the merchant had given these to my friend, Devadutta, last night, and my friend had given away the whole lot to me. Look, Devadutta is enamoured of the King, Devadutta, the daughter of Rasamanjari, has fallen for King Bhartrihari. But merchant Subhag Dutta would not let her go, he decked Devadutta with gold, he claims himself to be even richer than the King…"

Uddhav was startled. How inane he had been! Was he ignorant of the fact, that, Devadutta, the whore, was an object of enjoyment to the merchant? That was why, Dhruvaputra had left Avanti for good! He should have surmised much before. But how would he do that even? What was the reason behind Chaturika's donning the ornaments, presented to Devadutta? Chaturika's statement ran thus: Devadutta had lost all interest in jewelleries, especially if that came from the Merchant! She could not withstand the presence of the Merchant at all! Hence,she had given the ornaments presented by the merchant to Chaturika, with sheer disregard. To Devadutta, those ornaments had been a great burden. She would not be able to bear with such ponderous weight! She lacked in the courage to spurn the offer of the Merchant but she needed to purify herself with such stealthy rejections.

Uddhav kept pinning Chaturika with a keen stare, moving away from her, gingerly, tardily. What was the cause of such feminine wiles? Uddhav was boiling in anger. Chaturika went on narrating how Devadutta paid a visit to her, on the sly, immediately after the merchant left at the dead of night. Merchant Subhag Dutta sat up for playing dice with Devadutta. On being defeated repeatedly, he was adorning her with a piece of jewellery each time! Devadutta was yielding to an inchoate headache because of the ornaments, lying heavy on her. Her body seemed to burn at the touch of the jewelleries. The rage in Uddhav was growing keen as he kept listening to Chaturika's words. He kept reprimanding himself in his mind. He kept convulsing in anger. In his mind, he kept remonstrating, "Hey fallen woman, couldn't you tell me beforehand when I went bowing my head to your feet a hundred times, imagining sundry other things, inwardly?!" Pouncing on Chaturika, taking her by the tufts of hair, Uddhav threw her on the bed and said, "Hey you coquette, you should have said this earlier, thou have wasted such precious time of mine"!

Chaturika was frightened by the change in Uddhav! She began trembling in fear. All of a sudden, the desire in her had calmed down. The real face of Uddhavnarayan was growing distinct, more and more, it seemed. Uddhav gagged her mouth with the end of the stole, as she was about to utter something. Just in this manner, he had raped an adolescent damsel the day before, who was an immaculate virgin, untouched by any man preceding him.

"What are you up to"? Chaturika aimed at extricating herself from the clutch of Uddhav. Groans escaped from her throat. Uddhavnarayan thundered, "I have tamed a girl in this way last night, got me, Chaturika"?

The body, from head to foot, began to be limp. All her dreams she wove, all alone, since last night, began to disintegrate. Tears welled up Chaturika's eyes as she was being raped, even after having coition innumerable times, so far.

Uddhav stood exhausted much, much later. He kept on looking at the naked, raped body of Chaturika, pulling out the end of the cloth from her mouth that he stuck therein. Uddhavnarayan kept gasping and while feeling short of breath, he said, "This, too, is a way of coition, a mode of sexual union, Chaturika, the male gets gratified thus, you know"!

Chaturika did not lift her face up. Uddhav kept toying with the ornaments that stayed glued to her body all over, and said, "Please do not be angry with me, Chaturika, I am like this, I have again tested last night that my body gets satiated in this manner! But that woman cried her eyes out to mar all the pleasures of union though you have not done so"!

Chaturika got up from the bed. She was feeling chilly. Covering her body with a woollen shawl, she went to the end of the bed to sit. Now, Uddhavnarayan was changing the topic. Army Chieftain Kumar Bikram would be instrumental in getting him a hike in position soon. Then he would himself be able to deck Chaturika with such ornaments! Today Chaturika had made him happy! She was successful in exercising her wiles. A woman must be adept in amorous gestures and wiles, otherwise, what kind of woman would she be? He had tasted many a woman so far, but was he ever gratified to such an extent as today? He might have been so, but this day was an excellent experience, doubtlessly. He knew everything. Chaturika was just an ordinary whore, again she was the pleasure-woman of Uddhav! This was known to the Army Chieftain, the Merchant, one and all. Even the King knew that Chaturika , the harlot, was a keep of Uddhav only. Uddhav was perhaps acting his part, even after being cognizant of everything and all. This performance was also a part of sexual union! If he had not done that for so long, how would he have been desirous of raping her? How could he make good the ungratified desire of last night? The way he had engaged himself in sexual pleasure was a way improvised by himself alone. Thus, Uddhav was trying to justify his rape! Even the act of rape was an acting! Uddhav laughed. Then clutching the cascade of untied hair of Chaturika again, he said, "In the days of yore, the royal men used to attract the women in this way, this long hair of women, the enticing chignon, are all for facilitating the men to attract the women towards them, quite effortlessly! Uddhav drew Chaturika to his lap, sticking his hands into the woollen shawl, feeling the ornaments within, he asked, "Chaturika, who else knows about these ornaments"?

Nonplussed, morose Chaturika swayed her head.

"Are you sure that no one knows"?

Somehow Chaturika uttered, "Not even a crow does".

Taking off the jewelleries from the torso of Chaturika, Uddhav said, "These ornaments are to be properly taken care of, Merchant Subhag Dutta has presented his favourite harlot with these gems, it would not be wise to keep these with you, dear feline lady! And again, time is out of joint everywhere, one problem might lead to some other. I must have to think about you, if anything untoward befalls you for these jewelleries, would I even be spared? Merchant Subhag Dutta is a man without a heart, if the word makes way to his ears..."

Uddhavnarayan began to unfasten the Chadrahaar from her waist. While untying it, he went on, "Today you haven't served me with a betel leaf, Chaturika, the betel leaf of your mouth is my favourite, wait, as I haven't decked you up with these ornaments, I have to take these off - how can I divest thee of the jewels I adorn your body with"?

The oil in the lamp was about to deplete. The light flickered. Chaturika was feeling the bite of chill. Oh! How cold were the hands of Uddhavnarayan! They seemed like the hands of a dead man! Chaturika began to shiver. Keeping her eyes shut, she kept trembling in cold. Uddhavnarayan must not scorch her soft body, while divesting her of the jewelleries. The slut was overcome by fear! ////////////////////////

TEN

King Gandharvasen had two queens, had a pair of sons and a courtesan Rasamanjari, his aunt being cognizant of Rasamanjari. Harlot Devadutta, a renowned paragon of beauty and extremely gifted woman as known lately, was the daughter of Rasamanjari. This came as an information from Padmavati, the neighbour of Reba, just her age and proud of having a family comprising a husband and sons. While talking, she stuck the betel leaf inside her mouth, reddening her lips with betel-juice.

Reba listened to what she said. She listened to her, sitting at a distance. She was dying her cloth, ochre. Later, she would etch creepers and plants on the cotton attire, with the wooden dice. Her husband taught her this art. Kartikkumar was adept in many a thing. He was an expert in wooden carvings. This 'creeper-leaf' dice was completely improvised by him. Kartikkumar used to say that he would carve exact replica of fallen leaves, shrugged-off flowers, as in winter leaves began to fall off, he would create the exact impressions of fallen leaves being blown in the wind on the silk cloth. If the cloth was draped by someone, it would appear as though the spring was around the corner, even leaves fell off at the advent of the Spring! He would create the sorrowful note of falling leaves in her clothes. Kartikkumar assured, he would present Reba such a cloth on his return from war, printing thus and he would also take another one for queen Bhanumati to the Royal Court. A semblance of a pale smile flashed across the corner of Reba's lips, she was a soldier's wife, how could the same cloth be brought for both the queen and herself?! Would that ever be possible? Was it for this the man had never been back from the war? Reba turned to look at Gandhavati. Gandhavati got to her feet.

The woman Padmavati used to confide in was Parvati, an old woman, who was again Reba's neighbour! She was pretty old, lost her husband, a widow since ages. Slightly crooked by nature! Was more inclined to eroticism. Parvati, the wizened lady, rejoined to what Padmavati had said, "What kind of male would a man be if he fails to enjoy the company of sundry women? Gandharvasen had innumerable comfort-women, the queens were deprived of seeing their husbands on days like full-moon, festivals, so on. The men are just like that."

"No, no, why so, the Kings are exceptions!" Offering her view, Padmavati turned to Reba for support. Washing her hands with water, wiping the hands with the end of the cloth, standing beside Gandhavati, she asked, "Why did you get up? Where would you go"?

Gandhavati answered, "I am out to fetch water from the well".

"Yes, you will go, rest assured". Giggling, Padmavati spat in the spittoon, "Would you go to the well now to sit for long, hey Reba, the matrimonial alliance that has come now for consideration is quite tempting"!

Reba did not answer. She stretched her gaze to the sky. The first fifteen days of Ashwin were gone. Since quite a few days, summer-solstice of the Sun had set in. Though heat of the sun was yet to mellow, it would definitely slide up on the edge, on the passing of two lunar fortnights. And this was what had transpired indeed.

This year, the bite of chill was much less intense. The wind from the northern lands, ushering the chill this year, seemed to be less powerful, compared to that of last year. In this land, at this hour, the night's temperature dipped remarkably low, giving a fillip to the winter itself! During the night, chill grew severe, while in the daytime, the sunrays stood all-pervasive, making everything warm and cosy. This year, the days were warm though basking in the sun seemed impossible. The sun was there but its effulgence was missing. A certain turbidity engulfed the sun. Even the cerulean hue of the firmament stayed intertwined with grey. The people of Avanti were fond of the sun of these times. Basking in the sun in the afternoons, they used to chatter. For gossip, the afternoons were roomier enough to the women of this city. In Reba's courtyard, the three ladies continued to talk idly.

Casting down her eyes from the sky, Reba inquired of Padmavati, "Has wheat been grown"?

Padmavati shook her head, "As it grew in your land, oh Aunt, it had never happened so, go and have a peek into the wheat fields, Reba, you too, please"!

Reba had seen already. The wheat had been sown by the end of the month of Kartik. Last year, at least a little had been reaped, but this year they remained mostly un-germinated. Her father-in-law was talking about the scarcity of water on earth. At this time of the year, the wheat-fields wore a verdurous look. That green look had turned ashen, it seemed. Hither and thither lay patches of green wheat-fields while the rest was covered with ashen-black earth. How different the ambience, all around, looked! The trees of the cotton bushes looked lacklustre. None had ever seen such a dismal spectacle in the city of Avanti! Would flowers bloom in the Spring?

In order to veer the topic, Reba picked the issue of wheat. But the old woman, Parvati, wished to revert to the previous matter of discussion and said, "Gandharvasen had a desire for having pleasures but King Bhartrihari has no such fad".

"He is a poet, I heard", Padmavati inquired of Reba.

Reba replied, "Yes, I too heard the same".

"Like the great poet Bhasa"?

"That I cannot say".

Padmavati added, "I learnt that Swapna Basavaduttam had been penned by the celebrated poet, Bhasa, himself"!

Gandhavati joined the discussion at this point, adding, "You know, Aunt, there is a character named Padmavati in the play, Swapna Basavaduttam. She was the consort of Udayan, the King of Vatsya, the sister of the King of Magadh".

Taken by surprise, Padmavati expressed, "However, I knew that it was a tale of Basavadutta, the daughter of Pradyot Mahasen, the King of Ujjwain, and Udayan, the King of Vatsya. Is there anyone named Padmavati"?

"Yes, she is there, would you like to know"?

Old Parvati said, "Look, King of Vatsya too had married twice. Our King will not cast his glance at none else than his wife. Though childless, he will not marry again".

Reba cut her short, "Let it be so, Aunt! Please let go of the topic".

"Why would it be left at that? If the King is childless, what good will it be for the nation"?

"Okay fine, let us drop this topic, who are we to talk about such a matter"? Reba was in fear.

Old Parvati continued, "Who else will comment if not us? Even the King takes no fancy in Devadutta, the whore, how can a man stay without any crush on any woman"?

"Why? The queen is a paragon of beauty".

"The harlot is even lovelier than her, again, she has sundry qualities, hey Reba, do you have any idea about her"?

Reba's face darkened. She could guess the hint the old lady intended. Padmavati was not so capable in detecting all that. She was frank and open. She asked her, "Oh Aunt, what qualities does the harlot possess"?

The old woman flashed a toothless smile, "Which virtues, you mean? They attract the man, they know a good many things, do you know how to dance, how to compose and recite poems or how to play the sitar"?

"I do not know, but how come do they"?

"They have to know or why will the men pour all their wealth on them? But what has gone amiss with the King of Avanti? If the King stays childless, the city, too, would suffer the same fate".

Padmavati turned towards Gandhavati. The girl lost herself as she kept looking down the road. Padmavati tugged at her cloth, asking, "Please continue with what you kept narrating, the tale of Udayan and Basavadutta. Basavadutta was the Princess of Avanti. Wasn't she"?

Gandhavati responded, "Don't you know the tale"?

Padmavati answered, "I know, but I tend to forget, my memory gets jogged once you narrate it. Many of us can remember a barrage of things as you do, but I fail to do so".

Gandhavati had learnt about Udayan and Basavadutta from Dhruvaputra. Dhruvaputra had heard the same from Shivnath, Gandhavati's grandfather. Gandhavati remembered every detail of it as she heard, in verbatim, unaltered. She remembered that Prince Udayan, son of King Vatsya, used to teach the art of playing veena to Princess Basavadutta of Ujjwain. Then the two disappeared from Ujjwain to marry. A great conflagration broke out at Labanok, while King of Vatsya had gone out a-hunting! The devastating tongues of fire claimed the lives of Basavadutta and the minister of Vatsya. King of Vatsya kept mourning for Basavadutta of Avanti! One afternoon Dhruvaputra had narrated the tale, sitting by the river Gambhira. He talked about the sonorous Veena too. Basavadutta used to play that instrument. That Veena was found in the Kurchi woods, by the river Reba. Udayan seemed to hear the Veena, still being played in Ghosh raga. Gandhavati recalled how the eyes of Dhruvaputra reflected profound emotions. Dhruvaputra used to say, "Neither Udayan nor Basavadutta knew that both King Pradyot and the queen had given their consent to their wedding. They were utterly shocked when Basavadutta left Ujjwain with Udayan. They made the marriage happen with the aid of a priest by getting the portraits of the Prince and the Princess duly drawn. But did it ever happen? Truly? Would that wedding or the union have sanction of the scriptures? Gandhavati grew romantic inwardly. Shutting her eyes, she began to remember the countenance of Dhruvaputra! Dhruvaputra seemed to be Udayan, the King of Vatsya! Gandhavati imagined herself to be Basavadutta. No points of similarity the two tales shared, not in an iota, again would Dhruvaputra remember her at all? Perhaps not.

Padmavati accosted her, "Hey, why have you gone reticent"?

Old Parvati commented, "Who isn't familiar with the anecdote of Basavadutta? Everybody is. So let it be left at that. I mean to say, what sort of man is the King of Avanti? It seems, he is not a male. Oh! What are you saying, Aunt? Slandering the King is a sin"!

"Since long, the provisions stand exhausted, twenty-four months have slipped by in between, no clouds yet hovered over the sky only because our King is childless. Is it untrue? There's no millet, no wheat, what would people have to eat"?

Reba observed, "He has successfully subdued the revolt of the Huns".

Parvati inquired, "Will the Huns be back again"?

The heart missed a beat or two. Reba lowered her face to say, "No idea, for sure".

Did Dhruvaputra really flee to the Kingdom of the Huns? Old Parvati turned to Gandhavati, asking, "Hey maid, do you know anything? Where has that brat disappeared?"

Gandhavati expressed her ignorance. She turned her face aside. Her eyes moistened.

"You don't know, huh, how would you? Does that harlot know"? Gandhavati was shuddering, she did not reply. Have thou seen the whore, hey you girl? The old woman demanded, "How beautiful is she? Must be exceedingly so, why do the women who stay engrossed in dance and music look so attractive? Why at all? I have heard, she is beautiful as well as a maid of sundry qualities". Reddening her lips with betel-juice, Padmavati kept saying, "I had been to Mahakaal last full moon in Sravan and saw a whore, Aunt. And it was the maiden chance for me to come across a harlot".

"Devadasi"?

"Not at all, dear Aunt, she was a prostitute only"!

"They are harlots too", The old woman muttered under her breath.

"Why? Why would they be so? They serve Lord Mahakaal, the harlots do not. Yes, to return to my point, that harlot was not much beautiful. She was dusk-complexioned like us, the eyes were again feline, her appearance would betray that of a harlot though she dressed ostentatiously, however, she might not appear to be a woman of qualities but she knew how to dance and play Veena".

"Who have you seen instead of the one you intended to see?" Old Parvati vented out her doubt.

"No Aunt, all of them called her a harlot"!

"What's her name"?

"That I knew, but I have forgotten now".

"Are you sure that you haven't come across Devadutta"?

"Perhaps not, I heard her to be a real beauty, having a molten-gold complexion"!

"Who said"? The old woman asked.

"Who would tell me? Hearsay goes".

"From whom have you learnt it"?

"Forgotten, but someone or the other surely has told me"!

"Your husband"?

Padmavati stuck out her tongue and said, "Would he ever say all such nonsense? He hasn't said, though he might say, I can't recollect, he does not drop by a whore-house, for sure"!

"Then where does he go"?

"No idea"!

"He does for sure".

Padmavati burst into a peal of laughter, "What will you say supposing he does"?

Old Parvati said, "Your uncle used to share everything with me, never even thought of concealing anything. It was he who told me of Rasamanjari, and I was keen on learning Veena-playing under her tutelage"!

Padmavati giggled again, "Did you learn"?

The old woman nodded her head in the negative, "Would it be of any benefit at all as I was none but a housewife? My husband pointed it out".

"Did Uncle frequent Rasamanjari's"?

The elderly lady swayed her head, "How would he? Rasamanjari was the King's keep, he used to talk about her, that's it"!

"Did you keep hearing all"?

"Yes, listening to him, I often used to think that he might have been a frequenter of the red-light ghetto. Once I had been to the Kartikeyan Temple at Ramgiri and while passing by, my eyes fell on a hamlet of whores on the eastern end of Ujjwain, it looked sleepy and desolate and it was noon by then. Hence, all fell asleep and how godforsaken it looked"!

Reba raised her hand to intervene, "Let go of it, Aunt, my daughter is here".

"So what? Let her be here. Is she a baby, hasn't she come of age to be married off"?

Reba's face darkened. Gandhavati got to her feet again. It was quite in proximity. Her whole body began to stiffen as she lent her ears to the conversation between her grandma and the old lady. She left the place but curiosity kept gnawing at her bottom. She was between Scylla and Charybdis. Standing a bit off, she kept listening to the loud description of the red-light hamlet by the old lady. The old lady kept narrating how difficult it was for her to move on a cattle-cart that day! The trouble was for her husband indeed! The man used to frequent the bawdy belt for having whale of a time! If they possessed much wealth, if they were well-to-do, would her husband ever visit the brothel as a customer? While listening to the old lady, absent-minded Padmavati commented that her husband never used to go anywhere! It drove the sceptics to laughter!

Throwing a glance at the sky, Gandhavati walked up to the boundary of the house, lined by screw-pine bushes. Now the words failed to reach her ears. At times, only the sound of guffaws got wafted. Couldn't she learn the art of playing Veena or dancing? Or was it that these skills could not be mastered by anyone save a prostitute? She had never come to know that Dhruvaputra was enamoured of the Veena and dancing as well! Now she thought, if these art-forms could be mastered, then… Her inner being ached in utter desolation.

Reba beckoned, "Hey Sugandha, why are you standing there"?

Gandhavati, a girl of grit turned back and answered, "For no specific reason, Maa"!

Padmavati asked her to join them, "Please come here. You should know about these things".

What was she learning exactly? She was getting the reason of Dhruvaputra's falling madly in love with Devadutta, the courtesan! As though, she was listening to the history of the male proclivities! They are never gratified by one woman. This is what male nature is all about! The housewife must stay at home, give birth to children, and the man must keep visiting women, one after another. Was even Dhruvaputra no exception? Gandhavati's eyes clouded gradually. She felt numbed. Tears coursed down her cheeks on to her breasts. She could visualize everything with her mind's eye. Dhruvaputra distanced himself from her, being attracted to a whore, didn't he? That full-moon Chaitra evening, when the moon was reclining westward, Dhruvaputra stood in the waters of the Gambhira. She called out to him, for some time. No doubt, he came up like a man in a trance and walked towards the north-east! He cared not to throw a glance at her even! Reba rested her hand on Gandhavati and asked, "What's wrong"?

"What are you all talking about"?

"I am not saying anything".

"Was my father, too, like that, Maa"?

Reba waved her head in dissent.He was a soldier, he lost his way while subjugating the Huns! He was valiant, why would he visit such places, he was a man of absolutely different inclinations and proclivities!

While listening to her, Gandhavati could see her grandfather approaching. Shivnath was accompanied by someone. Gandhavati wiped her eyes with the end of her sari. Tamradhvaj? Yes, it was him, indeed. He took after a hunter in the forests, but how calm he was by nature! He came here just once. That was during the Festival of Lights! Gandhavati's heart quavered. Then, he must have come with the news of Dhruvaputra! Or, of her father? Gandhavati exclaimed, "He is none but Tamradhvaj, perhaps he is done with his calculations, oh my dear Maa"!

Gandhavati took note of Reba, slinking away from the courtyard, frightened. Her mother hid behind the pall of darkness, inside the house. She kept waiting, all alone. For the astronomer, from Dasharno.

Padmavati and old Parvati kept leaving the courtyard, deeply engaged in a conversation.

ELEVEN

Tamradhvaj had turned up at last. The afternoon of Poush was almost at its close. The sun was losing its effulgence slowly, gradually, its rays pervading all the ten directions. Tamradhvaj did not step into this hut. He walked towards the west along with Gandhavati's grandfather. Gandhavati was alone in the courtyard. She kept looking down the way, being nonplussed. Reba came out of the house as Tamradhvaj and her father-in-law had not entered. She came to stand beside her daughter. In a feeble voice she inquired, "Where have they gone"?

"Perhaps towards the Gambhira river", Gandhavati replied.

"Why? Why there"?

Throwing the query, Reba felt that it was perhaps directed towards herself. The dark which Gandhavati had been in, engulfed Reba too. Then she remembered the wheat field there. Did the astrologer-boy of Dasharno go to inspect the field?

Reba asked, "Is he here finally, with his astrological findings"?

"God knows"!

"Who knows what he has calculated"! Reba gibbered, "Results may differ if a little error creeps in the calculations"!

"Yes" … Gandhavati kept stretching her glance on the road.

"Whatever destined will happen. Is there any need of knowing the future"?

Gandhavati turned towards her mother and in a muffled tone said, "Are you frightened, Maa"?

"I do not know", Reba turned silent.

"Who knows, good news might even reach us"! Gandhavati muttered under her breath.

Reba was not talking. Gradually, the daughter too went speechless. Both mother and daughter kept looking up the road, stock-still. Reba had a hunch that they would be back right then. They would return and the news that the forest-frequenting man would announce, standing in this courtyard, like a hunter, would be far from happy! Reba had even thought that Kartikkumar would be back in a year, given the Huns had not imprisoned him and dumped him in a distant region. The Huns were an utterly ruthless, warrior-like race! If trapped by the Huns, he must be through an insufferable persecution! And if the words of Uddhav, the royal servant, would come true... Reba shuddered to think of it! She could never even imagine that the man would not return at all. It was just a matter of recent past when he left for Ujjwain, it seemed. Eyeing the Satavisha star, far-off, in the darkness of the evening, he walked out of this inner yard. He walked northward. Why hadn't he come back, given all auspices? Which luck had impeded his comeback from the war?

Gandhavati asked, "Why aren't they returning, Maa"?

Reba answered, "The dusk is approaching soon, light the lamp, blow the conch-shell, won't you tie your hair"?

"When again? Well Maa, it may be that Dhruvaputra has gone away in search of my father".

Reba stood startled. What do you say? What exactly? Carried away by emotions, the mother took her daughter in an embrace, "Would it ever be possible?"

"Don't you think so"?

Reba was driven to silence. Ahh, why didn't she think of this before? If such possibility dawned on her, mother and daughter would be able to stay in each other's embrace for life! It might appear as an unreal imagination, though it might not be untrue! Dhruvaputra's blood carried the hint of a Kshatriya soldier's wrath! Loaded with memories of sundry battles! He himself even said so. Dhruvaputra, humiliated by a whore, might have left the country! To pay back in gratitude, he might have set out in quest of Kartikkumar! What an amazing conjecture it could be! For the nonce, such an imagination helped Reba feel relieved of her anxiety! A thought flashed past her mind. Leaving her daughter behind, she walked towards her dwelling. While leaving, she thought, why would her words to her daughter prove false? This was nothing but the truth. Truth...truth...only the truth! God knew at which nook of her house, a venomous takshak stayed hidden from all eyes! Reba could hear it hissing!

The lamp was lit. Tamradhvaj stepped in along with the blowing of the conch-shell. An inexplicable charm of the gloaming stood all-pervasive across the ten directions, right then! The light that stayed on earth long after the evening was nothing but the light that embraced the ancient earth, so fondly! Standing by the hutment, Reba noticed that the young man of Dasharno had stretched his dust-laden feet on the low wooden stool. She had kept a water-pot by its side. It was not touched by Tamradhvaj, as he announced, "We have to go back again"!

"Would you like to sit in the courtyard in such wintry chill"? Shivnath worded his concern.

Tamradhvaj retorted, "Chill? But where"?

His weariness might have erased if he could sit washing his feet in water.

Tamradhvaj splashed water on his face and eyes, he held a tumbler in his hand, standing on the stone-slab, rested aside the Ketaki-laden fence. He cleaned his feet with water. What a strange man he was! Feisty! Smile sprang up at the corner of Gandhavati's lips. Wouldn't he purify himself, given the long journey he had undertaken? His thought followed a trajectory, he followed some other course of action. In fact, he wished to sit in this hut. Such was his wish. Failing to express it in words, he was afraid, if he would speak to the contrary.

Washing his feet, wiping it with a dry cloth, Tamradhvaj stepped in again to sit on the wooden stool. Shivnath said, "Dews will fall. Come, let's sit on the raised terrace".

"No, it is better to sit beneath the canopy of sky. Dewdrops are not that intense".

A lamp was lit in the dark of the courtyard. Tamradhvaj drew up his woollen wrapper on his head and mumbled, "I had no plan to come here, but suddenly I felt like coming over, why, I wonder".

"Are your calculations over"? Shivnath asked.

"Not complete yet, it would be the best if I could start tomorrow morning though the stars in the sky would conceal themselves, they stay lost during daytime. The night sky would be better if I could return at night, keeping an eye on the celestial bodies…what else may I want"? Tamradhvaj was groping for words though to no avail.

His words made Gandhavati laugh up her sleeves. Dhruvaputra used to say, the Arabian Sea lay so far! The merchant ship sailing on this sea, kept searching for a way by following the stars in the sky above. It fixed its gaze on the star, named Dhruva. Were Gambhira and Ujjwain frothy seas, that he would have to go back, tracing the stars by night? Reba sat squatting on the raised terrace, cogitating. Shivnath sat on another wooden stool, facing Tamradhvaj! Gandhavati sat at a distance. Both of them, however, were audible.

Tamradhvaj said, "I have really taken fancy on this Gambhira river, the wicker-plant has certainly withered and died in this severe winter but these creepers stay alive during monsoon, don't they"?

"Yes", replied Shivnath.

Gandhavati looked up at the firmament, bewildered. Her gaze stayed glued on the star, Dhruva, in the northern sky. Tamradhvaj's words cut through the darkness. How strange! It seemed, she had heard this voice even before. How sombre, how enchanting it was, as if Dhruvaputra was speaking! Was it exactly like that? Perhaps, he talked about the cane-clumps bordering the river, Gambhira, and hence the similarity! This river, the cane-woods, the sky, the millet-fields lining the bank of the river, Dhruvaputra was even under the spell of the cluster of clouds hovering over the river! Did Tamradhvaj know about it? Or did he come to learn? But how would he? Whatever little was known, it was known to Gandhavati only! None else knew. Did Tamradhvaj meet up with Dhruvaputra? Had he chanced upon Dhruvaputra standing beneath the rainclouds by the Gambhira, during the wet, rainy days? In the afternoon, he enjoyed the spectacle of flight of the herons! Did Tamradhvaj see all with the aid of his astronomical insight? Gandhavati fluttered like a leaf in amazement! Her eyes got filled with tears in the dark, as she cocked up her head to locate Dhruva, the star. How could Tamradhvaj bring alive those days? The cane-plants desired to drift down the gushing flow of the Gambhira. The clouds lay afloat on the waters of the Gambhira. Which era was this? Since aeons the clouds disappeared not to be seen for long thereafter! Dhruvaputra too seemed to have vanished along with the clouds from the city of Avanti, and he seemed to have returned to Ujjwain long ago, after the monsoon, and again in the morning of Chaitra Purnima. Which Chaitra Purnima was that? Alas, ages have sped by thereafter!

Tamradhvaj asked, "Do you still remember the day on which he left home"?

Gandhavati looked at him, startled, withdrawing her glance from the sky. On hearing Tamradhvaj, Shivnath turned to look at Gandhavati. Gandhavati, in turn, cast a glance at her mother, who sat squatting on the verandah. In the darkness, Reba drooped her head low.

Shivnath demanded, "Who are you talking about"?

"He who left home".

"Kartikkumar, my son, had set out on war, he had never left his home"!

"Dhruvaputra had left his dwelling behind", Tamradhvaj said.

"Yes, he had left almost a couple of years back, on the evening of Chaitra Purnima".

"Where was the moon in the sky then"?

Shivnath shook his head to say, "He left behind all eyes, leaving no hint,hence there's no idea about it. If it had been known beforehand, his mission of going untraced could have been stalled".

Tamradhvaj muttered for a while, "God only knew what", and then called Reba, abruptly, "Maa, could you give me something to eat"?

Gandhavati ran to her mother, thrilled. What did she hear? She was being confused by the words of Tamradhvaj, in the darkness. Wasn't this call very much like that of Dhruvaputra? Returning from afar, being utterly exhausted, he used to address Reba, her mother, just in the same manner.

Shivnath stood up to say, "We are really ashamed, are you hungry"?

"A cup of cow-milk would do", Tamradhvaj turned to Reba in darkness and requested. Reba went in a flurry, in an instant. He had asked for food, so frankly!

She went to sit by an earthen oven, at the corner of the inner yard, having instructed Gandhavati in a muffled voice. Gandhavati had gone to the kitchen, taking the lamp from inside the room. She came out with a bowl of milk in the dark. She stepped into the courtyard, with gingerly steps.

Reba was turning back to steal glances at Tamradhvaj, off and on. Affection for a child was writ large on her face! It was very natural for him to be hungry, he had come walking quite a few miles, to be precise. He seemed to be just like Dhruvaputra! Lighting up the dry twigs with fire from the lamp, Reba rested a hand on her cheek, leaving the milk-container on the earthen-stove. Gandhavati sat on her heels beside her. The fire in the earthen-stove leaped up. Wintry chill subsided, all of a sudden. Tamradhvaj spoke quietly, in an organized way though. Both mother and daughter were all ears to listen to Tamradhvaj!

Tamradhvaj said, "No doubt this is strange, no reason can be discerned for the lack of rains! Though the course of Nature alters owing to some serious reason, as a popular saying goes. When a messiah is born, or when the gods descend on earth from the heavens, the earth gets its harvests aplenty, downpour stands satisfactory and people are blessed with good fortune".

Shivnath observed, "This is no mere change in ordinary course, this is just a picture to the contrary".

Tamradhvaj replied, "Since the last couple of years, two months went without any shower, this Magh there is a possibility of a downpour. Has it ever happened that monsoon passed by dry, rainless, or without sufficient shower"?

Of course, it happened. And why not? Schedules stood altered, sometimes before or after the months of Asad and Sravan, or even after the so-called months of monsoon, in Bhadra. One crop had wasted, another crop grew instead, last when the monsoon came to stay no one remembered, the Magh preceding last year had seen scanty rains just for a day. Nature seemed to be empathetic, and it was perhaps the last monsoon, in Sravan, a few drops of rains drenched us, and then everything evaporated, all stood vacuous, desiccated.

Tamradhvaj said, "Even in Dasharno rainfall is scanty, I have got this news, this is the worst of times. This universe, even the life of humans, all seem to be governed by the star named Sabita. The astrologers of Ujjwain however are discussing a new star in its sky".

"Which star"?! Startled, Shivnath cocks his face high up to the sky.

"It is yet to make its presence felt, perhaps"!

Both Gandhavati and Reba were listening to Tamradhvaj. Milk was about to reach the boiling point. Reba took the container from the oven, clutching it with her cloth-end. The air was getting redolent with the fragrance of thick milk. A while ago, the milk was about to spill over. This is an auspicious sign, indicating prosperity and happiness.

Shivnath asked, "Are you ready with the computation"?

"I need to know which direction the man took, while bidding adieux to his residence as well as the river, Gambhira".

"Dhruvaputra"?

Yes, he has gone missing for almost a couple of years, and Kartikkumar, since the last five years. Dhruvaputra would definitely appear more distinct in my analysis than Kartikkumar".

Shivnath started. "'Would appear more distinct'-what does it mean?"

"I have seen indeed with my mind's eye! I have done the calculations on his birth-chart, reading and analysing the stars and planets therein, I have perhaps seen him standing in the cane-clumps, with thick clouds hovering over the sky".

"What are you saying"?

The milk-tumbler came. Tamradhvaj drank till the last drop, holding the vessel up to his mouth. Getting up in the dark, washing his hands and face with water, he came to occupy his old seat, and went on, "I have no faith in what the astrologers of Ujjwain say, but Acharya Brishavanu knows the firmament like the back of his palm.

Doubtlessly, he is striving hard to find out a chain of concatenation between the two: the visibility and non-appearance of the stars and planets and the vicissitudes of man's life. His research is going on uninterrupted, he stays up awake almost all night".

Shivnath asked, "But have you really seen"?

"I am keen on knowing the exact time of his leaving home, look this is not something bizarre to feel him. Like Acharya Brishavanu, I am trying to establish a connection between the sky-scape and the life of man, after all I am a bona-fide disciple of the Acharya"!

"How is it possible to know"?

Tamradhvaj replied, "It is the sky of Poush, in this sky none of the Seven Sages can exist, they are invisible - does it mean their ultimate disappearance"?

"Why so, during Ashwin they were there in the north-western corner of the sky"!

"It was about to set, it set down in Kartik, and again, would be seen in the north-eastern sky during the month of Magh, and then it will manifest itself gradually-this is nothing but a chain of system, if each man is governed by a galaxy of stars and planets, he, too, would be exposed to such vicissitudes in life, having a rise somewhere or setting down elsewhere".

"The astrologers corroborate that too".

"They do certainly, but they would fail to proffer any explanation. If the sky cannot be imagined, how can an explanation be put forth? Listen, Acharya Brishavanu could espy the seven saints, who stayed invisible, his sight would even expand beyond the bounds of this vast universe and reach the illimitable! He has taught me such wonders, and the star which stands hidden from our eyes, at night, can be traced if we would like to know. The Saint Agastya would spring up on the southern horizon in the month of Chaitra, just imagine how it glides forward! Though, through all seasons, Agastya stays concealed in the firmament, it is sure to stay elsewhere in this vast universe. If such a missing star can be traced, why can't we find out a man, who has gone missing? Just like Nature, man has a cycle of seasons in him, at the peak of Aghran starts a life which has its finale in Kartik. If such seasons can be divided in case of the humans the chain would surely be clear and discernible as long as he lives" Tamradhvaj fell quiet while explaining. In a lowered voice, he later demanded, "Am I being able to make my point clear"?

Gandhavati and Reba kept watching Tamradhvaj, utterly amazed. Glancing at Gandhavati, Reba said in a low tone, "When Dhruvaputra left, where did the moon stand then"?

Gandhavati hugged her mother's neck, put her face on her breast and blabbed, "I know".

"Really"?

"Yes, I do".

"Then tell him. He is a man of great wisdom".

Holding Reba's hand, Gandhavati walked forward and in a muffled voice said, "I know".

"Do you know"?! Tamradhvaj sprang up to his feet, "Then tell me, where was the moon, to which direction did he walk up, tell me. I have to leave now, again the chill is intensifying gradually".

Tamradhvaj looked steadfast into Gandhavati's eyes . In the dark, the starlight shone in the eyes of Tamradhvaj. Unable to bear the sight, Gandhavati drooped her head low.

TWELVE

The seven lakes of Ujjwain appeared as a garland bedecked with seven-layered wavy pearls around Avanti-Lakshmi's neck! Who said this? Dhruvaputra, who else? He used to pay frequent visits to the old soldier, Parashar, who used to while his time away on the edge of Ratnakarsagar. To the old man, the presence of Dhruvaputra was highly welcome! No wise man would ever come to sit beside the Kshatriya or a Shudra! To listen to the stories of his life, during the winter, or in a summer evening or in an afternoon in autumn. All of the Shudra locale used to look up in reverence to that handsome god-like youth.

The seven lakes of Ujjwain seemed like seven auspicious tithis. If circum-ambulated twice, it would be a Chaturdashi and then would come the full moon night. The endless blossoms of lotus on the seven lakes in moonshine, had the resplendence of seven million moons, right from the month of Bhadra to Aghran. Towards the east of the city lay Ratnakarsagar while Rudrasagar, another water-body, stood adjacent to the Mahakaal Temple in the west. The other five water-bodies lay strewn inside the city. Towards the south of the palace stood Pushkar lake, the inner haven of the palace had Ksheersagar, in its contiguity towards the north lay Gobardhansagar, in the further north stood Purushottamsagar, Vishnusagar.

Old Parashar was chanting the names of all the seven lakes. A road reached the palace through the southern end of Ratnakarsagar leading to the west. The road was lined by green grasslands and there stood the hamlet of the Shudras. Gazing at the lake, the old man was talking about King Gandharva. At the outset of his reign, a similar situation prevailed. A long absence of rainfall caused the ponds to run dry. That time too, there was dearth of the lotus flowers!

"Exactly how many years ago"? A youth threw the query.

"I do not keep the count, exact count, I mean... It seems, that year no lotus had bloomed at all", the elderly man mumbled and all of a sudden, the sky was overcast with clouds and water filled the seven lakes to the brim.

This Ratnakarsagar was meant for the Shudras only. Neither the Brahmins, the Kshatriyas nor the Vaishyas had their claim on this water. Ratnakarsagar, kept aside for the Shudras, had dried up, the little water it had, turned unfit for use, became muddy and turbid. Glancing at the water-surface, the old man was reminded of the memories of Purna Sarovar! He was quite aged. He himself did not know how old he was in years!

The old man recounted how he had gone to many countries to fight numerous battles, on behalf of King Gandharva. The King was a world-conqueror. Once the army had crossed the rivers in the south, Reba, Tapti and the Godavari, to reach further south by the side of the Cauvery river. Ahh, how picturesque that land was! In that land only, Agastya star rose and shone. It was surrounded on all sides by the coconut and the betel-nut clumps. Sandalwood trees were the speciality of that land only, where these grew and thrived. The retinue of soldiers reached the foothills of the Malay ranges. And how exquisite it was to spend the night on the lap of the Malay mountains. It was not a tale of this birth, it seemed. How wonderful were those starry nights and the air laden with sandal fragrance! It were as though the land of the Gods! There the Spring was eternal. Even in the month of Aghran, not a chill of winter was felt. All night was to be spent beneath the canopy of the firmament, and to walk along the galaxy, through the avenues of dreams. How enormous stood the Malay mountains! It seemed to proliferate in all the ten directions just like the clouds! Even till date, he was reminded of the Malaychandan ranges while the nimbus[rain-clouds] floated in his ken. The women of that land were so beautiful and how compassionate they were! Once when a soldier, indisposed by over-drinking had been left alone by his mates, who set out on another mission, a woman had taken care of him with motherly affection and brought him back to health…

The old man recounted many a thing. Since ages the sky showed no sign of clouds, hence, the Malay mountains made space in our tale. The birthplace of clouds seemed to be that land and as Agastya, the star, popped up on the horizon, clouds too piled up!

His life was chequered. And he never ran short of tales, having a bagful of it. Rainbow coloured those anecdotes. Those tales were bedecked with cascades of clouds just as the myriad-hued mountain ranges of the Vindhyas, the Satpura, and the Malay! He had witnessed rainfall in abundance. He had seen drought too. Lakes were dry, water was obtained by digging the sandy banks of the Gandhavati river — he was a treasure-trove of all such memories! The inner bosom of the river never went dry. River was just a mother! And again, this was the city of Ujjwain! The happy fields of Lord Shiva, the Mahakaaleswar! Here Mahakaal Shankara or Lord Shiva had slain Tripurasura! This mythological tale had been narrated to him by Dhruvaputra! In lieu of it, he used to listen to the resources as mentioned - the sandalwood forests in the southern territory, the moonlight-swept nights, the sandalwood-fragrance-laden wind across the Malay ranges, singing all night, sitting by the valley of those mountains. The forests of coconut and Guvak, the rivers like Reba, Tapti, the Cauvery, the Godavari, the wine made of the coconut juice, the walks along the Satpura massif, the cave in which the five Pandavas hid during their years of living incognito, and a lot more! Still now, Dhruvaputra's voice kept ringing in the ears of the old man,unawares! In this futile existence on earth, he had never found such a nice gentleman! Look, now he was recounting how the victory-chariot of Mahakaaleswar, Lord Shankar Mahadeva, was built by so many things together! This earth, the Mandar massif, all quarters of the universe, the sidereal system, the Ursa Major, the mythological Snake-King, the Himalayas, the Vindhyas, the rivers Indus, Ganga and Saraswati, day and night, and the parts of the new moon and full moon – all went to build that Chariot! The sun and the moon were the wheels of the chariot of Lord Shiva. Indra, Varun, Yamah and Kuver had been taken as the horses for His carriage. The flag-stand of that chariot was the Sumeru mountains. During lightning in the sky, his banner was like a ball of large cloud amidst the firmament... Parashar stopped short, while speaking. The listeners were all middle-aged, young and even some were just boys. All stood with an engrossed stare fixed on the old, wizened man of the village: Parashar. Parashar could easily carry on with the latter part of the tale taking up from the point he left, though it appeared somewhat unintelligible to himself! A whole year comprising six seasons meant one session of monsoon too, right? Then, how could it be the bow of Lord Shiva and how again would the inauspicious, stygian night be the string of that bow? He thought of getting an explanation from Dhruvaputra. But he had left the city of Avanti already! He let out a long sigh.

One of the listeners inquired, "The Sun and the Moon were the wheels of the Chariot, you say, could you please recount since the beginning, you old man, how the chariot was built, at what speed it ran"?

Parashar was about to answer when the hurtling of the chariot- wheels reached his ears. It came from the western direction indeed. In the west the palace stood, all the luminaries of this city resided in the west only, again the rivers Shipra and Gandhavati flew on, in the west. In that direction only stood the temple of Lord Mahakaaleswar. Yonder approached the chariot! Dust was kicked up to fill the sky. The western horizon was covered with dust just like clouds. All of a sudden, old Parashar stood up. Did clouds accumulate in the west? Was it the rumble of the clouds? Would there be downpour? But, at this time, no clouds swam in from the west! The rains during winter were caused by the nimbus clouds from the north, the clouds of the north-east drifted towards the west, to the Arabian Sea, to be precise. But if it surfaced, then? It was the Chariot, no doubt! Yes, the Chariot! Old Parashar's heart missed a beat or two. He was speaking about the chariot since long, the Victory-Chariot of the Mahakaaleswar, Mahadeva Shankar! Immediately after naming it, grating of the Chariot-wheels could be heard! Was then Lord Mahakaaleswar heading towards their ghetto? Was the wrathful, directionless Mahakaal rushing this way on His chariot? Did he turn inimical? If Lord Mahakaal turned his face away, this universe would surely face its doomsday! That was what the old, decrepit man learnt since ages. He, Himself, was coming to make His presence felt! The trance, in which the old Parashar was engulfed while recounting the tale of the Chariot of Lord Mahakaaleswar, alerted him of the imminent arrival of the Lord! Hence, the earth got enveloped by dust! Nay, it was not dust, clouds or lightning, but the pennant on the Chariot of Lord Mahakaal. Being a Shudra, he had never entered the temple of Lord Mahakaaleswar, Lord Shiva! He was not entitled to step in, rather! He had never seen how that image looked! Whatever he learnt, he heard it from Dhruvaputra! Was it a sin for a Shudra to utter the name of the Lord even? Old Parashar, in fear, cried out, "Escape, escape you all, he will survive who can flee, oh Lord, what have I done, Lord Mahakaal Shiva is hurrying towards us with His Chariot of Victory"! Bowing down to earth, touching it with his forehead, the old man shut his eyes pat and stayed stock-still as a stupendous hunk of a stone-slab!

In a few minutes, not a single soul was seen around. Only Parashar stayed alone in the field, still, unmoving, dark. Where had they all gone? Those who were there? Where had all taken refuge to? In which grotto, behind which banyan tree, in the dark of which twigs and foliage of a tree, like frightened birds? The trundling noise reached a higher decibel, gradually!

The chariot was approaching. In the desolate winter afternoon the chariot was inching towards the Ratnakarsagar, near Shudra locale. The hooves of the white horse of Cambodia kicked up dust around the chariot-wheel, in profusion. The two horses came to a stop by dashing and dragging their legs on the ground simultaneously. How robust the horses were! And how would the pilot of the chariot be? He hailed from the Kailash in the north. The chariot was gem-studded. This was not a war-chariot, just an ordinary one, yet it was extremely well-decked. Yellow, silk canopy, frills, and if the banner would have been a bit higher, it would easily pass for the King's chariot. The flag was white, immaculate, the brightness of the colour resembled the feathers of a swan. The chariot, high as ten men, one on the other, and wide as dozen blokes, standing next to each other, had a middle-aged man sitting stock-still, inside it. The silk attire was decked with gems, with a multi-appliqued, adroitly stitched, white silk shawl from Madras on it. Taking off the pink headgear in his hand, the man sitting in the carriage spoke in a deep, grave tone, "Hey Utanka, where have all the men gone"?

Utanka, the charioteer, replied, "They have fled away out of fear"!

"Utanka, call out"!

He did not have to shout. All were familiar with the name 'Utanka'. So, it was Utanka's chariot, that kept approaching! The chariot of the merchant, to be precise! The richest man of the city of Avanti, Subhag Dutta, came by driving his chariot like a conqueror, who had won the world! Subhag Dutta, the business magnate, seemed to come rushing his chariot like an enraged soldier! Parashar opened his eyes. He stood up instantly. As he got to his feet, Utanka laughed out boisterously and said, "Lord, here's one, who gets transformed into a man from stone"...

"Keep quiet"! Subhag Dutta reprimanded Utanka to silence. Utanka seemed to be deflated, standing on the carriage itself. Old Parashar was watching the chariot. He was inspecting the riders on the carriage. He should have an inkling that it might have been Utanka's chariot! Utanka's carriage ran at such a high speed usually! Whenever this chariot hit the thoroughfares of the city, the people used to make way for it, stepping off to the furthest edge. The chariot ran at a breakneck speed, setting all at naught! The wealthiest person of the city sat in it, quiet, still, only turning his head this side or that, to reconnoitre both sides of the road. This chariot was horrifying, no doubt! Fear-evoking, in the truest sense of the term! A couple of years ago, a village-youth flew to the front of this carriage and was left crippled by the kick of the horses and the grazing of the wheels. However, Subhag Dutta, the business magnate, had given three thousand and fifteen rupees to the boy with mutilated limbs. Since then, he was not seen on this path anymore!

Utanka helped Subhag Dutta alight from the chariot. The youth on the chauffeur's seat was quite handsome to look at. It was a fad of Subhag Dutta to be in the possession of valets of his choice. His house could boast of having a retinue of page-boys from various nations. Utanka hailed from the north-east. Merchant Subhag Dutta had brought the lad, Utanka, to Ujjwain, from the mountainous region, where cold-blasts were quite a regular affair. He turned into a strong, robust man, having fed on nutritious food. A mere glance at Utanka meant amazement at times and again fear took one in its grip, inwardly! The eyes were small, the eyebrows were almost vanished, the skin being smooth and bright, nose being blunt, losing its unique entity on the face. Subhag Dutta named him 'Utanka'. Vedic Sage Aydadhvam's disciple was Vedmuni. And Utanka was the disciple of Vedmuni. He was unparalleled in his devotion to his master! With him, everything lay safe, right from the women to the riches. Subhag Dutta, the master, could easily stay free from all worries, as was Vedmuni.

The business magnate alighted from the carriage and went towards the lake in slow steps. Mustering courage, old Parashar came to the fore to take a close look at Utanka. An expressionless face. Subhag Dutta's servant was stern and zombie-like, like a stone idol. Being a bit more daring, old Parashar began to stalk Subhag Dutta. With astonishment writ large on his eyes, he was looking at the merchant. Subhag Dutta turned towards him and in a low voice asked, "Ratnakarsagar has changed a lot...it's become waterless … but, since when"?

Without answering, the old man stood with his head, hung low. As if, he was solely responsible for the drying up of Ratnakarsagar. Walking towards the south, inching forward a little to the west, Subhag Dutta stepped in to the western bank. He was being followed by the elderly soldier. Again, Subhag Dutta turned back to look. He knew this man. Many years back, he was in the King's army. Almost all the youths of this Shudra hamlet used to come forward to hold weapons in times of the army's need. These warriors fortified the power of the King. Subhag Dutta was observing the aged man. Bare-footed, in soiled attire, even the cloth covering his body resembled a very old, badly-tattered saddle on the horse-back. A look of terror pervaded his eyes. The old man stood with folded palms. Subhag Dutta, threw a query abruptly, "Where's lotus? Why isn't it there"?

"No lotus blooms at this time", the old man's voice rattled, he kept muttering, "Ksheersagar, the pond adjacent to the palace, has a perpetual bloom of lotus over the year, I heard".

"But here too it bloomed"! Subhag Dutta's voice defeated him in decibel.

The old man kept gazing at the merchant, being astonished. He was embarrassed by such a trivial query from the richest man of this city! He knew himself quite well that the blooming season of lotus stretched from Bhadra to Aghran, only for these few months, the Ratnakarsagar stood replete with lotus.

Suhag Dutta asked, "Isn't there any lotus in the month of Poush? Yes?"

The old man, being nonplussed, could not find any answer to this question. Was it something new to find no lotus in Poush? It appeared from the words of the merchant that lotus should have bloomed at this time of the year! How could he say so? Didn't the trader know when the lotuses usually bloom?

In a low tone Subhag Dutta said, "Didn't you find, all the seven ponds had lotuses blooming all the year round, once upon a time"?

Now, the old man could get a drift of the merchant's statement. He swayed his head to support his view, silently. The merchant was an influential man of this city. He was the master. The Shudras were his servants. The Shudras were his loyal servants even though he hardly cared to look after them. The master's words never could go wrong. Supporting the master would mean well-being for the Shudras! Provision of rice would be there for them, year-round, they would be happy perennially, by the grace of the merchant! His words would never be otherwise, hence, lotus bloomed indeed, in this Ratnakarsagar, all through the year! The old man had not witnessed that himself, yet the merchant's words could hardly go wrong!

Subhag Dutta said, "Since a few years, it is being noted that lotuses are depleting soon. What would Ujjwain be left with, if the lake has no lotus in it"?

"It may be so", the old man maintained.

"Don't you know"?

"Yes Sir, I know".

"Have you apprised the King of this lotus-less plight"?

"No, my lord"!

"Aren't you aware of the reason of this lack of lotus"?

The old man threw all hesitations to the wind and answered, "Since long, there's no water in the pond, you know, my lord"!

"Why is there no water"?

"The sky has dearth of water hence the land too suffers the same fate".

"This lake, the seven water-bodies of Ujjwain, are they all nourished by the water from the sky"?

The old man went speechless. He knew that the water from the firmament only nourished all, irrespective of the rivers, oceans, water-bodies, so forth. As the sky ran short of water, the rivers, Shipra and Gandhavati too were getting emaciated, narrow! The soil turned stone-hard. The wheat cultivation became almost rare. No high-tide rose. The trees, woods, wind, everything seemed unusually heated! Even this winter, stones were getting scorched by the sun in the mid-afternoon! If it showered, it would never happen so. Soil lacked moisture, plants too lacked sap. The sugarcanes were devoid of enough juice this winter! His experience in life made him see that sufficient rainfall would definitely leave a sane earth. The workaday existence of man would have its own rhythm.

Finding the old man silent, Subhag Dutta again spoke up, "I have never seen that lack of rainfall causes the lakes to dry up, have you"?

Parashar was at his wit's end, he was groping for words. His memory brought forth waterless lakes, many a time. Again, a fresh rainfall filled the water-bodies to the brim. But the merchant maintained otherwise. Subhag Dutta stirred the silk-reticule suspended from his waist, Parashar was familiar with the jingle of the gold coins. He was thrilled. The trader kept the reticule again on his waist, dangling. The elderly man among all the villagers expressed, "Sir, I haven't seen such ever before".

"As lotus bloomed all through the year, this city was known as Kumudvati, 'kumud' meaning lotus or the moon".

"Yes, Sir"!

"Have you ever heard of this city of Kumudvati, devoid of lotus"?

Exactly the same question! The old man stood with folded palms. Now he raised his head to look into the eye of the merchant. He was waving his head. A faint smile flashed at the corner of his lips. Concealing his smile, he looked at the sky above and down to the pond. He kept swaying his head. Being worried, he looked at the old man and asked, "Tell me, what will transpire next"?

Parashar stayed silent. Subhag Dutta saw that a handful of men had assembled round his chariot. They were enjoying a close look at the chariot, going around it. Then suddenly, god knew why, they retraced their steps to the pond. All filed forward uniformly in a queue to reach the lake, one at the back of the other. They stood on the southern bend of the lake. Without approaching the merchant, who stood on the western bank, they set out to the eastern bank from the south. They seemed to reach the merchant on circum-ambulating the pond only. To his utter amazement, Subhag Dutta watched the men of all ages and appearances — tall, short, lean, obese, so on, going round the waterless Ratnakarsagar, in staggering steps.

Subhag Dutta turned to face the old man, "Is it any omen that the pond has gone waterless"?

"No Sir"!

"The sky is lacking in moisture, is it a good omen at all"?

"No Sir"!

"If the month of Poush witnesses such a predicament, I wonder what would await us in the terrible summer"!

"True, Sir"!

"Will Spring be here at all"?

Subhag Dutta looked worried as he said, "Spring only follows the winter, and ample of signs become prominent on its advent, can you see them at all"?

The old man muttered, "My master, you understand that much better than me, I am sure"!

Subhag Dutta was pacing up and down the room saying, "This year there will be no Spring, winter will yield straight to the summers"!

"How horrible will it be"! The old man's face betrayed signs of fear!

"Has it ever so happened that the ponds went waterless, rainfall ceased and the city of Avanti was aflame, perpetually"?

The old man shook his head in disapproval to say, "No, my master"!

The men had finished encircling the lake. All filed up in front of Subhag Dutta and held their heads low. Subhag Dutta threw the same query, "Have you seen"?

"What"? All the heads cocked up in a trice.

"Varundeva has left the land of Avanti"!

"No, my lord"! All of them cried out.

"Avanti will never have rain, the ponds would remain sans water, the sky too would be dry. Do you know that the sky running overhead is another ocean, gallons of water being there in the bosom of clouds"?

"Yes, my master"!

"Please accept this portmanteau fraught with gold coins, but what will happen to the ponds, lying dead as a possum? Any way out"?

"We want rainfall", all of them shouted in unison.

"No rainfall would ever occur", saying so, Subhag Dutta handed the reticule full of gold coins to old Parashar. He added, "You fought several times for saving the land of Avanti, so here I hand it to you. But why don't you know the reason of the disappearance of lotus in the ponds, where they bloomed throughout the year? Try to find out why clouds are on the wane, why wouldn't Spring be here again"? Subhag Dutta kept moving towards the chariot, while blabbing these words. While returning, he heard the Shudras hailing him aloud, honouring him with a standing ovation! It was just the old soldier who kept looking at the merchant with wide-eyed wonder. He was walking up to the chariot. Whatever he uttered might not be true at all, but how could the master lie? The old man, at this point, began to go down into the turbid, muddy water of the lake. How strange! Though the merchant claimed, he, himself, had never witnessed a lotus blooming in this pond, all through the year! As he said, his words would definitely prove to be true. He avoided telling a lie, even old Parashar was afraid of it. A fib would invite severe punishment! He wished to spend his last days in absolute peace sans worries. Parashar went muttering, Lotus would be in full-bloom, all the year round, from Bhadra to Sravan,the twelve months, to be precise! The merchant's words would never be wrong! It just could never be so!

Thirteen

The flames kindled by lust seemed to sway their body to the rhythm of dance. The evening ritual of showing lights to God by Dwijadev Brahmadev Bhatta, the Chief Priest, was about to conclude soon. In the evening, almost three hours got devoted to his worship of God, propitiating Him with lights. Perhaps, he was tired by now. Even in this wintry chill, drops of perspiration accumulated on his forehead. On his left, the devadasi, who drew fans for him with her thighs clasped together to look like an expanded altar, was fatigued too. The devadasi, favoured by God, who stood on the left of the livid-throated Lord Mahadeva seemed to be wearied by the three-hour-long evening ritual of worshipping God with lights. His hand worked incessantly. Rhythm struck his body just now, as he kept wielding the fly-whisk. It seemed that the rhythm would decide his emancipation.

The merchant was sitting outside the main hall, overlooking the door. He came just after the arati began. The flames of the five lamps leapt up and kept dancing in front of his eyes. The merchant was suddenly reminded of Devadutta, the courtesan. The glow of the flames resembled that of the yellow silk, that of the nascent moon, which just bobbed up. Devadutta seemed to be a radiant flambeau, clad in a yellow silk dress. The merchant had been a witness to her dance on this temple-ground. It was a Vaishakhi Purnima. The arati of Lord Mahadeva began. It seemed as though the courtesan grew into a flame to worship the Lord in the Mahakaal Temple. And then! The young lady turned fiery amidst the resounding timbrels and bells. Her two hands seemed to get transformed into thousand ones to swallow up the moonlit night. The King had come along with queen Bhanumati, the Chief of the Army had been there and he, himself, was among them. The merchant had taken Dhruvaputra along. And this proved to be fatal. The seeds of destruction had been sown in that amorous dance, that was on for almost three hours. The merchant was gazing at the devadasi. Young, well-poised, and, beautiful. Each of the damsels had been fit for an offering to the deity and the priest as well. The merchant grew restive within. He seemed to see Devadutta in the quivering flame of the lamp. This arati of Lord appeared to have mellowed into a flame of lust and passion. The Gods had no summer or winter, everlasting Spring prevailed in the Heavens where they reside. Only the flame of lust can perturb them. Swaying his head, the merchant wished to let go of the uncouth thoughts that cluttered his mind. But he got lustful again by the contortions of the body, the artistic postures of the devadasi who kept standing beside the deity. She was fanning the fly-whisk by bending a bit on the phallic image of Neelkantha - Lord Shiva. Her expanded hip, well-shaped breasts, body like a green stalk, and the thighs distinct through the mekhala — all caught the attention of the merchant. This young damsel had been chosen for the service of God for this season. She used to lie in front of the door of the main base-temple of Lord Mahakaal. At the behest of Lord Mahakaal the door opened wide.

The beating of drums could be heard. The bell and plates of bell-metal went ringing. Gradually, the sound of drums and bells reached crescendo. Arati was drawing to a close. To the north of the Mahakaal temple, the jackals in the forest of Mahakaal were to announce its conclusion, it seemed. The merchant observed the devadasi was convulsing along with the flicker of the flame of the panchapradip. The tycoon was watching how the stone-still image of the devadasi was swinging the fanning-wheel in her hand, sitting beside the chief priest. The dance, went beyond three hours on that Vaisakhi Purnima with perfect elan and was yet to stop, though the time assigned was nearly over. The chief courtesan was absorbed in her dancing. Her steps stirred sparks from the stones of the temple-yard. The torso, from the waist to the upper part of the body, shuddered. The pliancy, the chill of the south-westerly wind heated up, coming in contact with the flames of fire, and it spiralled to the sky. The moonshine heated up, the light manifested itself like dawn. Stirring his head, the trader again strove to drive away his unwelcome, uncivil thoughts. He stretched his gaze forward. Arati was about to end. It seemed that it would have been better if it hadn't concluded. The devadasi kept stooping low to the front of the phallic idol of Lord Shiva. Unfounded thoughts kept rushing in the brain, once again. The merchant closed his eyes sharp. He was sure that this young woman had definitely been stricken by lust. She was desirous of offering herself. Would God, the Mahakaal, come to life?

The boom of the conch-shell mingled with the beating of drums and the ringing of the plates of bell-metal as well as the bells. A couple of devadasis began to blow the conch-shell, skyward, standing outside the inner base-temple, behind the merchant. Conch-shells began to be blown on the temple-yard too. The pigeons who had taken refuge in the pinnacles of the temple or in the dovecotes of temple-turrets woke up instantly, kept flapping their wings and calmed down gradually after cooing for some time. The priest began to swing the flame of light in nimble hands. The body of the young devadasi who was working on the flying-whisk, kept bending more and more. The blood began to rush briskly inside the body of Subhag Dutta.

The merchant grew restless. His body grew hot, all of a sudden. His gaze was lapping up the beauty of the young dame, surrendered to Lord Mahakaal. The sound of the conch-shell had made his breathing to race. He was sensing inebriation deep inside his blood. It was as if the declaration of the hours of union. It was, as though, a call of the flame to its companion. To his utter amazement, the merchant found the restiveness of the young lady, fanning the whisk, to mount. He seemed never to have witnessed such a body, surrendered to God in full devotion, fraught with such supple poise. He had never seen such restless dance of the eyeballs, not even such lovelorn, sidelong glances. Her eyes began to reflect the lust of a woman, engaged in coition. He imagined as if the devadasi would merge her own entity to that of Lord Mahakaal. Merchant Subhag Dutta began to shiver severely.

The merchant hardly used to come to the temple these days. The chief priest used to contact him in case of need or an emergency. He would come with presents. Subhag Dutta could not even recall when he last sat through an arati session in the evening, with such deep involvement. The little he could remember was that of Devadutta, the whore's amorous, enchanting dance on a Vaisakhi Purnima. Even that too seemed to be a matter of the long-lost past. As though, before yawning eons! However, he was able to find both the evenings alike so far as the surrender, the offering to Lord was concerned. The pious dedication of those two devadasis had a striking similarity with that of Devadutta, being a glow of flame herself. He recollected how the moonshine of that evening had fallen far short of its effulgence compared to the beauty of the daughter of Rasamanjari. The spark of beauty of the pleasure-woman had covered the moonshine as it kept swallowing the starlight. Lord Mahakaal sprang up to life by her ardent devotion to God and her lustful dance as well. The temple-yard went abuzz. Subhag Dutta remembered an attraction just as a burning flame drew in the insects. Dhruvaputra had been enticed too. Dhruvaputra got scorched in that fire. He was still a-flame. His unmatched pelf and treasures, no doubt, kept protecting him, yet he was singed invariably. That night itself, he rushed to the brothel. The exhausted courtesan had turned him down, as she was sacrificing the night to Lord Mahakaal. Returning the gold-coin-filled bag, she requested him to leave, with folded palms. Since then, he was circum-ambulating the flame itself! The richest man of Avanti sat taut. Dizziness benumbed his head. It occurred to him that, the devadasi, dedicated to Lord Mahakaal, or devoted to the priest in service, was much richer in the treasure of youth than the chief harlot of this city! She was much younger in age! Who knew, her youth might have still been unexplored! The very glance made him think so. The merchant waved his head. It was unlawful to be enamoured of maids who were sacrificed to the Lord!

He would never have been enticed, but there was no gainsaying the fact, that the rhythmical swinging of the fly-whisk had driven him mad! The posture of her working on the whisk, the rhythm which was being created at each instant, seemed to be just another face of amorous dance-movements. The thighs, bending behind the mekhala, stood conjoined, kept expanding in front of the phallic image of Lord Shiva, and the shanks began to curve near the end of her thighs. Her waist, the tip of her thighs, buttocks—all kept breaking free from darkness to light, to the same beat, the same repeated, regular pattern of sound. Her body, from the waist to the upper torso, kept curving down on the Lord, just like the moon of Shukla Chaturthi! Deep, intense, heavy breaths bathed the phallic idol of Lord Shiva. The well-shaped breasts softened a bit to tighten again in desire, in keeping with the laws of rhythm. The devadasi's holding her body erect and upright and the noise of the anklets rising from the various poses of the body ruffled the calm of the merchant. The noise of intense breathing wafted to the ears of the merchant, with eyes half-closed. In imagination, he grew his wings again. The intermingled boom of drums, bell-metal plates and conch-shell had transported the devadasi to the height of excitement. The excitement had cast its shadow even on the young girl, dedicated to the priest. Nowhere the merchant was detecting any sign of devotion unalloyed of lust as he, himself, had transcended the limits of divine surrender sans desire! Merchant Subhag Dutta could sense a conflagration, keen on devastating a Poush night! The concealed fire had left the stony floor of the temple and the body of the temple-structure heated. Mingled crescendo of bells, conch-shells seemed to cover up an unworldly shriek of sexual delight! He seemed to be engrossed in a sudden sense of latent pleasure!

All of a sudden, the world came to an utter stillness. The all-pervasive noise that pervaded the large temple, the star-lit firmament stretched over the shrine, the darkness prevalent in the Gandhavati river, adjacent to the temple, in the courtyard, in the city of Ujjwain — all stood stock-still. Sound of conch-shell, bell and drums had stopped. The announcement of every three hours by the jackal in the forest of Mahakaal in the north was fading out. The merchant got to his feet. He had perspired profusely in the highly expensive indigenous woollen attire from Punjab. Removing the shawl, Subhag Dutta freed his chest to breathe freely. Now his breathing was slow, calm. He was exhausted. Fishing out the gold-coin-filled reticule from his waist in an indistinct voice he said, "Wonderful! Splendid is the swinging of the fly-whisk there, Lord Mahakaal would definitely be gratified, no doubt".

Being miffed at the plaudit of the swinging of the whisk, the old priest turned his head back, saw the merchant, Subhag Dutta, tried to conceal his disgust, replace it with mirth, got gratified and said, "Are you talking about that devadasi, Sir"?

The merchant failed to hear what the priest said. His eyes were glued to the reclining devadasi on the temple-wall, stretching beyond Brahmadev, the Chief Priest. The back of her head got hit on the stony wall, he could easily make out that. The noise had reached his ears. The fly-whisk slipped off from her hand. However, Lord Mahakaal would come to life usually as the lamp was shown while worshipping, and, it was now the time for His respite. But was the devadasi, whose youth bloomed fresh as the lotus-pond, really absorbed in self-surrender? Both her eyes were shut. Both her breasts, fleshy as nectarine fruit were heaving up and down with inhalation-exhalation, rhythmically. Being amazed by the graceful breasts the merchant yelled in a muffled tone, "What's wrong with her to find Lord Mahakaal fallen asleep lately"?!

"Mahakaal never used to sleep. Sleep was not for him, he used to stay awake as ever. At times however, he remained engrossed in meditation," saying so, the Chief Priest turned to Lord Mahakaal. The lady who served him ran instantly to hold the devadasi in both her hands. She had taken her head on her lap. The business magnate was annoyed. That coition-inducing posture made him passionate once again. Devadasi was thrown out of view by the youthful, serving maid. The other two devadasis, who kept blowing conch-shells, entered the base-temple, frightened, letting out inarticulate screams at the entrance. The Chief Priest emerged with the panchapradip in his hand, aflame. Golden flame was throbbing at the tip of the golden lamp. The Chief Priest placed the benediction on the forehead of the merchant, by floating the heat of the flame in his hand. And again, he repeated the action for himself. He called out to a young maid, "Take it, what's wrong with her"?

The intimidated maid who used to serve, placed the head of the devadasi down and received the panchapradip from the Chief Priest. The Chief Priest went admonishing her, "What about your duty? How could you keep tending her head, setting all your responsibilities at naught?"

What the fear-stricken maid replied, could not be made out. She kept holding the panchapradip firm, with gloom writ large on her face. The light of the lamp was about to be extinguished. Five wicks were aflame.

Just then, Brahmadev Bhatta, the Chief Priest, reprimanded her hard, "It is your good luck to have entered the base-temple, if you commit any blunder, you would be dumped straight into the litter-bin".

The young maid whispered, "Subhadra has lost her consciousness".

The Chief Priest answered, "She will be back to her health on her own. She is sheltered by Lord Mahakaal, Lord is keeping an eye on her, who are you to hold her"?

"She kept fasting all day long", the young maid muttered.

"She has to be on fasting". The Chief Priest came out of the base-temple. The man of business kept walking by his side. The Chief Priest inquired, "Are you gratified"?

"What for"?

"Observing Subhadra, the devadasi, I mean".

"The way she was swaying the fly-whisk was simply magnificent", pat came Subhag Dutta's comment.

The Chief Priest said, "I must let her know about you. It is by the grace of Lord Mahakaal, you have taken fancy on Subhadra…youthful, graceful, truly dedicated".

Both of them kept walking up to the room of the Chief Priest. A devadasi, with a lamp in her hand, kept showing them the way. She bent more and more, quite noticeably, to make the lamplight illumine the path. Moving forward, the Chief Priest demanded, "Are you desirous of Subhadra"?

"Let it remain as it is. She is protected by Lord Mahakaal".

As they kept conversing, the light in the devadasi's hand guttered. She was dragging her feet along to move forward. The merchant could hear the tinkle of her anklets in darkness. She was trying to steal a look at the devadasi, straining his eyes. Though in the dark, it was not clear whether she was young or elderly. The tinkling of her anklets made one imagine her to be a young lady. The merchant was observing how the soft, yellow blaze of the flame kept reflecting variegated shadows on the wall of the temple, on its roof as well. From the main shrine and the base-temple, the Chief-Priest's bedchamber was just a little bit off. Even that chamber was a part of the temple. A vast, rocky terrace and numerous pillars were to be crossed in order to reach there. The ceiling, however, was not too high. A little effort would be needed for the merchant to touch it. The shadow of the devadasi's hand grew prominent on that roof. Her reflection was a-quiver on the wall.

The business magnate asked, "Is she adept in dancing"?

"Would Lord Mahakaal be gratified sans dance"? Brahmadev replied.

"Where does this damsel hail from? Which nation? Which hamlet"?

"From Avanti, indeed. But a woman can hardly be bound by any rule, till she belongs to whoever she builds her shack with. Is there any inhibition in taking her as to be born in this Mahakaal only"?

Both of them stood at the threshold of the room. The devadasi had gone inside with the lamp in her hand. She was busy making the seat. The magnate could hear the jingle of the anklets. The anklets would mean the presence of a woman. Without the noise of the anklets, a lady's presence would be hard to ascertain. The sound faded off to silence. A few moments slipped by without noise. The Chief Priest in a muffled tone called out, "Hey, what's wrong? Why did you stop altogether"?

In frightened steps, the damsel emerged in the dark. Hastily, she ran to stand with her back leaning upon a column. A pale view affirmed her to be a young lady. The Chief Priest ordered, "Go, sit there and answer if called… Come in, Sir".

Both of them sat on two separate seats. On one corner, the lamp kept burning. The room was laden with the fragrance of joss-sticks. But some other smell was being wafted to the nostrils of the magnate. He could not however say whether the smell was issuing from within the smoke of the burnt incense. While lost in his inner musings, the merchant held out the silk-reticule from his waist and handed it to the priest for Subhadra, the devadasi.

Brahmadev, the priest turned radiant while accepting it. Feeling the weight of the reticule, he transferred it from the right to the left hand and exclaimed,"You are generous at heart".

The magnate's voice boomed as he said, "Listen Brahmin, I had gone to Ratnakarsagar, in the vicinity of the ghetto of the Shudras".

Hamlet of the Shudras! The Brahmin's face turned into a picture of abomination. He said, "Dhruvaputra, whom you sheltered, used to frequent the ghetto of the Shudras, even being a Kshatriya. And he had to face the music. Did you go there in search of any Shudra woman"?

The Merchant smirked, "Why? Is this city so impoverished that Subhag Dutta has to run after a Shudra maid"?

"Look, I heard the people there asking, why is the lake in such a deplorable state, which would never run dry so far, which again had lotus in blossom all the year round"?

"Has the lake gone dry"? Brahmadev inquired.

"About to"…

"Owing to drought, I mean, lack of rainfall"?

The Shudras of the hamlet kept saying, the water in the pond owed not solely to rainfall, even this place had witnessed such droughts before. But what had transpired now was just incredible!

The Chief Priest said, "But why would we take it from the Shudras,- both the women and the Shudras should stay silent — that's the edict of the society"!

The magnate cautioned him, "Please say it in a hushed tone. Ask your devadasi to leave, she is there, outside".

The Brahmin laughed, "Didn't I say that, neither the Shudras nor the women has any power, both the kinds are dumb like the inferior beasts, does the being who is sitting outside have any thinking power or any intelligence? Nothing at all she has, rest assured, not a faint possibility is there. They know, devourers are innumerable-- Lord Mahakaal, the wild beasts of the forest, the wolves even would have a feast on the delectable flesh — come on, keep talking, dear merchant"!

Subhag Dutta was drawing in the smell consciously. It was the odour of putrefaction of some animal-carcass. It might be a rat. He agreed, "Yes, your statement is true. But it is rather wrong to put the whole of the Shudra community in question for their women, as the Shudra male holds the weapon in favour of our army".

Hearing this, the Chief Priest's voice went a scale lower. Slouching a bit, taking the silk-bag from one hand to the other, he said, "I cannot fully make out your words".

Subhag Dutta said, "The Shudras comprise the lowest rung of the society. The grievance comes from among them, they say that Avanti had never witnessed such a plight. Has anyone ever heard of the sea going dry, has it ever happened that the whole city has gone lotus-less? Just think for a while".

"The lotus season is already over".

"But previously, the ponds used to stay crammed with white, blue lotuses irrespective of seasons, they say".

"Can't you remember"?

"Just guess, the complaint comes from a lower stratum, it may even be raised here, the forthcoming days seem to be really problematic".

"But in the months of Magh and Phalgun, rains pour", Brahmadev said.

"Since the last couple of years, rain eluded us and now also it may".

"Will Barundev be so ruthless? If the monsoon goes without rain, it will now shower, at this time of the year".

"Let Mahakaal be kind enough not to make the rain fall, such a natural disaster hardly occurs, not even just at anyone's will."

The eyes of the Chief Priest brightened, all of a sudden, he cried out, "Lalita, Lalita, where are you"?

Without getting any reply, he sprang up on his feet in an instant and rushing to the door called in a low voice, "Lalita, where have you gone, you slut, you keep rubbing your back against the wall! This harlot has an excessive craving for sex, I see".

The jingle of anklets could be heard. From far, the tinkling of the anklets got wafted beyond. The priest kept standing. He was excited by the words of the magnate. To alleviate his excitement, he stood up. The noise of the devadasi's anklets stopped. In a suppressed tone, he asked, "Where had you been"?

"Far away".

"Go and wait even further but make sure to answer as I call you".

Subhag Dutta rose up, "Which smell is this? It seems to be of a rotten animal, something has decomposed inside, it appears".

"Is it so"? The Chief Priest had grabbed the magnate's hand abruptly, "Forget that odour, Sir, do you want this drought to continue for a few more days in Avanti"?

"Yes, definitely, I want it. You will have everything you need to make it happen".

"To make Lord Varun adverse is a difficult task, even I may stand accursed, I may be brought to book by the King"!

"Rest assured, the Royal Treasury has gone bankrupt, the subjects' fields are sans harvest, at this moment the King himself is seeking my favour, the Royal Coffer is looking up to me for succour and this is an open secret".

The odour was growing pungent. The putrid smell of the decomposed creature was even superseding the fragrance of the incense. While talking at the threshold, they again stepped inside. The merchant demanded, "You will definitely be able to do it. Was the King asking for a yajna"?

"Hasn't asked as yet, perhaps he will".

"The financial support for the yajna will come from this Subhag Dutta. Please do mar the oblation, on the sly".

The Chief Priest was seized with fright, "I shall perform the yajna and I shall ruin it myself"!

"Yes, I tell you, this natural disaster will turn into a bliss to mankind sometime in future, nature has grown into our complementary force. The subjects are feeling irritated gradually, haven't you got a feel of that"?

The Chief Priest was petrified. He sat grabbing the reticule, heavy with gold coins, against his chest. He was also being overcome by fear. Subhag Dutta, the magnate, was loved by the King. He had limitless power in the Royal Court. The King would seek his help at times. He had not thought in his wildest dream that he would get to hear such bold words straight from his mouth! A few days back, Subhag Dutta had paid him a visit in the morning. Their conversation that day was all superfluous. Subhag Dutta demanded repeatedly, "What is the reason for such drought? Why has Nature turned indifferent? Who is responsible for this plight in Avanti and Ujjwain? Any way-out"?

The merchant was about to leave. In slow and firm steps, he stood on the threshold and said, "Let that devadasi, Subhadra, be with you, she is my gift to you, along with the gold coins. Please be firm in your aim, that's it. You are the Chief Priest of the temple of Lord Mahakaal, your command will be obeyed by all with reverence". Saying so, Subhag Dutta went on his knees and bowed down to touch his forehead on the stony ground. His ears were made to hear, "May you be victorious! May the Goddess of Avanti be more kind to you! May the city of Avanti be blessed, no path is to be avoided, keeping its welfare in view"!

Fourteen

The shadows kept oscillating. King Bhartrihari turned around, while standing. He flung open the leaves of the windows. In front of his eyes, the wide sky of Poush opened up. The light of the lamp swam outside in the darkness through the open casement. Bhartrihari fixed his gaze on the sky. The keen wintry wind was making an inroad. The King felt comfortable in a white woollen wrapper in the wind that blew. This was from Punjab. This had a magnificent embroidery on it. It was learnt that Bhanumati had the credit of making the woollen garments such ornate. At present, Bhanumati did not admit this. How strange! She said, A number of maids had been there in her paternal residence! And they had numerous qualities to boast of! Someone from among them might have sewn it. The King might go there to find out the woman who had sewn it. She must be exceedingly pretty with immortal youth. And again, what of that to the King? He has chosen the path of renunciation, for sure!

The King of Avanti was remembering all this. Through the open window, he kept watching the Ksheersagar, at a distance. The moon of the eighth lunar day, the dewy fog of Poush, and Ksheersagar lying in an abandon while darkness and light kept intermingling in it. It failed to be recognized, the location of the pond confused us. White lotus filled the pond round the year, numerous moons stood reflected on the eye of the water-body, it seemed. The still eyes of the King of Avanti had no light in them. He stretched a lightless glance through the darkness. It had never so happened that Ksheersagar could not be seen from this window. Ksheersagar had slid off the optical range. This was just a rare occurrence. Lotuses wilted in Ksheersagar, the petals dropped off too. But never all at a time. A few flowers bloomed round the twelve months. Some again bloomed from season to season. They bloomed through the monsoon till the autumn and even winter. But had it ever happened so that the pond went without water? No lotus was there in bloom anymore. The ducks who swam in water did not turn to that direction. When did the fishes in the water die? In which slush did they get stuck in, burying their heads, who could tell? The King wished he had turned round again. Now inching towards the window, he stood, turning

122

around. He closed the window. How evicted he felt within! He held the wrapper lose on his body. He turned again. He went moving forward. The lighted lamp remained behind. On the wall to his front swung the shadow of the King. As he stopped, the reflection too did. Eyeing the monstrous shadow, the King thought of paying a visit to Mangalnath. He had been there during a full-moon day in Kartik. And after that, a long time had sped by. It was the eighth full-moon day of Poush. It was drawing closer with only seven days to go. The King leaned back on the wall.

This was his study. Sitting in this room, he had composed the shlokas on amorous union. After their wedding, he had read them out to Bhanumati. Yonder lay the bark of the birch, the swan-quill, the inkpot. The King had thought of composing many more shlokas. Would those poems be again on sexual togetherness? Or would they be about love without coition? As his whole being stirred into emotional exuberance overlooking the dark universe, he could even take the emotions as the topic for his next lines. This poem would not be of bodily union, it must be of love only. But he could not write a single shloka so far. Who would inspire him in the dark ambience, in the moonlit nights, during twilight or even at the crack of dawn? The sadness of which estrangement from a beloved would make him create new and newer verses? The King's neck bent down. Bhanumati! Why not Bhanumati? Bhanumati had spread the darkness of a perpetual absence in his deeper within, it seemed. The new shloka would be written on that absence of light itself. In the dark void of estrangement from a paramour, it would be a tale of estrangement only. There was Bhanumati, sleeping, in the southern bedchamber. All alone. The King was here. Alone. Bhanumati lay alone on that vast bedstead. King Bhartrihari was alone with his pang of estrangement from his love. Loneliness engendered estranged feelings indeed. That bedchamber seemed to lie hundreds and hundreds of miles off. We are reminded of the way his young wife used to sit awake while poet Bhartrihari kept writing verses. She used to sit on the floor, at the other end of the door. How would the wife take to bed if her husband was yet to retire for the night, finishing off his writing? Again, how would it look if she kept sitting by the side of her husband? The poet sat deeply engrossed in composing his verses. That keen concentration might be intercepted by the proximity of his wife, who knew! Many an evening, many a night had slipped by while he failed to put a single word on the bark. The quill stayed dipped in the ink, but did not touch the bark at all.

The poet used to say, Man doesn't know the mystery of creation, even he who creates is not cognizant of it, yesterday I had composed a couple of shlokas. Today I could not write a single shloka.

The eyes of the young wife were awash with amazement. With wide-eyed wonder she asked, "If the creator doesn't know, how can creation happen then"?

"I don't know".

The wife seemed to fix her gaze on the sky through the open window and casting her glance on the planets, stars, and luminous objects, she inquired, "Take this Universe, doesn't the Creator know how He created it"?

The King rejoined," Perhaps he knows. But if he is aware of the form of the created object beforehand, what would he create then? That which exists is known to us, and, in bestowing existence on something that does not exist at all, lies the real joy of creation".

Bhanumati had an ocean of curiosity. How she used to stare at the poet! At the dead of night, staying stark awake, looking at the sleeping poet! Surrendering to the arms of sleep while observing the moonshine slipping bit by bit from the countenance of the poet and then relating the experience candidly, the following day!

Bhanumati said, "Oh King, even conceiving the child"!

The King replied, "No creation is greater than this! I shall never be able to make the dream of the child a reality, even after penning hundreds of thousands of shlokas"!

Bhanumati bombarded him with her query, "Does knowledge come first or the creation"?

The King replied, "Unearthing knowledge is creation indeed, and from the creation again knowledge results".

"Or is it then the knowledge inspires creation"?

The poet said, "Not so untrue".

"Then, the birth of knowledge"?

"That is not untrue again".

"Then which one is untrue"?

The King answered, "This universe, firmament, the vast earth—all are true, I do not know where untruth lies".

Bhanumati said, "If truth is there, untruth obviously be there too, that which ceases to exist now will be nothing but untruth ... what is the truth and what again is untruth"?

The King said, "Ignorance".

"What is ignorance"?

"That which is contrary to creation".

"What is creation"?

"Light, have you seen the light of dawn, Bhanumati"?

Listening to him, the eyes of Bhanumati got inundated with light. Slowly she uttered, "Oh King, I have seen myriads of lights, light of dawn, moonshine, starlight, the light of your eyes. But do you know, while your quill dances on the bark of birch etching the shloka on it, your eyes brighten up, and that light is also the glow of knowledge"!

Now the King's eyes were overcast with the melancholy of ignorance. The mind lay in disarray. Shlokas could not be composed in a confused state of mind. The King stirred as if it were the time to set out for Mangalnath. The two eyes would now stiffen in insomnia. Perhaps, the night would come to an end as sleeplessness would prolong. Inability to write the shlokas, the rejection of Bhanumati, getting lost in thoughtless sleep — all these remained cocooned in the disorderly mental plight. Emerging from the chamber, the King kept walking up and down the long verandah, enveloped in the chiaroscuro of light and darkness, though dimly illumined by the lamplight. The terrace was narrow, if two hands were stretched standing in the middle, it would not only get constrained by the walls but the hands would not be expanded fully too. The King was walking as a blind man. Three fingers of one of his hands were getting scraped on the stony wall, on one end. He came to a halt. On the right end, the bedchamber of the King and the queen stood. The King could visualize Bhanumati with his mind's eye.

Of late, King Bhartrihari felt no urge to touch the body of Bhanumati, her limbs still supple with the charms of youth. Pleasure and desire can hardly complement each other. Can gratifying the lustful desire be tantamount to pleasure? Could Bhanumati be the source of gratification? If so, Bhanumati would never refrain from repaying the love of the King. Did all joy remain in the body and limbs of a woman? In that case, neither the King nor the merchant should fall victims to melancholy. Was there any dearth of the gem called 'woman' in the land ruled by the King? A thirsty man would need cold water to slake his thirst, morsels of rice to alleviate his hunger gnawing at his entrails, and if a man was assailed by bodily desires, he would accept a woman, be it his wife or a whore. The flames of desire were no different from that of either thirst or hunger, which shot up temporarily. Hunger, thirst and lust were the essentials for a man to live by. Even the lesser creatures had the jab of hunger, thirst and passion. Just like the victuals that satisfy hunger and thirst, man and woman feed the urge for sexual union in themselves. These are the basic needs for sustaining life. But they cannot be components of living a life as happiness cannot be assured. Happiness is even more beyond living a life.

Rice, water, woman, man's hunger, thirst prove to be an antidote to the ailments of burning lust. Isn't man aware of all this?

King Bhartrihari had entered the bedchamber. At a corner of this room, a ghee-lamp was kept. That soft yellow glow had stretched up till the edge of the large bedstead. In the dark of the giant bed, Bhanumati lay fast asleep, with her mesmerizing, winsome beauty. Stepping in the room, the King had got a feel of that grace! Was this burn caused by fire? The flame of beauty! Or was this flame owed to desire? Or lust? Both the eyes of the King were closed. Though shut, he failed to remove Bhanumati from the range of his vision! If Bhanumati, the Lakshmi of Avanti, woke up to consciousness, he would have to keep looking on, mesmerized, into the pupils of both her eyes. It was as though, he was enjoying the sight of new stars, surfacing afresh in the sky. All new hues would keep engendering within him. New shlokas! If invited by Bhanumati, the King would move forward like a fly to the burning flame of that beauty! The King muttered under his breath, Alas, Bhanumati, call me, please, call me!

The King took up the lamp with both the hands. As taken to a height, the soft glow of the lamp could embrace the full stature of the sleeping queen, Bhanumati. The beauty that lay latent in the womb of darkness, stood manifested. It was as if the lamplight was the refuge for Bhanumati's exquisiteness. The King kept both his eyes wide open. What had he witnessed? A shadow of lapis-lazuli on a face resembling the gracious moon. Ponderous breasts, though covered with a winter-blanket betrayed the distinct lines. He grew anxious. Both his eyes got bedazzled by the beauty of Bhanumati. The exquisiteness of a sleeping woman which added an extra shade to her beauty mesmerized the King. He kept looking at Bhanumati, as though she belonged to someone else. In a muffled tone, he called up, "Bhanumati"!

Bhanumati's sleep was sound enough to be spoilt. The lamp in the King's hand was a-tremble. Putting the lamp back in its place, the perturbed King wanted to calm down. Standing in the dark, he again called out, "Bhanumati, get up, Bhanumati"!

The King could sense the surge of fire within him. Which fire? Was it ignited by Bhanumati's beauty? He was getting burned by that conflagration. He was the victim of his self-combustion. He failed to touch Bhanumati, though Bhanumati made a foray into his being, with all her essence and existence. The King had plummeted down on the stone-cold floor. He lay supine on the ice-cold stone. He stretched his pair of eyes towards rooftop. The flame of the lamp-wick was a-flutter. The King was keen on protecting himself. Gradually, the temperature of his body was slumping. Then Bhanumati had woken up on the royal bedstead, beyond his knowledge. Sitting up in her bed, she got to see the King. The King of Avanti was lying on the floor of the chamber.

Bhanumati accosted him, "What's wrong? Why are you there"?

The King lay still. His restless body was turning calm.

Bhanumati seemed hard to bear it, her voice was laced with a touch of harshness. She cried out, "Why such self-oppression? I shall not be able to sleep".

Slowly, the King sat up in that darkness. Then he stood up. To Bhanumati it seemed as if the King of Avanti had come up from the depth of the ground. It seemed to Bhanumati as though King Bhartrihari had raised his head, breaking the stone-slabs apart. As if from the void of the dark the King of Avanti had emerged — it appeared to Bhanumati thus. Bhanumati looked agape in utter astonishment. To her, Bhartrihari, the King of Avanti, Bhartrihari, her husband, seemed to be a stranger! Now he seemed no more the man who was close to her heart. It was hard to believe that this very man had composed the shlokas on sexual union of man and woman! Strange was it to find that the royal man of honour, once profligate, desirous of women, would lie on the cold floor to render himself devoid of all sexual passion. Didn't Bhanumati get the drift of this matter? Didn't she have the faintest inkling? And again, Bhanumati herself, felt no attraction to the King anymore! How strange! Life was thus! Once upon a time, this man's stentorian voice made her whole body resonate. She used to feel romantic by thinking of this man, deep down her own self. How unbounded were those love-laden days! The King had lain on the floor in such a wintry night! His body had surely warmed up somehow, which he was trying to cool down! Before going down on the floor, the King had stood by the edge of this bed, for sure! Then, Bhanumati lay fast asleep. Perhaps, the King had beholden her beauty as she lay asleep! It was a covert habit of King Bhartrihari! Many a night, the queen had woken up to find a pair of eyes, glued to her face! The King used to say that he loved to watch Bhanumati, without her knowledge. He was seized by that fad once again, perhaps. To gain control of his heated physique, the King had taken refuge to the ice-cold stone. Bhanumati's head swam. The King's love seemed unbearable to her. She cringed in disgust to surmise that the King had turned hot in desire, by throwing a glance at her sleeping body. Turning her face to the other direction, Bhanumati sat apart.

The King said, " With the seven ponds running dry sans water, the soil, the stones getting hard, with not a blob of cloud in the sky since ages, how can I lie on a floral bed"?

The queen did not stir. She felt like going off to sleep once again. If she fell asleep, the King would again keep beholding her beauty, with a lamp in his hand. He would again be seized by passion. In order to come out of that clutch of lust, he lay down on the ice-cold floor. The King lacked in the courage of touching her!

Bhanumati would wake up from sleep much before he touched her! How strange! How could Bhanumati sense everything even being dead to the world?

The King was saying, "Again a visit to Mangalnath is a must".

The queen did not move a bit. Bhanumati stood like a heap of darkness. She had almost erased her existence, it appeared. It seemed like King Bhartrihari was talking to darkness. He was speaking to himself. He was saying, Let us listen to what Acharya Brishavanu said, A new star was about to take birth in the realm of the firmament, and hence, such lack of rainfall resulted along with such dearth of harvest!

Bhanumati spoke up, "I shall sleep now".

The King was hurt, "Could you make out the significance of my statement, my queen"?

"What for"?

"You are the queen of Avanti, the Goddess of Wealth of Avanti, you will accompany me, we will go to the Mahakaal Temple after paying a visit to the ashram of Brishavanu. We will discuss the matter with the Chief Priest".

The queen had gone silent again. Unmoved, stock-still. She seemed to be shadowed by the growing darkness. In a low tone, the King was saying, "Such incident had never transpired here, ever before. All the seven lakes have gone waterless, not a single lotus has bloomed anywhere. I am the King of Avanti, how can I go off to sleep, even a bed of roses would turn to bed of thorns for me now! They would turn into ice-cold, rough stones. Avanti is now facing tough times, no field has crops, no wheat has been sown this time, no harvest of rice or barley is made possible..."

the King went on, "The astrologers in the royal court opine that a new star is being seen in the sky of Ujjwain. By the ominous influence of that stellar object, all rain-clouds have disappeared! The messenger of the Chief Priest of Mahakaal Temple had come, he was anxious, he begged for a little time. I said, I must see him in the dark hours of the night. Rumours would spread, if people saw the Chief Priest entering the King's court. Men are fond of imagining things..."

The queen took to the royal bedstead, slowly. King Bhartrihari could hear her inhalation in the darkness. In the dark, Bhartrihari could distinctly make out the contours of Bhanumati's body. Bhanumati lay turning to the other side of the bed. Gradually, he leaned over Bhanumati. Fragrance was being wafted to his nostrils. Fragrance of Bhanumati's body. The King suddenly felt giddy. In an inaudible voice, he called out, "Bhanumati, my love!"

Bhartrihari could not make out whether Bhanumati heard him or not. His whole being was getting numbed by the sweet smell of Bhanumati. Stretching his right hand, he wished to touch Bhanumati. He felt like scrounging another favour from Bhanumati. As if, again they would be each other's mirror. He was in terrible convulsion. In the darkness, he could clearly feel intense bewilderment engulfing the body of Bhanumati. Bhanumati's body was a-stir with intense breathing inside her woollens. He touched her. Now, Bhanumati could sense it and in a muffled voice expressed, "It's so cold, you can go but I am not coming along".

As the King touched Bhanumati's forehead, Bhanumati shuddered and sprang off, exclaiming – "Oh, how cold it is, just as a dead man's hand! Oh King, be off".

The King moved away. He was lost in himself. He walked out of the room hurriedly. This is the way when either of the couple, the man or the wife, gets piqued by the other. The touch of one appears to be corpse-like to the other. Bhanumati's rejection made the King move off from either the edge of this bed, or this bedchamber, or sometimes even from the front of Bhanumati's eyes, but at times, an explosion was an obvious outcome! And one such blast occurred right now. The presence of Bhanumati was still vibrant and vivid in this man's being! At this instant, however, he seemed like a dead man to Bhanumati. And Bhanumati, too, was acting the same by remaining irresponsive to all his approaches.

The King took the God's way, with a lamp in his hand. This stealthy way had led to the river Shipra on one end and the river Gandhavati on the other, both being contiguous to the shrine of Lord Mahakaal. Both the ways were deep and desolate. None knew about this path save the Chief of his Army, his younger step-brother, Bikram. While making his way into the darkness through the hidden lane, King Bhartrihari startled to an abrupt halt. It seemed as though the sleeping pigeons had suddenly woken up. Cooing in the drowsy spell, they again dropped off to sleep. Looking hither and thither, the King stepped into the temple-way with the lamp, held in his hand. He walked on.

Chapter Fifteen

The King walked through the temple-way. Lately, he had to follow this route alone. It never so happened before. Bhanumati, herself, had dragged him along to the

Mahakaal Shrine, at the dead of night. By the river Gandhavati, beneath the firmament, on a glowing moonlit night! They even had gone to the bank of the river, Shipra, by this way. But when was it? Before the last monsoon. When had the last monsoon hit? Last, nay, the Sravana before the last one, even preceding that by one year! Preceding that came Baisakh, perhaps in that Baisakh night, in the intense, desolate darkness, both held hands together to reach the Mahakaal, by the river, Shipra. Beside the river, underneath the sky, they had explored each other quite intimately, in the illumination of the stars. Many a night, the couple had lost themselves in each other, in that nonpareil silence! They seemed to hear the sound of one body mingling with the other. How melodious that sound had been! Each limb of one body resonated with the touch of the same limb of the other one. It was followed by the rains. Many a time the monsoon struck, the spring and the summer had faded out, bidding adieux to the land. Several times, the winter followed the monsoon, and the evening of autumn preceded the winter! Before autumn came the morning of early autumn. How enchanting that world had been! Spring, Summer, Monsoon, early Autumn, Autumn, Winter!

Bhartrihari could sense that the memories of that monsoon had gone grey too! That Baisakh, Jaisthya, Chaitra, Spring in Phalgun and the summer's memories had passed into nullity, the dreams of early and late autumn too had equally passed into oblivion. To which early times did all such memories date back? To which birth? From the temple-way, the King of Avanti had come up to stand beneath the sky. He left the lamp on that very way, behind a stone-slab. Now, he would walk down the path, lit by the stars in the firmament. He would get to know his path with the aid of the moon of Shukla Ashtami. Moonshine being coupled with fog had cast a turbid pall on the surroundings. Covering his head with his woollens, the King was walking away briskly in this strange universe, where it could hardly be discerned whether any other soul had been awake! Look, yonder that golden steeple could be seen. The moon was about to stand atop Mahakaal lately. The King stood to witness that rare spectacle! He bowed down his head in reverence. And again, he started walking with brisk steps. Swiftly. It was, as if he was out on a rendezvous. Just in this manner, the lovebirds of the city used to conceal themselves while going to meet their love. Walking by the river Gandhavati, throwing cautious glances hither and thither, he came up to the secret entrance of the Mahakaal Temple. It was customary to escape by this route during perils and the enemy-attacks. In slow steps, the King entered the darkness of the tunnel. Quite gingerly, feeling the path with his hands and feet, he came to the rear end of the shrine. Moving forward, he stepped into the terrace. He threaded his way through the narrow terrace, whose height too was low. This long corridor was known to him, he was familiar with each and every nook of this shrine. He had no issues with darkness. He knew the city of Avanti thoroughly too. He could walk down the thoroughfares of Avanti even in the dark. He knew the city of Ujjwain like the back of his palm. Closing his eyes, he could remember when, where, on which streets in Ujjwain the shadows fell, and when and where the shadows elongated! He knew which path in Ujjwain stayed inundated by moonshine and to what extent, on a moonlit night! Even he knew at which nooks and strips of this long terrace the first light of the nascent sun fell. Similarly, he was cognizant of the particular point on the other end of this terrace, from which the afternoon sunlight evaporated during winter. He knew even the spot at which the sunshine fell during an afternoon in Baisakh!

King Bhartrihari had almost reached the end of the corridor. He had his eyes fixed on the flame of a lamp. The lamp was burning like a lone star in the darkness. The flame of the lamp flickered as the oil in the lamp was about to deplete. The lamp was placed in the small niche on the wall. The dark space under the lamp was where the devadasi Lalita lay, on a makeshift bed. The bed was made of animal fur but was too rough, the wool might have been of an inferior quality. The tip of the bristles pricked all over the body.

The room of the Chief Priest was quite close by. Devadasi seemed to play sentry to his sleep. His sleep was quite elusive. Even such nights were not infrequent in which he had to get up every now and then. The Chief Priest used to suffer from a barrage of old-age-related ailments, as a consequence, his sleep was far from being sound. It was the responsibility of Lalita to ensure that his sleep would be unperturbed. By any means. It never so happened that the Chief Priest was awake and she had fallen asleep. Such instructions had not been issued to her, though. The Brahmin was the representative of Lord Mahakaal. His will was tantamount to the will of Lord Mahakaal! She was supposed to sleep only for the hours when the Priest would remain asleep. She was accustomed that way. Nothing otherwise should happen or she would be losing the right of serving the Chief Priest. She would not be allowed to stay there in the Mahakaal Shrine, if the Brahmin would feel offended. She could not even think where she would land up, if Lord Mahakaal abandoned her!

Slumber lay heavy on the eyelids of Lalita. She seemed to dream in the light spell of sleep. In her dream, Lord Mahakaal came to stand before him in a different attire. She could distinctly see that Lord Mahakaal was walking towards her, emerging from the base of the temple, taking to the long terrace. How dazzlingly handsome He looked! How radiant He was! Alas, Lord Mahakaal! I have sought refuge just at your feet. I have offered everything I possess, to YOU only!

The drowsiness of slumber was intervened by the abrupt footfall of the King, though that was so indistinct that it was tantamount to silence. But Lalita's sleep or slumber would surely be affected by that. Lalita used to sense even when the Brahmin turned on his back on the bed! Though not the silent footfall of the King, Lalita had definitely been aware of the tremor of the ground, like a wary reptile. Her panic was just similar. She sat up with a fear-stricken face, covering her body with a tattered woollen wrapper. Either she was shivering in chill or the presence of a man to her front had left her intimidated. From the tall stature of the man, she could make out that this was not the Brahmin. He was a man of short build. This was a different man! Someone else. But who? He was gradually becoming staid and numb with fear and bewilderment. Slowly, the trembling was calming down. She was flabbergasted to see that the covering on the head of the stranger was falling off. Her trembling did set in, again. Who was this man? The dream in which she was drowsily absorbed, seemed to make its presence felt before her, in the form of a human. The countenance of the King left her amazed, drove her at her wit's end. The lamplight had illumined the face of Bhartrihari. In that soft, yellow glow, the gladness of his face intensified even more. In a low tone, the King inquired of her, "Is the Brahmin asleep"?

Devadasi had bent down. She could not recognize the King. She had seen him for once, from far. Just once. While the King and the queen used to visit Mahakaal, the devadasis were not allowed to come close. She was tallying the signs in dreams as seen in a slumber with reality. She was stooping even more. She bent and sat with folded knees, in front of the King. In an inaudible voice, she shrieked, "Oh alas, Lord Mahakaal"!

Devadasi Lalita lowered her head to the feet of the King. The devadasi was shedding tears silently on the feet of the King. A few minutes later, the King moved away a little. The moan of the devadasi got wafted to his ears. He could discern the word 'Mahakaal' while the rest was her groan. Moving a little, Bhartrihari said, "Stop crying, you have to awaken the Priest".

Lalita, the devadasi, was convulsing terribly. She was striving hard to hold back her tears. But was failing to do so. Being an emotional damsel, she had taken it for sure that she had been able to bow down her head to the feet of Lord Mahakaal. She had taken it for granted, that, Lord Shiva, alias Lord Mahakaal, had come down trailing her dreams to stand in front of her. Who would have thought that such would happen to her in this birth? She had been here only for banging her forehead on the stones of the temple-terrace and thus wasting her youth away! Following this trail, many had gone out to the squalor of the red-light belt, off the city, utterly devastating their youth in here. Many of them had gone missing. But the one who had witnessed the Lord Mahakaal, had her life altered for good. She had no idea whether someone had witnessed Him, but she was sure that the old Brahmin, the Chief Priest, though a human in form was the real representative of Lord Mahakaal! He used to engage in conversation with Lord Mahakaal. The commandments of Lord Mahakaal got issued through him only. He was a pious man. He was a man of power. He was a man of wealth. He owned an immense store of gems and treasures. He had a palatial edifice in this very city. Who else would emulate him in happiness, in the city of Ujjwain?

Lalita, the maid, had prayed in an indistinct voice, "Oh Lord Mahakaal, be propitiated, be kind to this wretched woman, in utter miseries".

King Bhartrihari was getting embarrassed. The young woman's forehead was again touching his feet. He stood, budging a bit. By then, raising her head, Lalita had folded both the legs of the King in her two hands, breaking in heartrending tears, she had lifted the King's feet on her chest and kept sobbing, "This wretched woman is utterly destitute, oh Lord, You keep vigil on everything, nothing is beyond Your knowledge, this ill-fated wench is now the serving lady to the Brahmin; be kind to me, be gratified, I serve the Brahmin with all I possess, oh Lord, this life and youth are dedicated to his feet only, I learnt that if he would be happy, You would be equally so, though my mind never assents to it".

Breaking into tears, Lalita began to feel that the stone image of Neelkantha Shiva, was no more of stone. He had become flesh and blood. Lord Mahakaal stood in front of her, in the guise of a human. She was in an ecstasy. Her breasts were getting firm. Blood began to run in her blood vessels, speedily. God's delegate, another form of Lord, was the Chief Priest, the Brahmin. Lalita had to offer him this body of hers, by way of serving him. But that service stood governed by fear, by the diktats of a system. While the elderly priest's body entangled hers like an octopod, the blood in her arteries seemed to coagulate, no wave of romantic thrill seized her.

Her petal-soft body, seemed to be filled with liquid filth which was dedicated solely to Lord Mahakaal. She was getting impure. When the saliva from the mouth of the elderly Chief Priest drenched both her breasts, her body began to shrivel. She seemed to get metamorphosed into a saggy-skinned old woman, whose youth was spent. She lay devoid of any sense. On her benumbed body, the loose-fleshed frame of the Brahmin kept dancing. While the elderly Chief Priest kept toying with the lifeless body of a young damsel, he seemed to be inferior in taste to a pimp of a brothel or the ilk. The elderly Chief Priest was excessively lustful. A man of perverted desires. He would love to extract pleasure by oppressing, by molesting the object of lust. And once his gratification reached its limit, he would not hesitate to push the devadasi, the consumed object, off his bed. He used to kick the woman away, from his bed.

Devadasi Lalita was remembering all such things. Her youthful body was being pressed under the feet of the King, who was none other than Lord Mahakaal. Her pair of breasts had been touched by the couple of feet of the King. That touch enlivened her after a long interregnum. Her youthful body and mind never used to be roused here, in this manner. None could rouse it. Her body would never be roused, while being sheltered by Lord Mahakaal. The old Priest's molestation left her hurt, humiliated. She was in shivers. In each of her body-cells, an unimaginable excitement was taking its birth. She was a devadasi. She was dedicated to God. She had offered each of her limbs to the Lord, mentally, it seemed. But that was the limit. She was never brought to excitement by the Lord. Her body never aroused sexually, by thinking of the Lord. Stone! Just a piece of stone! Behind all eyes, she had touched the phallic image of Lord Mahakaal Shiva, in the base-temple. She had become restless herself, before touching it. But the male genital of that image was so cold! Almost like ice! Even it was devoid of any throb of life. As though, she had expected a lively stir while touching it. She had sprung out of the base-temple in fear. She had been caught red-handed by the old Chief Priest, the Brahmin. The coldness of the stone image of God seemed to paralyze her body. The old Priest had asked her to see him in his room. Her service to the base-temple got terminated that day. But the Chief Priest had taken her, in lieu of the Lord. He acted as the deputy of God. Lord Mahakaaleswar used to manifest Himself in him. All seemed sham, while Lalita, the maid, thought of his depraved lust.

Devadasi Lalita seemed to grow blind in emotional, desirous and unworldly joyful exuberance! Lord Mahakaal had assumed the form of a flesh-and-blood human to stand before her eyes! After such a long time, God had smiled upon her! Purblind Devadasi began to rise up with her desire-struck, emotion-rocked, piety-bound body! Oh Lord Mahakaal, please accept me. You have answered my prayers, please exonerate me from all sins, oh Lord…!

The roused 'youthful' body was hauling King Bhartrihari towards it. The lamp was about to snuff out. The King could hear, the indistinct voice kept chanting 'Mahakaal' incessantly. The King could feel that the corporeal frame of this devadasi was really exquisite! This lady, such youthful, was unaware of his identity. He was in delusion. Being distracted by the devadasi, he wished to obliterate his identity as the King of Avanti at that moment. The address that reached his ears was enough to leave him hesitant, yet, he failed to reveal his own identity! Devadasi had opened herself up in newly-blossomed youth before Lord Mahakaal. He was Lord Mahakaal Himself! Lord Mahakaal alias Lord Shiva! He was the blue-throated Lord Shiva! The King was feeling thrilled by the inarticulate chanting of the Devadasi! The young damsel was overpowering him gradually. The King seemed to come alive by the tactile propinquity of the devadasi. He was remembered of his deprivation, since long! Since long, he did not get the touch of such a youthful body of a young woman! Since long, Bhanumati lost her interest in him. Her soft voice cut into the darkness – "The Brahmin would wake up"!

"Oh Lord Mahakaal! All would happen according to Your will, whether the

Brahmin would come to senses or not would be on Your wish, oh Lord, I am here with all my entity awaiting you, oh Lord, since long I hadn't been able to see you for paying homage, by bowing down my head to your feet"!

The King had gone perplexed. His body had been racked by desire. And the young woman, too, was being oblivious to everything. Each part of the young damsel's body was growing distinct. The King was forgetful of his own position. It seemed as if the King would explode by an immediate contact with the youthful frame of the damsel. He remembered Bhanumati's face for a moment. And then in the intense darkness, he knew not where the queen of Avanti had drifted away! The King began to respond to the embrace of the devadasi. While reacting to it, he was being repeatedly reminded of the moments of heartless rejection of Bhanumati. Instead of going to Mangalnath, as already scheduled, he had been here at the Mahakaal temple. The queen was supposed to come along with him. He called for her but Bhanumati did not accompany him. Was it all in accordance with Lord Mahakaal's will? Or else, why would he stand here entangled in the mesh of enchantment with this youthful devadasi, on this terrace of the Mahakaal shrine? It would not be possible without the will of Lord Mahakaal. It would not be so. How dare a Devadasi claim the body of a King in order to satiate her own desire? She was a woman! Nothing but a woman!

Lalita, the devadasi was aroused. This whole universe, city of Avanti, Ujjwain, the King's throne, queen Bhanumati, the longstanding drought, the two rivers: Shipra and Gandhavati, waterless seven lakes, the Mahakaal Shrine, the firmament of Avanti, the stars and planets on the sky - all were losing their significance to the towering presence of the King. King Bhartrihari was mingling sexually with a woman, on the hard, stone-floor of the terrace, whose face was unknown to him as yet. He even failed to have a glimpse of the face. By then, the lamp, kept in the niche, had snuffed out.

Young devadasi was melting in gratitude. She could not tell the man apart from the God in the darkness of confusion. The King was feeling excited to think that the youthful lady was uniting with her God, she worshipped. The young woman was getting thrilled enough gradually, to imagine that the stony, hard, lifeless phallic image was growing warm, fleshy, and she kept whispering, "Oh Lord, how fortunate I am, I know not which virtue I possess, Oh Lord Mahakaal, be there with me in my respite, my dreams, do accept me, oh Lord Mahakaal"!

The night began to grow hot. Hundred eyes of the night stood open. They kept wide open. The union stood consummated. Long after, the King got to his feet. Devadasi Lalita was swaying between sleep and sleeplessness, fatigued by the labour of coitus, on the hard, stony floor. She was benumbed. She never had experienced such intense proximity, such thoroughness in coition in her life, so far. She had never had the true experience of sexual union, though she had been raped, time and again, day after day! Benumbed, like a dead possum, she had to open up her body to the old Priest. During the rape, wincing in pain, she used to hold Lord Mahakaal close to her soul. She used to remember Lord Mahakaal, inwardly. Lord Mahakaal would redeem her from this life of humiliation, ignominy and affliction. She had placed herself at the feet of Lord Mahakaal, she had none to turn to, save Him. In her utter satiety on union and the slumber that followed, devadasi Lalita could see how Lord Mahakaal was receding away with his towering manliness. Ah, how soothing was the touch of Lord Mahakaal!

Devadasi whispered, "Oh Lord"!

King Bhartrihari turned back. He would now return to his palace. That which transpired was something unthinkable! It was the first time in his life! Perhaps, he had been responsive to the call of a young woman for the first time in his life! In all unions preceding this, his own will only predominated. It happened thus always. He had not come here for getting his desire satiated at all. He had come to have a conversation with the elderly Priest. But he was going back to his palace, having sexual intercourse with a lovelorn young wench, instead. The young woman compelled him rather. He had not excited the young woman to action, rather it was she who roused him. None had aroused him thus before, rather failed to do so. No, not even the nonpareil paragon of beauty, Bhanumati, the queen of Ujjwain, to be precise. The King was feeling extremely gratified. He was forced to participate in coition. But that compulsion had overwhelmed him. Never before did he get to have a woman's body such completely. Never did a woman offer herself to him, with such no-holds-barred surrender. It was an amazing experience! Even with Bhanumati, he never had any such experience. Bhanumati failed as her love was not so immaculate unlike the commendable submission of this devadasi to her Lord Mahakaal! Even the deity of stone assumed the form of a flesh-and-blood being to come down to her, because of her fervent appeal to Him. Bhartrihari stooped low to sit beside the supine body of the devadasi. Taking the necklace off his neck, he kept it on the breast of the devadasi. Lalita could feel it, in the dark.

The King stood up. Devadasi had stuck out her hand to get hold of him again. The King did not stop anymore. To him, the city of Ujjwain, Avanti, the King's throne, the two rivers: Shipra and Gandhavati, lack of rainfall, the emergence of new stars in the sky—all began to resurface. He was being reminded of the fact that he was the Monarch of Ujjwain. The King began to walk at a brisk pace, emerging from the Mahakaal Shrine. King Bhartrihari seemed to walk in desultory steps, like a bird, flapping its wings, aimless on losing its direction. He stopped while walking. Yonder the golden spire of the temple of Lord Mahakaal stood! The moon had budged to the west from its pinnacle. The King bowed down. He touched his forehead to the ground. Dust and soil flicked past his temple. A little dust blew away. The King prayed to Lord Mahakaal, Oh Lord! Oh Lord, please bestow upon me the strength to make the rains cascade on the soil of Ujjwain, as if you trust a lesser mortal like me with your matchless power!

Even the King was not aware of the duration of staying in the posture, touching his head to the ground. The night kept yielding on to the morning.

Sixteen

It was an afternoon in the month of Magh. Gandhavati was inserting the rope tied to a copper pitcher into the darkness of the well. The water-level had gone down quite remarkably. As this hamlet, Gambhira, was on the bank of the river Gambhira, the water-surface was quite closer. From Chaitra, the supply went scarce, even the surface used to dip alarmingly. Again, if it rained in Magh, or in Chaitra, the water-surface shot up in a day. Yet in that month of Chaitra, the rope needed to be replaced, a much longer one than usual was required. This time, the surface of water dipped much lower. The rope had to be altered by the close of Aghran. Even that rope became smaller gradually. Gandhavati looked into the blackness of the well. She kept looking. Her face got covered in darkness. Even the dark entered into her mind!

This well was a gift from the King. Which King? Gandharvasen. Following the Dashpura conquest, King Bhartrihari had dug ponds in the village, planted trees, restructured all the wells in village after village, renovated all the shrines standing by the rivers: Shipra, Gandhavati and Gambhira. Gandhavati was cognizant of all such matters. She was just a wisp of a girl at that time. She was Sugandha. Sugandha, the daughter of Kartikkumar! Gandhavati could recollect a much-faded memory.

The people of Avanti used to pronounce the name of King Bhartrihari quite reverently. She heard of the King from Dhruvaputra. The King was scholarly and encouraged learning. On each full-moon day, he used to send his contributions to Sandipani Ashram. The King was enamoured of poetry. Dhruvaputra had recited one or two shlokas from the book of lyrics to her. The tip of her ears reddened, unawares. Was Dhruvaputra heartless? Was he nonchalant? Couldn't he guess in the least what went on in Gandhavati's inner recess? Her mate was reciting the shlokas on coition to her, though his heart rested on a whore. Gandhavati would go to Devadutta, the courtesan. She was keen on seeing her. She would measure her beauty with her own eyes.

Grim silence reigned supreme, all around. This corner of the well was secluded, indeed. Their courtyard was not visible from here. Mother sat alone. Reba, her mother, was falling silent with each passing day. This time, winter had not been so hard, yet not quite tolerable even. In this region, winter was too severe. Even that winter came to an end. The trees and the foliage looked limp, lifeless. All the creepers and herbs were almost devoid of life: Banyan, Indian fig-tree, Peepul, Ashoke, Neem, Sindhubar, so on. The leaves turned dull. It was the time for the leaves to fall off. Dust was kicked off by the wind and the falling leaves blew in the dust. Sal forest stood in the west of Gambhira. The trees which stood straight like the sages, engrossed in meditation, were being devoid of leaves which kept being shed.

The copper pitcher had almost touched the bottom of the well. Gandhavati threw a glance into the darkness. The rope was held tight in both her hands. She kept lifting the pitcher up, slowly, little by little. The empty pitcher came up effortlessly. Gandhavati took the pitcher in her hands and kept it by the side of the well. Where was the water? Gandhavati's face bore shadows of peril. She was flabbergasted to find that the little water she could draw up was mostly filthy, muddy, turbid. Did the well really run dry this year then? In her small span of life, she had no such experience before! She could not even think in her wildest dreams that the water in the well would ever deplete! Gandhavati emptied the water in the pitcher near her feet. Grains of sand got stuck to her feet. She kept driving the pitcher down into the darkness of the well, again. Throwing her glance, she went surmising whether water had been there at all. Darkness confused her. She failed to figure out anything. The splash, which issued as the pitcher dropped on the surface of water, did not reach her ears! It was the fragility of sound that was wafted to her auditory sense-organ. Abruptly, the pitcher had fallen on the hard surface of sand-and-soil. This sound was too grating! But while the pitcher slipped on to the water-surface, all of a sudden, or, while the pitcher danced on the water itself, how profound that sound would have been, how sweet and cool would be the charm of that stir! Once driven by wind into the ears, the river, Gambhira popped up before her sight. Gandhavati began to look for the water down in the crevice of the well, moving the rope with the pitcher tied at its end. Alas! Even the bottom of the earth had gone hard and dry! Lowering her head, she kept looking for the slightest signs of water. She failed. In the darkness, she called out: "Water, Water"! Ah—aah-aah! Echoed syllables came up to her! She kept swinging the pitcher in the dark void. The measurement of the rope certified that water was supposed to be there! But it was not. She kept lifting the pitcher up. Had the pitcher been filled with water? Putting the pitcher on the ground quite gingerly, after having it drawn up, she sat perching on the tips of her feet, going down on her knees. Whither had gone the crystalline water? Seeing the muddy, sand-soaked water, Gandhavati turned the pitcher upside down on the ground. She threw a glance at the sky. Had it ever been so before? Just fifteen days of the month of Magh had passed by. What days were ahead then? Her heart missed a beat or two. The firmament had now been a big void. Not a single flying bird came in view. In the great space, even at the end of human range of vision, a circling vulture could not be seen either. Gloom descended on the countenance of Gandhavati. This shadow was that of the mind. What would she do now? She would inform all, that the King's well had dried up. Didn't Dhruvaputra say that the King's well had been dug so deep that it would never dry up? Should Gandhavati go from door to door to announce that the King's well had gone waterless? Did the King lose his intent of slaking thirst of his subjects? Why only Dhruvaputra? Even Shivnath, her grandfather, used to say, that this well would never run bereft of water. King's power lay embedded in the depth of the well's darkness, the King had always striven to quench the thirst of his subject with that well, keeping it full to the brim — such thoughts would keep one's faith in the King unflinching, otherwise it would be difficult to breathe in a King's realm.

Gandhavati muttered, "Oh God, what's wrong? Even the King of Avanti has lost the power of slaking thirst of his subjects, Alack King, what a pity! The water You provide, oh Lord, would never deplete, we all are so sure!" Gandhavati would surely get an explanation had Dhruvaputra been there! She reminisced instantly,Would she ever have to sit before a waterless well, Dhruvaputra being there? Wouldn't the copper-pitcher splash down in the darkness of the water-filled pit? Would the sky of Avanti ever stand cloudless in the months of Asad and Sravan, Dhruvaputra being there? For two consecutive years? Where had gone those clouds, which the white rays of the Sun-God fed with white columns of water perennially? Dhruvaputra used to say, "The heat of the sun [with the help of air], culled water-droplets specifically from the ponds, rivers, the seas and used to pass them on to the blobs of clouds. The rains that poured down on earth, as a consequence, meant welfare to all beings".

Pressing the pitcher near her breast, Gandhavati looked up to the sky. Sans the cruel shadows she could see nothing up there. Like panic-stricken swallows, she allowed her gaze roam from the east to the west, imagined to traverse from the north to the south! Not a speck of cloud could meet her eye. Where would the huge reserve of water, which the Sun-God kept amassing since long, pour down? On which country? Her friend used to remark, the water which the Sun-God used to suck in from the earth with his heat, used to return to this earth, thousand-fold! Her friend was not there. His words too were going to be proved false. Rains eluded since long! In her mind, Gandhavati kept calculating when she had seen it raining last. It betrayed her memory. As it ran without rain or the sky without water, the water in the hell too stood exhausted. Alas, Dhruvaputra! Were you the cloud, yourself? Getting metamorphosed into cloud, you had left Avanti! Tears kept welling up to the eyes of Gandhavati!

Dear friend, do you know that since you left Avanti, this city has not yet witnessed the shadow of clouds, lambent on it? Those clouds— volcanic ones; the ones which issued out from Lord Brahma and again those which took birth from the lunar cycles – you used to talk about all of them! You said, that, the clouds used to manifest their glorious self with the aid of the thunderclaps, born of air and the lightning or taking birth from the fire. Oh friend, whither have gone your clouds, born of fire, Lord Brahma or the cycle of moon? Do you know that the people of Avanti are staying alive with only the memory of clouds? How magnificent had been that cloud-laden firmament of Avanti! Even till date, if I remember the clouds, you bob up on my mind's canvas! You are the son of Dhruva, your favourite season had been the 'monsoon'.

Monsoon was indeed the favourite season of Dhruvaputra! Dhruvaputra used to say, water constitutes the body of all earthly objects, animate, inanimate, all alike. While the static and the portable objects are consigned to flames, the smoke which spirals up to the sky is nothing but water. From that water, mica takes birth. As it does not glide past, the cloud is called 'Abhra'[mica]. Ah, what days had we spent by the bank of the river, Gambhira! The sky was overcast with Airavat-like balls of cloud and the universe stood enchanted by the patter of the rains. Being nourished by the water from the sky, river Gambhira rose inspate. With the shadows on its surface, the river flew with its eyes shut and aimless with intense inhalation-exhalation! The blue wicker-creepers bent down on the stream, and they kept a-flutter by the speed of the water-flow, all the time. As the rains stopped, the clouds kept thundering again and the peacocks flipped open their feathers in an orderly manner to welcome the clouds. Gandhavati had not seen such exquisiteness of the he- and she-peacocks, since long. Last monsoon, even the one preceding it, Gandhavati had no heart to go down to the river-bank. Both the years, monsoon surfaced to disappear, in no time. It was, as though, the clouds lost their way while coming here. It seemed as if Avanti was not their destination. Hence, the blue-cloud-hue of wicker-creepers on the bank of Gambhira had been singed by the scorching sunrays. Gambhira, the river, had lost its speed, ran like a woman, devoid of her youth, pulling it along, somehow, laboriously. It had been likewise, till date. However, those days were no exception too. It was the time when Tamradhvaj had left — that Tamradhvaj, the young astronomer, the disciple of Acharya Brishavanu! How strange it seemed! Why was she reminded of him? He had spoken of the monsoon itself, somewhat weirdly! He had described the appearance of Gambhira during monsoon, much later in the month of Poush! His words echoed those of Dhruvaputra! As if he had seen the clump of wicker-bushes on the bank of Gambhira during the monsoon, the blue of the wicker-creepers! Gandhavati was silent, gloomy, nonplussed — this afternoon was receding further, before her eyes, giving way to that evening of Poush when the milk in the pot stood ebullient in the dark! The young astronomer sat there. He was supposed to come here again. Why didn't he come? Why didn't he come for such a long time? Wasn't he done with his calculations yet?

Gandhavati had not noticed when the carriage-horse had drawn up on the road! She was not in herself at all. Lowering her face, she was engrossed in herself. Then, tying the horse to the mango-tree by the side of the road, Uddhavnarayan had walked in with majestic gait. He had a red headgear, had worn a blue silk apparel, on which he put a woollen shawl from Punjab. That cover was dusky like clouds. He had a garland of yellow, wild flowers, round his neck. The pair of footwear was embroidered with gold-threads. Uddhav was looking like a man of the royal court. He was drunk and it left its mark on his face and appearance. The horse drawing the carriage seemed to be a new one. It was quite robust. Around the neck of the horse too, there was a garland made of red, wild blossoms. Who knew, which female gardener had presented her with all such things?

Uddhavnarayan strained his throat to make a rattling noise and said, "I had not expected you to find here, hey girl, are you waiting for me, eh? You know that I take this path, but how did you know that I shall be crossing it now? Who told you, which popinjay"?

Startled, Gandhavati turned to look up. What a shame! Wasn't she thinking of that astrologer-cum-astronomer while remembering Dhruvaputra? And, was it the time for this heartless Uddhavnarayan to turn up? Casting a glance at Uddhav, she kept looking elsewhere. She was not replying to what Uddhavnarayan was saying.

Uddhavnarayan said, "I had decided already that today I shall be proposing this daughter of Gambhira, come on Sugandha, look at me!"

Gandhavati could discern from his voice that Uddhavnarayan had come there, being drunk. But it was not affable of a man to stand before a young woman in no way related to him, after swigging glasses of wine. She shrunk a bit instantly. Drawing the scarf, she tried to cover her torso, firmer. Uddhavnarayan was a royal employee. A royal servant was immensely powerful. She fixed her gaze on the horse, drawing the carriage. It stamped its feet to kick off dust. Gandhavati glanced into the vapid darkness inside the pitcher.

Uddhavnarayan inquired, "Today is the third day of the new moon, moon will make its presence felt in the first three hours of the night, may we meet then"?

Holding the empty pitcher close, with a perplexed look in his eyes, Gandhavati kept sitting. She was feeling threatened. The man had sidled up very close to her.

Again, Uddhavnarayan's voice reached her ears, "Hasn't Uncle apprised you of everything, is he there at home? Magh is passing by, this month is apt for seeing the ritual done. Where is Uncle, he has promised me after all"?

Mustering courage, Gandhavati looked up and answered Uddhav, "He is off to the city".

"He has gone to the city, what shall I do now? However, it is fine to see you, Sugandha, why are you sitting here like a nun"?

Gandhavati replied, "Please go down the way you came by".

"I have already come along the way, it is just my destination, Sugandha, are you aware of the position I hold in the royal court"?

Gandhavati chortled, "In the post of a royal poet perhaps, I heard that staking claim to that post is quite easy".

Uddhavnarayan was enthused,"No, no, why just a court-poet? I am in a higher post, you will come to know just after our wedding,I can let you know even now, though it is strictly confidential".

Gandhavati's smile had disappeared. Pressing the pitcher with both her hands, she tried to seek refuge in the vessel itself. Her mother had a word with her grandfather. Hadn't grandfather informed this man as yet? How terrible it seemed! The eyes of that man kept skimming past all over her body! Who knew, what plan had Uudhavnarayan had at the back of his mind, while coming in here? Her friend used to say that this man was just a dolt! No doubt, he had acquired a little knowledge, but it was devoid of imagination! A person without imagination would have all his knowledge in vain. Gandhavati cast a frightened, bewildered glance at Uddhavnarayan, who could tell what he had imagined?

Uddhav said, "This silk cloth is from Balkh, the woollen is from Punjab, the horse, drawing the carriage is from the Himalayas, which I bought lately. Did you ever ride a horse? Come Sugandha"!

Gandhavati replied, "You can proceed, I shan't go anywhere, you can go back with your horse, what do you have to share with a woman, in no way related to you"?

Uddhavnarayan seemed to be a bit dejected, he kept pacing up and down the road. The horse, drawing the carriage, came to stand beside him. He adjusted the turban, fished out a small silk reticule from his waist and took a gem-studded necklace on his fingertip. He kept looking at the gem-string with rapt attention. And threw a glance at Gandhavati, standing close by. He kept staring at her. In his stare, a touch of mesmerism stood distinct. The young damsel was extremely beautiful, such youthful possession might be the object of worship for any man. How could an ornament enhance her beauty by a few shades? He came to stand before Gandhavati slowly, with measured steps. In a low tone, he uttered, "I had brought a necklace for you, an exact replica ofMahalata, this is very costly, take it, it only befits the neck of the queen, such is its dazzle, its beauty! Suppose, this ornament is made to be sported on the neck of a princess, perhaps a merchant or a royal servant can only adorn her with it! Lift your face, have a look at the necklace"!

Gandhavati sat still with her face hung low, she spoke out haltingly, "I am no princess, I am just a daughter of an ordinary soldier, my father has gone to war and is yet to return, my dearest friend has left Avanti since the last two monsoons, I am anxious, worried, almost each night passes without sleep for me. you please go back, I am waiting for someone else, not for you"!

Uddhavnarayan was in the know of all these facts. Hence, he was neither flabbergasted nor dejected. He knew it well too, that, if one was keen on achieving his desired object, losing patience would be a strict no-no. And, if it meant a gem of a woman, then it would be a question of even more patience. He was drinking the nectar of youthful beauty with his eyes, beyond the knowledge of Gandhavati. Gradually, a pair of eyes kept turning into a hundred such sense-organs of vision! Even the beauty of Urvashi, the dancer in the court of heavens, failed in comparison with that of this woman! Lust got the better of Uddhavnarayan's vision. He began to lap in Gandhavati with his blood-shot eyes, overcome with lust! Gandhavati was a river. Dancing in ripples. It lived on the memories of rain. She was frightened by the glance of Uddhav! It occurred to her, as though the sky and the wind, all were aflame, all were getting scorched! She, too, would not be spared by the lolling tongues of this conflagration!

Uddhav came forward, in a muffled tone he declared, "It is the virtue of a valiant hero to outrage the chastity of women"!

Gandhavati was petrified! She was feeling stifled!

Uddhav grew sibilant, "I am the sessions-judge of the royal court, this position of a judge is much higher. What can't I do, I can even slay your grandfather, if so needed, and then, both the daughter and the mother will be enjoyed by the lechers, together"!

Gandhavati got immersed in sand. Eddying whorls caused cyclones in air while sands kicked off storms! All the rivers began to dry up, all ponds followed suit. Gandhavati sat with a lowered face. The tears which were about to well up, dried up in heat. Look Dhruvaputra, Uddhav, the sessions-judge of the royal court is touching me! Oh Dhruva, the star, I know not whether you still are there in the sky at this time of the day, Uddhav, the Judge, is pulling me by the tuft of my hair! Fiery breaths issued out of Gandhavati's body! She seemed to breathe among plethora of green foliage!

It was really a turbulent time! At this time, Dhruvaputra had gone missing with all the clouds - the Fiery, the Brahma-induced and the fifteen-day-spanned ones! Such droughts had not been witnessed by the people since long! Not even such lack of knowledge! Not a speck of light had been there anywhere, lack of knowledge had pervaded the sky of Avanti! All coffers of knowledge had been taken away by the Son of Dhruva, it seemed. That extremely handsome youth, that confidante of all the rivers: Gandhavati, Shipra, Gambhira, Reba, Betrabati — that companion of all the streams and rivers! Even Gandhavati was about to forget his face, it seemed! Yet, she kept calling him! The countenance of Tamradhvaj kept bobbing up inside his face! How bizarre! Whatever Dhruvaputra used to utter, Tamradhvaj spoke the same. Yet, would he ever turn into Dhruvaputra someday?

Gandhavati screamed in agony! She called out to the outer space lying cocooned in the folds of the firmament! She struck the ground with the palm of both her hands, blowing off the dust. The wind of Ujjwain wafted her crying, far and beyond. It was blown off far till it mingled with the heart-rending wail of affliction of Gandhavati!

The befuddled King of Avanti could hear the sound of loud sobs in the afternoon. Did the birds cry like this because of drought? And the trees? The King looked on the blank horizon through the open window. The horizon, it seemed, bore semblance of clouds! Not clouds, but the flock of vultures came swooping down! He was lending his ears to the screech of delight of the vultures! The wail of Gandhavati failed to make way to his ears!

The Chief Priest could hear the sound of her crying! Such wails and sobs were familiar to him. The raped woman would cry in that manner. The river, Gandhavati, flew by his temple. The wail emerged from the sandy banks of the river. With a smiling face, he turned to the merchant and said, "Can you hear that? No delay anymore, the time is optimum"!

The noise of crying stirred Reba, the mother. She was entering and emerging from the house. Her eyes seemed to be dazzled by gazing at the sun-inundated universe! Looking hither and thither, failing to control her anxiety, coming down to the courtyard, covering her mouth with her palms, the river-mother cried out, "Oh dear mother, my Sugandha, Sugandhaaa"!

The call of the mother was wafted by the wind, far,far beyond! From the city of

Ujjwain to the land of Dasharno to that of Bidisha! Ramgiri, Amrakut and many more mountains reverberated to the call of the river-mother! During lack of rainfall, the mother had to call out likewise. Otherwise, why would the clouds pile up? Clouds, clouds, clouds…! River was even the mother of clouds! Reba was like the mother of Dhruvaputra! Reba was calling out to her daughter. The cry reached the ears of Tamradhvaj! Or, anyone else too? That Son of Dhruva! He, who had flown off all the clouds along with himself! The cloud-mother was calling out to her offspring! Did Dhruvaputra remember that? Did he cherish all such memories? Or, had he now gone bankrupt of his memories? He was oblivious to everything! Everything that belonged to this Ujjwain, this Gambhira, this city of Avanti! Reba kept yelling at her daughter like a panicky bird-mother! The span of drought kept being prolonged further!

SEVENTEEN

Gandhavati was panic-stricken. How terrible a man was the royal servant, Uddhavnarayan! How ruthless he was!How mindlessly he said that her father, Kartikkumar had been slain in the Hun war! How nonchalantly he said that, Dhruvaputra, who went missing was sheltered by the Huns! He would be taken as a captive if he dared enter the city of Avanti! Smilingly, he announced, Dhruvaputra would be given capital punishment. Even though he was exempted from death-sentence, his right hand would surely be chopped off. Or, even an eye could be gouged out! Or one of the two legs might go incapacitated! Waiving all these, if the death-sentence stood final, he would be burnt to death in presence of the public! Or, he might be chopped to pieces to feed the jackals and the dogs! While saying, Uddhavnarayan burst into laughter. Laughing boisterously, he kept stamping his feet on the ground, how daring was that depraved fellow! He had been desirous of the whore who was meant to satisfy the lust of the merchant! Sheltered by the tradesman, how dared he desire his woman? Inane, poor Dhruvaputra!

Gandhavati sat silent on the raised terrace of the hut. Just at a little distance stood Reba, her mother. Being apprised of Uddhav's presence by Gandhavati, Reba too felt frightened. Uddhav was keen on possessing Gandhavati, by hook or by crook. What times lay ahead, who knew! Who would save Gandhavati, if Uddhav abducted her? Old grandfather, Shivnath? Reba was lost in her train of thoughts, with her head, drooped in front. She lifted her head to find Tamradhvaj, approaching. Reba turned her face to ask Gandhavati, "Please wipe your face off, Tamradhvaj of the Acharya Brishavanu Ashram is stepping in. Go, rather wipe your face with water, the cheeks bear marks of pain"!

Gandhavati got to her feet abruptly! Her whole body stood agitated! Tamradhvaj's arrival was certainly tantamount to having the news of Dhruvaputra and Kartikkumar! Consequently, Uddhavnarayan's announcement would prove false! Gandhavati stood there for a few seconds to stare at Tamradhvaj! No, he was not dressed in royal attire! Not even the young astronomer from Dasharno sat in any horse-drawn carriage! He came on foot, accompanied by her grandfather, Shivnath. Gandhavati calculated, he had come again just after one month! She was throwing curious glance at the ordinary cloth-draped youth, with a woollen piece left on his shoulder! Did he look like a hunter? Grandfather had said so. Tamradhvaj's looks bore the stamp of a hunter. Yes, exactly so. Tamradhvaj was headed towards their residence. But no, he wasn't! Grandfather was coming. Tamradhvaj took the path straight, veering towards the river, Gambhira, in the west. Gandhavati turned back to tell her mother, "Maa, water has depleted in the King's well, it was assured that the King's water-supply would never end, would never dry up, at least we all heard that. But the well is hard and dry, filled with grains of sand only"!

Reba was flabbergasted to learn this, "What do you say"?

"Yes, Maa"!

"Did you insert the pitcher into the well"?

"Yes, Maa, not a single drop of water is left in it".

Reba's face was overcast with the dusky shades of concern. Drawing her shawl around herself, adjusting her veil a little to the fore, she came down to the courtyard. She stepped forward. Fetching the stool to the courtyard, she moved aside with her head hung low. Shivnath came, took his seat and said, "Tamradhvaj has gone to Gambhira, he will join us in no time".

"Can't he come during daytime, it will soon be dark, how long will he talk then?" Reba inquired.

Shivnath smiled to say, "He says that if the sky above is devoid of stars, he feels like saying nothing. He loves to talk by looking at the stars and planets in the firmament - whatever suits one, you know. But he can even see in the dark, as he claims".

"What are you saying"?

"Yes, he finds it not at all difficult to walk through the dark, he had come to Ujjwain from Dasharno on foot only. It was Spring then, as he said, it was really a unique experience to walk on the thoroughfare on a Spring night, he used to walk mostly by night, resting all day long and again the sun during the month of Chaitra was scorching"!

Reba was lost in her thoughts, later she joined in to say, "In which Spring did he come to Ujjwain"?

"Perhaps the same Spring in which Dhruvaputra had gone away".

Reba spoke inaudibly, "On the night of Chaitra purnima, Dhruvaputra had left".

Yes, Shivnath was falling into a strange silence when he blabbed out, "Rightly said, it was the end of everything when Dhruvaputra had gone for good. But, Tamradhvaj is knowledgeable too".

Reba kept looking at the thoroughfare, being silent. Would Tamradhvaj be arriving here on completing his circumambulation of Gambhira? Dhruvaputra loved the bank of the Gambhira too. Shivnath said, "You know my daughter, he says that, if one walks into the night, he will surely hear the trees speaking, one tree calling out to the other, really Tamradhvaj is so imaginative"!

Reba came back again on Gandhavati's asking. She said, "You know, the King's well has gone dry".

"Oh God! Who said so"?

"Your granddaughter"!

"Alas! We are undone! Who will supply us water"?

Reba replied, "Gambhira... but the sandy surface has to be dug, father"!

Shivnath began to sway his head, "It had never so happened before like the present! But is drought anything new"?

Reba complained, "Uddhavnarayan had pounced upon Sugandha"!

Shivnath sank in the ground, "What are you saying"?

He failed to touch her, our girl managed to escape, "Have you promised Uddhav anything"?

"Not at all! He is a man of devilish nature, why should I give him my word? Even if you agree, I would never nod at it".

Reba said, "The daughter has come of age, grown nubile, so I uttered 'yes', but he is a crooked bloke, again a royal servant, if he abducts her, I am so frightened, father"!

Shivnath blew his top, "He will abduct her! How glibly you say, is it that easy? Is there no King in our land? I shall see the King!"

"What good would come of it, father, if you complain to the King against an employee of the royal court? Will he judge the fault of his servant at all? Other royal employees will protect Uddhav, have you ever heard that the royal staff has ever been punished"?

Shivnath was listening to Reba, speechlessly. It was true. Reba was really logical in her statements. Her husband had not come back from the war yet, five years have slipped by in the meantime. But Reba had never broken down in tears, she kept looking down the way, day in, day out.

The twilight was about to come to a close. Just then, Tamradhvaj stepped into the courtyard. In a low voice, he addressed, "Reba Maa"!

"Who's there"? Reba started. Whose voice would it be?

Tamradhvaj came to stand in front of Reba, "I am Tamradhvaj, from Acharya Brishavanu's ashram, have you forgotten me, Maa, as you look down the way"?

Reba receded with panic-stricken steps, drawing the cloth on her head, she said, "I had no idea that you would address me as 'Maa', come Sugandha, the astronomer is here. My son, please wait, let me fetch the seat for you".

Gandhavati fetched the stool. Putting another stool in the inner yard, she stood at a little distance. Reba came along with a water-pot. She asked Shivnath, "I am here with water, father, please clean your feet and hands, Tamradhvaj please do the same, whenever you drop in, the sun disappears from the sky, and, I have come to know that you are fond of night"!

Eighteen

It was Madonatsav that day. A day of full moon in the month of Chaitra. Youth fair and festival were in full swing in the temple of Lord Kamadeva. At early dawn, with the first light of the day, Dhruvaputra came back home. Gandhavati woke up much earlier, at the crack of dawn of Chaitra Purnima. It was also the day of Spring Festival, Basantotsav! It seemed, her mate's much-awaited presence would nudge her up from sleep and make her sit in the inner yard, facing the east in the hazy glow of the dawn. At that end of the sky, the Venus was a-dazzle, while on the southern horizon, the star, named Canopus or Agastya were shining! The stars were fading out of vision, gradually! Just then Dhruvaputra showed up. He was walking, bending forward. Perhaps, he had started off from Ujjwain at the dead of night. The nights in the month of Chaitra were usually cool. The cloth covering Dhruvaputra's body was soiled, the chest lay bare. His body looked emaciated, perhaps owing to rash lifestyle. Bloodshot eyes had sunken into the sockets. His face was looking gaunt and sickly, owing to a lack of shave. As Venus, the star, snuffed out, Dhruvaputra stepped into the inner yard. Gandhavati turned her face aside, in offence.

Gandhavati was in the know of everything. Uddhavnarayan was looking up at Gandhavati with lust in his eyes, since years! Uddhavnarayan, himself, had run in on the back of a mule to break the news to her grandfather. Dhruvaputra had kicked up storm in the city, by being enamoured of the Chief Prostitute! That whore, Devadutta, was the apple of Subhag Dutta's eye, it was an open secret! How inane the young man was to lay his hands on the gem of the trader's treasure-trove, even after winning a shelter from him!

Gandhavati did not believe, however. She had not liked the presence of Uddhav at all. Even the import of Uddhav's eyes was dubious. But grandfather had the wind of the same fact on reaching the city. He did not get to see Dhruvaputra. The merchant was puce in anger! It was not known whether he had left Ujjwain right then but he had come back again at the dawn of Chaitra Purnima. That comeback was forever,

151

thought Gandhavati. Or else, why would he return at the dawn of Chaitra Purnima? Alas, why had she turned aside to conceal her hurt feelings? If she had the faintest idea that her mate had come back for the last time to leave Avanti for good, would she ever allow him to go away? If she had turned her face to her friend, all his grief would have evaporated! He would have been absolved of all humiliation, all ignominy! Dhruvaputra had come in the room. He bolted the door.

"I know all these facts", in a muffled tone observed Reba, "Where is he now"?

Tamradhvaj said, "You are not supposed to know the whole of it, none does know that, not even Gandhavati, let alone Dhruvaputra himself".

"Then who does"?

Tamradhvaj said, "I know, Maa".

"Have you come to know through your calculations"?

Tamradhvaj smirked, "That is true indeed. Look at the sky, the unknown truths will dawn on the canvas of your mind"!

"But I cannot recognize the planets and the stars, save just a few".

Tamradhvaj said, "Millions and trillions of stars are there, who knows all? In the galaxy, thousands of stars, clusters of nebula exist, who can recognize all of them? But throwing up a glance at the firmament, looking up at the trillions of spots of light by night, don't we feel delighted within? Looking at the sky, keep thinking of that day. You cooked payasam for Dhruvaputra. He did not take that delicacy. He did not unbolt the door. The windows were shut too. Gandhavati called out many a time, but to no avail, her mate did not respond.

"I know everything".

"That which you have witnessed with your eyes, only that much is known to you! That which transpired behind your eyes, you hardly have any idea of that, Maa! I came by Gambhira, that river is lying waterless. Casting the piles of sand-grains aside, the rustic damsels and women are collecting water from the depth of the river. This is that river, in the crystalline water of which the shadowy clouds carved their niche intact. That moisture, that cloud — all are absent in the firmament of Avanti! Do you remember, Maa, how delighted this earth would have been during the monsoon, how pervasive the fragrance of honey would have been all around, how the scent rose from the earth, from the fresh trees, herbs and creepers, how beautifully the song of the ripples of the river mingled with the air, how the figs by the banks of the river and in the forests kept ripening, tardily, gradually"...

"How strange"! An indistinct note of exclamation issued out of Reba's throat, "Have you seen all such things"?

"Oh no, I hail from the banks of Betrabati river, Betrabati flows by on the south-western end of the city of Dasharno"!

"Then how did you come to know about the beauty of Gambhira's monsoon"?

"I know, Maa".

"Through your calculations, perhaps"!

Tamradhvaj answered, "Even the river, Betrabati, has dried up, it is sans water, rains eluded Dasharno too, this year. A forest-fire broke out far, in the foothills of the Amrakut ranges. That forest fire is still in flames, Maa! The fire is shimmering now. All the greenery is being devoured by the flames! The hunters who used to hover around the woods are showing a clean pair of heels. The animals of the forest are suffering sad demise, while escaping to the human habitats".

"How do you know"?

"I gathered, Maa, a group of traders from Amrakut were crossing Ujjwain on their way to Kankhal".

"How surprising! Reba's eyes opened wide in wonder, in the darkness".

Tamradhvaj added, "The river, Reba, issued out from that Amrakut itself. That river is dry, narrow, withered away, lately".

"And then"?! Reba's eyes turned tearful as she looked up at the sky.

Tamradhvaj said, "Coming from Amrakut, those merchants crossed the river, on their way to the North! Sands lie for stretches and beyond, drought persists, how shall the river, Reba, go in spate? Did Kadamba flower bloom this year? No idea! Did the earth-magnolia sprout on the moist ground? Haven't seen! Do you remember, Maa, that monsoon when the herd of cheetal deer was running under the canopy of clouds along the edge of the river and the scream of the peacock, eyeing the clouds hovering over the sky above? My land, Dasharno, is a beautiful place to live in, fenced on all sides by the bunch of Ketaki flowers. Dasharno is green with rose-apple, ripe rose-apples on trees, and again the birds have made their nests on those trees with twigs and small branches, Ketaki bushes are fraught with buds at the advent of monsoon. Betrabati stood full to the brim with water, how graciously meandering had been the river's movement — and now, it stands waterless"!

Reba sat speechless. She had no idea when Gandhavati came and stood near her, in the dark. Tamradhvaj could visualize the form of Gandhavati. Her eyes were a-dazzle like two dots of light, like a couple of stars! Tamradhvaj was talking about the Nichoih mountains. About the city of Bidisha, the capital of Dasharno! "Bidisha city stood on the border of the river, Betrabati. In its vicinity stood the Nichoih mountains. Lately, the intense silence around the mountains grew terrible, grim! The silence of the mountains had been the most favourite of all love-birds, doubtlessly! In the secluded mountain-gorges the lovers used to meet up and make the milieu on all sides resonate with their love-greetings and sweet nothings! The caves of Nichoih mountains remained redolent with the bodily fragrance of those lovelorn men and women! Now it is the favourite haunt of the jackals only, who hang about there in the afternoon. The gorges have now become the refuge of wild animals. I remember, during the fresh advent of monsoon, both the banks of the river Betrabati got laden with dense bushes of jasmine. In these bushes, the womenfolk used to come to pluck the flowers. Now the banks lie stark, desolate, only dust-particles keep flying over".

Gandhavati came forward and asked, "Who has told you of all these things"?

"None, I am from the land of Dasharno".

"But Amrakut ranges, the river, Reba?"

"The merchants".

"Do the merchants have such sweet way of looking at things"?

Tamradhvaj smiled, "How do I know"?

"Who has told you? Come on, tell me the truth".

Tamradhvaj looked up to the sky, pointed his forefinger to the stars in the sky. In a sunken voice, he said, "The stars of the firmament. Looking at the sky, I seem to visualize all these things only. I can also be witness to how Gambhira looked in that monsoon and who stood on Gambhira's bank at that time".

"Please tell me where my father, Kartikkumar, is".

Abruptly, Reba broke out in a muffled sob, saying, "No, let it be left at that, I do not want to know".

Gandhavati moved forward to touch her mother. She was convulsing alarmingly. It seemed as if her mother, Reba, came to know whatever Uddhavnarayan said. Mother had perhaps heard the rumour. But how would that be possible? Then, wouldn't her mother share it with her?

Reba composed herself. She said, "Continue with what you were saying, let me know, where and how Dhruvaputra is".

Gandhavati sat down in the courtyard, leaning against her mother. Mother and daughter sat next to each other. Tamradhvaj said, "He who is devoid of imagination can say no word of any value".

Gandhavati startled, whose words were those anyway? Her mate used to talk about Uddhavnarayan just in this manner. Alas! Who was then sitting in front of her?

Tamradhvaj said, "Do you remember those days, Maa, when the clouds, on their way to the Himalayas used to hover over this city of Avanti, city of Ujjwain, the spire of the Mahakaal temple, or on the top of the arrays of edifice"?

It was not Reba but Gandhavati, whose eyes began to shed tears. Did this man master the art of magic? These words were of Dhruvaputra! Dhruvaputra's, in verbatim!

Reba asked, In what way is Dhruvaputra related to these words? We are here to know of the whereabouts of Dhruvaputra.

Tamradhvaj replied, "Such a prologue is just to make a foray into that matter, listen Maa, your Dhruvaputra is no more. Avanti, Dasharno — all these regions are getting scorched by sunshine to the core, not a whit of cloud can be seen, any idea of the clouds, Maa?"

Reba maintained silence. It was beyond Reba's comprehension what Tamradhvaj was up to. How frequently he was deviating from one topic to the other. Gandhavati was thinking whether she was hearing right. Or was it absolutely the illusion of her auditory organ? That which she used to listen to, perching by the edge of the Gambhira or being laden with dust in this village, or weaving a garland with bakul flowers, seemed to be repeated in this darkness, and she kept listening. Even Tamradhvaj was talking about the clouds of three variations! It varied depending on its sources: Fiery clouds, Brahma-born clouds and clouds issued out of wings. Didn't Dhruvaputra say the same? Perhaps he did not, yet, whatever the astronomer from Dasharno was saying, seemed to be the same which she heard from her friend. Only her friend knew such things! None else did. But Tamradhvaj was here, uttering every word, stretching his glance to the sky.

"The clouds which eluded the sky of Avanti were either fire-born, Brahma-born or wing-born ones. The volcanic clouds are born of water. These clouds become distinct on the canvas of the firmament in the forms of ox, pig or mad elephant and unleash on earth. Such are the clouds. The earth is impregnated with life by them. These clouds sacrifice themselves to drench the universe. These clouds engender rains, silently. And these clouds which have thunder-like properties, keep rumbling across the firmament and that noise leaves the gaggle of geese pregnant, the clouds which are engendered from the inhalation of Lord Brahma, are Brahmaja clouds, to be precise.

These Brahmaja clouds keep thundering above the peaks of the mountain ranges, atop the lines of edifice during Sravan and Bhadra months! The earth grows blessed with harvests owing to the thundering of such clouds. Earth becomes beautiful! Man's relation with this cloud is really sweet! Maa, do you remember that cloud"?

In a faint noise, Gandhavati expressed her thrill, "All seems to me to have been heard of, long ago"!

Tamradhvaj went on speaking about the 'Pushkarbarta' clouds then. " was the other name of wing-born clouds. The highly mighty mountains had wings before. They used to fly from one place to the other across the world. The animals sought the intervention of Lord Indra in such an oppression. King of the Gods then cut off the wings of the mountains. Those snipped-off wings turned into water-filled clouds. Those clouds were named 'Pushkarbarta'. They had varieties of form. It is said, that, this cloud caused rains to fall at the end of a 'kalpa', which meant a day and a night of Brahma. Even the wildest of imagination could not have any room for Brahma's 'day and night'. It was, in fact, millions and millions of years! The wise men opine that, at the end of four hundred and thirty-two years, a 'kalpa' concludes. This cloud would cause rainfall at the end of an era. Likewise, sundry ages had slipped by, without our cognizance of the same! A thousand times this earth had been inundated by the rains only because of these 'Pushkarbarta' clouds"!

Gandhavati asked, "Will this year the earth be flooded by the rainfall from the 'Pushkarabarta' clouds? The age will come to an end, otherwise, why does the sky lie in such blind, slumbrous state"?

Tamradhvaj replied, "It seems to be so. Otherwise, why should it happen? Did Dhruvaputra say anything before leaving"?

Gandhavati said, "I can't recall whether he had said all these things, but now I feel that he had wished to share these facts too. Just these words, he was supposed to speak thus,on that evening of Chaitra Purnima".

"Are you telling the truth"?

"Yes, he, too, used to speak of the 'Pushkarbarta' clouds, those balls of clouds snuff out all fires, they stay in the refuge of a kind of wind named 'Parabaha' "...

"Tell me. Carry on, please". Tamradhvaj egged on.

"I do not remember all the words, but he used to speak of 'clouds' quite often, he used to speak of the position of all those clouds and in such positions, he used to speak of the four smoky columns, hogging all the four directions: Airavat[elephant], Mountains, Clouds, Snakes and the Nimbus to name a few of the major ones.

Tamradhvaj chipped in, "Yes, elephant, mountains, clouds and serpents have originated from the same family. The same water has given them birth. The water-bearing clouds and the elephants on the four corners cause snowfall during autumn for giving a boost to the harvest, even dewfall owes them only".

Gandhavati asked, "Will we now talk of clouds only?"

"Yes, precisely".

"I have already heard of all such things as you talked of, even before. I learnt them by the river of Gambhira as moonshine cascaded or while sitting in this courtyard. Otherwise, how could I talk of the Parabaha wind, how could I say that the wind harbours Pushkarbarta clouds"?

"Listen Gandhavati, let me tell you now about the rain during winter; do you remember in the north of the Himalayas, towards the south of the Sumeru range, stands a mountain called Hemkut"?

Gandhavati nodded. She whispered, "Perhaps Dhruvaputra used to refer to this on the night of Chaitra Purnima. Where is he lately"?

The words seemed to have eluded the ears of Tamradhvaj. He carried on, "A city had been there at the foothills of the Hemkut mountains, called Pundra"!

"Perhaps I heard of it"!

"Did I talk about it before"?

"It seems so. Gandhavati spoke in a low tone".

"Listen, if Hemkut mountain had snow-showers, the wind contained that water to flood the region stretching from the Hemkut to the Himalayas in the form of downpour. This rain even caused skimpy shower in the other regions as well, negligible downpour, though. That cloud used to glide down to the plains, crops grew by the effect of such clouds, the rains of Magh used to bring in good times, the soil being fertile and soft, facilitating the tilling with ploughs".

"Magh is heading to a close, will those clouds ever show up"?

Tamradhvaj cast his glance at the numerous stars of the firmament and in a muffled voice he said, "From Hemkut to the Himalayas, the wind wafted from the Himalayas at this time, crossing the lands of Punjab, Panchal, the river Indus, the five rivers, those nimbus clouds used to cause downpour along the banks of the Yamuna, drenching the dry edges of the Charmanvati river by that time. Even a crash, momentary shower would have been welcomed by the people. Those clouds used to float down to the sea from the Himalayas, concluding its journey down in the Arabian Sea".

"Is there any hint of that cloud in the sky"?

Tamradhvaj nodded in the negative: "No, it's not there".

"Then"?! A buried scream seemed to find a release through the bosom of Gandhavati! No haven anywhere! Uddhavnarayan was sidling close near her back. The devil was casting the shadow of his body. The water-bodies of the King's land had all gone dry. Sands were afloat in the air of Gambhira. Which times did they have to pass through lately? What was the way-out of this terrible curse? Where was the man who could prescribe ways of relief now? Where had he been?

Tamradhvaj said, "I have come to learn about those moments of his departure, please enlighten me as much as you can— he had come back from Ujjwain in the morning of Chaitra Purnima, right? And then?"

Gandhavati cocked her head up to the sky. That full moon of Chaitra began to make its presence felt, gradually, through the million stars. It was the day of Madonatsav. It was the day of paying a visit to the temple of Kamadeva. She dreamt in her heart of hearts of attending the Madan festival, holding the hands of her mate.

He came at dawn. Gandhavati turned her face aside in umbrage. Dhruvaputra had entered the room of his own. Yonder stood that room. The door had been drawn firm to keep it closed. Gandhavati never used to enter that room anymore. But didn't she ever sense that Dhruvaputra had come back to the room? Even sometimes, she leapt up to the raised terrace of that cottage to nudge the door open! Hushed emptiness ruled the roost inside. A musty smell lay heavy on the air. If Dhruvaputra failed to come back, that cottage would get razed to the ground, in course of time. Who would reclaim it? And that too, what for? Grandfather once said so. But he also had gone quiet thereafter!

Gandhavati threw a query, "Have you ever gone to the temple of Kamadeva"?

"Where"?

"It lies in the south-east from here".

"I know that".

"Why did you ask then"?

"Kamadeva temple is there in my Dasharno, in the city of Bidisha"!

"Have you seen Kamadeva"?

In an inaudible voice he rejoined, "Yes, I have seen"...

"When did you see, in your childhood"?

"No. I was coming from Dasharno to Avanti and on my way, I grew curious, was keen on going in to have look at Kamadeva. What a nice deity He is"!

"Hmm"…. Gandhavati gave a free rein to her gaze, skyward!

"How could youth be so dazzling? Dhruvaputra had attained that prime moment of his life, and Gandhavati, you too, have reached that dreamt-of instant"!

The sky grew refulgent before the eyes of the village-damsel!

Nineteen

Reba, the mother, had cooked rice-in-milk. The fragrance of that payasam had pervaded the room, the courtyard! The door being closed, the friend could not even feel it. He was fond of payasam, cooked by Reba, Gandhavati's mother. Mother called out to him a number of times, even Gandhavati shouted out his name, umpteen times! He neither opened the door nor cared to come out. It was Chaitra Purnima! Mother said, "Go, worship the deity at Kamadeva temple, old Parvati would escort you".

It seemed that mother had already planned for sending her daughter to Kamadeva's shrine. And Gandhavati, too, nursed a desire to have a look at the grace of Lord Kamadeva. She had heard of Kamadeva and Ratidevi from her mother. She also learnt how Kamadeva got burnt to ashes by the rage of Lord Mahadeva. Even, how Kamadeva had been absolved of that curse, by taking birth on earth! Ratidevi, too, had taken birth here on this earth for the redemption of her husband!

Old Parvati was a crooked lady. An ancient woman. With her eon-old widowhood, the old lady seemed to have a matchless far-sightedness. She seemed to have witnessed everything under the sun of this ocean-embraced universe! The land and the seas! What didn't she know? She spent her life with a curse of untimely widowhood, yet her words on men seemed to be the ultimate one! The wizened woman had gone to the Kamadeva temple umpteen times. She lacked colours in body, in mind as well, yet she used to pay a visit there. She got overjoyed on seeing Lord Kamadeva! Colours of her mind seemed to be restored. The old woman said, "Sundry hints of the union of man and woman could be detected in the temple of Kamadeva, on this day of Chaitra Purnima. It was even a pleasant spectacle! In this birth, I have spent my life on earth as Rati, in the next birth, I shall come as a woman of charms [mayavati]. I shall even get to see my husband, burnt to ashes, taking birth as Pradyumna, the son of Lord Krishna. Ah alack, what a pity! One who has none to turn to, must be assured of Lord Kamadeva with him or her; all one's desires will be fulfilled by Him" —

The shrewd lady held Gandhavati by hand and said, "Dhruvaputra has been won over by a courtesan".

Gandhavati got startled. Her face turned ashen in terrible shock. Oh God, all had come to know of this fact! All the creatures had learnt of it! Peacock, pigeon, the red-legged bartavelle and his mate, parrot, partridge — all the birds had come to know of it! Even the wild deer of the forest, the white cow had learnt of it. The river, Gambhira, the wicker-bushes by the river, the sand-basin of the river, the trees and herbs — all of them had come to know! The sky, the earth, the sun, the wind — all of them had learnt about it. As Gandhavati was on her way to the Kamadeva temple, holding the hands of the old woman, the noise of the falling leaves reverberated along the path. These leaves were falling off only in the grief of Dhruvaputra, who fell head over heels in love with a prostitute, erasing the memories of the daughter of Gambhira. She was heading towards the Kamadeva temple with her offerings, with a sad, pale face! The Ashok flowers in the basket, held in her hand, contained the reflection of her countenance. The flowers were turning black as did her face, her red lower lip!All nights went sleepless, the lower rims of her eyes certified that. This line of greenery and the elusiveness of sleep beside a dear one, had gaping hiatus in between! Her eyes seemed to have sunken deep in the sockets. She looked emaciated! Her body went out of hydration, she resembled a dry plant. A glance at her would aver her lack of mental happiness. The mind cast its shadow on her body too.

Old Parvati inquired, "Is it true that the whore had chucked him out after utter humiliation"?

Gandhavati's face darkened. Why did old grandma raise such an issue? What did she know of all such things? Didn't the old woman know that her mind burnt all day, all night, for her mate? The old hag went on, Courtesan Devadutta had driven him away like a street cur, like an uncared-for cat, he had even been beaten black-and-blue, no less than a thief!

"I know next to nothing, Grandma, most rumours are just baseless", retorted Gandhavati.

The old woman flashed a toothless smile. She said, "Why do you speak on the contrary? A widely-spread rumour has a considerable base in reality! A male must visit a whore, and topping all, the son of Dhruvadas, who is a bachelor, who has no idea of a woman, must have physique-related curiosity, again who would cater to his inquisition save a whore? It is because of such whores that a man in a family stays secure, lest no spinster, married or widowed women would have been spared by this male lust".

"Let it be so, Grandma, would it be of any help to know of all such facts"?

The old lady replied, "You are heading towards Lord Kamadeva's temple, you have come of age, now it is high time for you to know everything, you will have a family, you must know the tricks to keep your husband loyal to you, you should master wiles and if you fail to master it, the man will spend his hours at the bawdy house, will pour his wealth on the fallen woman"!

Gandhavati trembled. She shot a glance at the cloudless sky. Her eyes dazzled at the vacuous azure! Tears welled up to her eyes! Dhruvaputra was her mate and she his! The friend had no idea about how to bind her mate to her heart! Whatever she knew, had all been narrated to her by that mate of hers. Bringing her mouth to her ears, the old lady said, "Hey girl, what more do we need, now thou must be married off by your mother, by any means, if the beauty of youth wastes away without being appreciated by your man, then?"...

"Grandma, please stop all such nonsense"!

Old Parvati broke into a noisy laughter, "Look at my breasts, they had once been like those of yours, exactly like the full moon. Youth does not last forever, till it lasts, men, too, will be with you, like the lambs, they will grovel near your feet. Listen my girl, it's fine, you were not married, but didn't he love you"?

"Grandma"! Tears coursed down her cheeks! It seemed, the river, Gandhavati, bifurcated at a point to flow down on two sides. Old Parvati whispered in her ears, the wiles and ways of winning the hearts of the menfolk, her youth being so exquisite, so intact still! As Spring had been on her thus, why would a bumble-bee go elsewhere ignoring her? "Oh my damsel, this is the ideal time for enjoying, if he fails to enjoy with you, he is sure to leave. Listen my girl, the prostitutes know a lot of things, sundry forms of art, we can hardly think of! They know dance, music, veena-playing, laying beds, gleaning flowers, floral arrangement, even they can create sartorial wonder by sewing, they know the art of decking themselves well, so impeccably well — why on earth, would an ordinary girl of common household emulate a whore infallibly, adept in sixty-four ways of amorous union? But again, the thing that the domestic damsel possesses, the prostitute definitely lacks in, so never fear, my dear 'Maa'!"

Gandhavati replied, "Why shall I fear, Grandma? Please change the topic of your discussion".

Old Parvati touched her abruptly. She moved her hand lightly on her breasts. How terrifying was that touch! The girl seemed to throw up. It appeared that a reptile went slithering by, on her body. Pressing her tender breasts hard, the old hag placed her skinny hands on her buttock to comment, "Such being her youth, with such appeal of her flowery spring, why would she sit with a gloomy face, my dear girl? Even a whore has her youth, but that youthful charm gets the prick of hundred hornets, its honey being sucked by ten varieties of bumble-bee! But a homemaking damsel opens up her beauty solely to the man, to whom she is wedded, who bears her worldly responsibilities, she is just needed to gratify him with her charms. How could he go to a whore spurning such nectar-like lures of youth, and that too a courtesan like Devadutta! Devadutta is a courtesan, who is the keep of the King, enjoyed simultaneously by Subhag Dutta, the city-merchant! It is learnt that Subhag Dutta brings along chariot-loads of gold ornaments, she would like to have to her heart's content! Spurning all these aside, why would she fall for the words of the Son of Dhruvadas, who does not seem to have much money on him? Did he have the worth to meet all the demands of the whore? No, he did not have. Hence, he had been humiliated"!

Gandhavati could feel that the sunshine was becoming more intense gradually. The temperature was on the rise. The naked parts of her body seemed to be licked by the tongues of fire. Wheat fields on both the sides were almost bare, harvesting of crops was about to come to a close. One or two farmers were hanging about the crop-fields. The black soil seemed to suck in the light from the surroundings. The leaves were falling off from the trees, lined up along the edge of the thoroughfare. It kept being shed, incessantly. The noise of the falling leaves was growing deeper around her, it seemed. The old woman was again comparing her with a whore. The old woman was highlighting the capabilities of a prostitute. If needed, she would take her along to the prostitute. She would make her learn such esoteric knowledge by taking her to the whore, so that Dhruvaputra would stay enamoured of her, all his life! Many avenues of knowledge were there to keep a man under one's control and as the woman at home could not master such art, the man of the household would leave the house in lure of the outer world. The old woman was saying that she had seen Devadutta, the courtesan. On a full-moon day in the month of Sravan, she had gone to the Mahakaal temple. The old woman was describing the bodily charm of the prostitute. Devadutta seemed to be Ratidevi, in person. Her beauty was just tantamount to that of Kamadeva's wife. Her face and her eyes were both equally attractive! Old Parvati had even seen her mother, Rasamanjari, long back. Flame of her beauty was a notch higher than that of Rasamanjari's, whose fire was no less irresistible! That flame had singed many a man of Ujjwain. Dhruvaputra might burn to death by the lolling flames of that beauty! But Devadutta was not merely a powerhouse of lust, she was extremely talented too! Listen my girl, the way a prostitute would teach you the tricks of intimate union with your beloved, would be simply matchless!

Gandhavati kept crying profusely, "Why are you saying all such nonsense, I am his childhood friend, and he is mine, my friend has come back to his room".

"That I have seen already, the brat sits behind a door, closed firmly. Listen my dear girl, pray sincerely to Lord Kamadeva from the bottom of your heart, the man of your heart would surely come back to you".

Gandhavati fell silent. She seemed to know nothing about her reason of visiting the temple of Lord Kamadeva! Was it for bringing her companion straight under her control? Lowering her head, she was walking forward silently.

The old woman went walking, muttering to herself, "The man who is devoid of happiness in his household, would surely frequent a bawdyhouse to see a prostitute, and whatever the latter can satisfy him with. Will ever his wife be able to gratify him likewise? If someone had ever enjoyed the whore's sidelong glances or her irresistible charms — if anyone had been privy to the inebriating attraction of a fallen woman, would hardly come back without the blessings of Lord Kamadeva! If Lord Kamadeva had been kind enough to let him return to his wife at home, exercising mesmerism on him, he would surely come back. Your mother related every detail to me exhaustively, please pray to Lord Kandarpa from the bottom of your heart"!

"What has Maa said"? Gandhavati stopped short while asking! But her feelings could be gauged by that Old Parvati, who dragged it out into the open, and said, "Your mother has said that you have submitted yourself to Dhruvaputra in every way, both in reality and in dreams"!

The whole body of Gandhavati was set ablaze, it seemed. She knew not whether she had submitted herself to her companion, but her mind and body got soothed by the very sight of him. She had never expressed herself to her mate, explicitly. Yet, she could not deny Old Parvati's words. The old lady's hands rested on her waist while she kept saying, "Such youth, such face taking after the moon, such a flower-like body, how could a man turn to a slattern, leaving such a fragrant body, such nectar-dipped words?! Fie on that man who can do so"!

Gandhavati was getting burnt by the sun. Chaitra was about to come to a close. Black soil was sucking off all the grace of the earth! All flavours of the earth kept depleting, spring blossoms were falling off and turning black in the sunrays. Both of them sat on the way, under the shades of a bakul tree. The ground beneath the tree was covered with bakul flowers. The scent of bakul flowers lay heavy on the air. Nature was redolent with a pleasant fragrance. Nature was laden with the odour of sweet-scented blossoms. Black dust kept flying in the air. The Kamadeva temple stood at some distance on the way that stretched to the front. The river, Shipra, ran beyond the temple. The people of the city came to pay a visit to the Kamadeva temple, walking along the bank of the river, Shipra.

Tamradhvaj was listening to Gandhavati. Gandhavati kept saying that the more the old Parvati was cursing him [Dhruvaputra] for seeing a whore, the more she grew lovelorn for him. Since long, Gandhavati kept waiting to share her words with him. Who would listen to her? If she could make someone listen, the agony of her lover's absence could be alleviated a bit. The sunshine which had gone inside her on a Chaitra day, the heat of the burning universe which entered her, was yet to exhaust. What sweltering heat was it, how scorching it was! All her body seemed to get burnt! The burning which started off on the day of Chaitra Purnima had no sign of being soothed.

Tamradhvaj chipped in, "Please carry on. Dhruvaputra shall be traced amidst such narration".

Gandhavati muttered, "Let the old Grandma say whatever she wants to, Dhruvaputra is immaculate with a pure soul, a wise man cannot harbour an impure heart"…

Hearing that, the old woman kept giggling, "Who has said that he is impure, unholy? Men can never be impure, men have a right on all things on earth, he can lord over all women, he has the right to enjoy all womenfolk too. No one spends a single thought on whether he is seeing a slut or the wife of another man, it is the woman only who can be 'impure'! If a woman becomes a whore, she is undone, she renders herself as a woman of all men; menfolk, as a whole, has the liberty to enjoy her flesh - a woman has to balance all aspects of her life"!

Tamradhvaj retorted, "This is not untrue, such is the way of the world"!

Gandhavati whispered, "He used to say so, used to think in such vein".

Tamradhvaj answered, "Sometimes, men go astray, owing mostly to unruly thoughts".

"Perhaps, it happens so", said Gandhavati in an indistinct voice.

"And then what took place"? inquired Tamradhvaj.

Gandhavati shook terribly, as she was in tears. Her tears seemed to shatter her body! Old Parvati was making her see the point that to tame a man, Dhruvaputra, for that matter, the very first step was to attend the Madanotsav. She, then, felt herself small. She felt like dropping the idea of going to the temple of Lord Kamadeva. She felt like going back home and dragging her friend out, unbolting the door. She wished she could smear his body with colour-dust. The fascinating looks of his mate stood dishevelled by the storm. She wished she could make him regain his grace, by helping him have an ablution in the river-water. Gandhavati remembered. It was a day, long ago, when she was just a wisp of a girl! One evening, Dhruvaputra began to make her acquainted with the firmament, overhead. Pointing at the bright star on the northern sky, he asked her, "Can you recognize that star"?

"No, I do not".

"Dhruva…that star is called Dhruva"!

Gandhavati kept gazing at the sky, wonderstruck! Thrill seized her body, from head to foot. Was her companion born on that star? Her mate's father was Dhruva.Is he your father?

"Yes". She still seemed to hear that self-contained voice, "I am, in all possibility, the son of that very star, my father resides in that star, it seems I had descended on the bank of the river Gambhira straight from that star, you know Gandhavati, the sailors on the sea ascertain their direction with the help of that star"!

Gandhavati replied, "I was looking into its eyes, how radiant, how exquisite it appeared"!

"You have fallen head over heels in love because of that charm, lest many a prince would have sought your hands in marriage, Uddhav Das is a courtier, a man of the Royal Court - in which way is he lower in position than a prince? He is ready to marry you at the drop of a hat! If you agree, I can marry you off to him and slap that bloke hard with a befitting reply, do you agree"? Old Parvati was all hope as she demanded.

"How can you say, Grandma? Is he a man"?

"Of whom are you speaking? Uddhav?"

Gandhavati maintained silence. As the old woman held her firm, encircling her arms around, she commented, "I know, you would say so. That chap has asked me to negotiate, let it be over, let your friend be yours only, pray to Lord Kamadeva, He will fulfil your wish. Baisakhi Purnima is just a month away, on that day, it would be wise to make the wedding happen. Your mother has already made up her mind, the mangalsutra will adorn your neck that day, she will find peace by marrying you off to Dhruvaputra"!

Gandhavati had not the faintest idea of all these things. She was listening to the old woman, utterly surprised. She sat firm like a stone. The old woman kept advising to keep Dhruvaputra under strict observation from the day of Chaitra Purnima till that of Baisakhi Purnima, "Let him not leave Gambhira, do not allow him to travel to the city. The sluts are adept in casting charms. They fail to get a household, shack up with someone, hence, they draw out the man of the family; breaking a household, annulling the conjugal bond. A man will see the wily woman, again and again, as she will regale him with her illusory designs! In order to hold on to the man, a woman must have recourse to wiles, like a whore! He should be won over by her ravishing looks! Gandhavati would have to turn into a woman of charms and wiles too."

Gandhavati was listening. She was drooping under the blast of hot air. Fear was taking over as she was listening to the old woman. Then at one point of time, the old lady pulled her up. Both of them, again, resumed their walk towards the temple of Lord Kamadeva. Confusion crept in as an impact of the old woman's words, which she was keen to convey. Again, the old lady was praising Uddhavdas. Dhruvaputra was not a man of the Royal Court, rather he was condemned in the city of Ujjwain. The vilification of the prostitute was much more ignoble than the King's abuse at the Royal Court. Will ever Dhruvaputra win a position in the Royal Court? The old woman was quite certain about his failure to win so. With such a past, why would he be welcomed to attend the royal sessions at the court? Dhruvaputra would never be permitted to step into the King's palace! And sans the favour of the King, none had ever scaled the ladder of success or acquired certain power! Uddhavdas stood a fair chance of being blessed with a brilliant future, on the contrary!

Tamradhvaj asked, "Did Uddhavdas turn up today"?

"Yes".

"What was he saying"?

"Hasn't he given up his hopes as yet? I am so afraid of him, so very scared"!

Gandhavati had expressed her fear to old Parvati! Hearing this, the old woman laughed such boisterously! Uddhav, according to her, was a simple-hearted man, a good-natured innocent person. He would make Gandhavati, his queen! If Gandhavati agreed to meet Uddhav somewhere, the old woman was even eager to arrange it for her.

Tamradhvaj asked, "And what followed"?

Thereafter, Gandhavati and Parvati had reached Kamadeva Temple, on the bank of the river, Shipra. It was more of an arbour of youth than a mere shrine! Hundreds of flowers were in bloom on the way to the temple. Cotton balls were afloat in air, the bumble-bees were in flight, and the air was even saturated with the fragrance of the new shoots of mangoes! Scent of bakul flowers, strong fragrance of wild flowers whose name none was familiar with hung so heavy in the air. Stretching his gaze afar, it was discerned that a fair was on. The young damsels were pouring in, clad in colourful mekhalas and bright-hued scarves. They were stalked by romantic brats, just as swarms of drone in a honeycomb. Many among the young girls were urban housewives. Their consorts were walking by, holding their hands. The horde of singers kept filing in, singing, playing the tom-tom shaped percussion instruments. The palanquin drawn by eight bearers, brought in Bhanumati, the queen of Avanti! All let out joyous shrieks, calling out loud for joining the parade! They did not get any permission to enter the temple then. They had to wait for long! They spotted the King's sentry with the queen Bhanumati. The Army-Chief, Bikram, the King's younger brother was expected to grace the occasion, but the latter had suddenly been taken ill. Gandhavati and her associates had seen many newly-wed wives to turn up, holding their husband's hands. Many a lover had come, expecting to have a look at the face of their beloved. Many again had come all alone, to just say their prayers to Lord Kamadeva. A lot had come only in search of pure fun! Given an opportunity, they would shoot flower-arrows at the well-dressed young maids. All their attires were soaked in colours. Red, blue, yellow, green, pink, sky-blue. How colourful were the apparels, mekhalas, long scarves! The air was laden with colour-dust! Colour-smeared men and women were rushing towards the garden, looking for a cover. The young damsels were being chased by the youths, who tried to deck them with flowers. The Ashoke petals had filled the way with colours. A courtesan sat to play veena in the garden. No matter how melodious she played, many a person had stood around her, allured by the sonorous arpeggios of the strings.

From the unknown nooks of the flowery lawn, sibilant noise of pleasure was being wafted in. A strange fragrance hung in the air. What kind of smell was this? Old Parvati observed, "It was the smell of Kamadeva. On Chaitra Purnima, Kamadeva became all-pervasive, whoever could sniff that fragrance would turn fortunate".

"Have you ever seen Lord Kamadeva"? asked Tamradhvaj.

"Yes, I have seen."

Gandhavati lifted her face. She let her gaze dwell upon Tamradhvaj. Tamradhvaj had asked Gandhavati, stretching his glance to the sky, as though Gandhavati had been there, in the blue vault above. Gandhavati was readily impressed by looking at the disciple of Acharya Brishavanu. Brishavanu's disciple stood engrossed in gluing his vision to the azure canopy, overhead.

Only the fortunate could set her eyes on Kamadeva. Oh, how handsome he was! Old Parvati was absolutely right! The appearance of her friend was really comparable to that of Kamadeva. Did the old woman say or did she think so, herself? His nose was well-shaped, thighs, waist and shanks were round and fleshy. A golden yellow cloth had covered his waist. How expansive was his chest! That chest seemed to make Gandhavati feel secure, fearless. As if, to offer Gandhavati a safe haven! Any woman would covet such haven! The pair of eyes, the countenance, upper and lower lips, the base of his feet, nails — all were reddish in hue. Lord Kamadeva sat on the back of the mythological animal, Makar, his pet, amidst a pile of bakul flowers. He held floral-bows and floral-arrows in his hand. In front of him, a ghee-lamp stood burning. Worshipping Lord Kamadeva with Ashok and Bakul blossoms, she sat still, with a steadfast gaze. As if, the deity kept glancing at her. Tears coursed down Gandhavati's eyes by then.

She saw Tamradhvaj melting into the foggy darkness. The astronomer from Dasharno was leaving. Gandhavati came forward, all was yet to come to an end.

Tamradhvaj did not return. He walked on. He went past the courtyard.

Twenty

"Do you recall, that evening, on which Subhag Dutta , the merchant, had dropped in"? In a muffled voice, almost in a whisper, devadasi Subhadra said, His real age eludes us, it seems as if he is just a man of youth.

Lalita Dasi was taken by surprise to find the mark of senility writ large on the countenance of Subhag Dutta! Did it elude Subhadra's eyes? It was true that he was younger in age than the Chief Priest. But it hardly would indicate that he was just a youth in his heyday and the young devadasi had to nurture him in the deepest nook of her heart! How old would Subhadra be? Hardly eighteen or nineteen! Subhag Dutta was nearing fifty. Lalita Dasi threw a befuddled glance at Subhadra's face in the darkness. It was the day of Shukla Panchami during the month of Phalgun. And just then, the jackal had declared the third hour of evening. A crescent-moon, curved as a lance, had journeyed above the western forest of Mahakaal, lying quite far. Leaving her bed, Subhadra had woken up Lalita Dasi, lying fast asleep on the terrace near the priest's room and brought her along to sit on the commodious vestibule outside the temple. Lalita Dasi started at the touch of Subhadra. That night of Shukla Ashtami in the month of Poush was still vividly etched on the canvas of her mind. Did again Mahakaal ask for her? In the stupor of sleep, she had even called out to Lord Mahakaaleswar! But as she opened her eyes, her error stood rectified. A lamp, aglow, was held in the hand of Subhadra. She came to look at Lalita in the light of the lamp.

Now, both sat facing each other in the darkness. In the starlight, both of them stood manifested to each other. Subhadra was telling her, "The merchant had made a presence in her dreams, she had visualized the merchant in her dreams and that was why she was avid to share her inmost feelings with her"!

Lalita Dasi retorted, "Have you gone mad, Subhadra? Aren't thee the maid of Lord Mahakaal"?

"Whatever it might be, he was enchanted by my dance that evening, even my graceful body impressed him"!

"Who told you?"

"I had seen myself".

"But didn't you fall unconscious"?

"No, I had felt Lord Mahakaal that very day, intense joy had driven me senseless, this life seemed to be worth living, that evening only".

"That exactly happens", Lalita Dasi gibbered. That winter night flashed across her mind. Lord Mahakaal came to unite with him, on his own! The last remnant of ultimate joy of that union still stayed back with her. Till date, the tips of her breasts stood firm if she ever remembered that night! Hairs on the body stood straight, the pair of her eyes closed, slowly. If hunted, wouldn't she find a few nail-scratches on her breasts, bearing testimony to that nocturnal experience? Three fortnights had sped by, since then. Lalita Dasi seemed keen on holding back that mark all her life! But the touch was that of Lord Mahakaal. She was meant to be enjoyed by Lord Mahakaal. The maid of Lord Mahakaal as she was! She had offered her entire entity to Lord Mahakaal only. She knew quite well that the maid of Lord Mahakaal would never think of anyone else! But what was Subhadra up to?

Subhadra said, "My gaze slipped from Mahakaaleswar to the elegant merchant, Subhag Dutta, through the haze of the smoke of joss-sticks, he seemed to fix me with a wide-eyed gaze! As if, Lord Mahakaal had appeared before me in the form of the merchant, but he had not come thereafter".

"Why would the merchant come, the Chief Priest, the Brahmin, used to see him", Lalita blabbed.

"I am always reminded of that evening".

"This thought is just a sin, you are the serving-maid of Lord Mahakaal".

"Feeling him within, I swooned and then he expressed his concern. Yes, I remember everything".

Lalita smiled, "You have gone feeble owing to starvation".

"No, only I know well why I had bowed down to Lord Mahakaal so low"!

And Lalita Dasi had been driven to silence then. Being astonished, she was overcome by fear as well. How could Devadasi Subhadra be so desirous of the merchant, Subhag Dutta? So strange! No doubt, the merchant had loads of wealth but how about looks? Appearance? Where was his valour? A few years to go and he would be just the same as the Chief Priest! And why would the maid, who had been sacrificed to Lord Mahakaal, desire some other gentleman? It would then spell disaster to the prestige of the temple-family! The woman would be brought down to the status of a whore! If this news reached the ear of the Chief Priest, he would not waste the chance of humiliating her! The maid who had really been entrusted with the responsibility of cleaning the body of God, entering the inner base-temple of the Lord, would never harbour any other man in her heart, violating which the shrine would stand profaned! Alack! That would be simply horrifying! Only because of the sin of a devadasi, all would be taken as sinners in the eyes of the Chief Priest, the King, even that of the merchant!

Lalita asked, "Did you wake me up from sleep just for saying this"?

"Yes".

"Is the door of the base-temple open"?

"The Brahmin knows"!

"But, Bai, thou had slept by his door, hadn't thou"?

"Mahakaal would come to know", Lalita Dasi hissed out.

"Mahakaal is nothing but a stone-block"!

Lalita started and sticking her hand out, she placed it on Subhadra's lips to silence her, "What do you say? Uttering such words is a sin in itself! Lord Mahakaal is our refuge"!

Subhadra shook her head in the dark and unfastened her chignon. She kept toying with her hair, cascading it down absentmindedly, she said, "Many a time I had touched that image"!

Lalita started, "What do you say"?

"I scrubbed the body, the stone image stood ice-cold, touching it seemed to leave blood in my body frozen, how still, how motionless! Not a hint of life had been there"!

"Stop it"! Lalita Dasi reprimanded Subhadra, "Yhou have no limits to your sin, what stuff and nonsense do you utter"?

"Why? Haven't you rubbed and cleansed that idol"?

"When I was empowered to do, I did".

"How did you feel then"?

"Mahakaal is my haven, my Lord, I am blessed to have touched Him!"

"Tell me the truth".

"My mind was devoid of all sins while I touched Lord Mahakaal", Lalita Dasi said, "Lord Mahakaal blesses us by assuming a form, and, I am fortunate to see Him"!

Subhadra went astir, "Got to see Him, you, oh bai"?

"Yes, He has given me everything".

"What do you say, bai"?

"Yes, stone may be cold, of course that is to you, but I had received Him as a flesh-and-blood human, and oh, how warm was that divine physique! Oh Lord Mahakaal"! Devadasi Lalita bowed down to the darkness, with folded palms. And thereafter, she kept looking into the darkness with her palms, folded. It seemed to her that, Mahakaaleswar had emerged through the open door of the base temple into the darkness. He must have been somewhere, in close proximity. Lalita seemed to hear the sound of His inhalation and exhalation. It was just a typical human body. Lord Mahakaal had gone mad in an amorous union with her, on that night of Shukla Panchami! She got transformed into Uma, had gone emaciated because of her austere ascetic practice! Wasn't Subhadra aware of the ascetic pursuits of Uma? Was it so easy to win Lord Mahakaal? Would He ever be gratified so soon to bless anyone? Lalita Dasi was trembling vigorously. In her memory, that night grew magnified as an absolute reality. A certain thrill got the better of her corporeal frame!

Subhadra inquired, "How could a piece of stone become flesh-and-blood"?

"Never utter such a word of vice"!

Silence cocooned the two women in its folds. Lalita Dasi had been all ears, stealthily. River Gandhavati was flowing nearby in a thin stream. A nocturnal animal was moving from one end to the other. A rustling noise was being wafted in there. A field rabbit might have been crossing a wild stretch in the forest. Or was it someone else? Lalita Dasi was trying to discover the source of the noise, warily. Did any footfall come to life in the terrace? By which way had Lord Mahakaal come to her? Emerging from the base-temple, crossing over the terrace? Or did he rise up from the bank of the river, Gandhavati?

Subhadra quipped, "But the serving-maid of Lord Mahakaal is the Chief Priest's object of desire.

"He only serves the will of Lord Mahakaal by whatever he does".

"Who told you"?

"He himself does, he is in the know of Lord Mahakaal's will", Saying so, Lalita's voice got choked. She held back the affair of that Poush night to herself only. She never divulged to anyone that the well-ornate gold necklace was a gift from the One, the Virility Personified. She had stashed it away at a secret spot, outside the shrine, under a stone-slab. Danger would befall her, if she would keep it with her. Again, what was hers here? Not even a room was allotted to her. She had to be happy to lodge in the terrace. Initially, she had burnt desiring the Chief Priest in her sleep. She had learnt to believe that, whatever transpired in this temple was by the will of God. And that faith stood firm following her miraculous union with Lord Mahakaal, on that chilly night!

Subhadra blurted forth, "All the words of the Brahmin are false".

Lalita was overcome by terror, in a muffled voice, she said, "The stone of this temple, too, has ears, and the Chief Priest is even revered by the King, why do you make all these derogatory remarks against him"?

Subhadra charged her, "Don't you comprehend anything at all"?

"I am just an ordinary woman, sheltered by Lord Mahakaal, I have no mind for anything else save Lord Mahakaal, the Chief Priest serves Lord Mahakaal, he stands even a notch higher than the King"!

Subhadra kept mum. Lalita, too, trailed off to silence, while blabbing. She was really in fear now. It was beyond her comprehension that someone could even harbour such thoughts here in the city of Avanti or Ujjwain, sitting in this temple of Lord Mahakaal. If such words made way to the ears of any Brahmin, let alone the Chief Priest, would that man be spared? Subhadra would be thrown away into the Mahakaal forest. She would be the feed for the beasts in the jungle. Lalita Dasi intervened, "Enough is enough, now please go back".

"Are you afraid?" Subhadra inquired. She continued, "I have to see the merchant, I must have to meet him, he is superior to all in this city".

"Ask the Chief Priest".

"The Chief Priest himself had told me that the merchant had been impressed by my dance".

"Then"?

"Alas, Lord Mahakaal! Why is the Chief Priest, the Lord Brahmin, the custodian of all your powers, so ruthless? Why do such obscene words come out of his mouth"?

Lalita's hand sprang up to Subhadra's mouth. Subhadra bent forward. She buried her head in between her two knees, and said, "I must see the merchant. He is Lord Mahakaal to me".

Lalita Dasi remarked, "How would you get Him, being such insensitive? Whom would you approach if the merchant rejects you? Does the rich merchant have any dearth of women? Would ever Lord Mahakaal accept you, once dumped by the merchant"?

Subhadra did not raise her face. She did not answer even. Lalita looked at the Milky Way, turning her head up. The third prahar had sped by, long ago. Now dewfall got a boost. Lalita rose. Subhadra too did. Both of them came to stand in the dark of the terrace. Lalita said, "Waiting for the Lord never goes unrewarded, He must come to greet you, one day, just as I received Him".

Subhadra asked, "How is it that you got Him? But you are still a devadasi"!

"I am the maid of Lord Mahakaal, where shall I go"?

"The Priest deals heartlessly with you".

"Let him do so, he has no idea as to whose kindness makes me such strong"!

Lalita's face could not be clearly seen by Subhadra in the darkness. But she was feeling amazed by the depth of her voice. She observed, "If you knew, you could have been at a vantage position".

"No", deep and emphatic was Lalita's voice. "How can one be affected by the ruthlessness of the Chief Priest? Do you know what innumerable bad names he greets me with? You are the maid of the base temple, you are still exempted, but lately I have lost the privilege of dancing even!"

"Yet you say that Mahakaal is in your favour"!

"Yes, I got him on the day of Shukla Ashtami in the month of Poush, on a holy lunar day".

A shadow of humour toyed at the corner of Subhadra's lips in the darkness. In a humorous tone again, she said, "You had entered the inner base-temple, on the sly, and the door remained closed, eh"?

"No, He himself had come to me".

"Opening the door, you mean"?

"Cannot say". Mahakaal is omnipresent, He is in this darkness, inside the stone, in the firmament, even the moonshine is His abode, how can I say wherefrom he had come"?

"Did He manifest himself in a dream"?

"No, in the wakeful hours, and to your utter surprise, Mahakaal comes only thus"!

Subhadra had become quite sceptical since she had seen the merchant. While informing her about the merchant, the Chief Priest was gratifying his desire by pressing his favourite body-part on hers, she had lost all faith, absolutely. Though she used to perform the dance of dedication in front of Lord Mahakaal, she herself could feel that she was not left with the least of any emotions inside her! She seemed to attend to her duties only! She was just playing her role, shouldering her responsibilities! The Chief Priest had apprised her of Subhag Dutta, the merchant, being impressed by her dance, but Subhag Dutta had thrust the responsibility of enjoying her on the old Priest only! The merchant had given one hundred gold coins for Subhadra but in lieu of that the Chief Priest, Brahmadev Bhatta the Brahmin,, staked his claim on everything that Subhadra possessed. Alack, oh Mahakaal! All had been categorically related to her by the old Priest, in the manner of chanting hymns, sitting in the base temple only! The more he said, the more Subhadra had grown keen in love with the businessman. Without having anyone to bank upon, how would she live with such radiant youth of hers? Who would save her from this life of distress? If the old Priest indulged in lustful deeds, sitting before God in the base temple, then Lord Mahakaal, who do You belong to"?

Lalita Dasi asked, "Subhadra, would you please take me before the Lord in the base temple"?

"Would you like to go"?

"Yes, I shall go; since long I have not seen Him in seclusion, have not been with Him, and three fortnights have passed by after that night, Lord Mahakaal hasn't called on me even!"

Subhadra's curiosity mounted. She held the hand of Lalita Dasi in the darkness. In gingerly steps, the two women left for the Lord. In the lightless terrace, the jingle of their anklet-bells raised a faint noise. That very noise was enough to disclose their presence to the Brahmin priests! If they would wake up from their sleep, their life would turn hell by facing extensive interrogation! It took quite long for them to reach near Mahakaal, concealing the jingle of the anklet-bells. But on reaching the wide courtyard in front of the base temple, explosion of emotions got the better of him, shook Lalita Dasi and she blabbed out, "Oh Lord!"

Drawing her, Subhadra made Lalita enter inside the base-temple. She was growing intimidated, gradually, by Lalita's manners. If someone had an inkling of it! Scriptures had no sanction for co-habitation of two women in the base-temple together by midnight. Subhadra closed the door. The two damsels sat in front of Lord Mahakaaleswar, stretching their thighs as two altars.

The inner temple was redolent with sweet fragrance of the incense sticks. The air in the room was heavy with the fragrance of flowers. But the freshness of that sweet smell was no more. The fresh blossoms, offered for the day, were growing stale by then. Almost three-fourth of the pitch-black phallic image of Lord Mahakaal had been decked with heaps of flowers. The phallic image seemed to raise its head through those piles. This image lacked in limbs. Not even any of the three eyes had been there. This image showed neither happiness, nor morbidity. Not even signs of rage. It was embodiment of virility only. Being embedded in the source of creation, it contained the birth-seeds of the living world.

A lamp of ghee was lit in front of the Lord. The light of the lamp failed to reach all corners of the room, but it kept slipping off the oil-smeared idol of Lord Mahakaal. Tears coursed down the cheeks of Lalita Dasi, from her eyes, and they fell on her chest as tears of joy. Soiled woollen shawl and the covering-cloth had been taken off the body of the idol by the devadasi. Both her breasts quivered in excitement. Devadasi's body heaved like waves, in sync with the inhalation and exhalation. Subhadra Dasi glanced at Lalita in wide-eyed amazement. Were then her words true?

Lalita Dasi had entered the inner base temple after a long interregnum. She was desirous of offering herself to Lord Mahakaal through her dance, following the night of Shukla Ashtami. But it did not happen. The Chief Priest refrained from giving her the consent. Would she then bring Lord Mahakaaleswar to life at the dead of night? Would she awake Him by her dance of lust?

Subhadra wiped away the tears from Lalita's eyes, with her own uttariya and in a low voice she asked, "Wouldn't you tell me how you had won God"?

She must say. She was just all agog to speak out everything! On that holy night, she was blessed with an ultimate achievement of her life! She was turning her neck to take an exhaustive look of the base room. Square roof, a lone pillar, walls of pumice stone, and an unpolished floor. She slouched low, touched her forehead on the floor and prayed to God, "Oh Lord Mahakaal, I am here to narrate the experience of that holy night before you, taking you as a witness. Oh Lord, since that night, I keep remembering you alone and you have not come to me again, I feel all your caress on my body, oh Lord, both my breasts carry the mark of your love-making till date! Oh Lord, on that chilly, stone-cold night you seemed to have seen me, in that royal robe of yours"!

Subhadra was astonished. Subhadra's eyes grew wide in amazement, on learning Lalita Dasi's detailed account. Devadasi sat up. Moving aside the woollen shawl she freed the two breasts from the clutch of her bra. She had upheld her nudity before the Lord. She was describing the enchanting night, slowly, bit by bit. How strange! It was nothing but the account of union of the fondest souls. How gracefully was Lalita Dasi portraying the moment of a man and woman's union in words! On hearing, Subhadra grew excited. No such experience she had ever had in her life! The way in which the old Priest treated her should never happen even in the life of any lesser mortal. Even dogs were spared of such an existence. Subhadra's eyes got closed. Her mind would uphold the portrait of Subhag Dutta, the merchant, in a flash. Lalita Dasi's strange utterances were making way to her ears. Lalita Dasi was describing the amorous union with Lord Mahakaal, in a singsong voice of chanting mantras. Lord Mahakaal transformed that ice-cold night into a warm one. He seemed to unite with Uma, the daughter of the mountains in that darkness.

TWENTY-ONE

L alita Dasi, in a feeble tone, said, "You are right".

"How so"?

Wrenching her neck, the devadasi looked at the door of the inner temple. She confirmed whether it had been bolted firm. Then being free from worries, looking at the deity, she said in a lowered voice, "Just like you, I, too, used to think that Lord Mahakaal is just a slab of stone, He is just stone-cold".

"What are you saying"? Devadasi Subhadra was in for a surprise.

"Whatever I am saying is just the truth, Lord Mahakaal seemed to be inanimate, motionless, stone-like".

Subhadra's face got blanched in fear, she stood panic-stricken. The word which she herself had uttered outside the base-temple, sitting in the dark of the vestibule, she seemed perturbed to hear the same from someone else. This cave-temple was blessed with the presence of God. Lord stood in front of her. Whatever would have Subhadra said against Lord, had not been uttered here! That had been done there on the terrace of the temple in the darkness, quite at a distance from this cave-temple. Now, Lalita Dasi had again begun to speak on that matter taking cue from there. As if, she was keen on making Mahakaal listen to whatever Subhadra had said behind Him. It were as if Mahakaal was truly someone of flesh and blood. If He stayed in the base temple, He would continue to stay there, if He stood in the temple, He kept being there, as though, he could not stay outside the base temple, or the temple itself or even beyond the city of Ujjwain, for that matter. If He was placed below the glow of the lamp, certainly he could not stand in darkness. He was just collinear, like human beings. His abode was the base-temple hence devadasi Lalita had gone there to keep Him abreast of what Subhadra had said behind Him, outside the precincts of this inner temple.

Subhadra said, "Stop all these things"!

The words seemed to have eluded the ears of Lalita Dasi and she went on softly, slowly, "Your words are true, Mahakaal is just made of stone and nothing but stone"!

"No", Subhadra recoiled in panic.

Lalita Dasi said, "But life has to be breathed into the stone". That ice-coldness puts us to test, it seems. As if, Mahakaal wants to test how devout I am! Listen Subhadra, the Brahmin used to intimidate us by saying that, if we went into unholy practice or flouted his directives, the third eye of Lord Mahakaal will glow and we will be burnt to ashes"!

"Yes", Subhadra sat with her face, hung low.

Lalita's face was radiant with a sense of gratification. In a slow voice she said, "No, not really, when Mahakaal made off with my scarf, when He stole my mekhala, when I stood in front of Mahakaal, with my body utterly bare, I covered His eyes with my palms to save myself from dishonour. But He was Lord Mahakaal, a terribly desirous, lustful man at that time, his third eye lit up, and all my resistance proved futile, He began to behold me, the body which I used to offer Him so religiously each day, He went on etching lines of love-making on it"!

Subhadra shuddered. She looked at the phallic idol of Lord Mahakaaleswar in fear. Did that ice-cold stone ever spring up to life? Subhadra kept looking at Lalita with suspicion writ large on her eyes. Even in the light of the lamp, thrill could be clearly traced on the countenance of Lalita Dasi. She moved near Lalita. Keeping a hand on her back, she asked, "Who had come"?

Lalita stooped in obeisance to say, "Lord Mahakaal".

"Tell me the truth".

"Mahakaal is the ultimate truth".

"The Brahmin Priest, that old man"?

"No".

"The merchant"?

"No".

"Any courtier"?

"No".

"Any trader from the other land"?

"No", Lalita pressed her two ears to say, "I am not telling a lie"!

"Were you dreaming"?

"No".

"How was his appearance"?

"A man of strange, commendable virility"!

"Did you behold Him with your eyes"?

"No, I couldn't open my eyes".

"Didn't you open your eyes even for once"?

"It was stygian dark! He seemed to have merged with that darkness".

"Tell me the truth, whatsoever intense the darkness be, He had been on you"!

Lalita Dasi replied, " Please never speak in that manner, Subhadra, He is this Mahakaal, the deity I worship, to whom again, I have offered myself!"

"But all devadasis do that, is it anything new"?

"He can never be duped by wiles, being a serving-maid of Lord Mahakaal, it is a sin to express affinity towards the merchant, Lord Mahakaal knows everything".

"Lord Mahakaal never stepped into my dreams"!

"Why will He come if not prayed whole-heartedly"?

"Don't the others pray to Him, you mean to say? But all of them are enjoyed by others save Lord Mahakaal"!

Lalita retorted, "I do not know. All these should not even be uttered in front of the deity. Subhadra, if it had been that moment, I could have displayed the signs of His biting teeth on my breasts"!

Subhadra got thrilled once again. The bare breasts of Lalita shook as she breathed in and out. The circles round her breasts stood firm. As if, Lalita was burning in desire! She lifted up the lamp and kept inspecting Lalita in the glow of the lamp. Would ever the signs stay there for so many days? They must have faded out, disappeared. Her curiosity kept building up. Her breasts got swollen in the desire to know, it seemed. Who had come? Was it the merchant? She used to get desirous of the merchant in her deeper within. She had an inkling that the merchant had been carried away by her charms, her art of dancing. She knew, if she could be desired by the merchant, she would surely be spared the pains of serving this temple. Being subject to the perverted desires of the Chief Priest, she seemed to have lost all faith in God. She could not believe a single word of Lalita! All seemed to be begotten of Lalita's imagination.

Nowadays, she was not even entrusted with scrubbing the body of the idol. Yet, Lord Mahakaal came to enjoy her! Was Lalita driven out of her mind? Everything was imagined by her, whatever she kept saying, for sure. Or did anyone come to her? Who could it be?

Lalita came up, "I have a token of His presence".

"Where's the token?" Subhadra kept examining Lalita's breasts closely.

Covering her breasts with a woollen scarf, Lalita said, "He has left a token behind, His necklace, I am sure, you will believe me, once you see the ornament"!

Subhadra's eyes grew keen with intense suspicion. Then was it the merchant, Subhag Dutta? The merchant came to take Lalita Dasi? And, considering him as Mahakaal, Lalita had given him all that was hers? Lalita got to her feet, "Please come with me".

Subhadra followed her. Pulling the door of the base temple together, both of them stepped out in the dark. Lalita took the lamp which stood lit on the terrace in her hand. Saving the flame from the gush of air with a hand, she kept moving forward with the lamp in another hand.

Subhadra inquired, "But why haven't you spoken out for so long"?

"It occurred to me that Mahakaal had asked me to keep it a secret".

"Then why are you telling me now"?

"Let me stand forgiven by Mahakaal...but as you expressed your unfaith"…

Subhadra was all fear. If the Chief Priest would come to know of this fact, she would not be spared at all. The walls of this shrine had ears too. All words would reach the Chief Priest straightaway. The wind that remained locked in this sanctum sanctorum, be it of winter or of summer or of spring would surely tote the words to the Chief Priest! She was undone! Why did she open her inner desire to Lalita? If Lalita blabbed it out? Subhadra answered, "I am not sceptical. Please forget all these matters".

"What shall I forget? Whatever had happened that night"?!

"No, that of today", in an inaudible voice said Subhadra.

Lalita did not answer at all. They had come to the rear of the shrine. A considerable stretch of fallow land lay beyond the main temple. And then a wide rampart ran, which was about the height of one man-and-a-half. Behind the wall, flew the waters of the river, Gandhavati. The firmament of the cold night ran above. In the south-west, the Dogstar stood awake. Below that star stood another star, Canopus.

The moon was not visible. Standing beneath the luminous glow of the stars, Lalita said, "Following the evening lamp-ritual, the gate of the shrine stands closed. Hence, he who had come to me resides in this temple only".

"Where's the token"?

"My statement is true; none can come to me save those who stay within the temple"!

"The Chief Priest, the lustful old bloke"?

"No, He is Lord Mahakaaleswar"! Folding both her palms, Lalita Dasi bowed down and throwing a glance at the shrine said, "Yes, it is here".

Near the rampart, Lalita Dasi bent to sit low at the base of the Neem tree. Then, removing the stone-slab, she fished out the necklace. She unveiled the necklace in the darkness, wrapped in a torn piece of mekhala.

It was as if the flowers of light streamed down from the sky to form the garland in the vacuum. Subhadra was hushed to silence in utter amazement!

The golden necklace studded with diamond and other precious stones seemed to be made of the light flakes, drifting in the Milky Way. A stream of light flashed past before Subhadra's eyes. The musty darkness grew aglow! Subhadra's eyes got dazzled. This was just an invaluable treasure! What was this necklace called? Was this the one called Mahalata? Subhadra had heard of Mahalata, but had never seen it with her own eyes. Devadasi Subhadra felt an excitement as she was reminded of Mahalata. And how was it that such a necklace would come in the possession of a run-of-the-mill devadasi? Who could have given it to her? Subhadra grew agitated. Mahalata was no trifle to possess. She heard that Subhag Dutta, the merchant, had given Mahalata to his daughter, during her wedding. She also learnt that, Gandharvasen, the father of Bhartrihari, the King of Ujjwain, had given it as a present to his keep, Rasamanjari, a courtesan. All such information was culled from grapevine sources. Did that necklace change hands from Rasamanjari to Devadutta? And this necklace might have been there, in the possession of Bhanumati, the queen of King Bhartrihari! Or even it might be with Subhag Dutta. Or it might have also been possessed by an extraordinarily rich merchant or a tradesman. While thinking so, excited Subhadra snatched it off and kept running into the darkness.

"What have you done, bai? Return it. That has been given by Lord Mahakaal, that bears the touch of Lord Mahakaal"! With a muffled scream, Lalita kept chasing Subhadra. In a muffled voice she went on calling her, boiling in anger, cursing her, "Hey, you would be undone! Lord Mahakaal would perish you"!

Entering the shrine, Subhadra melted into darkness. Lalita kept chasing her, following the jingling of her anklet-bells. A darkness, she is familiar with; a terrace, known to her. Her assumption was correct, Subhadra had run towards the base temple. Running out of breath, Lalita came to find the door of the base temple had been bolted from inside. The lamp kept outside the door, in the niche of the wall, was about to snuff out. Lalita kept pounding the door. She called out to Subhadra, "Bai, please open the door, hey you,bai, it's a gift from the Lord". The noise of Lalita, crying, the sound of her knocking on the door, the jingling of her anklets— all kept pervading the quiet of the temple. By then, the pigeons who had taken shelter at the dovecotes on each arch of the temple, were nudged out of sleep. The flight of the pigeons went cooing, on being awake. As the pigeons cooed and flapped their wings, the birds sheltered on the neem, mango, jackfruit and wild-rose trees, on the boundary of the temple, chirped and trilled. The twitter of those birds bounded out of the temple-wall to reach beyond. Over and beyond the boundary wall, a parliament of crows, on an old sandpaper tree started cawing in the dark in fear, awakened from sleep by the shrill call of the other birds! Flapping their wings in the dark like sightless beings, they went back to the branches of the trees to cry out shrilly. The street curs got up from sleep by the caw of the crows and chirp of the birds. Getting up from sleep, they began crying out to the sky, venting out their doubt of losing the right direction. Only the planet- and star-studded night sky of Phalgun in its darkness was what they were familiar with. They knew even the planets and the stars of the sky. And as they knew them, they kept letting out their cries to the setting Canopus on the southern sky and above it, the brightly shining Sirius or the Dogstar. They went crying out, gazing at the Milky way. Through their cries, they seemed to call out to the Orion. They twisted their neck to the Ursa Major and fixed it with a steadfast gaze. They were struck with fear. The cry of the dogs awakened the inhabitants of the fishermen ghetto, bordering the bank of the river Gandhavati. They broke into a babel. They stared at the dark river, at the sky too. Did the enemy troops enter their city then? The Hun soldiers? Without being able to make out anything, they sat up straight for long, many of them together.

The Chief Priest was debarred from having a deep sleep. As he kept aging, sleep eluded him. He tossed between sleep and wakefulness though. He woke up from sleep. Being awake, the Chief Priest heard the dogs, barking. Why were the dogs crying into the dark? They had stopped by now. The pigeons were again trailing off to silence, while cooing aloud. The Chief Priest decided to rise up. Thieves might have barged in. But this was the shrine of Lord Mahakaal. The people of Avanti had an unflinching faith in Lord Mahakaal. The thieves would think ten times before entering the shrine. A few years ago, a thief was nabbed inside the temple. He was trying to enter the base-temple. Being caught red-handed, he was beaten black and blue, till he was half-dead. The Chief Priest, Brahmadev Bhatta, himself got him tied to the neem tree with the aid of the residents of the fishermen ghetto. Then came Utanka. Utanka killed the man alone, by agonizing him. Many had witnessed that death agony. The dwellers of the Shudrapalli were listening to the screams of death-throes, standing on the bank of the river Gandhavati. The man hailed from the Shudra ghetto itself. Since then, the temple had witnessed no troubles. Indeed, the shrine had no dearth of treasures and riches. All the ornaments and treasures were stashed away in a safe vault. The Chief Priest was in cognizance of that nook. Subhag Dutta knew that too. He had been informed by Brahmadev. He was compelled to share it with the King but the latter had no interest in it. Whatever Mahakaal received by way of charity or donation, went into the possession of the Chief Priest, indirectly.

Brahmadev woke up. Why were the dogs screaming thus, if it were not a thief? He wondered. What a whimpering noise, foreboding ill! Was it foreshadowing a fresh attack by the Huns? On waking up, he cried out from his own seat, "Lalita, hey Lalita...”!

He failed to elicit a response. Without getting an answer, the Chief priest got angry. He was feeling panicky. The screaming of the dogs subsided gradually, but the reverberation it had caused to spread over in the dark, was enough to make the hairs on Brahmadev's body, stand on their ends! His panic kept mounting. He feared as though the enemies might have made a foray into the city. If the Huns entered again, they would invariably rush to the temple first. Plundering the shrine they would win gold, silver, diamond, pearl and youthful devadasis. The Priest shouted, "Hey Lalita, hey slattern, where have you gone? Come here, listen to what I say".

Lalita did not turn up. The Chief Priest sat silent. He yelled again. At last, anklets jingled in the dark. Brahmadev's call had reached the ears of Lalita. She was walking in with brisk steps. She took the lamp from a niche. And then, as she came to stand at the threshold, the Chief Priest burst out in anger, "Where had you been"?

Lalita replied, "Mahakaal".

"What do you mean by Mahakaal"?

Lalita replied, "Master, I have got Lord Mahakaal".

Brahmadev got astonished, "What does it mean"?

"Lord Mahakaal came to me and this is the truth, my master!"

Brahmadev Bhatta called Lalita in, Lalita knelt before the Priest, keeping the lamp at the edge of the wall, touching his feet with both her palms. She said in a faint voice, "I am telling nothing but the truth, Sir"!

"Why do the dogs whimper"?

"I do not know, my master".

"When had Lord Mahakaal come"? Lifting one leg on the shoulder of Lalita and placing the other on her breasts, he demanded, "What for will He come to thee"?

Lalita answered, "This is the truth, my master"!

"For that reason, the dogs are weeping, hey slut, what do you mean to say, any idea"?

As her breasts hurt, Lalita broke into tears. Springing aside, she said, "Why the dogs weep, the dogs only know, but Sir, Subhadra has stolen all my belongings, please see to it".

TWENTY-TWO

Subhag Dutta came to say, "This ornament belongs to the King".

"What do you say"? The closed fist of the Chief Priest gave way.

"Yes, it has dropped straight into your hands from the neck of the King".

"Are you sure"?

"Yes", sticking out his hand, wringing the necklace out from the grip of the Chief Priest, tossing it from one palm to the other, he said, "When the King's coronation was on, while he was about to ascend the throne of Ujjwain, this necklace had been presented to him by the merchant of this city. I had gifted it to him, I can recognize but how has it come into your possession"?

Then, Brahmadev, the Chief Priest kept narrating about Lalita, Subhadra, et al, slowly, haltingly. He even touched upon the fact that Subhadra had snatched it away from Lalita. Subhag Dutta went asking at length and the Chief Priest kept answering. While hearing, Subhag Dutta asked him to call upon the two devadasis. Brahmadev pressed the bell. Lalita came in. Subhag Dutta startled to look at Lalita at the threshold, in a near-insane state. In a carelessly-worn attire, in dishevelled, unkempt, untied tresses, with a face marked by tears! The Chief Priest asked her to call for Subhadra. Lalita went off.

Subhag Dutta had dropped in. The Chief Priest had asked him in. What he had suspected came to be true. It was not just a wild guess, the gold necklace seemed familiar to him. The Chief Priest of Mahakaal Temple knew full well that Lord Mahakaal could never come there in person. He did not believe a word of Lalita and not even that of Subhadra. Subhadra was quite intelligent, while caught red-handed, she said that the ornament was a gift from God only. She had Lord Mahakaaleswar to aver thus, in the base-temple. Each word of Lalita was true to the core. Subhadra had no other way of saving both herself and Lalita, excepting this. She cried and kept saying, "Lord Mahakaal is just all ears to our prayers, Lord Mahakaal had given it to Lalita, Himself". Lalita remained silent, listening to Subhadra. She kept mum, very calm since quite a few days. Chief Priest could perceive that both the devadasis were in cahoots with each other in telling a fib, jointly. He himself knew how the deity was watchful! How the deity would step out of the inner shrine!

Lalita came back with Subhadra. Subhadra stood by the door, followed by someone else. Subhag Dutta saw Subhadra at close proximity. Before this, he had seen this damsel swinging like the flame of fire, during the evening rituals of lights in front of Lord Mahakaaleswar. Subhadra was looking at the merchant. Her heart was missing a beat or two. She was overcome with fear. Did she see this man through the haze of the smoke of incense sticks? Did this deity come to life through the gong of bells? She heard from Lalita that the merchant had come. The merchant was her Lord Mahakaal. Just like Lord Mahakaal, the merchant would make her drift along. She had not forgotten the merchant. She had woven many impossible moments inwardly. Now, she was getting to see the necklace in the hands of the merchant. The merchant's face looked cunning. The old Chief Priest sat beside the magnate. Both the faces seemed to have merged in each other.

The merchant was observing Subhadra keenly. Her newly-blossomed youth. The face was extremely exquisite. The eyes were so enchanting, she had such thick tufts of hair! Her hair cascaded on her back. She had bath in the morning. She would deck herself up as a devadasi, once the afternoon drew to its close. Her amorous adventure would begin in the evening after the sundown. The magnate had never seen these maidens in such attires before. The magnate asked, "Could you please tell me the truth"?

Subhadra tilted her head at one end. Alack, why had this man fitted himself into the same mould on coming in contact with the Chief Priest? Tears welled up in the eyes of Subhadra. Oh Mahakaal! Oh, the best of all men! You are my Mahakaal, indeed. But, oh the Lord of my heart, you are yielding to senility so soon! I can tell you the truth, but not here. Here the Chief Priest is present. Truth cannot be uttered before him! She would be harassed by the Chief Priest if she spoke the truth now, as prior to it she had told a lie! He would turn spiteful.

In a very soft voice Subhag Dutta demanded of her, "Tell me how did you get it"?

Subhadra lifted up her face and replied, "From Lalita".

"Or was it you who got it instead of Lalita"?

"To tell the truth, Lalita had kept it hidden as this necklace was a gift from the Lord".

Subhag Dutta said, "Think deeply again, uttering a lie is a sin in this shrine, and that sin may cause you terrible disaster"!

Subhadra repeated her answer. Subhag Dutta repeated his query. As Subhadra kept coming up with the same rejoinder, repeatedly, the magnate came to believe that she was not telling a lie. But then Subhadra said, "The Lord has ordered to return the necklace to Lalita". She had heard that sitting in the base temple that very night. On hearing so, she swooned. Lord Mahakaal, Himself, had presented it to Lalita!

The merchant again demanded, "Think it over".

"Whatever I have heard, I am relating that to you in verbatim".

"In this world, none else is stronger than Lord Mahakaal, such a stupendous temple stands nowhere else - Avanti, Vatsya, Saurashtra, Kosala, Magadh, wherever you go, nowhere you will find, I bet".

Subhadra had never heard such names. She kept quiet. The rough, stony floor had grabbed the base of her feet firmly. She was retaining the voice of the merchant in her ears, being all attentive. It sounded sweet. Oh you, great man! Devadasi Subhadra kept stretching her gaze down the way awaiting your footfall on it! Inwardly, Subhadra mused, Serving God will be worthwhile only if I can win you in my life. How tender, breeze-like is the sound of his voice. How soft and smooth is his glance.

Subhag Dutta asked, "Have you heard yourself"?

"Yes, Sir"! Subhadra lifted her face, her wide eyes met the eyes of the merchant! Tears were about to well up to her eyes. When would her deity come to take her away from this temple? Didn't the merchant know why Subhadra fixed him with such a steadfast stare?

Subhag Dutta asked, "Did you hear it in your dreams"?

"No, my lord, I heard while I was awake".

The Chief Priest grumbled, "She is trotting off a string of lies! This slut is honest, but I do not know what's wrong with her, again why she is repeating the same thing! I shall chuck her out of this temple if she does not tell the truth"!

"Please"! The Merchant held his hand up to stop the old priest. The eyes of the merchant were that of a lapidary, no doubt! No chance was there to dupe him with the fake passing as genuine. The gold could easily be told apart from the copper, even in bare eyes. But why just gold? For recognizing gold, the merchant needed no black stone-slab! The merchant could easily recognize a human being of worth. He seemed to get a feel of the mesmerized state of the devadasi. He said, "Many a time it happens that man fails to tell apart the dream from his wakeful state... did such a thing happen to you as well? It might have been so, tell me the truth, come on".

Subhadra could speak the truth! And that too, to the merchant Subhag Dutta only. Not in front of the old priest. Yet she retorted, "It might be so, but I think, it transpired while I was wide awake".

The merchant said, "How to differentiate between the dream and the wakeful state? If Mahakaal orders, it must be true in dreams, in reality or in wakefulness as well"!

"Yes, my lord"! Subhadra raised her face once again. She took a long look at her master to her heart's content, it seemed. Her heart went palpitating. Oh Lord, if only I could express my heart's desire! Doesn't the Lord know that? The merchant now called for Lalita. Lalita moved forward, Subhadra stood behind, touching her. Subhag Dutta inquired, "Think and tell me how this necklace reached your hand".

Lalita Dasi related the details of that cold night to Subhag Dutta, who kept asking while Lalita kept answering. But her answers were not enough to all the queries the merchant had. In the intense darkness, Lalita could not see the face of the deity, Lalita informed, crying bitterly. The merchant kept listening to her, wonderstruck. His attention was shifting to Subhadra, who stood behind, with eyes with concern. She kept looking! Both her eyes were awash with tears too. The merchant was keen on hearing of each moment of that ice-cold night. Lalita's voice was getting choked. She was withdrawing, being abashed. But the merchant was striving to tally his conjectures with Lalita's moment-by-moment account, for being confirmed.

Subhag Dutta ordered, "Tell me everything, see that nothing is left out by mistake".

"Lord"! Lalita's voice failed and her words too did. That moment of ultimate union was completely hers. She could not even share it with Subhadra. And how would he relate it to a man? She would never be able to give words to that sublime feelings, till her last breath.

"What happened, why are you keeping silent?" Subhag Dutta's voice sounded grating, harsh.

"Lord, that cannot be uttered", Subhadra answered from behind.

"Oh"! Subhag Dutta was visibly perturbed. "Why are you intervening? Tell me what followed, how did he take you in his arms, were you asleep or awake, did you know that he would come? Tell me the truth only".

"Sir, everything is in Lord's unintelligible scheme", Subhadra blabbed out.

The merchant thundered, "Who asked you to chip in? Shut up! Sundry activities are on in the temple, and everything will be passed on in the name of Lord, tell me, are God and man the same? Come on, Lalita, answer me"!

Lalita could sense that the soft veneer was about to fall off from the face of Subhag Dutta. Subhadra seemed to recoil a little. Did she think of this master in her deepest within? Are the two men the same: that man and this one?

"What happened, why don't you say whether that man and God are the same? Come on, Subhadra, tell me".

"No, Sir".

"Did God come or was it just a man"?

"God in the guise of a man", was Subhadra's rejoinder.

"A male of flesh and blood, come on Lalita, you had slept with him, tell me, was he like a man in the truest sense or like God"?

Lalita was trembling in fear, she failed to come up with a rejoinder.

"Did he behave as a male?"

Lalita lowered her head and in an indistinct voice said, "Yes, my lord"!

"Then how do you know that he was God, did he tell you Himself"?

Lalita nodded her head in the negative.

"Then why do you call him God"? The merchant thundered, turned to the Chief Priest and said, "He was no God but a sinner. He has left the shrine profaned. Give away the two damsels to some inveterate heretic. He will surely find out who had entered that night. Do I know too who had come? This is a dire sin, barging into the temple of Lord Mahakaal, enjoying His serving-maid like a detestable thief! Devadasi is again hoodwinking in the name of God! Shall I leave these two maidens with Utanka"?

Letting out a scream, Subhadra tumbled on the wall. Lalita held her firm. Subhag Dutta kept blowing his top. These two young maids would be taught right lessons if they fell in the hands of Utanka, his servant. He would simply thrash them out of their coquetry.

The Chief Priest asked, "What should we do now"?

Suddenly, Subhag Dutta became calm. "Nothing as of now. Let them be as they are, I know the owner of this necklace, they will come handy to make him stand accused".

"Utanka"?

"Let them wait, I shall see to it later. I have to find out who has taught them to put the blame on Lord Mahakaal. Listen, both of you may leave now".

As Lalita went away taking Subhadra as her support, Subhag Dutta bolted the door. His whole body kept trembling in excitement. He said, "The King had come to rape the devadasi in the dark of night! The devadasi had been outraged by the King of Ujjwain in her sleep! Such sin had never happened in Avanti! Oh, so horrible! Sky would come crashing on his head"!

"Are you sure?"

"Yes, none but the King! This had been there on the King's neck only. If the devadasi tells the truth, how will the King deny?

"Then"?!

Subhag Dutta said, "It calls for discussion. The King is childless and yet he… with a petty devadasi, in her sleep" …!

The old Priest feigned to plug both his ears with fingers in disgust, though he inquired again, "So what will happen now"?

"It should reach Devadutta"!

"But she is your serving-maid"!

"No, the King's. And Devadutta does not see any other man than the King, her pride must reach a blow"!

"Then what will follow"? The old Priest asked again.

"The King's deed will be known to all".

"Will it be circulated with drums"?

Subhag Dutta retorted, "The words will spread here and there at even a higher speed than the noise of the drums! Oh Brahmin, may I make a move"?

"As you wish".

"So, you are by my side"!

"Yes, I am", the old Priest cried out in affliction, all of a sudden! "What an awful humiliation! How dreadful a sin! Outraging the chastity of a sleeping woman? Not even the hell would accept this King of Avanti! This crime will surely paint the golden diadem on the pinnacle of the shrine black! I have no idea as to what can be done now".

TWENTY-THREE

Chaitra was aflame. Whirlwind was let loose. Just like cyclone, the scandal of the King reached far and wide. Apart from whispers and rumours, the disgrace spread far beyond the precincts of the city through verbal campaign.

The King stayed unsullied by any disgrace. Yet, it began to affect him. Didn't the moon have blemishes? Despite the stigmata, the moon looked beautiful. But the disgrace of the King failed to beautify him. It was sin. Sins engulfed this country, this city of Avanti.

As Phalgun Purnima ended, the fortnight of new moon began. Winter, this year, had come to a close much before. But, even on a Chaitra night, a bit of chill left its residue in the darkness. This time, not a trace of it had been there. The cloud-bearing winds that used to blow down from the Himalayas sometime in between Magh and Chaitra towards the Arabian Sea, causing drizzle or downpour on its way, stayed elusive this time. Wind forgot to turn back from the north-east. How would it return? Wind had not carried over nimbus during Asad and Sravan from either the Arabian Sea or the Amrakut ranges in the south-west to the Himalayas. The wind which had not blown across there would not return. Even in Magh or Phalgun, not even a few drops of shower did either the soil or the people of Avanti receive.

The dark night was sultry. Even nature during the daytime was suffocating. In such an atmosphere, rumours of scandal kept spreading like wildfire. Ujjwain's wind was rife with the King's vice. People thought, it was unbecoming of a King. He was the King of this holy land! The King was entitled to do anything. If he desired, the beautiful woman, the young maid would queue up to his gate. Was there any dearth of anything for the King? Anything under the sun, immovable or portable, belonged to the King only. Then why would he outrage the modesty of Lord Mahakaal's devadasi, on the sly like a thief? Why would he behave like a lascivious lecher? Such misgivings raised their heads in a few minds. Then they thought, he was the King of the land, the King could do no wrong! The King was above all sins. No crime could tarnish the King. The King was immaculate like the Sun. No blemish was blemish at all for him. The whisper went on thus. None could even think of disgrace! The King was the master of all. How would he harbour stigmata?

But the devadasi was being governed by Lord Mahakaal, she was an object of Lord Mahakaal's desire!Lord Mahakaal stood head and shoulders above all. Glancing at the peak of the temple it could be understood how great Lord Mahakaal was! How glorious was Lord Mahakaal! The spire of the palace bent low to the pinnacle of the Mahakaal temple! Why would the King enjoy the serving-maid of God? It was a question, no doubt. Many such queries were whirling in and assailing the minds of the ordinary populace.

Mahakaaleshwar Shiva was omnipotent! It was He who had freed this city of Ujjwain from the dragon-clutch of Tripurasura! The King himself was the worshipper of Mahakaaleshwar! How could he outrage the modesty of a maid, already sacrificed to Lord Mahakaal? Devadasi wept while being raped by the King. Devadasi said that she could not think of anyone save Lord Mahakaal! She had offered herself to God! Let the King save her from such molestation! The King hadn't cared to listen to her. He enjoyed her by coercion. Was this not an instance of abominable sin? What then sin would be?

How would it be sin? The King had enjoyed a young maid. The devadasi was none but a young maiden. It was lawful to apply force on a young damsel as well as a Shudra. Was there any importance of the willingness or reluctance of a woman or a Shudra? As a Shudra was born to serve the Brahmins, the Kshatriyas and the Vaishyas, a woman likewise should offer herself to satisfy the desires of a man! All women seemed to be female Shudras. Touching a Shudra might be a prohibitive act, but enjoying a female of Shudra clan was not so. Devadasi was just a woman like a female Shudra. She was fortunate that the King had just taken her as an object of lust! He had not thrown her away as a feed for jackals or the dogs! He had not even thrown her lifeless corpse into the Mahakaal forests! If the young maiden dared snatch the necklace from the neck of the King, she surely had done wrong! Who was that devadasi that would dare commit such deed? Enjoying a devadasi was the right of a King indeed. Who would dare raise a question on it?

But the King had awakened the devadasi in the guise of Lord Mahakaal. Words were trickling out of the Mahakaal temple, by degrees. The King had sought the acquiescence of the devadasi, feigning as Lord Mahakaal, in the darkness, just to gratify his instinctive desires! Perhaps the devadasi could recognize him or otherwise could have perceived that the assumed identity of Lord Mahakaal was nothing but a ruse. How would it be true? Lord Mahakaal was Lord Shiva, the God of Gods!

He would never desire a woman other than Parvati! Why would the Lord enjoy an ordinary maid-servant? Who wasn't aware of the hundred conjugal nights of Shankar-Parvati? Why would Shankar give up on Parvati in lieu of a trifle devadasi for physical enjoyment? No scripture had ever averred His lecherous union with sundry women. He was the lord of this universe. Who had ever heard that leaving Parvati, a woman of never-ending youth, Shankar had gone to copulate with a devadasi? This was the sin of the King. The King had desecrated the shrine by enjoying the devadasi, under an assumed identity of Lord Mahakaal.

A group of people were talking about the sin of the King. And another wing was incredulous about it. Some were saying that the mark of King's sin was distinct everywhere. Some again opined, King could not commit any crime. The sin in case of a subject would never be applicable to the King! King Bhartrihari was a human being. Even though, sin had touched man, the King remained beyond its impact. Again a few were out to say that, copulation hardly could be considered as a sin! Lotus is of red colour. Only because it is red, the bumble-bees fly around it. She was a young maid, though a devadasi. In a young damsel, there had been neither any nectar nor any gall. In copulation, she would taste like nectar. If on the contrary, she would be sheer poison. Alas! The King seemed to have drunk poison by seeking the company of a devadasi. Though a devadasi, she was just a youthful maid. What harm was there in having pleasure with her?

These words had made way from the ghetto of the Shudras to the Palace. They were heard on the streets of Ujjwain. Even in the red-light zone, one was whispering it into the ears of the other.

In the ghetto of the Shudras, few souls could be seen these days. Days of poverty had already begun! Almost every day, men and women went out in search of jobs. In the fields and lands, all might not be employed, but poverty had gone rare too. A little precaution would defer the want to the end of Asad. A few days ago, wheat, barley, legumes, mustard, the harvest of all was very poor, yielded very little, contrary to what was expected. Drought had left meadows and fields, thoroughly hard and dry. The crops sown in the land during Bhadra had withered in the land itself. The inhabitants of the Shudra locality were roaming round like whirlwind. They were hanging about the forests, the thoroughfares, the cities and were encircling the merchant's house, day in, day out.

On such an evening of Chaitra, the merchant's chariot had again drawn up to the edge of the Ratnakarsagar. The people were returning home by then. The day had expanded. The sun blazed in the sky for long. The merchant's chariot had been surrounded by the inhabitants of the Shudra locale. The merchant, Subhag Dutta, kept looking at the waterless aridity of the Ratnakarsagar. Not a drop of water had been there in the lake. Someone had sucked it up, it seemed. The merchant said, "Have you heard it all"?

Parashar tilted his head to one end. The old man had heard but had not believed a word of it.

"Why had the Ratnakarsagar gone dry, devoid of water"?

"It has gone dry, the Sun-God has sucked the water in", saying so, Old Parashar had bowed to the west. This time there was such scorching sunshine, which had never been here before. Since the last couple of years, water ran depleted.

"Do you have any wind of the Temple"?

"No, Sir". The old man muttered under his breath, "We are the lower castes, we are the Shudras"!

The Merchant said, "Since long there had been no rain, you know why"?

Parashar shook his head and then whispered, "Lord Mahakaal knows".

"Lord Mahakaal will leave everything topsy-turvy".

People of all ages with emaciated physique, looked on with frightened faces, at the merchant. They were panic-stricken but could not make out what to say. On a wintry afternoon in Poush, long back the merchant had come to distribute gold coins among them and now he had again come to their ghetto. Why did the merchant come? The man of his stature was not supposed to pay a visit to this Shudra locality, once again. The old man was being reminded of that afternoon. It was the month of Poush, this pond was nearly devoid of water. Seeing only the muddy water at the lees, they dreamt of the lake getting filled to the brim with heavy downpour. The merchant said, "We have to search for the reason behind the water evaporating, the lotus, being not in blossom at all". He advised them to go to the King's court. Could a Shudra ever approach the King? Old Parashar was spending his days by this lake! The words of the merchant sounded intimidating to him. How fierce his words sounded!

The merchant declared, "Lord Mahakaal has been displeased. Abominable incidents desecrated the temple, all will be torn asunder, all will be ruined"!

"Oh Lord"! Parashar kept trembling, folding his palms together.

"Can you sense that there will be no rain at all"?

Parashar kept quiet with a face, on which fear was writ large. The merchant went on, "The Sun-God will grow stronger by drinking more water, conflagration will ensue, and all will burn to ashes in that devastating fire".

"Oh lord"!

Merchant Subhag Dutta kept pacing up and down. All were watching that the tall frame of the merchant was growing taller. The shadows moving eastward kept circling the light, all around. The Shudras cowered into the dark of the shadows. Utanka, the charioteer, the servant of the merchant, stood in front of the chariot stock-still. Utanka never spoke much. There was no expression on Utanka's countenance, but anyone seemed to be frozen within, if he cast his glance at him. The merchant asked, "Why is Mahakaal cross"?

The Shudras were silent. They sat lowering their heads like criminals, without answering.

The merchant answered, "Sin has cast its shadows over the city, its consequences will be dreary"!

"Oh lord"!

"Does the sinner take the responsibility of his sins"?

"Oh lord"!

The merchant went on, "Immoral activities! The sin is of just an individual, but look, Ratnakarsagar has no water in it. Who does this Ratnakarsagar belong to"?

"It is ours, my lord"!

"Are you sinners"?

"No, my lord"!

"Who is going to shoulder the share of the sin"?

The concluding words left all of them panic-stricken. It seemed that the light of the eyes began to fade out. The merchant carried on, "Who has committed the sin, whose wrongdoing is causing the water-bodies to go dry is just a known fact. But who are being badly hit by it? Whose loss will it be if the crops wither away? Who will shoulder the responsibility of the bigwigs? Who?"

"Who, my Lord"?

The merchant smirked, "Who is being subject to the wrath of Lord Mahakaal"?

Old Parashar blabbed out, "Lord, we are ignorant"!

The merchant said, "But all the burden of sins lies on your head! The more the misdeed, the more is the sin, and the more the sin, the more it is ponderous! That burden will be borne by the people of lower castes, the Shudras, and such is the decree of God!"

"Oh Lord"! Tears kept coursing down the eyes of old Parashar, "Oh Lord, what is our fault, which sin have we perpetrated"?

The merchant remarked, "Even if not done, the load of sins must be borne! And the lakes must not display any lotus on them ever, the wells must be devoid of water, the rivers, Shipra and Gandhavati will run dry, all wheat must perish in the lands, and then what will be the consequences"?

"How will we survive, oh Lord"?

"You will not live, if only you stand against the sinner, you will".

Old Parashar started. Standing against the sinner would mean going against the King! Merchant Subhag Dutta was talking against the King. Or, the old man could not comprehend what the merchant kept saying. A rich man, rather the richest of all in the city, the most powerful man of the city, the merchant— why would he talk against the King? Then was the sinner anyone else? The words, spreading like wildfire all around, were then all a lie! Untrue, indeed. King would commit no crime, King could do no sin. Then who was the sinner? Whose burden of sin was to be shouldered— all the Shudras bewailed badly! Whose sin had caused the Ratnakarsagar to dry up? Whose sin had left all the crops dry and withered in the land again?

The merchant commented, "The rage of Mahakaal will be more stern, and alas what will happen then! Oh Lord Mahakaal, who has to drop dead and that too for whose crime! Oh God, please save the people of the lower rung".

Old Parashar's eyes were about to be clouded with tears. He marked that all around him kept shuddering in fear. Dark was about to wear on. The merchant began to move forward to the chariot in slow steps. The residents of the Shudra ghetto were close at his heels. Standing in front of the chariot, the merchant declared, "If you stand against the sinner, the wrath of God will alleviate".

"Who is the sinner, my master"? Old Parasahar demanded to know.

The merchant was taken aback. In keen gaze, he began to observe the old man of the village. The man seemed to be a man of evil intentions! He was eager to hear the name of the King from his mouth! He was all ears to hear the name of the sinner being uttered by the merchant! He threw an open query, "Don't you know who has committed the sin"?

"No, my master, whose sin is this"?

"Prick up your ears and you will get to listen, go inside the city, you will get to hear", saying so, the merchant walked up to the chariot and rode on it. As Utanka was about to strike the horse, the people moved away in fear. The horse neighed in pain as it had been flogged. It ran on. Utanka's strikes cut the air in a swishing noise. Its edge flicked across someone's arm-side. The man screamed in pain and sank into the ground. Darkness descended as the carriage pushed off. The stars lit up the sky. Old Parashar kept sitting by the bank of the Ratnakarsagar lake. He was reminiscing the days when he was with Dhruvaputra. It was Dhruvaputra who talked about Ratnakar, the robber. As none of Ratnakar's family shared the burden of Ratnakar's sins, Ratnakar got transformed into Balmiki. Dhruvaputra used to say that Ratnakar was, perhaps, their forebear. But now why would they bear the sins of the great men? Had Dhruvaputra been here, he could have come up with a befitting rejoinder. Fixing his gaze on the Pole star in the northern sky, Parashar called out to the missing man of virtues, "Hey Son of Dhruva, who else will answer this question but you"?

TWENTY-FOUR

Queen Bhanumati let out a cry of anguish on seeing Bikram, the Army Chieftain of Avanti, at her threshold, "Oh Prince, what am I hearing? Are all these true"?

The step-brother of the King entered the room. On a call from the inner house, he had come this afternoon to see the queen. This room was absolutely the queen's private boudoir. She used it for dressing up. None save Nipunika, her maid, entered this room. The King used to drop in, long back. His tiger-skin seat was there. The Prince came to perch on that seat. Before him, stood a huge mirror. It was afternoon, but the room was crisscrossed by light and darkness. A large lamp was lit. The Sun-God was yet to descend on the western sky. A little later, light from the west would creep in through the western window for some time. The Army Chieftain rubbed his hand on the tiger-skin and said, "This is true, my servant brought the news".

Turning her back to the mirror, queen Bhanumati sat facing the Prince. Today she was bereft of all her make-up. Whatever little she had, got smudged off, faded out. Her tears had washed all of it away. The queen again cried out, "What are you saying, Prince"?

Prince, Kumar Bikram said, "Yes, true in verbatim"!

"Who is that devadasi"?

"She is in the shrine. You can drop by to see her".

The queen touched her forehead and said, "Still alive, not dead yet"?

"Who'll kill her"?

"Why have you allowed her to live?" The queen grew agitated. Kumar watched, even the queen's reflection on the mirror was quivering. Or, was it that the mirror kept shaking? The queen was such a paragon of beauty that the mirror of this inner house felt honoured to hold her image up! Kumar had seen the queen. Intense breathing made her breasts heave, the tip of her nose had droplets of perspiration on it and both

201

her eyes set rolling, as observed the Army Commander. How beautiful was queen Bhanumati! How could the King settle for a devadasi leaving this beautiful woman aside? The beautiful lady had slouched in insult. She resumed crying again. The Army Commander kept his hand in hers and said, "Get composed, you are the queen of Avanti, an ordinary devadasi can never be the cause of your anger, envy or grief".

"But that has taken place, Oh! What a bad taste of the King"! The queen grumbled in rage.

The Chief of Army said, "Initially I did not believe this, but every word of it is true, I went to see the priest myself".

The queen thundered, "How dares she, go get the slut devoured by wolves and dogs"!

"What is her fault"? The Army Commander demanded.

"Fault"? The queen threw an astounding gaze at him. Tall, fair-complexioned, manly prince was really handsome like a swan! Droplets of sweat shone at the base of the prince's neck. Since how long she had been won over by the charm of the Prince, she could not remember. Since when, King Bhartrihari began to move away behind the shadow of his younger brother, Bikram, the queen failed to recall. Perplexity clouded her vision.

Kumar Bikram commented, "She is just a petty devadasi, no better than a worm or a fly, it is no great job to slay her but she has no capability of committing this crime"!

The queen inquired, "Who is the criminal"?

"You know the criminal, his sin cannot be covered up"!

"Sin"!

"Yes, outraging the modesty of Mahakaal's devadasi in His shrine is, doubtlessly, a crime; killing the devadasi will never put an end to the sin, it will rather stand firmer"!

The queen burst into tears and moaned, "While my maid Nipunika comes to relate the goings-on in the city, I cannot hold my head straight, Kumar! Isn't the King's disgrace, King's sin, tantamount to the queen's dishonour"?

The Army Commander kept shaking his head, " No, why will it be so, the sin of a man is his, his disgrace is his, I am being sad for you, the people of this city are sympathetic to you, they are feeling sorry for you"!

"Is the queen of Avanti at the mercy of the people of Ujjwain"?

The Army Chieftain smiled. He lowered the scarf on his chest. Beads of perspiration decked his wide chest. He went on whiffing. The queen moved forward. She began to fan the Army Commander's chest with her own scarf. She offered, "Let me call the maid-servant, she will fan".

"No, please stop it, the whole city is abuzz with public reproach".

"How could the people of the city come to know"?

"I don't know, but now this is a topic of discussion in the town".

Striking her head, the queen remarked, "But this spells disgrace to me as well".

"How so"?

"I could not hold the King back".

Army Commander remarked, "It is really difficult to keep such a man of perverted desire to oneself".

Queen Bhanumati pressed her ears with both her palms. It was unbecoming of a wife to listen to the calumny of her husband! But, instead of stopping, Kumar Bikram went on, "How could the King lose his sense? Even a dog would not mate with a sleeping bitch! Is he a male or just a creature lesser than human? Has anyone ever heard of a man, having sex with a sleeping woman"?

The statement did not sound logical. But it would seem logical if the memory haunted her! Hence the queen kept quiet. And if that would be true which was surmised to have happened, the King would really have behaved in an unkingly manner! The queen felt insecure. Her charms, her youth — all seemed to have wasted away. Bhanumati had been vanquished by the King. She had neglected the King, refused to share her bed with him. But how would she get to know that her rejection could ricochet so cruelly? Queen Bhanumati could never imagine in her wildest dreams that such retaliation lurked at the nook of the poet's heart! The maid was saying, "The ordinary devadasi's charm, youthful appeal had surely held out more appeal to the King far more than that of the queen's and hence the King of Avanti had offered himself to her. And who will aver whether the devadasi was asleep or awaiting the King's presence, lighting the lamp? What exactly had transpired was known only to that slut and King Bhartrihari himself".

The queen said, "I want to see that devadasi".

"Why"?

Queen Bhanumati could not reason for it though. Would she judge by seeing the devadasi, who was more beautiful between the two of them, and whose youth was more appealing? And why? Would she be calm at heart if she gave in to that defeat? Or if she emerged victorious? She was far more beautiful, that was averred by this Army Commander, the Prince! And she was the most beautiful woman of this city, according to Nipunika, her maid. Being the paragon of beauty numero uno, the queen had to accept defeat in the hands of a not-so-beautiful woman. And the maid said that the devadasi was just an ugly woman! Just because she was in her youth, she possessed natural charms to entice the King. Then what would the queen do by meeting her up? Triumph had no joy and defeat had neither, in this case! If discomfiture had to be brooked by a beauty, being compared to a bland-looking woman, the beauty herself would prove to be ugly, indeed.

The queen muttered, "What shall I do now, Kumar"?

"What will you do"?

"The King has shattered me to smithereens! My heart is broken, where shall I go now? The people think that the King has gone to another woman as I am incapable of satisfying his cravings. Do the men ever commit sin, Kumar?"

The Army Commander maintained silence. Age-old beliefs since birth, well-nurtured in his mind, did not allow him to say that if a man can be a sinner, a woman can equally be so.

Queen Bhanumati demanded to know, "What are the people of the city saying"?

"Ill-fame of the King has spread like wildfire in the city".

The common men say, "The queen failed to satisfy him, hence the King has veered his attention to the devadasi of the temple! Of what use is the queen's beauty if that fails to win the King's heart"?

Kumar Bikram holding out his hand, touched the chin of the queen, kept her face on the palm of his hand. In a tender though muffled voice he said, "The queen herself does not know for whom her charms are meant, let alone the city".

Bhanumati moved her face away. She bent down on the chest of Gandharvasen's son and heaved a warm sigh on the wide chest of the Army Commander. She whispered, "I know, but what shall I do now, Kumar, you go and throw that shameless she-demon into the dark dungeon"!

Kumar smiled, "Will you be pacified then"?

"Yes, I will be".

"But she is innocent, she was just lying asleep in the safe haven of the temple"!

"I know my King, he cannot force anyone to do anything, he just can't do that".

The Army Commander said, "You are trying to cover up the King's crime"!

The queen rejoined, "No, I am not exonerating him of his sin, but the devadasi is not telling the truth. Found guilty, she is trying to implicate the King wrongly, that scheming witch is really too daring"!

Kumar Bikram fell silent. Two possibilities flashed across his mind. This inner house was not at all an easy place. And just as the inner house, Bhanumati, its resident, was also complicated. Did Bhanumati seek the aid of the Army Commander in absolving the King of this blemish? Couldn't Bhanumati surmise why King Bhartrihari stood maligned in the eyes of the people of Avanti, knowing full well the intention of the Army Commander? If the Army Commander wants, the King can be cleansed of all such blemishes with the help of the devadasi herself! How long will it take in making this happen?

The queen asked, "Did she cry out in fear"?

"Why"?

"Silently the devilish woman got raped, and that too without anyone's knowledge"!

Kumar Bikram rejoined, "The Priest has come to know".

"Are you telling the truth"?

"Why shall I tell you a lie? But the old man kept mum in fear! As the King declared in darkness that he was Mahakaal indeed— his voice made him recognize the King"!

The queen kept shaking her head, "Can it be believed at all"?

The Army Chief said, "Let me push off then".

"Just now"?

"How can I stay back if I am not believed"?

The queen said, "Both the priest and the devadasi are telling lies, do shove the devadasi into the dark dungeon and warn the Priest".

"That is to be done by the King"!

"The King is in peril, don't you know your elder brother, Kumar, can he be harsh on anyone? He who can never be stern, who spends all his night sitting by the window if his wife doesn't welcome him to bed, can he outrage the modesty of a woman ever? The people of Avanti may not know him, but you know the King, in and out"!

"What do you want"? Kumar looked into the eyes of the queen.

"Let Ujjwain's throne be free from stain".

"This mark will vanish along with time, the throne is there since time immemorial, but how long will the King be on it"?

The queen did not start at his words, but, no doubt, she was overcome by fear. She could feel that the wind seemed to be suffocating, at any moment it could break into a storm. This plight was becoming intense, even more and more. Bhanumati's bosom kept palpitating. She lacked the courage to utter a word even.

Kumar said, " The King cannot go on committing wrong, being on the throne of Ujjwain".

"Shut up, I am in fear".

"The honour of the throne is the honour of the King indeed, but if he fails to respect it, then"?

"Shut up, keep the word of your mind locked inside". The queen broke into whispers and then blabbed, "The people of Ujjwain know their King well, you will be left exhausted, Kumar"!

The Army Commander got to his feet, "Tell me clearly, what do you want"?

"I do not know". The queen kept banging her head on the floor, crying. "I do not know what I want, I am empathetic to the King, Kumar! He, whom I could not tolerate before, is now evoking my pity, he is just a tender-hearted man, can he ever perpetrate such a heinous deed? But why is the scandal spreading like wildfire?"

"Why, don't you know"?

The queen stood up. "I know, but kindness is getting the better of me, please forbear, stop, put an end to all such things"!

Just as she uttered this, Army-Commander Kumar Bikram grabbed the two shoulders of the queen with his two paw-like palms, dashed queen Bhanumati on his expansive chest and said, "Sympathize, let the King be purified with your compassion, but the people of the city have begun to believe that a man can, of course, be despised, without forgetting the good deeds he has done".

"Oh alas, King"! The queen moved away. Shuffle of steps was being wafted to her ears from far. The prince smiled and listening to the loud lamentations of the queen, he blabbed, "But you have no way of retracing your steps, is the King blessed with your love"?

The queen kept silent. Her head dropped low. The Army Commander had touched her shoulders again, he was saying, " Going so far has been possible because of your indulgence, otherwise which man had ever dared enter the chamber of the queen of Avanti"!

"Shut up"!

The prince kept moving out. The queen came out of the door to step into the long verandah outside. The Army Commander was leaving. What a stature! How handsome he was! Casting bewitching glance at him, the queen, in a muffled voice beckoned, "Oh Prince"!

Kumar Bikram stood still, turning back. In a conceited posture of a swan, he held his head up to look at her, the wide eyes kept glistening in the light of the eyes only. He began retracing his steps towards the daughter of Kankhal, a paragon of beauty, more like a female swan! His body kept perspiring. The whole body kept pulsating with the inner store of fire!

TWENTY-FIVE

Chaitra was slipping by. Full moon night was coming up soon. And after a few days, the month of Baisakh would begin. On the eastern horizon, the Bisakha star was about to twinkle during night. Chitra, the star, had already been there, during the month of Chaitra. In the western sky, the seven sages were engrossed in meditation, the Agastya star was in the south. How distant was that south! In the land of origin of the star, Agastya, flew a river, named Kaveri. There had been the Malay ranges, the sandalwood forest—all she heard from the son of Dhruva! Now, Gandhavati kept reminiscing.

Mother and daughter sat on the raised terrace. Evening wore on slowly. Quietude ruled the roost all around. Both mother and daughter looked up to the sky. Chitra, Swati, Uttarphalguni, Purbaphalguni, Lubdhak, Rohini, Ardraa …Some of these stars had gone missing, just as Dhruvaputra went missing still and Bisakha remained untraced as well. The stars which had gone missing, would come back, as Bisakha, too, would. Even the Son of Dhruva was expected to be back. The stars which he had seen before leaving would surface again in each Chaitra. But would he not return? Not on the night of the full moon even! Not again on the day of Madanotsav? Memory stirred to bring back the river Gambhira of that full-moon night, the cane clump, the moonshine that flooded the universe, the river that flew along as a stream of light, only light! Could light then put things out of view? As it did in case of Dhruvaputra?! And in light itself, he went untraced! The man who was extremely wise but had taken a wrong course.

Reba asked, "When will he come back"?

"No one knows, Maa".

"Didn't he tell you"?

Gandhavati was speechless, as she looked on.Reba could read Gandhavati's mind. Reba smiled and said, "I am talking about the astronomer of Dasharno".

Gandhavati rejoined, "He did not tell me before leaving, Maa".

"He will be able to say.".

Gandhavati kept quiet. It seemed that Tamradhvaj would succeed. Yes, he must. But he had not come since long. Had he taken the way to Bidisha? Drought had left people restless. Gandhavati's grandfather was just narrating the other day: A man from some country had come to Ujjwain, after walking for seven days and seven nights! They thought that this part of the country might have been on rice. However, drought had left them starving! Grandfather was saying that, if it happened thus, men, being nonplussed, would move from one place to the other. They kept filing out and filing in. In the same hope, the people of Avanti used to move towards Dasharno. This influx and exodus went on. Did Tamradhvaj fall prey to such confusion to make a move to his own land? Did any news reach from Dasharno? Then, why was he not coming?

Human voice kept wafting in the dark. Both the mother and the daughter were all ears to listen. On hearing, they sat straight like a frightened deer. Then, did the astronomer from Dasharno come finally? Was his calculation complete? But it was not supposed to be so. Because he had not heard all of it, till now. Gandhavati could not share the happenings of that full moon night with Tamradhvaj, as yet. She stared down the road looking for him just to tell him everything. On learning every detail of it, Tamradhvaj would be able to finish his astrological calculations. In which direction was Dhruvaputra, in which again was Kartikkumar?

Reba alerted, "Someone is coming".

"One or two"?

"One is your grandpa's, that is, my father-in-law's, and another voice is someone else's".

"Who is the other one"?

Reba replied, "May be that Tamradhvaj then. He comes in the evening only".

Gandhavati grew restless, "Maa, he is coming from far".

"I know".

"He might be hungry in the ashram, he cooks his food himself". Gandhavati grew anxious.

"Yes, shall I boil the milk for him?" Reba asked in a mild tone.

Gandhavati lowered her head. Suddenly she grew conscious of her restlessness. Why was she getting thrilled? That man would come with the news of Dhruvaputra, may be that's why! He would utter the words of Dhruvaputra in the self-same tune and manner, that's why. Now, she had to narrate the tale of that full moon Chaitra night, of that ultimate exit of Dhruvaputra. Gandhavati surmised, perhaps Tamradhvaj knew everything. Tamradhvaj knew of Dhruvaputra — that night, river Gambhira, that journey towards suicide and all! And then? Rising from the river, that man seemed to have drifted along moonshine! He knew that too. But how did he know?

Gandhavati asked, "Shall I place the stool in the courtyard"?

Reba fell silent. Gandhavati grew all ears. She marked, even her mother was trying to guess the voice. The unfamiliar voice which was being heard, was not Tamradhvaj's. Then who was it? Gandhavati trembled. Yes, she could locate it. She could recognize. Her mother asked her to light up the lamp. Gandhavati said, " Maa, this is that miscreant"!

"Who"? Screamed out, Reba.

Then, in brisk steps, Shivnath had entered the courtyard in the dark. Now for the first time, his voice became audible, "No, no, please go away, Uddhav, you leave, it is rather better for my granddaughter to stay a spinster"!

Gandhavati and Reba, leaning their back on the wall of the terrace kept breathing, gingerly. They stood in hiding already. Uddhavnarayan stood in the courtyard. Before him, old Shivnath had gone on his knees.

Uddhavnarayan said, "You are getting agitated for no reason, Sir! Uddhavnarayan has brought a necklace, which is almost of the same worth as Mahalata, your granddaughter will never be so fortunate to touch this necklace even"!

"Whatever be it, please go back, I cannot trust her in your hands"!

Uddhav thundered in the dark, "You have to do it. Look, this necklace adorns the neck of the queen, it befits the neck of the top prostitute of the city, but I have managed it for Gandhavati, is it of no worth? Whatever Uddhavnarayan says, he does. How can you stop me"?

Shivnath folded his knees to bend, pleading. On the dust of the courtyard. Chaitra wind began to blow. Uddhavnarayan was pacing up and down before Shivnath. In the dark, his garb, his headgear kept dazzling. He was looking here and there in search of Gandhavati. Uddhavnarayan had drunk a little. Last time, Gandhavati had escaped to safety and Uddhav too let go of the jittery deer! Even a hunter would commit mistake at times. And such illusion only made the opportunity slip by. Today there would be no forgiveness, no compassion. He would return with the final word. He must seek Gandhavati's hands in marriage, in the month of Baisakh. If Uddhav failed to marry a young maid of his choice, what sort of royal servant would he be? If someone from the Royal court was refused by an ordinary rustic, that refusal would surely affect the King. Uddhav staked his claim to the soldier's daughter, but on which assurance? On the assurance of the King being with him! Being a man of the Royal Court meant he was protected by the King and in no way his claim would be challenged by anyone from the family of a missing soldier.

Uddhav said, "Look Sir, this is your good fortune that Uddhav is trying to stand by you, don't lose an opportunity, I tell you".

Both Gandhavati and Reba could hear the voice of Uddhav. Gandhavati was turning furious. She felt like registering protest by raising commotion, there and then. Whoa! How that old grandfather kept his palms folded before the depraved fellow! It seemed that Gandhavati could see the hapless face of her grandfather even in the darkness.

Shivnath replied, "You are crossing limits, Uddhav, before you had been appointed in the court, you used to move around aimlessly in search of job. I asked you to see the King and who knew such will be its consequences!"

Uddhav stamped his feet on the ground to kick off dust and answered, "Come on, do not try my patience by referring to such musty facts, I am dying for your granddaughter, and I am coming again and again for her, if you do not give your consent in this matter, I shall have recourse to coercion. I shall marry her by abducting, in accordance with the norms of the Rakshasha system. I shall take her away this very day and none can stop me! If the King of Avanti can go to enjoy Mahakaal's devadasi behind all eyes, his courtier would invariably possess Gandhavati! Let me see who comes in my way, this is the King's order, go, plunder and snatch whatever you like to"!

"Oh God! Alas, oh Lord Mahakaal"! Shivnath cried out in dejection! Then he resumed, "The father of this daughter has gone missing, Gandhavati is a soldier's daughter, who has left his family for good, for this city of Avanti, for our motherland!

Without letting him finish his statement, Uddhav broke into a boisterous laughter, "Fie on you, you old bloke, now I shall ask the King to arrange for a mass sraddh ceremony for offering obsequies to those who have not returned as yet, in assumption that they have all bidden adieux to this world! Do what I am telling you, you old man, call Gandhavati, that day I let her go, but today I shall not, I am armed with weapons, if resisted, I shall spell disaster on you all! Listen Gandhavati, sweet Gandhavati, see who has come for you, come Gandhavati, I am here to take you along…"!

Uddhav, in a nearly-choked voice, kept calling out to Gandhavati. It was crystal-clear that Uddhav had come here, highly drunk! His inebriation was escalating, gradually. Confusion was getting the better of him, terribly, bit by bit. Uddhav kept staggering. While losing his balance, he went encircling Shivnath, the old man. Shivnath clogged his ears with both his hands. Looking at the sky, he went mumbling to himself, "Oh Lord Mahakaal, leave me deaf! Oh God! Which era are we in, has the jackal's rule begun already"?

Uddhav kept clapping his hands and saying loudly, "Gandhavati, hey Gandhavati, your lover's obsequies too will be performed now, he had even dreamt of being the paramour of Devadutta, it is like aspiring for the moon, being a dwarf! Once that scoundrel comes to the town, I shall throw him into the prison, tying ropes around his waist! Uddhav will leave him dead by kicking hard, how dares he look up to Gandhavati, doesn't he know that Gandhavati belongs to Uddhav? Where is that Son of Dhruva, let him see his end today, I shall slay him today, I shall make jackals and vultures eat his flesh, it will be a grand feast…come, come, two corpses are there, have lumps of flesh, who will rescind the King's order"?

Reba could not maintain her calm anymore. For long, she pressed the mouth of her daughter and hid in the dark, like a piece of log! Shouting at the top of her voice, she jumped into the courtyard, roared like a madwoman, "Will you stop? Shut up"!

"Who are you, are you Gandhavati"? Uddhav looked into the dark, with half-closed eyes.

"No, I am her mother".

Uddhav broke into a noisy laughter and blurted out, " The widow of the soldier! I shall take the widow, too, to the city. I shall keep two women, with food and clothing, hey, you widow, call your daughter, let me have a look at her charming face, I, myself, shall deck her up with this Mahalata, anklets, gold anklets, call Gandhavati! Let her see which invaluable ornaments her husband, Uddhavnarayan, has brought for her"!

Reba sensed, Uddhavnarayan was grabbing the courtyard, the dwelling house, inch by inch, gradually! What an obnoxious stench was pervading the air. It reached her nostrils. All day this odour had not been there! Just now it could be had! The southern breeze of evening was wafting it in, perhaps. An animal might have died nearby, or might even be far away! Uddhav's delirium frightened her. Repeated utterance of the address 'widow' in the dark, intensified her fear. She recoiled in apprehension. Uddhav was throwing his limbs in air, obnoxiously. What would happen now? The man who sheltered them was growing feeble gradually, she felt. The man's strength had been totally sapped by the grief for his son who had gone missing, drought, lack of crops and the departure of the son of his dear friend, Dhruva! Lowering his head, Gandhavati's grandfather sat squatting! What would Reba do now?

Uddhav declared, "I shall help you get a lover too, hey you widow, you won't have to stay alone at such a young age! Let this old bloke count his days here, come, let me take both of you away, not just one, not one, but two at a time -ha, ha, ha, I shall give away the mother to the King of Avanti and the daughter will be mine, such is the King's command"!

At that moment, Gandhavati was descending from the raised terrace, in silent steps. She could feel that the way Uddhav's drunken state went beyond all limits, it would really be difficult to desist him. Support for a royal servant was always there! As he was a man of the King's court, none would stand by them to be a witness against him! She came to stand beside her mother, slowly. Her mother was shedding tears, covering her face with her sari. Gandhavati consoled her, "Maa, please don't cry. Can delirious ravings be ever true?

Uddhav had lost the hope of getting Gandhavati, even in the height of inebriation. He was suspecting Gandhavati to have hidden somewhere in the dark. A common practice as it was. For saving herself, she surely had gone into the woods or had sought shelter at some neighbour's. Who had even thought that Gandhavati would come in front of him to offer her hands? Gandhavati said, "Give me what you have brought along"!

"Will you take, will you"?

"Yes, I shall. Go away after handing it to me and later my grandfather will arrange for everything".

Uddhav was taken aback. Who had even thought that his mission would be fulfilled? He had dropped the necklace held in his hand into Gandhavati's. He moved the casket forward, which contained the anklets. Uddhav got free of all worries. Now there would be no impediment in winning Gandhavati.

Gandhavati said, "Now you must leave".

Uddhav moved to the other end of the courtyard. He was thinking, What more? Now he would come any day to ask her hands in marriage, in compliance with the Gandharva system. He was the King's courtier. Like the King, everything in the city of Avanti was in his possession, each object was known to him like the back of his palm. Uddhav melted in the darkness.

TWENTY-SIX

Shivnath had to face no trouble to find out Subhag Dutta's house in Ujjwain. The Merchant was known to all, who would dare not know him? The servant of the merchant, Utanka, was his charioteer too. His introduction might be necessary. How horrible was his stare! How speedy was the wheel of his chariot! From a long distance, the trundling noise of the chariot-wheel, the neighing of the horse and the sibilant noise of the whip could be heard. While the horses of the carriage kept galloping at their own pace, Utanka used to brandish the whip in the air, noisily. The speed of that whip was even similar to that of the lightning, flashing across the sky. It seemed, Utanka had some latent grievance against someone, who remained invisible though he wished to flog, making him bleed. Utanka, no doubt, had a reason for his wrath. And this had many tales to relate to.

When Shivnath reached the entrance of the Merchant's house, the sun was ablaze overhead. Behind Shivnath's silk-drapery, the gold ornaments were stashed in a silk-casket. All night he could not sleep. Why she alone, Reba, Gandhavati too failed to catch forty winks. In every hour of the night, Shivnath could hear their muffled voices. He heard the wailing of dogs afar and their barking in the darkness. He got scared right then, perhaps the noise of the hooves of the Tibetan horse would be approaching! Uddhavnarayan had come again, perhaps! What could the old man do if he abducted Gandhavati, at this horrifying plight of the city of Avanti? He was struck with fear. And then, the wicked man would take away Gandhavati forcibly, even marriage according to rakshasha style was not disapproved of. Uddhav's desire was becoming irresistible, gradually. That young royal servant was becoming immodest, more and more. All the royal employees had their greed and courage escalating, let alone Uddhav! The news regarding the King, which went rife all around, was enough to make one assume that the King's throne itself stood accursed! Alas! If the son of Dhruva would come to know of it!

At the entrance of the merchant's house, Shivnath had run into Utanka only.

His stare was bone-chilling! The man kept looking at him only. Lowering his head, Shivnath said, "I have come to see the merchant, I am in trouble"!

It was not clear whether the man had made out what he said. He was being struck by his unblinking stare! Shivnath tried to smile. The man did not smile back. Shivnath was feeling intimidated. Why was he looking at him in that manner? How desolate the merchant's house seemed! Was he not there then? In his absence, where would Shivnath go and to whom? He decided to hand the ornaments to the merchant and surrender himself. No other way had been there for him. Only the merchant could save Gandhavati. The merchant only could desist Uddhavnarayan. Experience had it that no complaint against a royal servant lodged at the King's court would bear any fruit. The King or the courtier saw just the interest of his loyal employee. Shivnath could gauge the enormity of royal power by encountering Uddhav! He was just a street-beggar and used to seek his help before being employed at the King's court! And now? Now, Subhag Dutta could only proffer refuge to this family, in peril. Only a man empowered by riches and position could oppose the royal power. Unsheathed sword, the edge of the spear or the lance could be gratified by diamond, ruby, gold, silver!

Shivnath said, "The merchant knows me".

The man seemed stone-like. No quiver was there in the lashes of his eyes even. Shivnath was waiting silently for his reaction. But he failed to elicit any response.

Shivnath did not know that if Utanka did not answer, it would easily be surmised that he had no consent to his proposition. The old man could sense that he was even sterner, much more dreadful, than the royal employee. He became submissive and implored again, "Our life is in danger, who else will save us but the merchant"?

Utanka was stock-still. A mango tree stretched its shade on his head. He stood alone in that expansive shade. Shivnath was being scorched by the sun. He felt like standing in that shade. But he dared not say anything. Utanka was not moving, hence Shivnath, too, could not stir. Shivnath turned his head up to look at the tree. Not a hint of mango blossoms was there. This was just a new, tender tree. Did it go fruitless this year? Or just infertile? By then he remembered. The air, in the long stretch he traversed on foot so far, was not redolent with sweet fragrance. Such a barren Spring we did not experience even last year, despite such drought! Wasn't there any flower blooming this Spring? No blossom could be seen, neither of mango nor of the neem. No, no blossom greeted his eye, on the way, not even bakul! Did it ever happen in his lifetime? Had ever such Spring come to Ujjwain, the city of Avanti, devoid of either fragrance or bumble-bees! Alack! Now the vultures of the sky had assumed the role of the bumble-bees. The vultures who were known to be drawn to the corpses kept flapping its wings on flowers, from one to the other, in lure of honey. Shivnath again said, "I need to see the merchant, I am an old man".

Utanka was motionless. His bare chest was hairless, smooth, fair in complexion. His hair was a bit reddish in colour. His body was brawny, muscular. His whole body was astir, because of inhaling and exhaling. His eyes, like two small insects, stood on his face. Shivnath could feel that this servant of the merchant hailing from the north-eastern region would not allow him to go inside. Apart from being a servant, Utanka was the merchant's bodyguard too. Shivnath heard that this servant was extremely ruthless in nature. The son of Dhruva had confided in him, indeed. He used to derive sadistic pleasure by inflicting oppression on men, for some reason or no reason at all. The merchant did not even reprimand him for this. His indulgence made Utanka so adamant. And if the merchant was indulgent, it would win the royal sanction too. Shivnath was in fear. Sense of jeopardy seemed to get the better of him. Would he have to go back, after coming this far? Whom would he approach save the merchant? He would have been free of all worries, if only he could hand these ornaments to the merchant! Keeping these jewelleries with him was tantamount to acceding to the demands of Uddhavnarayan! Rather sacrificing his granddaughter to that lecher, the inveterate, sinful bloke. Moving a step forward, standing on the border of the shade, he cried out, "Hey Utanka, oh Lord Utanka, my son has gone missing in the battle of Dashapura, I am in deep trouble, hence I am here to seek refuge to the merchant"!

A stir could be felt in Utanka. He was looking at the old man with utter astonishment. Shivnath sat on folded knees before him. He was not loosening his clutch on the silk cloth. He was in fear for the silk-casket. Shivnath hung his head low, in the sun. He felt like getting reduced to dust. He called out again, "Hey Utanka, Oh Lord Utanka, the merchant can save me from the wrath of the wicked man"!

Shivnath raised his head. Utanka was calling him. He motioned him to go inside. Getting to his feet, wiping the eyes with the edge of his cloth, Shivnath kept walking. He became like grass. He got transformed to dust. Panting for breath, he entered within. Beyond the gate lay a long stretch of a lawn. It was flanked by a patch of garden on both the sides. The garden was devoid of flowers. It looked somewhat drab. Walking, he came to stand in front of the chateau of the merchant. Why was it lying vacant, without any soul in it? He kept standing quiet.

Shivnath's every tender emotion had been broken to pieces and pulverized by Utanka. Holding the two silk-reticules in two hands, he was on the verge of crying, "Oh Lord! I stand jeopardized! I am coming from Gambhira, Dhruvadas was of my age, I am Shivnath, is the master in? Oh merchant"!

A young maid emerged from inside the house hearing the loud cries of

Shivnath. She looked at the old man, crying… Alack, what a pity, why is the old man crying? Oh God! What's amiss? What for does he cry? Where is Utanka? Where are the sentries? Today is our master's day-off. Today our master will meet no destitute or needy person. Today even no rice will be given to any poor. Then why has Utanka allowed this man to enter?

Hearing the commotion raised by the young maid-servant, the old maid had come out. She too stood astonished. Who could he be? Wherefrom had the man come? She inquired, "To which village do you belong? Why are you shedding tears, our lord is there, but today he will not give away alms. Today is not the day of serving the poor. And our master has already decided not to do so. That is the duty of the King. Go to the King's court, please. Go and see the King. The merchant is taking a break now".

Shivnath implored, "I am in peril. I am praying to the Master to save me".

The two maidservants looked at each other's face. Then they got aware of the silk-reticule, suspended from Shivnath's hand. Being self-oblivious, Shivnath had brought the reticule out in the open from the safe cover of his cloth, while crying. The young maid-servant demanded, "What's in there"?

Being overcome by fear, Shivnath went to hide it again behind the silk-linen. Noticing that, the two maid-servants grew more curious. They seemed to have got a hint of the presence of ornaments. The young maid came down to the compound — "What's there in that casket? The reticule seems to be familiar".

Shivnath again let out a loud cry, "Oh, you master, merchant Subhag Dutta…"!

Abruptly, the young damsel pressed Shivnath's mouth tight, and demanded, "Tell me, what's there inside, the master is in the inner house, your voice will not reach that far, who you are dear, come, come in, please". Saying so, the young maid squeezed the silk bag, held in the hand of Shivnath, right over the silk-cloth he wore. "Does it contain gold ornaments? This reticule is very familiar to me, but how has it reached your hands"?

Being more panicky, Shivnath intended to move away. But he failed. The physical strength of the young maid far exceeded his. And the young maid was shameless too. She took him in an embra, asking, "Come, come inside".

Shivnath tried to shout. He let out a groan from his mouth. Failing to do so, he moved away with a jerk. He called out, "Oh merchant, hey Utanka, please take me to the master, Lord Subhag Dutta"!

The young maid got frightened by the cry of Shivnath and sprang off. The old maid had gone inside. But a few more servants, male and female, had come out from within. Utanka was walking in from the gate, noiselessly. Shivnath was gasping, as he sat on the floor. Moving forward, Utanka observed him. And then he went inside. Watching Utanka approach, the other servants took alarm. They seemed to have stood still by the speechless gesticulation of Utanka! The young maid who had taken Shivnath in a clasp, seemed to disappear, where none could tell however. Now, in the compound, the old man stood alone under the sun. He pressed the silk-bag to his chest, replete with ornaments. The sun was setting his slouching body, ablaze. The heat was about to dwell on his backbone. The sagging skin on his body began to slacken more. No sound was reaching his ears. He seemed to have turned deaf! No sight was unfolding in front of his eyes. He seemed to have gone blind! His body had a little or no movement. His body appeared to have been immobile.

After long hours, no record of time had been kept, someone had come to place a hand on his back, as he lay in a state of stupor! This touch brought all his body parts to life! He got back his vision, he seemed to be cured of his deafness. Shivnath could hear that someone was calling him, "Hey you good man, get up, you have been called inside".

Shivnath saw the old maidservant standing before him. With a calm countenance. The old woman kept looking at him, surprised. He got up. He felt a surge of fear. Was it another ruse to make off with the ornaments? He turned his head around to find Utanka. Utanka was his master. Utanka was his saviour. He belonged to Utanka now. The Arab traders, coming from across the seas, used to say, 'Malik'. The lord was surely the 'Malik'! His friend Dhruva had learnt the word from the Barugaza port! Suddenly he remembered it. He saw his "malik' was looking at this direction with unblinking eyes, standing in the sun from the other end of the compound. The shade of the Ashok tree fell on him aslant. It was Ashok, indeed. But where were its flowers? Blossoms of Ashok? Truly so. He had come by walking such a long way, from Gambhira to Ujjwain, but he did not get to see any flower, shed on the ground! As the old woman was leading him to Utanka, he surely had been called in! Shivnath kept walking forward.

The merchant's house was sprawling and commodious. Shivnath could not say whether it would be called a palace. Once he had come here with Dhruvaputra, he kept remembering all! Dhruvaputra was behind the maid who was leading them and he followed Dhruvaputra. They went moving down the long verandah, on and still on! The servants were in the habit of walking speedily, in brisk steps. Their mode of work was like that only. Hence, they had to, especially he had to, rush at an unwonted speed. In the narrow corridor, he could not see the maid clearly. He was just getting to see the silky hair of Dhruvaputra, his tall stature. So many rooms had been there on both ends of the verandah! Some had its door closed, some again had it wide open!From inside some room issued the fragrance of a condiment, from another that of cinnamon, from another again the aroma of sandalwood, and from some other the scent of flowers hung heavy in the air of the dimly-lit corridor. Grapevine had it that the merchant's house extended gradually to the west, right from this end.

When this wing was being built, the merchant was just an ordinary one. He could not give up the old association. He kept all intact. Rather, this end of his house had made him so prosperous! So, all had been there as before. But that fragrance of costly spices, cinnamon, sandalwood or fresh blossoms had not been there anymore!A sultry ball of wind lay hanging heavy on the long stretch of the verandah! He had heard the coo of the nightingale from a distance, that time. It was then Spring too, as present. But now all kept strikingly quiet! That time, he could hear the veena being played on. He could not see the player, but the lilt reached his ears. Later he heard, that, in the merchant's residence, veena-playing was an incessant affair. Only the veena-playing would make one feel whether the merchant had been home. But what was wrong this time? Was this house in sync with the meadows and rivers of the city of Avanti? Or, was it because Dhruvaputra had been with him, he could get the sweet scent in the air or the strumming of veena-strings had made way to his ears in the dark! The old maid had stopped to say, "Go into this room, our master is here".

Shivnath kept standing. His heart was palpitating. It would have been better if he entered with the old maid at his heels. He had come to this end, negotiating sundry turns. How would he be back?

The old maid assured, "Go son, don't fear, Utanka is in your favour, as Utanka has been here with the message. You have no reason to panic, our master is kind-hearted, compassionate, believe me".

TWENTY-SEVEN

The son of his friend, Dhruva, was ungrateful, immodest and proud. He had been banished from this city. Wrongdoings of Dhruvaputra knew no limits. Did Shivnath, contemporary of Dhruva, come here to talk about that criminal? Did the youth want to come back? Was that knowledge-seeker enamoured of Devadutta? He had been banished. On his return he would be thrown behind the bars. The merchant grew angry as he kept on looking at Shivnath. He was reminded of everything. Subhag Dutta could go and stand beside Devadutta, the courtesan, in one cloth, giving up all the riches he had earned so far! A paragon of beauty as she was! He felt a romantic thrill all over, just as he remembered the face of Devadutta, no matter how long she stayed silent! The counsellors had asked him to wait. Even the merchant himself knew that he had no other option but to wait for her! One day, realizing his love for her to be unwavering, Devadutta would herself come to him in order to reciprocate.

Shivnath sat before the merchant, folding his knees. The merchant got excited a bit. What had the friend of Dhruva come to say? He must know that Dhruvaputra would be killed once he came back. Not much strength was needed to wipe off a man from the face of earth! He, himself, had sent Dhruvaputra to that courtesan to master the art of sixty-four variations of fine arts! He was permitted to learn the mystery of veena-playing, the mudras of dance, the hundred flowers in blossom, a few stars of the sky, even he was allowed to master the art of lovemaking, the laws of the union of man and woman! King Bhartrihari had learnt all the art of lovemaking from Devadutta's mother. Dhruvaputra was keen on learning intricacies of fine arts! It was through the son of Dhruva, the merchant was getting to know Devadutta, no doubt! In that pretext, he expressed his admiration for Devadutta by sending gifts to her. How anxious he was in gleaning all information of Devadutta from Dhruvaputra! But how ungrateful he was!

Subhag Dutta inquired, "Where is he"?

"Who? Who are you talking about, my lord"?

Fishing out the silk-reticule from within his silk-linen, putting it down before him, Shivnath said, "I am in danger, save me, oh merchant"!

The merchant did not hear Shivnath's words. He was taken aback to see the silk-reticule which was so familiar to him. While he pulled the casket, the ornaments got strewn all over. Startled, the merchant threw a quick look behind. Why, who could tell? He was familiar with all the ornaments. What was transpiring in that city was beyond his comprehension. It appeared to the merchant that the exiled youth had just been there behind him. How would then the gifts presented to Devadutta on the day of full moon in Aghran come back thus?

Faint light of day was there in the room. The window was not that wide. For more light, a tall lamp was kept aflame, at one corner. In the golden glow of the lamp, Mahalata, Chandrahaar, armlet, Swarnatilak, anklet, Swarnabalay—all the gold ornaments leaped up like lolling tongues of flame. Light inundated the room. Fire seemed to emit out of the edge of the ornaments, it seemed. That fire touched the face of the merchant. His eyes lit up. His wrath ignited like fire. What an insult! Could anyone be rejected by a prostitute, in that manner? The cause was none but Dhruvaputra! If Dhruvaputra had not made a foray into the life of Devadutta, victory would surely have been his. He had lost his battle to the youth! Devadutta was in love with the King as well as Dhruvaputra! That youth must have hidden somewhere in this city. And Devadutta was in touch with him! Lest how could these ornaments reach the hands of Shivnath?

Subhag Dutta asked him again, "Where is he"?

"Who, of whom are you taking about, my master"?

"Can't you understand who I am talking about? Of Dhruvaputra, that depraved hard-hearted man, he has certainly jeopardized your existence, you have to go to the prison for stealing these jewelleries"!

Shivnath kept banging his head on the rough, stony floor. While crying, he said, "Oh Lord, this came from the royal sessions-judge! I have no idea where Dhruvaputra is. Please listen to me, oh master, I am the father of a soldier, my son has gone missing, he has not returned from the war. Hun conquest has been celebrated, but he remains untraced till date, my granddaughter, Gandhavati is the only daughter of Kartikkumar, I am left with. Oh my master, please listen to me"!

While listening, Subhag Dutta asked again, "But where is that mindless villain? That ungrateful chap"?

"He is not here in this city of Avanti"!

"Haven't you come from him"?

"No, Sir"! Shivnath lifted his face. He kept wiping his eyes with the silk-cloth. "Then has Devadutta, the courtesan, sent you"?

"No, my lord! I am just an ordinary man,I do not know any courtesan".

"Then who has given you this jewellery"? Subhag Dutta kept throwing incredulous glance at Shivnath. He could not make out how the gift presented to Devadutta reached the hands of the foster-father of Dhruvaputra! How cruel the prostitute had been, how could she send the ornaments to him! The merchant was listening to Shivnath. He learnt about the sessions-judge, Uddhavnarayan. He did not believe him. In a sombre voice, he warned, "The consequence of talking ill of a royal servant is terrible, he may snatch your tongue off your mouth"!

"No, my lord, this is just the truth! Uddhavnarayan wants to get Gandhavati by coercion, she is just blooming into her youth, she is fond of someone else, if he does not return, he may stay a spinster all her life even"!

"How could Uddhavnarayan get hold of these ornaments"?

"I know next to nothing! Last afternoon, intoxicated Uddav entered the courtyard of my house with an overture of marriage, with this set of ornaments! He is an out-and-out depraved man! To whom shall I go, my Lord, who will save us"?

While listening, Subhag Dutta marked that Shivnath was addressing him as 'lord' by way of reverence. The way of Shivnath's talking was really very polite. The merchant could read a person. It did not seem that the person was lying. The men of his type were afraid of telling lies. A lie has to be fabricated. That art was not his cup of tea, it seemed. Yet he asked, "Are you telling the truth"?

"Yes, my Lord, this is the truth"!

"Haven't you had any contact with Dhruvaputra"?

"No, my Lord, though my granddaughter is waiting for his return".

The merchant was surprised. Just a nubile damsel, who had just crossed the girlish age, had an amorous yearning for Dhruvaputra! Dhruvaputra was in deep love with a courtesan. And the courtesan was enamoured of the King. The King wished the queen should think of Him only. She should bear his child in her womb. Queen Bhanumati did not even turn to glance at the King! She was won over by Kumar Bikram! A merchant in the midst, who could he be? He was head over heels in love with the courtesan! Perhaps, the courtesan failed to recognize him! His face had no room in Devadutta's mind. She was so rich! She had no dearth of anything - diamond, pearl, gold or silver! But would anyone spend sleepless nights for her in this city? In this city of Avanti?

"Are you really telling the truth that these ornaments have been given by Uddhavnarayan"?

"Yes, my Lord, he has threatened to abduct Gandhavati, and he demanded that these ornaments will suffice to make his proposition stand final. What will we do, my Lord, will that miscreant kidnap my innocent girl? Has it ever happened in Avanti"?

Subhag Dutta drew a long face. He was thinking inwardly,

Whoever might have given, Devadutta hasn't kept the ornaments to herself, at all! Didn't Devadutta know why he had decked her up with the jewelleries himself, with his own hands, on that full moon night of Aghran? Couldn't she guess why he had nursed such rage against Dhruvaputra? Dhruvaputra had expressed his amazement. He had let her know about his engrossing love. Devadutta is fond of the King and that is why his grudge against the King is mounting. The King has refused the invitation of the prostitute many a time, the King has never been enchanted by Devadutta, yet that paragon of beauty keeps awaiting the King and none else! He was instrumental in getting Uddhav into the King's Court. Uddhav is here to seek his favour till date. Does that Uddhav see Devadutta at her residence? How daring of him? Has the slut, surrendered herself to Uddhav, at last? She is a beauty of the highest order, is there any dearth of worthy man for her in this city?...

Sad merchant, sat with his head hung low.

Shivnath implored, "If you warn him, my Lord, Uddhav will stop doing it".

"Wedlock can certainly happen, he is a royal employee, in course of time he will be promoted to a higher position and the proposal is not that bad"!

"No, my Lord, she keeps waiting for Dhruvaputra"!

"Will he ever come back to this land"?

"Won't he return"? Shivnath seemed to let out a scream.

"He will land in jail if he comes back, and Uddhav himself will ensure that".

"Oh Sir, please let him be forgiven! He is young and this age is for committing mistakes. He has committed a blunder and comprehending that, he has left Ujjwain"!

"Has he then returned to Gambhira"?

"No, no".

"Then why are you saying all these things"?

"He hasn't returned yet, but he will surely come back"!

"Did he tell you before leaving"? In his mind, Subhag Dutta was getting anxious, it seemed. Again, even if Dhruvaputra had come back, what harm would it cause him? Did Devadutta accept him in absence of Dhruvaputra? Did she express her love for him? Yet he must not allow Dhruvaputra to enter this city! Avanti had abandoned him forever! If ever he would return, his place would surely be in the dark pit! If it reqires, his right hand would be chopped off. His eyes became bloodshot in envy! He had given him shelter. He had even arranged for his education. Yet it was he who had gone to strike at his weakest spot!

"Dhruvaputra is a lascivious man, attracted to a prostitute, why will you marry off your granddaughter to him"?

Shivnath rejoined, "He is doing wrong indeed. Oh Lord, please save us from Uddhav, he wants to outrage the modesty of a young maid by barging into the courtyard of a family-man, dead-drunk! This never had happened in Avanti before"!

Subhag Dutta visibly looked sympathetic. He became sad too. If Uddhav caused such an incident to take place, he must have done wrong! If the royal employees turned roguish, who would the common man approach for redressing wrong? How would the ordinary citizen stand against the royal authority? With the King being weak, such things would happen. In the temple, the devadasi would get raped, in the courtyard of a family-man a rogue would step in! Depraved he certainly was, otherwise how could he appropriate the ornaments from Devadutta, the courtesan, to present that to another woman as a gift? Didn't he ask the whore from whom she got it, while accepting? Certainly, he had come to know the truth. It was beyond his dreams, that, this man would come to the merchant with these jewelleries, seeking justice.

"Lord, Subhag Dutta"! Shivnath called out.

Subhag Dutta asked, "Will Dhruvaputra marry your granddaughter"?

"Yes, he will, my lord"!

"Then why did he turn to a whore"?

"Simply because of the collusion of the planets … all these are transpiring only for his absence".

"May be"… inaudibly uttered the merchant. If Dhruvaputra had been there and had not fallen for a prostitute, Uddhav certainly could not be so daring! Subhag Dutta got flung to fury. How did Uddhav dare have relations with Devadutta, the slut? How daring he had been! Everything was in for a change. Nature, man — everything and all. Uddhav came to seek favour from him. Even now, Uddhav sought his blessings.

All might be a ruse then! He employed sly tricks on getting an admission into the royal court! How strange! Hadn't this Uddhav come once to apprise him of the affair of Devadutta and Dhruvaputra? They sat behind bolted doors! Rasamanjari's daughter used to pick up new notes on her veena, making Dhruvaputra sit in front of her! She was about to create new 'mudras' for Dhruvaputra! They used to read the chapters on lovemaking together! The courtesan stayed engrossed in lovemaking with the young man: that Dhruvaputra! She was teaching Dhruvaputra the art of coition, ways, modes and skills of sexual intercourse! Learning it, Subhag Dutta had turned furious. While crossed, Dhruvaputra expressed his fascination for her! He had informed the friend of his father, how passionately he had been in love with her!

Now it occurred to him that Devadutta coveted new male, new virility. She had mesmerized an immaculate youth, Dhruvaputra, and now she worked her spell on an ordinary royal employee: Uddhavnarayan! When body and mind desired passionately, no difference between the master and the slave stood in the way.

"Lord, what shall I do"?

"Go back".

"And Uddhavnarayan"?!

"Let me see". Morose Subhag Dutta lowered his head.

Shivnath left. Now the merchant sat alone. On the floor lay strewn - Mahalata, Chandrachud, armlet, Swarnatilak! How beautiful did Devadutta look, bedecked in these gem-studded ornaments! These ornaments had been made by the jeweller on proper instructions. The merchant was looking at the sky through the window. The sky, being blazed by the sun had turned strangely askew. High above, the vulture couple kept encircling. Subhag Dutta moved away. Abruptly he yelled, "Utanka, hey you, Utanka"!

The merchant's voice reached the verandah across the room. That call was being carried by the fleet-footed maid from the corridor. "Utanka, hey Utanka, Utanka, my son, our master is calling you". On hearing the call, Utanka went walking in swift steps from the compound. The nature of the master's call could easily be construed from the voice of the maidservant. Anxious Utanka sprinted through the verandah. The balcony went abuzz with whispers-the master must have been angry, listen, the master's call was heard again; the merchant kept thundering, "Come Utanka, let me settle scores with that slattern, the King will not come to save her, come here, Utanka"!

TWENTY-EIGHT

Utanka's stare seemed to shed cold snow. Even Utanka's chariot was similar. It evoked fear on the main thoroughfare all the time. Who was not familiar with Utanka's chariot? The street curs used to know it very well. When Utanka's carriage with the master came hurtling down on the road, abruptly, like a whirlwind, a pack of dogs on the streets kept barking and running helter-skelter, losing all sense of directions. They seemed to sense the arrival of the chariot before it made its presence felt, with the horse from the Indus, the charioteer and the rolling wheels! That chariot had left many a dog, crippled. Subhag Dutta loved the maddening speed of the chariot. Even the King's chariot was not that speedy! Today the merchant did not feel like proclaiming his supremacy by his chariot's winged briskness, rather he discouraged his charioteer in a low tone, "Utanka, move slowly".

Just like the horse of the land of Indus, Utanka twisted his neck to look at his master. He sat hanging his neck down. His master looked dejected. The wrath in which he had called Utanka was now no more. Utanka could not make out what exactly had gone wrong that anger and exhaustion would dampen his master's spirits! It happened to him just after the rustic man left. As the master did not order him, he did not take him captive. And the man was quite innocent, Utanka used to know him. After the man's departure, his master, Subhag Dutta, looked edgy, restive. He looked even older. Whose ornaments and why again the old man brought these along? Utanka observed that the merchant sat, stooping low, to the front.

Subhag Dutta was silent. A yellow canopy stretched over his head. There was filigree of finely-cut ribbons all around the cloth. On the awning, the sharp sun of Chaitra hit hard. The fine-threads could not shelve the heat out. The heat came trickling down the merchant's body. A yellow glow surrounded him. Looking at the pensive face of his master, Utanka grew sad. Hardly he saw his master feeling so low. Since long, his master had not gone out on trade. On his trade-tours, Utanka accompanied him. The master used to set out on a journey for trade and commerce with a retinue

226

of his men, cattle-cart, goods, pigeons in cage, peacocks, and, a horde of servants and serving maids. On such a trade-tour, he brought Utanka from the north-eastern land. Utanka could faintly remember. During winter, snow stood thick all around. Eyeing the white cluster of clouds in the sky, he was reminded of that land. Collecting him, traversing many a land, Subhag Dutta had come back to Ujjwain finally. Heavy monsoon stood unleashed on the way. They were supposed to reach Ujjwain before the monsoon set in. But that did not happen. Didn't the master remember anything about the trade-tour? Didn't he remember anything of the Bay of Bengal? Soil of that land was soft, trees, dense forests surrounded the whole land. Coconut and paddy had been brought from that country. Why did the master engage himself in a conflict of love with just a boy, Dhruvaputra, being forgotten all about his trade? If his master so willed, would any woman dare evade his call? How long would it take to abduct Devadutta from the brothel to the master's house? Let the master issue an order.

Master's grief cast its shadow on the eyeballs of Utanka. He grew up at the merchant's house, he had travelled far and wide with the merchant. He was his loyal servant. When he would inhale, when again would exhale, fell in his jurisdiction, it seemed. He used to mind his duty.

Utanka pulled the reins of the two horses. Though this chariot was used for regular plying, it was mainly a war-chariot! It was of ten men's height and wide enough to seat twelve men, and, no doubt, it would be ideal for a battle. This was Utanka's favourite. In the whirl of the two large wheels of the chariot, in the emerging noise due to friction, Utanka grew more energized, more spirited. Then he would make the chariot speedy by thrusting the rein and flogging the Indus-horse mildly on its back and letting out a swishing noise by his flagellation. The enemy camp was in proximity, it seemed. The chariot would rush to upset everything! Utanka again stopped the chariot.

Subhag Dutta said, "I have to go to the brothel to see Devadutta".

Utanka noticed, the eyes of his master were bloodshot. He spanked his rein to make the two horses restive. Whipping them on their back, he gave a fillip to the speed of the carriage-wheels. The chariot ran, no doubt, but the movement was slow, no sign of unbridled passion had been there. Now, Subhag Dutta hurled a query at him, "What will be the punishment of an unfaithful woman"?

Utanka stood turning his neck back. Kohl adorned the rims of both his narrow eyes. How deep, enchanting his glance was! The master's grief had perhaps touched him. Melancholy was about to pervade his face, it seemed. Subhag Dutta was narrating the tale of the ornaments, changing hands. Saying so, he could sense that Devadutta would never be enamoured of him. Devadutta was never impressed by him. Could he force anyone to be inclined on him at all? Alas! Inarticulate pain was let out from the mouth of the merchant. He went speechless.

As the merchant stopped, Utanka grew ill at ease. His master was the best man of this city. And how would he regret for a courtesan of all persons! Let us go out on trade again, master! Utanka said inwardly. He knew that only a business tour could calm his master down. Then, which ornaments were presented by him, how they came back through someone else, who loved him, who did not – all would turn futile, extraneous. Utanka knew that women were commodities of enjoyment! It was unbecoming of a man to be sad for her, to go morose because of her, to be depressed for her cause. As the poor went crying bitterly for food and attire, his master was repenting for a woman likewise. A woman would just be a woman. How difficult it would be to own her! If the King could go to rape a devadasi, wouldn't the merchant be able to own that slut, by coercion? What if she was the chief prostitute, the merchant was no less, he was a gentleman numero uno, too! King would be the King, his master was also the possessor of immense wealth!

The merchant had never allowed his servant to go a notch higher in position. He had never discussed his personal matters with Utanka. Was a servant fit enough to listen to all that he said? But to abate the storm within, the merchant took Utanka to his confidence. He knew full well that there was no difference between Utanka and the Indus-horse! No word would spill elsewhere. Such a faithful, such ruthless a servant would be found nowhere, in no house of this city.

The merchant spoke out, "How dare-devil is Uddhav, the scoundrel? He used to live the life of a worm, that villain"!

Utanka was listening. He was not in the wont of answering back to his master. And now his master was lightening the burden of his mind. Yet, hearing the name of Uddhav, Utanka got excited and struck the horse lightly with his whip. He ruffled the air with a sibilant noise. He seemed to flog someone invisible with a whanging slash. The horses galloped. The trundle of the wheels grew strong. Dust was kicked off by the chariot wheels. Let Uddhav breathe his last! A detestable worm of all worms! He lashed the back of the horses again. The two horses picked up speed. Utanka went on flagellating, repeatedly. Then the merchant said, "Be slow, Utanka"!

He bridled the rein of the galloping horses. As he tugged at it, the horses came to a halt. Lifting the front legs up, they made a neighing noise. As the chariot was about to swerve at an end, the experienced charioteer, Utanka, began to control the pair of horses. But the neighing sound went on. Onlookers assembled on both sides of the road. Look yonder, a tall, lanky, dark man kept standing there. The pimp, Mahaparshwa seemed to have bent down. Looking at the merchant's chariot in panicky eyes, he began to wipe them. To someone he remarked, "The man has gone mad, Utanka is infuriated! Oh! Now he will surely make the pair of horse bleed, will transform them into donkeys, that ruffian had beaten me once! If Utanka turns furious, no one will be saved"!

Another pedestrian commented, "It's not Utanka, it's the horse of the chariot, if this animal gets flung to fury, no one can be saved".

"No, it's Utanka! The way he behaves seems like that of a madman, he keeps flogging like an insane".

"Flogging is needed to stop a madman".

"Then Utanka himself is fit for whipping", pimp Mahaparshwa spoke in a muffled voice.

"You are wrong, the two horses are mad, I have seen mad horse, haven't you"?

"No, you haven't seen a lunatic".

The passer-by said, "You cannot comprehend the ways of a mad horse, I see".

"You seem to be fond of Utanka, perhaps you are a servant of that cruel servant", as Mahaparshwa said so with annoyance, the pedestrian got angry. He pulled the cloth the tall, lanky man draped himself with and said, "Why are you here? Go, go to the brothel"!

"Why shall I go? Is the thoroughfare yours"?

The man then said, "I am going to shout at Utanka to tell him everything, first you have to say that the horses are mad, come on, say, I ask you".

The pimp freed himself at one jerk and said, "You are insane"!

Hearing that, the pedestrian again pounced on Mahaparshwa, "What have you said, you wicked man, am I insane? If I am insane, why do the horses of the chariot throw their legs in the air and keep neighing"?

A commotion broke out. Then, the merchant's chariot trundled out, asking for Uddhav repeatedly. The merchant was saying, Uddhav certainly has done wrong if Shivnath of Gambhira speaks the truth. First crime: Touching Devadutta's jewelleries gifted to her by the merchant, Second crime: Abducting the young maid of an ordinary family man; no moral laws stay binding in the Kingdom, the more the moral laws would be compromised, the more immoral practice would increase and the King would run the risk of being utterly ruined".

Utanka lost words. He was never in the habit of interfering with his master's words. Successful, supreme, rich gentlemen think themselves to be the best of the ilk. They take their own word as the final one. They stay firm in their decision. Keeping abreast of this truth, he was the best of all servants! He was the most favourite servant of the merchant; his power was illimitable. He was listening to the merchant's words, silently. The chariot was moving slowly. The merchant said, "The daughter of the family-man will be kidnapped, the crops will be plundered, the rainless land will be devoid of water, and thieves and ruffians will be let loose on streets — this city is heading towards that end"!

Utanka, twisting his neck, could see the silk-bag replete with ornaments, lying at the feet of the merchant. The merchant was not lifting it. His master was deeply hurt. Utanka, with the violent thrust of the reins, enhanced the speed of the chariot. The merchant was saying, "In absence of the King's control, the royal servant becomes a knave, all these responsibilities are that of the King. In case of the abduction of any maiden, or pillage or outraging the modesty of women, the sin of the King will go up. Just fine, let it increase, let Uddhav do whatever he feels like doing, how long will it take to squeeze Uddhav's life out, but let the King's load of troubles be intractable, even the royal courtesan is clinging on to the King's employee, turning blind eye to the King himself! This city is, no doubt, heading down fast to disaster".

The speedy chariot came to a grinding halt, quite abruptly. Look yonder, there was Uddhav! Riding a Tibetan horse, he moved with a mild swaying movement. Uddhav was crooning. Which song was that knave humming? He had been a village farmer once! A farmer who had not a single strip of land to call his own! That have-not had flaunted a silken headgear, draped himself with a silk cloth, displayed pearl necklace around his neck and had been out on a horseback, as though he was out to lead a procession of street-singers! But howsoever important a royal employee he might be, the rustic smell still had not left him altogether. Hence, he was crooning a rural tune. It was easily being heard, the tune of his surging happiness… "The pair of wood-apples are really sweet…the pitcher is even sweeter…oh dear, how honey-like is the wood-apple"!

The merchant roared, "That's Utanka, where is he going, what does he say"?

Hearing the roar of the merchant, Uddhavnarayan seemed to have gobbled the ripe wood-apple with its rind! He was in good humour. All his mirth got evaporated in a trice. Leaping off the horse, looking at the bloodshot eyes of the merchant he was overcome with fright. He said, "Lord, let me be forgiven, I am on my way to Gambhira, my own village, tomorrow I shall be back to touch your holy feet".

The tycoon was annoyed by the excessive modesty of Uddhav. He roared again, "Ask Utanka, why does he go to abduct the maiden from a family"?

Uddhav recoiled at these words. His limbs were going numb. He was afraid more of the tycoon than the King. He had not met the King in his lifetime being just an ordinary Sessions-Judge. How would that be possible? And again, everything lay in disarray now. Innumerable words were doing rounds in the city. Now he was almost an independent royal employee. He had hardly cared a fig for rules and ethics. He had an unencumbered entrance to the brothel. He was getting used to the behavioural wont of the royal employees of higher echelons, the Army Commander, the Chief Charioteer, the Superintendent of Merchandise, the Chief of Jewellers, the Chief of Landowners. He was enjoying the whores without spending a single coin, he was taking away this or that from the King's palace, was picking up goods of his choice from the shops—how pleasant a life he was having!

"Why doesn't he answer? From where has he managed the ornaments"?

Uddhav cowered in fear. His small stature looked even smaller. His countenance bore deep shadows of staying awake by night and dissipated existence. Now that had been mingled with worries and anxiety. Frightened Uddhavnarayan resumed, "Lord, that woman has on that wicked Dhruvaputra…!"

Without allowing him to finish the sentence, the tycoon interrupted to say, "Utanka, ask that uncivil bumpkin to see me at my house. Turn the chariot back, I demand to know, how he has got hold of those ornaments"!

In a jiffy, Utanka veered the course of the chariot. Now he knew what his duty was. To return home at high speed. His master issued an order. Utanka began to turn the chariot back, quite briskly. Circling a long stretch of road, Utanka made the carriage run at a breakneck speed. At the turn of the road, it went out of sight, gradually.

Uddhav kept standing for some time. To be frank and fair, what would he do now? He had to retrace his steps to the tycoon's house. He did not have that courage to drop the decision of going there. Oh God! Why did he have to run into the merchant at all? Otherwise, how smoothly he could have ambled down to Gambhira! He could have a relaxed respite at Gandhavati's courtyard. He had almost gone mad for that maiden. And by now, he had definitely staked a claim to her. As he had given her those ornaments, would it be long to have the damsel, adorned with those jewelleries? The tycoon talked of those very ornaments, right? Oh, what utter ruin! He had no inkling of what was underway and how! Instead of riding the horse, Uddhav was walking along, by its side. Walking on, he found Mahaparshwa, the pimp, lying supine on the road, and on his chest stood a pedestrian. On seeing Uddhav, the pedestrian leapt up to stand apart. The pimp then got to his feet, smiling, flicking the dust off his body. Coming forward, lowering his head, he said, "Why are you on foot, Sessions-Judge? What's wrong with your horse"?

Uddhav concealed his state of mind and throwing a stern glance at the passer-by, he demanded, "What's the matter? Was there any wrestling-session on, on the road"? The whore's agent smiled, "Let go of it. Oh Sessions-Judge, he is mad and what can't a madman do"?

Throb of life seemed to get restored to Uddhav. Mahaparshwa, the pimp, was sly, he was the master of guiles and tricks. Being solemn, he offered, "Come along with me"!

The pimp raised his hand, "Hey thou lunatic, go home, lest thou would be put behind the bars. Here's the Sessions-Judge from the Royal Court"!

The pedestrian walked off, hurriedly. He seemed to have almost escaped. Now, a small Tibetan horse, a short-statured Sessions-Judge of the Royal Court and an extremely tall pimp, Mahaparshwa, walked along the thoroughfare, slowly. Uddhav hawked.

Walking a few steps down, the pimp, Mahaparshwa inquired, "Looking anxious, eh"?

"No,nnno, why so"? Uddhav replied nervously, swallowing the ball of anxiety down his throat.

Why had the merchant turned back again? Mahaparshwa was striving hard to find out the underlying laws of cause-and-effect. The tycoon went back and just then Uddhav was seen to come, riding a horse at breakneck speed. Did the horse go lame? Tall, lanky pimp bent down to confirm. Oh where? No! Then why had he come down, walking? Why had the Sessions-Judge alighted from the horse? Again, where was he headed to?

Uddhav said, "To the merchant's place".

"What's the matter, Sir"?

Uddhav could guess that this sentry of the brothel could smell rat in it. Too cunning, after all. Even the reason behind his being engaged in a wrestle with the passer-by could be guessed by Uddhav. Surely he could, being too clever. No wonder, his head was stuffed with stratagems. Uddhav thought of consulting the pimp. Mahaparshwa was an authority on the ways of women, no matter a young maiden or an old hag, a homemaker or a resident of a brothel. Then, Uddhav kept narrating about Gandhavati, in a leisurely manner. No alternative had been there but to relate the matter to him. The problem would not be solved if he would share it with the horse - it would neither lift the burden off his heart nor pacify the tycoon.

Listening to him, Mahaparshwa asked, " Have you abducted the virgin maid, I mean, the damsel of Gambhira"?

"No, not yet".

"Fetch her to the brothel, go, welcome the tycoon, let him check on his own".

"What sort of statement is this"?

Mahaparshwa broke into a noisy, uncouth laughter and said, "The tycoon has made your fortune, and won't you be able to hand her to the business magnate? So ungrateful! The magnate has made you alight from the horse, now what if he snatches off the horse and the coronet"?

The words were really very pointed. Anger was building up in the mind of Uddhav. He felt like stabbing the pimp with a secret scimitar! He wished he could rip his belly open and take out the entrails to scatter them on the thoroughfare! But how could he deny the veracity of the statement?

Mahaparshwa said, "Go and find out whether the tycoon is seeing that woman, may be for that reason, he has kicked Dhruvaputra out of the city! Men of ripe age fall for young maidens, go, fetch her to our ghetto, new girls are a necessity. If one such could be had, new clients would surely drop in, the days are so barren! The prostitutes are sitting idle with all they have to offer, waiting eagerly, but none is there, the traders are not filing in, they are being plundered on the way".

Hmm, Utanka was lost in another thought... Has ever the merchant really seen Gandhavati? Otherwise, how will he know of her or the jewelleries, for that matter? Certainly, the news has reached him. Alas! To what exactly has he staked his claim? How will he be saved now?

Mahaparshwa exhorted, "Do whatever the tycoon wishes".

"How shall I make out what he wishes"?

Mahaparshwa broke into a noisy laughter, "This is the only medicine, offer your master to enjoy, do you have any dearth of women"?

"Can't say" … Just as Uddhav was about to mount the horse, in a worried face, the pimp demanded, "Please wait, give me a little money, oh Sessions-judge"!

"Money, but why"?

"We are going without rice, no customers are turning up, we are hanging about, no man of worth can be had and I have counselled you a bit, haven't I"?

Uddhav fixed him with a stern stare and said, I am going to see the tycoon, do not disturb me. Whatever I have said is not true. Is the tycoon such a man? He is in possession of Devadutta, the chief of all the whores, how dare you talk ill of him? And I shall marry Gandhavati"!

Mahaparshwa retreated by a step. It was surely a trick played by Uddhavnarayan! How could he be a man of the Royal court, if he remained unaware of guiles and pretexts? He was really too daring to have demanded money from a man of the Royal Court! On the contrary, he would get money from Mahaparshwa! Who wouldn't like to supply money to the Sessions-Judge? Unless they did so, they would have to land in trouble. Mahaparshwa folded both the palms and said, "Okay Sir, please move on, in fact, I am stricken by utter poverty, it is difficult to maintain my cool, all that I have said is wrong, please forget everything, my Lord"!

Uddhav left, riding his horse away. Mahaparshwa kept standing for some time. And then stamping his foot on the ground abruptly, he began to walk in the opposite direction. At least he had come to know that this day was an inauspicious one for Uddhav. How would he hold Chaturika in his clasp, without any effort? Today, the Sessions-Judge would have to face music, at the tycoon's. Indeed, it would be so. And the tycoon was so puce in anger! Uddhav: a nincompoop! Go thou to the merchant's place. Fie on thee! Spitting on, the pimp kept walking. None would be saved if he would deceive this pimp! Mahakaal would do the needful. Hearsay had it, that, the god's wrath would render the Gandharvas as pimps, in the next birth. After this birth, he would again become the handsome Gandharva! Many a beautiful maiden would be around him, serving. He would sit back happily, blessed always by the breath of the nymphs. He would float in the ethereal realm, singing incessantly. None would be more handsome than him either on the earth or in the heavens! Mahaparshwa, the pimp, began to droop forward, as he kept walking. Hunger gnawed at his entrails. His head throbbed on, he felt dizzy. Leaning against a neem tree, he kept on stretching a blurred glance at the thoroughfare!

TWENTY-NINE

The route of return to Ujjwain was not so short! The miles to return seemed to be even more than the onward journey to the place. The body was overcome with exhaustion, mind too was, as well. Worries subsided a little after handing the jewelleries to the magnate. But the elderly man could realize that his mind had gone bankrupt. He thought in one vein, it transpired just otherwise. He could not say anything the way he wanted to. All his allegations remained intact within himself. He thought, he would tell the magnate about Kartikkumar. It was, of course, the duty of the King to protect the daughter of a soldier who hadn't returned from the war. The Royal employee desired to abduct her— wasn't there any rule to stall it in the city of Avanti? Did the fact reach the King that his son had gone to war and went missing thereafter? Would there be no effort for launching a search for him?

He could not say the whole of it. The tycoon became furious on casting his glance at the jewelleries! While returning, Shivnath was really on the verge of collapsing. He was remembering the way he addressed the servant of the tycoon as 'Lord', going down on his knees! Even the way he greeted Subhag Dutta, a friend of Dhruvaputra of the same age, as 'Lord'! Such had never happened in his life! His heart was broken. His life would never be so insufferable if Kartikkumar had been there, or Dhruvaputra! Alas! He might not be rich, but the cup of his life was full to the brim. Did Gandhavati have any inkling of the fact that her grandfather was coming home today, destitute, losing plenitude of his life? Such sense of being utterly indigent had never got the better of this elderly man.

Reaching near the temple of Mangalnath by the river Shipra, he had halted. The sun had just tilted towards the western horizon of the sky. Its glow and radiance were extremely severe. The rage of the sun was such that it would burn the whole body to ashes! He sat beside the river. He stretched his body beneath a peepul tree. Only a vacuous look was there in his eyes. Bending his thighs and knees, he kept his face buried within, and looked on at the void of the river. The semblance of water was far-off. Sand, only sand! In the morning, he had seen the married women from the village were digging the sand to collect water from the bottom but now none of them had been there. Sun was setting the surface of the river ablaze. Seeing that, his mind began to feel void. City of Avanti had gone impoverished. Neither Kartikkumar nor Dhruvaputra had been there. It was devoid of clouds, crops, love in the mind of its people, kindness in their eyes, it had only combustion instead. The tycoon seemed to have been infuriated by looking at the ornaments! Tears welled up to Shivnath's eyes. He was the father of the hero: Kartikkumar. Even he had reared up Dhruvaputra. All his life, he had put in hardest of labour. He had snipped the crops, during harvest. With his own hands he had sown the crops, the seeds. He had never begged two handfuls of rice at any door. How could he, that same man, address the merchant's servant as 'Lord Utanka'! Shivnath was shedding tears. Profuse tears coursed down his chest. Long pent-up tears of affliction stood accumulated in his bosom. Such shedding of tears was next to impossible at home. There he would have to be like a banyan tree to offer protective shade to his daughter-in-law and grand-daughter. Reba used to weep surely, on the sly. Couldn't he make out that? Even Gandhavati, too, shed tears silently, behind all eyes, retreating to the reed-hedge. Was it unknown to him? He was not cognizant of his own tears! Shivnath never knew about the huge reserve of tears within him, held back secretly! He never admitted the fact that he had tears for his friend, Dhruva, who had passed away untimely, for his son who had gone missing, for the son of Dhruva who had been banished, for the acres of land lying sans harvest, for the river Shipra, gone waterless, for the singed soil, the sky, for the earth, for the water in the well, for the blossoms in Spring, for the fragrance of flowers with which the air stood redolent, for the lost hornets and bees, for the clouds which stood behind all eyes since long, for the perverted desire of Uddhavnarayan, the wicked man.

Everything stood devoid of grace! City of Avanti was just bereft of all its charms. Tears went coursing down Shivanth's cheeks, incessantly. He remembered Dhruvaputra. Remembered Kartikkumar too. Who knew that his life would turn out to be like this? The tycoon's servant had to be addressed as 'Lord'! He kept crying alone, sitting by the side of the river. He could not remember for how long he sat there like that! By then, did the shadows on the east stand elongated? Did the sun droop down to the west even more? Who could tell? As he felt a hand on his back, he started. That Utanka? Or Uddhav? Did Uddhav come again for Gandhavati? As he turned back, he got to see the youth from Dasharno!

Tamradhvaj went sombre, on seeing Shivnath shed tears, he asked, "What's up"?

"You"?

"The ashram of the Acharya is nearby, we met here one day just on this river-bank, don't you remember"?

Shivnath kept quiet. Tamradhvaj had not gone to Gambhira. Was he done with his calculations? Phalgun followed the month of Magh, even Chaitra was coming to a close. Could he find out completely, who had gone and where?

Tamradhvaj asked, "Are Gandhavati and Reba, her mother, keeping well"?

Shivnath thought whether he would talk about Uddhav. How powerful was Tamradhvaj to desist a royal employee? And these things are not to be shared with just everyone on earth. So, he did not answer.

Tamradhvaj said, "I thought of going there".

"Have you found them"?

Tamradhvaj asked, "Will you return"?

"I am on my way back".

"Come on, will it make any difference if you do not go back today? Why are you crying"?

Shivnath smiled sadly, "But none of them has returned as yet"!

Shivnath was coming back along with the astronomer from the land of Dasharno. He seemed to be a bit assured, on getting to see Tamradhvaj! He was an astronomer, not one of his relations, hardly familiar to him, a resident of another land, topping all, he was a young man! Uddhavnarayan would definitely control himself in front of him. Though Tamradhvaj was not a very stout and healthy man, he did not look feeble, lacking in physical strength. Shivnath twisted his neck to cast him a glance. The scarf on his body was not covering the whole of his torso, though at first glance he looked lean-bodied, a close look would reveal him to be a man of strong physique. Though his brawns did not stand out, novelty was there at its hint. Though Shivnath took Tamradhvaj to be a man of dark-complexion, he was not looking that dark now. Copper-complexioned, rather! What difference did it make between a fair- or a dark-complexioned male? His health, valour and knowledge only made him special. The curly hairs like a primitive hunter was so thick and close-cropped! The pair of eyes was so bright! Ah! Who was he? Mahakaal never left anyone wholly orphan. Kartikkumar, Dhruvaputra none of them had been with him, but at least this youth was there. This youth seemed to grow into their support, gradually. Shivnath was in two minds as to whether he should narrate Uddhav's tale to him. Couldn't Acharya Brishavanu report it to the King? Couldn't Tamradhvaj himself do? Didn't the King pay visit to Brishavanu's ashram?

Shivnath said, "I had gone to Ujjwain in the morning, now I am returning home".

"Oh God! What do you say? Did you have anything to eat"?

"I shall reach Gambhira before sunset, I suppose".

Tamradhvaj said, "I have come quite far from the ashram, fie on me, I have committed a mistake, I could have asked you everything in detail, why were you crying?"

Shivnath in a mild voice rejoined, "Doesn't man cry, when alone"?

"Why so, man becomes more focused rather".

"And the man who has tears deep down in his heart"?

I am just trying to make that point, anyway let it be left at that. You are hungry but I failed to guess, it is so bad, failing to know is my fault, Sir. Tamradhvaj began to shake his head, "Fie on me, fie on me, I am keen on knowing about the traceless stars and planets but I fail in feeling man's hunger, thirst, so on".

Shivnath grew emotional with the words of Tamradhvaj. They came to have respite beneath a mango tree standing by the road. The tree bent with blossoms which were shed in the dust, though. Seeing that, Shivnath pressed the hands of Tamradhvaj and said, "No one speaks in this manner. We are surrounded on all sides by knaves and I am accustomed to it. Let me return home and I must have whatever I get to eat and on my return from Ujjwain, as I stood at the entrance of a house for a glass of water, God knew why, someone had offered me a bowlful of sweetened rice-and-milk".

Shivnath deviated from the truth. But Tamradhvaj would not be pacified without a fabricated statement. He would keep on feeling sorry within. But the way Tamradhvaj was staring at him made it clear that he was in doubt. Shivnath was about to change the topic and said, "Have you seen anyone on this way riding a horse"?

"When"?

"From the morning till now".

"Whom do you expect to pass by"?

"No, I do not expect. Okay, let me tell you the truth then, do you know the Sessions-Judge of the Royal court"?

Whoever didn't know the Sessions-Judge? And this was the way he took for going up to Gambhira and returning, in a strange attire, riding a small horse. The very sight of the man was bizarre. Sometimes, he seemed to be in an abnormal state of mind. Tamradhvaj had never approached him. Rather he did not have any urge to do so".

"Was he supposed to go by the road"? Tamradhvaj inquired again.

"No, no, I was just asking whether he had passed by". Shivnath tried to segue on to another topic. In fact, the propriety of raising this matter created some confusion in him. Tamradhvaj was very polite too. Guessing something, he did not express his interest in it. If he would choose to depend on him, he must tell him himself, in case he had to say anything at all. Expressing curiosity would be just to put him into trouble.

Walking on for long hours, Shivnath was feeling exhausted. He was physically fit even at this age, no doubt. But the hunger sleeping in his entrails was about to make its demands within the body. To get rid of it, he had to be deliberately oblivious of it. If not so, it would pester him. Getting the better of him, it would render him motionless, numb. Shivnath said tenderly, "I heard, that the Sun is the creator of the clouds, water is filled into the clouds by earth and the sun again leaves the universe high and dry, by absorbing that water".

"This is invariably true".

"Wouldn't the water which the sun is sucking in, surface on Avanti's sky in the form of clouds"?

"That transformation is quite natural".

"Natural things are not taking place, that which is occurring is not supposed to happen".

"I know", Tamradhvaj whispered, "Ujjwain's throne is stigmatized, I heard. Is it true"?

"I heard this too".

"Abnormal happenings have every reason to be true".

Shivnath heaved a sigh, "If the city lacks in its guardian, if the clouds hovering over the sky fail to pour into showers, it only thunders and the rumbling of the clouds are heard,but the rains would never tumble down from the sky in absence of the King".

"Who told you"?

"I heard, and I even seem to take all these to be true! If the King does not care for the honour of the throne, if the King behaves in a way, which is unbecoming of a King, the revered loses his respect, the page-boy then has to be addressed reverently as 'Lord' and the elderly man is slighted by the young people"!

Tamradhvaj looked at him, "What's wrong with you? Why did you go to the city"?

Shivnath replied, "In absence of the King, joy never fills the heart of man, the gardens stay bereft of blossoms, the nightingales do not sing during the Spring, the bumble-bees are not seen humming around the flowers".

"That may so happen, but the King is there in this land".

"With the King being there, can a royal servant" ... Shivnath's voice trailed off to silence. His eyes met Tamradhvaj's. Tamradhvaj seemed to get the drift of Shivnath's statement. Royal servant referred to Uddhav. Gandhavati's grandfather was talking of Uddhav only. What had he done?

Shivnath said, "Royal servant enjoys liberty, keeps oppressing people".

"That may happen even in the King's presence".

"In that case, redress can be sought for, if it occurs at all".

"Doesn't it happen now, would you go to see King Bhartrihari"?

Tears, once again, clouded Shivnath's vision. He was reminded of an elderly peer sitting in front of Utanka, going down on his knees. An elderly man, before 'lord' Subhag Dutta, kept hanging his head low. He might have to grovel at the feet of Uddhav, who knew! If a King had been there in the kingdom, it would never have happened so. The people would not feel so hapless, if a King was there on the throne to rule. If the King ruled, why would Dhruvaputra be banished from Ujjwain? Why would there be no search mission for Kartikkumar?

Tamradhvaj again asked, "What's up"?

Shivnath mumbled, "In absence of a King, the river becomes dry, the wells fail to contain water, the sky stays devoid of rain, the heart of man remain desiccated. It was I, who was instrumental in sending Uddhav to the city, it was I, who advised him once to seek refuge to the tycoon.

Tamradhvaj touched the shoulders of the elderly man with both his hands and roared, "Tell me what had happened, tell me".

"You do not know, waterless river, grassless forest, a shepherd without sheep, a pair of eyes without light all these are common spectacles in absence of the King of a land. Listen, you astronomer, tell me the whereabouts of Dhruvaputra, lest dear Gandhavati will be undone".

THIRTY

On entering Gambhira, Tamradhvaj said, "Let me visit the river, please go home alone. Rest assured, I shall never divulge anything that I learnt, to either Gandhavati or mother Reba. They will be shocked".

Shivnath was impressed. The youth was truly considerate. It was true, that, if they would come to know that Shivnath had to address the tycoon's servant as 'Lord', going down on his knees, the night would be inundated with silent tears. If they would sense that Tamradhvaj had come to learn about the insolent behaviour of Uddhav, they would really be hurt. Who would love to share one's own insult with others? Shivnath knew not how to forbid Tamradhvaj to divulge it to anyone, after sharing everything with him. He was thinking that it would have been better if he never shared thus. But how would he stay without telling anyone? The words of one's own are to be shared with someone else. A helpless man would look up to someone for help, no doubt. He needed Tamradhvaj's help presently.

He was in need of Tamradhvaj's aid as he was a youth. His age was his sole strength. Tamradhvaj was knowledgeable. Knowledge was his valour. Uddhavnarayan was a youth too, but he was not a man of knowledge. King's power was his only strength. Only the wise could oppose the King's might! Dhruvaputra used to say so.

Tamradhvaj headed towards the river, all alone. As many times as he came to this village, he had gone to pay a visit to the river always. River was no less than one's mother, Tamradhvaj used to think so. His mother was no more. Long ago, after consigning his mother to the flames at the crematorium, by the Betrabati river and setting the bodily remains and ashes adrift in water, it seemed to him that the water of the river represented his mother's eyes. Mother kept looking on. He could notice his mother's tear-filled eyes everywhere — In the rivers like, Shipra, Gandhavati, Reba, Betrabati and Gambhira or the river coursing through the woods near Nichoih hills, proximal to Bidisha. The pair of eyes seemed to have mingled with water to be as pervasive as a river.

Tamradhvaj decided that he would never come to Gambhira again. He remembered that evening in the month of Magh: the evening air in the courtyard in winter was redolent with the surging milk, on the point of being spilled over, the light of the Pole star illuminating Gandhavati's face, who narrated the identity of all the clouds in the sky, which hovered over. All got mingled to cast a strange spell on him! His calculation was yet to finish. How would he finish his calculations, as the man depending on whom he made a promise, that Acharya Brishavanu was turning into a bundle of numb flesh, gradually! Last evening, he dozed off, while looking up to the sky. Those who had gone missing, if alive, would come back to their dear ones by sheer love of life indeed. This truth was known to Tamradhvaj! As Canopus[the star, Agastya] would come back to the sky in Phalgun, it must return thus. As Agastya, the star, disappeared from the Jaisthya sky, Dhruvaputra might have gone untraced likewise.

The reed woods along the bank of Gambhira had almost gone extinct. The firmament above was sternly desolate. Many birds used to fly in the sky, none of which could be seen these days. Far above, the flock of female vultures kept encircling the sky. Yonder, the swallow crossed over the sky from one end to the other, crying 'water, water'! Where had gone all the red-legged bartavelles, male and female? Tamradhvaj was looking for birds in the sky. Birds and clouds! Clouds were birds too, sans wings, however! Without wings, they would go flying! Tamradhvaj was observing that the river-bed had gone hard and dry. Sands were being blown off by the swoosh of the wind. At this end of the river, a narrow stream journeyed down, feebly. So little water! He stood looking at the river-bed. Here too his mother's eyes drooped in sleep. Tamradhvaj's own eyes smarted, became tearful.

The day was about to inch to its close. Tamradhvaj would now return to the courtyard of Gandhavati. Why was the name of Gandhavati being pronounced in the canvas of his mind, repeatedly? Tamradhvaj was retracing his steps, slowly. At the bank of the river, on the path, when evening kept descending, the heart went perplexed to the extreme. Whichever river it might be — Betrabati, Shipra, Gambhira or whatever. Acharya used to say, "Be it the Northern Hemisphere or the Southern, after sundown, the day enters into the night. And at sunrise, the night gets submerged in the water. As the night plunges into water, it assumes the tint of night during daytime, either it takes the colour of copper or looks bluish. And as day enters into night, the water-surface looks white, incandescent during night. Could the Acharya tell if the universe became waterless, where would the night go during daytime? And vice-versa — where would the day go at the advent of night?

The mother and daughter seemed to keep waiting for Tamradhvaj. Shivnath was resting at the raised terrace at the entrance of the house. After walking all day long, the body had gone limp now, looking for rest. Both the eyes of Gandhavati's grandfather were about to close in extreme fatigue. Mother and daughter had no idea that Tamradhvaj had come to Gambhira. Shivnath had told them nothing at all. Yet they seemed to wait for Tamradhvaj only. As though, he was to pay a visit to them that very day.

Reba said, "Come please, you had to bear much trouble".

"No mother, this much is the way and not more".

Reba was looking with surprise, at the youth of medium height, standing in the glow of twilight. The very glance averred that virility pervaded the whole being of this youth from Dasharno. All day long, she was remembering him only. He who would come to mind during the days of peril was the only one, a man could bank upon. Reba saw that Gandhavati fetched the stool. She offered him a potful of water. This water was brought by digging the sand of Gambhira. Tamradhvaj sat down. Taking the tumbler up, taking a gulp of water, he said, "Since long I had not come, today I suddenly remembered".

"Even we were thinking of you", Reba blabbed out.

Gandhavati went speechless. She was arranging her queries in her mind. Today itself, she wished to be certain whether Tamradhvaj would be able to apprise them of Dhruvaputra! Failing which, they would have to approach elsewhere. Somewhere a bald-headed ascetic woman had come, to whom the matters of past and present were just a child's play — she would then have to go there with her mother.

Gandhavati asked, "Have you forgotten your task"?

"No", Tamradhvaj smiled softly. He cast a deep glance at Gandhavati. She tied her tresses in a top-knot. Round the knot, a garland of wild flowers was wound. Even on Gandhavati's neck, the same garland was seen. Before this, Tamradhvaj had never seen Gandhavati to wear flower-ornaments. Yesterday, at this time, the ruffian had come here. For whom had the paramour of Dhruvaputra adorned herself today?

Gandhavati said, "I knew that you would come".

"Who told you"?

"None!"

"Then how could you feel, do you know the art of reckoning"?

Gandhavati retorted, "I also knew that Dhruvaputra would leave the house for somewhere else".

"Did he tell you"?

"No, the door of his room was shut all day long. He did not open his door even after we had been back from the Kamadeva temple. Don't you know anything about that day?"

"The previous day, the discussion hung incomplete".

"Yes, exactly"! Gandhavati, in an inaudible voice, answered. Her mother was not nearby. Yonder she was sitting at the other end of the raised terrace at the entrance. She was lighting up the lamp by striking the flint. Gandhavati seemed to be relieved. God only knew why! He would talk about the disappearance of Dhruvaputra, was it for that? Mother knew about it too. She knew, but could not explain why Dhruvaputra had gone towards the eastern horizon! Till date, the scene kept swimming in front of her eyes. Dhruvaputra was walking along the moonlit river-bank. Gandhavati cast a glance of astonishment to the way he took. She seemed to see a different man altogether. As though, someone unknown to her was leaving Avanti for elsewhere, some other strange land.

Tamradhvaj said, "How shall I finish my calculation if I do not know everything about Dhruvaputra"?

Gandhavati suggested, "Okay that can even be narrated later, before that let us finish the tale of previous day".

"Which had remained incomplete"?

"The identity of the clouds".

"How far had I gone?"

"Where is the Hemkut range located?" Gandhavati was eager to know.

"Please try to remember".

Gandhavati replied, "To the north of the Himalayas, to the south of the North Pole…"?

Tamradhvaj said, "I talked about the rains during winter. Listen Gandhavati, whatever I have come to know about the clouds is true. Let me talk about the rains now. The land is sizzling with fire, not a trace of water can be seen almost anywhere. Now if we do not learn about the rainfall,life will be more desiccated and dry".

Gandhavati was looking at Tamradhvaj's face with wonder in her eyes. In her eyes, two unknown stars of the firmament twinkled. Mother Reba was sitting at a distance, lighting up a lamp. Reba was listening to the conversation between Tamradhvaj and Gandhavati. Tamradhvaj was saying, "In fact, the Sun is the creator of the rains which in turn owes its existence to the Sun and in the wind the rains find an intermission. The heat of the sun attracts water from the sea, river or pond. Water then rises up to the sky being transformed to smoke. And thus, the clouds engender".

Gandhavati retorted, "I know… who doesn't"?

"Water contained in the clouds, comes down on earth, for its welfare".

"I know, you talk of the sun, of fire".

"Absorbing water for the clouds, the fire itself becomes a prelude to the rains".

"I know. Could you please give an introduction to fire"? Gandhavati asked.

Then Tamradhvaj stared at the dark. He kept quiet for long. Later at one point of time, Tamradhvaj kept talking about that fateful night. " All the surroundings stood enveloped by stygian darkness. Fire made its presence felt since the time when the creation was about to commence. Light got converted into fire. That fire was the earthly fire. The fire that remained in the sun and which produced the heat of the sun was just a holy flame. And this fire was fire of lightning indeed. Fire always would seem to have water within. The fire which set the Avanti city ablaze was founded on water too".

Gandhavati asked, "If it would have its base in water, why is then the fire so oppressive? Water is so cool and soothing"!

Tamradhvaj said, "Then learn about the real form of fire! Fire is thousand-footed and rotund like the pitcher. Fire has hundreds and thousands of rays. With the help of these rays, fire draws in water from the seas, rivers, ponds, wells, trees and herbs and life; the more the water is sucked in, the more the fire has the capability of storing it, almost hundred times – so now have you understood why is fire called 'water-retainer'?"

Reba was amazed. Who was she listening to? With whom did Gandhavati sit in discussion? Such a spectacle was familiar to her. Quite familiar. Reba was keen on clearing her confusion by looking into the dark. Had Dhruvaputra really returned? Since long, Gandhavati had such engaging discussions with Dhruvaputra! Since many births, perhaps. Alas Dhruvaputra! How could you forget everything?

Gandhavati asked, "Then? Our words are yet to finish".

Tamradhvaj said, "The sun is golden. For sun only, the earth has such heat, such cold, such rainfall. The sun makes the world warm with its rays, leaves it cold subsequently and floods it with heavy downpour. Rays of the sun are thousand in number, hence fire is thousand-footed".

Gandhavati looked at Tamradhvaj, mesmerised. Her gaze had gone vacant. She seemed to have felt that nothing in this world was meant for exhaustion. Such words could be heard from Dhruvaputra's mouth! How strange, these words were known to Dhruvautra alone! How could this man come to know?

Tamradhvaj said, "Listen Gandhavati, I am yet to finish my words".

Gandhavati in her mind mused, Words are not to be finished, dear friend!

Tamradhvaj said, The sun, fire, cloud, water – all are expansive like the earth itself. It is not possible to know about them in a day or two, even if we talk about the sun, fire and clouds all our life, yet it will remain incomplete. Still I shall say, among the thousand rays of the sun, cold-shedding rays are three hundred, these rays are yellowish, they are famed as Medhya, Bajhya, Hladan, Chandra, so on. And again, the three hundred white rays, shed by the sun bake the earth. These heat-inducing rays are known as Visvabhrit, Kakuv, Shukla etc. With these white rays, the sun nourishes and tends the paternal sphere, the abode of the gods and the earth: the sphere of human beings. As the sunrays slake the thirst on the paternal sphere by shedding water, they nourish the abode of gods with nectar and ply the earth with medicinal care — thus all the spheres are kept warm and taken care of".

Gandhavati mused, "Oh friend, your knowledge is stupendous! Your words, too, will never end all our life as introduction to clouds, fire and sun will never do".

Tamradhvaj said, There's more, Gandhavati! Now, let me tell you about monsoon. With four-hundred different-tinged rays, the sun floods the earth with the rains. Those rain-effecting sunrays are: Bandan, Bandya, Rhitosh, Nutan, Amrit, so on".

Gandhavati expressed her interest, "Where have those rays gone — Bandan, Rhitosh…"?

If that could be known, would these cities like Avanti, Dasharno just be heated thus? During the spring and summer, the sun emits three hundred rays to cause heat. In the monsoon and early autumn, it pours in rains through four hundred rays and during late autumn and winter it showers three hundred rays to make dewdrops and snow fall".

Gandhavati intervened, "Shall I fetch milk for you? Aren't you thirsty"?

"No, please be quiet".

Gandhavati sat, lowering her head. Last evening, the rogue, Uddhav, was letting hell loose in this courtyard by strutting viciously. Both mother and daughter went blanched in fear. Even grandfather was not within himself, he became nonplussed. And today though they assumed, the wicked fellow had not turned up. Instead, someone had come, whose presence was like the clouds in these dry days of drought! How cool and enchanting was the presence of Tamradhvaj! Gandhavati whispered, "You are just like my friend, Dhruvaputra"!

Did it reach the ears of Tamradhvaj?

He said, "Now you tell me about the disappearance of Dhruvaputra".

Gandhavati whispered, "What shall I say, how many times shall I say, I can't narrate anymore, my friend! You must get to hear it from my mother".

Tamradhvaj was watching Gandhavati in an unwavering gaze. Then Reba came forward with a lamp in her hand. She kept the lamp with its holder in between Gandhavati and Tamradhvaj. Gandhavati got to her feet to say, "Maa, please tell him about that full-moon night in Chaitra".

Mother dissuaded her, "If you don't narrate, it will not be complete".

A strange resonance rang clear through the whole of Gandhavati's being. Was he Tamradhvaj or somebody else? She shivered. In her mind she spoke out, Hey Dhruvaputra, in which form have you come here? Gandhavati could see Dhruvaputra in Tamradhvaj. Was it then the astronomer from Dasharno who could bring Dhruvaputra back to her, who had gone strangely missing?

Gandhavati whispered, "Dhruvaputra"!

Tamradhvaj looked on at the sky. In both his eyes, reflections of starlight could be seen. Gandhavati touched Tamradhvaj. Tamradhvaj hung his head low. He turned to look. It was as though the two were getting to know each other, as if they had remained cursed, since long. As if they were oblivious of each other since ages, since numerous eons.

Tamradhvaj asked, "Do you remember the monsoon"?

"Yes, I do".

"Of the clouds"?

"Yes".

"The clump of kadamba trees"?

"Yes".

"Gambhira river? Cane clump"?

"Yes, my friend. Both the eyes of Gandhavati were awash with tears. In the dark, Tamradhvaj stood witness to her silent release of tears"!

THIRTY-ONE

Gandhavati said, "It was Chaitra full moon night and I had gone to the temple of Kamadeva".

"I know it", said Tamradhvaj, "I heard of it".

"That very day, Dhruvaputra had come back from Ujjwain. Maa, you know quite well, please you narrate", Gandhavati asked her mother. In the dark, mother and daughter sat side by side. Tamradhvaj could see their faces in the dim light of the lamp. Gandhavati's eyes seemed to resemble a river. Water glistened in it. Reba's mother's eyes were similar too. But that river had gone devoid of water, owing to severe heat.

Let alone Chaitra Purnima, Dhruvaputra never used to stay outside Gambhira on any full moon night. When the moon used to bob up like a golden platter on the other side of the river, Dhruvaputra had been there. But in the preceding couple of years, he had not returned home on the full moon nights of Ashwin, Kartika, Magh and Phalgun. Uddhavnarayan used to turn up to talk about him. Dhruvaputra used to stay back at the bawdy house only. He was engrossed deep in pleasures and enjoyment. His acquisition of knowledge had gone fruitless. Calumny was doing rounds in the city. Such a man of perversion could not find his parallel in any other person, in the city of Avanti.

Shivnath had brought the news that Uddhav's words were true, the same had been doing rounds in the city. Heaving a sigh, Gandhavati's grandfather had placed his hand on his forehead. Reba and her daughter listened with faces, pale and darkened. They had learnt many a vile thing about Dhruvaputra. Old Parvati used to come to add fuel to the fire, by narrating many fabricated tales. Her words were more piercing than Uddhav's. She used to frequent this house as an emissary of Uddhav. Till now, that messenger had not lost hope. Even this morning, she dropped by.

Sleep had eluded Gandhavati on that night of Shukla Chaturdashi. Her inner self kept assuring that Dhruvaputra would return. He would come to spend the Chaitra full moon night at Gambhira. He would enjoy the rise of the moon at Gambhira. He would again narrate the tale of Udayan and Basavadutta, sitting in the courtyard, inundated with moonbeams that full moon night. He would talk about the river, Reba, the Moloy ranges, the stars, about the land where Canopus, the star, used to spring up on the horizon.

Gandhavati herself knew that sometimes her conjectures came to be true. Whatever she thought, came to happen in reality. Just as today, when she kept looking down the way, all day long. Time and again, she went to the edge of the courtyard to look at the end of the road, she had a hunch that the astronomer from Dasharno, the disciple of Acharya Brishavanu might turn up. If he failed, that wicked royal servant, Uddhavnarayan , would turn up instead. If he came today to abduct her—she would turn morbid in fear. Kidnapping her, Uddhav would force her into a marriage, as per Gandharva rules. Her inner prediction had corresponded with the reality. That day, too, her premonition had come to be true. Dhruvaputra had come back at dawn of the full moon day. He had come back, on foot, from Ujjwain, taking the way, lighted up by the moonshine of Chaturdashi. He had come fleeing, indeed - it struck her lately. At the close of night, when he stepped into the courtyard, the dog, familiar to her, whimpered twice and went quiet. Standing in the dark of the threshold, Gandhavati had seen his dust-laden body. Extraordinarily handsome Dhruvaputra had come back, dusty, soiled. Unkempt hair, untended physique, Gandhavati had even noticed his blue eyes, lined with marks of disgrace. Returning home, he had gone into his own cottage. Yonder stood that hut, with door bolted from outside. Gandhavati used to clean up the room every day. If she failed to do, Reba did.

Gandhavati said, " On Dhruvaputra's return, I went to Kamadeva's temple, it had been pre-fixed, I was chaperoned by old Parvati. Before leaving, I saw through the window that Dhruvaputra was lying on the ground. He was lying prostrate. His bed was at sixes and sevens.

Let him be asleep. That sleep was to compensate for many a sleepless night, who could tell how many? In the afternoon, she came back after her prayers. And she found the door closed likewise. Reba called, she even rapped on the door, a few times. Dhruvaputra did not answer.

And then...He unbolted the door in the evening. Dhruvaputra came out. He sat in the courtyard for long, Gandhavati placed ksheer-biscuit and water before him. Reba boiled the milk. She brought milk in a stone-bowl and kept it there. And a pair of bananas. Dhruvaputra sat speechless. He was in a trance. Reba came to stand before him, and called in a low tone, "Dhruvaputra, you haven't taken anything all day long, you must have been hungry by now. Today is a full-moon day, look the moon has bobbed up, look the moon is up, look there, if you don't eat anything, it would spell harm on the master of the house"!

Then, Dhruvaputra had cracked the ksheer-biscuit for having just a small piece of it. He fell silent again, after drinking water. Very silent. Shivnath then called him from far, "What's wrong with you, Dhruvaputra, why has your golden, glowing complexion burnt into such a tanned one? Be calm".

He sat motionless. Moonbeams slid down his bare body. Long after, he stood up slowly, and got back to his own hut. That cottage, yonder! It stood in the dark.

Tamradhvaj said, "Go Gandhavati and keep the lamp there".

Gandhavati got up with the lamp in her hand. Tamradhvaj cast bewitching glance at the paramour of Dhruvaputra. Gandhavati was walking along with the lamp in her hand. Reba noticed the enchanted eyes of the astronomer from Dasharno. How he kept looking! Oh God! What had it all come to? Reba knew those eyes, indeed. She knew the language of those eyes. Alas Dhruvaputra! Fire and clarified butter were encountering each other, face-to-face! Who knew what would transpire?! Did Tamradhvaj keep Dhruvaputra's whereabouts a secret, even after knowing it full well?

Reba broke the silence, "My daughter is my headache now, my Sugandha seems to burn in eternal fire, she cannot cast her eyes on anyone in this world, save Dhruvaputra"!

Tamradhvaj smiled, "I know, Maa"!

"Uddhavnarayan is so dreadful, do you know what he has done"?

"I know, Maa".

"Who told you"?

Tamradhvaj said, "I know everything, I want to know whatever I do not know, please tell me about Dhruvaputra now"!

"There my daughter is coming back, let her narrate".

Gandhavati returned. She sat beside her mother.

The lamp lit up Dhruvaputra's cottage, dispelling the darkness. Just a lone star, it seemed. When Dhruvaputra had entered his hut, Shivnath commented, "He is afflicted with remorse, let him be left alone, he will come free of this, gradually. There is no other man like him in this city of Avanti, so wise, so pure"!

Shivnath had shared something more with Gandhavati and Reba. "Knowledge is like daytime. And ignorance is like intense night of new moon. Ignorance likes to dominate over knowledge always. Does it succeed? No, it cannot. Dhruvaputra is achieving deliverance. He is coming under the influence of wisdom, bit by bit. None of us has no reason to be anxious at all".

Dhruvaputra stayed back in his room. Night began to intensify. All retired to their room, putting aside all worries. To Gandhavati, the Chaitra full moon looked pale. Devoid of joy. Far off, the foresters and hunters were celebrating joyfully, by sounding kettle-drums and horns. That noise was making way to her ears. Outside, milky moonshine was about to spill over. That light had made foray through the window to the room. Gandhavati could not sleep. In a while, she unbolted the room and went out. She went to stand in front of Dhruvaputra's cottage. And then, turning her head, looking straight through the window, she found him engrossed in meditation. Gandhavati had come back.

Gandhavati said, "After that I had fallen asleep. And my sleep got disrupted abruptly".

"What followed next"? asked Tamradhvaj.

Being awake, Gandhavati had heard the noise of opening the door. However, she was not sure whether she heard the noise on being awake or the noise itself had awakened her from sleep. It might be so, she might have nursed some fear stealthily, at the back of her mind. She sensed that Dhruvaputra was utterly restless, quite unsettled within. Leaving her bed, coming out of the room, Gandhavati had come to sit in the dark of the raised terrace. Then, Dhruvaputra had emerged from his room, unbolting the door. Sitting on the terrace, Gandhavati had looked on in amazement to find Dhruvaputra coming down to the courtyard. He gazed at the northern sky. The cloth covering his body was soiled, an end of which was skimming past the dust on the ground. Oh God! Dhruvaputra was leaving once again! Where was her companion going? To Ujjwain again? Once again to that brothel to see the whore? Had Dhruvaputra gone out of his mind? All the knowledge he acquired proved to be vain! All had gone to ruins. She would not allow him to go to Ujjwain, by any means.

Closing the door noiselessly, Gandhavati began to stalk Dhruvaputra. She would not let his friend leave. City of Ujjwain itself had ruined Dhruvaputra. Crossing the courtyard Gandhavati stepped down on the thoroughfare. Flooding moonbeams had illumined the streets just like daytime. Gandhavati was observing the footsteps which preceded hers. Those imprints were left by Dhruvaputra's feet. Gandhavati could recognize it. Many a time, she had found out Dhruvaputra, tracing those imprints on this dust!

Emerging outside, Gandhavati turned around. That way coursed down to Ujjwain. But none could be seen there. The road had gone straight afar. In the vacant road, Chaitra wind was kicking off dust. How far could he traverse in such a plight? And, Gandhavati had come close to his heels. Had she gone wrong somehow? Gandhavati looked down at the ground. No, Dhruvaputra's steps were not drawn down that way! Turning round, she stretched her gaze to the south-eastern direction. His companion had taken that way for sure! Her heart missed a beat. Yonder, there, at a distance, far-off, the shadow was moving down towards Gambhira river. Dhruvaputra was going away. His scarf had fallen off on the dust. Chaitra wind was flying it away. Gandhavati loped, kicking the dust off.

How strange! That night, not a single street-dog was around. Moonlight and silence were rife instead. Gandhavati controlled her desire of calling out to him from far! Her yell might have awakened the dwellers of the village. And that would be really embarrassing!

Walking, he reached the bank of the Gambhira. So briskly had Dhruvaputra walked! It was beyond Gandhavati to reach him! Though Chaitra wind blew topsy-turvy, the whole body of Gandhavati was clammy in perspiration owing to mounting tension. Almost running to the bend of the river, she saw Dhruvaputra going down into it. Into the water.

The river seemed to have slept that night. Even the moonshine had taken it in its folds to sleep. Gandhavati recalled. One evening, long ago, Dhruvaputra standing amidst moonbeams said to her, pointing to the expanse of the heavens, stars, rivers, meadows: "Sugandha, come try to learn, this is knowledge".

One day he demanded, "Tell me wherein lies the Orion? Can you tell me whether the star, Satavisha, has come to life or not, look yonder, Gandhavati, that's the North Star, Dhruva! While looking steadfast at that star we feel intrigued - did life sprout on earth like dewdrops from that very star? Is man's life the water contained in the stars? I heard that the water from the star, Swati, pours down like pearls in the sea…!"

In an indistinct voice, Gandhavati asked, "Is man really the child of the stars?"

"Exactly so … that is why, the star named Sun, keeps us alive, Gandhavati", said Tamradhvaj! He kept looking at Gandhavati. When Reba had gone away, none could tell.

Gandhavati whispered, "If not ours, his life definitely is the water of the Pole Star"!

"I know that. What happened next"?

What happened?... Gandhavati kept forgetting everything. She was free from worries by being sure that his mate had not gone to Ujjwain. Dhruvaputra had come for ablutions in the Gambhira river. Her grandfather was right. Dhruvaputra was getting free of all sins. He would begin his life anew, being pure again. Gandhavati was standing at the clump of canes. The twisted cane-leaves cast their shadows in brilliant artistic patterns. The moonshine was dripping down on the river from the cane leaves. That year, such drought as this had not been there! The bank of Gambhira was exquisite. The river was full to the brim with water, even during the month of Chaitra. The bend was quite deep. The moon kept floating on the river-water.

Going down into the river, Dhruvaputra kept moving towards the bend of the river. Once or twice, men got drowned in this unfathomable end of the river. Gandhavati guessed that Dhruvaputra had become perplexed. She saw Dhruvaputra going down into the sharp edge of the river. Was he sinking? Yes, yonder, he was. There he was rising up again! Gandhavati had stepped down into the river. Crossing the feet-deep, scanty water, she had run straight along the sand-bed, to the parallel of the deep bend of the river. Throwing her two hands above her head, she called out aloud, "You have gone out of your wits. Come up, Dhruvaputra, oh my friend, what are you going to do"?

Gandhavati was quaking in fear. Wasn't he bewildered? He had come to die. He had come to Gambhira to commit suicide! She sobbed out then, "Come up, Dhruvaputra, this river, this sky, moonshine, all these are knowledge in itself, you, yourself, have taught that. Dhruvaputra, please come up, let's return to the city"!

"Could he hear that"? Tamradhvaj asked.

"I do not know", Gandhavati said in an inaudible voice.

"And then what had happened"?

"He had come up, yes, he had. Just within the reach of a few arm-lengths, he stood on the sand-bed. From all over his body, moonbeams kept dripping like water. How dazzling those eyes were! I had never seen such wonder in anyone's eyes in my lifetime"!

Tamradhvaj got to his feet, "So I have heard you".

"But where is he"? Gandhavati, too, rose up, slowly.

Tamradhvaj replied, "I had no idea of this episode".

"The rest I could not get to say, as yet".

"So he had gone away, right"?

"Yes, he had walked past my side, on the bank of the river, got up, and then took to the north-eastern direction. I thought, he would be back home. But, in that very drenched attire he went walking, all alone. I failed to call out".

"Why"?

Gandhavati answered, "He seemed so strange, so unknown to me".

"Really"?

"Yes, it was someone else but Dhruvaputra, it seemed. Why couldn't I stand in front, blocking his way, that day"?

Tamradhvaj said, "The moon is up, let me push off".

"How long shall I wait again"?

"Why"?

"You have to come here with Dhruvaputra's whereabouts, once done with your calculations, won't you"?

"Yes, I will." With that promise Tamradhvaj set out, walking. He went beyond the dark courtyard.

THIRTY-TWO

Subhag Dutta said, "Let the city be ruined, let the country go to the dogs"!

"If Lord Mahakaal so wills, it will definitely happen so", answered the Chief Priest.

"I shall set out on trade but before that I want the throne to be free of all impediments".

"But the tycoon does not covet the throne", the Chief Priest smirked.

"If the King loses the throne that woman shall lose all her pride, I must take Devadutta, the courtesan, along"!

"Be calm, you are the richest man of this country, how can you be so perturbed by the nonchalance of a petty whore"?

Subhag Dutta said, "My supremacy has lost all its honour. She has given away the jewelleries, I had presented her, to an ugly-looking slut named, Chaturika"!

The Chief Priest asked, "Did you inquire into it"?

"Yes, I did".

"Is it then Lord Mahakaal's will"?

Subhag Dutta stamped his feet on the stony floor. His whole body was convulsing in anger. He had appointed Uddhav, the courtier, to fetch him the news. Then, he went to Devadutta's residence himself. He had just called for Chaturika there. Chaturika admitted the authenticity of the news and bent her forehead down on the merchant's feet, at the behest of Uddhav. Devadutta stayed silent. So reticent, that her breath, too, seemed to have stopped. Even her eyelids were not batting. What a pride! She did not answer any query, with care. Only if the King got dethroned, that pride might have a fall. How could she dare say that, she did not want to accept anything from anyone save the King? She was thus taught by her mother, Rasamanjari.

The Chief Priest said, "So would the King lose his throne for a whore"?

"Yes, he will lose it, then how do I stand supreme"?

"Yet, you are just a woman! If the merchant so desires, he can get as many women as he wants, and is woman a thing to be got with much effort in Avanti"?

"The King is just a rapist. He has outraged the chastity of a devadasi inside the temple and he must lose his throne for such a crime! Devadutta, the courtesan, is waiting for the King while the King goes to enjoy Lalita, the devadasi"!

"Will the throne be lost for an insignificant devadasi"? asked the Chief Priest.

"Yes, it will be lost, it will be, it will surely be".

"And won't it add much importance to a futile woman, a woman for enjoyment, won't it"?

Subhag Dutta trailed off to an abrupt silence, and threw an astonished gaze at the Chief Priest. What does the sly Brahmin mean? Then is he in secret truce with the King? The merchant stopped. He could not decide what to say. Then the Chief Priest smiled and said, "Women are the objects of pleasure, of enjoyment. She might be a Shudra woman or a Brahmin one, whatever- I am in no two opinions on it, do you have any"?

"No, but I am telling a different thing altogether".

"Take Devadutta away to your residence by coercion and press her".

"How can that be possible, she is the Chief Prostitute, paramour of the King"!

The Chief Priest smiled blunt, reddish, toothless gums could be seen and he said, "But the King is not fond of her, the King runs after the devadasis, robbing them of their modesty. He is of low, unrefined taste, even the queen is not fond of the King, I know this well, and aren't you even aware of the infamy, spreading like wildfire across the city? Both the King and the queen are objects of calumny now, in this city"!

"Does the Army-Commander know"?

"Bikram? Why won't he know"?

Does he know about the rumours regarding the queen Bhanumati? "The relation between Bikram and Bhanumati is no more a secret now"!

"So, what of that to him? He is a male - no stigma will tarnish his name".

The business magnate said, "But the King will not relinquish his throne for this reason"!

The old Priest said, "Drought is rife in this country, crops are no more, immoral practices are the order of the day and if such things be on the rise, if the city is torn with more immorality, more anarchy, the King will stand perplexed".

"What does Bikram say"? The Merchant asked.

"You talk to him. Initially he was hesitant about spreading rumours against the queen but I pointed out that our aim is nothing but the throne. In order to make the way to the throne, smooth and unencumbered, we would have to drag the queen down to the streets! And again, who is the queen Bhanumati to him? His brother's wife, and of course, a woman of no character. Otherwise, why would she enter into a relationship with her brother-in-law, leaving her husband aside? After all, she is a woman, it hardly matters whether a woman is a queen or a maidservant"!

The merchant looked on at the old Priest, dumbfounded. The scheme which was his brainchild, was being taken up for a proper shape by the Chief Priest himself. But would the courtesan, Devadutta, come into his possession, once the King lost his throne? Another misgiving was assailing him too, would the stigmata of both the King and the queen widen the Army-Commander's chance to attain the throne? And how much would it be?

The old priest seemed to guess the words he had at the back of his mind. He suggested, "The country is being torn by inveterate sins. And that is happening due to the King's misdeeds, go and set the Shudra ghetto ablaze".

"What are you saying"?

Yes, these are to be done as well! Only a juicy tale of illicit relationships will not make the people rise up in arms and the strength of the army is the Shudras"!

The merchant said, "What wrong have they done"?

"Do you want the Chief Prostitute to come in your possession"?

"Yes, I do".

"Why not change the King of Avanti then?

The merchant remarked, "Why are you being repetitive? It will make way to the King's ears. It may reach any sneaky ears, even the walls have ears"!

Old man smiled, "I had a long discussion with the Army-Commander".

"Yet, Bhartrihari is still the King of this land"!

"Damn it"! The Priest was annoyed. "You only came to advise that Avanti should be consigned to flames, it should go to the dogs! Send your servant to set it on fire. With no ponds having water in them, the merchant and the Army-Commander will stand beside the homeless Shudras and nothing will be there to fear".

The merchant felt that this old man was a great conspirator. He would have been rightly placed in the King's court instead of the Mahakaal temple. The tycoon was moving from one place to the other in utter perplexity, being dejected, insulted, thrown into anxiety by the indifference of the whore! He came burning in rage and now all the blaze of his anger seemed to have snuffed out, so abruptly! The Shudra locality leaped up before his eyes. Would just a few sparks of fire raze the houses to the ground of such an organized habitation?! No water was there in the lakes! Water in the wells was being exhausted soon. How would they extinguish the fire? Men and beasts – all would die together!

The Chief Priest said, "The number of people living will largely supersede those who will die".

"Why take the lives off, for no reason at all"?

The wizened man was irritated, "Why will it be for no reason? This is for making the King Bhartrihari lose his throne"!

The tycoon seemed to feel feeble. Was he trembling? What had happened to him! Devadutta's rejection seemed to have ruined his mental strength. He was left with no confidence at all. He muttered, "But why for no fault of their own, so many people will be rendered homeless, a few of whom will die even"?

The Chief Priest said in a nonchalant tone, "Not just human beings, as there is no sin in slaying animals, there is none in case of the Shudras too--all means are just fine in a bid to occupy the throne! Set the fire stealthily, send your men in pitch-darkness, as the King came in the form of Mahakaal to enjoy a devadasi, your men will assume the same form too to set the Shudra locale on fire, the cries of the dwellers of Shudra ghetto will rent the air of the city, the subjects will pay for the sin of the King, and King Bhartrihari will be left nonplussed".

By then, the tycoon was getting back his confidence. The temperature of his body was going up to reach the normal level soon. Yes, such was expected to happen. Let the jackals pace up and down the thoroughfares of the city during daytime, let vultures pounce, let plunders and pillage be the order of the day, let the knaves abduct the wife and daughter of the family men, let the royal employee take bribes for torturing the innocent people, let the Shudra ghetto be consigned to flames, and then the King's dethronement would be hastened, and as the King would be dislodged, Devadutta would be his, all her pride would be thoroughly pulverized. The merchant's breath became hot. He became inwardly desirous. Before his eyes, the body of Devadutta grew distinct. The breasts, the buttocks, well-shaped arms, the upper and lower lips... He let out a subdued whimper, "Fire will rage"!

The Priest was unmoved, "That will surely happen! I had a talk with Bikram, the Army-Commander, let the fire break out, the next responsibility is mine — there will be an oracle in the city".

The magnate asked, "Where is that devadasi now? After being raped by the King?"

"She now stays in the dark".

"Why in the dark"?

"She is desecrated, I despise an unholy menstruating woman".

Subhag Dutta inquired, "Isn't she pregnant"?

"No, but why"?

"The King enjoyed her all night. Then why hasn't she been impregnated?"

The Priest's eyes shone, "Would it be fine if it so happened"?

"Of course, if it would be so, we could have dragged the woman carrying child in her womb to the streets. Where would the King's honour stand, where would King Bhartrihari then put his shame"?

The Chief Priest said, "Why didn't you tell me this before"?

"What shall I say, I was sure that it would naturally happen, once the signs of her pregnancy would stand prominent, she would be taken before public eyes. But what's going on instead"?

The Chief Priest smiled, "You are talking like a child! It proves that the King lacks in such strength, an impotent King is sitting on the throne of Ujjwain, and if the King is devoid of the power of procreating his own children, why will crops grow, why will it rain again? As many times the queen will be impregnated, the country will be blessed with resources in abundance! There will be no more rainfall here in this land, till this King rules".

"Who told you this"?

"All are written in the scriptures".

"But did the King truly enjoy that 'dasi' of yours"?

"Not mine, she is the serving-maid of Lord Mahakaal"!

The tycoon said, "An impotent King has no right to be on the throne".

"No,he has no right".

"The city knows the fact that the King is impotent, the queen is sitting childless".

The Chief Priest said, "The city knows that the queen is powerless to give birth to children"!

"So, this is proved by Lalita that the King is impotent"!

"Yes, but why are you saying this, again and again"? The Chief Priest was irked.

"Won't it reach the ears of the courtesan, I mean, Devadutta"?

"If the whore comes to the shrine to seek my blessings, I shall let her know myself".

The merchant got excited. Why will Rasamanjari's daughter be enamoured of an impotent male? Oh Brahmin, could you please tell me how to make these words reach Devadutta's ears"?

The Chief Priest kept mum. The agitated magnate was pacing up and down the not-so-spacious room. The priest was an excessively cunning man. The merchant did not get to know the priest so well before. Now he felt like staying knelt down before him, all the time. The Priest took a little time to speak out, "The ornaments you had given Devadutta as a present have been given to the slut, Chaturika, for good"!

"Yes, Chaturika herself had handed it to Uddhavnarayan"!

"Or, was it stolen by Uddhav"?

"May be so".

"Only Chaturika can make the King's misdeed reach Devadutta's ears"!

Wonderful! The merchant seemed to chance upon a solution! As if, once Chaturika put the word into Devadutta's ears, she would be his. The merchant's age was really a matter of concern, at this age awaiting something to happen would be risky. Youth was about to decline and the period of his enjoyment too was getting circumscribed. Hence, failures were simply intolerable. He got up to say, "Let me go".

"Go you must, but if Devadutta asks for the proof of the King's impotence, then"?

"The proof is Lalitadasi, indeed"!

"You, yourself, has expressed doubt as to whether there is any proof of the King's outraging her modesty, and if the same query is raised by Devadutta"!

The tycoon smiled, "The King's necklace is on Lalita's neck"!

"But sundry reasons may be there behind it".

"Then"! Subhag Dutta's heart missed a beat or two.

"Are you thinking that Devadutta will come in your possession, just when she learns that the King is powerless to father any children"? The Chief Priest hurled a query.

"Yes, she will come, would any woman love to go to an impotent male"?

The Chief Priest smiled, "Devadutta's love is one-sided, King Bhartrihari is devoid of the power of lovemaking, he never comes near Devadutta as he will never be able to reciprocate. He wanted to check his strength by having sexual intercourse with a devadasi"!

"Then won't Chaturika inform her"?

"Yes, she will, but that will not bring you much profit, but well, if the fact of the King being an impotent spreads like wildfire, our way to success will be smoother".

"Then, what am I supposed to do"?

"Go, set the Shudras on fire, go, set them on fire! No other way than setting fire is there, go set the Shudra locality ablaze, let it be razed to dust by conflagration, let wails of loss and pain reverberate the city"…!

Loud lamentations kept hounding Subhag Dutta! He stepped forward!

THIRTY-THREE

Chaturika had come to the Chief Prostitute, Devadutta's house, as an emissary of Uddhav. Chaturika herself was fond of Devadutta who used to honour her as her friend. This house would always welcome her, but there was certainly a difference between today's visit and that of other times. She had come this day to break the heart of Devadutta, to scrounge the secret of her mind. She had to make Devadutta fall for the merchant, by praising him to the skies. Subhag Dutta was getting impatient. He was not willing to bide longer too. Though he was rich, he was very sad too! The price of a woman superseded even his riches. How strange! He failed to win the heart of Devadutta even after presenting her with diamond and other precious jewels!

There was no sentry at the entrance of the house. Very often, it stood unguarded. The pimp, that scoundrel, hailed from Saurashtra, dangling a scimitar from his waist, he used to display much hauteur! A man with a thick, bushy moustache, bloodshot eyes and almost always dead-drunk! The man would have been chucked out of service if his employer had been someone apart from Devadutta! She was weak on the men hailing from Saurashtra! Sometimes Chaturika thought that the man was not from Saurashtra, just to carve a niche in Devadutta's heart he had just proclaimed so. Perhaps, he was from some village in the vicinity. But again, how was that possible? At times, he used to sit there in the garden, crooning numbers, in a highly inebriated state. And those numbers were not from this part of the country. How unfamiliar was their tune, even the beats! If not from Saurashtra, wherefrom would he get that?

Entering the house, Chaturika found it to be very quiet. Usually it remained silent, yet the strum of veena-playing or the noise of the anklets used to be wafted to the ears. And the sound of hailing someone! Though all these were not regular affairs, today seemed to be a bit different! If the sentry had been there at the entrance, then too she could have felt so. In fact, since a few days, she was marking an overall change around her! The city was getting strangely quiet. The city-dwellers had no joy in their hearts. Uddhav was saying that it did not rain since long! Oh yes, right! Two monsoons had gone dry, without any downpour! Even after that, many days had sped by, but not a trace of rain dropped! No commotion seized the red-light locale as people were sad for the monsoon passing by, without rain. Joylessness was writ large on the face of the city and this house was no exception!

This was a path, strewn with gravel, flanked by garden on both sides. Was this garden so graceless ever? This path had gone straight into the house. Chaturika went a bit ahead to come to a halt. Was this that same arbour, where the courtesan, Rasamanjari, used to rock in a swing, King Gandharvasen used to help her oscillate, while the peacock and peahen used to caper around, the gander and the goose used to crane their necks to look at Rasamanjari, and the cuckoo went on cooing through the darkness around the Ashok tree. This garden had plethora of various flowers, trees, herbs and creepers. The trees were almost without leaves, during winter their leaves were shed and till now they were wilting. Yet there was no hint of any new foliage of Springtime! Blossoms were there on the Ashok tree, no doubt, but their colours were yet to be deep and pronounced! Chaitra Purnima had come to stay, though the Spring, the King of all seasons, was not in full bloom. While Uddhav swooned off at midnight, Chaturika opened the window to peep at the moon! How luminous it was! But who would ever tell by glancing at this garden that the Spring had ever been here to make its presence felt! Chaturika, to her utter dismay, noticed that the creeper had mostly got singed to look coppery, with just a part of it left yellow! She remembered, one day Devadutta had told her the names of all the creepers, all the trees, and she got her acquainted with all of them, while strolling in the garden. Her mother had taught her everything. Chaturika had forgotten all the names. If she could remember, she would have been the Chief Prostitute, Uddhav would then comply with her commands. Then, Chaturika would turn to the tycoon for proper attention. If not real love, she could have at least mesmerized him with dissimulation of love! The prostitutes were in the wont of practising all these wiles. But Devadutta had an unwavering determination… Why couldn't you make a deceitful affectation of love? The magnate would have just been won over by that. Potful of gold-coins, jewels and gems, diamond, precious stones — all would have made way into your house!

Chaturika remembered that she, too, had seen peacock in this garden. It was then, the blue-eyed, young Dhruvaputra had come over. At times, Devadutta would come down to the garden taking her along, she used to play veena, sitting beneath the Tamal tree. Dhruvaputra kept looking at her, in amazement, and, the peacock and the peahen, yonder at a distance, kept locking their lips with each other. Chaturika had not received their death-news, however. Then did Bandhul, that wretched sentry from Saurashtra, chop them off and eat up? Didn't Devadutta demand to know? Didn't Devadutta tend the garden? Could such lacklustre garden, the creepers and shrubs sans flowers, trees and plants co-exist in Devadutta's house? Wasn't she the best-ever beauty of the city of Ujjwain? The tycoons and rich men spent sleepless nights for her!

Devadutta seemed to have lost all affinity to this house. Which varieties of birds were there in this garden? Parrot, Chandana, Nightingale, Mynah, the male and female red-legged bartavelle, the male, female varieties of popinjay — all had been there! Where had all these gone? Only a pitch-black raven was there! It was watching Chaturika, perching alone on the branch of the pomegranate tree, with crimson eyes! Precisely like the man of Saurashtra! That man had a semi-dark complexion. In the alien land of the Christians and Jews, there had been such men with pitch-black complexion like dark night, like the black raven. Was this raven Bandhul then? Was he guarding this house assuming the form of a raven? Not impossible at all. In those lands, conjurors were there. They were adept in transforming a man into a crow. But one doubt still remained. The man was not that bad, why would he have to be changed into a raven, only because of the rage of the magician? Again, where was a magician in Ujjwain? He had never come to her place!

Chaturika made a noise to shoo away, "Go away! Get lost, thou inauspicious crow"!

The raven was very solemn. Dark of his complexion pervaded the garden. Chaturika was saddened. What sort of Spring was this? Where was the cuckoo who used to dwell on the Ashok tree and keep calling his distant mate, through all the twelve months of a year?

Chaturika knew that Uddhav was in great trouble. As you sow, so you would reap! God is there! And as God exists, Uddhav had been caught for snatching off such loads of ornaments! That Sessions-Judge had snatched off all the jewelleries from her by force, and had gifted it to a rustic girl! Her name was Gandhavati. That girl's grandfather, out of fear, came up to the merchant with all the ornaments and the latter, in turn, could recognize each of them! She was now guiding that Sessions-Judge. She had promised him to make Devadutta agree. If she succeeded, Uddhav would arrange for her redemption from this land of sin. Chaturika was sure that Uddhav's words were not true. He would never understand anything save his selfish interests. Yet, hope must be retained. If required, she would agree Devadutta to talk to the magnate. She would prefer to work as a maidservant at the merchant's house. She would serve Devadutta. She sought liberation from the clutch of Uddhav by any means!

How panic-stricken Uddhav had been! Day one: he came to torture her! Why didn't Chaturika name the person who had given her the ornaments? If any harm would inflict on him, he would not spare Chaturika. Accusing her of stealing Devadutta's ornaments, he would shove her to death, by immersing her in the river

Shipra, with a stone tied around her neck. However, Uddhav had become a bit calmer now. Chaturika was, in fact, the emissary of the tycoon through Uddhav. Uddhav did not have the courage to reach Devadutta the proposal of the merchant. Uddhav knew full well that if it made way to the King's ears, he would have to suffer a demotion. Didn't Uddhav know that the Chief Prostitute was bound to entertain the King only? If anyone would desire to cause an exception, wouldn't he flout the very edicts of the King? Chaturika again made the sibilant noise. The raven feigned not to hear, the raven was silent, very grave! Perhaps, the cuckoo had left the nest in fear of that raven!

The Champak, Sandalwood, Mango, Dates, Tamal, Kadamba, pomegranates — all the trees of the garden seemed to stand devoid of shades. The trees seemed to suffer laboured breathing, like the poor who went without rice! No hint of mango-buds was there! Just a few years back, she found the air redolent with the sweet scent of mango-buds. Spring was so abundant! A few names of the creepers which Devadutta told her the other day surfaced in Chaturika's memory but she could neither recognize the creepers nor the trees by name! She knew the grapevine, but where was it? It could not be found at all. She recalled, on a day of Spring, in the year before last, Devadutta plucked grapes from the vine, creeping over the Tamal tree, and kept handing them to Dhruvaputra! He was so handsome! If Devadutta was enamoured of the King only, then why did she grow restive at the mention of that youth? A woman's mind, after all! Chaturika heaved a long sigh. The Atashi bush seemed to be trampled by someone! Alas! Suddenly, Chaturika's heart grew heavy for that fair-complexioned man, for his pair of blue eyes, his charming glance, his amazing voice – alas, Dhruvaputra! Did you know that Spring had bidden adieux to Ujjwain?

Devadutta sat quiet, looking straight at golden peak of the Mahakaal temple. Chaturika called her, standing at the threshold, "I have come, my friend".

Without turning to her, Devadutta answered, "Please come in, Chaturika"!

Chaturika noticed that her friend's out-stretched feet showed no mark of alakta, her hairs stood unkempt, dishevelled, her attires were soiled, flick of colour was absent. She sat beside her. Her friend's countenance seemingly displayed the signs of a sleepless night. But Devadutta was not that sort of whore who had to entertain her guests all through the night. Who had come to her place? The King? But she had no idea about it. The Army-Commander? He would not come.

Chaturika asked, "Has my friend spent a sleepless night"?

"Yes, how painful such sleeplessness is"!

"Who had come"?

"Who would come"? Devadutta stretched her gaze at the sky.

"Why, the tycoon, who sits up sleepless for you and is eager on bestowing everything upon you"!

"If he wants to give, let him do. You will come to take it off".

Friend, I shall be undone in the same way again! Uddhav never brooks my possession of anything, he is my annihilator, he keeps vigil on me like the tame crow of Lord Yamah"!

Devadutta turned to her and said, "What would you do then?"

"What shall I do"?

"Where would you keep your possessions"?

"What do I have"?

"Whatever I shall give"!

Chaturika giggled, "It will be kept in the custody of Uddhav"!

"If I gift you all – this house, whatever I have earned so far"?

"Why will you give"? Chaturika grew panicky.

"Why? My wish. Handing everything to you, I shall be a beggar, a pauper"!

"Where will you go? You are the apple of the tycoon's eye, why will you be a beggar"? Chaturika blurted.

"Shut up"! Devadutta threw a fiery glance at Chaturika. "Are you his messenger"?

"What do you say, my friend? Then I must leave".

"No, why will you go? You should never utter the name of that old man, he has robbed me of my sleep by his sin, how fierce he is, he has driven away Dhruvaputra from this city. Does the city belong to that merchant"?

Chaturika answered, "Everything belongs to the rich indeed"!

"The very name of the person leaves the whole being profaned somehow"!

Chaturika made out that the merchant's matter would not hold water. If she praised the tycoon, she would be taken as a suspect by Devadutta. Oh! Uddhav had really trusted her with an uphill task! If she failed to carry it out, she would surely be ruined! Twirling the corner of his scarf, she said in a subdued voice, "Scandal of another person is now the talk of the town"!

"Who is he"? Devadutta started.

"Don't you know, my dear friend? Don't you know anything about the King"?

Devadutta heaved a sigh to say, "Let it be left at that, the King should not be vilified".

"Why will we vilify him? Haven't you heard about the devadasi? I am sure, you have".

"Then why do you bring up the matter again"?

"Do you know, my friend, that the King is impotent"? Saying so, Chaturika moved on. She could feel, that this was the best possible way to get the work done! A great job will be done if Devadutta would lose interest in the King! Alas! What a task she is assigned with! It would have been better if Chaturika would learn the art of arranging flowers or veena-playing from Devadutta instead"!

Devadutta said, So Chaturika, what have you come to talk about? Won't you practice dance"?

Chaturika said, "Dear friend, are you in a joyful mood now to ask for that"?

"Then keep quiet".

"I am keeping quiet but don't you know the fact about the King? Aren't you the King's favourite courtesan as your mother was"?

Devadutta kept measuring Chaturika with suspicious eyes and then asked, "Has your Uddhav sent you here"?

"Uddhav is not mine. He is an out-and-out villain"!

"Then tell me who has sent you? You have surely come as a messenger of the tycoon, otherwise, why are you talking ill of the King and praising the merchant instead? A King is just a King, howsoever his nature is; vilifying him will leave one accursed to lose his tongue. Tell me, Chaturika, tell me the truth"!

Chaturika was breaking down, from within. She could not control herself anymore. Chaturika was overly intelligent, she had made out the secret motive from the expression on her face! Chaturika cried out, "Oh my friend, Uddhav, that vile bloke does not allow me to stay calm".

Devadutta said, "A panic-ridden ambience is here all around, I have never witnessed such ever before. Tell Uddhav that it will need some time, ask for more time, let me wait, if he returns"!

"Who, who are you talking of"?

"Why, Dhruvaputra"!

"Then the King? You are the King's love, aren't you"?

In order to save myself from the tycoon, the King is just a refuge! Chaturika, a woman has to have recourse to sundry ruses to avoid a wicked man's clutch — I love Dhruvaputra, who has gone missing, I am awaiting him".

Chaturika's glance had astonishment writ large on it as she looked on at Devadutta. Was this a trick too, by which a woman would protect herself? The King's stigma was doing rounds now, by the spread of mouth! The King had committed sin! He had outraged the modesty of a devadasi in the precincts of the Mahakaal temple. Only for such a sin of the King, the land of Avanti had been subject to long periods of drought! No harvest resulted. All the seven lakes ran high and dry, sans water! The Spring had not manifested itself. The flowers did not bloom. The knaves were growing powerful with each passing day. At such a time, it was even a sin to express one's love for the King! Was she, therefore, referring to Dhruvaputra? Whatever might Devadutta say, 'talking ill of the King is an unpardonable sin', she now came to know in her heart of hearts that the King was now fit to be talked ill of! Wouldn't now this ill-speak cause the tongue of the speaker to fall off? But how would Devadutta keep the merchant at an arm's length by referring to Dhruvaputra? He had banished Dhruvaputra to take Devadutta in his possession. If he heard now that she was waiting for Dhruvaputra, won't it be enough to raise hell?

It was as though, Devadutta could fathom the goings-on in Chaturika's mind, she asked, "So you are not convinced as yet"?

"But you never said this before"!

"Yes, I did, you could not make out".

Chaturika blabbed out, My friend, the tycoon is mad for you, and he is the richest man of this city, loads of gems and jewels are there in his house. If he now comes to know that you are waiting for his protégé, it will be utter ruin"!

"Who is the protégé of whom"?

"Dhruvaputra had been here in this city owing to the merchant's kindness".

"His father was the merchant's bosom friend, the two had gone on trade-tours together, Dhruvaputra has legitimate claim on the merchant's treasures and wealth".

"Who told you, he himself"? Chaturika asked.

"No, I found out. The merchant is not that powerful to offer shelter to Dhruvaputra, this large universe is his refuge"!

Chaturika watched, the eyes of Devadutta glistened with tears. Did she feel like crying as the matter of Dhruvaputra surfaced? Was Devadutta really waiting for him or cooking up a tale just to hit the tycoon where it hurt him the most? Devadutta sat silently, lowering her head. Chaturika's head too hung low on her bosom, it seemed. Chaturika let out a sigh, Oh Lord Mahakaal! How helpless are the humans! Though rich, the tycoon was losing the battle to a man, once sheltered by him! Almost a landless person, who had not a single farthing on him!

Chaturika asked, "What shall I tell Uddhav"?

"You must tell him about Dhruvaputra, failing whose return no vow will be fulfilled"!

"How dreadful you sound, if it reaches the merchant's ears, hell will be let loose on earth"!

"Lord Mahakaal is there"! Devadutta uttered in a feeble voice.

Chaturika said, "I am not in it, if the merchant gets to know about Dhruvaputra from me, he will turn red in anger. So, it's better to say whatever you like and if possible keep Dhruvaputra's affair a secret"!

"Why"?

"Just to save the rich man's pride"!

Devadutta went on mulling over. But she had no soft corner for the rich merchant, rather she nursed a secret hatred. She must deal a blow to the merchant! No, she would not care a fig for saving his honour!

THIRTY-FOUR

Chaitra Purnima had come at the beginning of the month of Baisakh. Just after a few days, in the deep dark of the new moon night, conflagration broke out at the Shudra ghetto. The fire lapped up the thatched huts in an instant. Dry trees and bushes also got burnt up by the contiguity of the flames. The city sky was rent with cries of pain and of mourning. The greedy tongues of the flame seemed to touch the sky. Even the sky seemed to catch fire. Since long, the sky that stretched over the city of Avanti had gone waterless, dry! Fire had set it ablaze too.

There was no way to extinguish the fire. Where was water? The fluttering flames kept lolling threateningly, and at last, snuffed out on their own accord. Amidst such devastating fire, those who could manage to let go of their domestic animals like hen, pig, donkey, buffalo, lamb so on, did so in the dark. They escaped for life. Some could survive the fire, some succumbed to it. They got burnt in fire. A handful of humans too died. An old lady, unable to move, burnt into coal-like ashes. Old Parashar heard her loud wails. But none could move forward.

Such fire was never witnessed by anyone before. Fire seemed to leap up in all the rooms, together. The Shudra locality was almost in deep sleep. It was a lunar day of Krishna Navami! On the eastern sky, the moon had just bobbed up, red as fire.

At the wee hours of dawn came the tycoon. Close behind him came the Army Commander, riding a horse. It was pre-planned. All the people sat beside the Ratnakar Lake to lament. At a distance,everything kept smouldering. On the branches of the silk-cotton tree, fire kept dancing. Fire trickled drop by drop, on the burnt grass-blades. All around, the smell of fire pervaded.

The hurtling noise of the merchant's chariot announced his arrival. Standing on the carriage in the dark of the wee hours of dawn, the merchant let out a loud call, "Hey Utanka, go and find out the cause behind this conflagration"!

In the darkness, the whip in the hand of Utanka went cutting the air with swishing noise. Through the light of the smouldering flames, in the dying moonshine, the merchant was seen to descend from his carriage. On seeing him, hundreds of people of the Shudra ghetto cried out, "Utanka, Utanka has come. Oh Lord! Not a drop of water is there to douse the flames".

The merchant said, "Oh! The fire was such devastating that it could be seen from even hundreds of yards off"!

Someone said, crying, "Such has never happened in my life"!

"Then why did it happen now"?

"Oh Lord! I do not know who has survived and who hasn't. So many people have died! We are rendered beggars and all our belongings are eaten up by fire"!

"Why did it happen"?

"Someone had come to set us on fire. These words reached the merchant's ears in the dark. With such words doing rounds, the merchant became wary. He asked, "Who is saying so"?

No answer came from them. No answer meant that the person who uttered it, got alert. This alertness certified that he had seen or learnt something, which he feared to express. The merchant asked, "Parashar, where is Parashar"?

"I am here in the dark".

"Parashar, why did the fire break out"?

"I do not know, my Lord"!

"Did the fire bolt down from the sky"?

"No idea, my Lord"!

Someone quipped in the dark, "It has really descended from the sky"!

It was the same voice, which commented on setting the fire by someone. The merchant had a feel that Utanka, perhaps, could not hide himself from being spotted by someone. If it be so, that man would immediately be identified. So many men were there in the dark. All were talking aloud, lamenting! The burnt night was abuzz with the drone of men. How could that man be identified separately from this throng? The merchant demanded, "Who is speaking? Come forward".

None came to the front. The merchant, too, went silent. Waiting was the need of the hour. The word might not surface anymore. The Army-Commander, Kumar Bikram, was coming in. From tomorrow morning, rice and food would be given in charity! Then aid would have to be proffered. Along with that, the matter of the fire hitting down from the sky, too, would have to be given wings! It would spread like wildfire, all by itself.

Old Parashar said, "I had to witness it, standing here! What a devastating fire! Water from the tube-well had been taken in pitchers and poured on the flames but it evaporated as smoke, to our utter dismay. Oh Lord, how and why did it happen even after we all are devoted to you"?!

The merchant pressed his lips with teeth. Again, the doubt was surfacing. Did someone get to see Utanka? Utanka was silent but his presence itself was frightful, no doubt! What utter ruin! The tycoon shouted, "Utanka! Hey Utanka! Have thou fallen asleep again? Utanka had been in sleep since the evening, he does not want to come out in the dark by night, he says his vision gets feeble in the dark".

"Whoever doesn't see less in the dark"? An answer cut across the hum.

The merchant said, "I had seen from my window that the sky had gone crimson, and then only I could sense that you are on fire. I sent the maidservant to call Utanka, Utanka dillydallied in waking up. I know, he is afraid of the dark of the night"!

Someone chipped in, "All are afraid save the nocturnal creatures"!

The merchant went on, "What a deadly fire it was! The Army-Commander is coming, I sent him with this terrible news, but Utanka perhaps has fallen asleep again, Utanka, where are you? Where? Please come here".

"Let it be so, if he sleeps, let him continue with it, the very sight of him sends shudder in the body", old Parashar said.

"Let Utanka be there on the chariot, once the night is over, Utanka will lend his hands. Now tell me, how did the fire break out"?

The darkness was silent, the burnt smell hung heavy in the air. The west wind of Baisakh was driving the burnt odour towards the east. The red of the moon had now turned silver. The stars in the sky had disappeared from the vision because of the wisps of smoke, dust and wails of lamentation. Now, everything bobbed up to vision. Male, female, children, old men – all sat around the pond. But in the middle a deep, fathomless crater stood. It could easily be perceived that the lake was devoid of water as there was no shadow of stars and planets in the lake or that of the moon, which used to float on the water-surface all night. The darkness inside the pond seemed standstill, like burnt ashes. All were waiting for the night to come to an end. If the night did not come to a close, it would not be possible to approach that fire-pit. Now all was burning like the funeral-pyre in a crematorium.

The tycoon said, "I could not stay back anymore, I am neither your protector, nor the King of this land, but I was being afflicted within, your face popped up before my eyes, Parashar! Look the Army-Commander is coming, you are his soldiers"!

Someone observed, "We never light up lamp in our dwellings, my Lord, we do all our work under the moonshine, if any, lest we all finish our domestic chores in daylight. Not a trace of fire is there in our huts. So, how will fire break out if someone doesn't ignite?"

"Who can tell who lit it up"? Parashar reprimanded.

The tycoon said, "This fire might break out on its own even".

"Yes, yes, it can happen so". Old Parashar seemed to have got a way-out, I had seen it there in the jungle on the lap of the hills of Moloy of Southern Country, how fire broke out on its own accord".

"But my lord, the room in which the conflagration first set in, was one uninhabited by any human, lambs stayed in there instead. It is not possible for the lambs to light a fire! They are inferior creatures, after all".

The merchant observed that he, who was speaking, was firm on his point, he did not want to budge an inch from it. That was a pointer to his being cognizant of Utanka or some other miscreant, for that matter. But the spreading of fire on its own accord was to be made a case in point! Someone broke into wail there, at a distance! Now in the moonshine, the man standing in front, could be seen. He noticed old Parashar, casting a frightened glance at him, burying his face in the knees, sitting on the ground. Why wasn't the Army-Commander coming in yet? Once he would be here, they would all pray for provisions and be certain of its supply rather than discussing the mode of ignition.

The tycoon spoke out, "The Army-Commander is coming".

"Let him come, my Lord! Let him see what has befallen us, which sin of ours caused everything to be burnt to ashes, it would be better if we too would be consumed by the flames and transformed into ashes! What a relief it would be to us then"!

Someone began to mourn for a near one. In the dark, who could not reach this place stayed behind, in the fire!

Pacing up and down, the merchant said, "I have witnessed the devastating fire to descend".

"My Lord"! An indistinct voice reached the ears of the merchant.

"When the burden of sin reaches its limit, fire breaks out like this indeed".

"Oh Lord"!

The tycoon announced, "I shall give you money, do not panic, whatever is lost will be replenished".

"What are you saying, my Lord"?

The tycoon began to retrace his steps, as someone had begun to say again, that, "the fire had not broken of its own accord, it was the handiwork of some miscreant..."

Parashar was following the tycoon at his heels and kept saying, "Never mind those words, Lord, all these owe to the wrath of Lord Mahakaal".

"No"! Someone said. The tycoon heard, but could not identify the speaker. He was in doubt, whether someone had really said 'No' or it was an auditory illusion. Yonder, men like incorporeal spirits were filing in from the dark, burnt end of the ghetto and many more were even going into that direction. The soil was still in flames. The tycoon yelled, "Utanka"!

Where was Utanka? There stood the chariot. He was slouching inside the chariot. In the faint moonshine, the tycoon could read a shadow of fear, on the face of Utanka! Or was it not there? Or was it just a figment of his fertile imagination?

Parashar sidled up to him, "Lord! See that Utanka doesn't come here anymore".

"Why"?

"I cannot reason for it, but Utanka is dreadful"!

The magnate thundered, setting all his hesitations aside, "The reason for which the lakes have gone dry is the same for which the fire has broken out! Hey Utanka, have thou fallen asleep again? The night is heading to a close"!

Utanka raised his pale, bloodless face. Utanka seemed to be petrified. Or the pale moonshine rendered everything as dull as itself. The tycoon turned back to look. Old Parashar had come. He was standing just behind him. Wails of grief were being wafted from the edge of the lake.

"Utanka, let us go back", the tycoon called him.

Utanka alighted from the chariot. As he took up the rein, the pair of horses started whinnying. By then, they got frightened as well. While the tycoon was about to get into the carriage, Parashar said, "Lord, please do not come with this man. Oh! We are so scared of looking at him! We are ruined but who will benefit from our loss"?

"Why? But why"?

"That I cannot say, my Lord"! It seemed Parashar let out a scream of agony, in a subdued tone, "Which sin has caused us this ruin, we do not know, but we never had been so insolent to look up straight and talk to you, oh Lord"!

Lord Subhag Dutta got stone-cold, all of a sudden. Now it dawned on him, that even Utanka knew that they had recognized him! Undaunted to the core, ruthless Utanka, too, seemed to be on the point of collapsing. Could he hear the suppressed sobs of Utanka? Was he crying? The tycoon had never seen him shedding tears. But they did not name Utanka. They had not cursed Utanka! They only kept saying that he should not be there again. And only for this reason, this hard-hearted man broke down!

Utanka had returned with unbridled joy! It was he who had shown him the fire through the window. Both of them stood there for long. The tongues of flame kept licking the sky. The tycoon thought that, even a ball of truant cloud had been devoured by the fire! The tycoon did not want to come here at night. But Utanka was so enthusiastic! He was eager to check how far it got burnt! Utanka could not be happy without seeing his own handiwork with his own eyes!

Parashar said, "No worries, we are not that adamant to talk about the fire, but see that Utanka does not come here anymore. On seeing him all the people here will surely lose their calm"!

"Why, but why"?

"Lord, Utanka knows everything"! Whispering, Old Parashar said, "Please ask him, if you do not know at all. Alas! Oh, alas! When had such a day ever dawned in this land? Hey Utanka, go away with our master. Push off!"

Getting into the chariot, loosening the rein, Utanka started to brandish the whip and strike the back of the two horses. The neighing of the horses sent shivers through the night. Utanka's whip fell on the back of Old Parashar! With a muffled scream, the old man flew off aside. Utanka had taken his revenge! Gnashing his teeth, he made the chariot speed away through the moonshine.

The Shudra locality was left behind. Laments, cries — all receded at a distance, gradually. The burnt smell vanished from all corners. A cool breeze was greeting thetycoon's body. But the anxious magnate could not fix his mind on anything, he did not have the opportunity to shut his eyes too. He, in a suppressed voice called out, "Were thou seen"?

"Yes, my Lord"! The merchant got to hear Utanka's groan.

"Who saw you, was it Parashar"?

"Yes, my Lord"! Utanka lashed the two horses' back with his whip.

"Anyone else"?

"Yes, my Lord"! The tycoon heard Utanka's aggressive tone, swearing to kill that man, if permitted by his Lord!

Lord Subhag Dutta, cringed in fear and said, "What ruin have thou wrought? Now what would befall thee?! If it reaches the King's ear or the Army Commander's, hey Utanka… could all of them recognize thee"?

Utanka did not reply.

THIRTY-FIVE

Shudra women and servants were not trustworthy. Utanka had wrought utter ruin to the city of Avanti! A favourable situation had been made for usurping the throne, why would the Shudras go against the King, consciously? The Chief Priest was saying that a demon lurked inside Utanka. He, too, was afraid of Utanka. He, however, could not put forth any reason for such fear. Why did he feel so unnerved on seeing Utanka? He could surely see the inner demon in him with his mind's eye!

Now, only the Army Commander, Bikram, and the Chief Priest were there. The merchant was expected to join them though he was yet to turn up. Both of them were all ears to listen to the footsteps of the tycoon. Following the full moon, the new moon phase of Baisakh stood pervasive. The lamp was burning inside the room. In the light of the lamp, the shadows of the two men were cast enormous on the stone-wall and kept quivering. Nowhere any hint of wind was there today! In such sultry weather, this room appeared suffocating!

Bikram said, "All of Shudra ghetto have recognized Utanka, who has set them on fire. Nobody is saying that the King's sin has brought them misfortune. They all broke in agony before me, they could not say anything to Utanka in fear, as that servant of the tycoon is heartless"!

"Yes, whoever doesn't know this! The merchant has intended him to be like that"! said the Chief Priest.

"Why"?

"Such a servant is needed to protect his wealth and treasures".

"Then! Oh Brahmin! The opportunity is just slipping by, just before our eyes...", the Army-Chieftain halted while talking. He was lending his ears to the footsteps. The tycoon, indeed, was approaching. A devadasi usually would come with the noise of anklets. His conjecture proved not in vain. The tycoon entered. His face was tense, careworn with worries. The tycoon was not aware of the news which spread like wildfire! Being unaware, he rushed to the Ratnasagar Lakeside, along with Utanka. Taking his seat, he noticed worries, writ large on the faces of the Chief Priest and the Army Commander, Bikram. He kept two silk reticules on the floor. In an inaudible voice, he requested, "Please accept".

"Okay, these can be had… but what has Utanka done"? The Chief Priest demanded to know.

"I don't know whether they really had spotted him or by way of avenging, they are naming Utanka everywhere. Utanka is cruel and his beating has left many of them in pools of blood. The Shudra locale has made the best use of this fair chance".

"Or is it some kind of cruelty too?" Haltingly, said Bikram, the Army-Commander, "Lighting the fire before all eyes has caused the fierceness reach its summit and Utanka has done that precisely, he has set all belongings of the inhabitants on fire, by forcing them to face it – was there any directive like that"?

"Why will be there any such directive"? The merchant looked perturbed and annoyed too.

"Even after that, Utanka had driven you there, he was eager to see the impact of his cruelty and he was keen on making you privy to it too".

The tycoon went speechless. He was remembering how Utanka returned on horse-back, after setting the slum on fire. He was shaking in terrible ecstasy. He did not want to make late anymore. He was waiting, tying the horse to the chariot. He was sending the old maidservant to his master, repeatedly. His Lord must go to the Ratnakarsagar Lakeside, in the moonshine. Then the sky on that end of the city turned crimson.

The Army Commander, Bikram, warned that the opportunity was slipping by. Just this single incident was going in favour of the King. Such lack of rains, drought, lack of harvest, outraging the modesty of the devadasi, the childless existence of the King, his inefficient administration — all got wiped off by Utanka's ruthlessness. All were talking against Utanka. None was saying that it happened due to the King's sin. The servant of the tycoon was so cruel, the city-dwellers averred, that he had taken his master to witness the burnt locale of the Shudras, that very night! The tycoon was ignorant of it. If the tycoon would go alone, he could have learnt about Utanka's misdoings. Later that night, the Shudras went blanched in fear seeing Utanka again. Utanka seemed to be the embodiment of terror. The innocent Shudras failed to understand why Utanka behaved thus! Even if any destitute or Shudra boy fell in front of his chariot, his whip came straight on him. Why did Utanka set their hutments on fire?

The tycoon was miffed at the aspersions cast against the servant of his own making. The Army Commander maintained, "If the Shudras approached the King failing to get justice from him, things would come to a dreadful pass! If the King meted out proper justice to them, they would protect the King at the cost of their own lives. Though low in caste, the Shudras were not unfaithful, not traitors, they revered their master as God. Would it be possible to occupy the throne if the city-dwellers supported the King, disregarding the Army-Commander"?

The tycoon asked, "What is the way-out then"?

"Why is Utanka so cruel"? questioned the Chief Priest.

"This question is irrelevant, I think, without getting any proof at hand, they are keen on dumping Utanka on this pretext! Why will Utanka add fire in front of all? And in that case, why wouldn't the Shudras nab him and even if they failed to do so, why did they keep silent on this issue during my visit there"?

The Army-Commander said, "I have already explained it. Now, if that cruel servant is not punished, all our plans will go haywire".

The tycoon said, "For the well-being of Avanti, I can leave Utanka unto you. Now he is under house-arrest, glancing at him you will understand how innocent he is, far from the cruel you all take him to be, he is still crying since that night, at times he is going silent though. To strike a man and drive him to bleed and to set a ghetto on fire are not just the same. On setting the slum on fire Utanka has gone blanched in fear. He had no idea that fire could be so destructive, so devastating! A stupid servant, who had no idea how powerful fire could be"!

"What do you want to say"?

"I am not making any point. I just say that those who want to finish Utanka are the Shudras. Will you take the Shudras' words to be true? Henceforth, whatever be their demand, it will have to be fulfilled".

The Priest asked, "Isn't Utanka a Shudra as well"?

"He is a man of the hills".

"Aren't the hilly people Shudras? They are invariably the Shudras! As he is a servant, he is doubtlessly a Shudra. Why will a Shudra's words be paid heed to? The Shudra belt has been devastated by fire, all of them are huddling beside Ratnakarsagar Lake, they have lost all their belongings. Now, let Utanka die for establishing the justice meted out to them by the Army Commander. Though Utanka is the merchant's servant, Avanti will stand blessed if he dies. This is for the welfare of Avanti".

The Chief Priest's words sent chill down the merchant's spine. The magnate shivered. It was beyond his conjecture that the Brahmin would utter the death-sentence on Utanka! Utanka had gone to set the Shudra ghetto on fire, just complying with his order! It was said that he would come back after adding fire, stealthily. But he failed to do so. Now he was in peril. He was endangered because of a faulty implementation of the plan hatched by these three men. Wouldn't it be these three men's responsibility to protect him?

Perhaps, the Chief Priest could sense the goings-on in the tycoon's mind. In a soft voice he said, "I know, you will be hurt, the servant is loyal to you, courageous and even heartless, as desired. Setting the Shudra belt ablaze was in the aim of giving a fillip to the King's burden of sin. But tell me, could this truth be established that the fire descended straight from the sky? The childless, rapist King has desecrated the shrine of Lord Mahakaal. No redemption being there, the city of Avanti is going to be ruined by the wrath of Lord Mahakaal"!

"Can it be accomplished by the death of Utanka"?

It may not be so, but the Shudras will get to believe that Utanka had gone mad to perpetrate such heinous act and they will also come to know that Bikram, the Army-Commander is an efficient administrator, his justice has not spared the servant of the tycoon even! This will surely boost up the reputation of both the Army Commander and the tycoon. The city will rise, showering praises on you! Let him die then, let him be burnt to death"!

Tycoon Subhag Dutta sat lowering his head. Till date, Utanka had never disobeyed him. He raised no question at all. Whatever his master would say, would be the ultimate truth! If he had asked Utanka to kindle the flames by concealing himself, he would surely have done so. He did not warn him, he did not feel the need of it at all, for natural causes. And Utanka, too, failed to be under a cover, while going mad in a fierce spree of lighting fire! He fulfilled the wish of his master. As his master had asked him to burn the Shudra ghetto, it seemed as if the people of that locality too had their tacit nod to it. Such was the notion of Utanka! The tycoon had been in the grip of melancholy. He had raised Utanka according to his own set of values. He recalled how he had almost snatched off little Utanka from the lap of his poor parents on the hills.

The tycoon suggested, "What if Utanka leaves this city for good"?

"No, dying in front of everyone, that only will pacify the Shudra ghetto. In this case, dying by fire is the only judgment".

"Have the Shudras demanded thus"?

The Army-Commander reasoned, "No, they do not have that courage to demand the death of the servant of the tycoon, but in order to establish good administration and impartial justice, Utanka's death is a necessity"!

The merchant kept quiet. He had trained Utanka to be as cruel as a man could be. He had imparted lessons on ruthlessness to him. The merchant had made him grow the habit of eating raw meat. Utanka was so loyal to the master that he would not mind killing himself, if ordered by him. The merchant's eyes glistened. He remembered how the child Utanka turned puce in anger! A boy of the hills, would naturally be strong enough by birth to fight against all vagaries of nature! Adverse ambience was their all-time companion! Lack of food plagued the people of the hills, indeed. Yet, the child, Utanka, had gone without food for almost fifteen days since he had brought him here,snatching off the lap of his parents. Literally, he had snatched him off! Poverty-stricken mother of the hills did not want to part with her child, by any means. He had to impress his father with loads of goods, gems, jewelleries and madeira. That madeira had been made of grape-extract - it came as a gift from a merchant from the bank of the river, Kopisha. He could remember everything. Neither wine nor madeira could that man dream to have. He used to mind domestic chores and his wife, Utanka's mother, used to put her labour to earn rice for the family. That was the custom of that land. If he had not brought Utanka along with him, Utanka would have been like them! He had to live on rice, earned by the female member of the family. Being brought here, the child used to burst into tears for his parents, uttering unintelligible hilly dialect on many afternoons and at midnights. The maidservant reported to him that even in sleep he used to sob. Utanka had now grown up into an adult, burying all his past memories. Grew bold, undaunted. Only the brave could be ruthless. For fear of Utanka, no shadow of any thief ever fell on the merchant's house. Once he had put an end to a dog's life, by kicking it.

The tycoon had broken down, saying, "I never knew that I was so weak on Utanka"!

The Chief Priest commented, "Fetch another one from the hills".

"Now at this age I cannot risk rearing up a child anymore".

The Chief Priest said, "But you have to make such little sacrifice for this city of Avanti".

The merchant was heard to lament, "If I would have warned him to ignite, on the sly! Oh, alas"!

Now the Chief Priest was moved, he reasoned, "Hill boy, but after all, a Shudra! Why are you lamenting for a Shudra? You are the pride of this city, and as the Army

Commander, Bikram's glory would shoot up with this measure, yours will be no less, and it will help you to own that Chief Courtesan, Devadutta, even more easily"!

The tycoon answered, "True! But will it be justified to kill Utanka by fire, only to gratify the Shudras? Think once, please".

"Do not stretch your logic unnecessarily! Utanka has to die, lest Lord Mahakaal will be angry! The Chief Priest's voice reverberated, The sanctum sanctorum of Lord Mahakaal has been profaned by King Bhartrihari, our holy duty is to make him lose the throne, and for that, Utanka's death is a must, as if we are sacrificing the life of a Shudra to appease Lord Mahakaal. Lord Mahakaal, in turn, will pass the throne on to us, and Bikram will sit upon that royal seat"!

Magnate Subhag Dutta's neck drooped. Utanka had imprisoned himself behind the bolted door. It was as per the directive of the tycoon. Five days had sped by since that devastating conflagration. It had spread all over the city that Utanka, the pageboy of the tycoon, had made it happen. Only Utanka was exposed to bitter criticism, to harsh calumny, while the merchant was spared! Rather the people kept saying that the merchant had rushed to stand beside the endangered mass, that very night, setting food and sleep at naught! The rich would never be implicated or accused of anything wrong, hence no voice was raised against him. This incident proved once again how Utanka was hated by all and sundry.

The merchant said, "I accept your proposition, let it be as you want it to happen but ensure that he does not have to suffer the death-throes, kill him in some other way".

The Chief Priest laughed and said, "This is the only punishment for such heinous crime, won't you witness him being punished"?

"No".

"And you should not even mourn for him, Utanka's un-mourned death will catapult you to a noble stature, in the eyes of the people of this city" ...

No word of the Chief Priest was making way to the tycoon's ear. The Army-Commander kept an assuring hand on his back.

THIRTY-SIX

Utanka had been held captive. He had been surrendered by his master, Subhag Dutta! This news was doing rounds in the city. The conflagration in the Shudra ghetto and then Utanka being taken a prisoner had created stir in the city. But the city-residents would get enthusiastic on many issues and again would be blissfully forgotten about them! Utanka's imprisonment made them happy though none of them could hardly believe that Utanka could be punished! All were perhaps waiting for that day on which Utanka's chariot would run again at a breakneck speed on the main thoroughfare! His whip would be swishing through the air. The passers-by would be smeared with blood. The people hardly could believe that the servant of the richest man of the city, Utanka, would be penalised!

One day, at dawn, the city-dwellers were nudged out of their sleep by the booming noise of the conch-shell. The rhythmic beatings of the drums went on, a few had emerged out of their houses on the street, windows of a few houses were opened. The women of the city came to stand by the windows. The incessant piping of the conch-shell and beats of the drums compelled all the gentlemen to come outside unbolting the doors, and it made all the housewives, young ladies, and elderly women to line up before the light by the windows. Those men were all lately awakened from sleep and at the corner of the women's eyes or on their cheeks numerous signs of sleep and waking up, joy and sadness lay strewn. All of them stretched their astonished gaze at the thoroughfare of the city, fed with sonorous smorgasbord.

The conch-shell kept being blown followed by the drums and sometimes both of them together and lastly when both the conch-shell and the drums fell silent, the voice of the announcer could be heard. The conch-shell blower, the drum-player, the announcer all wore strange appearances! They seemed to be Shudras. Or, they might be hunters or forest-dwellers. They were dark-complexioned, wore animal-skin girdles around their waists, the rest of the body stood bare, their heads being covered with close-cropped, curly hair. Yes, they might possibly be hunters. Who else but a hunter could walk down the road, proclaiming death in such a solemn, spine-chilling voice! A small falchion, made of the horns of a buffalo, was held in the hands of the announcer. Lifting the falchion up, he went on relating the crime, committed by Utanka, the servant, in detail: " A cruel servant set the Shudra ghetto on fire. Now he has to die, being consigned to the flames only. According to the judgment passed by the Army-Commander, Kumar Bikram, Utanka has been sentenced to death! At dawn of the coming Krishna Chaturdashi, at the outskirts of the city near the Shudra ghetto, this servant will be thrown into the flames. City-dwellers, please take note of this announcement"!

After the announcement, followed by a little silence, the conch-shell boomed again. It was shrill and about to pierce the ear-drums! Inhabitants of the city were being pulled out of their sloth by the booming noise of the conch-shell. In the rhythmic beatings of the drums, the city-dwellers were raising themselves up from bed. After a long time, such noise had awakened the city! It reminded all of the Dashpura battle. The line of soldiers had gone for war, by blowing conch-shells and beating drums, in this manner. They had come back, waking up all the city-dwellers from sleep by blowing conch-shells. The women of the city were getting reminded of the ovation of flowers! At the wee hours of the night, they had been awakened from sleep by the deep sound of the conch-shells wafted from far-off and the beatings of the war-trumpets. Looking at the cool-bluish sky they surmised how long it would be for the night to end and how long again it would be for the sound of the conch-shell to reach the city! They could hear the rejoicing of the winners in that booming noise of the conch-shell. Naturally, gleaning the flowers, holding the windows wide open, they kept waiting for the retinue of soldiers, who had emerged triumphant! Then the elephant had stepped in, sashaying leisurely. At the heels of the elephant came the cavalry, followed by the infantry and the heroes in droves on the chariot. They were singing songs, lifting up their unsheathed swords, spear-like missiles, lances and falchions to the sky. In the light of the dawn, they glittered. Nascent sunrays were being reflected from those weapons, pointed towards the sky! Initially, flowers were being showered on their arms! Then the young maidens, housewives, and mothers were looking at the winners in astonishment. They were readily impressed by the bare-bodied, well-built, fine-statured soldiers and began to heap flowers on them copiously. The young maidens had seen King Bhartrihari on the chariot and Army-Commander, Bikram, on the horseback. That horse was white, Persian and vibrant with valour. Both the men were very handsome. On seeing them, the young ladies were carried away. Rejoicing, they took each other in deep embrace, smilingly. From the window, they kept greeting them with flowers, strewn from the window. It was Spring. That Spring, the God of the Seasons, pervaded himself with all its beauty over the sky and ambience of Avanti. The air was redolent with the fragrance of flowers. The young damsels gleaned many a flower— Ashokkali, Kurubok, Aparajita, Mandar, Bon Juthika and many more of familiar and unknown species from the forest. In the beating sounds of the war-trumpets, tom-tom, and the grave and solemn rhythmic noise of the drums, the lovelorn maidens had removed the veil from their faces. Their brassieres seemed to slip off, unawares.

And those who were mothers among the women, had seen the reflection of their sons in all the male soldiers. In the elderly bosoms, the feelings of a mother surged. They were those who showered flowers on the infantry soldiers. The infantry included the Shudra soldiers. They were strong, well-shaped, but were not handsome. But the mothers were greeting them only, from the core of their hearts considering them as their own children.

It was a tale of many moons ago. After that, they had not heard any blowing boom of the conch-shell. Since long, they did not come to stand before the open windows, hearing the noise of the drums and the tom-tom. Had not rushed to the windows being drawn by the blowing of the war-trumpets. The sound of the conch-shell which called them up today, came without any prescience. Who would come back triumphant as they had no knowledge of any soldiers setting out for war? Yet those who rushed to the windows had dishevelled look, hairs untied, marks of last evening's make-up left on their faces, here and there. And there was the fragrance of the bed, along with all such things. The odour of the husband's perspiration had still been there which was yet to disappear. The smell of 'imagination' pervaded the body of the spinsters. And, the elderly bodies were enveloped by fragrance-less nonchalance. They were all ears to the death sentence. In this Spring, when love and the welcome of new life were to sprout in Avanti, in the city of Ujjwain, while the announcer would proclaim the advent of Spring in a sentence like, 'Oh City-dwellers, listen to me, Spring is here', he kept announcing the death-sentence instead! The women's joy of waking up from sleep disappeared instantly. Terror, sadness filled them up, instead. At this pleasant daybreak, who came up with the news of death and why at all? Oh Lord Mahakaal! What had gone amiss with your golden Ujjwain? Neither bumblebees were there during the Spring, nor sweet smell of flowers, nowhere was any celebration of life in Springtime and who had come to talk about cessation of life? Since long, this city had gone rainless, it seemed as though the tenderness of man's heart had been stolen by waterless, dry city, and hence, hearing the news of death-sentence, yonder the men kept rejoicing, among whom were the fathers, sons, husbands, near and dear ones of all the women, queued up by the windows!

As many times, the announcer threw his gaze at the sky and pronounced the death-sentence, the men who assembled, went rejoicing, letting out shrieks of delight!

Whose death-sentence? It was Utanka's. Utanka, the cruel servant of the tycoon! Was it true? Or any namesake? Ruthless Utanka was being given death- sentence for the heinous crime of setting the Shudra ghetto on fire! Was it really true? Could this be believed at all?

The men, then, called out to the announcer or the drummers, "Listen, hey you men, come listen to us, we will pay you handsomely, come for a couple of words, we will gift you attires for covering the body. Whose death sentence are you talking about"?

The drums were beaten with fierce, sombre noise. In the sound of the drums, the domestic pigeons again kept encircling the sky. A panic-stricken pigeon went far away, flapping its wings. While the noise of the drums stopped, the announcer shouted at the top of his voice, "It is the death-sentence of Utanka, the servant of the tycoon"!

To be more certain, the men asked again, "Which tycoon"?

"Tycoon, but which one, I cannot say".

Is Subhag Dutta the tycoon in question? Someone had to ask, otherwise certainty about the identity could not be made. Was there any other Utanka in this city? Was he, too, a servant of some merchant? Merchant meant Subhag Dutta, all knew that, yet why such querying? There was a repetitive aim behind such inquisitiveness: the eagerness to learn about the death-sentence. Utanka's death news was, as if, an auspicious message to them! That was why, they repeatedly asked various queries to be certain about the news. How heartless was Utanka, many of them still carried the marks of his torture on their body! Many feet were injured by the wheels of that chariot! They, too, had come down to the streets with staff in their hands.

Someone threw a query, "Hey, why such death-sentence"?

"For setting the Shudra-ghetto ablaze"!

"Who had done it? Utanka"?

He, who was stalling the forward movement of the announcer by such queries was cognizant of everything. But he was trying to gratify his exhausted body consumed with subdued anger, by hearing the answer, repeatedly, from the announcer who looked like an accomplice of Lord Yamah. Now his query was, "Please tell us how he is going to be killed"!

"The servant will be consigned to the flames alive", saying so, raising his voice to the crescendo, he began to reach his words every ear, "The way he burnt all, he too will be burnt likewise"! Just as the words of the announcer trailed off, the conch-shell was blown, a sombre beating vibrated the drum: Ddum...ddum...

The men assembled there let out a cry of sympathy now, "Oh! Alas"! But their expressions bore no sign of pain. They were telling one another, "Oh! It would have been better if burning-to-death could have been avoided! That is really very painful"!

- "No, no, burning-to-death will be a befitting punishment for causing conflagration, indeed"!

- "He could have been impaled to death even"!

- "That is painful too. - "Death itself is painful — hey, what did you say, he will be burnt to death, alive??"

Then, the women of the city, who were standing by the narrow windows, plugged their ear-holes with both hands, on hearing the death sentence. It was rather ominous to hear the voice announcing death-sentence, accompanied by the booming noise of the conch-shells, war-trumpets and drums! They were terribly concerned with the welfare and misfortune of their families, as they used to stay with husband, children and the near ones. And again, they surmised that the sound of the conch-shell which woke them up from sleep after such long years, would definitely come with a piece of good news! Repeated death-news failed the women to hold on to their nonchalance. They burst into tears. Tears welled up in the eyes of a woman and taking cue from her, other women's eyes got awash with tears of affliction too. Tears did spread widely. The windows of each house began to close, one after another. With loud noise! Behind the closed windows, the women went breaking into tears. What a morning came, in which getting up from bed they got to hear the beatings of the drums, proclaiming a death-sentence! In this golden city, death-sentence was just an unusual happening. No death-sentence had been issued to anyone even during the reign of the King's father, let alone that of King Bhartrihari himself!

The announcer swinging the falchion made of ox-horn, began to notice with much surprise how the windows began to be closed! The falchion fell down from his hands. It too made him more embarrassed. Taking the falchion up, he thought that women of the city had turned their faces from him. Each window displayed the face of a woman, just awake! Those faces were exquisite, they bore marks of affection, their glowing eyes exhibited lovelorn glances! The hunter had noticed that, whoever a woman glanced at, that gaze had a mesmerizing touch, irrespective of her being in love with any other man or whatever. Eyeing the women's faces on the windows, the announcer was feeling enthused to proclaim the news of death, even more. Now, he was feeling lackadaisical. He thought he had witnessed signs of hatred towards him on the women's faces, just the instant before the windows were shut.

The menfolk shouted, "Why do you stop, carry on, keep saying...Keep announcing, keep proclaiming, let the death-news of Utanka spread all over the universe, across the sky and the wind"!

The announcer was looking at the closed windows, keeping mum. A faint noise of weeping was making way to his ears. He could feel that the women were crying themselves out, within the house, by closing the windows. Alas, Oh Spring! What Chaitra day it was, Springtime was getting awash with tears! Being a Shudra himself, he agreed to do this job in lieu of rice. He could comprehend, that, his announcement had reached pain to the minds of the women.

A man rushed to the announcer with a small reticule in his hand, "Please take this ten annas, distribute among yourselves, keeping three annas for each of you, please hand one anna to Utanka, ha ha ha, speak, keep saying where that rogue will be slain, listen dear, he was a sinner, the greatest sinner of all the Shudras, a greater sinner than a hunter, his death-sentence is more of tidings than a sad news"!

The announcer to his utter amazement had marked that, the men were rejoicing loudly, fighting off the initial inertia,

"…This is the consequence of a sin, sin ends in death, Lord Mahakaal is surely there"!

"…The merchant is noble,he has surrendered the servant immediately after learning the truth".

"…Grapevine has it, that, the Army-Commander has meted out this punishment, Utanka had not been taken to the King at all, it is rather preferable that the King would not judge the crime of a servant, the death-sentence of a servant could easily be issued by a petty employee of the Royal Court".

"…Hey, tell us again, won't he be flogged a hundred times by the city-dwellers"?

"… Firstly, both his hands should be mutilated and then he could be set on fire, alive"!

"…Hey, is there any chance of this punishment to be repealed"?

"- This man was terrible, a terrible man's death is always a spectacle, we must go to witness it, hey speak up, carry on"!

How strange! A death news regales someone, while it makes some other sad. The husband, who was commenting that death of a terrible is always a spectacle, had his wife lamenting in the dark of the room, "the man to be burnt to death would undergo such excruciating pain! Alas! Which Spring is here this year, in the city of Avanti"?

A faint noise of crying was causing heartburn to the announcer! He began to get singed within. This hunter was young in age, this hunter's eyes and mind were dipped in colours naturally, that youthful charm was getting drenched by the tears! Such rejection by so many women at one go, he could sense that the announcement of death-sentence was just the opposite of 'love'! When the women stood by the open windows, he observed that all were casting glances of amazement at his young, supple body, as if they had never seen such a youth! Thereafter, such amazement had disappeared, lamentation got the better of them and then contempt followed. The last damsel had shut the windows, being badly enraged. The morose announcer motioned at the drummer, Play on!

The drums repeatedly sounded. The loud rejoicing noise of the men and the sobs of the women began to be drowned by the rhythmic beating of the drums. The death-news eluded their ears. The drummer moved forward by beating his drums. Before him, the blower of the conch-shell took a step forward. In between the two, stood the announcer. The reticule containing the ten annas stayed unclaimed on the thoroughfare.

At that moment, an elderly lady had asked her daughter-in-law, "What have they said"?

"Haven't you heard, Maa"?

The old woman replied, "I have gone deaf. Lord Mahakaal blessed me with the power of hearing, He, himself has taken it away. So, what have they announced? Please whisper it in my ears".

The daughter-in-law wept silently, "How blessed you are, Maa"!

"Tell me who had come, who were they, Mahakaal had given me eyesight, but he has taken it back even, please whisper in my ears".

The daughter-in-law cupped her mouth in both her hands to say, "Lord Mahakaal is so kind to you, how pious you are, Maa, a man will be burnt alive and you do not have to witness that".

"Bring thy mouth to my ears, tell me for the last time, death is approaching fast, my days are numbered, let me know what is going on here in the city of Avanti"!

The sad daughter-in-law kept hanging her face low, she kept musing, 'You are a fortunate lady, your husband will never rejoice at the death of a man being burnt alive, without knowing such things, you will breathe your last, Maa, listen, Maa, listen…'!

The wife took her mouth near the ears of her mother-in-law, in a drenched voice while shedding tears, she said, "Spring hasn't arrived this year".

... "Who hasn't arrived"?

... "Spring, the King of all seasons, the Messenger of Death has come instead".

... "What do you say"?

..."No Spring, only Death will pervade the Springtime"!

The old woman smiled, "So what"?

... "Maa listen, this Spring has no joy in it".

... "Who is Joy"?

... "A call of Death has reached the threshold of the family man this Spring instead"!

"So what? What harm in that, my maid, what's wrong?" The old woman kept muttering, "Where is your husband, that man, which hell has he gone to"?

The wife cried out, "What are you saying, Maa? He is your child only".

The wizened woman was mumbling, "Lord Mahakaal has taken away whatever He had given. Who's your son, your son-in-law, who again is your daughter, your daughter-in-law, who is Death, who is named Spring, nothing you remember these days! Alas Oh Lord Mahakaal! Why had you given all, if you intended to take that back"?

THIRTY-SEVEN

How dreary death could be! Even now, Subhag Dutta was benumbed under the impact of the nerve-shattering groan of a dying man! Fettered in shackles, in a deserted hut thatched with leaves, Utanka had been burnt alive. Men in droves had come to witness that death. The merchant had no idea that his servant was an object of deep hatred to all! No one mourned his death! No one kept lamenting at all. All stood unmoved as if they were witnessing the death of an inferior creature. As a hog rent all ten directions with its cries cutting through the silence during his death, Utanka's shrill cries were just the same. As humans remain indifferent to the loud cries of a boar, the men witnessing the death standing near Utanka were nonchalant likewise. Subhag Dutta seemed to hear the wails of a hill-boy for his mother! He was reminded of everything in the past.

The city went all praise for him. The merchant had not forgiven even his favourite servant for committing a heinous crime. He did not want to conceal the crime rather he surrendered him to justice. It was he who first made out that, cruel Utanka derived joy from ruthlessness for no reason, just for a similar delight he had set the Shudra ghetto on fire, in the dark of a night. The people of the city were showering praises on Subhag Dutta, the tycoon, and the Army-Commander, Bikram. How noble were they - the merchant and the Army-Commander! They stood beside the Shudras, who were rungs lower in caste. The Shudras' huts were set ablaze by another Shudra who had to pay for it too, with his own life! Hail to thee, Subhag Dutta! Utanka's demise helped the inhabitants of this city to breathe in peace, once again. The tycoon had no idea of how ruthless this servant was! If he knew before, he would surely have been slain, long ago! After a long time, the streets and thoroughfares of Ujjwain became safe. Utanka's lash from the chariot would not come on anyone abruptly, none would have to lose his life under the wheels of his carriage, none would have to continue living on earth, being maimed.

Three days were over since Utanka died by burning. The magnate had kept himself confined indoors. He was spending sleepless nights and days, mourning, behind all eyes. His own greed had snatched the life of his servant, who was truly innocent! It occurred to the merchant, rather painfully! He was even sadder to learn that his name was being uttered in the city with much reverence! All news reached Subhag Dutta while he sat back in his room.

King Bhartrihari had sent for him. The tycoon had declined it, very politely. He heard that, the King was not averse to him as the city-people had not been so. All were happy. They all were rejoicing, right from the Shudras to the Brahmins. Right from the royal employees to Mahaparshwa, the pimp. Such expansive delight was beyond the tycoon's imagination.

Now he felt that Utanka's death had saved him! Just for Utanka, the common populace was going against him, gradually. As Utanka was no more, the city-dwellers were pouring in to greet him, to bless him. They kept saying, perhaps Subhag Dutta had been absolved of all his sins. Unknowingly, he had given indulgence to a demon! Rearing up Utanka was his sin, indeed. That sin had been washed away by Utanka's death. Utanka, the inveterate sinner, had gone again to listen to the people's laments after setting the Shudra ghetto on fire! That fire itself seemed to have swallowed Utanka! For one sin, the Shudra locality had been burnt to ashes, for another, Utanka had to die!

Now lolling tongues of fire enveloped the city of Avanti! Here, only fire was the omnipotent force. In this city of Avanti, none had been there who could encounter the fire! In fact, none was against the fire here! No clouds, no shades, all seemed to have threaded their way to the gaping mouth of the fire itself. As all day Nature remained dreadful, no wonder, fire would gobble up the ghetto of the Shudras! It might be so, that Utanka had only carried out the dictates of Fire! And hence, he had been abducted by the fire itself! Utanka the sinner, the ruthless, the heartless was perhaps thus predestined to be burnt to ashes!

The tycoon did not respond to the call of the shrine of Lord Mahakaal even! The messenger of Army Commander, Bikram, had come to find aggrieved Subhag Dutta in self-exile. How could a man be so attached to another man! He, himself, could not be cruel, the very sight of blood made him recoil in disgust, then how could he transform an innocent hill-boy into a ruthless, hard-hearted being?

Night was dark and intense now. Sleep eluded the merchant's eyes. All wings of the mansion were enveloped in silence, all inmates were fast asleep. No servant boy or maid lay awake. Subhag Dutta had come to stand in the open terrace. The sky of Baisakh ran above his head. The cluster of stars and planets stood sleepless. Yonder, high above, the northern sky, the Ursa Major had drooped down from the north to the south, sidling up to the west on its journey. Yonder was the way of light — the Milky Way! In the north, close by the Galaxy, the star, Brahmahriday, was sparkling. Looking at the constellation of stars, the rich, lonely man broke into tears! Utanka's demise had left him friendless in this whole universe, he felt. Utanka was his servant. He had no idea when and how this pageboy had grown so intimate to be a part of his life! The merchant had never thought in his wildest dream that a Shudra from the hills would be so dear to a rich Vaishya like himself!

Utanka was not there. It seemed as if none had been there in this chateau! As presently, he stayed up awake while all others in the house had been fast asleep. While alive, it never happened, that Utanka would turn blind eye to his master, spending a sleepless night! It had never so happened that he would stand all alone in this terrace and Utanka would not be there close by. Utanka's olfactory organ was extremely strong! He would have sensed all indeed.

"Utanka, hey Utanka"! Sobbed the rich merchant, once again.

"Master"! The blue darkness seemed to answer back.

"Is it very painful to die, Utanka"?

"Yes, as my master wanted"!

"Has the fire eaten thee up, Utanka"?

"Oh yes Master, it is really painful to die"!

"Too painful? Very much"?

"Master, it is just the same as a boar dying in pain""""!

"Were thou reminded of thy mother, Utanka?" whispered Subhag Dutta.

"Lord! My master! Why did I die"?

Subhag Dutta kept quiet. A pair of his bewildered eyes kept piercing through the darkness, from one end to the other. He called out again, "Utanka, hey Utanka"!

"Master, why did I die"?

"Thou had set the Shudra ghetto on fire"!

"What happens if the Shudra locality is torched"?

Subhag Dutta kept silent. If Shudra ghetto is set on fire, the Shudras die. That is why, Utanka has died. Utanka dear, couldn't thou come out of the combustion?

Utanka cried out, "Oh Lord, my Master, why have I died"?

Subhag Dutta said, "For the city of Avanti, for the welfare of Avanti"!

"Why did I set the Shudra ghetto on fire, my Lord?"

Subhag Dutta replied, "That's for the welfare of Avanti".

"Why do people rejoice on my death, Master?"

Subhag Dutta answered, "That too for the welfare of Avanti."

Subhag Dutta heard, "Let Avanti be blessed, I pray for the well-being of the King"!

"Well-being of the King will spell doom to Avanti"!

"So, the King's misfortune will cause welfare of Avanti - is it true, my Lord"?

"True"! The millionaire merchant was shrinking while saying, "Utanka, thy death leaves me in pain".

"The people of this city rejoice, why do you feel sad, my Master"?

"Utanka dear, your death is nothing but me getting burnt in fire"!

"None feels so, why do you? And it was you who sent me to die, my Lord"!

Subhag Dutta covered his face with both his hands. It seemed that Utanka had come to stand behind him. He could hear the deep and intense breathing of Utanka! Utanka turned to stand before him and said, "After a long time, I had again gone to the mountains in the North, my Master"!

"What did thou see there, Utanka? Have the peaks been capped by snow lately"?!

No, my Lord! Water has coursed down in the form of rivers, a terrible conflagration has sucked in the water of the rivers to the sky, not a drop of water is left either in the water-bodies, lakes, rivers, streams or ponds. Oh Lord, neither my mother, nor my father is there"!

"Where are they"?

"My mother has gone to a far-off land in agony, and my father has breathed his last in sadness, without having anything to eat".

"Utanka dear, I am really hurt, really pained by thy demise"…

"These are not true at all, my Master, you had brought me along from the mountains only for such a death, my mother is there no more, she has left for some distant land in grief and my father is dead and gone, being sad and even sadder for his son"!

"Stop Utanka, why do you say that again"?

"No, my Lord! If my mother comes to know of such a death news, my mother will go far and far, even further, and my father will die again, again once again, and he will be left with none but death itself"!

"Hey Utanka, if the whore loved me, such would not happen at all"!

"Do you know that, my Lord"?

"I know, but I do not run after the whore's love anymore, the Army-Commander covets the throne".

"The richest man wants the Chief Prostitute".

"That is the reason behind thy death".

"Have you come to know this, my Lord"?

"Yes, I have learnt, Utanka, no one should die like thee".

"Every day many a man dies likewise! Oh Lord, please set sail for trade"!

"Yes, I shall go for trade, yes, I must set out".

You are a merchant, you had to witness Utanka's death as you are here in the city, if you had gone out on trade, Utanka would have been alive! My Master, without setting out for trade you made Utanka a cruel being and you made Utanka burn by fire"!

Rich Subhag Dutta held his head low. He could sense that staying in this city would be difficult for him with each passing day. Utanka's chariot used to rage through the roads of this city! That chariot stood forsaken in the garage. The new chauffeur would not drive that carriage. He would drive an ordinary carriage through the main thoroughfare at a low speed. The pair of horses of Utanka's carriage was from Persia. They had become so quiet. Repeated lashes of Utanka had excited them to run berserk. Even in respite, they used to ruffle the darkness of the night by their abrupt neighing! Subhag Dutta could understand that he would have to set out on a journey. Let the courtesan wait. Now, he could realize that he had committed a blunder. He had lost Utanka because of Devadutta. The Chief Priest remarked, "Shudra and woman, both are to be abandoned." Knowing each word of the Chief Priest to be true, he never could stay without women around him! How could a man live without a woman? All the flavours of life remained cocooned in the women only! He had his wife, children but life without Devadutta would be scorched by sunrays, would transform into coal, by burning. Again, he could now sense that the woman was the chief cause behind the destruction. He had sent Dhruvaputra far-off on exile, for Devadutta. Alas! Oh Dhruvaputra! Oh my friend, Dhruva! I could not protect your child, could not let him live, with care. I do not know about his whereabouts,I cannot say whether he is alive or dead. All had happened because of that whore! She still would dazzle me with her beauty, day and night, just as ever!

"Lord! Please set out on trade. If you stay back in the city, you will be the servant of the prostitute".

"What do thou say, Utanka"?

"I speak the truth, my Master, already you have become her servant, if you don't leave this city, you will not be spared by that woman."

"It is not the truth, Utanka, I am nobody's servant," Subhag Dutta protested.

"You are Devadutta's servant"! That's why, you have made Utanka commit sin, then you got him killed by burning him alive. Utanka had not gone to the Shudra locality to set it on fire. You demanded and your order was to be carried out with reverence by him. No doubt, all these owe to Devadutta, but that lady knows next to nothing about all such matters."

Subhag Dutta replied, "Devadutta does not want me".

"Yet, you are her servant, as the Army-Commander has become the servant of the queen. The Army-Commander desires the throne for the queen, Bhanumati, the woman and the throne getting merged with each other. Please, my Lord, go out of Ujjwain at your earliest, go out on business, oh Master, you have burnt Utanka to death, and if you stay back in this city, you will set so many things on fire, oh Lord! Do not allow yourself to be burnt anymore!"

Subhag Dutta said, "I must go for trade".

"Then go, please. You are yet to see many lands! Go, my Lord, go for trade, go and find Dhruvaputra, then only Utanka will be saved from this sense of burning, burning still as I am"!

Subhag Dutta sat down in the darkness on the singed grass-blades of the field. He was crying, covering his face with both hands. Utanka sat before him, firm, as an embodiment of darkness, he kept whispering, "Cry, my Master, shed tears to douse the fire, let me cry too, my Master, let me alleviate my pain by weeping. Oh my Lord, you have not reared up Utanka as a human being, hence at his death, all are rejoicing, as if another boar has burnt in fire, a jackal has died, a tiger has lost its life, as though, a mad dog has breathed his last. Oh Lord, the men say, 'Rightly served! Utanka is no more'! As men utter words of relief, I burn within, I get singed, no, the fire has not been extinguished! Oh Lord, neither water, nor cloud is there, I am getting dried up, I am dying, why did you make me so cruel, why did you get me a heart of stone, tell me, Oh Lord?!"

Subhag Dutta apologized, "Forgive me, Utanka"!

"Can forgiveness alleviate the sense of burning, now I feel that I had no pity on men, I was delighted to see blood, I was happy to hear cries of pain. My Master, did you derive similar pleasure too"?

"No Utanka, no".

"Of course, you did, then why didn't you forbid me ever, why didn't you stop me"?

"Shut up, Utanka"!

Utanka went on, "You did not teach me what it meant to be compassionate, to be kind, I learnt them after my demise. I really take pity on you, my Master! You have sent the son of Dhruva on exile for the whore, you have slain Utanka, you do not have kindness, my Master! Set out on business, then you will get to know compassion, kindness, lest people will celebrate your death too, they will keep rejoicing"!

Throwing both his hands up, Utanka cried out in agony, "Stop, Utanka, stop! Thy fire has encircled me, don't thou have an iota of compassion in thy heart? After all, I am thy Master"!

The universe sank in silence thereafter!

THIRTY-EIGHT

King Bhartrihari was going to see Acharya Brishavanu. It was the second prahar of the night. The city was enveloped in pin-drop silence. And off the God's way, just on the bank of the river Shipra, stood the temple of Lord Mangalnath. The way leading to the ashram of Brishavanu was desolate and not even a street-cur was lying awake, it seemed. It was the day of Krishna Chaturdashi. Moon was absent from the sky, the light reflecting from the Milky Way, helped him move along the road. Starlight was there to help the King see the road. He had left the lamp, held in his hand, concealed behind the God's way. Now nothing could be taken for granted. Day by day, the King of Ujjwain was shattering inwardly.

Long back, he had paid a visit to the ashram of Acharya Brishavanu. As far as he could recall, it was the full moon night in the month of Kartick. Five full moon nights had sped by, since then. Even after such a long interregnum, Acharya could not enlighten him of anything substantial at all. He would tell him the reason behind such drought! King Bhartrihari felt like being in the clutch of peril now. Previously, he could conjecture everything, just a word from the mouth of his dear ones or his courtiers would be enough for him to comprehend their state of mind, but now every assumption was eluding him. Many things remained indistinct, hazy. A man he was familiar with, seemed unknown to him. Queen Bhanumati seemed to be quite distant a relation to him. He failed to understand Bikram, his younger brother. Merchant Subhag Dutta appeared to be volatile at times. Topping all, he could not find any explanation behind all the happenings, either in his own life or in the city itself. Wouldn't the Acharya be able to explain it? This, too, seemed quite strange to him. How was it that he could not read it anymore even after knowing the firmament like the back of his palm? Then what would befall this city, this country? Where would the lives of the meek and mild populace of Ujjwain head on to?

The city was ablaze because of drought. But why? The Acharya consoled that he would glean the information from the sky. From all the stars like the Orion, Arundhati,

Brahmahriday, Bishakha. From the stars of the zodiac signs. Had he done that at all? He, himself, had gone out to meet Acharya Brishavanu. But which destiny had taken him off to Lord Mahakaal's temple that night? Before he could reach the Chief Priest, while entering the Mahakaal temple, a devadasi had stopped him midway. Romantic feelings got the better of him as memories of that night came to his mind. Who was that devadasi? He had not even looked at her face clearly. His unsatisfied desires of life found fulfilment that night, it seemed. But that incident had been doing rounds in the city lately! Who divulged? That devadasi? But that night, he had not seen her face clearly even! That woman, resembling the Earth, had borne Lord Mahakaal on her! He was reminded of the inarticulate groan, she let out. In the dark, if she again called Lord Mahakaal, would he be able to recognize her at all?

All seemed so strange! How could he have sexual intercourse with a woman he had never seen before, who was just an absolute stranger to him? And again, how did she recognize him as an impersonation of Lord Mahakaal? Was it really difficult to recognize the King even in the dark? It had never happened in his life. Sometimes, it seemed, as though, he had gone to rape a hapless woman like a lecherous male. This incident really went against his grain. Do such things happen when the nature gets averse, the sky goes cloudless, when the rivers and the water-bodies run devoid of water? Did his own nature become so unintelligible as the greater Nature had turned different? He had never felt so complete in his life! How replete with varieties was life! How strewn with surprises could life remain? And how did destiny stand enveloped by darkness and mist?! Did he have any dearth of women? The paragon of beauty of Ujjwain, the Chief Prostitute, Devadutta, used to look forward to his much-awaited visit, though he used to find peace in declining her. But didn't the beauty of Devadutta charm him? Again, queen Bhanumati never cared to turn towards him at all! God only knew why such things happened in a single lifetime?

Army Commander, Bikram, had burnt the servant of the tycoon just a few days ago. The tycoon was again present in such celebration of death! He had seen Utanka. Utanka was the most trustworthy follower of the magnate. Utanka's past was not unknown to him. It was also doing rounds that the incident of combustion at the Shudra ghetto was the handiwork of Utanka! Why did he make that incident happen? Did he go out of his mind? Did he set the Shudra locality on fire, for no reason at all? Could it be so? Or he did not cause it to happen at all! In these days of scorching heat, the fire broke out for some unknown cause! Such incidents of conflagration might happen because of man's inadvertence. He thought of finding out the source of the incident with the help of the city-cop. But everything came to the fore even preceding that. Utanka had died too. Everything appeared to be blurred to him. The merchant himself had surrendered his servant to Bikram though it sounded quite strange! The

Shudra ghetto had been burnt by fire. Why did the merchant hold his own servant responsible for that? Was he so kind to the Shudras? Was it credible? Did the merchant act befittingly?

No one was acting of his own accord. Neither the Army Commander, Bikram, nor queen Bhanumati! The Shudras were the strength of the armed forces. It was really true. But after the incident of conflagration, implicating the miscreant soon and burning him alive seemed somewhat unnatural too. The queen was to be beside the King. But Bhanumati seemed impregnable! Why did it so happen? Were all these owing to the drought? Lack of rainfall might cause such things to happen. The universe along with all the living things stay alive because of the clouds in the sky, rainfall, sun, cold, fog, light and darkness. Would such irrelevance mark man's behaviour if the Nature turned adverse? How strange! It was in the air that the witnesses expressed delight at Utanka's demise! Not a single soul of the city was sad for Utanka's death! On hearing it, he, himself was being drawn into mourning! Utanka, as grapevine sources went, died of excruciating pain. Did kindness, compassion evaporate from the human mind? Was this the manifestation of Nature's fury too?

The people of Ujjwain were never like this. Why had they been so? He would demand to learn all explanations from Acharya Brishavanu. Who else would explain all such things save him? He had not inquired of the devadasi! He did not even care to know her name! Now he felt like knowing that. It was being learnt that, that night's incident had reached the ears of all the city-dwellers! He was feeling withdrawn after learning it. Who could tell where his destiny was leading him to?

Shipra river flew by on his left. That river was now plunged in darkness. He remembered of gazing at the reflection of the stars on the water-surface of the river on such a new-moon night! It was long, long back! Now the sky was studded with stars but the bosom of the river failed to hold their reflection on it.

He came to stand before Acharya Brishavanu's ashram in the dark. Not a single whiff of wind was there today! He ran into Tamradhvaj at the entrance of the ashram. Holding the lamp in his hand, he welcomed the King, "You are welcome to this ashram"!

"Acharya"?

"He is there…yonder he is sitting in the dark". Raising the lamp, Tamradhvaj illumined the courtyard. The King moved forward.

Was Acharya Brishavanu asleep? So silent, motionless he was! The King turned to look. Tamradhvaj said, "Acharya is in meditation".

"When will he be back in his senses"?

"Surely, he will… Oh King, please come to this end to take rest. Would you like to go inside the ashram"?

No. The King walked in slow steps to the paved bank of the river, Shipra. Tamradhvaj followed him with a lamp in his hand. The King sat on the floor, Tamradhvaj stood and kept waiting, leaving the lamp at a small distance. The King too fell somewhat silent. The King of Ujjwain was looking up at the dots of light, on the sky. Tamradhvaj kept observing the King.

A little later, the King had been back in his senses. The disciple of the Acharya was standing for his command. He turned towards him. Last time when he met the youth, he took him to be intelligent. Being curious, he asked to be introduced to Tamradhvaj. The King took fancy on Tamradhvaj as he introduced himself, bowing down his head. He said, "Why are you standing there, be seated"!

Tamradhvaj sat on his knees in front of the King. Staying for long in the dark, light of one's eyes makes everything clearly visible. Tamradhvaj could espy the bottom of the waterless river. He said, "Oh King, in our country, the river, Betrabati, too, is almost dried up".

"I know, the news has reached me".

Tamradhvaj inquired, "There wasn't such a drought ever before, was it there"?

"I have not witnessed, King Bhartrihari replied in a feeble voice, I had asked the Acharya to find out the reason behind such lack of rainfall".

Tamradhvaj kept quiet. He wanted to say something, but was feeling hesitant. He wished to inquire about Dhruvaputra. Did the King know him?

The King was taken aback. "Who are you talking of"?

"The son of Dhruva! Dhruvadas was the merchant, Subhag Dutta's bosom friend".

The King said, "No, I can't recall".

"It is not you who will remember this, it is a tale that dates long back. Leaving a one-year-old son, Dhruvadas breathed his last. Even while giving birth to the child, his mother kicked the bucket too. That orphan boy had been reared up by a man of Gambhira village".

"And what next"?

"Dhruvaputra was a man of knowledge, the merchant had taken the responsibility of educating him", Tamradhvaj went on. The King kept listening with rapt attention. Tamradhvaj was describing Dhruvaputra slowly, in accordance with

Gandhavati's description of him. Then all of a sudden, he said, "Since he has gone on exile, rainfall has vanished from this land".

"How so, even your Dasharno is equally affected by drought"!

"Dasharno, Ujjwain…all share the same sky, oh King"!

"The whole world shares only one sky"!

"I cannot talk about the whole world, but I haven't heard of any downpour anywhere"!

"Are there no clouds in any land"?

"No, my King! A group of men have moved towards the east, thinking that the east had rainfall, another body of people came to this end from the east, surmising rainfall in here, the men from the north are shifting to the south and vice-versa, people have gone restive, oh King, restless men do not want to halt anywhere".

The King said, "Perhaps I know next to nothing about all those matters".

Tamradhvaj said, "You know! You cannot afford to be ignorant of anything! You are the King"!

Wrenching his neck, the King threw a glance at Tamradhvaj. He could not turn a deaf ear to the firmness of voice of this youth. For once, he felt like asking more about Dhruvaputra. He had just heard the name and nothing more than that. But the way Tamradhvaj described Dhruvaputra, it seemed, he should know more about him. But what would it amount to? His mind was going restless. He failed to concentrate on anything. Tamradhvaj's words were making way to his ear. He was saying, "All night people keep moving down the thoroughfare, if you want to notice, oh King, you can go and stand there, on the road"!

The King stood up abruptly, "Has Acharya woken up"?

"He is lying awake, indeed".

"No, it doesn't seem so, it seems that he is still asleep".

Tamradhvaj retracted a little. It was not that such words did not strike him! But the very thought unnerved him. Was the Acharya engrossed in meditation or sleeping instead? The King rose. He stepped forward towards the ashram. Tamradhvaj was following the King. Moving to the fore, the King stopped abruptly, turned back to look at him, "You have talked of a strange matter"!

"Which one"? Tamradhvaj was taken by surprise.

"I think, I have seen Dhruvaputra"!

"May be", Tamradhwaj answered in an inarticulate voice!

The King said, "Man's heart is loaded with love and compassion. Without affection, love, this world cannot keep going; the man of the West thinks that rains, crops, happiness – all are there in the East; the King thinks that all pleasures lie contained in the subjects' life, while the subjects think just the contrary".

Tamradhvaj said, "Yes King, this is just an old saying, an old adage that everyone knows".

The King said, "My mind has become restive and once it is so, the people of the East cannot keep on living in the East, they shift to the West, come please, ask Acharya to wake up from sleep"!

Tamradhvaj informed, "He is in meditation".

"I am restless, how long will Acharya take? The city of Avanti is ablaze, is getting singed, today I must return with the answer," saying so, the King moved forward in long steps. He came to stand in front of Acharya Brishavanu, who sat in deep meditation. Starlight fell on the countenance of the astronomer, who was lost in meditation. His eyes were closed. Restive King, knelt down and said to Tamradhvaj, who was standing behind Acharya, "Planets and stars are studies in calculations, how does meditation help it"?

"Yes, venerated King, Acharya knows that, meditation can solve everything, when calculation loses direction, only meditation can help".

The King called, "Acharya"!

The King heard the noise of deep breathing. Only a man, fast asleep, can breathe thus.

The King said," Acharya, I am the King of Ujjwain, I have come to know the outcome of your calculations, since long this land is in the clutch of drought"!

Acharya, who was in deep meditation, stayed unresponsive. The King kept looking. This was the appearance of a man in sleep, no doubt! His conjecture was not incorrect. The King produced his hand, touched the chest of Acharya Brishavanu and immediately the earth seemed to quake. The still stature of Brishvanu moved. He started to open his eyes. Opening his eyes, he saw the King in front of him. Both his eyes widened. An expression of being in peril became prominent in his widened eyes. He had a hunch that the King would come. There was no other way for the King than to come. No rainfall happened as yet, in Avanti! The city was ablaze, the villages were being scorched. The earth kept cracking. The King had faith in the Acharya who would come to know the reason behind Nature's fury! He came to get the wind of the words against the King which was rife in the city. King could only be saved by the clouds of the sky now! Good rainfall owed to the piety of the King, the people used to think. Good shower would definitely lave off all the sins of the King! It had washed off evil, it would again wash it off. The throne would remain safe and sound. Otherwise, bad and false rumours would do rounds. The heat of the sun would burn off all the good deeds of the King!

The King demanded, "Have you chanced upon any solution to the troubled plight, Acharya"?

Acharya shook his head. In a pained face, he replied, "I do not know".

"Don't you know"? The King cried out in desperation. "Haven't you found out even after so long, which planet or star of the sky would be held responsible for the drought in Avanti"?

Brishavanu replied, "No".

"If Acharya Brishavanu fails, who will succeed"?

"I don't know", the elderly astronomer sat drooping his head low. He spoke in a sibilant voice, "I cannot come up with a joyful news for you, dear King"!

"Then what shall I do"? If there is no rainfall in the city, the rivers like Gandhavati, Shipra – all will dry up. The Seven Lakes have almost dried up. Now people will set out on an exodus, leaving this city. How dreadful you sound, Acharya"!

Acharya Brishavanu stood up slowly. He moved forward into the darkness. Raising both his hands, he looked up to the sky, in a broken voice, he kept saying, "This world has turned into a place of unhappiness to me, oh King, to whom have you come? To my eyes the sky looks awry, it has cracked up like the earth"!

The King came forward, "What are you saying, Acharya"?

Acharya called Tamradhvaj, "Come here".

Tamradhvaj came and in a grave tone said, "You look as if you are in danger, Acharya"!

Brishavanu said, "Look up to the sky, the northern sky, I mean".

Tamradhvaj could locate the Orion in the northern sky. Like the hook-like tendrils of the wild creeper, the seven stars stood piercing the sky. Near the north-eastern horizon, the second star of the cluster of seven was Basistha. Acharya asked, "Is Basistha there"?

"Yes, Acharya", Tamradhvaj got thrilled, just after saying so. Why this query?

He himself was gazing at it. Didn't Tamradhvaj have any idea about the seven sages? Then Acharya demanded to know, "And is Arundhati there, beside Basistha"?

Gazing at Arundhati, Tamradhvaj was reminded of Gandhavati. He was casting a steadfast gaze at the tiny star. He seemed to have seen the face of Gandhavati in the sky. Just then he heard the call of Acharya, "Can you get to see Arundhati"?

"Yes"! Staring at the sky, Tamradhvaj answered.

"Oh King, can you locate it"?

"Yes, Acharya"! While answering, the King found that fear was writ large on the face of Acharya. Even in the dark, it was quite vivid. The King could see quite distinctly.

THIRTY-NINE

The King could see that the frightened Acharya had turned his face aside. The King moved around to stand face-to face with Brishavanu once again. He saw that both the eyes of the elderly astronomer were wide open. The King could sense that Brishavanu was trembling. He could not decipher the reason however. He stood in front of Brishavanu, being somewhat perplexed. Then, Tamradhvaj came forward. Perhaps, he had a premonition that the Acharya was about to fall down. He caught hold of him, clasping him, he queried, "What's wrong, Acharya, are you feeling out of sorts"?

Acharya lowered his head, he began to nod.

"Rather you take rest", the King advised.

In a broken voice, Acharya Brishavanu said, "But I cannot locate Arundhati at all".

Tamradhvaj startled, the King shuddered and both of them seemed to exclaim in unison, "What do you say, Acharya, is it the truth, or any imagination, originating from despair"?

Acharya's neck lowered, he kept whispering, "Arundhati has gone far removed from my eyes, I perceive the sky as a wave and that wave is of a river of darkness, I have never seen such in my life, what sort of truth is this?"

Tamradhvaj was frightened, he let out an agonizing scream, "What are you saying, my Lord? Is it true"?

"True".

"How can it be true,this is a terrible revelation"!

Acharya whispered, "Since the last couple of months, I am not finding Arundhati anymore, Tamradhvaj, each night is being blurred before my eyes and at last I have surrendered myself to sleep,I have come under the spell of sleep, and the sky has turned a stranger to me, dear! Narrating so, the elderly astronomer sat down on the ground".

The King said, "I do not believe this".

That will not alter the truth though, "Oh King, can you espy the little star beside Basistha"?

The King tilted his head. Then Brishavanu went on haltingly, "While researching the reason behind the misfortune of Avanti,I have come to know about my death, which is imminent. You know, my King, if Arundhati remains hidden from someone's eyes, his death approaches fast and this is for sure. I can clearly see that my death is inching closer".

"Oh Lord, please be calm", Tamradhvaj implored.

Brishavanu got to his feet. The light in both his eyes was really about to die. The Chief Astronomer was looking like a blind man indeed. He went on, "I shall go, leaving Avanti behind, I can visualize my own death, Oh King"!

Tamradhvaj said, "Lord, please be composed. In Dasharno, my homeland, by the side of the river, Betrabati, a plant grows, whose juice can cure blindness almost near-radical, the vision gets crystal-clear, I shall go there to fetch it".

Brishavanu began to shake his head, "That would not work

anymore".

"Why, my Lord"?

"That creeper is available in the forest, on the other bank of the river, Shipra. Do you think I did not try it? But drought has taken off the light from my eyes, Tamradhvaj you better bring me my books".

"What use are these books"? Bhartrihari demanded to know. His voice seemed to sound ruthless.

"I shall take them along".

"Along with you, you mean. But what for"?

"I do not know, but to be frank and fair, my Lord, if any miracle comes my way"!

"Miracle"?

"Yes,if I bump into a man who can restore light to both my eyes, I shall again get to see Arundhati"!

The King kept silent. Could it ever happen so? Would there be anyone who could nullify his senility? Tamradhvaj had gone to fetch the box of books. Underneath the sky, the King and the purblind astronomer stood facing each other. The King was looking steadfast at the face of the Acharya! Slowly he said, "Does such miracle ever happen"?

"It may happen so. Do we know everything of this universe or are we familiar with each individual"?

The King muttered, "I heard that the men belonging to a pure religion are capable of exercising such powers".

Brishavanu lowered his head. "Are you going in search of such a man of pure religion, who is well-versed in tantra as well"?

Brishavanu did not raise his head. "Do they really do it, are they really capable of such powers"?

Brishavanu cocked his head up and said, "I, too, have heard of it".

"Can they bring down rains"?

"Who knows, perhaps they can"!

"Have you ever heard of anything as such"?

"I can imagine, I can hope, in that hope I take to the streets, bidding adieux to this city. Shall I not get anyone in the villages or towns who can bring back light to my eyes, let him be a man of pure religion or a Brahmin, a Shudra or whatever! Oh King, I am going away in search of that man who can even usher in rains, he, who knows the whereabouts of the clouds. I shall come back to this city along with such a man"!

Tamradhvaj was listening to all that he was saying. He handed the small box of books to old Brishavanu. But as Brishavanu, holding the books near his bosom, was about to set out on his journey, in stumbling steps, Tamradhvaj could not hold himself aloof, he sprang up to stop him, proffering his hands. The King desisted him saying, "Wait"!

"Is he leaving truly"?

"Let him leave".

"He is just a blind man, shall I let a blind go all alone, on the road"? Acharya halted. Tamradhvaj called out in a scream of agony, "Where will you go, my Lord"?

The King again stopped Tamradhvaj by saying, "He is going out in search of something which will bring back vision to his eyes and as he will get back his eyesight, the period of drought in this country will come to an end".

Tamradhvaj, in a muffled voice said, "You are so cruel"!

"Cruelty? Where exactly do you find it, you, young man"?

"You think, the rain will be made to happen by some miracle, Acharya will come back with such a man of unearthly powers, but will it ever come true"?

"It can come to be true, if he chances upon a man who can bring back a blind man's vision, can cause clouds to form in the sky, which in turn will cause rains, it will be good for him, for Ujjwain, and the city of Avanti as well".

"Oh King, is there any such man in reality"?

"Might have been there, who can tell, but hearsay has it, indeed".

"So, at last, the King has to count on a blind person, leaving aside everyone sighted! Shelving youth aside, old age comes to be your chief support"! Uttering these words, Tamradhvaj had a hunch that it was not worth doing in front of the King! He lowered his head. The King put his hand on his back, and whispered, "You are the Acharya's disciple, mind you"!

"Yes, my King"!

"Do you know calculations"?

"A bit, but the mystery of drought is something beyond the jurisdiction of my knowledge".

The King heaved a sigh and said, "Acharya Brishavanu had given me his word, I depended on him but I had no idea that he had undergone such transformations by now"!

Tamradhvaj said, "Where has Acharya Brishavanu gone in this darkness"?

"I am sure, he will come back. Is drought the reason of his being blind"?

"That is possible, drought is ushering in blindness here, even though not in sight, but certainly in mind"!

King Bhartrihari had thrown an astonished stare at Tamradhvaj. He had taken fancy to the statement. He became saddened. He looked at the expansive sky above. He went listless, he threw a glance at the sky. He remembered the queen. Of the devadasi. What was her name? Lalita Dasi. The King remembered the whore, Devadutta. Then all went blank, nothing was there on his mind. Being oblivious of all, he kept gazing at the sky. Tears welled up in his eyes. Oh! How stark alone he was! None would be such lonely as a blind man. He could not see the sky, the light, not even any near and dear one. The King felt that, in this large universe, he was alone too. None had been there in this world. He began to shiver visibly.

For quite long, the King and Tamradhvaj stayed quiet. In between them, time was flowing past into eternity, it seemed. Endless silence enveloped the two. After a long pause, Tamradhvaj called, "Oh King, why are you silent"?

The King downed his head from the sky, and in an inarticulate voice replied, "I was gazing at Arundhati".

Tamradhvaj said, "Blind Acharya had walked past, all alone, by the bank of the river. You, being the King, did not desist him in a desire of something illusory, but is this the virtue of a King"?

The King fixed Tamradhvaj with a long stare, saying nothing.

Tamradhvaj remarked, "Blind, sick and distressed are protected by the King. To a King there can be no distinction between the blind and the sighted, the rich and the have-not, the wise and the ignorant, the beautiful and the ugly—all are just equal to him".

The King took time to speak haltingly, "I have allowed Acharya to leave, prioritizing the well-being of this Kingdom, the King can hardly stay impartial when the polity gets scorched by the scourge of drought, he has to judge who is sighted and who is blind. As an able-bodied healthy man is a need in the time of war, likewise, a man with proper eyesight will be the refuge for the King, during such unprecedented natural calamity, the terrible disaster in the world of nature"!

Tamradhvaj inquired, "Is this disaster natural"?

"When Nature turns adverse"!

"Oh King, the people think this is the wrath of Lord Mahakaal"!

The King opined, "This Nature is Mahakaaleswar [Lord Mahakaal]. I hope Acharya Brishavanu will come back. His eyes will then be aglow and the sky over Ujjwain will be overcast with rain-bearing clouds".

"When the disaster is natural, who else but Nature herself has to bless us with the clouds"!

The King remained reticent. Swaying his head, he went on, "Yet man awaits some surprise. Something may abruptly take place which he had never thought of, in his life"!

Tamradhvaj said, "If someone waits for a miracle to happen, he evades the responsibility of working towards some end on his own". The King maintained silence. Tamradhvaj could feel that the King of Ujjwain was being assailed by his inner conflict. He was tender-hearted. Though jeopardized, the King Bhartrihari had helped the blind astronomer to set out on a journey, on a rugged way, in quest of such a man whose existence on this earth was questionable. Who would make the downpour possible? Who was so powerful save and except Nature? Tamradhvaj could feel that the King, pinned down from all corners, was perplexed regarding what to do or what exactly to articulate. He asked again, "Did you think that the expulsion of Acharya would bring welfare to Ujjwain or did you seriously expect Acharya to return with any sorcerer"?

The King started. Leaning back on the wall of darkness, he lowered his head. He gently came up with a rejoinder, "I have no idea what leads to what else, Ujjwain is being shoved inch-by-inch to death by drought, drought itself is death, Acharya said that he seemed to sense death on losing his eyesight and again blindness spells death to an astronomer indeed! Hence, I thought, if he would leave this city along with his 'death', this city would be blessed with rainfall and signs of life would abound, everywhere".

Tamradhvaj could sense that the King was a drowned man. He, himself, could not feel what he did or thought. But the King was a wise man. Strange! Despite being wise, why couldn't he understand that the expulsion of an unsuccessful man would not cause any leaf on the tree to quiver or the dust on the road to blow? Whether Brishavanu would leave or not, it would hardly affect any change in Ujjwain in the least! Then, why was the hapless man allowed to leave? Perhaps, Acharya talked about his blindness just to cover up his failure! As he failed to chance upon anything with his calculations, he took his exit from the city on the ruse of being blind! And, in order to fortify that reason, he imagined a conjuror, who would bring his vision back and cause the clouds to surface in the sky with his magical power. Tamradhvaj kept looking into the darkness. The Acharya had melted into the air walking along the riverbank, and this particular way was even taken by Dhruvaputra. A road that led to the east. Tamradhvaj uttered the words softly, "Even though not in this manner, but the other one had taken that direction to the east for sure - none other than Dhruvaputra"!

"Who is Dhruvaputra? Why do you draw his instance"?

"He is not in this city, after his exit, the sky of Avanti has gone without clouds"!

"Many people have left, many again have filed in, leaving-and-coming in is an incessant and regular affair, what does it have to do with drought, with lack of rainfall"?

The matter was clear indeed. Yet Tamradhvaj said, "Oh King, I have researched and come to know that, if drought is death, the day it rains is the day of birth, and it occurs to me, rain can just not be equal to birth, it is wisdom as well while drought is lack of wisdom. Dhruvaputra was a wise man, in the truest sense"!

The King protested, "Just incredible! Then, has wisdom disappeared from this city"?

"Yes, oh King! You have marked how Acharya has yielded to senility, losing all his knowledge, oh King, you take a comprehensive look all around and just think, if not ignorance, then what for all these events keep transpiring in this city"?!

"Which incident"?

"Try to remember"!

The King asked, "But who are you"?

"I hail from the land of Dasharno…I have told you already, dear King"!

The King cast a flabbergasted look at Tamradhvaj. This youth seemed to be familiar to him! Did he ever see him? Though he could not recall when and where. This was happening lately. Amnesia was setting in, too often, quite alarmingly.

FORTY

The most noted of all merchants of Avanti, Subhag Dutta, would set out on a trade tour. This was a breaking news at Avanti! The people of Ujjwain could not remember when Subhag Dutta had last gone with his retinue of traders to a distant land! As though, this prolonged drought was the reason for such amnesia!

Subhag Dutta would be going to the land of Balkh, on the lap of the Caucasus range, far to the north-west! Whether crossing Purushpur, Gandhaar to Balkh or a place somewhere in between the five rivers and the river, Indus, in Punjab, Subhag Dutta had doubts about it. Many a man had many a tale to narrate. None was there in this city who had been to that land or was in the know of that place! Acharya Brishavanu of Saandipani Ashram had set out to an aimless destination, he was aware of the whereabouts of the firmament. Couldn't a man who knew the ins and outs of the sky tell anything about the earth? Perhaps, Acharya knew where the land of Balkh was located. The city of Ujjwain took alarm at the news of Acharya Brishavanu's sudden disappearance. If he, who was aware of the sky like the back of his palm, he, who acquired all possible knowledge, would leave the city, the city would surely be plunged in darkness. Perhaps the age of ignorance had already begun. The glory of Ujjwain seemed to have been lost. Clouds would never hover over the city anymore. The dry wind of drought would blow over the city forever. The richest merchant had not gone out on business expedition since ages, was he going away with all treasures and riches of Ujjwain, finally, never to return? The city of Avanti would be left devoid of all its splendour, with a burnt sky overhead!

Subhag Dutta said, "I had a desire since long, to fetch yellow silk from Balkh, but I am aging, oh King, and after this it would not be possible anymore, the longing itself would die out".

The King came to know about the tycoon's business expedition. The King had sent for the rich tycoon, Subhag Dutta. Subhag Dutta kept saying, he had heard the description of that land from the Ionian Greek traders. It was a strange tale. In that land, situated on the lap of the Caucasus range, Alexander, the great valiant hero, had expanded his empire. Consequently, many people of Greece had stayed back in that land. Though Balkh was a land of Greece, it never had been the primordial land of the men and women of Greece at all. That land was far-off, across the seas, dotted with grapevines. He had gleaned all information, as needed. The merchants knew all. It was them who would bring all the news. Tycoon Subhag Dutta said, "All these had been narrated to him by another individual, he was Dhruvaputra"!

King Bhartrihari got startled, "Who is Dhruvaputra"?

"The son of my bosom friend".

"Where is he"?

"He is not here in this city. He was erudite, wise".

Saying so, Subhag Dutta lowered his head. His voice kept sounding grave. He had confined himself in his house after Utanka's death. After almost a month or more, he had come out in the open. He would set out on a business trip. He would be going to the distant land of Balkh. The King was remembering Tamradhvaj. He had heard of Dhruvaputra from him indeed. He asked, "Was he sheltered by you"?

"True, my King".

"Have I ever seen him"?

Subhag Dutta retorted, "I cannot say if he had come on his own, but I had never brought him along".

"Was he handsome"?

Subhag Dutta went silent. In a little while, he said, "He was in full bloom of youth, youth is beautiful and he was knowledgeable and knowledge has its own beauty too"!

"Such a man would have been the pride of Ujjwain"!

Subhag Dutta maintained his silence. What rejoinder would he come up with? Knowing full well, knowing that his father's mate, tycoon Subhag Dutta was enamoured of that devadasi, how could Dhruvaputra fall in love with that woman? Ungrateful to the core, no doubt! He had been fostered by him only! If he would stay back at Gambhira, he would either have been a royal employee or a sentry of the hamlet or a soldier at the most! If an ordinary soldier, he might have gone missing like Kartikkumar, Shivnath's son! Subhag Dutta's mind got filled with disgust once again.

The King said, "If Dhruvaputra had been here, he could have answered all your queries".

Subhag Dutta stayed mute. Perhaps the King's saying was true! Again, it would not have been true too. Some incidents had transpired in Ujjwain just for Dhruvaputra, which were simply undesirable! Just for Dhruvaputra, Devadutta, the courtesan, had rejected him. Now that the slut said she was fond of the King proved to be just a facade of falsity and nothing else! In fact, she was awaiting Dhruvaputra's return. She feigned to be enamoured of the King, just to slight the tycoon, Subhag Dutta's advances. This was her strategy of living her life. Subhag Dutta could divine that. But if the harlot would really love the King, would the King have to go, on the sly, to the shrine of Mahakaal to desecrate it? Would he then have to be physically intimate with an innocent devadasi, impersonating as Lord Mahakaal? This happened just because the harlot refused to win the King as her own, with her charms. This was his duty, no doubt. It could not be possible because of Dhruvaputra. If Dhruvaputra had not made her fall for him with his attractive virtues, he would be able to exercise his authority on Devadutta himself! If that would have happened, he did not have to enter into a collusion with the Army-Commander, Bikram, the younger brother of the King. Neither conflagration at the Shudra ghetto nor Utanka's demise would have to be engineered. All owed to the rejection of the prostitute. It was the root cause, to be precise. And at its base stood the unseen influence and invisible presence of Dhruvaputra. And now after witnessing the gruesome spectacle of death, tycoon Subhag Dutta was no longer reminded of the face of Devadutta. No woman would ever be able to alleviate his mourning. Neither a woman of this earth nor the nymph of the heaven, none of them! He would not be able to come out of this grief even at the cost of a block of diamond or gems and pearls. He had sculpted Utanka with his own hands. He had shaped him into an obedient servant. He had bestowed his own ruthlessness upon the creature, he brought from the hills. He had snatched off the child Utanka from the lap of his mother! Even at this moment, her deathly wails kept ringing in his ears! All this had happened because of Devadutta. Subhag Dutta had enveloped his own life with melancholy, just to establish his claim on a woman! Dhruvaputra was the sole and invisible cause of such sorrow and gloom.

The King said, "The city is ablaze, and not a hint of clouds or rain is there, since long! And in these troubled times, our tycoon is going to leave this city, couldn't he postpone his journey at all"?

Subhag Dutta moved his head. He had had to go. Even the arrangements for the journey were also nearly complete. Long, long back, he had set out to the northern states, went to the Himalayas, brought Utanka along. Then, he had gone to the east, till Pataliputra, to Barugaza at the south west, he had connections already with the Shurparak port, he had been to Dasharno, to Vatsya, but was yet to journey to the north-west, across the river, Indus, to Purushpur, Gandhaar, Balkh – the land of yellow silk. As he expressed his desire, the small and notable group of merchants had assured of accompanying him. They would be taking along the merchandise of Ujjwain and Avanti - fine muslin, fine and coarse cotton garments, and those would be both white and of varied colours! They would be toting along gems, jewels, peacock, pigeon and a flock of other varieties of birds, sugarcane, sandalwood, so on, so forth. The day of journey too nearly approached and now how would the King stop him? In this city, at the dead of night, magnate Subhag Dutta could hear the loud wails, heart-rending death-throes of Utanka! As the night intensified further, Utanka would come to stand in front of him. Subhag Dutta could now smell the stench of burnt flesh of humans, in the air of this city. Now, this city was no more a peaceful refuge to him. The fragrance and refreshing ambience of yore, had lately become a thing of the past. Signs of combustion stood pronounced, all around.

The King chipped in, "Now is not the befitting moment for business expedition"!

"I know".

"If monsoon strikes midway, you have to come back"!

"I am aware of that".

"Then why are you leaving now"?

Subhag Dutta answered, "Oh King, I am sick and tired of everything here! Since the last one month, I am spending sleepless nights. I must have to go for a change, leaving this city behind".

The King remarked, "Is it because of the death of your servant-boy from the hills"?

Subhag Dutta replied, "Nothing is supposed to remain beyond your knowledge"!

"Of course, all remained beyond my cognizance, I still do not know the reason for his death-sentence"!

"Haven't the King heard anything of the deadly conflagration at the Shudra ghetto"?

"Yes, I witnessed it that night! But this is not unusual during droughts"!

"But Utanka himself had ignited the flame"!

"Why"?

"No idea, my King"!

The merchant's servant was served with a death-sentence, yet why hadn't the merchant intervened to exonerate him? If the Army-Commander failed, the King would definitely have forgiven him!!

Tycoon Subhag Dutta kept mum. Without being able to elicit a reply, the King said, "I know next to nothing about this judgment".

Subhag Dutta replied, "Whatever is done cannot be undone, my King! Utanka will never come back alive. Hence, I have to set out on a trade-tour".

The King exclaimed, "Judgment was issued at such remarkable hurry, a death-sentence had been served, the convict was burnt alive, yet the King remained ignorant of everything! But why"?

Subhag Dutta remained speechless. He was not at the helm of judgment, it was done by the Army Commander, Bikram. Only an Army Commander was entitled to such power of judgment. He had that right. But this matter was supposed to stay confined in between the King and the Army-Commander. The King would demand an answer of the Army-Commander as to why had this matter of judgment and issue of death-sentence been kept beyond the knowledge of the King? Why the merchant? He was not at the helm of administrative affairs of the Kingdom! The King did not entrust him with any sort of responsibility! And it was not even expected of him! The state-power was to be enjoyed by the King, right from the Army- Commander to Uddhavnarayan! All powers of the tycoon remained restricted to his riches and treasures. With that wealth, he would buy the administrative power, by bits. Uddhavnarayan used to grovel at his feet just in lure of that! The Army-Commander sought his aid in unctuous diction, to realize his aim of ascending the throne! And again, with the power of wealth itself, he wished to buy the company of the Chief Prostitute! But why would the King ask him about 'judgment'? His loyal, tamed, loving man was no more! He, only, was in mourning!

The King said, "I have been utterly astonished by the incident! It was not at all pleasant to me"!

Subhag Dutta maintained silence. Faintly he surmised that the King might have learnt something! The King, perhaps, got the wind of the fact that the incidents like the combustion at the Shudra ghetto, Utanka's death-sentence were all a part of a collusion against him! Just mere thought it left Subhag Dutta perspiring! The maid who was fanning her with a palmyra fan had increased the speed too as she got the feel of the matter.

The King demanded, "The Shudra ghetto at the border of the city, would be burnt down for no reason and immediately after, the miscreant would be sentenced to death in no time, and the King would have no information of anything at all, but why, why will it be so? What for?"

Subhag Dutta lowered his head. He seemed to understand that the King had sent for him after coming to know everything and all! The King had no interest in his business expedition but Utanka's death-sentence had made him suspicious. The people of the city were all praise for the Army Commander and the merchant, as well. The Army Commander had identified the criminal and sentenced him to death and the merchant had not given his servant any protection, as he was the miscreant. The King had taken umbrage as these words got wafted to his ears. The King had read ample of books, his power of conjecture was quite keen, it was as sharp as his olfactory sense! The King had sent for Subhag Dutta for cross-examination, just out of suspicion. And again, it was true that the King had his followers strewn across the city, hadn't he? Perhaps, the King was in the know of everything that had transpired! Was the King engaged in a game with tycoon Subhag Dutta just as a cat would toy with a half-dead rat? Did the King's resistance begin, stealthily? Would King Bhartrihari pass the throne of Ujjwain on, so easily? All these were there, a-jumble, in his mind. Subhag Dutta was being overcome by fear in his mind! He had immense wealth, he had no dearth of gems and jewels. His own wealth would amount to almost the same as that in the coffers of this kingdom. But he was not the King, by any means. By the order of the King any soldier would unsheathe his sword. He, of course, was not empowered that way! Subhag Dutta lost the peace of his mind.

After a long time, Subhag Dutta had a feel of standing in front of the Arabian Sea. During youth, he used to spend time with his companion, Dhruva, by the sea! Facing the sea, they used to think of themselves as little drops of water. It seemed to Subhag Dutta that he was sitting under the star-studded sky of the night, glancing above! All around him stood the stillness of an endless meadow. His friend Dhruva was an amazing person! Throwing his gaze at the firmament, he used to say, 'man is nothing but dust in this wider universe, don't we think ourselves to be just dust particles while looking at the sky'? With the King in front of him, Subhag Dutta was returning to that truth, it seemed. Though he might be blessed with immense wealth, the King had the throne! In the cities of Ujjwain and Avanti, King Bhartrihari was the Supreme Lord, Mahadeva, he was the representative of Lord Mahakaaleshwar! Lord Mahadeva himself had freed this city! This city was a heaven beyond the Heavens. It could be considered at par with the Heavens!

The King spoke out, "I heard that Utanka was a man of hard-hearted nature"!

The merchant now seemed to get a straw to catch, as a drowning man would. He said, "Yes revered King, his ruthless nature was the real cause of his setting the Shudra locale on fire"!

"But why did he set it on fire, that too, so abruptly"?

Subhag Dutta shook his head, expressing ignorance.

"Setting Shudra ghetto ablaze and issuing death-sentence, both are mysterious! If the Army-Commander would judge in absence of the King, it would make sense! But I am very much here in this city"!

The merchant went in studied silence. He could feel that no truth was hidden from King Bhartrihari! Gleaning all information, the King had called for him. He could not see the King eye-to-eye.

The King said, "Utanka hailed from the hills, he was a man of the forests"!

"Yes, my King"!

"But they are hardly of such cruel disposition"!

"Utanka was so, he was just an exception"! The merchant said.

"But why would he make such fire break out"?

"I do not know, my King"! The merchant got to his feet. He was feeling very small himself. For the King's voice or his power, he would have to ascend the throne. But he would never be capable of doing that. Rather, he would just assist the man who would be usurping the throne! Army Commander, Bikram, to be precise. That consent he had given to King Bhartrihari too. He had donated numerous gold coins to the King! He had presented the King such precious gifts! The gem-studded necklace which the King had adorned the devadasi with, was his gift to the King! But all these donations were nothing but to buy the royal power! But the power of the King could hardly be won thus!

The King inquired, "Will you really go out on business expedition"?

"Yes, King, I shall go. Everything seems so unbearable to me, I had reared up Utanka myself, I had brought Utanka from his mother's bosom"!

"Why had you made him grow to be such cruel"?

Subhag Dutta started and replied, "He had grown up like that"!

"Was there an ambience of ruthlessness around him?"

"No, my King! He was surrounded on all sides by this city only"!

King Bhartrihari grew sad, he cast a glance at the distant sky through the window. It was all vacuum, only the wings of the female vultures looked like black dots, flapping. The King said, "These rivers - Shipra, Gandhavati; the Mahakaal temple, Saptasagar lake, the pursuit of knowledge, music and percussion - how can one who grows up in such an ambience be cruel, so hard-hearted"?

"But it was so"!

"Weren't you aware of this"?

"Yes, I knew", Subhag Dutta whispered, "I never thought that things would come to such a pass"!

"What had escaped your thoughts"?

"That he would have to die for it".

The King was talking with his eyes glued to the window, "Are you aggrieved by his demise"?

"Yes, my King"!

"If you begged for his life, he would have been spared, but you didn't ask for that, did you"?

"I could not understand that I would be so shocked by his death, I just demanded the punishment of the criminal"!

The King said, "Even a slight harm to the dog lying in front of his house makes a man anxious and he tries to protect it. You could have approached me, you are the most prominent tycoon of this city, no other merchant in this city would dare emulate you in riches. Would the Army-Commander ever object to your wish"?

The merchant sat speechless. He thought, he had been spotted. Why was Utanka so cruel? Why had Utanka died after setting the Shudra hamlet on fire? If the King inquired keenly of all such things, he must be able to know everything. The King would come to know that Utanka used to brandish the flog, perched on the chariot, by his command only. Even Utanka's cruelty was his desired intent. The tycoon sat hanging his head low.

The King said, "With the Shudra ghetto torched and the death that follows—what exactly is there behind such incidents? What are the city-dwellers saying"?

The merchant kept standing on his feet. He was waiting to hear the ultimate truth from the mouth of the King! The King had certainly come to know about the intention of the priest, merchant and the Army- Commander!

The King said, "You can set out, you revered gentleman! You are going on an untimely trade expedition. But can you be sure that the bank of the river Indus or Purushpur will have downpour though Avanti goes without it? When you are leaving the city behind, the city-dwellers are in utter peril, such drought had never been experienced by this city before! Please set out on your trade-tour, the onus of this city lies on me, I must see the end of this drought and then I too..." King Bhartrihari left his words hanging in the mid-air!

The tycoon's head was dropping low and lower. He could feel that if he would want to live respectably, he would have to set out on a business expedition, without fail. Would his pre-eminence remain unaltered, if he postpones his business-tour with humble subservience to the will of the King"?

FORTY-ONE

The span of drought, lack of rains was stretching from long to longer! The best astronomer, Acharya Brishavanu had left Ujjwain. Some said, he had gone to the east, according to some, he had walked up to the west. Some of them were even coming up with views like, he was seen at the wee hours of the morning, walking along the meadows on the other side of the river Shipra, crossing the river itself and melting in the vacuum, just as the stars of the night melted away in the daylight. And Tamradhvaj, Brishavanu's disciple too had gone away somewhere else! Did he go off to the city of Bidisha, his own land, or was Acharya's way his own? He was, perhaps, stalking him, behind all eyes! However, Tamradhvaj had still been there, in the Ashram, even after the sad exit of the Acharya! Then after a few days, he also had gone missing. The city-residents were commenting variedly upon Acharya's journey to no destination! They were into assuming, they were into imagining.

After Acharya Brishavanu's exit, it was in the air, that tycoon Subhag Dutta would set out on a business tour. He would be accompanied by a few traders of Ujjwain of mixed status! Even his business expedition was also triggering conjectures and imaginings among the people. Many words were having wings! The city-people surmised that the magnate was leaving this city for good. Acharya left, Subhag Dutta would be leaving, - would this city be a void, gradually? Ujjwain was illumined by the presence of these people only, if they would leave, whom would the glorious history of Ujjwain be written upon? What would happen to this city if the rain-clouds never surfaced?

Baisakh was drawing nearly to its close. The days were being spent under sweltering heat, setting everything ablaze. As nights were not so long during this season, the sense of being burnt by sun remained for long. The sun-baked daytime became a thing of terror. Though the night was cool, how long would it persist? No sooner did it begin, than it hurried to its end! Now all day and night, many words were getting ``wings in the city, many were being made anew to fly off to the people,

322

and the residents in turn were cooking up more words with those ingredients to be catered fresh, to all and sundry. Some remarked that the golden days of Ujjwain were no more. As this drought was getting prolonged, its meaning lay deep, more intense. This lack of rains was an indicator to a devastating deluge, which would continue till endless eternity. Who could tell where would it lead to? None could tell for how long the city would keep burning thus! Acharya Brishavanu had gone away, the other astronomers failed to detect anything at all.

A city-resident said, "As Lord Varundev has become dissatisfied, things are coming to such a pass"!

"Tell me about Varundev", asked an elderly man, the owner of a pearl-shop. They two stood face-to-face on the street of this city itself, in the twilight. Twilight being over, darkness had descended. The moon shone in the mid-sky. The full moon was just a few days to go. On that very full-moon day, Lord Buddha had been born. He was none but the incarnation of Lord Vishnu, they learnt that way. But those who had followed him, were still just outcasts. The shaven-headed ones were the objects of suspicion of the people of the city, including the Brahmin priests.

The wise city-resident said, "There's no way if Varundev gets dissatisfied, as He is the God of rains, He is one among the ten deities presiding over the ten quarters of the globe, the Sun being His eyes, His chariot being golden and his residence being at the converging point of the sky and the sea".

"Have you seen the sea"? The middle-aged man inquired.

The wise city-dweller swayed his head and said, "No, I have not seen but have heard of the sea that it is blue in colour, it is full of water, it has neither any beginning nor an end".

"The Saptasagar of Ujjwain has gone bereft of water, what has happened to the sea"?

"The sea would have been devoid of water, too, if it was here in the city of Avanti"!

"Where is the sea"?

"It is there, somewhere across Saurashtra"!

"How far is that"?

"It might be about fifteen thousand miles off, seas are all around, as Saurashtra is on our west, it is there, it is there again in the east, in the south too, but I do not know whether there is a sea in the north, it might be there. No idea"!

"In the north, there are different mountain ranges, snow-covered lands"!

"Even across that it might be there, the sky bends low over the sea"!

"Who has told you"?

"The merchants talked of such things".

They began to exchange views on the sea. While walking, they came to a unanimous decision that there had been seas on all the ten ends, and high above ran only the sky, which was again a sea. And the sky was invariably the sea, as water poured down from the sky, unhindered, on the earth, and who didn't know that the sky was blue? There was sky above and down in the hell there was sea too. Otherwise, how could water come up from the hell? How could water spurt out once the earth was dug? As the rivers were fed by the water of the hell, the water in the well too got siphoned from the seas in the hell!

The middle-aged man said, "But most of the wells have gone dry, so does it mean that the drought has caused the water in the seas of hell to be exhausted too"!

The wise man replied, "Then how could water be procured by digging the sand-bed by the river"?

Exactly, the elderly man nodded and asked, "Has the sky-ocean too dried up"?

"I cannot say, it may be so".

"Then where has that water gone"?

"It has dried up because of the sweltering heat"!

"How dreadful"- stuttered the elderly man. He went on, "All are taking place beyond our knowledge, and we are not getting to know anything"!

The wise man waved his head, "Man cannot know everything, he just suffers the consequences".

"Is there no remedy at all"?

"Which remedy are you talking about"?

"Man must know everything and thus be forewarned".

"Man is too trivial; the vast Nature, oceans, mountains, rivers, wind, planets, stars—all are much, much bigger compared to man, the whole of the stupendous Nature is impregnable to us"!

The aged man kept swinging his head, "You are right! Man doesn't know about himself even"!

"Exactly so! But a man can be wise if he harbours love and affection in his heart".

The elderly man could not make out the purport of his statement. He was roaming around the thoroughfares of the city since the afternoon. A lot many were hanging about likewise. As the sun went down, all of them seemed to be out in quest of clouds, to find out how long it would take for monsoon to arrive or why such drought at all! But within this lay embedded numerous queries, sundry words. They knew not how to speak out. He looked up at the stars of the night. How clear it was! How bluish the moonlit sky looked! He kept on gazing. He was trying to make out the last statement of the wise man.

The knowledgeable man said, "The watery sky is now just a memory of the past, all the seven seas seem to have gone waterless perhaps".

"In Ujjwain, as seen by all, not even one of the seven lakes shows any sign of water"!

"Yes, now I am thinking thus, if the seven lakes of Ujjwain go high and dry, how would the seven seas stay filled with water"?

"That sea is not here in Avanti but you have said that blue water still flows there".

"No doubt I said, but now I am doubtful of my assumption, because this land is blessed by Lord Mahakaal, if it goes without water, if all the water-bodies here turn waterless, if Ratnakarsagar, Vishnusagar all dry up, then the seas elsewhere would definitely turn dry, become waterless".

The elderly man kept quiet. He was again listening to the tale of Varundev. At other times, standing on the merging point between the sky and the sea, Lord Varundev used to baulk at the sun's trajectory but as he stood apart lately, there was no hint of cloud anywhere. How dreadful had become the plight here in this city, in this country! As the Mahakaal forests suffered lack of water, the wild animals began to die. The thirsty animals were coming out of the forest by night, by day even. As they emerged, they were being killed by the hunters. On the way to the Mahakaal forests, animals lay dead here and there. The she-vultures were swooping down from the sky, all the time. The scorching sunrays were taking lives of both humans and the animals. A hunter was heard to lie dead on the other bank of the river, Shipra. Such horrendous incidents were the order of the day!

"What next"?

The wise city-dweller said, "The sky, the seas, all surely have gone devoid of water. The heat of the Sun was causing the sky to be curved slowly, bit by bit, following which, the sky too will crack like the earth one day, though tardily".

"Where? But why can't we see that"?

"I have witnessed". Putting a hand on his chest, the wise man said effortlessly, "If the sky cracks, fire will start emitting from that fissure little by little, and in the daytime the same is happening! Don't you think that the billowy fire cascades down from the sky as rains did, during monsoon"?

"Yes, this is true, it seems to be so", the elderly man mumbled.

"Tell me, why did Acharya Brishavanu leave this city"?

"Why"?

"Why?! He had come to know of all these matters! Who but he could detect the curve on the sky, much before? He sensed that Ujjwain was turning into a dreary Land of Death"!

How dreadful it would sound! The elderly man had an eerie sensation as he kept listening. What was he hearing? Acharya was just like an ant! As ants get the signal of the onset of monsoon before all, he too left the city likewise, having premonition of a prolonged phase of lack of rains, of severe drought. He came to know that rainfall was nothing more than a sweet memory of the yesteryears. In the womb of the future, rain-bearing clouds would be absent, hence he went away.

"Did the Acharya really come to know of it"?

"Yes, that is true, for many more years this land would not have any rainfall".

"Then"? The elderly man asked.

"There would be no shower, all will dry up to be waterless".

"And then"?

"Even later, there will be no downpour, soil and the trees will stand sans water and the rivers, ponds, wells and lakes have already gone dry, I can easily take note of it".

"Then, what will happen"?

"Then man will suffer the lack of water, true, they will not get any water to quench thirst and all the plasma in man's body along with blood and marrow will be desiccated like dry logs of wood".

"And then"?

"Tears will be shed to get depleted too".

"Oh, how terrible! Could Acharya Brishavanu come to be aware of all such things"?

"Perhaps, there will be no drop of water anywhere, and that's the truth".

"What next"?

"Then, the earth will be fiery and turn skeletal, man being desiccated, all will be exhausted, all will transform into a vacuum, all will be a zero"!

"After the zero, what will follow"?

"Then incessant rain will set in, it will keep pouring, knowing not where to stop".

"Are you sure? When will that happen"?

"May be thousands and thousands of years, but that downpour will not be pleasant".

"At least, this drought will no more be there!"

"Yes, it will be so but again rainfall will begin like the ancient times. After each kalpa, the Pushkarbarta clouds start unleashing rain incessantly and that period of uninterrupted rain continues without cessation" ...

"From whom have you got such information"?

"I know", that wise city-bloke placed a hand on his chest and muttered, "Rains will not begin until this drought ends, and the span of drought will come to a close at the completion of a kalpa".

"You are saying so but when will kalpa be over"?

"One kalpa means one day and one night of Lord Brahma, the day is over, the night is now heading to its close".

"When will it end"? The elderly man of the city demanded again.

"Yes, it will end, and that very day the downpour will start off incessantly, with no end in view", replied the wise man.

"Let it not cease, let it continue, oh God, all are getting dried up, sapless"!

"Rain will continue unabated".

"Let it continue, one day it will surely cease".

"Aye no, the Sun-God will hide under the cover of clouds".

The aged city-dweller asked, "So will there be only shadow of clouds on earth"?

"Only that will remain", the knowledgeable man answered.

"And sunlight, won't it be there"?

"No, it will not. Again, light will turn dim, the rain will continue till the end of the epoch. It will keep pouring".

"Ah! That would be just amazing"! The elderly resident of the city looked up to the sky. He asked, "Kadamba flower will bloom then."

"It will, but due to excessive rains the new blossoms will wilt away soon".

"Will the flying geese be impregnated by the clouds"?

"May be, but the geese will leave this country".

"Who told you"?

"They will be rendered homeless, the trees will be extirpated and fall on the ground, it will be a frightful time, all will be submerged in water"!

The elderly man said, "We will seek refuge in our houses"!

"The houses, too, will be under water".

The aged man heaved a sigh while saying, "Let it be so, yet, we will be saved from this sweltering heat! When will this kalpa come to its end"?

"It will be, but I cannot say how long it will take, how many days or whether thousands of years or even millions! Who knows how much of the kalpa has already been over and how much has been left as yet! Perhaps, this birth will be over, by then".

"Yet how much is left, can you assume"?

The wise city-dweller mumbled, "Much is left indeed, all the signs of drought are yet to be distinct, the rudimentary hints are just being noticed, all the saps and flavours have not yet faded out from the bosom of earth, we are still living, aren't we"?

FORTY- TWO

Conversations were on. Everyday. During each twilight. Every evening. At night, the noise of conversation reached its crescendo.

One day, that elderly person, the proprietor of the pearl-stall said, "Everything is being ruined. No sap is there at the root of the grass, a good number of trees are wilting up and if this continues for a few days, all will face death"!

The wise bloke said in response, "Many more miles even to go now, Earth's fluid might be depleted, but what about the milk of human mind: compassion, affection"?

"It can't be understood, what does drought have to do with it"?

"The tie is deep, kindness, love and affection—all are like sap, like water, that have started to exhaust lately, you get to see, and it will also be followed by the dearth of knowledge in this city".

The elderly person became nonplussed somehow by this rejoinder, he said, "Still I cannot make out".

"Think a while, can you love as before"?

"Whom shall I love"? The elderly man mumbled, "My wife has passed away a couple of years ago, she suffered a lot before her demise, a deadly malady had spread its tentacles in her body" …

"Do you remember her"?

"I am reminded of a diseased woman with dreadful looks, though she was a beauty once, to my utter dismay, how it got ruined! In my early youth, I had loved her, but was there any love later? Or, I just pitied her". Tears welled up to the old man's eyes.

Then the wise man said, "As you are crying, it proves that you have kindness and affection in your mind still. When all these will disappear, right then the kalpa will come to an end. I mean to say, the earth will be burnt to ashes by being scorched by the heat of the sun, only fire and sunlight will be eternal".

The elderly city-dweller listened, he wiped his eyes with the corner of his scarf, slowly. Then, all of a sudden, he turned stern and said, "No, I do not have any kindness or any affection, my life is a desert"!

"Why didn't you marry again, only a woman can bring calm to a man's life".

"I have done but it was a mistake".

"What mistake did you commit"?

"She is a young damsel, perhaps she is in love with someone else, I never get hold of her mind, let alone her body".

"Are you telling the truth"?

"True, her youth attracted me once and then I cannot say what went wrong with her"!

"What does she say, does she chant words of love"?

"Nothing at all, she stays reticent almost always".

"You certainly cohabit, what does she say then"?

"Nothing at all, she stays calm in bed".

"Is she adept in the art of copulation?" asked the wise man.

"I cannot make out— she is never aroused!"

"Are you still capable of sexual intercourse"?

"I do not know". The aged bloke turned his face to the other side and said, "If the woman does not excite you, how can the union happen"?

"Try to recall".

The middle-aged man said, "Yes, I feel the surge of desire! But she remains as cold as stone".

"She behaves thus because of drought, may be".

"Are you telling the truth"?

"Yes, true indeed, from the mind of that young wife all sap might have evaporated, love, desire, kindness— all these virtues adorning man's mind have gone to pieces, all the sterling virtues like compassion, affection, love, might have taken a backseat now, might have been dumped as things of the past".

The elderly man became sad. He asked, "Why such drought then"?

The wise man swung his head and muttered, "I don't know that but a reason must be there, hearsay affirms that, the wheels of Sun-God's chariot were stuck, hence daytime will be unending now".

"Okay, let us drop this matter now", the middle-aged man was frightened.

"The Sun-God will destroy everything with the fire of his wrath, the chariot will lose its power to move. How will the Kingdom survive if the King stays engrossed in luxury and merry-making? That is why, Acharya Brishavanu has left".

The aged bloke shook his head and mumbled, "I am not at one with you, the King can do no wrong, the King is beyond all sins, the King is the pure man"...! Saying so, the man walked down the moonlit road. Even this night was so unbearable! Not a whiff of fresh air was there, the sultriness was intolerable! The main thoroughfare was made of gravels. It was yet to be cool. The heat as absorbed by the earth all day long, was being emitted, very slowly. Hot steam was rising from the earth on both sides of the road. The man reached his home on foot. The young wife with a pensive face had fixed a steadfast glance at the moon in the sky, through the open window. The elderly man called out to his wife and asked, "What were you watching in the sky"?

"The moon".

"Keep watching. If the wheels of the Sun-God's chariot get stuck, there will be no nights, moon will also not come up, only noon will prevail on earth...getting sad eh... but why"?

The wife replied, "Since long, I have not seen clouds in the sky".

"What if there are no clouds at all"?

The young maiden did not answer. She stood in front of her husband, with her face, lowered. Her husband was irked failing to elicit an answer. He cautioned, "A housewife should not stand by the window, it looks odd".

The wife kept quiet. Seeing her speechless, the husband began to fume, gradually. He said, "You look at the other men standing by the window. In the evening, the street abounds with lecherous folks".

"No, my master, I have no idea of it at all".

"Whenever I come back home, why do I find you standing there"?

"I just await your return. I came to stand here just now", the maiden retorted, untruly.

"I have heard that the passers-by watch you, they look at you".

The maiden kept mum. She was overcome by fear. Day by day, the mien of her elderly husband kept changing. She had marked that cruelty was being writ large on his facial expressions. She loved to see the passers-by, chariot-drawn individuals, horse-riders, right from the courtiers to the hunters — all from her window. This house was very dark, desolate and none had been there to talk to. A maidservant was there, but she was past her youth. That maidservant used to narrate her days of youth, about how and when her husband paid heed to her in her young days! In order to prove herself to be true, she used to narrate in detail how her husband used to behave in the bed. And how it thrilled her! Finding her narration to be incongruous with her own experience, she got enveloped by an all-pervasive sorrow. She used to stay in this house, being in dumps all the time. It was a welcome relief to look at the sky, streets and the people therein!

Her husband said, "If clouds hover over the horizon, it could easily be felt without even standing by the window."

"Yes, my master".

"The thunderclaps can be heard, the wind blows cool".

"Yes, my master".

"If it rains, the dust and soil get drenched and the smell reaches your nostrils as you lie in bed or sit in the verandah".

"Yes, my master".

"If it rains, its noise can be heard, right"?

"Yes, it can be heard".

"Then what do you watch stretching your gaze at the burnt sky, the she-vultures circling around"?

"No, I do not watch the she-vultures at all, the maiden got frightened by her husband's rude, peevish voice".

"You watch the jackals on the street, the youthful men are nothing but sort of jackals"!

The maiden did not say anything. She felt weird within. Her husband's turbid eyes seemed to blaze and throb. Cruelty was writ large in his vision. Why was it happening thus? Tears clouded her eyes. Did she ever shirk the duty of serving her husband well? She was always meticulous about the comfort and care of her old husband. She used to provide her husband in the way he would love to be cared for. Then why was he behaving thus?

The old man said, "Youth is to be hated. I have understood it after crossing that age".

"My master"! The young wife broke into tears.

"If any woman behaves falsely with her husband, if she is not transparent, this span of drought will get prolonged! Never in the pride of youth, you should feel that youth is to stay forever"!

Frightened, the young wife fell on the feet of her harsh-tongued husband, imploring, "Why are you saying so, my master"?

The people of the city are saying that, this drought is because of the sin of unfaithful, adulterous women! The sky is being heard to crack because of the blaze of the sun, and, once it crashes, you will get to feel.

Signs of fright stood visible on the face of his wife, poignantly. On seeing that, the middle-aged husband grew more joyful. A dreadful smile stood distinct on his lips. He used to get cold response from his wife almost every night. In order to gratify his physical desire, he got this young wife, but his body had lost its sexual urge, by then. He thought, his wife's ice-cold attitude was responsible for it. Eyeing the frightened look on his wife's face, the aged man said, "Now the sky will come crumbling down on the soil of Ujjwain, the adulterous women will serve as food to the vultures, their bodies will be afflicted with malady. The span of youth is to be hated".

"What are you saying, my master?" The innocent maiden cried out. It was beyond her, why her husband was intimidating her almost every day? Why was her husband changing altogether? Why was he growing suspicious of her? Even if she got to see any youthful man while standing by the window, she used to conceal herself in fear of her husband finding it out. She wanted to cry aloud. But she could not, because of fear. From deep down her bosom, tears welled up. In the mind of the aged man, violence seemed to scale high. He was the only person who had the foremost right to touch this young maiden, in whichever way he liked, with his feeble body. However, she didn't grow responsive at all. But why? She definitely longed for a youthful man. The very thought infuriated him. He said, "From now on, if I see you standing by the window, looking at some other man, you will be punished severely, here in this birth, in death as well".

The wife was shedding silent tears. But no tears could be seen in her eyes. All seemed to have dried up. Her husband kicked her, accused her straightaway, objectionably, "Who do you think of, in bed"?

"No, my master, this is not true"!

"Of which jackal? Thou vulture, a sow"!

The wife hung her head low. She could feel that her middle-aged husband had gone out of his mind. What would she do? She did not have much to do in the bed. Much later, when she grew warm in bed, the middle-aged man slept off, being exhausted. How she felt pity for him then!

The elderly man said, "I have grown weaker after coming in contact with thee, hey witch, thou must be knowing the art of conjuring like the shaven friars, I must put an end to thy life, beware, thou slut"!

The elderly man began to shower torrents of obscenities on the young wife. He began to feel certain pleasure, while upbraiding her. While talking ill of the youthful wife's body, while cursing the young wife in abominable diction, he kept drooling.

The wife could gradually feel that such outbursts might be due to the prolonged span of drought. At the advent of monsoon, her elderly husband would change perhaps. Again, he would turn affectionate. And then? She closed both her eyes. When would this man breathe his last? Then only she would be saved. And just then the monsoon would be here.

The elderly man abruptly asked, Do you pray for my demise?

The damsel started, how could he read her mind? She went speechless, and the elderly man cursed her for that, A deadly disease will befall you, your youth would die an early death, what will you do then? Who will you spend your life with?

The damsel fell crying. While shedding tears, she was praying, Let clouds hover over, let it rain even though after a long interregnum, let Kadamba flowers bloom, let peacock hold open its plumage! She prayed to her old husband, groveling at his feet, My master, let the drought come to an end, let monsoon be here, my master, please fetch clouds to the sky of Ujjwain, oh my master, you can only make it happen, you can only make us hear the thunder of the clouds, my master, I offer you my everything, just annihilate this phase of drought!

The elderly foul-mouthed man calmed down, temporarily. He took himself to be Varundev! Perhaps he could make it possible. He began to turn ruthless by degrees and devoid of compassion like God. It was difficult to be a deity, without being devoid of kindness. Man was more familiar with God's wrath than His kindness. The elderly husband wished to emphasize his unification with God, he said haltingly, My days are numbered. But you are still young, you will have to experience old age during youth only! Turn into an old woman, be an old lady soon!

The young woman hung her head.

If Sun-God gets static in the sky, if the chariot-wheel gets stuck, you will burn more, you will lie dead as a possum, on turning into an old hag!

My master, be calm!

The young wife's ardent prayer pervaded the full-moon night! That night, the inhabitants of Ujjwain had dreamt of clouds. Such dream, too, eluded them since long. A dream could even turn into reality. Of man's dream, indeed, the reality is begotten!

FORTY-THREE

As the elderly man retired to his house, the wise man was left alone. He could not decide upon anything being alone. Where would he go now? He began to walk aimlessly. The path was illumined by moonshine, no wind blew, the evening being over, the nature was cooling down. He drew up to the front of the brothel, in slow steps. Chaturika was waiting at the entrance of the house. Looking at the middle-aged man on the threshold, she welcomed her in, "My Lord, please come and have rest at Chaturika's residence. I am Chaturika".

The man stood. Listening to the call of Chaturika and noticing her, God knew what seized him, he entered.

He washed his feet in the courtyard with Chaturika's help. Then, sprinkling water on his neck and head, he heaved a long sigh and craned his neck to look up to the sky.

Chaturika called out to him, "Oh Lord, would you like to sit here or inside"?

The man did not answer but kept muttering to himself something unintelligible, instead. The words eluded her. Chaturika asked, "Lord, have you come from any foreign land"?

"Why, what of that to you"?

"Has there been rainfall in that country, have you seen clouds on your way"?

Shaking his head, the man said, "You witty woman, do you still have humour in your mind? Do you still feel joy in your heart?"

Chaturika could not make out. She asked, "What do you mean to say, oh Lord"?

"Don't you know me"?

Chaturika shook her head and said, "No, I don't know you, Sir!"

"I have come to the bawdyhouse for the first time in my life. I can feel the dreariness of drought, this city is on the verge of ruins, understood"?

Chaturika was taken aback, but she was not afraid. She kept watching the man, from head to foot. His words appeared unnatural. Was he insane? His appearance was just like that. Otherwise, why would he come to a whorehouse to share his thoughts? Did anyone ever come here, spending money, with such irrelevant talk?

The man said, "There's no rainfall, no clouds since ages, tell me why"?

"I do not know", Chaturika gibbered, "This year there had been no Northwester, no hailstorm too. Otherwise, the heat would have lessened".

"When did you see it raining last, oh harlot"?

Chaturika tried to recall but failed. Then she thought, even if it rained in her sleep, could she not feel it on waking up? Again, she might not sense even. In an inaudible voice she replied, "It might have rained, but when I cannot say exactly".

"Are you telling the truth"?

Chaturika removed the scarf from her breasts, "Phew! Then, you lewd man, are you not from the city but a village bumpkin?" Saying so, she became alert. She might be mistaken. This man might be a trader or a merchant even! Scraping an acquaintance preceding love-making differed from person to person. In which way could one be gratified physically and mentally, who could tell?

The man said, "Please be quiet, you whore, Ujjwain has not witnessed rains since many years"!

"How many years"?

The man answered, "Some thousand years"!

Chaturika giggled and said, "Sir, would you listen to my veena"?

Why, why are you talking about playing the veena?

Chaturika came up saying, "I am just twenty years of age, just a wench of twenty years, I have seen rains quite a few times and you are talking of thousand years, who are you, man"?

Then the city-dweller turned serious, he said, "I have also witnessed that rainfall, I am talking about the future. In future, someone at this time will come to say here at this brothel that drought is continuing since thousand years"!

Chaturika again thought that deriving joy from something varies from person to person. Verbal humour differed in appeal from one individual to another. She again took up the scarf and spread it over her breasts saying, "Shall I live even after thousand years, my Lord"?

"You may not be there, someone else will".

"Will you be alive, my Lord"?

"If I do not live, someone else will, he may be just me in the next birth, this very Ayuputra"!

Chaturika was astonished, "Lord, are you Ayuputra"?

"Yes, Nahush Sharman, I belong to the lineage of physicians".

"But didn't you say, Ayuputra, Lord"?

The man laughed, "Hey whore, do you know mythology? Ayu was the son of Urvashi and Pururaba, the son of Ayu[Ayuputra] was Nahush, he had even ruled the realm of Gods for hundreds of thousands of years. At that time, Indra, the King of Gods had swooned himself, after killing Britrasura.

Chaturika folded her palms and in a mesmerized voice asked, "Oh Lord, who are you"?

"I am Nahush Sharman, my father was a physician. I am one too, but I had killed a boy while treating him".

"Lord"! Tears leaped up to Chaturika's eyes.

"That boy was my own child, since then, I have thrown away my pestle-and-mortar, stones, plants and leaves, creepers, roots into the litterbin. Hey whore, the forthcoming days are dreadful, do escape".

"Why, my Lord, what will happen"?

"Lack of rains will continue till thousand years".

Chaturika, the slut, made it out to be the raving of a lunatic and said, "There are people in the city, if they live, I shall also live".

"None will live! Have you heard the name of Acharya Brishavanu"?

Chaturika tilted her neck in deep reverence, and said, "Yes, my Lord, I have gone to the temple of Lord Mangalnath quite a few times, had even gone to the front of the shrine, paid my respect to Acharya Brishavanu, standing outside".

Nahush Sharman informed, "Acharya Brishavanu has left this city and now the magnate, Subhag Dutta will follow suit".

Chaturika mused, "Saved are we, exit of the tycoon would come as a relief to

Devadutta". Displaying false astonishment on her face, she kept looking at Nahush Sharman, the physician, and said, "I heard that his servant, that cruel Utanka, has been burnt alive"!

"You have rightly heard".

"The city-people have been saved", Chaturika muttered under her breath. Then she offered, "Lord, shall I perform lustful dance? This maid of yours has mastered both dance and veena-playing!

The middle-aged Nahush Sharman felt agitated as he said, "Is it the time for dance and playing the veena? Let me tell you, you whore, if possible leave this city, even tycoon Subhag Dutta is going away, don't you know that"?

Chaturika now got to understand that this man had not come to her, he had come to deliver the alarming news to just any whore, he would come across. She retorted, "Okay, if such is destined, I shall die at the feet of Lord Mahakaal. Now you can leave, Sir"!

Those words made his face blaze in rage and he warned, "You wench, you have gone to the dogs, just minding your calling of prostitution! You haven't kept abreast of the world and the times, this drought is a dreary indicator of a terrible rainfall, do you get me"?

Chaturika, the public woman, emerged out of her tenement. She began to shout, "Hey Mahaparshwa, hey brother, Mahaparshwa, where are you, here's a madman in my room"!

Mahaparshwa, the pimp, did not have to come. As the word reached the ear of the man, he leapt out of the room to hold the hand of Chaturika, who stood in the courtyard, and say, "Hey whore, why do thou shout? I came to warn thee, I came to tell thee that thou would be saved if thou go away serving the traders, journeying on to Balkh! Hey profaned woman, go along with them, thou would be saved"!

"To which country will they go"? Chaturika frowned and looked on at the face of the elderly man, throwing the query. Why the countenance of that elderly man looked so pitiable, who could tell! Chaturika softened towards him, "To which country will Subhag Dutta go"?

"To Balkh, it is far-off, beyond the river Indus, Purushpur, Gandhaar, it is a land where yellow silk is available".

"Will you bring that yellow silk for me, Sir"?

"Who will fetch it?"

"Why you, won't you go?"

"Why me? Why shall I leave"?

"All of them are leaving, won't you, too?" Chaturika hurled her query.

Old Nahush Sharman kept shaking his head and then said, "You accompany them, then one day rain will tumble down on Ujjwain, never to cease again".

"When will this rainfall happen, Lord"?

"Hundreds of thousands of years of drought will be followed by hundreds of thousands of years of rains! Alas, oh alas, whoever I share this news with fails to get me, but why? Then why has Acharya Brishavanu left this city? Why are the merchants all leaving"?

Shaking his head, the man went forward leaving the moonlit courtyard behind! Chaturika stopped him, saying, "Wait, my Lord, let me fetch a lamp".

"No, do what I asked you to do, you whore, go away to the country of Balkh, here you are serving the men, there too, you will serve the traders, and 'women' are a must on a journey, they will take you along gladly and now you are in the full bloom of youth. How long will the adult men be able to spend days without women"?

Chaturika grew suspicious, she kept thinking… Has then this man been sent by Subhag Dutta and other merchants? Can it be so that the tycoon is now longing for Chaturika, giving up all hopes for Devadutta? Who knows?

As this made Chaturika go beside herself with joy, she took alarm too, inwardly. She asked, "Will you now leave, Sir"?

"I have come to leave only. I haven't come here for mere enjoyment, oh slut, have I? I am asking you to leave this city, this city stands ruined and I can clearly see everything that will follow hereafter".

"What will happen, oh Lord"?

"Yes, the swallows! All the inhabitants of this city will run in search of water, all day long, like the swallows. Water will be made available to the King, queen, the Army-Commander and the tycoon; all others, in their emaciated appearance will be like the swallows, swallows, swallows!" Saying so, elderly Nahush Sharman, crossed the courtyard on foot.

Chaturika sat down in the courtyard.

All day long, no gentleman came to pay her a visit! Uddhavnarayan was not yet expected. And the man who had come was either a madman or a spy of the merchants.

So, Subhag Dutta was keen on leaving Devadutta! Chaturika was thrilled. Then lady-luck smiled on her! She would be spared from the grip of that colluding man of pervert tastes, that Uddhavnarayan! Oh Lord Mahakaal! Turning towards the west, Chaturika bowed down to the shrine of Lord Mahakaal, which stood beyond her range of vision. Oh Lord, just make it happen! Let the merchant, Subhag Dutta, take her along to that foreign land! What was the name of that country? Balkh, Balkh! Chaturika kept pronouncing the name, just to hold it back in her memory. But, Nahush Sharman, the physician had just left! She had neither said 'Yes' nor 'No' to him. Then, what would happen? Would Nahush Sharman go back to report harlot Chaturika's dissent? She stood up. She needed the man just then. No, she would not stay back in this city anymore. She would not stay to be beaten by Uddhavnarayan. It was far better to accompany the tycoon, Subhag Dutta, on his business expedition, as his serving-maid than rot away in this squalid ghetto! Devadutta was a fool! She kept waiting for that ignoramus Dhruvaputra, here in this city, just because she was a nincompoop! Would he come back at all? No way, he would never return! Perhaps, at long last, he would even cease to exist! Perhaps, he had gone to the Kingdom of the Huns! Could he come back to Avanti again, this being an enemy Kingdom? Devadutta's never-ending youth was wasting away, unawares. Being excited, Chaturika rushed out. The road lay vacant. In the empty thoroughfare, noise of horse's hooves could be heard. And indistinct voices could also be heard. Walking down the moonlit way, covering her face with the scarf, as she moved to the fore, she saw something which she had expected, Uddhavnarayan was approaching, humming a tune, riding the little Tibetan horse! He was a bit tipsy from drinking wine. Chaturika stood on the edge of the road, hiding her face behind a veil. She was freezing in fear. Uddhav must not be able to recognize her! If he could, it would spell disaster for her! But her hopes were belied. The royal sessions-judge sprinted down from the horseback with a near-extinguished flambeau in his hand. In an inebriated voice, he ranted on, "Who are you, oh maiden, out on your love-tryst, standing on the edge of the road? Who are you, hey whore, hanging about this road by night"? Instantly, Uddhav clasped her hand.

FORTY-FOUR

Chaturika said straight that she was on her way to the merchant's house. It might not be true, not even untrue! As she was out on the road, she might go to the merchant's house or might be looking for the renowned physician, Nahush Sharman. The merchant's residence was not far. She did not know the exact corner of this city, where Nahush Sharman resided, but she knew the location of the merchant's house. Perhaps, Nahush Sharman had gone there. It might not be so, even though there was no such problem in imagining it! Such imagination would have driven her on the way to the merchant's residence. He had come with the message from the merchant for sure and now it was his responsibility to return to the merchant with Chaturika's whereabouts. Chaturika could have covered a considerable distance, if Uddhavnarayan had not detained her, blocking her path.

Chaturika's rejoinder caused Uddhavnarayan to lower his hood. As the black cobra slithered to its pit, slowly, pacified, Uddhavnarayan staggered to stand at the other end of the horse. Now the horse stood hanging its head silently, in between the harlot and the sessions-judge. All came to a standstill. The nimble-footed animal lost its speed, the moonshine stood still as well, like the two humans. Uddhav was looking at Chaturika, blinking. Was this the same slut or someone else? Was he getting confused? Delirious stupor might lead him to confusion. He might confuse the directions, even could fail to recognize the humans. Wasn't this Chaturika? Or any other woman, from a respectable family? Or, harlot Devadutta? He had seen the face just for once, was he wrong? Now, the woman had again covered her head and face with her scarf! Alas! What a pity! He had undone himself. He had humiliated the merchant's ladylove, going on an assignation, on the road. If this news reached the merchant, he might have to face the same fate as Utanka. Would Uddhav be spared, while the merchant did not save his own favourite servant from being burnt or try for his pardon? Uddhav had witnessed Utanka's death by fire! Uddhav was getting blanched in fear. The road was desolate. Faint moonshine lay on the thoroughfare. At a considerable distance, Utanka seemed to make his presence felt. He buried his face in both his hands.

"What's wrong"? Chaturika asked.

Uddhav came to recognize her again, by her voice. He removed his hands from his face. In a feeble voice he tried to confirm, "Chaturika"?

"Can't you recognize me, when inebriated"?

"What did you say?... Where are you going"? Uddhav asked, rubbing both his eyes.

"To the merchant's house, he has sent for me".

"Is it true"? Uddhav's eyes widened in astonishment!

Chaturika giggled. Without answering him straightaway, she said, "You are dead-drunk, Mr. Sessions-Judge"!

"Are you going on a rendezvous"?

"Exactly so, the merchant has sent for me", said Chaturika in a muffled voice. While saying, a thrill pervaded her body. Ah! Let these words be true!

Uddhav kept looking again. All went beyond his comprehension. Yet, his grey cells were not dead and defunct! His grey cells remained alert all the time. Plethora of diplomatic strategies, wits and schemes clouded his grey matter always, he could not tally this incident with anything in reality, to be precise. His serving-maid, his object of pleasure, a petty harlot was going, on an assignation of love to the house of the merchant!! Or was he going wrong somewhere? This woman was not Chaturika, someone else, some aristocratic housewife, being caught red-handed, she had to assume the identity of Chaturika! He was at his wit's end, for being heavily drunk. He might have been mistaken somehow. He was even mistaking one's voice for another's! Whoever this lady could have been, she was the merchant's ladylove! Throwing the flambeau away, he folded his palms and gibbered, "Please come along, I shall drop you at the merchant's place, the road is desolate, who knows which peril lurks"!

Chaturika chortled again, "The source of danger is YOU, Sessions-man"!

The voice was exactly Chaturika's! But she was not Chaturika! Those who went on love-tryst could do like that. Uddhav heard that the lover-women could assume many forms with the help of 'yoga'. They could also make themselves invisible by applying magical powers!

Chaturika said, "Follow your own way, you took".

"I am heading on to the brothel" …

"But the whore is on her way to the merchant's house".

Uddhav said, "Why will she go? You must be some woman of noble, dignified lineage".

Chaturika remarked, "Really you are dead-drunk, Mr. Sessions-Judge"!

Uddhav again heard the voice, which was just the same as Chaturika's! But it was nothing but his auditory illusion. Being speechless, he kept looking. The desolation of the moonlit way had extinguished his flambeau. An eerie feeling got the better of him. Perhaps, this lady was not even a ladylove but something else! Perhaps an evil woman adept in witchcraft. He had been caught in her web. Alack, oh alas! Since long, he used to saunter around either on foot or on horseback. In moonshine, being on horseback he had some valorous delight within. Today he had that feeling. Hence, without thinking twice, he had blocked the way of the ladylove! However, making such a thing happen was nothing new. Very often, he used to nab one or the other! If he had not been the Sessions-Judge of the Royal Court, if he would not go out on nocturnal rounds, he would never have come to know the housewife in particular, who used to go to the man of her choice for love-making, again that young maiden who would get involved with that gentleman in secret rendezvous! How respectable those families were, to which the ladyloves used to pay visits or how dignified these women themselves were, no matter whether daughters or housewives, it left Uddhav flabbergasted, as the truth would dawn upon him. He used to keep some information of the strange, secret incidents which transpired every day in the respectable households of this city, as the Sessions-man of the royal court! And so many nubile women were nabbed by him by night! He, too, grabbed the opportunity, coming his way! He used to drink the honey of youth, in midway! At times, he would take off the gold chain from the neck or the gold-ring from the finger of these women. The women out on rendezvous, could neither report of this oppression anywhere nor could they cry. They used to accept it as sheer misfortune! Of course, Uddhav would not do anything at all, before being doubly certain!

Chaturika demanded, "Why have you gone silent"?

"Are you really Chaturika? I mean, Chaturika of the brothel"?

"Then, who am I"?

Uddhav began to shake his head violently. He could comprehend that he was being deceived by some sorceress, who is out on a romantic assignation. If not a sorceress, how could she go to the merchant's house on a rendezvous?

Uddhav said, "Who will know, none at all".

"All will come to know - you will divulge it to all".

"No, no, no"!

"Yes, you will, sitting in a tavern, you will make it public"!

"Then I shall not be allowed to live".

That's true, indeed. Chaturika was growing courageous gradually. She could understand that it was the only way to get rid of Uddhav. Otherwise, that dead-drunk fellow would drag her to bed, with such malodorous body of his. Then she would have to serve that drunkard all night. Throwing up all over, he would defile her chamber. Phew! This very thought left her emetic. While thinking of his vomiting, Chaturika felt deep hatred pervading her senses! Right at this moment, for the first time, Chaturika was aware of this feeling of contempt. Today whatever she gathered from Nahush Sharman, seemed to be true now. Really true. If Subhag Dutta had not been desirous of her, why would the medic enter her dwelling and why would he exhort her again and again to accompany Subhag Dutta, on his business tour? If this was true, why would she be afraid of Uddhavnarayan? Fear begets respect. As there was no fear, no respect too was. In lieu of respect, there was only repugnance. Since long, she used to clean the chamber, left dirty with Uddhav's throwing up, without a single word of objection, considering that to be her duty. Today, the very thought left her overcome with aversion.

Chaturika said, "Go, where you intended to".

"I was on my way to the brothel…"

"No, go to your own house".

"The brothel is my second home", Uddhav folded his palms again.

Chaturika said, "No… but I shall not return".

"Are you Chaturika, really"?

"Then who am I"?

"Aren't you somebody else"?

Chaturika smiled, this needed to be reported to the merchant that the Sessions-Judge had hallucinations, when drunk.

Uddhav found her to be none but Chaturika. Strange! How terrible! Did Chaturika frequent the residence of the merchant? Or, somewhere else? She might tell lies, being caught red-handed. Now, Uddhav's grey cells were being active. His wits and strategies began working once again. Why would the whore, enjoyed by Uddhav, be called upon by the merchant? In a sombre tone, he said, "Let me drop you at the merchant's place".

"No, the merchant will be angry. The beloved on assignation always makes it alone".

"Or, were you going somewhere else"?

Chaturika could sense that Uddhav began to grow suspicious, it meant that he was coming out of the spell of intoxication. Uddhav was a highly suspicious fellow. If he really took her to the merchant's house, then? Nahush Sharma might be right, and wrong as well. If untrue, it would cause dreadful consequences to be faced. Then?

Uddhav said, "You must have managed to have another paramour, I am sure"!

Oh! Chaturika knew that Uddhav had to be bridled right then, otherwise, this knave would turn furious! Coming forward, she said, "Come, take me to the merchant's place, let me ride the horse's back, it is already late, I am afraid, he must have fallen asleep by now"!

"Where"? Uddhav's eyebrows curved into a frown.

"To the merchant's place. Let me go and tell him everything".

"What will you tell him"?

"I shall say that I am late because of Uddhav".

Then this is true! Uddhav mumbled. This is really a dreary trouble! Chaturika's words might be true, might be untrue even. If untrue, Uddhav would be spared, he might punish her for telling a lie, but what if it was true? And how great an ordeal he would be in! The merchant would make him burn alive. Uddhav kept both his hands on the horse's back. He mused, "What shall I do now"?

Chaturika could hear him, she said, "Come, lead me to the merchant's residence, let me clear your doubts".

Chaturika could feel that no other way did exist save this. If Uddhav would take her, fine! If Nahush Sharman's words were correct, she would also be able to take revenge on Uddhav! Otherwise, death would be inevitable. Though she was no better than the dead!

Uddhav declined, "No Chaturika, you go alone".

"How shall I go alone, it is already late, look yonder, the moon has begun to wane, the merchant has gone to his empty bed being tired of waiting for me by the window-side, looking down the way. If I rush there on a horse, it would save me a little time".

Uddhav was visibly in fear, "No, I shall not go, better you do".

"If you don't, I shall not go too".

"Why? Won't you go to the merchant, though sent for"?

"No". Chaturika began to walk in reverse direction, in brisk steps, raising her voice, she kept saying, "If you block the way thus, all romantic assignations will come to a halt in the city. Has it ever happened"?

Instead of jumping on the horseback, holding the rein in his hand, he went pulling the horse, following Chaturika and calling out to her, "Come Chaturika, do not retrace your steps back".

"No man, I shall not return, why have you blocked my way"?

"It will not happen anymore".

"Please bear the brunt of whatever has happened, Nahush Sharman might come again for a follow-up"!

"Who"?

Chaturika looked up. She felt giddy. She had a sensation of terror. The evil man might run to the place of the Chief Physician on his horseback. There is no reason to believe him. Could Uddhav get to hear the name?

Uddhav asked, "Who had come as his messenger"?

Chaturika said, "Not a male, but a female messenger had come".

"Who was she"?

"Why would you know that? Do not come to me today. Even the merchant might come, he will take me along with him on his business expedition".

Uddhav stood still. Chaturika was walking towards the bawdyhouse in nimble steps through the desolate road. Then Chaturika's words must be true! How would he confirm: true or untrue? Who would he find it out from? Mulling it over, pulling along the old horse like a burden, Uddhav kept moving forward.

FORTY-FIVE

For the next couple of days, Chaturika went into hiding. She kept waiting for the merchant's messenger in her room, quietly. She could not dare leave her room lest that Chief Physician, Nahush Sharman, or someone else would come and leave, without seeing her. Even Devadutta had called for her but she refused, saying, she was down with illness, she would see her later.

The maidservant sent by Devadutta went speechless, surprised, as there had been no sign of illness anywhere on her face!

Chaturika smiled, sitting at the corner of the wall, saying, "Yes, it's there, thou may not trace it".

As the maidservant left, it occurred to Chaturika that, Devadutta perhaps would have been happy on learning it. It would be the best, if she could apprise Devadutta of it. She had much intelligence, she even used to hate Subhag Dutta, the merchant. Devadutta might have advised her on how Chaturika would unite with the merchant!

But why would Devadutta hate the merchant? Was Subhag Dutta a man to be abhorred? Was he even inferior to the Shudras? Being the richest man of the city, to whom the King, the Minister, all owed a lot, how could he be looked down upon by Devadutta? How daring could she be? Though the Chief Prostitute, yet, she was just a petty woman! Could ever such pride befit a woman? Devadutta would surely be brought to book, if Divine Justice worked! But this was even true that Devadutta had no mind for the merchant, hence he had to veer his attention to a petty harlot. Chaturika was aware of everything.

She grew restive after meeting Nahush Sharman. She could not pay heed to anything. Concentrating on anything was just next to impossible for her. Lord Mahakaal was there, hence, such an amazing incident transpired in her life! Chaturika had not even imagined such a consequence ever. She had not approached Subhag

Dutta on her own and now he was sending for her! It happened only because Lord Mahakaal had remembered her.

The Chief Physician came that day to drop the news, but went away never to return. Not even sent any other messenger later! But again, Uddhav, too, stopped visiting her. That meant, Uddhav had come to learn that he had blocked the way of the merchant's beloved. Out of fear, he had stopped dropping by. Fear was natural, no doubt. Didn't Uddhav get a lesson by leaving her bereft of all the jewellery, adorning her? The ornaments were enough to prove that she was in touch with the merchant. Just then, Chaturika could have made out how the jewelleries belonging to the merchant went back to him again! Her brain was not functioning. All appeared to be perplexing. Did then Devadutta know everything? Knowing all, the womanly envy had held her back from divulging anything to her! Did Devadutta, being rejected by the merchant, grow averse to him just to gratify her own hurt feelings? That would invariably be so. While the bigwig of the city would veer his attention from the best paragon of beauty, a prostitute of numerous virtues, to one of her followers, then what would Devadutta be left with other than hatred to retaliate her disgrace? Learning about the weakness of the merchant on her, Devadutta had given all the jewelleries to her only: Mahalata, Chandrahaar, armlets, anklets, gold bangles, so forth! She might have even given her all such valuables by order of the merchant himself! Oh God! How could such strange things happen? So, a human got wings to fly in the sky. Chaturika kept toying with numerous puzzling thoughts in her mind. She could feel that she failed to get the drift of anything at all, as she was simple, innocent and a damsel of little intelligence. Being simple-hearted, she could not recognize her lover. Now it was clear to her, why beautiful, qualified Devadutta had offered her heart to a tramp, like Dhruvaputra! What did the son of Dhruva have? Nothing at all, neither he had money, nor he had the pride of having noble lineage! He was not born in a royal family even. Men like him used to hang about hither and thither on the roads of Ujjwain, for no reason whatsoever. If the banks of the rivers, Shipra or Gandhavati, were ever visited in the late afternoon, one would find many indifferent souls, sitting there with their glance glued to the sky above. Now, it seemed that Uddhav Narayan was far more worthy than the son of Dhruva! After all, he was a man from within the King's Court! Royal power was his chief support! He used to roam around the city with commendable authority! If Devadutta would ever offer her heart to Uddhav! Alas Devadutta! Tears shot up to the eyes of Chaturika, as she kept thinking about the misfortune of Devadutta and the joy of good luck of her own! Even after mastering almost the whole corpus of fine arts, Devadutta got to win the heart of nearly impecunious and orphan, the tramp, Dhruvaputra! Devadutta must be knowing who the merchant longed for, and just on learning it, she began to mourn for Dhruvaputra, who had gone missing, to cover up her dejection!

Sankranti was over! Today was the first day of the month of Jaisthya. Chaturika had come out of her room. Keeping her hair unfastened, she was looking for the pimp, Mahaparshwa, standing on her threshold. The pimp was the only help she could now look up to. The merchant had sent for Chaturika, and now it was her responsibility to mind her duties. Wouldn't the pimp be able to fetch the news of the merchant's setting out on a business expedition? Rather the pimp should go and find out the doctor, Nahush Sharman! Chaturika would scrounge all information from him only. She would ask him to reach the merchant, her desire to be his serving-maid, his companion. Chaturika would be his ladylove, going on an assignation to him. Let the Chief Physician fetch the details to her - which day, when and where would the merchant keep waiting? The leading physician came like a squally wind, like a gust of air, and disappeared almost immediately, throwing Chaturika in the vortex of a mental storm! What would Chaturika do now? Would she call for Uddhav through the pimp? Uddhav would just be the right person to fetch her each information. Perhaps Uddhav was in the know of everything. Being the King's Sessions-Judge, how would anything escape his knowledge? Udhhav himself used to say that he would be able to have the information regarding the date on which a young maiden started menstruating for the first time, if he so wished. Now Chaturika could feel that as Devadutta had veered her attention from the merchant to Dhruvaputra mentally, Uddhav also was looking for another damsel knowing her inside out. Being inane, she could not get the wind of anything at all!

All day long, she kept moving in and out of her room. Neither the pimp, nor Uddhav came into her sight. The whole city was reeling under the sweltering heat of the sun. Chaturika's house too seemed like a blast furnace. Chaturika threw her gaze at the sky. Her eyes got dazzled. All kept burning. The swishing noise of loo reached her ears. Heated air blew with a swoosh. Streams of fire kept surging through the city of Ujjwain. On the edge of the road stood a neem tree on the branch of which sat an enormous raven. Every now and then, it kept cawing. Chaturika covered both her eyes with her hands, she did not want to see the crow. The grave and serious caw of that crow was tantamount to the call of death! That crow was ominous. Chaturika clucked to shoo it away. The crow did not budge an inch at all. Rather it kept cawing to a crescendo. Chaturika entered home in fear. She had fear writ large on her face. The noon was so long! At noon, no voice of any human being could be heard. Desolation ruled the roost. The raven went on cawing, cutting through the seclusion.

The noon seemed never to have an end. The stillness seemed to be unruffled. Chaturika stayed inert in that stupor. Afternoon being over, just at the advent of evening, Chaturika saw Mahaparshwa to return. How deplorable the sun-burnt man's plight had been! The tall, lanky stature had bent like a half-singed corpse. It looked as though, Mahaparshwa had come up straight from the funeral pyre. The eyes had sunken deep into the sockets, the reddish hair stood on their ends, the cloth girding his loin was soiled, ragged. The dirty scarf that was meant to cover his body, was worn around his neck, like a noose. Mahaparshwa was walking at a great speed. He was about to cross Chaturika's house, while he halted being accosted by her.

"The time is out of joint, Chaturika, there's no use sitting by thy door".

"What's wrong, please stop here, Mahaparshwa, my brother"!

Mahaparshwa stopped, threw a look at the scythe and said, "It's almost dark, though the moon is yet to rise, I am night-blind, you know, Chaturika"!

"You are not night-blind! Please go, once the moon comes up. Any news about the city"?

Mahaparshwa squatted, began to shake his head, "No, the city-news is not heartening, Chaturika! We have to escape, leaving the city behind. Days of terror are ahead of us".

Chaturika smiled and said, "In this plight, the merchant is setting out on his business tour, just imagine"!

"What"?! Mahaparshwa got startled. He kept looking at the harlot in surprise. Was it Chaturika who was talking about the merchant's tour?! What of that to her, whether the merchant set out on a business tour or not? He said, "What do we, the paupers, got to do with a rich man's business expedition"?

Chaturika retorted, "Why? He is going out on a business expedition after ages"!

Mahaparshwa laughed noisily and said, "Let him go, but trade and commerce in this city is in doldrums! Nowhere a man who desires a woman can be found, such has never happened in this city. Go away, otherwise thou shall die miserably in hunger".

"Go, I must"! In a muffled voice, Chaturika seemed to grunt.

Mahaparshwa shook his head, "Go thou must, but where, from every corner only disheartening news gets pouring in, all are burning under the sun, rice can't be had by begging, hereafter".

Chaturika seemed not to hear his words at all. She said, "Brother Mahaparshwa, do you know any physician named Nahush Sharman? The Chief Physician, I mean".

Mahaparshwa found darkness ruling the roost, all around. Ah! Now their body and soul would cool down. Again, he heard Nahush Sharman's name. Turning around, he stared at the face of Chaturika. Doubt was writ large on Mahaparshwa's face, he was trying to tally one with the other. He asked, "But why"?

"I need to know".

"Why such necessity"?

"That you will know later, hey brother, do you know anything about the merchant's day of journey"?

Mahaparshwa touched his cheek with a palm, he failed to make out the exact query of Chaturika and asked, "Which news do you want Chaturika, of Nahush Sharman or of the merchant"?

Chaturika became wary. This pimp, Mahaparshwa, was a cunning fellow, he was adept in making a mountain of a mole-hill. She said haltingly, "Could you please ask Nahush Sharman to come here, brother Mahaparshwa? I need to meet him".

"Who are you talking about"?

"Nahush Sharman, the Chief Physician".

Mahaparshwa smiled, "How do you know him, Chaturika"?

"Do you know him, brother Mahaparshwa"?

Mahaparshwa broke into a cackle, "It seems that the lunatic had come here to your place just a few days back. Didn't you call me, Chaturika"?

Such were the words of Mahaparshwa. Addresses like 'Thou' and 'You' would alter very often. Chaturika said gently, "Yes, Mahaparshwa brother, I need him only".

"What's wrong? Mahaparshwa grew suspicious. Why do you need that physician"?

"Well, he came here with a piece of news".

"Have you contracted any disease, Chaturika"? Mahaparshwa stood up abruptly, narrowing his eyes, receding a step further. Chaturika was frightened, "What nonsense are you talking"?

"Don't hold back from me, that will be of no help, tell me, what's wrong with you"?

Chaturika said, "I need him, I am telling you".

"He is just a mad doctor, how can he treat you? Tell me Chaturika, how far has the malady spread over? It is my responsibility, lest I shall be accused of neglecting you".

Chaturika grew impatient, "What are you saying, brother Mahaparshwa, the Chief Physician was here with some news, I want to hear that news again".

Mahaparshwa kept swaying his head. He was not believing Chaturika. His suspicion was intensifying. The maladies with which the harlots were affected in this bawdy house were deadly. If such an ailment was even heard of, she would be driven away from the brothel, lest it might affect others. It was more of death in itself than a disease! Mahaparshwa's mother, too, had died of that disease. Mahaparshwa was reminded of his mother's sickly face, reflecting death. He was just a boy of ten at that time. Popular belief ran that it was a disease that involved secretion of morbid things. When all the blood in the body stood contaminated, it could hardly be concealed. The ailment began to spread all over the body, originating from the genitals. On face even the symptoms of the malady stood prominent. Mahaparshwa remembered, how blood was about to spurt out from his mother's face! A dwelling was set up for mother at the outskirts of the city. Mother had gone somewhere else from there, where no one knew. Grapevine sources had it that, his mother had entered the Mahakaal forests. The God of Death resided in there. The wild animals had a feast on his mother's body, afflicted with maladies.

Mahaparshwa said, "There's no gain in holding it back from me, Chaturika"!

Chaturika was overcome with fear now," What are you saying, brother Mahaparshwa? The Chief Physician had come here with a proposition". Mahaparshwa said, "That Royal Physician? He is a madman, in his hand an awful death had occurred, a seven-year-old boy had died after having medicines prescribed by him. I heard that he had given up treating patients since then"!

"No, not for treatment"!

Mahaparshwa smirked, "Then why will a harlot look for a doctor? I learnt from hearsay, that the eccentric doctor kept treating patients, secretly, he had been here even, I had no idea at all. Had anyone asked for him"?

Chaturika was now truly panicky. If this pimp divulged the matter to anyone else, she would be in for trouble! The lie would spread far and wide and then none would judge its veracity or falsity! City people were just like that. Just a savoury topic would do, they would keep analysing that, all day long! Then what would happen? Darkness of terror intensified before the eyes of Chaturika. Nothing would be impossible for Mahaparshwa to accomplish. Perhaps, he would keep sharing this matter with various people in the city, the whole day. Again, the assumption was just his own. Chaturika was only asking for the Royal Physician, Nahush Sharman, that was all.

Mahaparshwa grew curious then, "This is your right age, come, come along, your youth is yet to mellow, who has passed this disease on to you, does the Sessions-Judge, Uddhav, know of it"?

Chaturika, grabbed the hand of Mahaparshwa, abruptly, "I did not say so".

"What didn't you say"?

"About the disease".

The pimp turned furious, "Then did I tell you? You would harbour disease and I would make it public! Would anyone believe me"?

Chaturika assured, "Brother Mahaparshwa, I haven't contracted any illness".

The bent body of Mahaparshwa sprang up straight as he stamped his feet on the ground, "Only the physician can tell whether you have any disease or not. This disease can hardly be hidden. My mother had succumbed to this ailment, and Uddhav, the courtier would throw you there in the jungle"!

Chaturika could sense that the peril was just in front of her. Mahaparshwa was toying with her. Mahaparshwa was very sly, he kept on indulging in doing things by evil means and at an opportune moment he would raise his hood! Chaturika said, "You know quite well that I am unaffected, I am just fine. But if you utter such words again, I shall go and see the merchant, I mean, Subhag Dutta".

Mahaparshwa laughed noisily, "Alack, what a pity, you are the maid-servant of the merchant! Would you be able to reach the merchant's chamber or Uddhav will take you to the jungle to throw you off, well ahead of it? If you folks fall ill, the whole city would be in danger".

Chaturika bowed down and asked, "What do you really want, brother Mahaparshwa"?

"What will you give me, Chaturika"?

"Whatever I can, I shall give you, brother Mahaparshwa"!

Mahaparshwa said, "Your youth holds out no appeal to me, I am sick and tired of seeing women. Again, if you have any disease, I shall have to go to the jungle too".

"I have no disease". Chaturika then cried out, "What do you want, brother Mahaparshwa, do not utter such words again, I shall have to die then".

Mahaparshwa asked, "What do thou have? Do thou have gold in thy house"?

"It's there, just a little bit though".

"Is there silver"?

"Yes, a bit of it".

"Gems and jewels"?

"How shall I be left with any such valuables, as the Sessions-Judge comes and snatches off whatever belongs to me"! Saying so, she kept shedding silent tears, burying her face in her palm. It was evening. Light was not there.All signs of light kept dying gradually. While weeping, Chaturika could sense that, this man would not let her go. As a cat plays with a rat, he had a game-plan likewise. Again, Mahaparshwa was born in this brothel. A bawdy house would make a man such heartless.

Mahaparshwa said, "Do something, whatever you earn from the clients visiting you for the coming seven days, will belong to me"!

"The Sessions-Judge comes to take his share, how can I hoodwink him?" While saying so, Chaturika kept wiping her eyes.

"Well, whatever remains, will be mine".

Chaturika, taken by surprise, looked at Mahaparshwa. After the Sessions-Judge's grabbing of his share, what more would be left for Mahaparshwa? Whatever would remain must serve her with rice. Would he like to take it? Mahaparshwa seemed to sense her agony and said, "But you would not be allowed to remain in fasting, whatever left still would be mine".

Chaturika inhaled freely and asked, "What would be left, even after"??

"That which still remains, I live on left-out food only. Get ready tomorrow at dawn, I shall take you to the mad physician, Nahush Sharman!"

Tears coursed down the eyes of Chaturika, in gratitude. The pimp, Mahaparshwa, again sat squatting on the threshold and said, "Roaming around under the sun inhibits the grey cells to function properly. At times, I think, I shall cause harm to men, let men go to the dogs and let me derive joy out of it, just as the servant of the merchant died, being burnt alive, crying out like a boar. Let all men die likewise. Just as my mother had undergone pain, had entered into the forest on her own, let all follow suit. But later I think, what good will it fetch me? If an epidemic breaks out in the city, shall I be spared? Oh! What a dreadful heat! Hearsay has it that daytime will last long. Daytime will continue uninterrupted, all day, all night. Only sunlight! Previously, it was so".

"How was it"? Asked Chaturika, in astonishment.

FORTY-SIX

It was a terrible morning! It was more an afternoon than a morning, the heat being so oppressive! Scarcely had the night's darkness dispelled before the afternoon seemed to have happened. How little in span was the night, the day seemed too expansive in comparison. The day was getting prolonged gradually. While walking, Mahaparshwa, the pimp said, "Now that era has begun in which there would be no night at all".

"What do you say, brother Mahaparshwa"? As the tall and lanky pimp, Mahaparshwa, loped through quite a long stretch, with his long steps, each step covering a considerable distance, Chaturika had to lag behind, nearly running after him. In that state, she went on continuing a dialogue with Mahaparshwa. Every now and then, Mahaparshwa slackened his pace to be in sync with Chaturika's. Mahaparshwa spoke in a muffled voice, curving his body, "Yes, Chaturika, is the sun budging in that direction"?

"Which direction"?

Folding his palms, Mahaparshwa touched his forehead to say, "Mahakaal knows everything, everything happens according to His will. Look Chaturika, the shrine has been defiled, hence the sky is dry, the sky has bent low due to lack of water".

Chaturika looked up to the sky for some time. She could not comprehend the drift of his statement. She was now going to meet the Royal Physician, Nahush Sharman. She could not even confirm that Mahaparshwa's doubt had been cleared completely, though watching numerous men and women till this middle-age, he got a rudimentary instinct of identifying the people telling a lie as well as the truth. Hence, he had taken Chaturika along. Sometimes, he took the harlot's words to be true, and sometimes again, they appeared to be elusive. When a prostitute sought help of a physician, secretly, the purport would surely be just unitary. And the physician was Nahush Sharman of all persons! None took him to be a doctor at all. Throwing away his pestle and mortar he had taken to the streets for the whole day, just a madman lately! Madman, no doubt, but his diagnosis was known to be infallible, he knew such rare medicines! He did not apply his knowledge though, he gave up everything just for one mistake!

Mahaparshwa called out to Chaturika, "Are you coming along, Chaturika"?

"Yes, coming"! The whore replied while running behind. She implored, "Please walk a bit slower. It is really difficult to catch up with you, brother Mahaparshwa"!

Mahaparshwa turned his face back, grinned with a flash of his reddish teeth and said, "If the heat of the sun goes high, none knows where Nahush Sharman would escape"!

"What are you saying, brother Mahaparshwa"?

"Yes, it is so, if the sun scales high, his temperament will touch high too, his eccentricity will increase, then he tends to forget everything. Come, walk faster".

"Yes, I am walking", Chaturika replied in an inaudible tone. And then asked sotto voce, "That man, I mean, the merchant's messenger"?

The query escaped his ears, while walking. Mahaparshwa threw a glance at the sky again. The western sky was before his eyes. Though not certain, being an ignoramus, he failed to notice that the heat of the sun was causing the sky to bend, losing its shape. True, the sky was creasing up at its edge! This fact was doing rounds. All were concerned, secret discussions were rife, in the taverns, on the streets, by the riverside. If not true, wherefrom did the fact make a dent in the society? What would take place hereafter? What if the sun stood straight up in the sky all the time? The night was gradually being smaller. No sooner the city cooled down than the darkness of night evaporated. It was also doing rounds that the night would merge with the day, later on! Again, hearsay reached such a limit that there would be no nights, only days would prevail. If there were no nights, trade and commerce would go to the dogs, who would visit the brothels during daytime? Where would one hide in the broad daylight? Who would come to the brothel without any fear, if there would be no cover to hide their face? Mahaparshwa walked forward, shaking his head.

Chaturika was watching how the city stood static during dawn, as was usual in a brothel. It seemed to her that the city stayed awake all night, to fall asleep now. The dozing city was inching towards a sleep presently. The trees lining the road were almost leafless, the grass on the ground got singed to red. By the roadside, many a flower used to stand in bloom despite neglect: jasmine, tagar, bel, champak, aparajita , red amaranth, so on, soforth . But now, not a hint of these blossoms had been there. The city seemed to be devoid of flowers. The whore's face went gloomy.

Both of them had reached the marketplace of Ujjwain. The commotion in a rural market at dawn was absent, the way in which the rural market would come to life after a night's sleep and respite seemed to be missing. By this time, all the shops were to open. But some shops were opening, some were bolted, some were about to up its shutters! The owner of the shop, which opened, sat such motionless, looked so lifelessly still taking after the stationary, lifeless eyes of a dead animal, as if all his sales and transactions had already been over and he would love to walk home, downing the shutters. Not many souls had been there out on the road. The people were not at all interested in shopping, for whom would the shops open then? What for would they open at all?

Mahaparshwa said, "A large share of the customers were the traders from alien lands, how would trade and commerce run if they did not pour in"?

"Why aren't they coming, brother Mahaparshwa"?

Mahaparshwa rejoined, "Henceforth, the sun will not set in Ujjwain, daytime will last the whole day, it will be afternoons only".

"Who told you?

"That is why, Acharya Brishavanu has left the city for good, he has left us informing this fact".

"What are you saying"? Chaturika was visibly anxious. "Won't there be nights"?

"No, we will have to miss out on nights".

Chaturika broke into a giggle all of a sudden, "How will that be possible, if there's no night, when will the lover come to see his beloved?"

"That is their concern, walk faster now".

Chaturika stood still. It was not easy to keep pace with Mahaparshwa. She was panting for breath. She was feeling restive. Again, she was not in the wont of walking so fast. Though morning, the soft glow of the sunlight was absent. The heat of the sun was being well-perceived. It was the time for his deep sleep. At night, someone or the other stayed with her. If none would be there, that knave Uddhav would come up, being drunk. Then he would have to be taken inside. Chaturika missed out on her sleep if anyone would be there in her chamber though the man remained in a stupor under the impact of wine. But whoever would come to her place for merrymaking - be that the son of a rich man or a merchant hailing from a far-off land, they used to leave at the crack of dawn. Uddhav, too, did the same. Chaturika was standing, looking around at the desolate city. She was gazing at the noiseless shop-lined ghetto.

Mahaparshwa said, "Why have thou stood still, Chaturika"?

"Let me wait, oh God, the long pace at which you walk"!

"If thou tarry on the road, the sun will rise high and the lunatic physician will move from one place to the other, without leaving any clue".

Chaturika said, "The shops are still closed".

"Yes, something seems to be wrong at this hour of the day, the shops are usually abuzz with various noises issuing from the smithy, the brazier's corner, the stall of the conch-shells. Look there, all these shops are closed".

Chaturika inquired, "The pearl-stall"?

Mahaparshwa broke into a noisy laughter, "What of that to you"?

"The flower-stall"?

"The female florists used to sit huddling together. I come on frequent rounds at this corner, Chaturika, such a spectacle never met my eye, see yonder, just a single florist is sitting with her flowers".

The sunrays drove Chaturika into an irritation in her head. She had a thick tuft of hair. If she let her hair down, it would fall down,beyond her waist. Those tresses were tied into a chignon. Since a few days, the tension and worries had stopped her from oiling her head or sprucing it up with a comb. With all ten fingers of both her hands, she began to comb it.

Mahaparshwa said, "The door of the tavern is yet to open, the tavern does not open so soon though".

"The longer it does not open, the better; brother Mahaparshwa, if there would be a few jasmine, bel or tagar flowers, I could have taken some, to weave a garland"!

Mahaparshwa loped in giant steps towards the old florist woman. He came back, too, after casting a cursory glance. Coming back, he began to shake his head in disapproval and say, "All these are stale flowers, who knows from which garbage pit, she has gleaned"?!

Chaturika said, scratching her head, "Why will they be stale"?

"There's none to buy flowers, tell me, do the men drop in at all in thy chamber"?

Chaturika retorted, "Let's go, Mahaparshwa brother, standing here makes me get scorched, from head to feet. Oh, I have an itching sensation in the upper part of my head"!

Mahaparshwa said, "That's for lice".

"Lice means"?

"Thou have lice in your head"!

Chaturika replied, "I must wash my head with fuller's earth, all these have turned blood-suckers, getting the sun"! Saying so, she grabbed a louse with her forefinger and thumb and kept killing it on her nail.

Mahaparshwa asked, "Who has gifted you these lice? Is it that Chief Physician"?

"What do you say"?

"Was he there in your room lately, Chaturika"?

Chaturika shook her head. Mahaparshwa kept walking tardily. The whore kept following him, noiselessly. The sun had left the worms in a tizzy, they hid in the dark of her hair in such a manner that Chaturika thought of untying her hair, undoing the chignon. Shaking off the dry hair, she felt like shedding the lice.

Mahaparshwa asked, "Will the Chief Physician give thee the medicine for lice"?

Chaturika came up to say, "No, he is a messenger".

Though Mahaparshwa was expected to hear the words, he feigned not to take them in his ears. Walking, they left the shops heading towards the west, making way through the hamlets. Chaturika saw a few people were on their way to the river, with empty water-cans in their hands. Some preceded them, some were behind them. They would also walk towards the river and then would head more towards the west by the bank of the river Gandhavati, in order to meet Nahush Sharman.

Chaturika called out, "Mahaparshwa brother, did you hear me"?

"What am I to hear"?

"Of Nahush Sharman, the Chief Physician"!

Mahaparshwa said, "Once we reach him, we will get to know when night will come to an end for good, yielding to an unending day instead".

"Can that ever happen"?

"That is happening in reality, have thou ever seen the shops downing their shutters and the traders not lining up? They, too, keep abreast of this news".

Chaturika said, "But at this time of the year, the nights are generally short in span".

Mahaparshwa pulled his own hair, the lice in his head grew restive, it seemed.

Scratching his head, he said, "Not such short-lived and who again says that the nights turn short-spanned? They remain as they are".

Chaturika went speechless. It seemed that the pimp, Mahaparshwa, might be correct.

Nights would remain the same as before, though this year they were getting short-lived, gradually. The sun was hitting harder along with time and Chaturika could feel that. Her back was getting singed. The tender beauty of the morning which used to pervade all around, remained absent. By this hour of the day, the ground was getting scorched by the sun. The heat was smoking its way through the surface of the ground. How strange! Where were the birds? The chirps and twitters of the birds were meant to fill this morning! But they were not there. Chaturika looked hither and thither. At last, she could spot the flock of the vultures, just like a black dot, far-off in the sky.

Mahaparshwa, the pimp, kept walking, talking to himself. He was muttering, "Various people were to be seen in the morning, they were there to keep all in good humour, cracking jokes, engaging all in joyous piffles, but nothing happens now. Rather mornings, these days, have lost all charm to make all such things happen as they did before. But if it is not so, then what kind of morning is this?" Mahaparshwa used to make a little money by nabbing the man, who used to return home stealthily, emerging from the brothel. After the night's revelry and entertainment, they would return home, dragging their feet, utterly exhausted. Demanding money then would surely bear fruit. Phew! The pimp kept stamping his feet on the ground and grumbling – "The whores of Ujjwain have all gone devoid of their charms as downpour is denied, if such be the state of this city, if such azure sky, such firmament with cloudy shades, if that star-studded vault of the sky gets bent and twisted by the oppressive sun, if senility grips the sky, all women would be prone to age untimely, too. All the bawdy houses of Ujjwain has got replete with old, elderly women. Hence, the traders in droves are not making a beeline to the harlots, at all. Even the householders have left visiting them, on the sly. As they are not pouring in, the nights are becoming shorter in span".

Chaturika said, "What nonsense are you saying, brother Mahaparshwa"?

Mahaparshwa did not turn to look back. He kept moving both his hands, wrenching his body. Scratching his head with one hand, he went on, "If the men lose interest in women, whose fault is it then, of the men"?

"The time is out of joint".

"Time is occasionally out of joint. Then, more wiles, more strategies to attract men are to be employed. Who will approach you, Chaturika, if you sit at the threshold with a lice-laden head"?

Chaturika replied, "Yes, they will come".

"Who"? Mahaparshwa turned back to look.

"You will come to know of him, take me to the Chief Physician, please".

"I am taking thee along, but tell me, do thou really have no disease at all"?

"I am telling you,I don't have any ailment. Tell me, how many times am I to repeat it"? Chaturika drew all her hair on her breast and then said, "Let everything be over , brother Mahaparshwa, you will be rewarded, I shall take you along too".

Mahaparshwa was taken aback. Without getting the feel of anything, he kept walking faster.

FORTY-SEVEN

Chief Physician, Nahush Sharman, was found in the west of Mahakaal Temple, by the river Gandhavati. Across the river stretched the Mahakaal forests. Instead of entering the forests, the Chief Physician got down into the river, thought of crossing it, leaving the city behind. Just at that instant, Mahaparshwa and Chaturika appeared before him. Old Physician had descended on the bed of the river, while Mahaparshwa loped and nearly ran to stop him, demanding, "Where are you going, Chief-Physician? We had started hours ago just to meet you, the sun has left us with a torpid sensation in our head, here this woman has taken recourse to you"!

Chaturika was looking at the river, lying waterless, like a half-dead snake. River Gandhavati was usually narrow to look at and now it lay almost stagnant, without any stir. The sand was shining like the edge of a knife under the sun. Hardly one could keep staring at it. It seemed that the heat would rise from the river to dazzle the face. On the east of the river, the end at which the Mahakaal Temple stood, Chaturika bowed a little in reverence, "Oh Lord Mahakaal, please save your serving-maid"! Chaturika was shivering in excitement on finding the Chief Physician, on getting to see him. Now, she would come to know of the merchant, whether the best merchant of Ujjwain had asked for her at all!

Chief Physician Nahush Sharman pushed Mahaparshwa with both his hands, "Who are you, and who again is she? I shall leave Avanti for good".

"Where will you go, Sir"?

"Where there is the sea, have you ever seen an ocean"?

Mahaparshwa retorted, "No sea has any water, all the seven lakes of Ujjwain have gone dry, which sea are you fording on to"?

"The High Sea, the Ionian Greek trader told me".

Mahaparshwa quipped in, "Please be calm, Sir! If you leave, who will save these orphaned women, as here's Chaturika, she has come to you for holding on to her dear life. Come Chaturika, tell him, what's wrong with thee"!

Chaturika was coming up from the river-bed, with a lowered face. Before her, were Mahaparshwa and Nahush Sharman! By the river bank, under the shadow of a banyan tree, the Chief Physician was gasping. He was looking at Chaturika in opaque, dull eyes. Suddenly he was reminded of the damsel, "You seem quite familiar, dear girl, now tell me, where have I seen you"?

Chaturika did not have to rejoin, preceding that Mahaparshwa introduced her as the mistress, the keep of Uddhav Das, the King's Sessions-Judge. Then, he began to introduce Uddhav Das. How powerful Uddhav was in this royal court-politics of power, the position he held, what he himself did, so on, so forth. Mahaparshwa was in no doubt that the Chief Physician could easily scrounge a position in the royal court if Uddhav so wished. Only the Chief Physician would have to cure this slut of her venereal disease!

Hearing him, Chaturika let out an indistinct scream, "What are you saying, Mahaparshwa brother"?

"I am just referring to thy misfortune, prostitution has its bright aspect, it has its drawbacks as well. If thou are down with venereal disease, then as a whore thou stand undone, losing all thy possessions, I know that well, none else does so, thou have to die, being burnt, inch by inch, bit by bit".

The maid, Chaturika, now snarled out for saving herself from such false imposition, "Did I ever tell you of any disease? Beware Mahaparshwa, I have been coveted by the greatest of all merchants, Subhag Dutta. You shut up!"

Hearing this, throwing both his hands up, the pimp, Mahaparshwa, seemed to defend himself. He could not make out the whole of it. Things were not falling in place. What! How could the merchant ask for Chaturika? Why? Was the merchant not getting proper supply of beautiful women in Ujjwain? What nonsense was on, in here? Again, the King of Avanti had gone to the shrine to enjoy the flesh of a devadasi on its terrace like a petty thief! Was there any scarcity of women for the King? The queen was such a paragon of beauty, the whore Devadutta had been there, even a bevy of young damsels, charming daughters of rich men were there too. If the King desired, they would be going on love-tryst almost hiding the lamp under the corner of their saris, tying the anklets of both feet with the end of their saris. And now, Uddhav's mistress, Chaturika, the whore, was bragging of being sought after by Subhag Dutta, the merchant! Mahaparshwa was on the verge of bursting into a laughter. Such was beauty! If youth waned, none would be interested at all. And did the merchant really covet this woman? If the object of pleasure for a King would be a petty devadasi, no wonder, the merchant would express his interest in Chaturika. Mahaparshwa was suspicious about the veracity of the statement, which might be true or otherwise. True or false, whatever it might be, he would take the side of convenience and opportunity.

The manners and demeanours of the Chief-Physician, Nahush Sharman, did not tally with Chaturika's statement or Mahaparshwa's thoughts. The old man was observing Mahaparshwa and Chaturika with suspicious eyes. While doing so, he clasped his kinky hair abruptly, and in a rattling voice said, "What has happened, tell me"!

"What would happen"?

"Hereafter there will be no nights at all! Last night, sleep eluded me".

"Why"? Chaturika demanded to know.

"It is being learnt that the sunlight will no more fade out, there will be no afternoon, not even morning, oh what horrible day is ahead, go, escape, gentle lady"!

Mahaparshwa said, "And me"?

"Where will you go, none will take you, I know you well. Lady, I have recognized you"!

"Lord"! Chaturika lowered her head to the ground,in a surge of emotions, "Lord! I have come to you to know about that only".

The elderly Chief Physician broke into a noisy laughter suddenly to say, "Who am I? My pestle-and-mortar are in the garbage-bin, Acharya Brishavanu has escaped, leaving the city behind. What more do you want to hear, you woman"?

"Lord, where shall I go"? Chaturika's heart missed a beat or two. In a whisper she said, "Won't the great merchant, Subhag Dutta, send his palanquin to my house"?

Mahaparshwa was all ears to take the words in. Now Chaturika's movements seemed quite dubious. With whom did Chaturika tie amorous knot, stealthily? Subhag Dutta? He felt a shudder down his spine. A weird sensation got the better of his whole body. Was Chaturika not really unwell then? Who was this Chief Physician in reality? Why was Chaturika asking this man about the merchant? Was this eccentric physician a messenger of the merchant? But why, none knew about it! He, himself, used to hang about the city, all day long. Since the afternoon, he used to stay near the brothel, guarding the door, to be precise. The arrival and departure of the visitors were within his grasp. Who told him of this matter of 'having a mirror in one's nails'? A female friar from an alien land, adept in charms and incantations, perhaps. She did not teach Mahaparshwa the 'mantra', though. Now he was regretting. Then he would have known everything by casting a glance at the nails of a person. He wished he would catch hold of that female friar. But she was here at the outskirts of the city for just one evening. If the Chief Priest of Mahakaal Temple would have come to know of her, he would never have burnt anyone alive. Mahaparshwa was being assailed by varied thoughts. And after much thinking, he came to a decision that, this must reach the ears of Uddhavnarayan. He was the man of the Royal Sessions Court, after all. How could a whore of this city go to the merchant's place without his knowledge? Was it ever possible?

The Chief Physician said, "You are supposed to escape, yes, now I remember, we met that evening, but who are you still waiting for"?

"Lord, for the merchant".

"Catch up with the merchant on the way, he will be going to the west, crossing the Indus, he would go to Purushpur, Gandhaar, and beyond that, to the river Oxus, to Balkh, go, walk along that route, you can meet him on the way".

Chaturika said, "Lord, the merchant covets this maid, doesn't he"?

"You need not know what the merchant does or not, hereafter, the day will neither be longer nor shorter, the sunrays won't be softer, the Sun-God is getting stranded at one point, his chariot-wheel is getting stuck, terrible times are ahead, go, flee away, you whore"!

Mahaparshwa asked, "Who catered this news to you"?

"How would you understand who catered, I am now crossing the river, I had set out on my journey, you all dragged me back again".

Mahaparshwa asked, "Whom does the merchant covet, Chaturika"?

Chaturika hung her head low. As she was not replying, Mahaparshwa said, "Uddhav must know the whole of it, he is none but the Sessions-judge of the Royal Court, thou are his mistress, not the merchant's".

"That man knows it already", Chaturika mumbled.

"Does he know? Whoa! He too knows! Only I do not know, the merchant covets thee, zounds! What isn't transpiring in this city, this is the last phase of Kalyug, indeed. The merchant is running short of women. Mahaparshwa grabbed his hair with both his hands and then said, "Give me my dues, thou whore, before leaving! I want a gold necklace, a silk scarf, since ages I dreamt of draping my body in a pink scarf, and, my headgear would be yellow".

Listening to Mahaparshwa, Chaturika's shapeless face was growing into a beautiful one. In the tawdry eyeballs, shadow of clouds seemed to intensify, the eyes became black, her complexion began to glow like Devadutta's, all the lacunae on her body started being cured. After such a long time, it seemed to be clear, how plain-looking she had been, and how beautiful she could be, in a trice, it seemed as though, she would be able to master all the sixty-four fine arts, all rules of amorous art, all the postures of sexual union, all the 'mudras' and she would be able to create a new dance style even. She would rule solely over the courtyard of the merchant's house with her footwork during dance, with the graceful movements of her arms, and the whole ambience would be joyous with her charming presence. She would begin her dance recital on a full moon night, remembering Lord of the Lords, blue-throated Mahadeva. Being mesmerized by her dance, the merchant, Subhag Dutta, would turn into her man of errands. Then, Chaturika would shoo away Uddhavnarayan from the King's court. If the merchant willed, that would easily happen. Thinking thus, tears seemed to have flooded both the eyes of Chaturika. Downing her face, she kept looking at her expansive thighs, her two arms right from her breasts. Glancing at those limbs, she thought she had to add fragrance to her hair, had to take bath, smearing her body with sandal-paste, she would have to rub off the dirt from her feet for over long hours. She would have to dry her hair sitting in the shade, with the smoke of joss-sticks and many more tasks to accomplish. She must take lessons from Devadutta.

Mahaparshwa said, "Oh revered Chief Physician, is it true that wheels of the chariot of the Sun-God are getting stuck, are all that you say, true"?

"Check the truth as it happens, whoever, in this city, doesn't know this"?

"But I do not know".

"Being an ignoramus, thou do not know. Can thou tell me, how many horses does the Sun have?"

Mahaparshwa kept on glancing, agape. He did not know. Till date, he had no need to know this. And again, how would he know? Did any such incident take place before? He knew superficially that the Sun-God used to traverse from the east to the west on His chariot, but he had never espied the carriage of the Sun-God! And how would a sinner like him witness such a spectacle? He did neither have that sight nor the inner vision. And he had never thought of seeing it either. He did not have much time indeed. At dawn, he had gone to the streets to find many men bowing down to the Sun with folded palms, with their face turned to the east. They kept chanting hymns gazing at the just-bobbed-up crimson Sun in the sky. He had never felt any interest in the mantra, they were chanting. Did he even know the significance of worshipping the Sun-God? However, he thought, that those rituals should be done or observed.

Turning towards Chaturika, he asked, "How many horses, hey Chaturika"?

Chaturika's face turned sullen. She had no idea. Devadutta, perhaps, knew. Devadutta knew so many things: river Oxus, Balkh country! She had heard of all these names for the first time from Devadutta. But not this one. This topic did not come up, hence she did not learn, if it did, she would obviously get to know of it. If the merchant now asked her, what would she rejoin? This very day she would have to know everything. But it might so happen that, instead of asking all this, the merchant would ask for something else! Then who would she approach to learn? Devadutta? Ohh! It was heard that the merchant was enamoured of none but Devadutta and his mind was now concentrating upon this wretched Chaturika! Would the tycoon desert her because of her ignorance? No, why would that happen? Those things were known to the wise men, even the old Chief Physician knew so much. Then, the merchant might send for this elderly Chief Physician. Smile flashed at the corner of her lips. Chaturika decided that she would offer her youth to Subhag Dutta, the tycoon. Would Subhag Dutta ever inquire all such things if he became keen on enjoying her youth? Could anyone look at the sun for long, so that he would be able to count his horses? Wouldn't the eyes dazzle? Chaturika told Mahaparshwa the same. Hearing so, Mahaparshwa was beside himself with joy. Exactly so, the Sun can hardly be glanced at for long, dear Chief Physician!

"Thou fool"! Chief Physician Nahush Sharman cried out. And then replied, "Seven horses"!

"Seven! One, two, three…amounting to s-e-v-e-n"?

"Naturally, that is how to count! Would you like to know its history?"

"Which history, Chief Physician"?

"Of the horses of the Sun-God, of His chariot"!

"Of course, let the merchant's matter be over", Chaturika suggested.

"Which 'matter' of the merchant? He is going to Balkh, to the distant bank of the river, Oxus, and there as we know, traders of Ionian Greek origin rule".

"May I ask you, when shall I be sent for by the merchant"?

"That he only knows, whether he will call you or not, whether he will take along sluts or pick them up on his way, I have no idea! In this world, many things are scarce, save women, right? Women can be had in times of need, what do you think, Mahaparshwa"?

Mahaparshwa could not make out. He began to sway his neck, knowing not why... Just now, Chaturika said that the merchant coveted her, while the Chief Physician came up with the substantial truth, is there any dearth of whores ever? Really, the world abounds with floozies. The merchant could have anyone on demand, why Chaturika alone? Why again had the King seen Lalita, a devadasi?

FORTY-EIGHT

The Chief Physician, Nahush Sharman, said, "In the city of Avanti, Ujjwain… all are blind. He who could visualize the Sun's chariot has left this city for good. After Acharya Brishavanu's departure, no one could see anything".

"What"? Mahaparshwa asked, failing to make out anything.

"Through the Acharya's eyes, the sky could have been watched, hearsay has it that the wheels of the Sun's chariot are sinking down into the earth. The seven horses have crossed their prime. Even after much effort, the wheels cannot be pulled up".

"What are you saying, Sir"? Watching the sky, Mahaparshwa asked with much surprise.

"Whatever I say is right, what will you get by watching the sky, will you ever be able to watch the wheels of the chariot? You are just blind! Oh, what a disaster! What strange happenings are on in this city of Avanti"!

Rubbing both his eyes, Mahaparshwa cast his gaze at the river, the other bank of the river, the banyan tree and its base, the sun-baked meadows, all at one go. What led to what exactly, was way beyond one's comprehension. The Chief Physician claimed himself to be blind though he could see everything clearly. Mahaparshwa knew that all of the Physician's words were not to be taken seriously. And again, it was true that, the Physician's words were not to be pooh-poohed away. Acharya Brishavanu had left the city without apprising anyone of anything, but why had he gone away? Some serious reason must be there behind his leaving. The things which were not to happen in the city kept happening and there could be no denial of this fact. Was the King supposed to enjoy an ordinary devadasi? Was this Chaturika quite apt for the enjoyment of the tycoon? What did Chaturika have at her command? Neither she had knowledge, nor intellect nor she was an enchanting beauty! The whore's wiles, postures and youth were enough to make the merchant forget everything! Shame, shame, shame, Avanti had to stand in disgrace! The King, the merchant, all had lost

370

their wits. The sky being devoid of moisture, the earth remaining starved fordrops of rain from the sky would leave all, in such a state,perhaps. Mahaparshwa was thinking thus. He kept wondering, why did the Chief Physician call him 'blind'? What for? He said that after the departure of the Acharya all had gone blind, but what for? What did it mean at all? Was it just a stray saying without much significance? Throwing away his pestle and mortar, Nahush Sharman had become insane! Were these words just stuff and nonsense of a lunatic? While thinking, he asked Chaturika, "Are you seeing all, Chaturika, with your eyes"?

"What"? Chaturika started. She was a bit morose, all were not happening in accordance with her imagination.

"All are blind… what does it mean"?

Chaturika shook her head. She wished to ask the son of Ayu, the Physician-super Nahush Sharman, more clearly. But hesitation stopped her and again she was accompanied by this apish pimp, Mahaparshwa! It would be better if they had not come together. She could have gone to the merchant along with the Physician!

Without getting any rejoinder, Mahaparshwa began to think again, how could this be public that the chariot-wheel of Sun-God had got stuck and the senile horses could not draw that anymore? And what did it really mean? He started visualizing everything in his stupor. The sun was ascending high, by degrees. The temperature was escalating too, gradually. Heat of the blazing furnace seemed to pervade all directions.

The Chief Physician, Nahush Sharman, said, "Such days are near at hand, when there will be no nights".

Mahaparshwa tilted his head, "Yes, it is doing rounds, I have heard that too".

"Tell me, how large is the chariot of the Sun-God"? the old man threw this query.

"No idea", rejoined Mahaparshwa.

"Do thou know"? The Chief Physician demanded of Chaturika.

Chaturika shook her head in the negative. She had no knowledge of anything, at all.

Stretching both his hands wide on both sides the elderly person said, "Fifty thousand miles is its width, do you know the names of the seven horses"?

"Sorry, I do not know, you tell us", Mahaparshwa bent forward. How strange! Life was moving on, quite comfortably, without knowing all these things. But now he felt knowing was no loss, rather a gain on the contrary. Once learnt, it brought some other comfort, some other happiness, beyond explanation! Without knowledge, it seemed as if he was just a have-not!

Elderly Nahush Sharman was laughing out noisily, "All are devoid of wisdom, all have turned blind, they cannot even conjecture what sort of days lie ahead! The seven horses are seven rhythmic variations: Gayatri, Trishtup, Anushtup, Jagati, Ponkti, Brihati, Ushnikâ…

Mahaparshwa was amazed. A thrill seemed to electrocute his whole body. How enthrallingly the old Physician was deliberating! Were all these true, or just nonsensical utterances of a lunatic? But was it not sounding true? He kept muttering, "Gayatri, Trishtup, Anushtup … and what next, Chief Physician Sir"?

"Don't have to know, you don't have to know any more, what will you get by knowing, all will get burnt, all hours will be daytime, yet man will remain blind, man will not be able to see anything".

"Really"?

"Neither death, nor birth will be witnessed by anyone, man will not be able to identify the hour he is in, neither will he be able to guess what will happen nor remember what had happened and when"!

Mahaparshwa clutched his hair with both hands and muttered, "Gayatri, Jagati, Anushtup"…he bowed down to touch the feet of the Chief Physician, "Please tell me again".

The old man replied, "In the city of Avanti, there will neither be monsoon, nor spring, not even late or early autumn".

And then …? By that time, Chaturika seemed to get back her wits and she could take note of the measure of the diction, the trajectory the words were following and even could feel the fact that she could not make out the import of the old Physician's words that day. Signs of panic stood on her face eventually. All kept being revealed to her, gradually. Her imaginings regarding the tycoon were then baseless. Though baseless, she had become amorously engaged with the tycoon, on the sly. In this universe a large number of things took place, which were not scheduled to happen. A great number of strange events were seen to transpire. Such drought, such lack of clouds and rains had never taken place, but now it had begun to happen. The wisest man of the city, Acharya Brishavanu, has left the city forever, paragon of beauty, Devadutta, the harlot, had refused to respond to the call of the tycoon for a lowbrow indigent like Dhruvaputra. Leaving his extraordinarily beautiful queen, forgetting Devadutta, the whore, the King had gone to a devadasi, in the dark. If all these facts were true, her dream would come to be true too. Her imagination might turn into reality. Was there any dearth of strange facts in the world? Did ever anyone think that the fierce servant of the merchant would be burnt alive? Could she, too, ever think that she would be able to desire the tycoon in her imagination? She was afraid of him! If her desire were true, the merchant would definitely take her along on his business expedition, may be. On the way, they would make love. Her dreams of love would be fulfilled. This wizened Chief Physician had opened the floodgate of her imagination. She was nothing more than the serving-maid of Uddhav! Uddhav's repeated rape was eroding her, bit by bit, every day. Suddenly, she was reminded of Devadutta's prediction made in the past, someday Kumar Bikram or the tycoon would be enamoured of her! Devadutta's conjecture had come to be true! Chaturika was trembling. Her mind was filled in gratitude for Devadutta.

Mahaparshwa called her, "Are thou listening to the words"?

No word was making way to her ears. Chaturika was under an illusory spell. She was thinking that anything would be made possible by love. Devadutta had remarked as if she knew this truth. If she thought of the merchant, the merchant, too, would harbour her in his thoughts. But how? Chaturika was in a fix. Did the tycoon, Subhag Dutta know her at all? How did he know her? When? Perhaps the tycoon had ensconced her in his thoughts, without her knowledge, just by seeing her! It was because of the merchant's order, Uddhav had sent her as a messenger to Devadutta! Then why wouldn't the tycoon remember her? Who could tell, how one would respond to love?!

"Why aren't thou saying anything"? Mahaparshwa asked Chaturika.

Chaturika said, "Now is the time for going back".

"Where would thou return"?

"Why, to my own house"?

"Thou must return to the brothel, Chaturika! Again, the Chief Physician is saying that all will be ruined to nullity, all will be burnt by the heat to destruction, no nights will be there, the sun will stand still at a point, as it happens when the wheels of a chariot are stuck".

Chaturika heard once again. She heard the same even before, but she could feel nothing unusual at all. In her mind, love had taken birth. Love! Love itself had made her so extremely courageous! She could not think of anything save the merchant!

Mahaparshwa said, "But we have to leave this city for good".

"Now at least, let us retrace our steps back home". Chaturika stood up. She was getting impatient. If the messenger of the merchant would come with the palanquin to the brothel! Without getting her, they might think that Chaturika had escaped. As a few were leaving the city, she too, perhaps had stepped into their shoes. She called out, "Mahaparshwa brother, the sunshine is mellowing, let's go".

Mahaparshwa said, "Let's sit for a few minutes more".

"What good will come from sitting here, I need not to be here anymore, you have come here for me".

Mahaparshwa said, "If the Chief Physician has something else to say"!

Chaturika shook her head, "If you don't come, I shall go back all alone".

Mahaparshwa said, "But the words are true, no morning will be there, no early evening too will follow, only afternoons will remain static, neither the daytime will reach its acme, nor touch its nadir".

Chaturika said, "Let it be so, let us go back for now".

"Then what'll happen, Chaturika"?

Chaturika began to walk. She felt uncanny while listening to the old Physician's words. Though she was thinking of the merchant, the words of the Physician were entering into her ears too! She was overcome with fear. Fear would sit firm instead of being quelled, if she stayed back in here. Besides, her mind grew restless. Another thought troubled her inwardly. As this royal physician had made her free from fear by opening the barred gates of her mind, he was also speaking of fearsome things! Just as he had instilled in her the desire to lead her life anew, he was even leaving her panicky, by spreading the fear of death in her mind. Chaturika turned aside to cast a glance at the old man. Sitting under the shadow of the banyan tree, he was looking at them, bewildered. Chaturika said, "Chief Physician Sir, we are leaving."

"Won't you stay back"?

"Where to stay"? Chaturika demanded.

"Won't you come along"?

"Where will we go"?

The old doctor said, "With me, across the river".

Chaturika shook her head, saying, "We are expecting a guest to drop in, Sir"!

"Thou have taken in many a guest, thou whore, now live by thyself", Mahaparshwa exhorted.

Chaturika said, "If you want to stay back with the Chief Physician, do so Mahaparshwa brother, but I have to leave, who knows, perhaps the palanquin is awaiting my return".

Mahaparshwa could make neither head nor tail of what she said, he felt such things would happen if the wheels of the chariot of Sun got stuck! Who would send a palanquin for such a run-of-the-mill harlot? And again, what for? The tycoon?! He felt like breaking into a guffaw. Rather it would be better if she could be saved from the jaws of death. He went up to hold the hands of Chaturika. "All are untrue"!

"What is untrue"?

"None is going to send a palanquin for thee, it would be better if thou come along with us to the other bank of the river, Chaturika. Stay with us".

"No}, Chaturika wrenched her hand free.

"If it is 'no', I shall have to go back there with thee".

"Why, you better go to the other bank with this old man"!

"No", Mahaparshwa again took Chaturika's hand, "if thou don't come, I shall not go".

"Why"?

"I don't know, Chaturika, I could never enter thy room, even after going to stand before it, for fear of Uddhav!Come to the other bank of the river, come, no Uddhav will be there".

Chaturika was looking at Mahaparshwa, utterly amazed. What was this scoundrel pimp, the page-boy of the harlots saying?! Was he saying, 'for fear of Uddhav'?? Oh, how strange! So, such things did still happen! So,the pimp, Mahaparshwa, had harboured such thoughts in his mind??Did the ape have a mind then? Did really the mind of this apish rogue contain a yellow yolk like an egg? If such be true, then what impediment would stop the palanquin of the merchant drawing up to her door? It could easily come. If the pimp, Mahaparshwa, could grow amorous of her behind all eyes, she too might wait for the words of 'love' by the merchant!

Chaturika rejoined, "I shall go back to my room, Mahaparshwa, the time is not yet ripe for going to the other end of the river"!

"But there is Uddhav in the city"!

"Let him be there, if you are so afraid of him, you can listen to the expatiation on death from this elderly man." In a muffled tone, Chaturika went hissing. She did not want to stay back anymore, she longed for rushing back towards the city!

Mahaparshwa asked, "Hadn't thou believed my words, Chaturika"?

Chaturika rejoined, "Yes, I had, such things happen when the wheels of the Sun's chariot get stuck"!

"How will it be"?

"It will be of many kinds, come Mahaparshwa, behind me, come thou ape, trace thy path following my shadows"!

Hanging his head, Mahaparshwa said, "Yes, coming"!

"Thou should not come back to that old man anymore".

"All right"! Mahaparshwa began to follow Chaturika. Seeing both of them leaving, Nahush Sharman got to his feet and asked, "Where are thou going"?

None of them answered. Then the old man covered his face with both the hands, clung to the reflection of the banyan tree. Chaturika and Mahaparshwa walked quite a bit forward, leaving the river behind. While walking, Mahaparshwa called out, "Listen to me, Chaturika"!

"I have heard whatever thou had to say"!

"The old physician was speaking of death, no doubt, but the city-dwellers are also talking about the continual presence of daytime and the abolition of nights! But as the old man talked of the seven horses, it occurred to me that for fear of Uddhav I cannot approach thee! Listen Chaturika, at last I understand my own mind and dare speak my mind out, only after hearing the seven names of the seven horses"!

Walking briskly, Chaturika said, "Got thee! Fetch water from the river, Shipra, for me today, won't thou, Mahaparshwa"?

FORTY-NINE

The wisest man of Ujjwain had left this city, this country, by the night of Chaitra Purnima, a couple of years back. He bade adieux to the rivers Shipra and Gambhira , Mahakaal Shrine, Sapta Sagar, seven pleasant lakes, to this golden city to set out on journey to Terra Incognito. He had gone untraced. Parashar used to know that handsome youth, Dhruvaputra. It was heard that Dhruvaputra had fallen in love with Devadutta and this had infuriated Subhag Dutta, the tycoon. The merchant was secretly in love with the Chief Courtesan, Devadutta. Again, Devadutta never thought of anyone save King Bhartrihari, but the King had no affinity towards this paragon of beauty. The King had lost his sense of judgment. King Bhartrihari had been sexually united with an ordinary devadasi named Lalita, at the temple-yard, at the dead of night. How terrifying this incident had been! It had never happened before. Had ever the Mahakaal temple been defiled by anyone of the Kingly status before? The King's heart was filled with kindness and tender feelings. It was never learnt that he was lustful! But now everything was coming into the open. Even the words were making their way to the Shudra ghetto. The King and the queen were childless. If any childless King would sit on the throne, the land would surely be sterile. All creative endeavours would end up, turning abortive. Crops would be destroyed, water-bodies would go dry, love would fade out from the hearts of the subjects, humans would rush towards utter ruin.

All strange incidents were taking place, one after another. The best merchant of Ujjwain, Subhag Dutta's servant had gone insane, as grapevine sources affirmed. If not so, why would Utanka go and set the Shudra locality on fire, in the dark of night, for no reason at all? But his death was even more strange! It had never happened in this country that the merchant's servant had been accused of oppressing the Shudras and the merchant hailing from a respectable origin stood in support of the Shudras! The servant Utanka had been sentenced to death. But that death-sentence itself was assailing the elderly soldier, Parashar, as a ghastly memory. How gruesome that death had been! That cry of death, that loud wail for living alive on earth! Even till date, Utanka used to pop up in his nightmare as he lay in a daze of sleep. His body was burnt by fire. Like dying embers, the fire was smouldering. Stench of burnt flesh kept spreading all over. Why did they all have to witness such a death? The hunter had announced the death-sentence and in that declaration lay a hint of witnessing the death. Old Parashar had gone to distant lands like the bank of the river, Indus, to fight as a soldier in the King's army or got engaged in face-to-face tussle with the Huns, but he had never watched such cruel, blood-chilling death! He had witnessed many a death in the battlefield, but he had never been so aggrieved before!

Old Parashar was saying, "Since Dhruvaputra has gone away leaving this city, things have come to such a pass that the sky stands bereft of all clouds"!

"Didn't the clouds disappear likewise, ever before"?

Parashar was shaking his head. During his lifetime, he had never seen such a face of nature, had never witnessed such a deplorable, disastrous plight this city was in!

Subhag Dutta was going to leave this graceless city. Was it an optimum time for setting out on a business expedition? But the merchant was going to the country of Balkh with his retinue of traders! All were quitting this city, Acharya Brishavanu too did. Old Parashar was striking his chest in despair, looking at the dry, waterless Ratnakasagar, in the dark of the evening, even Acharya had left! The city of Avanti had never been so impoverished like this.

Since a few days, old Parashar was being reminded of Dhruvaputra. Had Dhruvaputra been here, he could have explained the reason for this drought! His advice would surely be effective for overcoming this state of peril. In fact, when man loses his sense of direction, gets nonplussed, losing all confidence in himself for keeping alive, he needs someone else to help him out. Flouting all norms, Dhruvaputra used to come and sit here by this Ratnakarsagar just to talk to Parashar. Parashar could vividly remember, yonder would sit that youthful gentleman! How soft, how loving and kind he was! If not so, then why, being the most revered man of this city, the wisest person, would he come daily to the Shudra ghetto? This never had happened before, never would happen again as it was in case of Dhruvaputra!

Parashar said, "If Dhruvaputra had been here, such an incident would not take place".

Someone remarked, "But he was the first to leave this city of Ujjwain"!

Parashar retorted, "If he had not gone away leaving Avanti, such incidents would never take place, Ujjwain would remain as it had been as ever"!

Another person commented, "Perhaps he had an inkling of this matter much ahead, hence, he left this city before all".

Parashar shook his head, "No, being humiliated, being harassed, he had left Ujjwain, was there anyone else who had been just as wise as him or is there one even now"?

All kept quiet. Regarding knowledge their idea was very little. They did not know what knowledge meant, at all. They were fond of Dhruvaputra's appearance: semi-golden hair, fair complexion, blue eyes— as if an Ionian Greek tradesman had come to the market place of Ujjwain! Or quite different? Were Dhruvaputra's eyes bluish? Was his hair golden, or did it turn reddish by negligence, being over-exposed to the sun? Did he really have the same white complexion like the Greek men? Or was he a bit copper-complexioned? Getting sun-burnt, that copper-complexion had turned into black, perhaps. Even that look was no less exquisite. Dhruvaputra used to circumambulate this city and its surroundings on foot, disregarding the raging sun overhead. In the raging afternoon, he could be seen traversing the field towards this direction. Coming to this end, he used to enjoy respite in the shadow of the tall Peepul tree. Now, that tree stood half-burnt, Utanka had set it on fire. If he ever came here in the evening, or in the late afternoon, he used to sit by the side of this Ratnakarsagar. Then the 'sagar' stood filled with water, the breeze was cool. Many a person used to throng around Dhruvaputra, on this side as well as the other. But howsoever good or generous he had been, how could he be taken as the greatest of all wise men? Was the King less wise?

Parashar said, "I cannot pinpoint or elaborate but he was the wisest of all"!

"How could you feel that"?

"It can be understood, the light of wisdom is something typical, you know"!

"How's that"?

"It seemed to orb around Dhruvaputra, it seemed".

Then all began to imagine how illumined Dhruvaputra's surroundings had been! Some of them even thought that it could really be seen around him! While Dhruvaputra used to visit this Shudra locale disregarding the dry wind of the summer heat, stepping on the hot cauldron-like ground, both his feet remained dusty, twigs, straws, dry leaves got stuck to his hair! His face looked red in the heat of the sun … and? Was there any orb of light at the back of his head? Someone hurled a query, "Was Dhruvaputra very fair, I mean, white in complexion"?

"Haven't you seen him"? asked Parashar.

"Can't remember. Nowadays I tend to forget everything".

Someone else then demanded, "What is Knowledge"?

"What are you saying"?

"I mean, how can we understand that a man is wise, knowledgeable"?

Parashar maintained silence. He was thinking how to make him understand the true nature of a wise man. Cogitating for a second, he said, "He who knows everything is wise".

"Did Dhruvaputra know everything under the sun"?

"I think so, otherwise why would he come here to see us"?

"As he used to come to this ghetto to see us, the downtrodden ones… that's why he was wise?!"

Parashar said, "If not wise, why would he pay us a visit"?

"Why would he come even though he was wise"?

Parashar was driven to silence. In the darkness, throwing a glance at the man, he thought, was he averse to Dhruvaputra? Lest why was he raising so many queries? The man sat at a little distance. In front of him, one of his relations sat, naturally he was not getting a full view of the man, though he could recognize him by his voice. This might be the son or grandson of the man Parashar had at the back of his mind! Again, it might be the other way round, that man might be this man's father or grandfather! If the middle one would be taken into consideration, he might be his father or even son. Sundry possibilities cropped up in Parashar's mind. Yet he asked, "Haven't you heard of Dhruvaputra"?

"Heard of him… yes! But then I never thought of anything otherwise"!

"Didn't Dhruvaputra speak in a different vein"?

"Yes, he did, but was it enough to prove that he was the wisest person"?

Parashar answered, "If he did not leave Ujjwain for good…"

"This is your opinion, but he left before all did, that means, he was assailed by fear before all".

Parashar said, "May be, may not be, I have never seen another man in my life like him, my eyes opened by conversing with him — I came to learn a lot".

"What did you come to know"?

"Whatever I learnt I am now getting oblivious of it, I think, if a wise man is harassed, humiliated, wisdom itself goes to ruin, and that is taking place all around".

Piercing darkness, the man's voice surfaced, "What does this mean?"

Failing to hold his emotions back, old Parashar said, "Dhruvaputra used to know everything, don't you all remember him"?

A few blurted 'yes'. Some of them maintained silence. One from among those who kept quiet asked after a little while, "What did Dhruvaputra say usually"?

"Have you forgotten?" Some other person charged him.

"Do you remember"?

While recalling, he felt that he failed to arrange Dhruvaputra's words in a perfect order! He, then, asked Parashar, "What did he say generally"?

Parashar rejoined, "Do I remember everything"?

"Well, please tell us how Dhruvaputra was".

"Don't you remember"? Parashar asked.

Then, those who thought of Dhruvputra's looks to be similar to that of the Ionian Greeks a little while ago, stuck to their opinion, though others maintained a different view… Quite different. Absolutely different. Some reminisced of his fair complexion, blue eyes and golden hair. Some again talked about his copper complexion, reddish hair, black eyes! Again, someone else said, "No, no, so far as I can remember he was of semi-dark complexion, had close-cropped, thick, black hair, a bit curly, just like the hunters". Someone else added, he was of medium height, some again refuted him, He was tall in stature. Someone said, his voice was grave and solemn, like the roar of thunder. Some again opined, "No, not so, it was a bit musical, if heard abruptly it might appear to be a woman's voice, though firmness could be detected even in that soft, womanly, dulcet voice! It was very pleasing to the ear". Wise men are just like that. They are remembered thus, no doubt!

Parashar was being taken aback. He thought, both were correct. All their views were correct! Dhruvaputra could be white, or even copper-complexioned! Again, why not dark-complexioned? He might even be like a hunter. Again, he might not be so. The tone of his voice was solemn, it might be both manly or singsong and charming! All seemed to be true. Long ago, Dhruvaputra used to come over at this ghetto, and then he left Ujjwain for someplace else. Sometimes it seemed that, Parashar had never seen him with his own eyes, he had only heard of him! Listening to others describing Dhruvaputra, was just the same as listening to Dhruvaputra, talking about the stars and planets, oceans, deserts, the great poet, Bhasa, the love affair of Udayan, the King of Vatsya and Basavadutta, the Princess of Ujjwain, King Dushyanta and Shakuntala, the foster-daughter of the sage Kanva at his ashram. Did Parashar learn about Dhruvaputra's complexion, colour of hair, the tinge of the eyeball, tonal texture of his voice, so on, so forth from Dhruvaputra himself? Did Parashar hear in some way while the others in some other manner? Couldn't they see Dhruvaputra or just imagine him by hearing about him so often? It might be possible. Perhaps, this could be true or even untrue.

Parashar said, "Who, from among you, was talking of knowledge"?

"I, we" … the rejoinders flew in, through the darkness.

Then Parashar said, "I may be wrong, but I had talked to him for hours, listened to him speaking incessantly, day in, day out, under full-moonshine, in pale new-moonlight, beneath the clouds, in sunshine, amidst the cosy shadows..."

"All right, tell us what you heard".

"It seems, Knowledge is Truth"!

"What is Truth"?

"If Truth had not been ruined, this Ratnakarsagar would remain filled with water to the brim".

"Since long, there is no water in this lake"!

"That means, Truth is absent here".

"Do you know it for sure"?

"I think so, he used to speak like this, where there is Truth, Knowledge is there. If Knowledge is there, wise men are bound to be at that place, and their presence ensures abundance of water in the lakes even during sweltering heat of the summer, clouds hover over the sky, the clouds even cast their shadows on the ground, crops abound in arable lands and the rainfall is quite timely"!

"How strange it sounds! Now things can easily be sorted out".

Parashar was getting amazed by his own words. The things he kept uttering, were not known even to himself. He, himself, had never thought in this vein. How could he speak out which he never had thought even? How was that possible? Yet, to his mind, the words sounded true. Parashar went on, "Truth itself is Knowledge, if Knowledge prevailed, our Shudra locale would not be perished by fire. And what did Utanka gain out of it? Why did he set our dwellings on fire? There was no bad blood in between!"

"This means ignorance, untruth"! someone spoke out.

"Yes, ignorance got the better of him, that is why, he had to lose his life by being involved in such a heinous activity", Parashar kept mumbling, and then in a very soft tone, he added, "And the way he had been slain, failed to establish the Truth, could not even remove ignorance"!

"I am being surprised", wonder rang clear in a voice which said, "I, too, had thought similarly, can true judgment be solemnized if a person is burnt alive? Ujjwain's judgment is the most revered one in the world and I heard from a number of people that injustice does not exist here, and it never was there in the past too".

Parashar said, "Ujjwain has nothing to boast of as Dhruvaputra is not here, everything has gone bankrupt, clouds have disappeared, the man, committing crime is being burnt alive, the screams and cries of pain of the criminal while dying stops me from sleeping, till date! I am earnestly looking for the return of Dhruvaputra. May be on his return, everything will revert back to its normal state, as before".

They kept conversing thus. They knew they would not be able to think of anything else save this. No way was there to think even. They knew of Dhruvaputra only. They were inhaling and exhaling in the hope of seeing everything catapulting to its former state on Dhruvaputra's homecoming. A man, coming from far on foot traversing miles reached Ratnakarsagar. The middle-aged man, panting for breath said, "Have you heard that the wheels of the Sun-God's chariot are getting stuck, have you got any hint of this"?

"What are we hearing"? All of them stood stock-still. They all shouted for life in unison, "From where did you get this terrible news? Who told you? Oh Lord Mahakaal! What are we getting to hear"?

The middle-aged man rejoined, "The city is abuzz with this news, the word is spreading its wings from the city to a far distance, even the people from afar get to know of it, why don't the inhabitants of the Shudra ghetto know anything at all"?

All kept silent. The man went on, "If the wheels of the Sun-God's chariot really get stuck, there will be no end to daytime and this night will be the last one..."

Hearing this, all got panic-stricken. One from among them started running abruptly, letting out screams in fear, "We have to flee! All are escaping from this city, if we stay back, we will get burnt to death by the oppressive sun, in course of time"!

One kept muttering, "In some other country, there must be clouds and water, youthful maidens and all. I shall make a journey to that country, where there are water and waves in the river, I shall have to flee, lest my wife will follow me with the child on her lap"!

Suppressed uproar prevailed, someone else opined, "If this be the last night, then it would be better if we can escape as far as we can till the night lasts, it may certainly be true, this afternoon I had seen a peacock, on the verge of dying in the meadow, and I had a hunch that something evil was about to take place."

"Whose peacock was that"?

"Who knew whose, it was circling in the meadow, alone".

"Was that peacock from the jungle"?

"Maybe so".

"Small peacock or a big one"?

I do not remember in such detail, I have to flee with my wife and children, we have been orphaned, none is taking care of us. Since long, there is no cloud in the sky, no water in the ponds, the King could have done something, but he hasn't, as yet".

"We have no one"… Someone was heard wailing in the darkness, "If there is no night, if only sunshine rules the roost in such fierce manner, none of us will survive, we still get to live during nights, when a little calm soothes us".

"Really, we do not have anyone…the King is not thinking for us".

"For how long will the King keep sitting on the throne, as all are going to leave this city"!

"Alas"! Parashar had struck his chest, "the day Dhruvaputra had left, I thought it was ominous and now that has come to be true"...

If there is no rainfall for a long time, if crops are destroyed, if water-bodies run dry, if no hint of clouds is there in the sky, if the sun dazzles us, man's cogitative faculties function improperly. Man feels threatened. And that fear would turn fierce if the tale of the Sun-God's chariot wheels did rounds from ear to ear. The city of Ujjwain stood forlorn, desolate. The residents of the Shudra habitat thought that it was impossible to survive if they did not leave the city for elsewhere. That very night, a large number of them had left. A few more had stayed back to usher in the following day. Next day, too, hearing the intimidating words of fear, they left by night. Thus, a lot of them kept evacuating the city. Only old Parashar was wondering how far he would go by walking, in such a feeble and decrepit body of his! It would be better, if he would wait for Dhruvaputra sitting in the half-burnt shadow of the half-burnt Peepul tree, when the day would be unending. His experiences in life certified that nothing in life occurred in a certain way, changes were inevitable, no doubt. Wouldn't then Dhruvaputra come back? Parashar kept thinking thus, in the dark of the night sitting by the Ratnakarsagar. Someone had spread a rumour that there had been cloud and water in another country, hence some of them were escaping on their own, all by themselves. How would he save this Shudra ghetto?

FIFTY

Last Spring, Tamradhvaj had come by the end of Chaitra. After that, for long, he had not been seen. Were his calculations yet to be finished? Again, the sky had burnt incessantly, to turn almost black. The trees stood shorn of leaves, with each passing day. Even the sap, cooped inside the earth was being sucked in by the fire of the sun. All were on the verge of dying, it seemed. Human beings, too, would dry up to take after the dead trees. How frail that girl had been! Reba put her hand on her daughter's body. At this age, the body would look charming and gracious, but Gandhavati seemed to become lean and emaciated.

Reba asked, "Do you look at yourself"?

Gandhavati shook her head to say, "What shall I look for, Maa"?

"Your body? Your health"?

"What can I do, Maa"?

Reba's eyes got filled with tears. Supply of rice was on the verge of depletion. From somewhere, a peacock had strutted in. It must be from the forest. Gandhavati had sheltered it in shades. Just in a couple of days, the peacock died in the afternoon, circling in the meadow. Oh! How that day had been! The sunshine seemed to incise the body in pieces like a sharp sword. Gandhavati had cried her heart out that day! All night, she kept weeping. And the night was not long at all. Yet, howsoever long it had been, the maiden did not have her forty winks!

Gandhavati charged, "You ask me but have you looked at yourself, Maa"?

Reba kept mum. She knew that she was becoming a bag of bones. Not a little sap had been there in her. It seemed as if the blood in her body was evaporating like water, owing to the sweltering heat. She had become feeble. Reba could not bear herself anymore. What would happen? Worries kept her awake all night. Even though, sleep would come, it would be dotted by nightmares, strange nocturnal visitations.

Fearsome! One night, in her dreams came Dhruvaputra, dying of thirst. How terrible that dream was! After she woke up, it seemed to her that someone was really going away, being disheartened for not getting any water, which he begged repeatedly. But alack, what a pity! Never in her dreams, she got to see rainfall! Last night, in her dreams, she had seen the sandy river, Gambhira. She kept on digging and digging the sand, but to no avail. No hint of water was there. She kept on removing the sand from the river, with both her hands. How panicky she had become after that! And the nightmare came at the wee hours of dawn. Dreams in the dawn are said to come true. If it so happened, then? Now, she had only to depend on the sand on the bank of the Gambhira! Even at the close of day, by digging the sand and ascertaining the water-level, water was procured and sifted before being brought home. And again, during the crack of dawn one had to go there. What if, the river-bed really went dry and not a drop of water would be had even after removing the sand for a whole day? Then!!

Old Parvati had come. The old hag, the messenger of Uddhav had taken after a singed wood now. Being bent and incapacitated, she had taken a stick. She had turned hoary-headed, and all those tresses kept flying, being scorched by the sun. The old woman did not even care to tie it by a ribbon. Now the old hag was not talking about Uddhav! She stopped, as Uddhav asked her not to say anything. Being an employee of the royal court, would he have any dearth of woman? Perhaps, he got someone worthier than Gandhavati. Various categories of whore were there in the brothel of Ujjwain and Gandhavati would not be able to emulate them in either beauty or quality! What did Gandhavati possess save grace and youth? Was she adept in tricks and wiles? Again, her charms and youth were waning day by day. Hereafter, when all day long, the sun would rage overhead, all the nights would be replaced by daylight, what would happen then? The universe would take just a day to burn out to nullity. The old woman called out, "Yes, Reba, have you heard"?

Reba kept quiet. Her curiosity was lessening now. Nowadays, she was not reminded of Kartikkumar or Dhruvaputra, at all! Being disappointed, Reba had lost all her interest. Would her husband ever return? Or, would she take to widowhood on the completion of twelve years? And what difference would it make in assuming widowhood or not? Again, what happiness was she in now?

The old woman was scrutinizing the mother and the daughter, perching on her stick. Making a clacking sound with her tongue and lips, she said, "Alas! Where has vanished such dazzling beauty like Rambha, Menoka"?

Gandhavati flared up, "Shut up, do not speak a single word"!

"Are you looking down the way"?

Gandhavati did not answer. Failing to elicit a rejoinder, the old Parvatidasi circled the courtyard in the raging sun, keeping the stick leaned against the elevated verandah, she scrambled up to the shadows on the raised terrace. Being seated, sticking her tongue out, she kept panting for breath. Saliva kept drooling from her tongue on her soiled ghagra.

Reba asked her daughter, "Where is that astronomer from Dasharno"?

"How do I know"?

"What did he tell you before leaving"?

"Will certainly return"!

"Who will return"?

Gandhavati restrained herself as she was about to blab out, "Tamradhvaj will be back"! But she said, "Father and Dhruvaputra", instead.

"But you did not tell me that his calculations had been complete".

"It was yet to be finished".

"Then how could he predict that they will return"?

Perhaps he had said so, it occurred to me, Maa. Okay, let him come again, this time he will surely come with the correct news, won't he, Maa?

Reba cast a glance at her daughter. Gandhavati seemed to be more anxious about Tamradhvaj's imminent visit than the news of either Dhruvaputra or Kartikkumar! The very thought startled Reba. Why would Gandhavati be avid for Tamradhvaj's visit? Tamradhvaj would come with the news of Dhruvaputra on the completion of his calculations, - for that only? But since long, Tamradhvaj had not come there. Calculations were yet to be finished, so what? Couldn't he come just for paying a visit? For Gandhavati! What the hell was she thinking of? Why would Tamradhvaj come, knowing full well that Gandhavati was awaiting Dhruvaputra's return! Was this the reason for not coming of the youth of Dasharno? He was aware of the affair of Gandhavati and Dhruvaputra, wasn't he? Nothing was held back from him. Then what was wrong with him? There, Gandhavati was throwing a steadfast gaze at the sun-baked, dust-strewn way! Was it for Tamradhvaj? Or in the hope of Dhruvaputra? But at that moment, Tamradhvaj stood a fair possibility of coming back than Dhruvaputra!

Parvati, the old hag, stretching her legs forward, scratching her head with both hands asked, "Who will come, of whom are both of you speaking?

Failing to elicit a reply, the old woman said, "People are escaping from this country, why will they come back, see whether they have started a new family in the other land or not"?

Reba shivered, she screamed in fear, "What do you say"?

"Male nature is like that"!

"No, don't you know how her father was"?

"Then why is he not coming back"?

"He only knows, who can tell whether he has been held captive by the Huns or not"?!

"Calm thy mind with such thoughts! How many men have you seen in your life, how would you know of which nature they are, getting a new woman they tend to forget everything, in fact, 'forgetting' is their wont."

"Leave it"! Gandhavati intervened. "Let it be left at that, Granny"!

The old woman kept tracing the lice in her head, by mere guess, then she asked Gandhavati to come near her, "Come here!

"Why"? Gandhavati was afraid of the old woman, what ominous would she whisper again, taking her mouth near her ear? She would become jittery to hear all those things!

Old Parvati offered, "Come let me pick the lice".

Gandhavati retorted, "But I don't have lice in my head"!

"What, don't you have lice"?

Reba turned stern then, in a bit harsh voice, she rejoined, "Aunt, why do you make me listen to all such ominous things? Is it good to have lice"?

"Which good is happening to us, tell me, when Uddhav wanted, if our girl would give her consent to it, she would be saved. Now, Uddhav is no more needed".

"We are saved", Reba interrupted.

Oh God! What a pain! The old woman kept picking lice from her head, with the tip of her ten fingers, making guesswork guide her, and muttering, "They are in droves in my head, you all have too, many a time they go undetected, their existence cannot be felt if the mind remains busy with the thoughts of a gentleman"!

Reba thought of asking the old hag to leave. But she would kick up an uproar! She would shout at the top of her voice, assembling quite a few souls, unnecessarily. She would speak ill of her. It would be far better to keep silent.

The old woman said, "The peacock you caught from the forest has died, evil has already been let loose, dear! Is it possible that you don't have lice in your head?"

"Why in your head then"?

"They harbour in my head, but now I feel much pain because of them", saying so, the old woman took a louse picked between the nails of her two fingers and squeezing it to death, distorting her face, distending the toothless cheeks, she said, "During summer, in this excessive heat, they get always restive. Sucking on my head irritatingly, they keep crawling down the roots of my hairs".

"How disgusting"! Gandhavati let out a muffled scream!

"You shall have it too, if one does not get her man on time, she has to entertain a louse called 'husband' in her head"!

"What are you saying, aunt, and to whom"?

"This is for that maiden, if a louse grabs her, it will suck to the core, it won't allow her to sleep at night, and once asleep, it will threaten her with nightmares".

Reba recalled the incident of removing sand. She turned grave and solemn. She kept on looking at the crone. The old woman slaying lice on her head, said, "Just after a couple of days, we will have new-moon night, then again full-moon, who knows whether new-moon will be here again or not"?!

"Why"?

"Haven't you heard"?

Reba and Gandhavati exchanged glances. Yes, they had heard certainly. One day, Shivnath came to narrate but they did not believe him as these words appeared incredible. And now the old woman was repeating it. Folding both her palms, bowing down to the sky, the old woman went narrating the fact of the chariot wheels of the Sun-God, getting stuck. What would happen to this old woman? If the daylight persisted without being snuffed out, the lice would go crazy and impatient, under the scorching heat of the sun!

The old woman said, "I shall get my head shaven by a barber".

Gandhavati smiled mischievously, "Will you turn into a clean-shaven anchoress"?

"But there is no other way of killing the lice-family"!

Gandhavati said, "Okay have it shaven, I shall have a look at it".

Old Parvati quipped, "You all have to undergo the same treatment, no alternative being there".

Gandhavati kept imagining, how the old woman would look with a clean-shaven head! During her heyday of youth, this old woman was heard to be breathtakingly beautiful! Mother used to say so. Mother had not seen her herself, she heard it from her father. Father again learnt it from his mother. She had charms, that could still be found in traces. Getting burnt under the sun, that remnant too was about to fade out. Last winter, the old woman was about to die. She lay in her room, shrivelled up. The winter being over, she was back again to health.

Parvati, the old lady, said, "Now Lord Mahakaal will put an end to everything"!

"Never say so, I am in fear", Reba mumbled.

"This is true, Uddhav has said so, just yesterday he was going back to the city".

"Did he come"?

"Yes, he comes often, and now his position is higher than before, he is a trusted aide of the Army Commander. He left saying, Grapevine has it that the chariot wheels of the Sun-God are getting stuck".

"Did he come to tell you"? Reba demanded to know.

"Yes, he had come to tell me, he is the Royal Court employee. His duty is to keep abreast of everything, who has come from where and gone whither and when, on which day, all he gathers to inform the Royal Court"!

Reba said, "Fine, let him do so".

"He has come to know that if the chariot-wheels get stuck, the Sun will not follow the trajectory from the east to the west, the daylight will remain just the same, oh God, how will that be"?

Gandhavati rejoined, "This is not true. It cannot happen thus".

But this is happening thus. When did it rain last?"

Gandhavati asked, "But how does it relate to that"?

"I have never seen the Sun sucking in all water in my lifetime. Yonder Reba, look, look, how strong the sunshine is! It is smouldering, dazzling, it seems to be fuming"!

Reba allowed her gaze to move far across the courtyard! Yes, it seemed to be in tune with the old woman's words. Reba came down from the verandah to the sun-baked courtyard! Old Parvati also came down bending on her stick. Gandhavati was the last to descend. The wizened, decrepit old woman lifted her face up to the sky and said, "Look, the sun stands dead-still at that point of the sky, since ages! Such sunshine seems to be there for years together"!

Reba, Gandhavati, in an inaudible voice exclaimed in unison, "Is it so"?

"Yes, it is. Since eons, the Sun has not gone off to sleep, has it"?

Reba and Gandhavati whispered, "Yes, true. Yes, right, whatever Uddhav says is always true. Uddhav's words are tantamount to the King's words, the words of the Royal Court, such a news has reached the King! The chariot-wheels have begun to get stuck inside the earth. Alas, oh Lord Mahakaal! How long would such sunshine rage?" Holding the stick in one hand and scratching the head loaded with lice, the old woman said, "All are fleeing, birds and their ilk are taking flight. Since how long was it going on, tell me, such daytime, such unmitigated heat!"

Tears welled up to Reba's eyes, she said, "Since long".

"Don't you see nightmares in your sleep"?

"Yes, aunt, I do".

"Then my words are true! True! True!"

Reba and Gandhavati hugged each other in fear. Such wide daylight, yet they were utterly in fear! Darkness wore on, it seemed. Who knew that the light had such a fearsome face? The eyes were growing dark. The old woman kept sauntering in the courtyard and saying, "Decide what thou would do, Mother and Daughter, put thy heads together to think, would thou like to live for eating, wearing clothes, just for the sake of living or for being burnt to death, by degrees"!

FIFTY-ONE

Reba was feeling giddy under the sun. Gandhavati held her to make her sit on the raised terrace. Old Parvati was standing in the sun, her tresses were being tousled by the hot air. Hollow cheeks and sagging skin seemed to lend her a ghastly look. The old hag was saying, "No other way-out is there, it seems that the Sun-God will come to a standstill within a day or two or perhaps it has done so and the daytime will never end from now on".

"Stop you, Granny"! Gandhavati embraced her mother to ask softly, "Will you have water, Maa"?

"Ask her to leave", Reba gathers her strength to utter somehow.

Gandhavati asked her accordingly, but the old woman smiled at her. Stamping her stick slowly, she came to sit on the shadow of the terrace again to say, "I am leaving, but what will happen to you"?

"What do you mean"?

"You will be burnt to ashes, don't I understand the excitement of youthful passions"?

Gandhavati said, "Granny please go home. Never utter such words".

The old woman kept scratching her head with both her hands, saying, "There is a rich man in the city of Ujjwain, a bit older in age, but he has enough wealth, he is looking for a young maiden, the young wife of his is a profligate one, the rich man wants to marry again. I thought of you, you came to my mind".

Gandhavati's eyes seemed to emit fire. With anger in her eyes, she kept looking at the old woman. But the hag's facial expressions remained unaltered. She turned a blind eye to the fire of Gandhavati's wrath. She said, "Why do you stare at me like that, oh girl, what will happen to thee, who will take you and for what"?

"Shut up, be off, oh aunt"! Reba seemed to be back to her consciousness while she spoke slowly.

"If so wished, I can go away! Now there is no fear of getting dark, no advent of evening, no approach of night, no crack of dawn, no morning will be there, I can go if I wish but none will be spared from the rage of the sun ever"!

"Then please leave, do not wait for the turn of the clock"! Gandhavati replied.

"I shall go, but when, I cannot decide, I have been here since long, look yonder at the shadows of the neem tree, the shadows are not getting elongated".

Gandhavati started. She looked at the kadam tree, standing at the corner of the courtyard. A little shadow lay there on the ground in the east. That certified the position of the sun in the west. But could ever the words of the old woman be true? The shadows were not getting elongated as the sun stood still. Everything appeared strange to her. Sunshine, trees, shadows, heat all seemed to be stagnant to her. None exhibited any stir. She asked, "Granny, have you really seen"?

"Why would I say, if I hadn't? Now, the Sun-God's movement is just like an old man's, He is moving slow and thus He will come to a standstill in the sky itself, then shadows will not be long, will not get shorter even".

Gandhavati thought, it might be so. The eyes were getting dazzled while gazing at the sunshine. Was the shadow of the tree getting much shorter? Would all the shadows in the world vanish, being short, even shorter? Nowhere any shadows would exist, just sunshine would be there instead! Her grandfather had changed into a different person altogether. With a long, dejected face, he used to roam about, from one place to another. He was looking for Tamradhvaj. Acharya Brishavanu has left. Did Tamradhvaj also follow suit? Gandhavati remembered, Tamradhvaj's wild appearance took after that of a hunter, though no mark of wildness had been there on his face, the expressions brought the very thought of a hunter usually to our mind! Gandhavati reminisced, Tamradhvaj used to come to stand there, at that point, every time at sundown, their hut being on the western end of the courtyard, with shadows pervading there. Shadows and Tamradhvaj both figured in Gandhavati's memory, almost simultaneously. She was being repeatedly reminded of Tamradhvaj as she remembered shadows and the evenings, which cooled down gradually. His hairs were close-cropped, curly like male hunters, a bit cat-eyed, how nice it would seem when Tamradhvaj kept looking. He was of tall stature. Tamradhvaj was perhaps a bit taller than Dhruvaputra. Lean-bodied, no doubt, but how wide his chest was, how masculine his build was, how brawny he looked! Tamradhvaj said, he would be able to walk up to Dasharno, without stopping anywhere, without having respite at night, rather he would be able to curtail the length of his route, by walking speedily by night! Did Tamradhvaj take that way then? He got the news that this city of Avanti would never witness sunset!

Old Parvati came forward to touch Gandhavati's breasts, rather unawares! And Gandhavati recoiled by that touch and sprang aside. It seemed to her to be the touch of someone like Uddhav or any other miscreant. The old woman kept laughing noisily as she went scratching her head standing in the sun, "Your breasts are getting dried up, oh you damsel"!

In shame and fear, Gandhavati withdrew asking, "Please go away, oh aunt"!

"Yes, I shall go, of course, I shall, how succulent as mango, your breasts had been, now they are dried-up because of continuous exposure to the sun, all juices have evaporated".

"Stop it, aunt"!

"These are now like an old woman's, why would any man take you, you wench, your mate is not turning up just for this reason"!

"Will you stop"? Gandhavati thundered.

Squatting under the sun, the old woman said, "So soon your youth has disappeared, oh girl, you could not even get any time to enjoy it! Ask me, I shall plead with the rich merchant, Durmukh, to send his wife to her parents and come here to marry you! Let him enjoy your youth, you would be the wife of a well-to-do man, on his death you would inherit his properties".

Gandhavati ran to her mother across the courtyard, while she sat on the elevated terrace. She clutched her mother with both her hands. Her mother seemed to have fallen asleep. In the scorching sun, in the torturing heat, because of the enraging remarks of the old hag, Reba, Gandhavati's mother, lay numb, in half-consciousness. Sitting in the shadows of the raised platform, Gandhavati closed her eyes. Just then, old Parvati, sitting in the sunshine of the courtyard said, "This raised terrace too will be devoid of shadows when the Sun-God will come to a halt. Look yonder there is sun, was there any sunshine towards the north"?

Starting, Gandhavati marked with wide-eyed wonder that the north of the terrace, running North-South lengthwise, displayed a sliver of glittering sunlight! The sunshine made her imagine a decrepit witch, slouching there. Even a little while ago, there had been no patch of sun. Wherefrom did it come and what for? Gandhavati was oblivious of the fact, that, it was the time of the Summer Solstice for the Sun-God! At this time, that corner of the verandah would hold the rays of the setting sun in the west, for a little longer, every day. During the Winter Solstice in winter, the sunshine lingered at the southern corner of the verandah! Gandhavati was blissfully forgotten about how her mother, Reba, and she herself used to touch the sunrays, sitting on that southern end of the verandah during winter. But they never had felt the sunshine on the northern corner. They did not even notice that the sunshine, like a fierce old hag, used to come to stay there at this point of time. There, at that end, stood the dumping ground. Gandhavati looked at the sunrays with fear in her eyes.

"What do you look at"?

"You"! Gandhavati whispered, "Who are you"?

"Death"!

Gandhavati asked, "When have you come"?

"Now dear, just at this moment".

"Be off"!

"I haven't come to be off, I shall enter your room".

"When have you come"?

"Now".

"When will you leave"?

"Now".

"Who are you"?

"Death! The shadows in your hut will burn out, I am here to enter your room".

Gandhavati kept looking at the patch of sunshine, in almost weird eyes. The sunshine kept transforming to become more like old Parvati. Did the old woman stand there? Yes, she stood. Death stood leaning on the wall. And now bending her waist she would come in this direction!

Being afraid, Gandhavati asked again, "Who are you"?

"Death! The Sun will burn your terrace, your room - everything and all. The Sun will not set down ever again".

Gandhavati screamed in fear and took her mother in a bear-hug, "Mother, mother, who is she"?

Reba opened her eyes, wiped them and said, "Where? Who"?

"There, Maa, yonder, look"! Gandhavati turned her mother's head. Turning it, she saw a terrifying patch of sunrays spread more on a small part. Then was it true? Sunshine was coming to eat up this part too. That witch of sunshine had a lolling tongue, grey hair loaded with lice, sunken cheeks, turbid eyes and a twisted body.

"Who are you"? Reba asked somehow, in sleepy eyes. Her weary body was shivering.

By then, old Parvati had come up to the edge of the elevated terrace and all of a sudden, had caught hold of Gandhavati's scarf, off her guard, saying, "Hey you girl, listen to me"!

"Who"? Gandhavati sprang off screaming, "You be off"!

"Why shall I go, I am here for you only, if youth wanes, what will happen to you"?

Now Reba opened her eyes. She saw the old hag laughing with her ugly appearance, her grey tresses were being blown by the southwesterly, just as the cotton seeds did. She caught hold of the old woman in a trice, "Will you go"?

"Of course, I shall go, give me your daughter first"!

"What do you mean by 'give me'?"

Rich merchant Durmukh is on the look-out for a young and gentle bride, he is ready to offer acres of land, gold jewelleries and diamond nose-pin, and he will take you along with the bride to the city.

"Tell me whether you will leave or not"! Reba stood up suddenly, leaped down into the courtyard and said, "If you do not leave, I shall call people".

"Call people! Your daughter had charmed that Dhruvaputra, who went to Ujjwain to have an affair with a prostitute even after enjoying her and now both of you are after another man! I shall make it public in the village, don't I have a mouth"?

"What are you saying, older sister"? Reba seemed to cower down.

"You have got it, I am sure, who comes to this place"?

"Who? None at all".

"No, no one comes! A hunter-like man does, doesn't he"?

"Where"? Reba was keen to avoid her.

Then, Gandhavati came down into the sun and said, "Yes, an astronomer from Dasharno comes"!

"Not at all, he is just another gentleman, all will leave you as a husk, otherwise how do you have such a haggard look"? Again, the bony, skinny hand of that decrepit woman pawed on the breast of Gandhavati in the flash of a second! Gandhavati wailed in pain. How dreadfully manly was the squeeze of that old Parvati's hands! The old woman seemed keen on tearing off her breasts, her nipples! Gandhavati pushed the senile woman with both her hands, "Go, I say get lost"!

The old woman kept panting for breath. Saliva kept drooling from her tongue on the ground and she said, "You got nothing, at this age you should have more, much more, and then men will take fancy on you. The new man will also leave you, take it from me"!

Hanging their heads in shame, the mother and the daughter came to sit on the raised terrace. Old Parvati went on speaking ill about Tamradhvaj! When did she come across the young astronomer from the ashram of Acharya Brishavanu? Such obscenities the old woman was uttering! She had no control over her tongue! Mother and daughter hung their heads in shame. Abruptly, the old woman announced her taking leave. She said that in a few days, the Sun-God would stand stationary in the sky, if they made up their mind by then, they could send for her.

That rich, old man would keep both the mother and the daughter with him. Nowadays, many men were going for trade to the country of Balkh. It would be led by the chief merchant, tycoon Subhag Dutta. Many other traders would accompany him on this tour. One of those businessmen was this old Durmukh. It would be a long way, taking longer to reach. All were asking for stout, healthy, young serving-maids. This rich old man was looking for a young maid. If he liked her, he would keep her back as his wife, otherwise he would return her with profuse presents. If he would get a new wife, he would drop the idea of going on this trade-tour.

Mother and daughter kept listening. The words of the old woman seemed quite explicit and comprehensible sometimes, and sometimes again they appeared to be confusing. Gandhavati had pressed her ears with both her hands. Both mother and daughter were tired. So exhausted were they that, they failed to react violently to the words of the old woman as they did some time back. That harshness had died out. Their spirits seemed to have flagged. She felt that old Parvati would not leave them soon. Old Parvati had pressed both of them with her saggy, wrinkled hands. The old woman would go back fulfilling the mission on which she had been there.

Reba asked, "Of what else did you talk with the old merchant"?

"Uddhav hasn't told me anything about that".

"So Uddhav has sent you here"?!

"No, no, why will Uddhav send me, he just asked me to find out".

"Did he talk about us"? Reba muttered, while asking.

Old Parvati was very sly, "Why will he talk about you? Does your daughter possess youth anymore? She is shorn of youth now, haven't you marked it"?

Reba looked at her daughter with fatigued eyes. Her daughter had buried her face in between her knees. Her two ears had been pressed by her two hands even a few seconds back, now that resistance too seemed to have been withdrawn!

Old Parvati, in a suppressed tone said, "Does a young maiden of this age have such an appearance? She is just a bag of bones now, if there is no flesh, what would allure the groom towards her"?

"Then"! Being utterly nonplussed, Reba seemed to surrender herself to Parvati!

The old woman simpered, "Okay, I shall make all arrangements, if she gets proper diet comprising rice and water, milk and ghee, she will again get back her lost beauty. Again at this age, the body desires a man's touch, doesn't it"?

"Yes", in an indistinct voice Reba answered, and then asked, "What is the age of that merchant"?

Parvati swung her head, "What? Who knows that exactly? Does a man's age count? He has enough wealth and treasures"!

"Old merchant"?

"Old or young, how does it concern you? He's a diamond merchant, dealing with pearls and other gems. These merchants are usually quiet, very calm".

"Who told you"?

"I know pearls are obtained from the sea and the sea is very calm".

"In which sea are the pearls available"?

The old woman shook her head and asked, "What do you mean by 'which sea'?"

Reba said, "Have you seen pearls"?

"Certainly I have, why not"?

"Where have you seen"?

"In the hands of Uddhav, there is a pearl in his ring, a white one".

Reba said, "Dhruvaputra knew about these pearls".

The old woman laughed aloud and said, "Again, you talk of him! Oh Lord! That rogue has tied you with illusory bond, thinking of him, both of you, mother and daughter, are dying together, aren't you ashamed of naming him? Hey Reba, speak out"!

Being utterly perplexed, Reba kept looking at that old hag! What sort of statement was this? What did the old hag want to say? Reba's face darkened with insult and shame. How dreadful were the old woman's words! The old hag was saying again, "Dhruvaputra has won the hearts of both the mother and the daughter with magical charm. Both of them think of that gentleman together, at the same time. Dream of him. Don't you see him, Reba? Doesn't Dhruvaputra visit you in your dreams? There, your daughter, she is ruining herself for Dhruvaputra"!

Reba cried out, "What are you saying, aunt"?

"Don't I understand anything, don't I see both of you? Your husband did not return after going to war, what happens in a household without a man has just taken place here, even you have fire of youth within, it's there, it is, still now".

"No"! Reba broke into sobs. Tears kept coursing down her cheeks in multiple streams. She lowered her face. Shattered Gandhavati then lifted her face to say, "Please leave now, Granny"!

"I shall leave. Am I here to sit back and relax"?

Gandhavati took her mother in an embrace to say, "Do not cry, Maa, he will not come back perhaps".

"Of whom do you say"?

Gandhavati said, "Dhruvaputra! He will not come back, Maa, perhaps for this reason he will not be back".

"Which reason?"

Gandhavati whispered, "For this reason… now I get it, why he is not coming back"!

"Do you disbelieve me"?

"No, Maa, you are my mother, after all"!

"Then why do you speak so"?

Gandhavati cried, she said, weeping, "I don't know why I have said so. If this old granny does not leave, I shall not be able to say even, I am afraid of this old woman"!

Old Parvati was swaying, looking at the sunshine. Her face was being pointed, growing fierce gradually! She had been successful by now, it seemed. The old woman was humming a song in delight to celebrate her success in planting suspicion in the hearts of the mother-daughter duo:

"No husband at home, youth's lost in weeps,

Oh Sun God, sit back, shall offer you in heaps!

My hubby is no more, no one is at home,

In my dreams I see a male lying on my bosom.

Fire burns in my room, that fire singes me" -

"Which song is this, Maa?" Gandhavati whispered.

"Everything is a lie, I have no one but you".

"Maa, the courtesan, whose beauty he had fallen for, was even older than him, you know"?

Reba said, "Who can tell what entices a man and what doesn't"?

"Maa, will you tell me the truth"?

"What shall I say"?

"What did his gaze mean when he glanced at you, Maa"?

"He is just like my child"!

"Did you ever sense anything? Is it because of that shame, he is not coming back? That shame had dragged him to the prostitute of Ujjwain, Maa, who knows, what can win a man, will you tell me the truth, Maa"?

Then, humming a tune, old Parvati went down into the sun. She was leaving for the nonce to come again later.

Fifty-Two

Old Parvati had left by then. Mother and daughter now sat at a distance from each other, isolated. Such a long time! The sun was about to set. That day, the Sun-God did not stay back in the sky. The fear which assailed them was over. It was believed that, the speed of the chariot of Sun-God was on the wane. Perhaps, a few of the horses of the chariot of Sun-God had become old. The troop of horses which was supposed to have unending lease of life lost the strength of their legs, the vigour they originally had. They were taking much longer to see the Sun-God drifting from the eastern horizon to the western! Now at the advent of darkness, the mother and daughter would seem to be relieved. They would not have to see each other's face. None could tell where Gandhavati's grandfather kept hanging about, all day long. The old man was driven to his wit's end on witnessing everything all around.

Reba called out to her daughter, "Won't you get up"?

"Where shall I go, getting up"?

"Won't you go to fetch water to Gambhira"?

"You go".

"Shall I leave you alone"?

"What will happen to me? I shall not be gobbled up by any jackal even, rest assured".

In a sad voice Reba said, "Why are you talking thus"?

Then Gandhavati raised her face, saw her mother eye-to-eye and said, "But Dhruvaputra had not talked about pearls with me".

"I was asking your grandfather for a seven-stringed necklace for you. He had been there, and his knowledge in pearls impressed us."

"Maa, you never told me that he lectured on pearls"!

"What to say, I never felt like saying this"!

"Did he tell you separately"?

Reba got startled, she said, "Have you taken the old crone's words to be true"?

"That may not be true, but you never talk of father, Maa"!

"What shall I say and to whom"?

"Why, to me"?!

"You must reminisce about your father!"

"I do indeed".

"Thus, I talk about Dhruvaputra who has gone missing too"! Reba said.

"Why do you talk of Dhruvaputra"?

"Shall I not say? It pacifies your mind, doesn't it"?

"It won't be calm again, Maa, my mind is set on fire now"!

"What are you saying"?

Now Reba grew restive, "What sort of girl are you? Who knows what's there in store for you? If he comes back, then how will you stand before him in such a state of mind? He is just like my own child"!

"Child? Is it true, Maa? But he is the son of my Grandpa's friend"!

"Though the son of your Grandpa's friend, his father was just older by a few years than your father, in fact, he is like a grandson to your Grandpa"!

Gandhavati said, "But he was blindly fond of you, Maa"!

"Naturally, I am just like his mother"!

"Doesn't your heart palpitate as you say so, Maa"?

"What are you saying, my girl, have you gone mad"?

"Now I can make out the purport of his varied demeanours". Muttering, Gandhavati descended on the courtyard, sat slouching on the dusty ground, and sitting thus, she raised her face to her mother, saying, "He was just devoted to you only, Maa"!

Reba said, "Sugandha, you must change the topic, let go of these things, I don't like to hear all such nonsense. She, who loses her husband in a war, to which he had gone never to return, is left with none in this world. I do not have anyone. I had a daughter, she too is far removed from me, that far".

Gandhavati blurted out, "Thank God, night is here".

"You shut up"!

"If there had been no nights, where would you hide yourself, Maa"?

"You have full faith in the old woman's words, but I, who bore you in my womb, don't you find my words true by whit, even? Which sin have I committed"?

Gandhavati was drawing lines on the dusty ground with her forefinger. She was trying to recall old memories while etching the lines. When there had been no such glare of the sun, when clouds were not there in the sky, when winter had been there, fogs too were there, when autumn, spring, Dhruvaputra, all had been there— Gandhavati was trying to remember those times in the past but failed. How strange! Nothing came to her mind! Whatever she could recall was snippets of Dhruvaputra's conversation with her mother! Alas! She could not make out anything, the old crone could, instead! Now she could see the truth, Dhruvaputra had surrendered himself to the whore of Ujjwain, just to avoid the mother and the daughter! Then being humiliated there, he did not stay back even after returning home, only for her mother! If any relationship really did bloom with Reba, her mother, it would be a matter of utter shame. Dhruvaputra would not come back to Ujjwain for that disgrace. It was a terrible sin! Addressing as 'Maa'... Gandhavati found Reba sitting there, with her head, drooping.

Gandhavati said, "May I ask you something, Maa"?

"Please ask, ask me whatever you want to know, these are all retribution of the sins I had committed in my previous birth. I have to suffer now in this birth".

"You might have committed the sin in this birth even"!

Reba held her head up and in a broken voice said, "Yes, it can be so, as you are saying, I can only be acquitted of this by death"!

"Maa, never say so, to whom shall I go if you die"?

"If you know that, then why do you utter all such stuff and nonsense"?

"Maa, confide in me as your friend"!

"I have nothing to say".

"Do you remember my father, Kartikkumar"?

"Yes, I do".

"Does your husband appear in your dreams"?

Reba moved her head slowly, whispering, "Why, no, since long he hadn't appeared in my dreams"!

"Dhruvaputra"?

Reba inquired, "Doesn't Dhruvaputra figure in your dreams"?

"I do not know, Maa, so many images line up in my dreams, I cannot remember everything".

"Doesn't he figure in your dreams at wee hours of dawn"?

"Tell me about yourself, do not hide anything, do not deceive me, Maa"!

Reba kept lowering her head, then said, "Yes, he had come".

"When? But you didn't tell me"!

"I had forgotten, and again it's a matter of dreams, it is not reality".

Gandhavati demanded, "How did Dhruvaputra figure"?

"Coming to the threshold, he called out, Reba Maa, please give me water".

"Strange! He called you 'maa' and you … or was it him"?

"Shut up, Sugandha, never think of such sin, he came here exhausted, shrivelled, his body seemed to be in dire need of water! traversing a long way, he had come to me for water, how poorly was Dhruvaputra looking then! I had never seen him so distressed"!

"Then?"

I could not give him water though.

"Oh Lord! Why"?

"Nowhere was there a drop of water, as in the city of Avanti we suffer now".

"Where was I then, Maa"?

"You were fast asleep, lying beside me".

"Then is it true that he came here, secretly"? Gandhavati questioned.

Reba muttered, "I am telling you it was the dream in the wee hours of dawn, on waking up I found light was about to crack, the birdsong could be heard".

"Did he come in the dark of night"?

Reba felt that Gandhavati was not believing her fully. She was narrating her dream to her and Gandhavati thought that she was trying to cover the reality with dreams. Reba mused, "Nowhere had there been a drop of water, he left without getting a single drop of it".

"Why didn't you keep him waiting"?

Reba withheld her rejoinder. Gandhavati wanted to see her mother's face clearly in the dark. She could not make out which line was growing distinct in her mother's eyes. Her mother's face was becoming more blurred in the starlight. Gandhavati asked her again, "Why didn't you wake me up by asking him to wait, Maa"?

Reba was not being able to answer. So, this incident was not a false one, was it then true?! She was feeling somewhat confused. She could not tell apart the reality from the unreal. Was she talking about the dream or was she narrating the fact as it had transpired? Gandhavati was muttering, "Why didn't you wake me up, Maa, I could have fetched water from the river, Gambhira".

"You were sleeping"!

"When did he come"?

"In the wee hours of daybreak, hearing his call, I came out to see a poorly beggar, sitting in the courtyard. At the close of night, moonbeams had been there, it was the new-moon fortnight, I saw him in the light, but it was just stupor in a dream!"

"No, he came, whatever the old grandma has said is true"!

Reba said, "I know about dreams only"!

"Do not cover up the truth like this, Maa, since long a search for him is on, we all are awaiting him, the astronomer from Dasharno would calculate and tell us about his whereabouts, where he can be lately. And he comes here, behind all eyes, to see you"!

Reba asked, "Doesn't he come in your sleep to stand before you"?

"No, Maa, how will he come? He knows only you"!

Reba touched her forehead with her hand. Her grey cells were not functioning. She could not get the drift of Gandhavati's words. She, herself, could not understand whether the incident she was narrating was real or just a hallucination! Dreams are illusory. Dhruvaputra had charmed her with illusion! Reba was fearing, were then the old crone Parvati's words coming to be true? Long back, when she had dreamt of her husband, Kartikkumar, who went missing, she could not recall. But Dhruvaputra used to haunt her, almost often. Why did he come at all? Could anyone deliberately haunt someone in dreams? Could he enter into a dream to make his presence felt? What was it that Dhruvaputra could not speak out, explicitly? Reba shivered. She could not think of it at all!

Gandhavati said, "For how long was he here"?

"I do not remember".

"In which direction has he gone"?

"Crossing the courtyard, he stepped into the thoroughfare".

"Then? Couldn't you stop him"?

Reba said, "Let go of it, Sugandha, stop all such things".

Gandhavati in a sad tone added, "I shall not await him anymore, Maa, he comes to you and leaves, and never asks me for water"!

"Oh Lord, it was trance in a dream, being cocooned in sleep"!

"I, too, have sleep, have stupor, but he never comes in, since long, he has not turned up, I shall not look down the way awaiting him, better you do".

"What stigmata are you referring to, my girl, what about your father"?

"You keep looking down the way for both of them, Maa"!

Then Reba said, "You are making me feel guilty just for no reason whatsoever, my girl, not seriously, yet if I say that you are inclined towards that old, pearl-merchant, then"?

"What do you mean, Maa"?

"Did that old crone, Parvati, tell you before"?

"Yes, she did, just the other day she took me out separately to Gambhira to narrate everything"!

"But you didn't tell me"?

"I didn't, I was afraid to tell you".

Do y"ou know the pearl-trader"?

"No, Maa, how shall I know him"?

"Is he Uddhavnarayan himself"?

"How can I even know that, but he is rich and is quite elderly".

"How is Uddhav involved in this matter then"?

"He is out to impress the women".

Reba plugged her ears with both her hands, "How can you forget Dhruvaputra just after hearing about that pearl-merchant? if it is true, then why did you get flung to fury at the crone's words? I am getting bewildered".

Gandhavati hung her head low, for long. Mother and daughter went speechless for a long while. Darkness began to intensify between them. Much later, Gandhavati whispered, "I called him several times, now I can make out, why he hadn't come back"!

"No, he had come in the trance of my dream, that which you are thinking is not true"!

Gandhavati said, "He had gone away by the bank of the river Gambhira, turning deaf ear to all my calls, he does not love me at all, that is why, he appears in your dreams".

"Do you love him"?

Gandhavati mumbled, "Is there any worth of unipolar love, Maa"?

Reba said, "This is our destiny! if thy father is still alive, why doesn't he return? If he has started a new family elsewhere, we just keep wasting our time thinking of him! Come Sugandha, let us go away with that old merchant, both of us, mother and daughter!"

Gandhavati retorted, "But you said you would talk about the pearls! Of what else did Dhruvaputra talk to you"?

"Of horses, of elephants, of the yellow silk from Balkh, of various gems and jewels"!

"When did he talk of them"?

"When all fell asleep, even you slept off, just then"!

"But you never let me know of it"!

"I didn't say, as I was sure that he used to tell you everything – of that Tamraparni river in the land called Pandya, and the pearl of Tamraparni, found at the point where the river met the sea, the Haimavata pearl originating from the Himalayas, Maahendra pearls begotten of the sea near the Mahendra mountains, the best of all pearls: Indrachchanda, Bijaychchanda, Nakshatramala, so on, so forth!"

"I know next to nothing, Maa, I have understood by now why he has left, you and I, both are more responsible for his leaving for good, than the whore".

"I am not to be accused,he was like my child".

"I have lost all faith", Gandhavati seemed to burst into tears.

Outside the courtyard, Shivnath, the grandfather's voice was being heard right then... Someone was accompanying him. Who was he? Dhruvaputra? Or the old pearl-merchant or Uddhav once again? Or? Gandhavati's heart missed a beat or two, it convulsed. Then did Tamradhvaj come? His voice too seemed to resemble that of Dhruvaputra! Today, it seemed a bit different! Mother and daughter got to their feet. They were relieved. They were entering into intense darkness, more and more, gradually, since that afternoon. Since evening wore on.

Gandhavati ran fast, "Who's there"?

"You haven't lighted the lamp, Gandhavati dear, please light it up, the disciple of Acharya Brishavanu has come, let him be seated, offer him water, he is thirsty".

Gandhavati could not decide whether to light the lamp first or fetch water for him!

Fifty-three

Why did Tamradhvaj come by night? Now for how long would he sit here and when again would he leave? As the question surfaced in Reba's mind, the disciple of Acharya Brishavanu seemed to sense it. Smiling sweetly in the darkness, he said, "Don't you know, Reba mother, that I can see through the dark"?

Reba replied, "Yes, I know. But, fierce night-faring animals generally get active by night, again robbers, thieves are already there"!

Tamradhvaj said, "But I have nothing on me, what will they snatch off"?

"Yet, I fear".

Tamradhvaj laughed up and said, "I prefer walking by night, the physical exertion becomes minimum at that time, the stars in the sky show us the way".

Reba smiled and said, "Everything is so different with you"!

When such exchanges were on, Gandhavati kept sitting behind her grandfather, Shivnath. She was looking at the astronomer from a distance. Tamradhvaj was truly thirsty, her mother brought him water to slake his thirst while she lit up the lamp. Her mother had scrounged the happiness of offering water to a thirsty man, depriving her, it seemed! The lamp was lit up just for nothing. It got snuffed out by wind. And so little time was taken for lighting the lamp! Mother had handed the nectarine to Tamradhvaj for satiating hunger. Mother gave herself, Gandhavati was not even asked for handing it to him. Now she was getting to remember how Dhruvaputra had been taken afar from her, secretly, by her mother. Had been taken away, indeed. Sitting up all night to listen to the tales of gems, horses, yellow silk of Balkh…Gandhavati grew anxious. Now, Tamradhvaj would announce the findings of his calculations, he would let them know where Kartikkumar had been, where again Dhruvaputra! Gandhavati threw a glance at the sky, looked at the Dhruva star in the north. While looking, she could hear her mother and Tamradhvaj's merry exchange and laughter. She could not understand what her mother was up to. Didn't mother want her husband to return? Was she forgetting about her husband who had been to an alien land? Gandhavati stood up, in silent steps she walked up to her mother. Dhruvaputra had come to her mother and asked for water. Mother failed to offer him. Did her mother offer water to Tamradhvaj in her own hand to slake his thirst just to atone for her past failure and thus assuage her grief? Was her mother envious of her? Did her mother want to put her off the track as she did in case of Dhruvaputra? Gandhavati remembered Dhruvaputra. Again, she flared up in the fury of wrath. Dhruvaputra did not see her or recognize her on that Spring night, it seemed. Sense of guilt had goaded Dhruvaputra to flee away from Ujjwain. How could he come back again? He used to love Gandhavati, but if Reba Maa stood as a wall on his way, if Reba Maa wanted to draw Dhruvaputra towards herself, pushing her daughter aside, how could that wise, exceedingly handsome man return again, getting the wind of that?

Gandhavati put her hand on Reba's shoulders. Reba got startled by the touch of her daughter. She turned around and looked. She saw her daughter's eyes were aflame. The breathing of agitated Gandhavati was audible. Reba felt that Gandhavati was still enveloped by the galled vapour of the afternoon! She lowered her head and left the scene. What would she do with herself? Her daughter's youth was turning fruitless, wasting away, to be precise! That failure had left her daughter weak in mind. Feeble mind is an easy breeding ground of diseases. And that had happened in her case. Lousy, old Parvati had imbued her with wrong misgivings.

Gandhavati said, "Go and sit there, Maa, I shall ask him about Dhruvaputra, if you are interested to know about father, please come, or I can know from him as well".

Being seated on the wooden stool, Tamradhvaj could not get the drift of the conversation between Gandhavati and her mother. She saw Gandhavati's mother was retreating before his eyes, noiselessly. Gandhavati sat face-to-face instead, in the dust of the courtyard. She sat with her head hung low. She seemed relieved by taking Tamradhvaj under cover.

Reba sat on a stone slab, a few hands off from Shivnath. Shivnath told her, "Perhaps, he has been able to trace Dhruvaputra"!

"Could he trace him"? Reba was delighted, "Did he tell you"?

"He didn't, it's just my guess, let us see what he says".

"Why didn't he come for so long"?

"May be because of unfinished calculations, and the news of Acharya Brishavanu left him dejected. The Ashram is lying vacant, after all".

"Where has the Acharya gone"?

"He had gone out in search of Acharya".

"Didn't he get him"?

Shivnath nodded in the negative and then said, "I think, Tamradhvaj himself had left too, Ujjwain would be devoid of its residents gradually, not a single soul would be left behind to stay in here".

"This city of Avanti, you mean"?

"Perhaps even Avanti! If the river Gambhira goes dry, how would people stay in here"?

"Will the river turn waterless"?

"May be! Without rains, how long can it flow by with a gush"?

Reba said, "Do you know about the chariot-wheel of Sun-God? Have you heard, father"?

"Yes, I have heard. Let us hear what Tamradhvaj says".

Reba asked, "Why again does he come back after leaving for once"?

Uttering these words, Reba bent down and took the soil of the hard ground of the courtyard in her two hands. Her query was not relevant. Wasn't she happy because of Tamradhvaj's arrival? Tamradhvaj would come with the news of famished Dhruvaputra! Now Reba was thinking, perhaps that was not a dream but reality! Dhruvaputra had come, being oppressed by the sun, being thirsty. He had gone back, without getting a drop of water! The grief had cocooned her, on the sly. It kept doing so, since long! Did the secret grief fill her with some sort of pleasure? Dhruvaputra had visited her in her dreams. Her dreams alone. Gandhavati could not talk about any dreams at all. Reba could not decide what she desired. Who was Dhruvaputra to her? Dhruvaputra was her daughter's lover. Gandhavati was getting emaciated with each passing day, awaiting Dhruvaputra's return. Tamradhvaj's arrival meant arrival of some news regarding Dhruvaputra! Would she tell Tamradhvaj of her dream?... Dhruvaputra was like my son, he came to me thirsty, without approaching

Gandhavati! Was it then because of his being oblivious of Gandhavati?... Late into the night, one day in the past, Dhruvaputra narrated the tale of King Dushyanta, of the lineage of Porus, and Shakuntala, the foster-daughter of the sage Kanva, at his ashram, situated on the river Malini, and Gandhavati had slept off, in fear, while listening. Had Dhruvaputra forgotten Gandhavati like that King? Hope he hadn't. King Dushyanta, fearing public disgrace, had been oblivious of his wife, Shakuntala, along with her son. Dhruvaputra had said something else. It happened because of the curse of the sage, Durbasa, on Shakuntala! Being engrossed in her husband's thought, Shakuntala could not hear the call of the sage, Durbasa! Because of that sin, Dushyanta had forgotten Shakuntala. Was Gandhavati accursed? Was she herself accursed as well? Hence, Dhruvaputra, Kartikkumar, both had lost the remembrances of these two women!

Shivnath had the headgear on his lap whose colour had faded out. As Shivnath was growing old, he was becoming more seized by a stubborn resolve! He was running from pillar to post asking after Dhruvaputra and Kartikkumar! How far could Dhruvaputra have gone? Sometimes, he would get a hint from the traders and merchants. But one's description would always cancel the other's, again and again. Shivnath was in search of the merchant Manibhadra from Pataliputra or Brikodar! Brikodar had said, that, he would surely get to meet Manibhadra in the tavern of Bidisha. It was news since that Deepavali! Didn't Manibhadra get anything to know, since then? Today Shivnath would tell Tamradhvaj about Manibhadra. Manibhadra would take the way to Ujjwain, through Dasharno and Bidisha, or he might take another way, yet in the tavern of Bidisha he would surely come to know that someone was awaiting him in Ujjwain. It was Manibhadra, who had seen Dhruvaputra, journeying.

Reba asked, "Father, do you know whether he is done with his calculations or not"?

Shivnath shook his head," No, I haven't asked him. The days are growing so terrible, Reba Maa! Don't even know what will follow next!"

"Won't the daytime really terminate ever"?

"I cannot say, but the King has desecrated the shrine of Lord Mahakaal and this is true".

"Then what will we do"?

"I don't know, someone was saying that when daytime will never end, in terrible heat, in fearful light, all the people will turn blind"!

"What are you saying, father"?

"Such words are doing rounds, I think, merchants will never come to Ujjwain. I thought, Manibhadra would perhaps pass by this way towards Saurashtra, before monsoon. Could you guess which Manibhadra I am talking about, Maa"?

Reba tilted her head. But she could not make any head or tail as to how that merchant who had been here last Bhadra, would come up with any fresh news of Dhruvaputra! He had seen someone like Dhruvaputra on the way to Shurparak port, as he claimed! But he never knew Dhruvaputra! God knew whom he had seen! But Gandhavati's grandfather stayed in high hopes. He had again sent news through someone that Manibhadra must come to Ujjwain this time, along with Dhruvaputra! Reba took sympathy on this old man. Could it ever happen so?

Shivnath said, "If the merchants come to know of the present plight of Ujjwain, if they know that Sun-God is ruining this golden city, where daytime will never end, the degrees of sunshine will neither decrease nor increase, all will come to a standstill, will then any of them be interested to come here"?

"I heard that the merchants are going away, leaving the city", Reba said in an inaudible voice.

"Yes, all remain panic-stricken".

"Isn't there any way to be saved from it"?

Shivnath said, "The King has defiled the temple of Lord Mahakaal and the throne! This is the wrath of Lord Mahakaal, and people are witnessing how severe the fury of God can be!

Reba asked, Will the subjects pay for the sin of their King by losing eyesight?"

"Yes, they will, as the act of piety of the King causes welfare to the subjects, Maa"! Saying so, the old man kept his face lowered, kept gibbering, "So many soldiers had been lost in the Hun war, which brought us victory but none thought of them at all. Just think for how many days the victory fest had continued! Are all this just? Where exactly the soldiers got lost, did they die or are still living as prisoners of war at the enemies' — none cared to seek any information at all"!

While hearing, Reba's eyes got moistened with tears. Reba asked in an inaudible voice, "If we leave, will they come back to meet him [Kartikkumar]"?

"No, that won't happen".

"Then what will we do, father"?

"If really the wheels of the Sun God's chariot get stuck, we will have to leave".

"Where will we go, with the merchants"?

"Why so, we will go on our own, towards Bidisha, Maa" !

"To Dasharno"?

"Yes, to that land, Tamradhvaj will surely come along! It is doing rounds, in fact, Acharya Brishavanu has said that, once the Sun God's chariot gets stuck, the daylight will remain just the same, it will be dazzling, neither it will decrease nor increase, then Maa, time can hardly be ascertained".

"How will that be"?

"It will be dreadful without an afternoon, a morning or a dawn, even the twilight! Only noon will rage, a terrible noontide"!

At the mention of noon, picture of the noon that slipped by lately, bobbed up in front of Reba's eyes. Under the blinding sun, the old, decrepit woman, Parvati, was searching lice among her grey strands of hair. In the blazing sun, the lice on her head grew restive. The shadows of the tree had died even, because of the oppressive sun.

Reba spoke under her breath, "Only noon"!

"Yes, just that, how moments or days had passed by"!

"Strange! How is that time"?

"Tamradhvaj will be able to say".

"Don't you know"?

In the dark, Shivnath felt ashamed, "He knew it in totality".

"Who, who are you speaking of"?

"Why, the son of my friend, Dhruva, who told me perfunctorily".

"You? Why, when, at what time"?

"When both of you fell asleep, then perhaps some time at the crack of dawn, before the crows cawed, even preceding the daybreak"!

"But we do not know"!

"I haven't told you, have I"?

"Why didn't you say"?

"Just for no reason. I did not tell you, it's just like that".

Reba expressed an inarticulate amazement and feebly said, "Did he then narrate about the universe, separately to us"?

"Yes, listen Maa, the son of my friend, Dhruva, was truly wise, now it occurs to me that perhaps he had come to know of the future of Ujjwain. Hence, he left".

Reba shook her head and haltingly said, "No father, I think just otherwise, as he has left, Ujjwain has fallen in such trouble!"

Who knows! He had woken me up on a winter night all of a sudden and his exit had taken place on a full-moon night, when he was fresh from Ujjwain, even one-and-half-month ago.

"What next"?

"In the dead of that winter night, he said that he would talk about Time"!

"What? But we are ignorant of it"!

"You don't know! And why will you? He did not tell you, if he did, you wouldn't be able to ascertain the age of either yourself or your daughter"!

"What relationship is there between wisdom and age"?

"When man attains age, as I can feel after crossing so many years on earth, time appears like the moment it takes for batting of an eyelid, even fraction of that moment! I had just taken birth flipping open my eyes, I got to see the light pervading the city of Avanti, how the golden light reflecting from the gold pinnacle of Mahakaal temple kept inundating the city of Ujjwain during dawn, had bath at the river Shipra, went to marry the damsel from the Western part of our country, Kartikkumar took birth, my friend Dhruva breathed his last, Dhruva, my friend, was much younger in age but he was my soul-mate. How long did it take all these incidents to happen in my life, tell me? I think, time got lost in itself as I opened my fist, this realization would have eluded me unless I had attained this age"!

"Dhruvaputra is very young, tender in age, how would he think in this vein"?

"He was the only one who made me think, he was a remarkably wise man, and wise men are to live endless, our one day is a year to them. Listen Maa, late into the night, he woke me up to expatiate on Time, then Eternity stopped short in the darkness and mist. He said that, In the one-fourth time of batting of an eyelid lay the inception of Time, that moment when I was born, I opened my eyes and then shut off my eyelids immediately after... it was long back! The shortest span of Time was that little time, one-fourth of a moment, and then it began to increase, Time flew by, proliferated,- Time taken for batting an eyelid for once[nimesh], Kashtha[a small unit of Time], Kala is almost 8 seconds in time-scale, Naalika is a small measure of Time, Moment, Former Part of the day, Latter part of the day, Day, Night, Lunar Fortnight, Month, Seasons, Ayan, the interval between two Solstices, a Whole Year, Epoch...

Reba asked, "Did he tell you all this"?

"Yes, Maa"!

"But we do not know, either me or my daughter"!

He said, "Mutual exchange of knowledge makes it complete".

Reba looked at Tamradhvaj and Gandhavati in the darkness. Their words failed to reach her ears. Reba thought of calling Gandhavati there. Alas, my daughter! How she had been torn asunder by Gandhavati all through the noon. How her daughter was burning in deadly poison! Didn't Dhruvaputra tell Gandhavati that exchange of knowledge made it complete? If he left saying so, then why was she burning thus? Would folks turn into such insensitive beings if rains failed to pour since eons?

Fifty-four

Gandhavati said, "You look much emaciated!"

"No, it's nothing", Tamradhvaj threw a gaze at the sky.

"Your body seems to be singed, if you come having a bath in the river, it would make you feel cool and pleasant".

Tamradhvaj said, "Coming back, I shall scrounge water from the bosom of the river Shipra and have bath".

When Tamradhvaj entered, in such fading twilight, Gandhavati had noticed that the cloth with which he swathed himself was soiled, the thick, curly hair turned reddish by over-exposure to the sweltering heat, and being burnt by the sun, the man had become darker in complexion.

Tamradhvaj said, "Those words are not true, they cannot be true."

Tamradhvaj replied after a long pause. Gandhavati had asked initially, whether it was true that the chariot-wheels of Sun-God were getting stuck! How it would be, if the conjecture which was doing rounds would come to be true! Wouldn't the daytime ever come to an end? Would all men turn blind?

Tamradhvaj did not answer. He maintained silence. Tamradhvaj only answered whatever Gandhavati demanded to know. At this instant, he replied to the query asked of him much before.

Gandhavati said, "As the rumour spread like wildfire, almost all souls are leaving Ujjwain now".

Water is scarce, clouds are in dearth in the sky, crops have been destroyed and hence all are leaving Ujjwain. Does the Sun shower its rays only on the cities of Ujjwain and Avanti?

Gandhavati kept looking at Tamradhvaj with eyes glowing with amazement.

417

Dhruvaputra used to speak thus! Tamradhvaj inquired, "Didn't Dhruvaputra speak of the Sun"?

Gandhavati nodded in the negative and said, "No"!

"Don't you know that if the Sun stands still, time will come to a halt too"?

Gandhavati was listening to Tamradhvaj. What did he mean by 'Time coming to a standstill'? Won't there be any night by the end of the day? Old Parvati had already said so. But then, the matter of an old pearl-merchant gained prime importance! Gandhavati asked, "Will day stay unaltered, won't there be nights"?

Tamradhvaj smiled, "That may be so. Won't time advance then"?

"How's that"?

"Didn't Dhruvaputra tell you about Time"?

"The country had not fallen in such troubled times then"!

"Which troubled times you are talking of"?

"There was no fear of sundown, with sun itself being annulled"!

Tamradhvaj shook his head to say, "All this is untrue. Many, many miles far-off is the star, Savita, it emits heat to keep all beings in the universe, warm. Does Savita, the star, stay in the sky of Ujjwain only"?

"Not so"?

"Didn't Dhruvaputra enlighten you on such matters"?

"Why? No"! answering him, Gandhavati sensed that her rejoinder was not true. She had heard all such things in different diction, but without further discussion on these matters, she was about to forget them all, in course of time. Slew of information slipped off from her memory! Now, it would be fine, if Tamradhvaj could bring alive everything to her memory!

Tamradhvaj asked, "Dhruvaputra used to talk so elaborately about planets and stars, didn't he talk about Savita, the star? Didn't he say that the star Savita is the source of all light, all heat"?

Gandhavati tilted her head and whispered, "Perhaps he said".

"Yes, he said, you are being forgetful of everything".

"May be, please tell me again", Gandhavati said, in an inarticulate voice. She felt a thrill while saying so.

Tamradhvaj said, "Umpteen conjectures are doing rounds in the city, if there had been a downpour, all rumours could have been silenced to the utter relief of mankind".

"How will monsoon happen"?

Tamradhvaj sadly said, "Not a hint of cloud is there in the sky, God knows what will happen! But you are not asking me anything about Dhruvaputra?!"

"Tell me".

"I wonder how you believe in the stillness of Savita star! If the Sun comes to a standstill, we can't have any nook to go, in the universe. Either dreadful daytime or black, intense night will rule the roost in the city of Ujjwain and also across the globe".

Gandhavati raised her face, she said in a whisper, "Strange! I used to know this"!

"You knew, did you forget then"?

"Can't say! Was it you who said this"? Gandhavati looked up to the sky to ask.

"May be, we discussed many a thing, didn't we"? Tamradhvaj answered.

"Sitting in this courtyard"?

"That's possible", came Tamradhvaj's rejoinder.

"In the evening"?

"May be. Perhaps it was an evening like this", Tamradhvaj said.

"Is this evening a rehash of that one"? Gandhavati asked him.

"Perhaps" Tamradhvaj was watching Gandhavati's face in amazement. He was wondering whether Gandhavati was keen on taking this evening in tow with another evening in the past to say that Time was standing still! That evening of the distant past was still all-pervasive. If the Savita star would come to an abrupt halt, that evening would stand stationary forever! The Sun itself is the source of day and night, the root of creation of the morning and the evening! The Sun is the source of Time indeed! If noon could not be told apart from the afternoon, how would man feel the drift of Time? If the soft glow of the dawn could not be told apart from the strong light of the noon, how would man differentiate between the presence of a morning or a noon? If noon persisted it would continue to be so, if the evening did, it would also remain forever.

Gandhavati asked, "Is it the same evening around us that happened many years ago"?

"I had not come to this country leaving Dasharno, since long"!

"I know this evening as one from the distant past, when I heard of the star named Savita, heard that because the motion of Savita occurred day and night ... past, future..."!

Tamradhvaj smiled, "Exactly so, if Savita would come to a standstill, all time would have been the happening present, no past would be there, and sans past what would we do, Gandhavati"?

Gandhavati rejoined, "We would then forget the past and would not be able to think of the future"!

Tamradhvaj said, "True! Man would surely be oblivious of his past, would have forgotten to imagine the future; memory, amnesia, imagination—all are controlled by the star, Savita"!

Gandhavati asked, "Then man has no fear"?

"No, no fear is there and if the rains pour, all fear will definitely dispel".

"Could Dhruvaputra be traced"?

"Are you awaiting Dhruvaputra's return"?

Gandhavati shivered, she could not utter anything. She wanted to think about Dhruvaputra, she tried to remember his face but failed. All seemed to be enveloped in darkness. Was then the past fading out from her? Was then the Sun really coming to a standstill in the celestial system? She asked, "Where had you been for so long"?

"I went out in search of the Acharya".

"Was the Acharya turning blind"? Gandhavati asked.

"Who told you"?

"I do not know. No one told me. It just struck me".

Tamradhvaj said, "If the earth remains heated for long, if rainfall is withheld since ages, such things cross our mind, many facts are just cooked up. The Acharya had become very senile and naturally his eyesight had become feeble, old age had told upon his body".

Gandhavati said, "Without downpour, man will not be saved".

"Rains will happen, surely it will come in torrents someday".

Then, Shivnath and Reba had come to stand behind Gandhavati. Tamradhvaj said, "Please sit down, let us rather discuss how this city can be saved from this threatening peril"!

Gandhavati was flanked by Reba and Shivnath on both her sides, Shivnath sitting a bit askew, thus completing a circle of four. Reba asked, "Did Dhruvaputra talk of Time to you, Sugandha? How does Time flow"?

Gandhavati turned around to look. She seemed to pierce her mother with her eyes. She did not reply.

Reba said, "He told your grandfather. Strange! Dhruvaputra did not share these things either with Sugandha or me. He told father, and again what he told me, he did not share with either of them and whatever he used to tell Sugandha we have no clue of that" …

The glitter in Gandhavati's eyes dimmed. She was listening to her mother, in utter astonishment. While listening, she seemed to be a bit aloof. She could not think what would be the befitting rejoinder to her mother's words. Then Shivnath talked about that night of severe chill in which Dhruvaputra had explained the imagined seventeen-layered chart of Time, nudging him out of his sleep.

Tamradhvaj asked, "Did he tell you how the measurement of Time is determined"?

Shivnath got startled, shook his head and said, "He talked about Tut, Lav, from trice to moment, day, he even explained how one-fourth of time taken by the batting of an eyelid helps to determine a smaller portion of Time and he talked thus".

Tamradhvaj said, "Didn't he talk about determining Time by shadows"?

Shivnath nodded in the negative, "No, Sugandha did you hear, Reba, you"?

Morose Gandhavati shook her head. Reba said, "Dhruvaputra used to tell three of us separately, of the mysteries of the universe, and now I am getting to hear of Time for the first time"!

Tamradhvaj said, "May be, as it is not possible for an individual to have nose for all aspects of knowledge, Dhruvaputra had not talked about everything".

Gandhavati thought that the words were meant for her. Tamradhvaj had come to know what was going on in her mind since this noon. It seemed as though he had come to get wind of her suspicion too. She hung her head low. She had lost her wits perhaps. She could not understand how Tamradhvaj had come to know of the noontide. She was sitting face-to-face with Tamradhvaj since he came into this courtyard. Gandhavati stood up. Reba asked, "Where will you go"?

Gandhavati did not reply. She could feel that she was to Dhruvaputra as much as her mother and grandfather had been to him. Like all others, she was just a run-of-the-mill presence to Dhruvaputra. But the others were not awaiting Dhruvaputra, why then would she? Even Dhruvaputra did not care a fig to appear in her dreams, then why did she wait for his return? Gandhavati went to the other end of the courtyard all alone, noiselessly. Without being lonely, it was not possible to know oneself. Gandhavati sat down in the dust.She looked at the star-studded sky, as though, she was casting a gaze at her own face in the mirror. She could sense that the ignorance which made her look at her mother with suspicion, this afternoon, had engendered her lack of trust in Dhruvaputra, herself and her mother. It had made her own lack of self-reliance appear more vivid. Gandhavati could feel that whatever Dhruvaputra had narrated to her had all slipped into oblivion. Her eyes were getting drenched, silently. The stars in the sky were blurring. They were merging with nullity. Did she come to know lately, after such a long time, that Dhruvaputra had left her in the lurch? Dhruvaputra had not remembered her at all! Perhaps he had not kept Ujjwain in his thoughts. Dhruvaputra had gone away never to return. Gandhavati stretched her gaze to the dark ground, hanging her head low. She was trying to trace Dhruvaputra in the terrain of her mind, though failing in her efforts. Sitting in wait for Dhruvaputra, Gandhavati had rendered her mind vacant, she could not sense that she had already lost Dhruvaputra! She was feeling ashamed, even repentant.She thought that she had laid herself bare to him. Dhruvaputra was a heartless man. She should have made a decision just when he had surrendered himself to a courtesan, deserting her. Mother could have told her! Mother could have made her understand. In fact, a man's crime would not be a crime at all, a male might easily have committed such blunder during his youth, being polygamous, it was natural of him to fall in love with some other woman! Was she not wasting her youth in having blind trust in Dhruvaputra? And such unflinching faith had kept her mother waiting too, she waited for the moment when that ruthless, polygamous, harlot-addict male would seek her daughter's hand in marriage! Tears from Gandhavati's eyes fell into the dust of the courtyard. The ground which had not been wet by the drops of water from the great void of the sky since ages, was getting drenched to the bottom. The earth went restive in the dark. It was as though, the dust particles were running helter-skelter and were whispering to each other, 'The rains would be here'! Perhaps, a downpour was imminent! Being quiet, they all were praying in the dark, 'More water, give us more water'! They were praying for an incessant downpour. Gandhavati was weeping. She herself had no idea that so much tears had been there, concealed in her eyes. She was feeling lighter gradually, shedding stealthy tears.

Then all three got up to circumambulate her before they sat face-to-face. Tamradhvaj called out to her, Gandhavati, "Won't you hear about the Acharya"?

Gandhavati had heard the noise of their breathing. She wiped her eyes with her scarf, still keeping her face down, restraining her tears, which were about to well up.

Her eyesight was getting feeble.

Gandhavati said, "I surmised, you have also corroborated".

Tamradhvaj said, "Such unfounded fears will rush in to cloud one's mind, loads of strange thoughts will leave him perplexed as the earth stands heated for such a long time"!

"But I know this", Gandhavati grew impatient!

"The man's brain fails to function properly; the number of lunatics shoots up".

"I know, I know everything".

"Who told you"?

Gandhavati swayed her head, "Why will anyone have to tell, this can easily be understood on one's own!"

Tamradhvaj's face brightened up in the dark, he said, "You know, Gandhavati, the Sun-God's chariot is one-wheeled, riding such carriage, drawn by Arun, he sucks water with thousand rays daily, in his diurnal transit. He gives back that water in the form of rain, moving around in that carriage. That rule has been flouted it seems. But as the Sun-God has taken in water, He would surely give it back too".

Gandhavati said, "I know, didn't it ever happen thus? Since many an eon, many a great epoch, the eternal Time remains pervading the animal world! It had certainly happened in some country or some city".

"Strange! How do you know and who told you"?

"None, Maa! It is possible to know".

"How so"?

"From the depth of one's own self it can be construed. Providence is there, its slips will be there too. Can ever a day be just the repetition of the previous one"?

"Strange again! From whom did you come to know, was it Dhruvaputra"?!

Gandhavati shook her head and said, "He will never be back".

"Who will not return? Who are you speaking of"?

Gandhavati said, "Dhruvaputra! My father Kartikkumar, Dhruvaputra, none of them will return! Never ever they will".

Reba glanced at Tamradhvaj! Did Tamradhvaj come to know anything as such through his calculations? Did Gandhavati leave as she learnt that Dhruvaputra would never be back? But no, Tamradhvaj had not told them any such thing. What heartless news had heard her daughter, Sugandha! Throwing Reba into utter surprise, Tamradhvaj declared, "But my calculations are yet to be finished, now I doubt, whether it will work thus".

"Then how do you know"? Reba demanded of Gandhavati.

Gandhavati replied, "You also know this much, Maa, if your husband had remained alive, he was supposed to have come back by now"!

"Then"?! Reba cried out.

Gandhavati said, "Don't you know the truth, Maa? The men are usually very cruel by nature. It is quite likely of him not to return even though he is alive! Dhruvaputra was interested in many women. How was my father, was he like Dhruvaputra?"

Fifty-five

Reba sat gloomy, sullen. Her daughter's words seemed to have made way into her soul. Tamradhvaj marked it and said, "Gandhavati is just a slip of a girl, do not take her words as true, truth is to be perceived".

Gandhavati lowered her head. After letting the words out, she thought that it would be better if she had not said this at all. Was the statement true? The possibility of its being untrue was more indeed. Even though Dhruvaputra had forgotten, why would her father be forgetful of the household of his own creation, this house, this village, this country? He did not come back after setting out for war! If the greatest possibility in not returning from war had really happened, she would then have obviously disregarded her father! Could such words be uttered against him, who died in the war? Such words demeaning him, who had been taken as a Prisoner of War to rot away in the enemy camp, would submerge one in sin! Gandhavati had recoiled! Dhruvaputra had breached her trust, did her father do so? Perhaps, no.

Tamradhvaj said, "Your words have hurt the feelings of your daughter!"

"But she has said just the truth, the men are like that".

"Have you ever seen, I mean, seen anyone of the sort"?

Reba kept mum.

Tamradhvaj said, "Are all men like that Sessions-judge Uddhav or Subhag Dutta, the merchant? One is an evil soul sheltered by the King and the other is a rogue swollen in pride of possessing immense wealth! Did either Dhruvaputra or Kartikkumar have the pride of royal power or that of wealth"?

Reba intervened, "Please drop this discussion".

Tamradhvaj rejoined, "If it is left at that, you will get burnt within, day in, day out, Gandhavati will burn in contrition, neither Dhruvaputra nor Kartikkumar was similar to either Uddhav, the sessions-judge, or Subhag Dutta"!

Reba inquired, "Then why did they forget us"?

Tamradhvaj said, "That again is a hard truth, it is very difficult to come to terms with the truth, take it from me, Dhruvaputra has certainly lost the memories of this city of Avanti, Ujjwain, along with the two rivers: Shipra and Gambhira"!

"Have you divined it"?

Cocking his neck up, holding the stem of throat straight like the horse of the Ionian Greeks, Tamradhvaj said, "Yes, I have certainly come to know of it"!

"Known by your calculations"?

"Knowing can happen on its own, Maa, the truth can be perceived and is there any need of calculations for that? It is not that Dhruvaputra had gone to war planning not to return! He has left behind all at his own sweet will, and preceding that he had been humiliated in the city. Do you know the merchant had a servant called Utanka?"

Shivanth started. Though sitting among the four, he was just a lonely listener. He said, "Yes, I have seen him, he was furious, I heard of him to be ruthless"!

"When did you see him last"?

"The day I had gone to the merchant with the ornaments given by Uddhav!"

Tamradhvaj listened. Reba, Gandhavati too did. They grew sad while listening to him. In the presence of Shivnath, Tamradhvaj said, "Hope Utanka did not beat you"!

"No, no"!

A lowborn Shudra or the hunter, whoever used to come in front of Utanka's chariot, used to be flogged by his rein to bleed. Till date, the form of Utanka brandishing the whip was a menace to all!

"What's wrong, why bring Utanka into discussion"?

"Dhruvaputra had been beaten by him"!

"What are you saying, Tamradhvaj"? Reba let out a scream in fright!

"Yes, many in the city knew of it, the day being Shukla Chaturdashi, as he was returning from the brothel and everything could be distinctly seen in moonlight on the road"!

"And then"?

"It was just a couple of days to go for Chaitra Purnima and numerous people were out on the street of Ujjwain, all had witnessed how Dhruvaputra had fallen on the road, by the whiplash of Utanka"!

"And then what happened"? Reba asked.

Those who had witnessed the scene went in hiding, out of fear, all could understand that the wrath of the merchant had driven Dhruvaputra to such a sorry state! Utanka was only obeying the order of his master!

"Didn't Utanka know Dhruvaputr, or did he take him to be one from among the Shudras by mistake"?

Tamradhvaj shook his head in response to Gandhavati's remark and said, "But I heard of Dhruvaputra and the merchant's friendship, the people of Ujjwain haven't yet forgotten the spectacle of Dhruvaputra sitting beside the merchant in the chariot, talking intimately. Utanka's chariot was circling the city in an ambling pace, a lot many are witness to this sight and no one has forgotten anything at all".

"Have you seen yourself"? Gandhavati inquired.

Tamradhvaj shook his head, "I did not take note of it, perhaps I had seen or hadn't. But I had come from the land of Dasharno much later, if I knew Dhruvaputra so closely, I certainly would have been a witness to the sight, but I just heard of it".

"Then, did Utanka…"? Reba left the sentence hanging in mid-air, unfinished.

"Yes, by order of the merchant he had beaten Dhruvaputra and he had been driven out of the merchant's residence, do you know that"?

"No", Shivnath said. "Staying far-off, I know next to nothing about it".

"Did you know that he had lost his refuge at Sandipani ashram by then"?

"No, how could we know"?

"Where had Dhruvaputra sought shelter, any idea"?

Shivnath said, "We know next to nothing, and that is why we have sought your help, you, young man, he was our dear one, we were extremely fond of him, if you ask I would say, he was like my child, even Reba Maa's"!

"In the Shudra ghetto, very cautiously, avoiding all eyes… how daring Dhruvaputra was"!

"Shudra ghetto? Alas, oh Lord Mahakaal"! Reba let out a cry of dejection!

Tamradhvaj said, "This is the truth, indeed"!

"Did you come to know everything by your calculations"?

"No, I had to investigate quite stealthily, a few from the Shudra ghetto were cognizant of this fact, though not all, everything had been kept under such cover! He had lost all rights of staying in the city by then, the merchant would surely have slain him if the Shudras had not offered him shelter at that time"!

"Shudras are rungs lower than the ordinary folks, they are untouchables, their touch is considered as all-desecrating and he had sought refuge with them!" In a strangely despondent tone, Reba uttered, "Was he then banished from the city for this reason"?

Tamradhvaj said, "He did not have any refuge save this, many of the city liked him, they looked up to him for words of wisdom, but none had the courage to stand against the merchant, and Ujjwain is ruled by the merchant lately, none can approach the King, the merchant and all his loyal staff take revenge".

"Did the merchant know that Dhruvaputra had taken shelter at the Shudra ghetto"?

"I don't think so, again he might know. Now I think he obviously knew about it. Otherwise, why would he set the Shudra locale on fire, appointing Utanka for this deed? Again, it occurs to me that, if the merchant knew of this before, he could have taken an action at that time itself, why so late? Two, two-and-a-half years have sped by, why then without any instigation would he harm the Shudra ghetto so badly by fire? Now, the shadows of Dhruvaputra are absent in the city, even the people are about to forget him"!

Shivnath quipped, "But you have come with a terrible news, oh the astronomer from Dasharno, being so wise, so knowledgeable, had Dhruvaputra really gone to the Shudra habitation for seeking refuge, only because of being emotionally attached to a prostitute"!

"Yes, this is the fact"!

"Fie"! Shivnath spoke out in an indistinct voice, "We all are shocked, extremely shocked"!

Tamradhvaj said, "But the Shudras are the chief pillar of strength of the armed forces"!

"Yet, the company of the Shudras is to be shunned by all means, always!" Reba remarked.

Then Tamradhvaj added, "Maa, do you know that our scriptures have put the women and the Shudras on the same pedestal"?

Reba's face turned even more pensive in the darkness. She sat lowering her head. But Gandhavati hissed like a young she-snake, and said, "And that woman is a whore, that is the only truth"!

"Who told you this"?

"Dhruvaputra"! Gandhavati's reply came pat.

"No, Dhruvaputra has not said this, whatever the scriptures may aver, there is no special mention of the whores in it, the women as a whole have been referred to".

"What do you want to make us understand by this"? Gandhavati stood up, infuriated. "Then why have you come? Go and stay in a secluded place sans woman!"

Tamradhvaj smiled, The Ashramites stay only thus, and I too do, Gandhavati! But let me tell you something, whatever the scriptures may say, can man abandon his mother, sister, wife, beloved, female relatives, well-wishers or do they ever do so? Didn't the savants composing scriptures know that the world will turn lifeless, insipid without women"?

Gandhavati charged, "Then why did you refer to such a mention in the scriptures"?

Tamradhvaj said, "Reba Maa was saying that the company of the Shudras is to be shunned by all means, always, but along with that, the scriptures also bear the mention of such views. Look Maa, Dhruvaputra had flouted all such regulations and forbiddances"!

Heaving a sigh, Reba said, "I think, the whore had applied the charms of mesmerism on him, and I heard that these prostitutes are armed with such skills, rather they cannot do without it".

Tamradhvaj remarked, "Dhruvaputra had done such things which could legitimately be done".

"What could be done"?

"One could save himself by going to the Shudra ghetto even"!

"Why can't that be done? Will we allow the dicta of the scriptures go wrong? Now it is clear to me that he had really gone astray, we are waiting for him in vain! That Dhruvaputra, whom we had sent to the capital for becoming a real man, had been driven out of the city and then had been beaten like a lowborn man! Who can say what consequences has he got to suffer"? Saying so, Reba broke into sobs and asked, "Did you know of this before"?

"I learnt, gradually".

"From whom did you learn such facts"?

"Going to the city, I came to know".

"Do the city-dwellers know that Dhruvaputra had taken refuge at the Shudra ghetto"?

"A few know, a few again don't".

"This can never be true"! Shivnath objected and got to his feet, "No, no, you came to learn all fabricated lies, all engineered by none other than the merchant"!

Then Tamradhvaj rejoined, "Would you like to come along with me"?

"Where shall I go"?

To the Shudra ghetto, lying beside Ratnakarsagar. Let us go and learn what they are saying. Look Sir, even everyone from the Shudra belt did not know that he used to stay back there for the night, he had their rice, their water along with them though this fact had been kept a high secret! Dhruvaputra was trying to save himself from the wrath of the merchant just after falling in love with Devadutta. He used to pay a visit to Devadutta's place, even used to return home at the dead of night! The merchant had no control over the inner house of a prostitute, let alone the Chief Prostitute, Devadutta's!

Gandhavati had pressed her ears with both hands. The words of Tamradhvaj appeared like gall to her! How dreadful the words of the astronomer from Dasharno sounded! And he would tell them the whereabouts of Dhruvaputra, where he had been to, how he was doing, so on, so forth! But he was making them listen to such facts instead, which they were not supposed to know!

Shivnath offered, "Would you like to come along with me now"?

"I can accompany you, in fact, we should go now, if Parashar also leaves Ujjwain for good, the facts will remain beyond our knowledge, forever"! Tamradhvaj reasoned.

"Are they leaving Ujjwain"?

"Yes, because of drought, scarcity of water, lack of harvest to be reaped, and such natural disasters, the city lies vacant, men leave for elsewhere, bidding adieux to their own country"!

Then Reba asked, "What good will it be on your visit there"?

"Truth will dawn upon us", Tamradhvaj replied.

"The truth you have come to know already"! Reba said, "You don't have to venture into the dark"!

Tamradhvaj said, "I have to go without fail, I shall return, I feel comfortable in the dark. I heard that Dhruvaputra had come back alone to the Shudra ghetto that night, with a blood-splattered body! And from there he started for this end of the river, Gambhira!"

Reba spat, "Let it be skipped, do not speak of Dhruvaputra anymore"!

Gandhavati too cried in unison, "Yes, not any more, no more please"! Gandhavati sobbed.

Reba said, "If you go to the Shudra ghetto, more perhaps will come up, such facts will surface which we may not like to hear at all! Why then? We do not need him anymore; he does not know that one must be grateful to the person who shelters him. It is, no doubt true that the merchant had helped him with a shelter".

Pacing up and down in the dark, Shivnath suggested, "No, you stay at home bolting the doors, I shall set out with this man, I shall have to learn whether the servant of the merchant, Utanka, had really beaten Dhruvaputra or not"!

Tamradhvaj then broke the news of Utanka's death! Shivnath was aware of that. He said, "It was not Utanka, the merchant himself had flogged him, how would a petty servant dare throw Dhruvaputra's blood-smeared body on the edge of the road without his master's indulgence? Please come, I shall go along with you to the Shudra ghetto".

"What benefit can be reaped out of it, dear father? I want him not to return, who used to have rice at the Shudra ghetto! His departure is good for us"! Reba blabbed out.

Gandhavati then looked up to the sky. Gandhavati went speechless. It could not be ascertained whether she was listening or not. How strange her silence had been! Tamradhvaj observed her, sprang up on his feet and said, I am even feeling curious to know how the last days of Dhruvaputra had really been spent and the knowing is an urgent need. If not explored, we would never be able to find out where he is now and how he fares. Is he returning here or has gone distant even more, or whether he is keen on going away to a far-off land, for good! Let's go"!

Reba declared, "I am not interested in anything else. He should not come back to Ujjwain, that's it"!

Tamradhvaj smiled and said, "Your husband had gone out to war, he had fought his enemy standing just beside a Shudra soldier, he had to share his rice with them at the end of the day, and such is a common practice, Maa"!

Gandhavati got startled to look around. The voice seemed to be wafted from near-past. She found Tamradhvaj standing tall in the dark. What a strapping! What a height! His eyes seemed like two new stars which had fallen straight from the sky! Gandhavati looked on.

Reba said, "Maybe it was because no rules and laws were mandatory in the battlefield"!

Tamradhvaj rejoined, "Necessity flouts all norms and regulations. Please come along, let's move forward, the residents of the Shudra ghetto will be leaving the city. Will the old soldier stay back if all go off, leaving the city? I met him once by the river, Shipra, and learnt that Dhruvaputra used to frequent that place. Let me get it corroborated by him, whatever I am hearing lately is true or not. Then I shall be able to finish my calculations".

Both of them melted into the darkness.

FIFTY-SIX

The darkness was turning soothing, gradually. Without the cognizance of both the men, the Krishna Chaturthi moon bobbed up in the sky, and was ascending, by degrees. The desolate universe was getting transparent under the light. While walking, Shivnath said, "I thought, it would be too dark".

Tamradhvaj said, "Night, moonshine— glancing at all these we never would be able to guess that this country is heading on to a terrible disaster!In the darkness it seemed that, there had been water at places, there had been downpour a few days back and everything was just perfect".

Shivnath said while walking, "Every now and then, a bizarre idea crosses my mind".

"Which idea"?

"Is there any relationship between Dhruvaputra's exit and the lack of rainfall"?

Tamradhvaj said, "If the sky remains cloudless for long, if the lakes dry up, such thoughts creep in, a support of logic is what we look for".

"There had been no downpour after Dhruvaputra's exit".

"It might have happened even if Dhruvaputra had been here! The two incidents coincide with each other, that's it".

"But even the presence of some person is again an indicator to good and ill of the nation, some faces make us glad and some again intimidate us, as that of Uddhavnarayan or of Utanka, as it had been"!

Tamradhvaj said, "That's true, but how does it relate to rain and lack of rain"?

"I don't know, it's my notion", Shivnath mumbled, throwing his gaze to the moonshine-laved meadows.

The night was quite cold. The wind too cooled down. It seemed soothing to the body. Tamradhvaj had taken the loincloth on his shoulders, to walk with a bare torso! While walking, a little later, Tamradhvaj said, "I think there is no connection between Dhruvaputra's departure and the drought, even if Dhruvaputra would have been with us now, he would have spoken in the same vein. This vast universe, the star, Savita, the celestial galaxy — all seemed to be clubbed under one system, hence the change of seasons, the advent of monsoon and winter— there's a rule somewhere, a change in which has occurred and that is not unnatural!"

"Can it thus occur?" Shivnath was taken aback.

"Yes, a merchant from the East told me that the same had happened in their country too, hasn't it ever happened here in this land? Try to remember"!

"Perhaps, it happened! But that did not last for so long, whenever it was felt that the animal world was seething in trouble, just then, Mahakaal had brought clouds, rains tumbled down, man could not remember that drought spanning for over a short period!"

"In the eastern country, the plight was just the same as Avanti, many people had left the villages and cities, owing to the lack of rainfall, the villages had been ransacked, people had been struck with dearth of food and all the land and habitable spaces lay evacuated."

"But I haven't heard it".

"I have heard", Tamradhvaj said. "Then the hunger-stricken people began to live on leaves of trees, all grew emaciated and feeble, right from the child to the old, wizened man, the roads were a pile of dead carcasses, the children died in their mother's lap, again beside the dead mother the innocent child used to cackle and humans turned into bags of bones, hanging about, begging rice, even a good many of them breathing their last by that time!"

"How will you know? This is the tale from the eastern country, alms were in dearth and the King had hiked the tax just at that time. Lack of rains had caused lack of harvest, no crops had been produced, even trees went sans foliage, no blade of grass grew on earth."

"What are you saying"? Shivnath got frightened, "Is this our future? Will it ever happen in Ujjwain?"

"A prolonged lack of rainfall would bear such consequences only!"

"Alas! Oh alas! Then let me leave this land with my two dependents!"

"Why will they be dependents?"

"Sometimes I think so, lest why am I to take care of all these matters at this age? Those on whom I used to depend, have slipped off into oblivion, leaving me alone! What am I to do now? I am not even left with enough time, contemplating God."

Tamradhvaj said, "They are your near and dear ones. Your blood is flowing in Gandhavati's veins!"

"True, but I am now an old man and years are adding up leaving me older, quite alarmingly. You know, if there is no rainfall for a long time, even us, the elderly persons will certainly have no leisure and the missing persons will not return home".

Tamradhvaj said, "May be so, during drought, all troubles seem related to lack of rainfall only. Listen Grandfather, the eastern country had been affected by such dearth of harvests that it cast a meaningful influence on the people, even it is learnt that the women could not be impregnated properly. Since many days, the cry of the new-born could not be heard".

"What an unnerving information!" Shivnath trembled, "Let it be left at that, do not speak more".

"I am just saying that such an incident had really happened."

"But if such a thing happens in this country?"

"No wonder! Perhaps, the country is heading on to such consequences."

Shivnath said, "Acharya Brishavanu might have told us about the way-out from this ordeal, and now who knows what will happen to this country in his absence?"

Tamradhvaj did not reply to this dubious statement. Tamradhvaj came to an abrupt halt after walking for some length and said, "I traversed such a long way, without any anxiety, people have just begun to leave the country, our land is yet to pass on to the robbers and thieves, as had happened in the eastern country".

Shivnath said, "Though Uddhavnarayan is a royal staff, he is no less than a robber"!

Tamradhvaj said, "Time is there still"!

"Though time is there, it cannot be put to right use by humans, they are really quite hapless. If God from the heavens would not descend to our rescue, we would never be saved from this plight. What can we do on our own, what can the King do even?"

Tamradhvaj went speechless. He had accepted the words, it seemed.

Shivnath said again, "Yet only the King can do, if the King stays beyond stigmata, if He would follow rituals and perform yajna, and if Lord Mahakaal would be duly propitiated, why would this country burn in drought? Don't you think that the King needs to remain pure and immaculate?"

Tamradhvaj said, "True! But these measures of judgment of purity-impurity leave room for suspicion too. I know the heart of King Bhartrihari to be pure, one day I had talked to him in our Ashram, and that was the day on which the Acharya had left the Ashram!"

Shivnath had gone silent. Talking ill of the King is an abominable deed. It's a crime, indeed. Being reminded, the old man recoiled. Even the colonnades of trees lining both sides of the thoroughfare seemed to have ears, Shivnath thought.

Tamradhvaj said, "Do you know that the merchant, Subhag Dutta, is setting out on a business expedition?"

"Yes, I know, and knowing it I am in fear as Uddhavnarayan will turn demonic, once the merchant leaves the city!"

"The merchant is not our guardian, the King is there!"

Shivnath said, "The King is not accessible".

"I shall go, you need not worry. The day when Acharya had left the Ashram, the King had visited him by night, I spoke with him and found him to be a man with a tender heart and logic-abiding!"

Shivnath heard without any comment. Now the river Shipra fell on their right side. Shipra river was calm, immobile, it seemed to lie like a dead reptile under the moonshine. Both of them stood facing the river. Their breaths were audible to each other.

A little later, Tamradhvaj said, "I had not come to your residence since long. I had not been here".

"Yes, I know, I came in search of you to no avail".

"Won't you ask me, where had I been to?"

"Did you go to Bidisha?"

"No, look Grandfather, we all are in peril."

"What are you saying?!"

"I had found the observations of the people of the eastern country to be true while I was out looking for Acharya. I had gone away leaving the Ashram for Acharya Brishavanu."

"Which observations are you talking about?"

"Man has become skeletal in frame, birds, beats, human beings, all are dying together."

"We are becoming skeletons too, don't you see Gandhavati and Reba?"

"Is this place facing low supply of rice even?"

"Yes, we are facing it! Last year, there had been no harvest of crops. For two consecutive years, there is no rice, wheat nor maize!"

Tamradhvaj said, "We should do something, by tonight a decision has to be reached, on my return to Ujjwain, gleaning news from all fronts."

"Which decision?"

Tamradhvaj rejoined, "The eastern country had gone desolate, many people had died, the vultures had come down from the sky to perch on the hut-tops!"

"That has not taken place in our country, however!"

"Going to happen, I had gone far towards the north. Are you aware of this fact that Acharya has left the city, being blind?!"

"Blind?!" Shivnath let out a scream of fear, "Then is it true that the heat of the sun leaves man blind? Then is it true that nights will terminate and the days will never end?!"

Tamradhvaj jerked his head and said, No, his eyesight became feeble because of senility that debilitated him. This is the law of nature. Acharya failed to recognize the stars anymore, he failed to espy Arundhati star, his blindness would never be similar to ours. Look Grandfather, while I had been out in quest of the Acharya, I had come across even more horrifying plights affecting the far-off hamlets and habitations in the north, where drought was more extensive, more pervasive, casting its more intimidating, taller shadows! And that too, long before the exit of Dhruvaputra, the skeletal frames were roaming around, all had become emaciated, thin and lifeless — oh, what a dreadful experience it had been for me! How terrible!"

"Would you please tell us what exactly you had seen there?" Shivnath implored humbly.

FIFTY-SEVEN

Acharya Brishavanu had gone towards the north. His hermitage was on the eastern bank of the river, Shipra. Walking along the bank, he had gone to the north of the river. But how far would he proceed? In the North, just after a way stretching less than five miles, a tributary had slipped down towards the south. If he had not crossed the river at that point, the way to the north would stand blocked. Tamradhvaj had surmised that Acharya would definitely walk towards the north crossing the river and then he would move towards north-east, taking the way to Koshala, Sravasti. Later he found that, his conjecture was not at all wrong.

The Himalayas lay far, far-off, by many miles! The Himalayas, the abode of God, had encircled a part of this world. It ran gradually from the North-East to the West. The Himalayas stood quite distant across Mathura, Surasena, Matsyadesh, Indraprastha in the North-West! Rather, the distance was much less from the north-east. The merchants used to opine thus. The merchants from Sravasti used to make a beeline to Ujjwain, they mentioned the time they needed to reach there with their retinue. It was much less than the time reported by the merchants and pilgrims who used to come down from the distant Himalayas, crossing Indraprastha!

Once the Acharya had expressed his desire of walking towards the Himalayas with Tamradhvaj, at the fag-end of his life, when death would be imminent. If death would be so kind to spare him for some time, he would walk up to the Himalayas to surrender himself. The Pandavas had found the way to the Heaven on that very mountain range. That way was still there, it was not lost. Somewhere the path lay alone, desolate, like the wayward, stray traveller lying down for respite. On both its sides, flowers of variegated colours lined up, and the deep, blue sky ran overhead. No noise was there, around. Silence was, no doubt, the shapeless form of Death! Acharya used to think that he would move towards that path, if it welcomed him at all.

Acharya thought thus. He did not think about old age. He expected Death to sidle up near him, abruptly. Acharya was mistaken. In fact, man would inch towards

438

that stupendous destiny in the form of Death, towards that unending darkness, on his own. And Acharya Brishavanu was oblivious of this. Either he had forgotten or he did not want to remember. Setting out for the Himalayas with Death as his companion or awaiting Death by the side of the river Shipra - in neither of the two thoughts, Death figured in the least. Rather it contained an impossible manifestation of Life! Wise astronomer could not have an inkling of himself moving towards Death! That deep, desolate path filled with silence had accepted him since the moment of his birth. Just after birth, man began to start off with his journey on that path!

Tamradhvaj had waited for a few days, in the hope of the Acharya's return. Coming back, he would sit by this river, Shipra, to surrender himself to destiny. But in a few days, as the chance of his coming back stood annulled gradually, Tamradhvaj grew restive. Actually he, too, could not believe that the Acharya might go away, for good. Failing to save the city of Avanti from drought, it was beyond the conjecture of Tamradhvaj that the Acharya would really leave this hermitage, Mangalnath Temple, river, the river banks lined with Banyan tree, Peepul tree, Neem and Wood-apple trees! At last, he also went out one night, tracing the way by moonlight. Going quite a bit along the eastern bank, Tamradhvaj had gone down into the river, at the mouth of its bend. The surroundings stood awake in a sleepy abandon. Tamradhvaj had a stick in his hand, and at its tip suspended a bundle of food and a few clothes. He was moving forward with the pole on his shoulder. Save the sudden attack of ferocious, night-faring beasts of prey there had not been any other fear at all. When the forests went waterless, the fierce animals used to draw up to the human habitations in search of water.

Crossing the river, Tamradhvaj had walked towards the north-east. During daytime, the sweltering sun, the heat, the fiery gusts of wind rushing from the desert lands in the west had compelled Tamradhvaj to stop. It was fortnight of full-moon then. He used to walk in the moonlight. Thus, walking for nearly fifteen days, he came to a halt. The shadows of the banyan tree where he had halted during afternoon, nearly thirty men and women assembled there, their appearance resembling that of the hunters. Tamradhvaj had seen a huge slab of stone at the base of the banyan tree. Eyes had been painted on that stone with a piece of chalk. The piece of stone seemed to throb with life, eyeing him. The men were astonished to see Tamradhvaj there. Tamradhvaj's appearance had a faint resemblance with that of the hunters. But those male hunters lacked in the wild grace as Tamradhvaj had. They were almost like a ramshackle shrine. Absolutely skeletal, with dull eyeballs, shrunk into the sockets, the close-cropped, curly hair, fallen off from most heads.

Tamradhvaj had moved forward towards them, and asked, "Who are you"?

An elderly man rejoined, "We hail from this village, who are you?"

Tamradhvaj asked, "What are you doing here"?

The aged man said, "Since long, water has dried up, the sky gets ripped open to disgorge fire, do you have any information regarding water in the sky?"

Tamradhvaj perched upon a root of the banyan tree. Then he heard the beating of drums. Five men or so came up to stand there, blowing bugle and beating drums, along with a peacock and a peahen. They came walking through the field. One of them was toting a deadly axe in his hand. Tamradhvaj got to his feet, "What's about to happen here"?

"Offering blood to the goddess, it has to be poured on the earth. Then only we can have water".

"Who has told you so?" Tamradhvaj asked.

"Who will tell us? Such is the order of things". The old hunter came forward once again, "If rains fail, the goddess demands the blood of the peacock and peahen, she protects our village, look at her, she is Kalamukhi!"

Tamradhvaj saw that the eyes of the stone-block went astir. The peacock and the peahen shrivelled in fear. As if, they could sense what would follow in a few moments. Tamradhvaj asked, "Does rain happen in this way?"

"May not happen anywhere, but it will surely pour down on our Kalamukhi hamlet, she is Kalamukhi Goddess, the deity of our village, if she is propitiated with blood, clouds will hover over the sky."

Another one added, "Monsoon comes only for the peacock and the peahen when they are delighted to see the clouds in the sky, the peacock mates with the peahen, if the blood of peacock and peahen is offered, clouds are sure to surface".

Someone said, "Clouds only look for peacock, if monsoon fails, the offering of a peacock would surely usher in the downpour".

"But clouds are yet to surface", Tamradhvaj answered.

"The clouds, this time, demand a peacock and a peahen, if that fails, humans are to be offered, Kalamukhi will never be propitiated without the offering of blood. Even the sky will not be gratified. Sans blood nothing is possible. But who are you, Sir?"

Tamradhvaj replied, "I am coming from the city of Ujjwain".

"Where is Ujjwain"?

"Haven't you got any idea of Ujjwain"?

"Perhaps we know, again we cannot demand that we know for sure", the old hunter retorted.

"Ujjwain is the capital of Avanti".

"Where is the city of Avanti"?

"This is Avanti only".

They shook their heads to say, "How can that be, this is Kalamukhi village of Kalamukhi goddess, the city of Kalamukhi, why will it be Avanti?"

Tamradhvaj asked, "Have you heard of the temple of Mahakaal"?

"We know of this Kalamukhi, if Kalamukhi gets angry such calamities happen, rains do not pour, the wilderness remains devoid of wild animals, the crops wilt away, the women face abortion, on its own…"

Tamradhvaj reiterated, "Lord Mahakaal is there in Ujjwain, he is the greatest of all deities, please set the peacock and the peahen free".

"No way! Kalamukhi asks for blood, the soil too demands it, Kalamukhi had drunk it even before. Once she had devoured a pigeon, then a dog, and now she is going to have this pair of peacock-peahen. If blood is not offered, water will be denied by the Goddess".

Tamradhvaj pleaded, "Let go of the peacock-peahen, if they scream out to the clouds, clouds will invariably gather in the sky".

All came yelling at him, "Who are you? Why are you speaking wrong? Kalamukhi wants blood, come on, carry on, beat the drums, blow the bugle!

Their musical instruments were frightful! Their sound began to remind one of the thundering of clouds. The people began to dance. They were mostly inebriated. Someone tore off the throat of the peahen. Blood spurted out in profusion. The stone-piece had an ablution in that blood. The sight of blood had driven the people crazier. Tamradhvaj hid his face behind both his hands. He heard the throat of the peahen had been torn off and the peacock was to be sacrificed. Piercing through that blistering afternoon, the heartrending scream of the peacock reached his ears. The cry drove them even madder.

Tamradhvaj opened his eyes to find that men grew in number. The peacock lay on the lap of the stone-block, with its legs tied up. The old hunter sat on the seat of the priest. The mantras were being chanted. That mantra was really strange—

Old hunter called out, "Kalamukhi, fierce Jwalamukhi, what for are you sitting here?"

Another one took the cue and added, "No clouds, no rains, heart too breaks…"

"Kalamukhi, fierce Jwalamukhi, why are you sitting here?
Have blood, drink blood, wallow in blood, revered dear!
Check Kalamukhi's tongue, no saliva drools,
Sans water, red ant dies precariously in pools,
Red insects, blue worms, the ash of blue flies,
Kalamukhi, fierce Jwalamukhi, either eats or dies."

The old hunter thundered, "Kalamukhi wants to eat, wants a pair of pea-hen, wishes to gobble up both the peacock and the pea-hen, it will satisfy her hunger, leave her cool to the core, she has terrible thirst, we want water, the Woman needs to slake it with blood, She will bless us with water after having her fill of blood. Look, the man who has come, I have heard about his country, he hails from".

"How did you learn, did you go there?"

"No, I heard, I came to learn that no rains are there at your place too, for rains a man has been burnt to death, hasn't he been?"

Tamradhvaj had been taken aback. Dumbstruck, with astonishment! How could Utanka's death-news make all the way to this country! The man was senile. Below his nose grew a thick, grey moustache resembling an annular structure of grey jute-mesh. His hair was all hoary. Skin on his body sagged, the eyes looked turbid, and a red loin circled around his waist. Many of the hunters had bark of trees around their waists. The cloth which they used to wear grew threadbare by then. All of them looked agape at the senile hunter, who had seen the olden times.

The old hunter said, "I heard that many bigwigs reside in the city of Ujjwain, numerous gems and treasures are there, In Ujjwain, the pinnacles of the temples are nearly sky-high, all the people live happily in Ujjwain."

Tamradhvaj said, "True!"

"In Ujjwain there's no dearth of anything".

"That is also true".

"In Ujjwain, all the houses keep elephants as tamed animals".

"That is not untrue too".

"The men ride white horses".

"That is also true".

"The women who live in Ujjwain are extremely beautiful."

"True indeed."

"Their complexion is like that of moonshine, their eyes are wide like those of a deer, their laughter takes after the casting of pearls."

Tamradhvaj smiled, "Certainly true".

"Tears never well up to their eyes, their minds are never affected by sorrow".

Tamradhvaj tilted his head.

"In Ujjwain there is no sorrow, no pain."

"Perhaps true."

"But in Ujjwain there is no rain."

"Yes".

"Since many days rains are not there."

"Yes".

"Then a merchant of Ujjwain had scattered the dust in the fields by burning his servant alive."

"Who told you?"

"Tell me whether it is true or not, we are offering dog, pigeon, peacock to Goddess Kalamukhi, Lord Mahakaal of Ujjwain has eaten up a whole human being!"

Tamradhvaj said, "Yes, it is true."

"But ashes were spread on earth instead of blood. That ash flew off from one house to the other of Ujjwain, a river named Kshipra flew by, the ashes blew on its water too, yet Lord Mahakaal was not propitiated, the people of Ujjwain had no sorrow in their minds but rainfall is a must and they crave for rains".

"Who told you all?"

"He forbade us, we should not say anything."

"Who is the man?" Tamradhvaj became restless.

"It is forbidden to say anything, listen you all, in the city of Ujjwain there are seven lakes, all are devoid of water presently, the wells all around run dry, hence on the faces of women the smile is absent, they cannot have bath, stigmata have smeared the women who are as beautiful as moonlight, the black of the ashes".

Tamradhvaj asked, "Did that man tell you everything"?

"Who knows, he told a bit, and held back a little, I am telling you, conversations run like this, in this vein. I am talking about the women of the city of Ujjwain, whose faces light up with a smile like that of the clouds of Ashwin, the tresses are tinged with the colour of clouds, but that beauty is on the wane now, with each passing day and now none of them can boast of their beauty anymore."

Tamradhvaj said, "How strange! Who told you?"

"He, who narrated, had forbidden us to divulge, let me tell you, as the women are bereft of their beauty, the men are naturally unhappy and for this reason the King of Ujjwain had taken a serving-maid of Lord Mahakaal for his pleasure, in darkness, on the sly! It is learnt that Lord Mahakaal demands likewise, if Lord gets a woman with auspicious signs, He would enjoy her all night, the people will know that the King had enjoyed a young serving-maid of Lord Mahakaal but in reality, Mahakaal himself had assumed the form of the King!

"Who told you all such facts?"

"He has forbidden us, he has told me to relate this to a soul from Ujjwain, if I ever would bump into. The fact which people know is not true, that which they do not know is true on the contrary."

Tamradhvaj was feeling a shiver within, on seeing the old hunter-leader. The old man kept fixing him with a stare and said, "If you can disseminate this information on your return to the city, it will be saved. The King of Ujjwain is good hence all are good, if the King bears a stigma it will affect all as well. Listen, this man is from that city of Ujjwain and ask him to tell us about Ujjwain!"

Tamradhvaj asked, "From whom have you heard all?"

"That old man forbade us, since many a night he narrated to me about Ujjwain, the river named Kshipra, the pinnacle of the temple in the city."

"Where has the elderly man been to?"

"I cannot say, he left at the wee hours of dawn when I was sleeping like a log. If awake, I would have tied the old man here, many facts of Ujjwain he had shared, really!"

"Even about the stars in the sky?"

"No, not at all, he did not mention it even for once."

FIFTY-EIGHT

Tamradhvaj could feel that the old hunter was talking about Acharya Brishavanu. The old man of the village, the chief hunter, was speaking slowly, while opening himself up. Tamradhvaj was relieved of all worries to be sure that Acharya was somewhere down this way. His assumption was infallible. He inquired, "When did he leave this hamlet?"

Someone answered, "Perhaps when the moon was thin, narrow and curved!"

"No, no, the moon was half-filled then, then it began to fill up and full moon emerged".

"No, no, it was half-fleshed then, it began reducing to make a new moon night happen, and how inebriating that new moon night was, new moon nights are stygian dark these days".

"No, no, after full-moon, the moon was getting smaller… When was it then?"

Tamradhvaj was busy in calculating, mentally. The day Acharya had left the hermitage, it was Krishna Chaturdashi. The moon on Krishna Trayodashi stayed back in the sky almost all day long, it set down in the afternoon, and that moon had surfaced again with a lean body in the wee hours of night on the eastern horizon, when the night was about to come to a close. The narrow moon set down in the afternoon after remaining in the sky for the whole day, the night went moon-less, such was Krishna Chaturdashi! Acharya had set out on his journey in the dark of Krishna Chaturdashi itself! Afterwards, the moon began to grow by bits, gradually. Full moon night came. After that full moon night, new moon fortnight had begun once again. So far as lunar day was concerned, this day was Krishna Saptami! Tamradhvaj calculated, it would be almost midnight when the moon would surface and now at this hour, the moon must have set down. He asked the old hunter, "When did the Acharya leave?"

"He, however, did not stay back, he just took a day-long respite. I still remember it was a full-moon day, it was just a day in therecent past!"

"Yes, yes, it was a full-moon day "— all chimed in unison. They were certain about the lunar day, which was a full-moon one, by the words of the elderly man. Tamradhvaj kept thinking inwardly, So Acharya, even though burdened with age, was walking towards the north-east like him, in almost the same pace as his. It seemed as though the Acharya had no dearth of strength in him!

The old man of that hunter-tribe asked, "Who is he"?

Who knew what the man of years kept thinking as he introduced the Acharya formally? He maintained silence for some time, and then asked, "Does he know all the stars of the sky"?

"Yes, I know likewise".

Then, someone had remarked, "The sky is known well to the birds like pigeons, parrots, and vultures."

Tamradhvaj did not reply. He could feel that these folks could not get the Acharya. They had not even understood him. How would they locate him, they were just blind, though two-eyed? Kalamukhi hamlet might be a part of Avanti, but the light of Avanti, even by a bit, had not reached here at all! These eyeless, plebeian people were blissfully ignorant even of the name of their country being Avanti! Another name of Ujjwain, the capital of Avanti, was Vishalanagar. They were ignorant of the fact that another name of Vishalanagar was also Padmavati, as Goddess Lakshmi, seated on lotus flower, had her resort there. Again, they were unaware of the fact that, the city of Padmavati was also known as Kumudvati, because the blood-red lotus remained in blossom all year long in the Seven Lakes. With 'Kumudvati' Ujjwain city, the city of Amravati was often brought in comparison. Just like Amravati, the capital of Indra, the King of Gods, in the capital of the city of Avanti no trace of mourning, sorrow, senility and death could be found. As Amravati was the dwelling-place of the gods, in Ujjwain, the capital of Avanti too, they used to reside, being accompanied by the nymphs, whose dazzle of beauty made the city shine and glitter. Like the city located in the mythological mountain of the heavens, even here at some corner stood the five trees of the gods' abode, Mandar, Parijat, Santanak, Kalpavriksha, Harichandan. As these hunters' tribe of a distant land was almost in the dark about such things, they even did not know that the present-day Ujjwain had nothing in keeping with the past. They were not even interested to know that the glory of Amravati was lost in course of time and none would now be able to trace those five trees of gods' realm. Padmavati Lakshmi had left the country, hence the city of Ujjwain bore the mark of deplorable plight in each corner. No hint of red lotus was there as the water had dried up in the Seven Lakes, hence none would ever pronounce the name, Kumudvati, again!

Tamradhvaj asked, "To which direction has he gone"?

Old hunter shook his head, saying, "Then he had put me to sleep!"

"Didn't he tell you of his intention?"

"No, he only talked about the city of Ujjwain. After the servant's death there had been no hint of water, even after the sexual union with a devadasi with auspicious traits, no water could be had".

"What more did he say"?

"He talked of the city of Ujjwain, said that Lord Mahakaal was quite a living deity!"

"Yes, indeed He is a watchful God!" Tamradhvaj bowed down to Lord Mahakaal, turning towards the distant south-west and said, "May Lord save Ujjwain!"

"Wasn't the young maiden auspicious in her looks"?

"Who said so"?

"Then why isn't water there"?

"What are you saying?"

Elderly man of hunters' tribe said, "Water may come thus, but the union occurs in our arable grounds, crop-fields, and that maiden has to be virgin, unscathed, the man has to be pure as well, the one who has not touched a woman till then—isn't your King married?"

"The queen is there, the King bears all auspicious signs, King can do anything".

"But I heard that he was Lord Mahakaal in appearance of the King!"

"May be."

"Do you know?"

"I know next to nothing", Tamradhvaj said.

"How can you evade it saying so? If the King is not pure, if he indulged in sexual intercourse before, then how would water come to the sky, and the maiden was to be taken to the crop-field, why in the temple?"

"I don't know".

"If you offered a human, why didn't you sprinkle his blood on the arable pastures, it would surely usher in rains, who asked you to burn him to death?"

Tamradhvaj said, "I have no idea. Perhaps I was not in town then."

The old hunter came charging, "What do you know then"?

Tamradhvaj smiled, "I am out in search of the man who came to your village."

The old hunter said, "This is really strange! He had come, I had witnessed that, but when he had left, I cannot say, now it seems that he had never been here."

"Then how did you see him?"

"Did I really see him?"

"If not, how did you know all those facts?"

The old man rejoined, "May be in my dreams. Better speak about the city of Ujjwain".

Tamradhvaj asked, "Doesn't anyone from among you know, in which direction had he walked up?"

"He had disappeared, that may even be possible".

"Possible? But how?"

"I heard that it may happen so. The friars and female ascetics can do so."

"But he was not that".

"I can't say"!

A maiden giggled to say, "Suppose, he didn't turn up at all".

"Then who had come"?

"None had come at all". The old hunter said. "You tell us how do you know that this village of Goddess Kalamukhi is in Avanti?"

Tamradhvaj knew that the boundaries of Avanti were quite sprawling. No walk, stretched over six to seven fortnights, even could make one cross this country! Even his land, Dasharno, had borne allegiance to Avanti. A merchant said, starting off from his Vatsya he reached Avanti within a fortnight, then autumn slipped by, winter sped by, he reached here after visiting many lands, all being under the rule of Avanti! All showered applause on the King of Avanti, though a King had been there to rule that land, all talked of Avanti only!

Old hunter said, "So the King of Avanti is the King of the Universe?"

"Yes."

"Does he reside in the city of Ujjwain?"

"Yes, exactly so."

"Go and tell the King that our village is burning"!

"On my return, I shall tell him."

"Go and tell your King that there's no water anywhere".

"Shall tell him".

"Owing to lack of water, animals, trees and humans are dying".

Tamradhvaj asked, "When and where"?

"Come on, take that direction, to the north-west, you'll get to see."

Tamradhvaj inquired, "What shall I get to see?"

"Dead beasts, the vultures from the sky swooping down, people dying daily, once dead, we drop the corpse at that end, let the vultures live on them."

Tamradhvaj saw that the eyes of the hunter were sans any expression. With eyes taking after those of a dead animal, the old man went talking. The old man was saying, "Tell the King, there's no rice in any household".

"I shall tell him".

"If there is no woman with auspicious features in the city of Ujjwain, we will provide, let the King drop in here, these meadows and grounds are lying fallow for him".

"What are you saying?"

"I mean it. So many acres of land! There's no water, even the grasses are dying".

"It's the same everywhere".

"Ask the King to come to this Kalamukhi village from Ujjwain city riding his chariot, these fields and crop-fields are awaiting him, there is a virgin maiden, whose limbs are not passionately touched by any man as yet, we have kept her aside for the King"!

"What for?"

"The King has enjoyed the serving-maid of the temple, but the sky still is going cloudless, the maid has not told the truth for sure and why didn't the King take the maid to the crop-field?"

Tamradhvaj went speechless. The brain of the old hunter was not fertile. He was reiterating the same thing. The elderly man was even forgetting what he had said, what he hadn't even. He was repeating it. But Tamradhvaj was wondering at the explanation the Acharya had left them with. Utanka's death and the King's sexual intercourse with the devadasi in the dark of the temple, behind all eyes,both these incidents are the stigmata of Ujjwain, no doubt. But Acharya Brishavanu had nurtured that stigma in the deepest nook of his own heart, in a different way altogether. He,himself, had failed in transforming the period of drought to one of good downpour. That was why, he had considered Utanka's demise and the outraging of the devadasi's modesty as a functional correlative of the possibility of downpour. This was nothing but sheer failure of the Acharya! But the Acharya had never expressed such faith to him, then how could these hunters learn about such things from the Acharya! Or, Acharya talked of Utanka's death and the misdeed of the King, he talked of the cruel heart of mankind, he narrated the terrible outburst of man's desire—and all those had been construed thus by the old hunter!

The old hunter said, "A bath is a must, here we do not have any river, water-reservoir is there, the water from underground can be siphoned up, sacred man and woman must have their bath in that water, then mantra of goddess Kalamukhi will be chanted, thereafter the man and the woman will unite in the evening, the optimum hour for the sexual union of a couple. Whenever the time of union approaches, tell your King, the Kalamukhi village is dying, the vultures are coming down day in, day out, even by night the vultures keep vigil on the dead corpses, let him come here to enjoy our maid on the meadows of Kalamukhi, his land will be blessed with rainfall, once again!"

Tamradhvaj said, "Let it be so, it can be related to him".

"Tell your King that owing to lack of harvest, there is no crop, no rice, if good rainfall helps us reap crops, rice still goes lacking, good rains or drought, they are just the same, just a mere guess".

"Why?"

"The plunderers come to rob us of crops, I have just learnt of having a King, but our King had never protected us till date. Why are we in such a bad plight even after having a King?"

Tamradhvaj assured, "I shall inform the King".

Then the old hunter kept looking at him, fixing him with his dead-beast-like stare, holding the eyeballs still. Looking at him for long, he said, "Aren't you our King by any chance? He described our King thus only".

Tamradhvaj startled, "No, no, how shall I be so"?

"I heard that the Kings go out to have a look at their country, they take the guise of a pauper to witness the joys and sorrows of their subjects, being wary of no one recognizing them as Kings".

Tamradhvaj smiled, "True".

"We have never seen our King, we had no idea that we had a King, then how would we recognize our King"?

"A mere glance at him will help you recognize him".

"How will that be possible"?

"It will be possible, the King can be recognized even if he comes to stand among thousands of men".

The old hunter said, "Won't the King be like an ordinary man"?

"Of course,a man, a man only becomes the King of men".

"Strange! Then how can we recognize him?"

"Just glancing at him you will feel that he only can be the King, a class apart from the rest of the people".

The old man fell silent. Tamradhvaj was contemplating, his looks had similarities with that of the hunters; curly hair, copper-complexion, hence even after taking him for a King, the thought had been annulled by the old man. Now the old man was nonplussed to imagine the looks and appearances of a King. If the King would just be a man, how could he be distinguished from among other men? Again, if the King was a man of flesh and blood, how would he be a King?

A little later, the elderly hunter said, "Tell us about the appearance of a King, come on"!

"A young maiden broke into a sudden giggle, Does a King have a horn on his head to differentiate himself from the others?"

Tamradhvaj looked at the damsel. Dark-complexioned, round-faced, slit-eyed, her forehead smeared probably with red sandalwood-paste. She was in full bloom of youth, but lack of rice caused a dent in there. The maiden was laughing and her whole body kept shaking with the vibration of her laughter. Tamradhvaj was reminded of the spate in the river Betrabati of Dasharno , during heavy monsoon.

The laughter of the young maiden annoyed the old man who reprimanded her, "Stop thou Kalamukhi, the King will come to this country, first came that old man, now this gentleman has turned up and now the King will come finally. If the King visits us, clouds will hover over the sky, downpour will begin, the King can usher in the clouds!"

" Yes, yes, this is true". Tamradhvaj was taken aback, all present there shouted in unison, "Yes, this is true indeed, if the King comes, the clouds will come close at his heels, we have our King, when the King will come here from the city of Ujjwain, Kalamukhi village will be inundated with water!"

Tamradhvaj closed his eyes to listen to the sombre declaration of the people! He too was won over by the belief that the words were true! He joined the chorus, adding his voice to theirs. He began to speak of a wondrous possibility. If King Bhartrihari could ever get to hear such words, he would feel blessed, it seemed. In the city of Ujjwain, he was vilified terribly. Drought, the incident with devadasi Lalita at the Mahakaal temple, so on, had made him quite small in the eyes of all. Men were tallying one incident with the other.

Old hunter said, "Let the King come, we will offer him the flesh of a calf, pulao and the delicious meat of the calf will fortify his valour and he will be able to conquer all the three realms: the Heaven, Hell and the Earth!"

The elderly hunter again added, "Let the King come, we will offer him the biggest peacock we have".

Then, after a pause, the old man continued, "We will offer him a maid with good omen, who will be adept in the art of copulation, who will serve the King best! We will donate all to the King, we will gift him all the animals of the forest situated on the western nook, let him step in, let there be a downpour".

It seemed as if the words of the old man were making way through the pores into the body of Tamradhvaj. He could feel a thrill all over his body. Tamradhvaj observed that, along with the declaration, the facial expressions of the men and women who assembled there, kept changing! Tamradhvaj listened to the words, they seemed to him like an occasional thunderclap of the clouds, staying latent at some corner of the sky.

FIFTY-NINE

That evening, Tamradhvaj had gone out walking again. Throughout the night. At midnight, the moon rose. Then, in the last hours of the night, the moon of Krishna Saptami had leapt overhead. Tamradhvaj had reached a human habitation. As the sun was getting more intense, he reached another village. Going there too, he learnt about the Acharya. The Acharya, all through his journey, kept talking about Ujjwain. About the city, the temple of Lord Mahakaal, the union of the King with devadasi Lalita, the death of Utanka, about the drought, about the King.

The hamlet seemed to pant for breath. The inhabitants of the village were almost skeletal in appearance. But they had welcomed Tamradhvaj in the same way as they had welcomed the Acharya. They were perhaps thinking at the back of their mind, that, someone would be there in their hamlet, who would be able to usher in clouds in the sky,overhead. They had heard of the King from Acharya. Just a few days back, Acharya had come here. None in that village knew about the King. Through the narration of Acharya and later that of Tamradhvaj, they were getting to know the King, gradually.

Tamradhvaj could make out that these plebeians had taken the King as an immaculate, spotless man without any blemish. Acharya had informed them thus. They had taken the physical union of the King with the devadasi Lalita as a measure to make the earth blessed with abundant harvest of crops. Profuse rainfall would cause good harvest of crops and the people would thus be saved. They had assumed that the death of the hill-boy Utanka, the servant from the north-east, had been made to happen just to stall the drought. Tamradhvaj came to learn that the people had expected the King to come soon. On arrival of the King, the days of drought would come to an end. Even in each village, a nubile maid with auspicious signs would be waiting for the yet-to-be-seen, almost superhuman King! By the evening, she would have physical union with the King to bring thunder-clouds. If clouds failed to gather in the sky, it would shove all to their end.

While listening to all that he was saying, Shivnath intervened, "So did you get to meet the Acharya"?

"No".

"Then"?

"Third night, perhaps Krishna Navami, the moon rose to make its presence felt in the small hours of night. I found myself in a large tract of grassland while the night came to a close. At dawn I got to see the skeleton of a human being".

"Oh Lord!" Shivnath screamed in fear.

"Yes, all the flesh of his body had been devoured by the jackal and the vultures, though the jackal was moving elsewhere in despair, on sniffing a bone, may be to a distant place in the morning. The dead man had nothing to offer to the living beings anymore".

"Where was he heading on to, who was he"?

"A traveller". Tamradhvaj muttered. Shivnath noticed that the Acharya's disciple had bent down under some heavy burden. Shivnath produced his hand in the dark. He touched Tamradhvaj and slowly said, "Raise your face up, it is night time, you are not being clearly visible, tell me, who was he"?

"That wayfarer was traversing the huge grassland to head on to the north-east. I think, he lost his way, and perhaps the directionless old man had collapsed in the field, being worst-hit by the deadly sun. He was straining himself to walk, putting more strength than he had in him and he failed to move anymore with his decrepit physique though there had been ways to save himself."

"Was it there?" Shivnath asked.

Tamradhvaj said, "The field was not at all a desert, within it a water-body had been there quite near, in a short distance stood a huge Peepul tree, in its shadow the fierce dogs and vultures, male and female, took shelter. The traveller could neither approach the shadow nor reach the water-body. It might be so, that, he had truly been blind, and that was why he failed to witness the dreadful spectacle of sunburnt Nature, though he could feel its heat, being burnt in that sweltering temperature, craving for a shadow, sensing not where exactly it lay, he collapsed ultimately under the blinding, scorching heat of the sun!"

"How could you identify him by just looking at his skeleton"?

"Why, his silk apparel, the small bundle of his books, which had not been touched even by the carnivorous animals and the flock of birds of prey"!

"Then"?

"Wrapping the few bones in the silk cloth, I began to trace my way towards the river, Shipra, I had to walk for a few days, through the night, and then reached the bank of the river Shipra, with the bones of the Acharya, burnt the remains at the dead of night without informing anyone. My heart was on the point of breaking, how could that great man had such a disastrous end?!"

"Didn't you observe the period of personal impurity on his demise?"

"No, I wanted to keep the death of the Acharya, a secret. Doubtlessly, he was a great teacher! But who could tell whether his living body was about to be devoured by the male and female vultures, the pack of dogs or even if not so, they had definitely slain him and the Acharya, while still alive, could hear the spine-chilling shriek of delight of these dogs and vultures! Such pathetic death would better remain concealed from all, beyond everyone's knowledge".

"But the death is the truth!"

"This death exceeds the truth even, now the King, the Kingdom, the capital, all are in peril, if the death-news of the Acharya reaches now, people will feel even more endangered, the King would be terribly shocked too, if obsequies had been performed, the death could not be kept a secret at all".

"Then where had you been to?"

Tamradhvaj said, "On cremating Acharya, I had gone out again, I had seen how the whole of the country was in jeopardy. As far as I had gone, there had been no sign of any rains anywhere, men were leaving their ancestral hamlet, habitation, they were setting out for an uncertain destiny and those who were staying back, they thought this was not the right way to live life, change is inevitable."

"What change"?

"If clouds hovered over the sky, that would be a change too, someone told me of a new star surfacing in the sky causing such disaster to follow".

"I haven't heard of any such thing", Shivnath said.

"Rumours are having new and newer ramification, the tale of the chariot-wheel of the Sun-God getting stuck was doing rounds in the other part of the country. In fact, I heard of it for the first time there only. Later the tale had been rife in Ujjwain. Had the Acharya been here, such words would never be spoken!"

"And what more did you hear?"

It goes like this: The people of north-east, over a stretch of few furlongs, kept waiting for the King, they hoped that according to the Acharya's prediction, the King would come there to put an end to drought and the inhabitants of the south-east were of the opinion that the new star was throwing everything topsy-turvy. On the other end, the Army-Commander, Bikram, had gone towards the Shurparak port with his regiment, crossing the river, Reba"!

"That Shurparak, you mean, on the bank of the Arabian Sea?"

"Yes, had you ever been there?"

Shivnath replied, "Yes, I had gone during my heyday of youth, now the days of youth seem to be sometime from my previous birth!"

Tamradhvaj said, "There robbers and thieves have grown extremely active, the Ionian Greek merchants used to come to Ujjwain from Shurparak, Barugaza etc. They have left quite a few tradesmen bankrupt. This has adversely affected the influx of merchants to Ujjwain".

Shivnath said, "Now the climate has clemency and they can come in droves, later the monsoon would be here and the paths would turn inaccessible. Then we would have to wait at the port itself, the thoroughfare usually crossed in one day would need three days to traverse"!

Tamradhvaj said, "While leaving, the armies warned that till the new star appearing in the sky of Ujjwain stands firm in its own position, such drought and lack of rains will continue unabated. I got my first lesson of astronomy from Acharya Brishavanu, but I know next to nothing about any new star".

"What did the Acharya say"?

"I am reminded of something, the Acharya had left Ujjwain failing to locate the little star, Arundhati, beside Vasistha, the noted savant among the great Seven Sages. The Acharya feared that this failure of not espying Arundhati would forebode imminent death. His fear came to be true."

Shivnath, who had lowered his head, said, "I do not get to locate the Ursa major anymore, nowadays, I hardly cast my gaze at the north-west sky, in fear."

Tamradhvaj said, "I cannot say which leads to what, but I have seen many who cannot see anything, have been struck with senility, incapacitation, blindness, yet they continue to live in the country of Dasharno. At the outskirt of my city, Bidisha, stays an old man, who is known to have crossed hundred years, long ago".

Whoever keeps the count of age? I had learnt from Dhruvadas during my youth long back that, as the Arabian Sea brought forth the Ionian merchants during this time to Shurparak and Barugaza, our city of Avanti used to get gravid with harvest of crops by the wind likewise, gushing in from that Sea and that wind blew off the clouds in the direction of Ujjwain".

"I know, I know, that wind is called by the Ionian merchants as 'Mausam'."

"Yes, Yes, Dhruvadas certainly used to talk about it, now I remember, the Ionian merchants used to claim, smilingly, that they used to bring in 'Mausam' in their trade-boats. Is it true?"

Tamradhvaj looked on into the darkness. He had gone silent, all of a sudden. He kept thinking— This large universe, those million stars in the sky, drought, rains in limit, excessive rains, trade-winds, 'Mausam' — how Lord Mahakaal had arranged all the things so amazingly! The Sea yonder, is known to be directionless, devoid of any banks, yet it too has shore and that shore is dotted with numerous countries. Tamradhvaj nursed a secret desire, none knew on which shore of the Sea stood grapevine-lined land of the white Ionians, if the Greeks could come to this country from such a long distance, why wouldn't he set sail with his trade-ships to their land? The chief reason behind his mastering the art of Astronomy was just that, being familiar with the stars in the sky, knowing their trajectory of movements beforehand, one would surely be able to set out on a voyage! Tamradhvaj imagined, he was floating in the boundless sea and the night sky stretched overhead. As the sky stood expansive on the vast field, the same would surely apply to the sea too. Then, in the darkness of night, nothing would be visible save the stars, with which he had not been familiar as yet. Getting to know the stars, he would set sail on the boat. In late autumn, immediately when 'Mausam' returned with the Ionian Greek merchants, Tamradhvaj's voyage would kick off to a start. Would a day like this await him really in future? Stupendous life like the Sea, endless existence like the Space! Far-off from Dasharno, Tamradhvaj kept on thinking, all alone, during night. Sleep eluded him since many a night.

Shivnath asked, "May I dare to say something"?

"Speak out, no reason is there to be overcome by fear"!

"None knew who stood where in the dark, the trees looked like human beings erroneously. Look, as the dacoits and thieves robbed the traders and wayfarers of their belongings, the soldiers too never lagged behind! The armies, too, did the same".

"Your son too had been there, in the army".

"Let him be there, as heroic, courageous soldiers are there in the army, greedy, mean plotters, knaves too are there as well. The power of the weapons is a great strength, the pride of arms is a towering gratification, again that pride makes the royal servant, and the army, oppressive! Haven't you seen Uddhavdas?"

Tamradhvaj rejoined, "True, but not absolutely so"!

"I have seen how robbing the merchants of all their belongings, taking their share of booties, the battery of armies got engaged in petty squabbles, their chiefs encourage them in such misdoings, don't the armies abduct women?"

"Perhaps they do."

"As they do, the royal servant too follows suit, his power is no less than that of the King, Uddhavdas becomes an arrant knave, boastful of being strengthened by that power. I think, you know, the merchants really used to usher in monsoon winds from the Arabian Sea, though they did not bring it on their own, they used to send it to this direction, as Dhruvaputra once narrated it. Oh Lord, how he knew so much! That which he did not know distinctly, he would bring it alive with the aid of his imagination. Now, the retinue of soldiers have lined up there to save the merchants, won't the line of soldiers stall the monsoon clouds, wind or 'Mausam' there in the north-west? And if they do so, will ever the period of drought come to an end?"

Tamradhvaj said, "Will ever your words be true? They will never be."

"Why? The armies with such weapons, such wrath, such lust, such greed, such desire, such inordinate will to occupy—won't they succeed?"

"You know well that they will fail! All are controlled by Lord Mahakaal, the regiment of armies can in no way stand in comparison to the power of Lord Mahakaal, the man has no right at all on the sky way, does man have that strength, can he have so? As man is not omnipotent the world gets saved! If man with power would know how to control the rain-clouds, the country of the powerful would have destroyed the world of the weak and the feeble! The cloud, rain and sunlight obey the will of Lord Mahakaal, hence the Kalamukhi village is so enchantingly beautiful!"

Shivnath became quiet. It seemed to him that the battery of armies had progressed along that way, in which the advent of 'Mausam' would happen, the monsoon wind would gush in with the footfall of the Ionian Greek merchants! The march of the regiment of soldiers meant destruction, pillage, murder, rape — transcending all, would it be possible for well-wishing cloud or wind to reach this land? To make a foray into this firmament of Ujjwain?

SIXTY

The line of armies had marched down to the other bank of the river, Reba, towards Shurparak port, situated in the southwest, on the shore of the Arabian Sea. There the Ionian Greek merchants had disembarked from the trade-ships with the collection of saleable commodities. The armies would protect them and usher them in the Ujjwain city. The rain-clouds might come at their heels. Shivnath said, "The advent of the monsoon clouds would be stalled by the platoon. The armies wished the drought to continue for long in this country, with the order and discipline crumbling down. Hence in the name of quelling the robbers and thieves it would be easy for them to subdue the innocent citizens, the perplexed merchants, so on, so forth. The plunder would continue unabated.

Tamradhvaj inquired, "Will the monsoon clouds flow only from the Shurparak port"?

Shivnath was silent. Shivnath was realizing gradually, that it was perhaps not right to express his baseless imaginings in that manner. Tamradhvaj had not offered him unconditional support rather Tamradhvaj's appearance certified that he was quite mature and he talked on proper judgment and analysis. Who was Tamradhvaj? He was an astronomer from Dasharno, the disciple of Acharya Brishavanu. The King had a sweet relationship with the Acharya. The King depended upon the Acharya, he had thought, perhaps the Acharya himself would search for a way-out from such dreadful drought. The Acharya would tell them why the drought hit them hard. He failed and hence he left the city. This youth,too, being the disciple of the Acharya, enjoyed a nice bond of friendship with the King. The King knew him personally, it seemed. So, it was a blunder to utter ill against the regiment of armies before him. No one knew how one's word would be taken in by the other! Casting aspersions against the King's army was tantamount to talking ill of the King!

Failing to elicit a rejoinder from Shivnath, Tamradhvaj said, "The birthplace of the clouds is that Arabian Sea and in the south-east there is the Eastern Sea, even much down to the south of Shurparak the clouds formed. And do you know that the clouds, climbing up the valley of the Malay mountains in the south-west, rush down towards Ujjwain?"

Shivnath nodded in the negative and said, "How shall I know? When my friend Dhruva had come back from Shurparak he also told me the same, he was then struck with a deadly disease yet he never missed out on a chance to be humorous. He said, the Ionian Greeks had reached Shurparak by sailing their trade-ships in the favourable direction of the wind, bearing the clouds!"

"Strange! Was he Dhruvaputra's father?"

"Yes, my friend Dhruva, he was just like my younger brother. Though younger, he was much superior in knowledge and glory, even at that age!

He spoke with elan, Acharya used to say, that it was the wind which used to allure the Ionian Greek merchants to trade and commerce, they used to sail down the seas. However, Acharya had heard this from a merchant and that merchant kept abreast of much of the astronomical news.

Shivnath said, "I veered to some other topic while talking about Dhruva, my friend. I commented on something which I would rather not do, so please forget such things."

Gandhavati's grandfather could feel that Tamradhvaj had been seized by a sudden panic. He got withdrawn somehow. He seemed to have recoiled. The moon was gliding towards the west, it would be morning once it set down. Moreover, it would stay in the sky for some time. If there had been no moonbeams, the old man could have talked on, without being much worried. In the dark, one would get to reveal oneself much more! Yet Tamradhvaj sensed that Gandhavati's grandfather was not being able to depend on him absolutely. If he failed to offer him support, where would the old man turn for help? To whom would he run being dejected? Who would he await, looking down the road? Being reminded of all such facts, Tamradhvaj stretched his gaze to the other bank of the moonlit river. He wondered, why he was being so concerned about Shivnath?! Even just a few months back, he did not know this family and how could he win the right of offering them support by now? The other side of the river appeared hazy before his sight. A little could be made out, though mostly unperceived. Straight across the opposite bank stood a young banyan tree. In the play of light and darkness, that tree seemed to be a huge one. Tamradhvaj took off his eyes from the other bank to concentrate on the surface of the river. He was reminded of a dead boa-constrictor! That huge snake had breathed its last slithering by the base of the Nichoih mountain, in the vicinity of the city of Bidisha. On his own, being old and decrepit. Perhaps, it had come down, leaving behind its age-old dwelling. From above the mountain. And then he was inching towards the wild river. It might have been thirsty. Tamradhvaj seemed to look at the gargantuan creature, lying there, dying of unslaked thirst. Long drought had left the river dead, it seemed. Alack! What a pity! On looking at the river, Tamradhvaj felt emotionally attached, this speedy, smooth-flowing river, made both its banks impregnated with abundant crops, since time immemorial! This river, since its inception, had kept the city of Avanti alive. Still now, the inhabitants of Ujjwain were taking water by digging into its bosom. To the last point of its ability, the river would strive hard to save both its banks. It seemed to Tamradhvaj that the river Kshipra aka Shipra, kept eyeing him with its morbid physique, with its everlasting thirst. The river begged for water. The speedy Kshipra river was now stationary owing to its senility, it was gasping for breath! It appeared to Tamradhvaj thus. Perhaps, the river sought for his help at this point of time. If she had been saved, she would save this country in turn. Avanti would again thrive with harvest of crops. Throwing a look at the river it occurred to Tamradhvaj, that, if all would be mutually interdependent during this drought, this famine, it would save us ultimately. All would have to build that strength for offering support to each other.

Tamradhvaj glanced at the sky. Looking up at the star-spangled sky this youth from Dasharno seemed to pray for strength. Man was the child of the cluster of stars, of the galaxy of lights of the sky. Emerging from the stars, the life of man descended upon this earth like a drop of water into the darkness. Life meant nothing but light! From the dot of light, man's life took birth. The stillness of the earth was broken by man's inhalation and exhalation. The light of the eyes dispelled the darkness. Contemplating thus, Tamradhvaj prayed for strength staring up to the sky. Then he spoke out, "Are you getting afraid, Grandpa"?

Shivnath replied, "No, it's not that, But I wanted to talk about my friend, Dhruva, I spoke a lot, please forget what I have said".

"What shall I forget, what shall I keep back in my memory again"?

Sad Shivnath said, "I got agitated abruptly, lest why should I say so? My son too had gone for war with the regiment of soldiers, hadn't he? ..."

Tamradhvaj said, "Steer clear of all worries, these words will remain here only, will stay locked within me, you are not in danger alone, when Nature turns inimical, its impact falls on everyone alike, the King is not happy just as his subjects. If there had been downpour, all our bodies would have been calmer, cooler, you alone are not getting burnt because of drought, the trees, all animals, rivers, soil — all are on fire".

Shivnath kept mum. If Nature turned hostile, the whole animal world would be in jeopardy. Even the insects and worms. But because of the hostility of Nature, as ordinary people were made to suffer, as the animals were pained by thirst, would the King suffer likewise? The King was omnipotent. Who would put him in danger? No calamity would ever be able to perish him. Tamradhvaj was young. He would have to take lessons from this life even more. Man would never be truly wise unless he attained age. But when years advance and age ripens, the experiences of life pile up, strength diminishes, courage flags. Such is man's life.

Tamradhvaj reverted to the former topic taking a detour through something else and said, "The clouds being blown from the end of Shurparak fort cause rainfall at Ujjwain and again causing downpour on both the banks of the river, Charmanvati, cross the river, Yamuna. Making rain happen in Indraprastha, they again float further to the north-east and to the other end, like Haridwar, Neeldhara Ganga, to Gomati river, lying more distant, and there the Himalayas begin to run along. The Acharya had followed that way, rather he wanted to."

"On the way of the clouds?" Shivnath asked.

"Yes, but clouds are not there, who would show the path to the Acharya? And the clouds being blown to that direction, reverted its course to the earth again. They would never evaporate like man, on their journey to the Heaven."

How strange! Shivnath was thinking that he could hear the voice of Dhruvaputra quite distinctly. This boy's knowledge-trove was no less rich too. Tamradhvaj was lecturing from there, — "From that end of the universe, clouds again retrace their path towards human habitation. Why would the clouds take birth, if they fail to drench the people in the villages and cities, if they fail to bring the dry grasslands to life, if they would not be able to render the narrow, morbid river into a lively, fleeting, youthful one, once again? Why would the clouds be born, if they fail to produce crops, if they would not succeed in adorning the plumage of the peacock or instilling desire in the mind of the lovelorn lover, staying far from his beloved, or if they fail in etching the sketch of the path of return, in the eyes of the lovelorn maiden waiting for her lover or her husband? The clouds never would undertake a lonely journey towards the Heaven after reaching the Himalayas, but they would return to the human habitation in the north instead. Skimming past both the banks of the Ganga and that of the Gomati. Traversing both banks of the Yamuna, they would meander into the country of thirsty soil. In the distant northwest, these clouds used to make the rivers: Sutlej and Bipasha, run full to the brim..."

Tamradhvaj was speaking slowly. Shivnath was listening to him, mesmerised. A thrill was what he felt. The memories of the clouds kept surfacing in his mind. Tamradhvaj was saying, "The clouds sailing towards the north and west were growing weaker. Gradually, they got totally annihilated, after drenching both the banks of the river, Indus. The clouds from the south-west journeyed towards the north-east in the month of Asad." In the far north-east, Red river was flowing by, Tamradhvaj had heard about it from the merchants who hailed from that country.

"The land of Guvak, you mean"? Shivnath said.

"Do you know?"

"Well, Dhruva, my friend, used to trade Guvak with the Ionian Greek merchants! He talked about the Red river to me and I shared it with Dhruvaputra. That Red river would grow dreadful in the month of Asad and it can hardly be guessed how much water the river would remain. It used to resemble the sea in this month of Asad."

Tamradhvaj was whispering, "On the valley of the Red River, thousands and thousands of Guvak trees used to stand tall touching the clouds in the sky. Only clumps of bamboo and Guvak trees abounded in that country. The Guvak trees were tall, straight and lean in appearance. They used to sway in the cloud-toting winds".

Shivnath asked, "Have you seen the Guvak trees"?

"No, I learnt from the merchants that they resemble the coconut trees in appearance."

"Have you seen the coconut trees?"

"No, I heard them to be like the Guvak trees only, they go up straight like a banner towards the sky, their tip is leafy, I can draw if you want."

"Without seeing it, how will you draw"?

"The merchants from that country made me acquainted with it by drawing the same in the valley of the Red River, the clouds would hover over the Guvak tree-tops, the fragrance, too, began to waft in, who could tell whether the clouds arising from the Eastern Sea made way to the bank of the Red river"?

"Dhruvaputra narrated about the Eastern Sea", Shivnath said.

"Yes, wind from that Sea reaches the Country in the East, the wind from the Arabian Sea does not blow that way hence the cloud-toting wind has to swish down to the South, then again it whirls round to the Eastern country, a strange connective link bobs up in my mind, Grandpa!"

"Which link?"

"Perhaps, it was you, who made me see this connective link".

"Which link, I am just an ignoramus".

"Cannot say 'ignoramus', but I think there is a secret link between the cloud-toting winds and the entry and exit of the group of merchants."

"You only say this, you had said already that the Ionian Greek merchants used to bring along with them, the cloud-bearing wind: 'Mausam'."

"You, yourself, knew this. I think, I heard it from you!"

Shivnath nodded to differ, "But I heard it from you!"

"No, didn't you just say that the regiment had gone to Shurparak, Barugaza ports to plunder the merchants, to prolong the period of drought?"

"I did not want to say in that vein", Shivnath said in an inaudible voice.

"I said that the statement is not wholly true, again not false even. The retinue of soldiers marched towards Shurparak, there the Ionian merchants used to disembark from the business-ships, they were accompanied by clouds, the strutting of the armies was just to stall everything. It seems to be true, may be partially true, that the clouds had a close bond with the merchants…"

Shivnath kept quiet. He could not understand what Tamradhvaj was hinting at. It was not clear whether he was supporting him or speaking against him or was trying to read his mind by offering him support. Shivnath listened to the words of Tamradhvaj, quite attentively.

Tamradhvaj was saying that he met the merchants from the east in mid-winter, they journeyed towards this end after the autumnal harvest, culled 'guvak' in the month of Ashwin, by that time, 'guvak' would ripen fully, collecting 'guvak' and paddy, when they headed towards the north-west, their destinations would be Shurparak port, the city of Ujjwain, then the clouds seemed to accompany them to return to the Arabian Sea, the Eastern Sea, the clouds from the north-east caused the winter monsoon to happen here, in this country.

"This time, there had been no rains during winter."

"No, it did not happen, the merchants too came fewer in number. They are not coming here from any direction, the information has reached them that Ujjwain is burning in drought".

"Would the clouds pile up, if the merchants had turned up"? Shivnath asked.

"God knows, but it seems that they are the controlling bodies of the clouds and rains. Lord Mahakaal himself is the controlling authority of clouds and rains, of Nature as a whole, to be precise. It was you, who said so."

"I know that indeed", Tamradhvaj said, "but we do not know everything,

Grandpa, the merchants visit many places, they are followed by the clouds that flow on, the clouds seem to direct them on the right path to reach here, the clouds and the gush of wind that begin to be annihilated while reaching the Eastern Sea or Arabian Sea , soften the hard soil. Naturally men get engaged in agriculture, if cultivation runs well the merchants benefit out of it, their trade runs well, they can carry the crops from one country to the other or beyond, men can buy or sell, even barter".

"Drought spells bad times for the tribe of traders too.

"Yes, so strange, the merchants from Ujjwain are about to set off, leaving the country now! Would the clouds and rain which used to float in, on the sly, fly off with them, then"?

"Where are the clouds and the rain you talk about"?

"Are they then carrying the wind of drought along?"

"But how can even that be possible?" Shivnath voiced his doubt.

"Won't his trade-tour be a failure, if he takes along the winds of drought?"

"That is expected naturally".

Heaving a long sigh, Tamradhvaj said, "All are just mere conjectures".

Dawn was about to break. The birds were waking up. Another day of scorching sun was about to begin. Both of them began to walk. They were headed towards the Shudra ghetto. The ultimate news regarding Dhruvaputra was there. Before exile, before returning to Gambhira, it was essential to know whether Dhruvaputra had taken refuge at the Shudra ghetto.

While moving forward, Shivnath stopped, "If I take your word to be true, then?"

"Which word?"

"Dhruvaputra had been there at the Shudra ghetto indeed"!

"Won't you come along"? While asking, Tamradhvaj could feel that the old man had woven complex woofs of suspicion in his mind. Gandhavati's grandfather was being unable to accept the fact of scrounging a shelter at the Shudra habitation.

Shivnath said, "Man's life is dotted with numerous incidents, such is the flow of life, why think upon it unnecessarily"?

Tamradhvaj said, "His father's friend, merchant Subhag Dutta, rendered him shelter-less being blind in desire for Devadutta, the courtesan, who had surrendered herself to Dhruvaputra and even loved him!"

Shivnath's head hung low. By then the bluish glow of dawn was disappearing to give way to a bright light that spread evenly, all around. In the light, the river, the banks of the river, copses and bushes, the fields afar and even the sky were looking graceless, bland. Old Shivnath closed his eyes, withdrawing his gaze from the decrepit, no-youth, stooping, senile stature of Ujjwain, resembling a dust-smeared old crone. He wondered how he had been connected to the son of Dhruva! The courtesan, the Shudra ghetto—all had marred the immaculateness of Dhruvaputra, straightaway!

SIXTY-ONE

Shivnath had seen the Shudra ghetto from outside. Neither did he have any need to go inside the ghetto ever, nor did he feel like going in. He had not an iota of interest in Shudra locale. Now, along with Tamradhvaj, he had stepped into a squalid, poverty-stricken habitation. It was true that the city of Ujjwain, Gambhira and the surroundings were going lack-lustre gradually, but the Shudra ghetto was never decked with grace. Hence how could it be lost to give way to something grimmer? When a graceful human gets worn-out by disease and other ailments, grace can yet be traced in his or her graceless appearance, which would never be erased out. Though the cities of Ujjwain, Avanti had lost their former grandeur due to drought, a look at it would definitely make us feel how these cities had been and would be again, after a shower, leaving everything cool and pleasant. Shivnath was feeling squeamish, on casting a look at the Shudra ghetto. He had to sit up all night for nothing at all. All night he seemed to have journeyed to the distant horizons, sometimes with Acharya Brishavanu, sometimes being accompanied by his disciple, Tamradhvaj, sometimes at Shurparak port with the clouds, and again in the hills of north-east, in the Arabian Sea, in the Eastern Sea. He was feeling tired now. That fatigue was even mounting on seeing the huts, left behind by their residents. They had smashed the earthen-ovens on the courtyard before leaving. Though they did not demolish the huts made with clay, earth and stones, the huts were crumbling down on their own, as was usual in the absence of their occupants. A tree stood, burnt black by the fire. Suddenly, it occurred to Shivnath that it got burnt by the flames of the sun itself. Could it ever happen that unbearable heat would set the clump of trees on fire? As it happened sometimes at the close of the winter. In dense forests, up the hills. He asked Tamradhvaj, "Have you ever witnessed forest-fire?"

"This fire had been kindled by Utanka, don't you know?"

"Yes, I know, I heard, but why did Utanka do so?"

Tamradhvaj shook his head and said, "I have come here also in quest of that".

467

Shivnath asked, "Have you ever been here before?"

Tamradhvaj nodded his head in the negative, "No, I had no such opportunity, I am thinking of it since long, I would come here to know, what attracted Dhruvaputra to this place!"

Shivnath did not like his words and quipped in, "Then you have to pay a visit to the red-light area as well".

"I shall go".

"Really, will you?"

"If not, how shall I know the truth?"

"All truths are not to be explored, a few truths are to be left in the dark".

Tamradhvaj maintained silence. Shivnath noticed that the news of their presence had already made way into the locality. An old man, thin-built, tall, dressed in a loincloth save which he had nothing to drape himself with, came forward and asked, "Who are you? What are you here for? It seems that you hail from respectable families!"

Shivnath was charmed by his words. He cast an amazed look at the emaciated person. Then Tamradhvaj said, "We have come in search of Dhruvaputra".

Old Parashar got startled, then sensing something, he joined both his palms to bow down and asked, "Who are you? Why will Dhruvaputra be here?"

Tamradhvaj tried to make his point clear, "We have come in quest of Dhruvaputra and Utanka".

"Are you the King's men"?

"No, we are coming all the way from the Gambhira village".

"Are you the Army Commander's men"?

"No, he is the friend of Dhruvaputra's father".

"Has the merchant sent you here?"

"No, WE are looking for Dhruvaputra".

Parashar replied, "We know next to nothing".

Tamradhvaj sat on the root of the banyan tree, with Shivnath by his side. At a little distance, the old village-headman, Parashar, sat squatting. Many faces peeped from behind Parashar, different in looks, of various ages, with varying expressions writ large on their faces, right from the fear-mingled curiosity to blank, nonchalant and variegated.

Shivnath asked, "Did he frequent this place"?

"Who, Utanka?"

"No, Dhruvaputra."

"Yes, Utanka used to come, but he set everything on fire, look at that tree, how it had contracted fire. Oh! Such flames, such all-devouring fire!"

Tamradhvaj said, "Talk about Dhruvaputra!"

"But we do not know"!

"Did Dhruvaputra come here often"?

"We do not know".

Shivnath said, "I am a friend of his father, he had been reared up by me, he left without letting us know anything, we are on the look-out for him, we are in trouble by his absence".

"But he is not here".

"But he was here, didn't he come over frequently to this place"?

Tamradhvaj assured, "Tell us, you have nothing to fear".

"We know next to nothing".

"Then we cannot bring Dhruvaputra back".

"The merchant sent for the news, Utanka said"… Parashar left his sentence unfinished.

"What did he say"? Tamradhvaj inquired.

"We have forgotten Dhruvaputra".

"No, you haven't forgotten. Tamradhvaj bent down to say, We are neither the King, nor the merchant, nor the Army Commander, we represent no one, we seek the well-being of Dhruvaputra".

"No, we haven't forgotten"! Parashar broke down. Both his eyes glistened.

Shivnath could feel that Dhruvaputra had left deep impressions on the hearts of these people. They were not unfamiliar with Dhruvaputra. Dhruvaputra used to come here. Look yonder, tears kept streaming down the eyes of that old man. The old man was saying, "It was dawn when Dhruvaputra had come here, for the first time, to sit upon this very root of the banyan tree"! Right at the place where Tamradhvaj sat, there! Why did Dhruvaputra come here? Why did he come very often? What exactly did he need here in this Shudra ghetto? Had he taken fancy on some young maiden, even in here? Women had no differences: whether of higher or lower castes. What had happened to Dhruvaputra?

Old Parashar said, "They had rescued Dhruvaputra from the city. When was it? No, it was before his exit. It was perhaps the Saptami tithi or it might even be the Ashtami tithi of a full-moon fortnight. The crescent moon hung from the sky. Late into the night, on their way back home, two of them had found him lying on the edge of the road, in a pool of blood. Utanka had flogged him".

"Why, what did Dhruvaputra say?"

"Nothing at all, Sir!" Parashar folded both his palms.

"Who had rescued him?"

"None of them is there, all of them have left their dwellings behind, the city would burn out by the fire of the sky, they say."

For some time, all of them sat silent. A profound silence stood pervading the shadows of the banyan tree. Old Parashar sat with his head lowered. The persons sitting at their back, had hung their heads in shame. All the faces were dark. Shadows were now sad in appearance.

After a small length of time, Tamradhvaj asked, "And then what followed?"

"Nothing at all, two days later, Dhruvaputra had gone back to the city again".

"And then?"

"Utanka had come to forbid us not to say anything regarding Dhruvaputra, and we did accordingly. Utanka was very ruthless".

"What more did he say?"

"Dhruvaputra should not get any refuge, he was highborn, offering him shelter at Shudra ghetto meant insulting the respected families. The merchant would not brook it".

Shivnath was growing impatient. He found these words irritating. It would be fine if he could clog the ear-holes with his palms. In which web was Dhruvaputra entangled? Which sorcerer had made him forget all: his own dignity, glory and identity? It was being clear that all his learning became fruitless. And they rescued him to this ghetto, bringing him in here! He lay unconscious by being flogged black and blue by the servant of the merchant! What tragic end of a man of such noble stature! How could he become the eyesore of the merchant, even after being an apple of his eye, since long? Was it just for being the whore's love or was this Shudra ghetto another formidable cause too?

Shivnath asked, "Why was he in the wont of coming here?"

"He knew that better", Parashar retorted.

"Did you ask him to come?"

"No, he used to come on his own."

"But he was not supposed to come over here", Shivnath charged.

"Yes, Sir"!

"Then why did he frequent this place, for whom did he come?"

Parashar had gone silent. He was trying to get the intention of the man, hurling queries at him. Just in this way, Utanka, one day - no, he had a touch of cruelty in his voice which this man did not have. But the question was the same. Parashar was trying to make out the intents of these men!

Shivnath knew that these Shudras were fond of Buddhism, secretly. The friars and monks of this religion were adept in numerous magical tricks and esoteric art. Was Dhruvaputra caught in the enchanting spell of someone here? The reason of his frequenting the red-light locale could be understood, but why this place? Did the merchant abandon him for his attachment to the courtesan and hence got him drubbed by his servant or was there any other reason behind this?

Shivnath stood astounded, "How did he come here initially"?

"That I don't know".

"Did he come on his own or someone had brought him in here"?

"I know next to nothing about it, Sir, but none had brought him in here, I had never seen him before, never heard of him too, and how would we hear, at all? We are an ignorant lot. Who will talk to us of Dhruvaputra? We don't know anything, none tells us anything even, if anyone goes far-off, news reaches us through him, otherwise how would we know of anything at all? We never used to know him before".

Shivnath could feel it to be an impregnable conundrum. As Dhruvaputra's exit had become a highly complicated mystery to him, this matter too was no less. All of a sudden, Tamradhvaj asked, "Are a few from among you leaving this colony?"

Parashar answered, "Some are leaving, all will follow suit."

"Drought is raging through all places".

"How do you know? Has the sin of Ujjwain defiled all other places too?"

"Which sin of Ujjwain?"

Parashar grew alert, he said, "That I do not know, Sir, the rumours are rife that the Sun-God will stop budging an inch, the sky will keep disgorging fire all day long, that fire will be caught by trees, dwellings, even the earth!"

Tamradhvaj could sense that an all-pervading intimidation was there to rule the roost. Who could save them from this? Only the Nature, only the clouds in the sky could come to their rescue. It would have been divine, if the Ionian Greek merchants could really usher in clouds! If the merchants from the East would come being accompanied by clouds, the city of Avanti would have been saved. Tamradhvaj thought inwardly, let the traders roam round with clouds, let them begin transaction of clouds! Lest, the heat of daytime would be enough to set the trees on fire. That burnt tree seemed a pointer to the future form of the city of Ujjwain. Tamradhvaj felt a shudder within as he kept looking at that tree. He seemed to be panic-stricken, inwardly.

Shivnath asked, "Tell us the truth, why did Dhruvaputra come here frequently?"

"To witness our lifestyle".

"Is it credible?"

"I do not believe this even, said Parashar".

"Then why did he come?"

"To see all of us, it seems as if he used to come to see all— the boar, dog, peacock, he used to enjoy respite sitting back in here, we all used to assemble, as we are here today."

"Do you have any enchantress among you?"

Parashar shook his head, "Sorry, I have no idea!"

"They are adept in mesmerizing people."

"No idea at all."

"What was Dhruvaputra's attraction here? Didn't he know that the Shudras are always to be shunned?"

Parashar hung his head low and muttered, "We stay far-off, we hadn't called him to join us at all. One fine morning, I found him in a white attire, white scarf, how gracious were his looks! The place he would be in, would stand adorned with an orb of glow, he was seen traversing the field to come here and sit at the base of this banyan tree".

"Did he know that it was a Shudra ghetto?"

"He knew and in spite of that he used to come here. He would come here to listen to the tales of war".

Shivnath held his chin up, his spine grew taut, he asked, "Are you telling the truth?"

"I do not know."

"Then are you telling a lie?"

Parashar drooped his neck to say, "That too I don't know, now it seems that neither is the truth."

"Neither is the truth!"

"Whatever I had said about Dhruvaputra!"

Tamradhvaj said, "We have come to know about Dhruvaputra, it would perhaps be easier to find him out if we could know his whereabouts, tell us just the truth!"

Parashar said, "Now all appear to be untruth to me! Perhaps we had imagined him, imagined a person like him who would listen to our tales, day in, day out, of the Indus river, of the Malay ranges!"

"From whom did you learn these names"?

"Perhaps Dhruvaputra, or perhaps I knew on my own, but all seem to be blatant lies, perhaps Dhruvaputra had never been here, perhaps I had seen him once on my visit to the city, long ago, perching on the chariot of the merchant while the scarf on his body was a-flutter in the wind".

"Then?" asked Shivnath.

"I do not know, now all seem to be the illusions of my old age, why will Dhruvaputra come here? In our habitation, we do not have such a nubile girl to offer him for his pleasure. The best prostitute stood ready for him... why will he come here at all? We do not have gems and treasures even, so that he will come in lure of it!"

"Then didn't he come at all?" Shivnath asked.

"He hadn't come, but I had seen him here at the base of this banyan tree, by the edge of that Ratnakarsagar, Sir, witnessed his entrance into this place traversing the field and his exit by the same way!"

"What are you saying, speak clearly, explicitly!"

"Why will he frequent the Shudra ghetto being such a wise man? Neither do we have such a girl amongst us to impress him nor a sorceress to win him with magical tricks."

Shivnath was trying to make out what he wanted to say. Tamradhvaj could see him sitting by the side of Ratnakarsagar or this banyan root, quite clearly. All stood vivid in front of him. Even the domestic pets of the Shudra colony had filed in. Tamradhvaj was trembling. His head was throbbing. He could feel that he came to know more than he could find with his calculations.

Parashar said, "All seem to be a dream, it was my dream, the dream of an old, wizened fellow"!

"Oh, I see!" Shivnath, in a low voice, uttered. "Did he partake of rice here, in these Shudra dwellings?"

"Dreams, all are dreams!"

"Tell us if he did."

"Dreams! Lest why would he take rice in here?"

"Did he have rice"? Shivnath screamed in disgust.

"Cannot say, perhaps he was not Dhruvaputra!"

"Wasn't he?"

"No, someone else perhaps… so many souls are there in this world, so many of them walk through the field, so many take respite perching on the root of the banyan tree! Utanka had scourged so many of them, even had beaten a good many of them to death, he was very ruthless, he had brought someone here like him, can't it be so? And the man he had brought along wasn't perhaps Dhruvaputra at all!"

"Strange! How can that be?" Shivnath spoke up.

"If …perhaps, it may be so"!

"But you all said that he was none but Dhruvaputra!"

"No, now it seems that he was not Dhruvaputra, someone else perhaps, we are ignorant, we took him to be Dhruvaputra, Sir! You came here to drag us out of that wrong notion. Hailing from a highly respectable family, being so wise, why would Dhruvaputra come to this Shudra ghetto? It is an extremely abominable act, the act of an ignorant person, he was no fool, that was why, he never came here."

Shivnath sat speechless. Tamradhvaj kept staring at the old Shudra. The man stood up. Shaking his head, he turned around.

SIXTY-TWO

Parashar said, "We will go now".

"Where"? Tamradhvaj asked. Will all of them go away? Had they come to stand at that crucial juncture when the Shudra ghetto was going to be totally evacuated? Perhaps so. The flock of boars, the pack of dogs, the cocks, peacocks, donkeys all were there. Now it would be better to begin the exodus with the animals, domestic pets, women and children. The children were there. The women were not there, perhaps they had not joined them because of the male strangers. The women might have stayed back in their huts, managing their respective households. If the old man would call out, all would emerge outside. The old man seemed to be the Chieftain of this Shudra ghetto. The elderly men of a village would gradually turn to be so. Tamradhvaj was reminded of the herd of elephants. As the elephant led out the herd, this old bloke would also go likewise. Tamradhvaj was reminded of the forest-path of Dasharno. He was transported mentally to the herd of elephants thinking of a new journey, standing motionless in the forest of Dasharno. Exactly in the same manner. Tamradhvaj grew sad. If such exodus of people happened, what would be the future of Ujjwain? Even the incident of conflagration had not left the Shudra ghetto so evacuated as the drought was making the city of Ujjwain, a land, devoid of human beings.

He told Shivnath in a low voice, "They are leaving".

Shivnath lifted his head to say, "Let them go".

"Why? The city would turn into a land of no souls".

Shivnath softly said, "The city can do away with the Shudra ghetto. It is for the city's well-being".

Tamradhvaj looked, cocking his neck. He found the Chieftain to have turned around. He had moved away towards the shadow of the banyan tree. His face was turned to the west. Shivnath in a mild voice said again, "I can comprehend why the merchant had been angry with Dhruvaputra, there was reason enough for his wrath".

"Why"? Tamradhvaj asked.

Shivnath had wiped off the sweat from his forehead with his scarf and under his breath said, "How could the merchant brook the fact that a high-born man would be in close contact with the Shudras? I know him, he is quite a devout man"!

Tamradhvaj said, "But it is not clearly known whether Dhruvaputra had come here, the man said it could be someone else as well".

He replied as he could comprehend his mistake, "Otherwise how dare they serve Dhruvaputra with rice? Dhruvaputra had taken rice at the Shudras, can you imagine how hurt would be my daughter-in-law and granddaughter if they come to know of this"?

Tamradhvaj said, "But they were saying…"

"Whatever they might say, that would be a logic in favour of Dhruvaputra. If Dhruvaputra ever returned they should not offer him either shelter or rice. If the priest came to know about his crime, an unpardonable crime of taking rice at the Shudras…this would pose a threat to the society, making it crumble down. Did Lord Mahakaal create the four varnas for no reason at all"?

Tamradhvaj kept quiet. Coming to Ujjwain, he found that everything was related to Lord Mahakaal! But looking at the phallic image of Lord Mahakaal, Shiva, it occurred to him suddenly that it was just an idol of a hunter! Strange! Looking at the image of the union of the woman's womb and phallus, it never struck him that this deity might be fond of the Brahmins, Kshatriyas or Vaishyas. Even in that Kalamukhi village he had seen the phallic idol, beneath the Peepul tree amidst flowers and the holy leaves of the wood-apple tree — it seemed like a little version of the idol of Lord Mahakaal! Tamradhvaj jerked his head. These thoughts were immoral. It would be better not to think in this vein. Sitting in the far-off city of Bidisha, he had heard of Lord Mahakaal. All the merchant-groups used to head towards Ujjwain always. The reason was certainly the Mahakaal temple. Visiting Mahakaal was a holy act of piety and that would make them earn success in their business tours. All the buying and selling of goods could successfully be done in Ujjwain itself.

Shivnath asked, "Are they the followers of Buddhism? Followers of the friars and monks with tonsured heads of this religion, I mean?"

Tamradhvaj got startled. He marked a secret doubt in the eyes of Shivnath. While Dhruvaputra lay in the pools of blood on the main thoroughfare of the city, it was they who had brought him here to nurse him back to health again. It was they who offered him rice to eat as hounded out of the city but Shivnath was not grateful to them, in the least. Rather, he became angry, why the Shudras had proffered refuge to Dhruvaputra to make him almost deviate from his own religious belief! It was not widely publicized. Or was it so and hence Dhruvaputra had been banished from the city? May be for this reason, the merchant had driven him away! Perhaps this was the chief cause of his ouster. The whore's love had no base, it was not true even. In order to cover up this reason, his love of a prostitute might be a rumour spread by the merchant. Thus Dhruvaputra was saved from being fallen for his intimacy with the Shudras! Shivnath was turning stern. He thought, it was necessary to go to Ujjwain for a secret survey. A visit to the whore was essential too. Then, all would dawn on him clearly. How could his heyday of youth be tarnished by his hobnobbing with a courtesan? It was the duty of the whores to entertain the men! For deriving such pleasure, Dhruvaputra used to visit them. The pleasure, denied by the wives of the men in the household, which they would not expect even, the whores were there to regale them with it! If Dhruvaputra went there, how could it be a crime? If Dhruvaputra took the primary lessons of the fine arts or the art of sexual intercourse at a brothel, then what crime was that for which the merchant had driven him off, got him flogged by his servant, tried to slay him, and finally banished him from the city? Real truth lay elsewhere. Shivnath was trying to tally the facts. So long, he did not think about this matter so deeply. Today as if the curtain on his thoughts was being lifted. Alas! Gandhavati knew that, on being attracted to a whore, he had forgotten her! What did it mean by attachment to a whore? The raison d' etre of the prostitutes drew Dhruvaputra to them, that's it! Wouldn't he know everything on his arrival in the city? A saying went thus: if a prostitutewas not seen, many a lesson in life would remain incomplete! Why would his love for Gandhavati diminish because of it? But ascribing the stigma to him, which was far from a blemish, rather the pride of a male, the merchant had saved him from the fire of wrath of the Brahmin priest, of the bigwigs of the society, so on. Would ever Dhruvaputra be able to return to Ujjwain, if he had been made to fall from the faith he usually practised? Once fallen from his own religious belief, would ever Dhruvaputra be able to come back to Ujjwain? Or could he rub shoulders with the high society of Ujjwain, at all? His knowledge, intelligence—all would have been perished! Knowledge, intellect, poetic talent would never flourish without royal patronage. Could ever a man fallen from his religious faith be blessed with royal support? Oh alas! Tamradhvaj had heard everything. Dhruvaputra used to have rice here. He had been nursed just here! If these words became public, what would the consequences be?

Tamradhvaj said, "Buddhism has the curtain dropped on it, friars and monks, the shaven-headed lovers of Lord Buddha, residing anywhere have gone into hiding,

I haven't heard of anyone staying back in Ujjwain, though I have seen them in my village hamlet".

"What have you seen?"

"The followers of Buddhism, tonsured, fond of the teachings of Lord Buddha, both male and female, go through the city of Bidisha to the woody hills of Sanchi."

"Where is that hill located?"

To the South of Bidisha, quite proximal, while reaching Ujjwain, all have to take a turn from the Sanchi hills to the West, if one walks towards the east of Ujjwain, he would reach the Sanchi hills, yes, even to Bidisha, in fact, the hill is located in the outskirts of the city of Bidisha.

While speaking, Tamradhvaj marked that, the old Shudra fellow had turned to them, being curious. He was listening to their conversation. Tamradhvaj was saying, "In the caves of the Sanchi hills, the ascetics of the Buddhist order, stayed in hiding, they were the followers of Lord Buddha after all".

Shivnath inquired, "Have you ever been to that hill?"

"I had gone there, a Buddhist hermit had taken me along, on the sly. The hill is covered with dense forest, and the forest is quite perilous. However, the inner region of the hills is clean, there the worshippers of Lord Buddha reside. There is a secret entrance in the southern end of the hill, a tunnel in the rear, to be precise."

"What did you see?"

"In the stones, on the walls of the cave, the life of Lord Buddha was etched."

"But you had never shared these experiences!"

"No need was felt so far."

"Do you know that though Lord Buddha is an incarnation of Lord Vishnu, his followers are depraved, they do not abide by either religious principles or the four 'ashrams'[varna]".

"I know that, they claim their religion to be a different one".

"They speak wrong, they are ignorant hence they say thus. I have heard that those who practise that religion are ferocious in nature, they have a close contact with the ghosts and evil spirits, they are well conversant with strange scriptural rites."

"May be, but that hermit was sweet by nature."

"You have been saved by coming to Ujjwain from Bidisha, lest they would have hypnotized you and you would have been left with no way of return."

Tamradhvaj maintained silence. Then Shivnath in a muffled voice said, "I think the followers of Buddhism are staying at many places, with their own identities concealed".

"I know next to nothing about this".

"The King must pay his attention to this fact".

"God knows!" Tamradhvaj was not happy with this conversation. Yet, he was fond of Shivnath indeed. It was not that he was the grandfather of Gandhavati, but he was just a common man, sans greed, of a simple and plain disposition. And was fallen in difficult times, no doubt. His son went missing and Dhruvaputra had gone untraced too. Again, was he capable enough to trace them alone, all by himself?"

Shivnath said, "I have heard that the followers of Buddhism stay such mingled with us, that it is very difficult to recognize them, and I have learnt that all the Shudras have taken to Buddhism. Is it true?" Shivnath threw the query.

"I have no idea".

"In that religion, there is no differences between the Shudras and the non-Shudras, it had never been there, it is they who have offered him rice to eat. Have they imbibed the courage from Buddhism then?"

"What are you saying?" Tamradhvaj was startled. He was frightened. Instantly, he took a look at the Shudras. Did they hear his words? Tamradhvaj found Shivnath's expressions to have undergone a sea-change. Gandhavati's grandfather was seething in rage.

In a muffled voice he was heard to say, "Mostly the Shudras were there among the Buddhists, I doubt if Dhruvaputra had come to know anyone fond of Buddhism, for that matter!"

Let these matters be shelved aside. Looking at the expressionless faces, Tamradhvaj thought that they were listening perhaps, but had no courage to react to it.

"Dhruvaputra had journeyed towards the east, as Gandhavati said confidently".

"Yes, I had even heard that".

"Then, has he gone towards Bidisha, to the Sanchi hill"? Shivnath asked.

"Why, that is the refuge of the Buddhists".

"You can't get it, perhaps Dhruvaputra had fallen for a Buddhist worshipper,

I mean someone of that religious bastion, whatever we may say, they are still there, though quite secretly".

Tamradhvaj nodded in the negative, "No, that is impossible".

"If not so, then why did the merchant set this ghetto on fire?"

"Fire was kindled by his servant."

"Without his approval, how would Utanka, the servant, dare add fire?"

"Why did he do it?"

"These people would offer rice to a highborn man and cause him to be expelled from his own caste, they might be secretly Buddhists or how could they dare offer him rice! Dhruvaputra could have remained dead by the roadside. It is said that, dying in one's own religious faith is much, much welcome".

Tamradhvaj said, "One would continue to live, would it be better if he had died?"

"At least he would not have been fallen from his own religious faith!"

Tamradhvaj heaved a long sigh. He was afraid of Shivnath's words. Shivnath certified that the merchant was devout and meticulously observant of religious rites. Perhaps, the merchant had come to know about Dhruvaputra's hobnobbing with the Shudras. If it would be a case of an affair with a Shudra woman, it would have been definitely different and the merchant could have tolerated it, but taking rice at the Shudra ghetto - it was just an unpardonable crime! Just as it was Dhruvaputra's crime, it was that of these Shudras as well. They were secretly in touch with the religion of the shaven-headed friars and monks, otherwise they could not do this. And that was why, Utanka had set their dwellings on fire, at the insistence of the merchant.

Then Parashar turned round to say, "Now let us leave".

"Where will you go"?

Parashar said, "Sir, you will not accept our hospitality even, what shall we offer you then? I can understand that a crime was committed".

Shivnath asked, "Was he really Dhruvaputra, the man who used to come here?"

"I have already told you, Sir, he was just one among the many who used to enter and leave by the way of that field!"

"But no one was Dhruvaputra!"

"No, Sir, whatever you say is true indeed."

"Dhruvaputra had not taken rice in here, right?"

"No, Sir."

"Dhruvaputra did not come here, did he?"

"No, Sir!" Parashar was in fear.

"Could Dhruvaputra have the rice offered by you?"

"No Sir, he could not."

"Can you offer him rice?"

"No, Sir, we cannot."

"Can you offer him water?"

"No, Sir, no, the water offered by us would not be fit for him to drink."

"Do you follow the religion of the shaven-headed friars and monks?"

"No, Sir, no", being frightened, Parashar let out a scream.

"Why then had Utanka set the ghetto on fire, being aware of everything?"

Parashar said, "I have understood. Sir, let us take your leave, heat of the sun is on the rise!"

Then Tamradhvaj got to his feet and said, "Who will stay back in Ujjwain, if all of you leave? Today it may not rain, but tomorrow it will, surely".

"Yes, it will", Parashar threw a glance at the distant sky.

"Once it rains, there will be no unease", Tamradhvaj said.

"True, we won't have any discomfort, the lakes will be filled to the brim."

"Then, why leave? Ujjwain will turn absolutely desolate".

"Yes, Sir! Dhruvaputra has left it to utter nullity" … mused Parashar.

"You should not speak of Dhruvaputra, do not take his name even".

"We will not say, hey you all, never take the name of Dhruvaputra"! He made others listen, and added, "Dhruvaputra had cast magic charm on us"!

"Let the matter be left at that", Shivnath said.

"Let it be so, Sir, let's go now," Parashar folded his palms again.

"Where will you go, to which land?" Tamradhvaj demanded to know.

Parashar smiled, "Where will we go, Sir, nowhere at all, we all are heading to the Ratnakarsagar. Which place is left for us to go? There is rain nowhere".

Tamradhvaj asked, "Is this Sagar one of the seven lakes"?

"Yes, Sir, the King had made it available to us, hail to the King!"

"Is there any water now?"

"No, how is that possible, nowhere else there is water, save the river."

"Then what's the need of that dry lake?" Tamradhvaj questioned.

Parashar said, "We are digging".

Tamradhvaj and Shivnath got startled together. They kept looking at the Chief of the Shudras, that old man, with their eyes wide with wonder. He appeared like the Chief of the tribe. All had come to queue up behind him. It seemed to Tamradhvaj that this elderly person was much happier than the King of Ujjwain. All stood behind him, the whole colony, to be precise!

Shivnath asked, "What will you get by digging"?

"If there is water in the hell, it will come up".

Shivnath said, "The hell is an ocean, the firmament is an ocean, there is water nowhere".

Old Parashar joined both his palms again, "Digging the river will fetch water, Sir!"

Shivnath failed to answer. Tamradhvaj marked, as the captain elephant led the herd away, this old man too went along, in the same manner. It seemed as though the whole locale was following the Chief of the Shudras. They were heading towards the waterless lake. He was being followed by the team of boars, herd of donkeys, flock of cocks, the pack of dogs, the pride of peacocks and the line of kids. The old man seemed to set out on a long journey with all in tow. He walked forward in slow steps. He began to walk close to Parashar and asked, "Who advised you to dig"?

"None".

"Dhruvaputra"?

"Sir, we do not know Dhruvaputra"! Folding his palms, with tear-filled eyes, the old soldier, Parashar, kept looking on.

SIXTY-THREE

Tamradhvaj asked, "Can the water surface by digging"?

"The lake would be deep, at least during monsoon it would be capacious enough to hold more water."

"Who suggested this digging… Dhruvaputra"?

Parashar stood a while and said, "We haven't seen him ever, as lower-caste people, we are not entitled to know him, we do not even have the right to offer him rice".

"Then have you thought of digging on your own"?

"No", Parashar nodded his head in the negative, "Not me even".

"Then who thought, who told you"?

Parashar said, "People are leaving, assurance of a drop of water would hold them back, hence the digging has begun, with a hope of water to surface. The people have stopped leaving as they seem to find a ray of hope".

Parashar was moving in slow steps. The people had moved forward, at a brisk pace. Quite at a distance, Tamradhvaj could see the elevated bank of the lake. The people were moving in that direction in long steps. The animals, too, were heading on to that direction. Strange! Even they could sense that water might come up. They were in real trouble because of lack of water. The people quenched their thirst with the water they used to collect from the far-off rivers. Did the thirst slake at all? If it slaked, why did the donkeys bray, looking up to the sky, in the afternoon?

Parashar said, "The people were left with no hope at all, Sir! They thought that all the living creatures would die of dried-up bosom, along with them they themselves would die too. Hence, they grew panicky".

"Has this fear subsided now"?

"Fear is still there, if the Sun-God comes to a standstill in the sky, there will be no nights, no full-moon, no nights of moonshine in which all the hours can be devoted to digging the earth by the lake. Don't we have fear, Sir? Of course, we do have, if ears are pressed to the chest, it can be detected"!

"Then how about your hopes being raised"?

"People were at their wit's end, news from all corners poured in to confirm that not a speck of cloud would be there in the sky! Then what will men do, even the King is not capable of bidding clouds hover over the sky, let alone the merchant or the Brahmin Priest of Lord Mahakaal shrine! Hence people would not be left with any other choice but to die. How dreadful the days are, Sir!"

"Then you mean, no hopes are there"?

"No. Hope is there, I am yet to finish my words, fear pervades all around. An old, eccentric Ayurvedic physician, Nahush Sharman, is there, who is spreading the rumour that when daytime will stop to terminate, people will lose their sleep with nights vanishing, though not death. And all the people will turn blind."

"These are baseless thoughts."

"All said that they would leave, but where they did not know! They are in two minds! They are keen on leaving and again deciding otherwise, the very next moment. They are heaving sighs throwing a wistful gaze at the sky, they are praying to Lord Mahakaal! But why would Lord Mahakaal listen to our entreaties, we do not have any participation in that temple, we are debarred from entering it, the people cannot pray to Lord Mahakaal with all their hearts, such is the practice, Sir! But who are you to Dhruvaputra, none but Dhruvaputra would want to hear us!"

"What did Dhruvaputra want to hear"?

"He used to say and we used to listen to him!"

"What exactly did he say"?

"Nothing Sir, whatever I have said is wrong, we have forgotten him, we do not know him."

Tamradhvaj assured, "But Grandpa has left, so speak just the truth."

Parashar swung his head and said, "I am extremely frightened, what for had Utanka added fire, being a servant himself? If the merchant bade him to kindle fire, why had he not saved him then, from the clutch of death? Now I get to see that Dhruvaputra is omnipresent in every way, though absent physically".

Tamradhvaj nudged him, "Won't you speak of Dhruvaputra?"

"No, I shall speak of water, will he even figure in my expatiation on water"?

"Did he ever talk about digging?"

"Yes, he did", Parashar tilted his neck to one end to continue, "I do not know whether he said or not. When digging started off, an old man called Dikpati told us one day. It was the month of Phalgun, it might be that Phalgun preceding the Chaitra in which Dhruvaputra had left, or it might be some other Phalgun as well or it might not be any Phalgun for that matter! Old Dikpati can retain nothing in his grey cells, he might mistake the month of Asad with Phalgun, he might take you to be Dhruvaputra, he cannot see, he is hard of hearing too."

To Tamradhvaj, it occurred, as if the old man was swallowing his words, even disgorging them the next moment. He wished to speak out, again fear was getting the better of him. And he was narrating a fabricated tale. While narrating, he was losing the trail even. He, himself, could not even comprehend what he was saying. Tamradhvaj asked, "Then what had happened?"

"After what?" Parashar kept looking in a nonplussed gaze.

"Who talked about digging when all hopes for rains stood belied?"

"We floated the idea, all joined us".

"How could all speak the same in unison"?

He said, Suppose, if someone advises to cut the soil in the hope of water, then all would join in the demand, let the earth be dug in! When the people were threatened with the possibility of the drought continuing for years, with the rivers drying up gradually, with no sign of water left anywhere, with the exodus of the King, with the merchant leaving the city along with his retinue of traders, the Army Commander along with the soldiers, even Lord Mahakaal! At that moment if anyone suggests, "Let the lake be dug deeper, the water is there beneath the surface of earth", then all would cry out in unison, "Yes, let it be dug"! One Phalgun, after having his bath, Dhruvaputra said, The water-level drops during the months of Phalgun and Chaitra, "Let the water remaining in the lake be siphoned out and let the pond be dug deeper so that the water from the nether region comes up and again it would be able to contain more rainwater during monsoon".

Tamradhvaj's query was put, "Then what followed"?

When the matter of digging the pond arose, everyone was sure that water would come up and if so happened, all would be saved. All were apprehending that Nature would provide us with no water, the water underground even belonged to Nature alias Lord Mahakaal! Those who were talking about leaving, they kept thinking of death, giving up all hopes and watching the vultures in the sky, they said, "Let us try for once. It made the people think that something effective could be done, if water could be coaxed out! Sky, too, would be kind enough to bless us with a downpour".

"Will it surface"?

"Yes, that is our assumption. The sky will have its mirror to look at its own face in the lake, and the lake in turn would get to see its face in the sky, as there's no water underneath, there's no water up above as well, none loves the other, Dhruvaputra is not here anymore, people have nothing at all."

Tamradhvaj thought that, Dhruvaputra had gone away in such a manner that his departure was being reminisced by all and sundry, at each moment. That's why, though he had left, he was still there among them. The Chief of the Shudras,the old man of the village was then sitting beneath the Neem tree, on a flat slab of stone and kept saying, "He used to sit here too, if I would come, he used to make me sit here and he, himself would sit on the ground below".

Tamradhvaj looked up towards the sky. Cloudless, thoroughly hard and dry, how lighted was the distant field, that being the east. Tamradhvaj thought, it might be that Dhruvaputra never used to come here, all these are cock-and-bull stories, wholly cooked up by the village-Chief. While thinking, Tamradhvaj became anxious. Dhruvaputra was in no way comparable to anyone, at all. If anyone would come to the Shudra ghetto to have rice, it would be none but Dhruvaputra.

Tamradhvaj asked, "Under such heat of the sun, how is the work being done"?

"In the morning a spell of work will be done, then again in the afternoon. Just a few days back, it was full-moon, the work continued through the night, that day itself the work had begun and all were relieved to be assigned with this task".

"How were they relieved"?

"All have come to understand that there is a possibility of water welling up from the nether region of the earth, if so, they will lift it, the water will be of everyone, the pond will be deeper, rainwater will be stored in there during monsoon. But who are you, Sir? You talk very much like Dhruvaputra."

"Did Dhruvaputra speak like this"?

"Yes, he did, he used to ask us minutely, no point could be glossed over. Go and see, Sir, numerous stone slabs are there, a large slab has fallen, that has to be removed from there".

Tamradhvaj began to walk towards the lake, slowly. Many men had been on the edge, many of them thronged below. Black soil was coming up from underneath—soft, moist— that soil was getting deposited on one end of the edge. The two sides of the lake were high while the other two were a bit low, in the west the soil on the acclivity had gone steep, the nature of the land was likewise. The water from the other end came to be accumulated in the lake from the inclined margin, the eastern side was broken and hence a bit depressed and from that end the earth was cascading down. As Tamradhvaj went to stand at that end, everyone's work had come to an abrupt standstill. Nearly twenty men were chopping earth with axe, digging tool, lance. Some of them even had proper earth-cutters too, a spade, for example. All the men kept looking at Tamradhvaj. Someone in a low voice said, "Lord"!

Tamradhvaj replied, "I am none".

"Lord"! The men, being surprised, bowed down to Tamradhvaj, in respect.

Tamradhvaj said, "Do your own work".

All began to mind their work of chopping earth, bending their bodies. Five men were trying hard to remove a huge chunk of a heavily charred stone but kept failing to do so. The old Village-Chief was talking about that stone only. Tamradhvaj called out, "Listen, everyone"!

"Tell us, oh Lord!" All of them stopped working again.

"That stone has to be removed".

"Let the earth be chopped a little more", someone from among them spoke out.

"That stone has impeded the water from flowing, it seems".

"Water! All the men expressed their delight in unison".

Tamradhvaj asked, "How did the stone emerge, has it come up from underneath the earth, was it lying covered?"

"Yes, my Lord!"

"Can you remove the stone?"

"It is very heavy! We've tried our best",someone put forth.

Tamradhvaj got to understand that it was a giant stone, almost like a knoll. It stood hidden under the earth. It was ashen-red in colour and it bore numerous scars on it. It occurred to Tamradhvaj that perhaps water would surely spurt out if that stone could be removed. Again, it might not happen. The lake had been dug anew. But no trace of water could be found. Tamradhvaj had a fear that no water would ever re-surface. Water had been sucked inside the hell, perhaps. While chopping off the earth, these men would get fatigued at one point in time, they would feel dejected, then? Then how would the Village-Head stop them? Just for a few days they had worked, such a big pond would need much longer to be dug for making it deeper. But moist clods of earth had surfaced already. Were these moist clods the memories of the lost and happier times of Ratnakarsagar? Or did it bear the sign of water, latent in its womb?

A horde of men kept chopping the earth. Another team kept throwing the earth on the sides, fetching them in bamboo- and wicker-baskets. There were even women who were lifting the earth. Tamradhvaj heard some of them crooning, while chopping the earth. Another one was singing in unison with the former. Thus, one after another began to join in. They kept singing in chorus. Unintelligible song, Tamradhvaj could not understand, but it had tune in it. That tune reminded him of Kalamukhi village. He seemed to listen to the same number, as heard in that village. The same tune seemed to have come down as a tradition. In keeping with the rhythm of the song, the lance, shovel, axe and spade began to strike together. The people with earth on their heads began to come up in queue, in droves, singing. They began to ascend, synchronising their physical rhythm with that of the song. Among them, someone began to cry out in his own language, a peculiar harmony was created in that language too, in his shout, a tune seemed to be heard. Some of them began to join him in his singing. While mingling voices, someone came apart to expand his hands to the sky, Tamradhvaj looked to find her to be a young maiden. Pouring the earth on the edge of the lake, she sang out in a melodious voice,

"No water, no cloud, no man of my heart inside my mind— no, none, dear"!

Almost everyone sang in unison with her. Thus earth-chopping went on. From one number to the other, from one tune to another, the working men kept drifting along. Tamradhvaj raised his hands to bid goodbye to them: "Let me go".

The people, busy in digging the ground, stood up and said, "Come again, my lord"!

"Come again, Lord!" Twirling his neck backward, Tamradhvaj noticed that the old Village Headman was greeting him, "Will the water come up, Sir"?

Tamradhvaj rejoined, "Yes, it will".

Parashar then cried out to say, "Our lord says that water is not far below, come, dig the ground, without water there's no meaning of existence."

From the hollow bosom of Ratnakarsagar, the people shouted, "Water is not far off anymore, Lord knows all, Lord says!"

Tamradhvaj was coming down from the edge of the pond. Parashar was at his heels. While descending, without turning back, Tamradhvaj said, "If the water doesn't surface"?

"Please Sir, do not say so". He got to hear a muffled cry of anguish.

"If it happens thus?"

Parashar went on, "If water comes up, it is for the well-being of one and all, not just the Shudras will be saved, all of Ujjwain will spring up to life!"

"Who will take water from this Ratnakarsagar lake, from this Shudra ghetto? Which Brahmin?" Tamradhvaj turned around after throwing the query.

They had come down from the edge of the pond. The Village- Headman's face seemed to be strangely aglow, he said, "The other six ponds which are there, need to be dug up then!"

"And if water is not found even then?"

"None will be here anymore!"

"Where will they go?"

"Someplace else, to some other city or village, and men are fleeing, on the sly!"

"Why on the sly?"

"The man is being followed by his wife and children, hence he is escaping stealthily, on fleeing he thinks that wherever he would go, everything must be there. Even the merchant is escaping, oh Lord!"

Tamradhvaj came to stand in the shadows of the Neem tree. There, yonder there, Shivnath was seen to sit back and relax upon the banyan roots. Sitting up straight all night, he seemed to gain strength. Shivnath stretched his legs. It was so soothing beneath the banyan tree! A gentle breeze had left Shivnath's body numb, indolent.

Parashar said, "They think that they will be able to go somewhere else, unaffected by such drought. Rice, young maiden, fallow, arable lands will be there along with forests, rivers, ponds as in here, but to their utter dismay, they will go there to find nothing at all"!

Tamradhvaj asked, "If water does not surface, will the men flee away?"

"If they escape, they will face death, I have to find ways to hold them back here. I am the man who is here for most of my life, much earlier than almost all of them, I was born in here, I had a job with the royal battery of soldiers here, I know if something is missing in Ujjwain, it cannot be had anywhere else. If Ujjwain is cloudless, where else on earth can we find clouds? Come on, tell me, oh Lord! If something is not available in Ujjwain, nowhere else it can be found. So, who will go to which place?"

"Tell them so."

"No amount of narration will do, the people are saying that they will go for a makeover, the men are thinking of grabbing this opportunity, a couple of men have been caught red-handed while escaping, leaving their wife and children behind. They say they will begin life anew."

Tamradhvaj looked at them with wonder in his eyes. The Village-Headman went rocking as he kept uttering these words, while speaking he halted and kept resuming. If drought happens or rainfall becomes scanty, such things are known take place. Men think in sundry ways, dream umpteen alike. Men thought they would flee off from here to start everything afresh. Young maidens with auspicious omens, clouds, rivers, lakes full to the brim, fields abounding in crops, seemed to await them. Alack, this is man! Inwardly, they knew that they were inching towards death, again each day, surprisingly, they were dreaming of having a rebirth. If Parashar failed to keep them back in here, with whom would he stay himself? It was just finding out such tricks to save oneself! If water did not surface, he knew of nothing else but dying! In which way else could he remain alive?

SIXTY-FOUR

On his return from the Chief Physician, Nahush Sharman, the pimp, Mahaparshwa, seemed to be deployed as the sentry of Chaturika's dwelling. What else could the pimp do? The people from the other countries were dropping by in the city. All day long, he would have to hang about the streets and stand dust-laden. It was rather more comfortable for him to sit at the threshold of Chaturika's residence. In the meantime, Mahaparshwa had performed a deed one evening, while sitting in a tavern to drink, he had informed Uddhavnarayan that his mistress had vanished. Uddhav should not dare look at Chaturika anymore.

Uddhav was taken aback, "What do you say, hey bastard"?

"I am speaking just the truth."

"Have you ever spoken the truth in your life?"

"Listen you Sessions-Judge Sir, the merchant is now fond of Chaturika, and why not, she is so youthful, so charming!"

Uddhav then tried to make out, who the pimp was referring to. He heard the name but in a fit of inebriation, something else he might have heard. He asked again, "Which whore are you talking of?"

"Why, Chaturika, the whore, lady-luck has smiled on her at last"!

"Oh, that she-cat, you mean the pussycat! What's wrong with her"?

"Nothing as such! She is accompanying the merchant on his trade-tour, the tycoon is taking along women, by selection."

Hearing this, Uddhav was about to choke and hiccup. Did the merchant lose his mental balance or was this rogue lying? Was there any dearth of beautiful women in the world? That pussycat, at last? No doubt, she was youthful, but during youth who didn't have the charms or the beauty? The female donkeys, who used to walk

491

down the road, looked no less charming, they would sashay and jig their ears while walking, but would they draw any attention at all? He could not believe him. He, after all, knew the ways and demeanours of this pimp! That time, when the merchant had almost forced him dismount from the horse on the main thoroughfare, this pimp came up with vulgar, nasty remarks! In fact, Chaturika was a part of that incident too. The ornaments he made off with from her house landed him in trouble, to be precise. Uddhav, however, had successfully managed all by himself. Being suspicious, Uddhavnarayan had asked Mahaparshwa, "Who told you"?

"Why, the merchant had sent his emissary".

"Tell me the truth!"

"I am telling the truth in the name of Lord Mahakaal!"

Hearing that, Uddhavnarayan felt withdrawn. His hunch was that it might have been true! The ornaments which the merchant had offered, adorned Chaturika, after all. Chaturika was not her former self anymore. The way in which she looked, the diction in which she spoke were all strange to Uddhav, he could not understand the head or tail of it. She had learnt a few dance 'mudra's even, she was mastering the art of Veena-playing too — all these might have been for the merchant only! None would ever be able to predict who would fall for whom! Uddhav must have to be cautious from now.

Mahaparshwa became successful. Uddhav had stopped dropping by. He had already been irregular as Chaturika's income had touched a low, he failed to extort much money. And on learning this from Mahaparshwa, the venomous serpent had gone into hibernation, underground. Till the drought was over, he would not be back to his former self again.

Sometimes on Chaturika's threshold, sometimes on the edge of her courtyard, beneath the kadam tree Mahaparshwa was seen sitting alone. Chaturika was sure that the sly, malicious pimp had no courage to enter her room. She knew him quite well. She knew him intimately in the earlier times, though that had nothing to do with his present self. Really the man had undergone drastic change! Perhaps such would be natural if clouds remained absent from the sky for long! The merchant felt a prick of love for her and Mahaparshwa, the pimp, changed into a better leaf!

Chaturika watched the dark face of the roguish pimp. He seemed to be happy just with her flash of smile, a call, or the tinkle of the bells of her anklet. Happy! It was as if the purpose of his existence would be fulfilled if he could get a glimpse of Chaturika's face. However, Chaturika knew what sort of man this pimp was! As the drought was telling upon his destiny, the pimp stayed like that. He would become a real man in course of time. How long would a man be content on getting to look at a woman? Sly men are like the vultures in the sky! The adjutant storks would swoop down on the earth, waiting for the dying creature to breathe its last. Once done, it would inch towards the dead being. The vulture knew that the waiting was worth it. It would reap him good result.It might get a whole corpse even, men are mostly like that. Some are fierce dogs, as the Royal Sessions-Judge Uddhavnarayan, once seen he would pounce upon to have a feast on the beast of prey's flesh, and some are like adjutant storks, as Mahaparshawa was. Mahaparshwa knew that if he hurried, Chaturika would slip off through his clutch. Chaturika would never look for his service.

Yonder, Mahaparshwa sat like a servant. Today he was a servant, tomorrow the table might turn, and Chaturika might be his serving-maid. For her, Mahaparshwa used to go to the river to fetch water, at the crack of dawn, before the sunlight made its presence felt. Chaturika knew well that she would not be getting such service from Mahaparshwa all her life. Given an opportunity, he would hiss up, holding his hood straight. She even knew more, that she had been kept under strict vigil. He would never allow her to move away beyond his ken. It made Chaturika sometimes angry, sometimes empathetic. She would take bath sitting in the terrace. Why would that scoundrel keep ogling at her, while having bath? Just after she thought that he was her servant, he would carry out her orders. Presently, such was going on in her life. Hence, it hardly would matter whether Mahaparshwa watched her or not. Rather, if looking at her he served her more, that would certainly be her gain. One day, she called out to Mahaparshwa, who was sitting idle, "Hey you rogue, come here".

Mahaparshwa started, "Are you calling me, Chaturika?"

"Why do you sit back like that?"

"I love to do so."

"Come here, rub my heels with this pumice-stone, come!"

Strange! Mahaparshwa did as she ordered him. He did not cast any glance anywhere else save the heels, even by mistake. While she removed the cover from her breasts to pour water on them, Mahaparshwa did not raise his head even after sensing it.

A while ago, she called Mahaparshwa in the afternoon and said, "Hey you knave, come listen to me, why doesn't the barber's wife, the female-barber, come?"

"I can't say, perhaps she has left, people are leaving, you know."

"Who will help me to paint the borders of my feet with lac-dye?"

"Shall I be on the look-out for her?"

"No", sticking out one foot, Chaturika said, "You have cleaned heels with the pumice-stone, it would be better if you paint the edges of my feet, if the merchant drops in".

Mahaparshwa smeared lac dye on her feet. He decorated her feet. Superseding the female-barber in skill, he asked, "So, is it fine?"

"Yes, this much will do, after all you're a male".

"Okay let it be so then?"

"Do not escape, you rogue, if the merchant comes over!"

Mahaparshwa tilted his neck like an obedient servant. Chaturika had seen how Mahaparshwa was trembling while daubing her feet with the lac-dye. His body was visibly perspiring. His eyes were narrowing, his breath was quickening, as men usually have during sexual union. Chaturika knew that the pimp would draw a line here and now, as he was keeping quiet in fear of the merchant, Subhag Dutta. Otherwise, he would have a feast on her flesh as a tiger. After all, the pimp was a man! He had enough strength in his sinews. But how could anyone else be so cunning like him? If he failed, he would call for either Uddhav or the ilk. He would have incited them to attack her! She would be happy to accompany the merchant now. How long would she keep the teeth of a mad dog at bay?

Chaturika would go away, leaving the city for good. After such a long time, at last, her God of Destiny, Lord Mahakaal had been kind to her, finally. The merchant had called for her. Chaturika could feel that her life was changing after a long wait. The drought had come to her as a blessing in disguise. If there had been no drought, would the merchant set out on trade at this time of the year, after such a long interregnum? No, he would not. He was carrying on business transaction with the foreign traders, being here in Ujjwain. That fetched him heaps of gold coin! The merchant was setting out on this journey under compulsion. The city was getting evacuated gradually. Some were leaving stealthily, some did by blowing a bugle aloud, as the merchant was heading on to Balkh. There were clouds in the sky of that land, there was thunder in those clouds, there was rain. In the rivers of that land, water coursed down, the acres of land had crops aplenty, people had abundant gold coins and mohurs pouring in their coffers. Chaturika knew that she would be free again once she went to Balkh, along with the merchant. In that land, a handsome Ionian Greek youth was awaiting her. None would be there like Uddhav. Now the journey was about to begin. This city was not a place to inhabit anymore. She was lucky, drought continued. Clouds were not there. Clouds did not surface. If clouds would be there, would they be able to alter her fortune? Certainly, the merchant would not call her then. Long drought would be like this, many inched towards death, luck of many again altered too. As there had been drought, she could bid adieux to this ruthless existence, this fire-burnt city, this habitation of Alakshmi. This city had been engulfed by shadows of sheer misfortune, death had come to rest on its crown, now an escape from here would be the only solution. Ah! When would she reach that magic city, where abundance was the watchword, where life was blessed with joy!

Chaturika called out to Mahaparshwa in the evening, "Mahaparshwa, brother Mahaparshwa"!

Standing on the threshold, Mahaparshwa objected to it, "Why do you call me 'brother', Chaturika?"

Chaturika smiled to say, "Then let me call you 'lover', oh my lover, go and find out when the merchant will set sail".

Mahaparshwa retorted, "He will send a messenger once he decides to leave!"

"No, no, he has called for me, if I do not ask, he may think that I am rejecting him like Devadutta!"

Stamping his feet on the ground in the dark, Mahaparshwa said, "No, no, why will he think so?"

"Go, reach him my concern! And ask him."

Yet Mahaparshwa hummed and hawed, "Would it be wise to ask of our own accord?"

Chaturika got annoyed, she said under her breath, "You would come to feel when I shall keep you twirling on your toe! Before I leave, I shall ask the merchant to flog you, pinning you down on the street of the city, if the merchant comes to know that you drink the nectar of my beauty secretly, he might even set you on fire to get burnt to death like Utanka, who can tell? Being a dwarf, you dream of reaching up to the moon! For you, a washer-man's female-donkey would suffice or at the most, a hen! Phew!"

Watching Chaturika to maintain studied silence, Mahaparshwa again added, "If the merchant takes you along, he will definitely send his litter borne by four bearers or a chariot for you, why would you have to go yourself to confirm?"

Chaturika thought that Mahaparshwa was mocking at her. "'Litter, borne by four bearers or a chariot'"! As if, she was no match for him at all! Let the palanquin or the chariot wait, she must go to the merchant's house, on foot. She furiously snapped at Mahaparshwa, "You don't have to think so much, you arrant knave, do as I ask you to do or else get lost from my sight, if ever any work is done by you properly!"

This medicine only worked wonder. In the dark of the evening, Mahaparshwa set out on his journey. The moon was yet to rise, but he started off. He had no trouble in walking in the dark rather he used to see through the darkness better. Sending him, Chaturika kept waiting for his return, for the news he would fetch! What would he say, what would he get to learn?

The way stretched quite long. No doubt, tall and lanky Mahaparshwa walked at a fast pace, with his long legs, but it would take long as he would reach there, wait for the merchant and again retrace his steps back home. Chaturika might have to wait all night. When would Mahaparshwa get the opportunity to talk to the merchant, who could tell? Chaturika began to gaze at the stars in the sky.

After a long wait, lady-luck at last smiled on her. Her fortune began to be kind to her! She was going to be free of all bonds with this city. Getting free of this city would mean being free of this squalid life! Chaturika's eyelids began to droop as the southern breeze blew. She learnt that whatever this city of Ujjwain lacked in, Balkh had all that to offer. Clouds,rains, lakes full to the brim with water, flower arbours – everything . She heard that in that land, there was no difference between the beautiful and the ugly, between the cat-eyed and the blue-eyed! There no one was a prostitute and again all who were so, enjoyed the status of Devadutta! There the royal servants were gentle in nature, kind-hearted. No one would be there like Uddhavnarayan to snatch all she would possess. Chaturika kept praying silently- let the drought continue. The merchant might postpone his journey if it rained and later would the merchant ever think of her?

Mahaparshwa came back quite soon. Then the moon was up in the sky. The moonbeams had cascaded down on her courtyard. Mahaparshwa was panting for breath. He sat at a little distance, squatting. He kept quiet. Even Chaturika stayed silent, looking at him. A little later, Mahaparshwa said, "I went almost running and came back running too".

"Did you cover such a long distance by running?!"

Mahaparshwa rejoined, "I said 'almost running', don't you know how fast I can walk!"

"Any news?"

"Yes, got it". Proffering a curt rejoinder, he fell quiet. Chaturika felt enthused at his reticence. Then, Mahaparshwa had really come back with an authentic news! Mahaparshwa did not want her to leave Ujjwain along with the merchant. Chaturika felt at the end of her breath, avidly waiting to listen to Mahaparshwa. Mahaparshwa seemed to doze off, as if he was reluctant to come up with the news.

"What news you got, tell me"! Chaturika demanded of Mahaparshwa.

It seemed as if Mahaparshwa was nudged out of sleep to rejoin, "That Chief-Physician is really a madcap, his words are not true!"

Chaturika's face dimmed to darkness, losing its glow. She began to watch Mahaparshwa, quite minutely. The knave was yawning. Did he go there to bring such news? The moon seemed to have slipped behind an unfamiliar tree. And amidst all these, it drooped down. In a harsh voice, Chaturika charged, "Did you go there at all, Mahaparshwa, tell me the truth, come on!"

"Yes, I did."

"Whom did you meet"?

"The merchant".

"Did you get to see the merchant?"

"Yes, I did."

"What did the merchant say?"

"The Chief Physician is a madcap".

"Swear in the name of Lord Mahakaal and say that you had got to meet the merchant"!

Mahaparshwa kept mum. The doubt seemed to be true. Sitting there, glum and reticent, for quite some time as he was about to get to his feet, Chaturika thundered, "Hey thou scoundrel, sit down, tell me is it a lie?"

Mahaparshwa kept quiet. What to say being caught red-handed? And it drove Chaturika to be certain that, Mahaparshwa hadn't gone there apprehending he would come to know about the date and time of the merchant's departure. Mahaparshwa knew everything. He used to roam around the city all day long, why wouldn't he know? Chaturika roared, " Thou shall never come to my place anymore, must not sit here, make sure that I never see thy face".

Mahaparswa got frightened. If he was debarred from coming here, to Chaturika's place, if he was disallowed from fetching water for Chaturika, if he was not allowed to see Chaturika having her bath, if he could not feel blessed by looking at Chaturika's moon-shaped face, then what for would he continue to live? He, too, would leave the city for somewhere else. Many people were leaving, he too would follow suit. Go off he must, but how would he leave Chaturika alone? Chaturika would continue to stay in Ujjwain, and he would leave in search of rain clouds to some other city, where abundance of resources was assured!! All would be there, save Chaturika! Absence of Chaturika meant a big vacuum to him! A sense of nullity! Mahaparshwa looked on at Chaturika with a dark, gloomy face.

Chaturika roared, "How dare thou hold the truth back from me?"

Mahaparshwa said, "No, I shall not do it again".

"Thou can't be trusted, thou, the filth of garbage bin, are thou fit enough to sit in here, thou are the dust from below the feet of the merchant!"

Mahaparshwa reasoned, "I was about to go, but while approaching, I found the chariot of the merchant was heading towards the King's palace!"

"Why didn't thou stop the carriage carrying the merchant, Utanka is no more, hope thou know?!"

"None was there in the chariot, Chaturika!"

"Then who was there, how did thou recognize it to be the merchant's chariot?"

"I know it, again who doesn't know the chariot belonging to the merchant, even the vacant chariot would leave no chance for any mistake!"

"If a 'vacant chariot', then why did thou come back?"

"I understood that the merchant was there in the palace"!

"Again thou are lying"?

"No, Chaturika!"

"If thou lie, be sure to find me dead!"

Immediately on hearing such words, tall and lanky Mahaparshwa broke down, seemed to collapse on the ground, bending down to cry out, "I hadn't gone!"

"Then where had thou been for so long?"

"I sat there, by the meadows in the dark and decided to return just as the moon would be up in the sky".

"Really? Telling the truth?"

"Yes, just the truth, if thou leave with the merchant, where shall I go, Chaturika?"

Chaturika said, "If these words reach the merchant's ear, will thou be allowed to live?"

"No, I shall not be allowed to live", pat came Mahaparshwa's rejoinder.

"Thou must go tomorrow morning quite early, lest forget to see my face!"

Mahaparshwa said, "If I fail to see the merchant"?

"Thou should keep waiting, but make sure to bring the news"!

Mahaparshwa drooped his neck on one side. Chaturika was ordering him, and he was waiting for her command since long, it seemed. Mahaparshwa thought that he was the serving-boy to Chaturika, servant of all servants. He would do as Chaturika would command. He would be able to put up with Chaturika's kick, such was his allegiance to her! It would be great pleasure if a man would become the servant of the woman he loved. The life would be blessed with a sense of fulfilment. He muttered, "I must obey whatever be thy command!"

"Then be off now".

"It is night now, look how the moon rising so late has reached the mid-sky and now it would roll down to set".

"Whatever it is, the merchant will now be back from the palace"!

"Who told thee"? Mahaparshwa was taken aback.

"Thou said now, that the empty chariot was heading on to the palace!"

Mahaparshwa answered, "That's a blatant lie. I didn't tell thee the truth"!

Chaturika began to sway her head from one end to the other, being flummoxed, "No, the way thou said, if it be a fib, how could thou utter it?"

Mahaparshwa smiled, "The moon was yet to bob up, how could the chariot run in the dark? And why would an empty chariot run, was it then the merchant who had gone to the palace on foot?"

"Why so, he must be going there by his chariot! Lighting a flambeau, he will go!"

"If he would go by a chariot, it would wait for him there in the palace itself", Mahaparshwa wanted to make her understand.

Chaturika said, "I don't know such things. Thou must go and find it out. If needed, go and lie down in front of the entrance of the merchant's residence. Whenever he will come in or go out, be it this evening or tomorrow morning, thou would kneel straight on his feet".

What would now Mahaparshwa do? He was in a real fix. Perhaps, loving a woman would land a man in such trouble! He had never thought of any woman in that manner. He was nothing more than a sentry guarding the entrance of a brothel, why would he take fancy on a woman, at all? But it had happened. This was passed on to him as a wont from his previous birth. While walking, Mahaparshwa kept thinking so. Mahaparshwa thought, In the previous birth, I had been an extremely handsome Gandharva. Falling in love was my destiny. I can even die for Chaturika. Chaturika, I want to be thy lover. How can a beloved hurt her lover so deeply? Or, did real joy in love rest in its pain?! Extremely lanky Mahaparshwa kept walking alone, in the desolate thoroughfare, in wobbly steps, in the moonlit night. He halted while walking. He kept thinking, Who will know whether I sat before the merchant's house, through the night or went off home to sleep the night away? Rather, I shall go back home. If I go there in the morning, that will suffice.

Mahaparshwa did not wait anymore. He came to the front of his hut taking a detour and felt utterly relieved. He sat stretching his legs to the fore. And then lay on his back in the courtyard. He slept off, lying supine. But that sleep was interrupted abruptly. He felt a combustion in his stomach. It was just as the roads and thoroughfares of Ujjwain getting heated up during noon. But he had no provision of meals at home. All day long, he remained engrossed in the beauty of Chaturika's face. And today, that whore hadn't even asked him to have anything. Mahaparshwa got to his feet. His grey cells used to work erratically if hunger gnawed in his entrails. What would he do now? Would he go to the harlot's place? Let me have something to eat, Chaturika, let me have rice and water, I am thy most obedient and humble servant, I am thy lapdog... Mahaparshwa staggered forward.

SIXTY-FIVE

Mahaparshwa was in deep trouble now. He could understand that Chaturika would not listen to his irrelevant lies anymore. So strange! Chaturika used to detect all his lies. Again, was there any other person in this city to emulate him in the art of lying? Mahaparshwa knew full well, that, even if he got to talk to the merchant, Subhag Dutta, he would not be able to tell her the truth. His words would remain in his mouth. He would cover them up with some other words! He would love to fabricate tales, his tongue would itch to blab it out! Then it would be Chaturika's duty to extract the truth through cross-examination. Chaturika was adept in it. Only to Chaturika, Mahaparshwa could not hold on to his fib for long! After all, he was in love with Chaturika!

He was Chaturika's servant and he was in love with her. He used to fetch water for her from far, at the break of dawn, when the sun was yet to announce its presence. As a crow looked for the leftovers, he used to sit likewise for having a glimpse of Chaturika's graceful face! And for listening to her voice. For being called by her! For being asked to do this or that for her! But he could not accomplish the chief task as yet! He was telling lies and was being proved a liar each time! How would he be able to do this? He promised to go to the merchant's residence, but being alone on the road his mind changed abruptly! It kept happening so. Was it natural for a person who was in love? Or was it because of the drought? Would this drought take Chaturika away from him?

Day before yesterday, he came back to Chaturika's place at the dead of night, driven by pricks of hunger! Then moonshine had receded from her courtyard. Lord Mahakaal had robbed the light, which originally was His! Standing in the darkness like an otherworldly spirit, he cried out, "Chaturika"!

The whore seemed not to sleep at all. A single call woke her up to make her unbolt the door and emerge out of the room to stand outside with a lamp in her hand to rejoin, "Who calls me at this odd hour of the night, who, is it the Chief Physician"?

Hungry Mahaparshwa's hopes were belied once again. She lay awake all night, hoping for a call of the merchant! Again, the lunatic Chief Physician would come to inform her when the merchant would call her, where would he wait for her in the evening! Mahaparshwa could feel that his rival was the merchant, Subhag Dutta. Being a tycoon, his wealth knew no limits! And he was just a beggar down the street. Mahaparshwa begged, "This is me Chaturika, all day long I got nothing to eat!"

"Mahaparshwa! Didn't you leave?"

"I had gone, but it is hunger that made me retrace my steps".

"You had gone and come back again?"

"Yes, Chaturika, can you offer me something to eat"?

"But didn't you go at all?"

"Yes, I did".

"Again, you are lying — tell me the truth"!

The truth was to be said. Strange! Without chiding him, Chaturika offered him to eat. Milk, sweetmeat made of powdered til, pulverized barley, sugarcane molasses and ripe plantains, were all she had to offer him. While having all the delicacies, Mahaparshwa thought that Chaturika definitely loved him and hence she could extinguish the fire of his hunger, so affectionately! Such was love! Finishing the food, while washing it away with water, he felt that he was longing for such love only! Who would feed him with such care? Nobody on earth. To douse the flames of hunger burning his entrails, a woman was the one, a man would turn to! Nobody else would be able to do it. He would not allow Chaturika to leave along with the tycoon. If needed, he would fall on the tycoon's feet to beg. Then he, himself, would leave this city with Chaturika! This city would not let him live happily. There was one Uddhavnarayan, if he would come to know each detail, he would again start dropping by! His wrath was dreary! He was no less cruel too. It would be far better to start life anew, going elsewhere, to escape his clutch. As Ujjwain kept reaching her such trouble, Chaturika would stay happily, in some other city. And he, himself, along with Chaturika! Mahaparshwa had thought of building a shack on the bank of a river. There the sun would be soft, the breeze would be cool, pleasant. The crop-fields would lie there for them, the clouds would hover over the sky, the rains would be generous on their fields and the royal servants would be suave and polite. The retinue of soldiers. The virtuous King. None would ever turn their eyes to them, none would mean any harm to them. That city would not have any brothel, any whore, and hence there would be no accursed Gandharva, no pimp. In that city, there would be no sly, damned liar like him! Such absence would surely make him come clean out of his nature. Being released from the curse, he might again get back the previous form of a Gandharva. Once he was back in the former shape, Chaturika would look up to him as a man. As a 'man' to be coveted. Chaturika would cast amorous glance at him. Chaturika would fix him with a desirous stare. She would grow fond of him. It all might happen if the merchant spared Chaturika to go along with him to the country of Balkh. Then, Chaturika would learn to depend on him. She would then want to live, falling back on him for support.

Mahaparshwa failed to go to the merchant's house though he came out saying so. He was hanging about the streets of the city. What would he do? He could neither go back to Chaturika nor approach the merchant for scrounging the information regarding his date of setting sail and the day on which Chaturika would come and join him.

He was dozing, slouching beneath a kadam tree, by the road. Sleep was eluding him at night. During daytime too, he was not getting any respite. What would he do now? Right then, two men, one elderly and another young, came to address him, "Do you hear, Sir?"

Just beneath the kadam tree 'Sir' sat, only to listen to them. Mahaparshwa sat up straight. His sly eyes could make out that they were not well conversant with the goings-on of the city. They were new to the city. But his memory was too sharp. He thought of seeing them before. Perhaps, days ago, in the streets of Ujjwain. Though not from the city, they hailed from its vicinity. Each day, people used to come to the city, in droves. Either to the royal court or in search of a royal servant or for trade or for buying and selling. And again, many of them used to come for no reason at all. To explore the city, to go around the city. Many again used to come to say their wish to Lord Mahakaal, to bow down to Lord Mahakaal. After a cursory visit to Lord Mahakaal, they would look for a brothel. The variety of entertainments this city had to offer would in no way be emulated by any other place. Lately, owing to drought, people kept escaping this city on the one hand and many kept pouring in, on the other. They came hoping, as Lord Mahakaal was there, as the King resided there, the city must be blessed with clouds and good amount of rainfall.

Mahaparshwa asked, "Any need"?

"Do you belong to this city"?

Mahaparshwa answered, "I think so, this is my place of birth, my workplace as well".

Tamradhvaj said, "We are here on a purpose".

"Who are you, wherefrom are you coming, what for are you here, whom do you want to meet?"

As Tamradhvaj kept introducing himself, Mahaparshwa sat up taut and said, "He has left the city. I heard that he had gone to Kalinga in the North."

The speaker's depth of knowledge impressed Tamradhvaj. The city used to abound in such men. They would pretend to know a lot but in reality, knew nothing at all.

He said, "But Kalinga is in the South".

"No, it is in the North, I heard it from the Army-Commander and the King corroborated too".

"What do you say"?

"He has gone to the North, to Kalinga, I heard myself, but what is your purpose"?

Tamradhvaj took him to be a depraved man, who used to live on mean ways to earn his bread. How would he help them with any information? But such men would while their time away on the thoroughfares. They used to take note of everything. They were curious to know about everything they would come across. Such men would be of help to let them know what had taken place that day. How had the merchant's servant struck Dhruvaputra? How far had Dhruvaputra been involved with Devadutta? The merchant had banished Dhruvaputra from the city, but why? Was this banishment accorded to him by the King or the Army-Commander?

Mahaparshwa felt that they were not ordinary citizens that he would con them to earn some quick money and disappear! If he could be of some help to them, he would be able to get something in return. After such a long wait, he got something worthwhile to do. How long would he sit beneath the kadam tree? He would have to get up from there in sometime to roam around the city, aimlessly, under the blinding heat of the sun! For a while to the merchant's house and again to the main thoroughfare! Where else would he go? Chaturika, perhaps, had relaxed on the bed to catch her forty winks by now, in a dark room! In her sleep, she might get to see the merchant even! But Chaturika would not get to see him though she intended to do so in her dreams. Even after losing herself in sleep, thinking deeply of the merchant, she might see Mahaparshwa in her dreams! Perhaps, she was getting her body scrubbed by him! He might pour the sandal-scented water on the naked body of Chaturika. Perhaps, he was daubing white sandal paste on the two breasts of Chaturika! In her youth, Chaturika would have no parallel! Even the Chief Prostitute, Devadutta, would not be such titillating in her sex-appeal. Such was Mahaparshwa's view! He had never raised his head to look at Devadutta. He did not have that courage at all. Devadutta was a star, far-off in the sky, hardly visible, Chaturika was the moon instead. If thought of, she would be a tangible reality. She could be touched in his dreams. In the moonshine she could be bathed, though not belonging to him, he could take her as his own.

Tamradhvaj asked, "Do you remember Dhruvaputra, the son of Dhruva?"

Though he remembered well, Mahaparshwa feigned ignorance and asked in turn, "Whose son?"

"Dhruvaputra, who had been here, sheltered by the merchant!"

"Oh, yes! That nincompoop who had been beaten black and blue by Utanka, he would have been killed if I had not intervened by stopping the lash, however those things are long over, Utanka also is no more, the merchant is also setting out for Balkh with Chaturika, the whore. This drought spelt disaster to some and to some again it was the best of times!"

"Could you please introduce yourself?" Shivnath requested.

"How to introduce myself, if taken to the King, He would recognize me, the merchant too would, the whores too, even Devadutta would— that is what I am."

"Where does she reside"? Tamradhvaj asked.

"Who is this 'she' you are referring to?"

"Devadutta, the whore!" Tamradhvaj inquired again.

Mahaparshwa tried to get the import of the question, remaining silent. Did these two men begin to beat about the bush? Actually, they wanted to know where the courtesan Devadutta resided. Hence such circumlocution, while trying to scrounge one information, deviating his attention to some other! Who could look for Devadutta's residence? He, who would be able to pay her handsomely. For that, being rich was a must. But these men were not looking rich, though Mahaparshwa, the pimp, knew that the affluent ones from the village would never show off their riches. Their appearance would never testify to the wealth they possessed or how capable they were of maintaining a number of prostitutes for themselves! Hence, Mahaparshwa became wary and said, "Sirs, what do you want to know? Of whom? How can I answer if not spoken specifically?"

Tamradhvaj said, "Whereabouts of Dhruvaputra… please help us, you will surely stay blessed."

Hearing 'stay blessed', Mahaparshwa was suddenly impressed. He would then have Chaturika, 'staying blessed' would surely mean it. The Merchant would abandon her. He would leave this city with Chaturika. As he learnt this in the prime time of morning, it would surely come true. He asked, "Why do you need to know of him"?

Tamradhvaj explained the exigency at length. He introduced Shivnath to him.

While listening, Tamradhvaj thought, whether he would speak the truth or a lie! A fib could easily be fabricated, but would that be of any help to these men? They said that if he helped them, it would fetch him good fortune. If he wished for his own well-being, he would never be able to lie. But what would he say at all? Dhruvaputra was sheltered by the merchant. And was fond of Devadutta, the whore. Usually, the men would have a mistress as his keep but as he had become the servant of Chaturika, likewise Dhruvaputra was heard to be devoted to Devadutta, almost like a servant! He also narrated what he knew, whatever he had witnessed during his rounds in and around the city. He had not seen anything from close quarters but from a distance! He heard all from far too. The truth which floated in the air of the city-roads and lanes with ramifications and embellishments, would hardly reveal the basic truth which lay inside it, hidden somewhere and it was really difficult to find it out. Men would always speak out their surmises. Would the manner in which Chaturika kept oppressing him, day in, day out, sending him for gleaning information about the other men, making him work as a lady-barber, tally with the case of Dhruvaputra and Devadutta? Could Devadutta make Dhruvaputra work in the same manner? No, it hardly seemed to be so. The merchant was caught between the two whores. One was, harlot Chaturika, who had almost given up food and sleep only for the merchant, the other was Devadutta, the courtesan, who used to treat the merchant as Chaturika treated Mahaparshwa! Weighing thus, Mahaparshwa thought that the merchant could not win the heart of Devadutta even after coaxing her with whatever he possessed. Then why would he be blamed? He had nothing save his mind, a heart and the right to love and this unwieldy,fear-inducing stature of a lanky man!

Shivnath said, "What do you know of Dhruvaputra, Sir"?

"I know indeed".

"Did he frequent the Shudra ghetto?"

This was new to him. How would Mahaparshwa know all such details? His whole day would have been spent in managing clients for the whores! At that time, traders, foreigners, scions of rich families used to come over in search of pleasure and leave this city thereafter, quite regularly. The brothel ran with elan and was abuzz with clients. No room lay unoccupied. In the evening, all the rooms were lit up with lamps. Sandalwood, the scent of aguru ruled the roost, while during monsoon the air stood heavy with the sweet fragrance of swarnachampak, jasmine and malati. Once taking the path, the men from other lands used to reach the brothel, enticed by such sweet fragrance. Those days were golden indeed! Tears welled up to Mahaparshwa's eyes. During monsoon, winter or Spring — people had no dearth of joy at any moment. Would ever those days come back again? Then too, Chaturika had been there! But

Mahaparshwa used to feel no attraction towards her at that time! He did not have much time then! He used to be on the road almost late into the night. Which man of which house was enjoying secretly the woman of which other place, he would have to keep abreast of all such information to extract money from them. Now, everything had stopped. He had almost run out of business. As he had no work in hand, his love for the whore was soaring, day by day! If there would have been no drought, this situation would never arise then! Drought had ruined him, for sure. Again, drought had spiced up his life with a different sort of feelings. Sometimes, he would think that life without love was so ugly! But because of Chaturika's neglect, he was even looking for a gradual relief from love as well.

Flicking off the dust from his body, "Mahaparshwa said, Of course, he used to frequent there, and topping all, he had become an obedient servant of the harlot, a trusted servant to be precise"!

"How so"? Tamradhvaj was a bit flabbergasted, he had never heard of such a thing before!

"Look, in absence of a serving-maid, he himself used to paint the feet of the woman with lac-dye. Preceding that, he used to rub her heels clean with a pumice-stone! Fie on him!"

Shivnath had shrunken in disgust, he asked, "What all nonsense you say? Oh God, he had such a downfall! Knowledge, pursuit of learning — all got razed to dust!"

"Yes, everything got ruined! Attraction of a woman could annul every other thing! And again, if the woman kept playing, taking him as a pawn, then the whole affair would be a miserable mess. If a woman could not be tamed, the life of a man would go in vain, a few men were there who would turn into faithful slaves of the women, they were no less than domestic pets like cats or dogs in real life."

Shivnath stopped him short, "Stop it, don't go ahead, are we in the city to learn such abominable things"?!

Mahaparshwa heaved a long sigh, seized his hairs in a tight clutch with both hands and said, "Again, can a woman be really like that? If we so desire, we can enjoy five women at one go, we can even outrage her modesty by dragging her down to the woods, and as we do it, the women stay meek and polite, a rung lower in status. But what had gone wrong with your Dhruvaputra, he was no less than a woman himself! The whore used to go naked in front of him but he had no right to look at any of her limbs, let alone touch it."

Tamradhvaj asked, "Are you speaking the truth"?

"Is there any other way than telling the truth, Sir? Can't you see what's going on around us, now we all have to speak the truth only, in the hope of altering the situation with the force of truth! In this city, not a whit of fib is doing rounds anymore. Only the truth has to be spoken, none is lending any ear to anything but the truth, whatever you will get to hear now in this city should all be true, just true!"

"I haven't heard of any such thing,I keep coming to this city"!

"Then lying was the order of the day, people grew into blatant liars, you hadn't heard any truth at all, your Dhruvaputra had been lost in the charms and beauty of the fallen woman, he used to walk down to the river or the lake to fetch water for the harlot"!

"But there was no dearth of water at that time"!

"It was there and he danced to the tune of the courtesan and who won't ever do that? Obeying commands, one after another, of the harlot kept him always on his toes. He had no time for a little respite"!

"Really, so strange, we haven't ever learnt such things so far"!

"How will you know? But I know, he was mad for the whore, but the whore used to send him to the merchant, to the King and to all other men"!

"Oh Lord!" Shivnath's face got distorted, "Why didn't he escape then?"

"He was planning to slink away, but the attraction of a woman is so irresistible! The woman can play magical tricks on a man, can transform a man into a cow or a goat even! What would be the way-out then?"

"Then what followed?"

"What more would happen, he had to roam on the streets of the city, at the behest of the whore! If ever he longed for coming back, she would again send him for an information to the merchant or to someone else. Would ever any man love to see another man for a reason or no reason, just being directed by the woman he has fallen for?"

Tamradhvaj was growing suspicious. His words seemed to be far from true. Again, they might be true too. But Devadutta was fond of the merchant, then why would Dhruvaputra hang about the roads in search of the merchant? He said, "Will you please lead us to Devadutta's residence? We do not know where she lives".

Mahaparshwa felt relieved. After a long hiatus, he was being able to do his work. His duty was to manage clients from the road and take them to the brothel. He was back to his own calling. He took them along.

SIXTY-SIX

While stepping into the bawdy house, Shivnath had thought that he must have a dip in the Shipra river while returning and should go back home pure in body and mind. All night, sleep eluded him. Even there was no respite as yet. It seemed as if Tamradhvaj was showing him around the hell! He was talking about the hell only.

Thus, ruminating a host of puzzling thoughts a-jumble in his mind, he entered the inner court of the bawdy-house. The elderly man had been enchanted by being face-to-face with Devadutta. He knew the harlots to be of one category, but he found this woman to be a class apart. He knew the prostitutes to be shrewish, but this one was very courteous and meek, just like the monsoon clouds, the moist, dense green forest, the trees and herbs. He was of the notion that the whores were foul-mouthed, cunning, given an opportunity they would leave a man impecunious, absolutely bankrupt. The scriptures had described the women as the gateway to the Hell and these women must be the whores, Shivnath was cocksure. But now he came to see that this woman would be unparalleled as a honey-tongued, soft-spoken lady. Where was her attire like a hot-dressed prostitute? This woman looked like a hermitess, unadorned with ornaments. Shivnath was reminded of Uma, the ascetic.

The sly man on the road, who led them here was waiting near the entrance. Introducing himself, Tamradhvaj said, "We are here obviously in quest of him, he can't go missing, so abruptly!"

"No, he cannot be", rejoining inaudibly, Devadutta bowed her head down to the earth to honour the two stranger guests and then raising her head, she said, "So many days have passed by in the meantime! How strange, none looks for him, none has come here even to ask after him! I thought he had none of his own, anywhere, since seven generations! But man is not born like a tree, after all!"

Tamradhvaj said, "Yes, he was like a tree only, having none of his parents alive."

"Was he a friendless man, didn't he have any well-wisher"?

Tamradhvaj said, "Cannot say whether he had any such friend in the city, but I had gone to the Shudra ghetto to see his friends and this man, his daughter-in-law and granddaughter are good friends of him too".

Devadutta let out a long sigh. Her apparels were almost plain, lacking any colour. And the house was marked with silence. Maid servants were invariably there, at the threshold a sentry from Saurashtra was posted, who helped them reach this far, but all seemed to be under a spell of melancholy. Was it because there had been no downpour or Devadutta herself was somewhat morose?

Tamradhvaj inquired, "How was he"?

"Don't you know that"?

"What had gone wrong with him?"

"Don't you know that even? So many days have sped by in between, is there anything concealed or unrevealed"?

Shivnath asked, "My daughter, how did you take him to be"?

Devadutta kept on looking in a vacant gaze. She was thinking whether Dhruvaputra narrated about this man's family to her. He used to speak of these men only. She asked, "Has he returned, who had gone to war?"

"You mean, my son, Kartikkumar? No, he still goes untraced".

Devadutta elongated her gaze at the void of the sky through the window and began to croon abruptly:

"On my husband's chest lean my pals, all the neighbour women;

My own husband was in an alien land, like a lost cloud, by then!"!'

"What are you saying?" Shivnath asked.

"These couplets he used to recite, while reminiscing of Reba quite often!"

"What did he say?" Shivnath was frightened. What more would he have to hear? Knowing the truth was always unnerving!

"That song, Reba used to sing, does she even now?"

Shivnath said, "But I have no idea! What kind of song is this?"

"I heard it from Dhruvaputra, I had almost forgotten it, suddenly I remembered it, you know, if I could get to see Reba!"

Shivnath retorted, "But how will you see her? She is the Goddess Lakshmi of my household, she is my daughter-in-law, whose husband has gone to another land.

How can she come here, to this place?"... Would you like to get up now?

Tamradhvaj replied, "Please do not be so impatient, sit down, nothing is here to be afraid of."

Devadutta asked, "Grandpa, would you have water here"?

Shivnath shook his head. He sat straight and stiff. A man cannot be understood by just a mere glance from outside. Who knew how Dhruvaputra had grown up behind his eyes? He talked about Reba to this harlot, in this bawdyhouse! What he had said only Lord Mahakaal would know. But Reba was even more like a mother to him!

Devadutta said, "Please be composed, Grandpa! Reba Maa had reared him up, Reba Maa used to sit up awake all night, her husband being off to a foreign land, how could she put up with such pain? Dhruvaputra used to feel for her and say..."

"What did he say"?

"He used to bow down to Reba Maa in reverence, sitting here, getting ready to play Veena. he used to touch the instrument after offering his respect to Reba Maa. Look Grandpa, he grew up by listening to Reba Maa's songs".

"But I never heard her singing songs!"

Dhruvaputra had heard:

"Blossoms sprout on mango tree,

Ashok flowers are being shed,

My husband's off to another land

I remember him, instead."

Devadutta lowered her head, while humming the tune. She whispered, "Did I guess ever before that he was composing the tale of my future?"

"Is this his composition?"

"No, this is Reba Maa's, whose husband hasn't returned as yet".

"But, how strange, Reba Maa never sings this song!" Tamradhvaj quipped in.

"The woman, whose husband does not return after going to a foreign land, sings inwardly. Who will feel her pain? None, perhaps! If anyone felt for her, it was

Dhruvaputra! I had forgotten all, I was trying to forget Dhruvaputra, but again I am reminded of everything."

"Which other song did he talk about"?

"Just a line or two, again a line or two more, I used to teach him how to play Veena, he used to tell me about the woman whose husband had been off to an alien land. I heard that during the days of clouds hovering over the sky, she used to be overcome with pain, but I see her suffering no less during the time of drought too…

"Who has sent you to war?

The war is my co-wife,

She's snatched my man, so far,

Mind's joy is lost to strife,

My husband is in a land, afar,

Poverty is at the door,

hounding his wife!"

Tamradhvaj asked, "What had happened to Dhruvaputra?"

"I don't know, he had mastered the art of Veena-playing quite well."

"Then why did he go away?"

For quite some time, Devadutta sat lowering her head, and then haltingly she said, "The merchant had sent him to make a truce with me. I hate the merchant, a mere glance at him sends shudder through my spine. What to say, this is the truth!"

Tamradhvaj thought his assumption was quite similar. Devadutta continued to say that, she had a latent hatred, an intolerance towards the tycoons. A rich man's wrath had left her mother, Rasamanjari, widowed. The tycoons seized the world in their clasp, only because of their power of wealth and riches. They took their gifts to be the only truth in this universe, all else would be subservient to it: concern and affection, love, kindness, sacrifice, all…Hence, she kept on repudiating the offers of the merchant, Subhag Dutta, always. She was supposed to be faithful to the King! But she could not remember whether the King of Ujjwain had ever cast a glance at her. Thoughts of Dhruvaputra still sent shivers through her body. At midnight, she would wake up from her sleep!

"Didn't Dhruvaputra talk about Gandhavati?"

That damsel! A strange smile flashed across the corner of Devadutta's lips. She said, "Oh certainly he had talked about that wisp of a girl whose father had gone to war never to come back, her mother kept looking down the way awaiting his return, imagining her husband to have lost his way, roaming in different paths, or smearing ashes all over his body, he was so engrossed in war which was yet to draw to its close! She guessed that her husband would come back on horseback, nay, riding a camel or like Lord Mahakaal, Shiva, on the back of an ox:

"My husband went missing, to become Shiva, the Lord,

Smearing ash and dust all over his body,

By the path I sit and think Time is naughty,

Won't he be back, isn't it time yet, Oh God?"

Shivnath asked, "Is this song yours?"

"No, Dhruvaputra's."

"How is it that we failed to read him?!"

"Even I failed! I used to think, who the merchant has sent to me for negotiation? The merchant's letter reached me through him and I blew them off through my window. He used to talk about Gambhira, the foreign traders who used to come to Ujjwain, the Ionian Greek merchants, he talked about the rivers like Shipra, Gandhavati, Gambhira, Reba ... he used to talk of the river, Reba:

"The damsel is now in her youth,

The youth brings in bumblebees,

My youth is bidding adieux, so uncouth,

Fading in the dark, in the late night's trees.

My husband on a full-moon night left,

My youth stands useless, of all joys bereft"!

"Stop it now! All of a sudden, Shivnath grew impatient, what kind of remark can it be on one's mother?"

"Can't a mother be in her youth?" Devadutta muttered under her breath.

Shivnath plugged his ears with his hands and said, "Stop it, my girl, no need to proceed any further, he was a difficult man to understand, now I get it, he used to cast evil gaze on Reba"!!

Devadutta said, "No, he cast no evil glance at anyone! Sans her youth, how can a mother bear the child in her womb, and if that youth dries up, wastes away, won't she feel sad"?

Shivnath retorted, "Let go of it, young lady! You used to learn such facts from him! Your duty is to create an illicit relationship or let it happen. Dhruvaputra was just a young man, you nursed grudge against the tycoon and he was pontificated on the altar of that wrath"!

"How dare the rich merchant banish him?"

"But he had been banished by him, hadn't he?"

"Dhruvaputra left the city, taking umbrage."

"For which hurt feelings?"

"That I do not know, I learnt that he had been ruthlessly beaten black and blue by the servant, Utanka, and thereafter he did not come to me, I cannot say when Dhruvaputra had left!"

"Was he in the wont of visiting the Shudra ghetto?"

I don't know, he used to talk about the Shudra habitation, many of them hadn't been back after going on work, the women used to shed tears while singing songs, he shared even all this with me. But I wonder, why Dhruvaputra used to talk repeatedly about those wives whose husbands had gone abroad! He used to quote them in verbatim— where has he gone leaving me alone like a wife whose husband stays abroad, I always am all ears to listen to his footfall, I was familiar with the shuffle of his feet. I used to know the odour of his body, none would ever be able to kiss like him, the way he used to offer me his love was nonpareil, none would be able to arouse me like him, letting me have the carnal pleasure in the maximum, none but he knew how the life would taste such nectar-like!"

Almost about to plug his earhole with both his hands, Shivnath was being silently impressed by the whore's words, as he kept listening to her. He was being thrilled. What strange words were being uttered by her! How brazen she spoke, though the words were not sounding shameless! The words had sweet, honey-like appeal in them. Shivnath began to get the feel of that sweetness, it seemed.

Tamradhvaj asked, "Then he used to go to the Shudra ghetto, you mean to say?"

"Yes, he did, otherwise how could he sing Shudra ghetto-specific songs?"

"Did he take the rice offered by the Shudras?" Tamradhvaj hurled a query.

"Yes, he did, he was free of all prejudices, to be precise."

"Had the merchant beaten him for that?"

"No, the rich tycoons are usually very hard-hearted, the merchant is even more cruel than his servant, he flogged Dhruvaputra just to teach me a lesson, to hurt me severely."

"Was he really wounded?"

"Yes, he was, if he stayed back in Ujjwain, he would have been more wounded, even more, Utanka would have whipped him on, for the pleasure of the merchant!"

"Is this your conjecture"? Shivnath questioned.

"The tycoons are ruthless in every sense of the term, I am reminded of my mother, Dhruvaputra might have been slain in the hands of Utanka, the servant, as the rich tycoons do! My mother, Rasamanjari had come fleeing from Saurashtra, my father was a foreigner, an Ionian Greek, who hailed from the land beside the river, Oxus…"

Devadutta went on in a low voice. While continuing, both her eyes were getting awash with tears. Shivnath sat with lowered head. Shivnath wondered, if Tamradhvaj hadn't brought him here, with which truth he would have to spend the rest of his life! Devadutta informed, that Dhruvaputra had not left the city because of any fear of being slain, but he did so for being utterly humiliated, for having his feelings hurt! But as he left, his life had been saved! If Dhruvaputra hadn't lived, whom would she keep waiting for?

Mahaparshwa, who sat outside the door, was getting impatient gradually, as the conversation was on among Devadutta, Shivnath, Tamradhvaj. He was feeling the growing advent of hunger in his entrails. The daytime was at its peak. The sun grew raging more, outside. The conversation was not coming to an end yet. Mahaparshwa had thought that Devadutta and this pair of elderly and young men would engage in a bitter altercation. Dhruvaputra was a yet-to-mellow, idiotic nincompoop, and these men had come all the way for him! What Mahaparshwa could understand was that, Dhruvaputra had become the bête noire to the merchant. The merchant would kill him if he had not escaped. Even, his plight was the same. If the merchant would come to know that he was the lover of Chaturika, would he spare him? He would crush him to death like an ant. What would happen to him, who could tell?

The two were yet to emerge from the house. Hence, Mahaparshwa could not leave. Would they pay him a little for his service, won't they? At least, a couple of silver coins. Or at least, make an arrangement for his afternoon repast. He felt small to stand before Chaturika's door, asking for food repeatedly. Everything said and done, she was just a woman! He, himself, was a man in its truest sense. In his mind, he knew himself as an accursed Gandharva, an angel of Paradise, adept in music. Was it becoming of a man to remain in control of a woman? He went to the door, by dragging himself on the floor. If one could eavesdrop the conversation among people, it would be to one's gain, never a loss, for sure. Mahaparshwa could hear about the river, Oxus. Learnt about the land, beside the river, Oxus. In that land, only the gods seemed to reside. In that land, all her forebears had been there – her father was still alive in that place, all were there— her grandfather, her great-grandfather, even the relatives who were no more. Devadutta was saying that her mother, Rasamanjari, had died long back, she, too, might have been there by the river, Oxus. There, the men were like Gandharvas, the women were beauties like Urvashi, the nymph. Her mother, Rasamanjari, was just like them. Mother wanted to go there but failed. Even she wished to go.

Tamradhvaj said, "The Ionian Greeks look just like gods!"

Shivnath said, "I heard it to be a land of the Gandharvas, the handsome angels of paradise."

Devadutta said, "My mother used to say, you have surely heard this from Dhruvaputra."

"Yes, he had said so once upon a time."

" He heard it from me, my mother used to say that my father was a brilliant singer. He could paint pictures, sculpt idols, weave silk and used to roam round the cities with the silk apparels, my mother had taught him how to play Vallaki and Veena. He used to play … he was full of love like the Gandharvas, the land on the bank of the river, Oxus, was the land of the Gandharvas."

Being mesmerised, Tamradhvaj said, "How beautifully you are narrating"!

"I know that only, the Gandharvas who come in the form of man, only return to that land, comprising the river Oxus and a hill, a grassland, the rainbow in the sky, sweet fragrance in the air, the twang of Veena being played, and, the songs brought from the land of grapevines. Alexander, the valiant hero had founded that land and he was the scion of the Gandharvas too" … Devadutta heaved a long sigh. She lowered her head.

Then, Mahaparshwa was calling from outside the door, "Maa, are you done with talking?"

"Who's there"? Devadutta became alert.

Mahaparshwa drew up to the door and said, "Maa, I am Mahaparshwa, the pimp! Maa, have you finished talking about the Gandharvas? May I add, Maa, I heard that some of the Gandharvas, descending here on this earth, I mean, from their own abode, become like the men residing on earth. For instance, this pimp, who has no tune in his voice, no charm in his looks, no knowledge of Veena playing, no rice to eat, is just a servant of a whore…!"

Devadutta asked, "Who are you?"

Mahaparshwa said, "I am Mahaparshwa, the pimp! Presently, I am the servant of Chaturika,the whore, but as a matter of fact, I was a Gandharva in my previous birth, and that Chaturika was a Gandharvi, my companion, now we are in deep trouble, I am in real ordeal, I have no rice to eat, no water to drink…!"

Devadutta was taken aback, "Does Chaturika have a servant? But I have no information of him!"

"Well, I have joined her as a servant willingly. How will you know that her life is also a very sad one? We want to be liberated together, we want to go back to the abode of the Gandharvas, Maa"!

"Will you go?"

"Yes, Maa".

"I shall go too".

"You! But you have no dearth of anything, Maa! You have rice, water, you are blessed with happiness and comfort"!

Devadutta said, "I have nothing at all, I want to feel relieved by going to the bank of the river, Oxus, I hate to live on the kindness of the King or the charity of the merchant!"

Mahaparshwa kept quiet. He believed nothing that she said.

Then, Devadutta came up to add, "It may be that Dhruvaputra has gone away to that country! He was like a Gandharva too"!

"That's no wonder"! Shivnath's hopes seemed to be belied.

"Yes, that is possible, he had heard of the river, Oxus, from me!"

"Then, what will happen?"

"No one ever returns from that country."

Then, Tamradhvaj was thinking-Is it true that none comes back? If Dhruvaputra does not come back, will Ujjwain hasten towards its ruin by being burnt with drought? He said, "Dhruvaputra is like a ball of cloud, he can drift anywhere though he can come back even, just as the clouds do. Your words are not true, revered lady, we have taken to the streets in the hope of tracing Dhruvaputra, please let him come back to us."

Devadutta kept looking at him, with surprise in her eyes. Tear droplets glittered in both her eyes. Could she bring back Dhruvaputra? From where would she fetch that blue-eyed youth with a divine appearance? She hung her head low and lost herself in the memories of Dhruvaputra!

SIXTY-SEVEN

By the afternoon, Mahaparshwa came back to Chaturika. Chaturika dressed up. She adorned her chignon with a string of wild flowers. Her mekhala was dyed in raw turmeric. Her brassiere was of saffron colour, her scarf seemed to be dark crimson, dyed in lime and catechu. Lac-dye stayed back on her feet since a couple of days. Now in the west of the courtyard stood sun-tanned Mahaparshwa, an old shadow-like presence in her life. The shadow lay limp, morbid. It would breathe its last in a few seconds, it seemed. Chaturika sat upon that dying shadow, and at a little distance on a shadow, stood Mahaparshwa. Sitting there, drawing a breath, Mahaparshwa said, "Let me tell the truth,Chaturika. I have come armed with it, if you allow me to speak, I can tell you."

"Haven't you gone to him?"

"No".

"Did you reach his threshold"?

"No".

"You are a cheat, a deceiver, you would live on my money and would never go on my errand. Go, get lost."

Mahaparshwa came prepared. He was not frightened, rather kept waiting for her rage to alleviate. Once excited, Chaturika seemed to puff up her cheeks like a female cat, an agitating one. Her breasts seemed to swell up more. In her inhalation-exhalation, the whore seemed to assume her real form in front of Mahaparshwa's eyes! Chaturika became quiet gradually, while scolding him. What would she do without stopping? Even the huge cataclysm comes to a stop at one point in time. And she knew even if she asked him to get lost, her only hope was Mahaparshwa. In these times of upheaval, what would she do if that scoundrel would not be there beside her? For her, it was difficult, rather next to impossible, to unearth the news. And as this news reached Uddhav's ears through Mahaparshwa, he had even stopped dropping by at hers. Chaturika was lining up her logic systematically, at the back of her mind: the merchant was the tycoon, numero uno, of this city, his wealth had no limits. Was it so easy to meet him? Mahaparshwa was just an ordinary man. He would not be able again to curry favour with the merchant! Mahaparshwa would take his time, no doubt. He was biding his time for visiting the merchant and thus kept building courage within. One day, he must get to see him, rather unexpectedly. To obey her, Mahaparshwa used to hang about the roads, all day long, looking for an opportune moment to meet the merchant! Chaturika felt for him. The man returned, being singed by the raging sun outside. He needed to be offered a little water too! Let it cool his bosom and then conversation might ensue. She offered, "Would you like to have water"?

Mahaparshwa moved his head and said, "Let me tell you the news first."

"Must tell me, but get soothed first, Lord Mahakaal would slay all the people, the flames of a crematorium seem to have been lit up".

Mahaparshwa said, "Listen Chaturika, you should know this".

"Yes, I must know, but take rest presently, sitting in this shadow".

"Have enjoyed respite, now look, the merchant is a heartless man!"

"What do you mean"? Chaturika got startled, suspicion was writ large on her face, "What do you say?"

"Just the truth, the merchant is very cruel, in fact, the tycoons are ruthless usually"!

Now, Chaturika's entrails seemed to be on fire! It seemed to her, that, Mahaparshwa was planning to prop up logic against his not paying a visit there! And, he was baulking any future chance of going there too, putting forth his sharp logic. The knave always nursed evil thoughts within. Sometimes, he felt horny on seeing her too, she suspected. He used to cast desirous eye on her limbs, inwardly, it seemed. Let him do so. But he was hatching out a different plan, it seemed. A trick to debar her from approaching the merchant. Setting the merchant at naught, she would land in this depraved scoundrel's bed instead, what a desire! Fools rush where angels fear to tread!! Go to the dogs! Get lost! While muttering, Chaturika flared up abruptly, she said, "You have come up with a great news, let me cook 'paramanna', let me anoint you with sandal-paste, let me take care of you".

"I am telling you the truth only, Chaturika!"

"If the merchant comes to know, what your plight will be, guess"!

Mahaparshwa said, "But I have told only you, how would it make way to the merchant's ear"?

"In sundry ways it can happen, he is not a depraved being like you, he is the richest man, he has no dearth of anything, whatever he will desire, he will get hold of that. If he calls out, hundred women will go to make a beeline to his door seeking his attention, what won't he get, if demanded? Lord Mahakaal has poured down all wealth on him!"

Mahaparshwa said, "Your words are not true".

"Not true, you mean, all lies"?

Mahaparshwa said, "Will there be clouds in the sky of Ujjwain, if he so desires"?

"No wonder, it may happen".

Mahaparshwa smiled and said, "Chaturika, he is too ruthless, he aimed at slaying Dhruvaputra, by his servant, Utanka! He did not even step forward to save Utanka, while he was dying! Despite possessing fabulous wealth, does ever the Chief Prostitute respond to his call?"

Chaturika said, "He is magnanimous, otherwise, he could have imprisoned Dhruvaputra, even the Chief Prostitute would have suffered the same fate, is his kindness indicative of his inability?"

"Devadutta has said that the tycoons never ever meant any good to anyone".

"Untrue, but how did you hear this?"

Then Mahaparshwa said everything, quite slowly. While hearing, Chaturika began to tremble in rage. She said, "She is overly conceited, after all, she is not a man but a woman, the women must not brag, many a time the merchant had called her, he came with sundry gifts, yet she refused her.So what? She rejected his offer and he has come to me! Have you shared this with anyone that the merchant has called for me?"

"No, I did not say, I just listened to what they said".

"Well done, strangers had been there, I suppose!"

While speaking, Chaturika was breathing quietly. The little bird in her breast seemed to have fallen asleep. She was becoming calm, devoid of all anxieties. Since the last few days, she was having an apprehension, if Devadutta would turn soft to the merchant, after all, it was a woman's tender heart! A prostitute needed a man always to depend upon, not like Uddhavnarayan, but rich like the merchant, the tycoon, who would cover her with gold and jewels, all over. The King was not interested in Devadutta and Devadutta would not look at the man who clamoured for her attention!

Dhruvaputra had already gone away leaving the city. What would be the future of Devadutta? The city was turning desolate like a crematorium, along with time. If the day's fire did not extinguish, none would stay here, where would then Devadutta go? Let Devadutta be there. Chaturika said, "The merchant was very good at heart".

"Not good, Chaturika, I know."

"Do you know, really, do you?"

"Yes, I know, he spurns the woman away from his bed, after enjoying her to his heart's content".

"Who said such words? This is a lie".

"I know he, who said this, is not there in the city".

"You would be undone,you should not speak anymore".

Mahaparhswa said, I am just an ordinary wormlike being! How accursed shall I be? And again, I am a male and it is them who spell disaster in others' lives!Being a woman you stand threatened, think of yourself, Chaturika!

All suspicion which Chaturika might have had in her mind began to dispel. As Mahaparshwa was trying to detain her, it was a big proof of the merchant coveting her! The scoundrel pimp never used to believe this, and, now learning this, he was trying to stop Chaturika in some way or other.

Chaturika said, "Since when you are so honest in your intentions! Your duty is to mean bad to others, to deceive them"!

Mahaparshwa said, "How far am I able to accomplish, Chaturika? Such is my deplorable state that I spend my days in hand-to-mouth plight. Though I deceive men much, I wonder how does the rich tycoon get the money poured on him, just so spontaneously? The rich tycoon never takes a human being as one of its kind!"

Chaturika was visibly annoyed. In a subdued voice, she chided Mahaparshwa, "If you speak so ill against such a man, you would be a sinner, none can get so much unless Lord Mahakaal is not kind to him! He is blessed by Lord Mahakaal!"

Mahaparshwa said, "The merchant thinks as money can buy silk, pigeon-peas for horses, ornaments, it can buy a human being likewise and ornaments can buy women. He considers human beings as horses and silk."

Chaturika went wide-eyed in wonder on hearing this. What sort of words did he utter? Who had taught this knavish pimp such words? She had never heard such words in her life! She thundered, "Stop you, Mahaparshwa, if you fail, you can leave, stop uttering slander about a man of such a high stature, it is a sin, heaping words of calumny on some bigwig will surely mean misfortune to the culprit and you feign to be a wise man, I see."

"I haven't said anything at all. These are from Devadutta, I just listened to whatever she said". Chaturika boiled in rage, "Why had you been to her, you inveterately sinful bloke?"

"You have heard the reason of my going there, haven't you"?

"You mustn't go there, Lord Mahakaal would be angry with you, you would be ruined, you knave, and the greatest ruin would befall Devadutta, my friend. Such pride is not good, in her pride she swells up high, though the sky lies far above one's head! What makes a woman proud, she lags behind the men, once she loses her youth all lose interest in her, if she falls ill who cares for her? Men are kind, if we talk ill of menfolk, we will stand cursed."

Mahaparshwa maintained studied silence. But he was far from believing whatever Chaturika kept saying. He believed all that he heard at Devadutta's house, sitting on her threshold, nearly all afternoon. As Chaturika was talking about male and female, those two men and Devadutta did not speak that way, at all. He had taken fancy to whatever Devadutta had said. Mahaparshwa was waiting for Chaturika's excitement to subside. Glancing at Mahaparshwa sans an answer, Chaturika came to an abrupt halt and asked, "Why have you kept mum?"

"Go, see Devadutta and listen to her, Chaturika!"

"Why should I go and listen to her?"

"Once you do, you would believe me, the merchant adds no extra value to humans, setting fire to the Shudra ghetto with the help of Utanka, his servant, he sets him ablaze to death only! To him, Utanka was not valuable more than any dry straw or twigs".

Chaturika was again annoyed and said, "Danger will befall my friend."

"Who"? Mahaparshwa's eyebrows knitted up, "Are you talking of Devadutta?"

"Yes, the merchant, who is as rich as the Jews, never sleeps all the time. Did you know the two men who you took along to my friend's chamber?"

Mahaparshwa stopped awhile and kept looking at Chaturika's face, "They are travellers, from somewhere outside this city, but the faces seemed to be familiar, I might have seen earlier!"

Chaturika said, "You would be ruined too, my friend is the Chief Prostitute, the King is an admirer of her, but who are you, hey depraved bloke"?

Mahaparshwa said, "Tell me clearly what you would like to say".

"I say,those two men might be the spies of the merchant, or that of the King, who are out to find out who speak against the King or the merchant"!

Mahaparshwa was visibly frightened," But they had come in search of Dhruvaputra, one of them being the disciple of Acharya Brishavanu".

Chaturika said, "Brishavanu himself is not there in this city anymore, how can you talk about his disciple? Do you know him?"

Mahaparshwa shook his neck. Chaturika put her hand on her cheeks to say, "All these words will be transmitted to the place that matters, no rain is here, the city goes aflame like a funeral pyre, now would we talk ill against the respectable men of this city?"

"Isn't it right?"

"Not at all. It will trigger uprising of the subjects"!

Mahaparshwa was visibly frightened, "But we haven't discussed such matters".

"What did you say"?

"I was just at one with whatever they said".

"If they throw you into the prison, would you ever be able to come out of it?"

Mahaparshwa thought that Chaturika's words could not be wrong. Really so, why then would a couple of men come to the city asking after Dhruvaputra? And again, coming to the city, why would they grab him? Now, the drought was on. And during the drought only, the subjects could be up in arms. And that could be quelled by the spy of the King, by roaming on the thoroughfares. Alas! Oh, alas! This was not right. He could not make out the head or tail of anything, but kept nodding continuously in approval of whatever the two men said".

"Then what will happen to me, Chaturika"?

"You would die, the merchant would put you on fire too, like Utanka"!

"Oh God! How painful it would be! I heard the screams of the man in death-throes, it could be heard when a boar is put to death, he died like a boar".

"He did not commit much crime, he only set the Shudra ghetto on fire, your crime would be more horrifying, if you speak ill against a respectable person, you would be thrown into the hell, your singed body would be fed to the dogs by the merchant"!

Mahaparshwa cried out in pain, "What are you saying, Chaturika, what have I done? I dozed off, sitting beneath the kadam tree while the couple of men pulled me out of sleep, I hadn't called the spies in!"

"Both your hands can be chopped off by the hangman, do you know that?"

"But I haven't committed any crime!"

"You are a criminal down to the bottom, you had taken them to Devadutta's house, talking ill of the merchant and the King!"

"No, I did not do so, I did not talk on the road."

"If the spies report that you did, then?"

"Why will they say so?"

"They will, just to ensure that both your hands and legs are mutilated by the executioner, you would be punished as a thief, the merchant would feed you alive to the wild dogs, a terribly wrathful man as he is!"

"I know that, he was heard to have killed Dhruvaputra if the latter hadn't gone away."

Chaturika said, "Utanka was really innocent, he had committed no crime at all! Did he set the Shudra locality on fire just for no reason, you mean to say? Yet, he had to suffer severe pain, while dying."

"Yes". Mahaparshwa's neck drooped. He said, "Such matters only were discussed".

"Such things are a sin to harbour in one's mind. The merchant would sense it however, if it surfaced in one's mind, blessed as he is by Lord Mahakaal"! Chaturika kept whispering, "He is saintly to the good, he would cover the servants with gold, if otherwise he would burn them to death, without any iota of kindness! Beware, Mahaparshwa!"

"What shall I do now?"

"Where have the two spies gone"?

"They went in search of the merchant, in the hope of meeting him up."

"There you are, they will make him listen to whatever they have learnt, and that too, today itself!"

Mahaparshwa was at his wit's end, knowing not what to do. Chaturika only could save her. The merchant had taken fancy on Chaturika. At her insistence, the merchant could have pardoned him. Mahaparshwa was recoiling in fear. He was being reminded of the groans and cries of dying Utanka!

Chaturika said, "All the powers rest in the wealthy tycoon himself"!

"I know, your friend too said the same."

"If he wills, he can put a man to death, reaching him excruciating pain, no matter he has any fault or not. I've also heard that he is extremely ruthless".

Mahaparshwa was overcome by fear and said, "You keep repeating our words"!

Chaturika swayed her head and said, "He is kind to me but if he so wishes, he can rejoice by slaying a human"!

"During noon, we were discussing these things only".

Chaturika said, "Uddhav had said all this, I must let the merchant know of Uddhav, he will kill him by rendering him to the status of a beggar, just go and tell him about me, Mahaparshwa, ask him when Chaturika, the maid, will come to see him!"

Mahaparshwa asked, "If again a spy intervenes, then?"

"I could have taken them to be spy at just one glance, couldn't my friend get it?"

"No", Mahaparshwa muttered, "You can see your friend and ask her who had come and what for?"

Chaturika assured him of going there the following day. The pimp and the ugly, cat-eyed Chaturika, the apple of Uddhav's eye, had almost the same level of intelligence. They went on discussing the merchant and the spies quite nonsensically, right from the evening till late into the night.

SIXTY-EIGHT

Chaturika said, "Dear friend, your words have come true at last, my luck is smiling on me now!"

Devadutta was etching a man on the floor with the help of a piece of chalk. Completing the painting to her satisfaction, she was driven to elation. The man drawn with a piece of chalk could not be recognized, but one could have a guess, no doubt. That face was not of the King. Wherein lay the glory of the King? The King's diadem, sword or the bow-and-arrow? That face was of a common man. Seeing so, Chaturika seemed to be relieved. The face was not that of the merchant even. And it was not supposed to be the merchant's too. Yet a slim apprehension had already been there at the corner of Chaturika's mind. The merchant desired Devadutta, if she agreed by any remote chance, the tycoon Subhag Dutta, would not ever care to glance at Chaturika. But why was the merchant desirous of a woman who loved to build castles in the air with an utterly ordinary man, would love to remain engrossed in his thoughts? Wasn't there any glory in his wealth, treasures and riches?

Devadutta was amazed, a little annoyed even by the joyous presence of Chaturika! Yet, concealing her feelings behind her facial expressions, she asked, "On whom does luck smiles upon? What's going on in the city?"

Chaturika touched her own bosom and said, "On this wretched wench… but dear friend, who have you etched in here, who's that lucky fellow, that handsome man, who has been drawn by Devadutta, in her solitary hours…?"

Before Chaturika could finish her words, Devadutta began to erase the picture she had drawn with a piece of chalk, with her own scarf, slowly. Knowing everything, Chaturika was feigning ignorance. Chaturika had become even more clever. But did Chaturika know that too much of cleverness would be proved to be idiocy in the long run? Etching Dhruvaputra, in her own style, all by herself, and remaining engrossed in him, was her mind's play. In that game, another picture was there, too. But she never sat to draw that image with reality as her base! Sometimes, Dhruvaputra, sometimes a riverbank of dreams, small huts, massif at a distance, - she grew busy with such portrayal of nature. River Oxus, the banks of the river, the mountain range far-off, the forestland … and many more! As Dhruvaputra was relegating to a vain existence to her, along with time, likewise, the river Oxus had remained as a mythical truth to her, since her childhood. But all these were her own chiaroscuro on her mind's canvas, she never wanted that anyone else would be privy to it. Devadutta was more vexed, within.

Chaturika said, "What's wrong, dear friend, why are you wiping it off?"

Devadutta, avoiding a rejoinder, asked her in turn, "What about you?"

"As you used to tell me, dear friend, that either the merchant or the Army Commander or otherwise a tradesman from an alien land or a royal servant, would surely take fancy to me and Uddhav will never be able to oppress me forever, that has been proved, your prediction has come true, you know"!

"I predicted, didn't I?" Drawing new lines on the floor with a piece of chalk, Devadutta asked, "So, has any royal servant shown up, is he a prince of any land?"

Chaturika seemed to stoop low, in bashfulness. She said in a low voice, "You had said that my dance would be able to win the heart of either the merchant or the Army Commander or the King himself".

"Who is impressed"?

Chaturika rejoined, "The merchant, the tycoon, Subhag Dutta".

How strange! Devadutta began to scrutinize Chaturika. But where was the sign of prosperity on her appearance? Her face bore signs of worry. All women would be radiant with the beams of full-moon, if she would win a man of her choice in life. She would be complete. But where was that sign in Chaturika? Perhaps it was there, her vision missed it somehow. She heard that the merchant Subhag Dutta had called for Chaturika. After such a long time, the merchant had gone quiet at last. The news came as a relief to Devadutta. But was this news worth believing? How would the merchant be won over by this ordinary beauty of Chaturika? Was there any dearth of beautiful damsels in this city? Did drought render a person blind by mortifying his senses to tell bad apart from good? Otherwise, why would the merchant covet Chaturika? Or was it his whim of some sort? Being rejected by Devadutta, it was a kind of revenge to call Chaturika of ugly appearance, instead. Both Devadutta and Chaturika became equal in status to him! By accepting Chaturika, Devadutta had been somehow demeaned, as if there was no difference between Chaturika and Devadutta. Or, the tycoons were just like that. The pride of wealth would come in their way of taking a human as a human. Or why would he welcome Chaturika? Was there anything in that feline Chaturika which could charm any man? Buck-toothed, pout-lipped Chaturika, with heavy breasts and ponderous buttocks, was just a bundle of flesh! But in the long last, flesh only would win a man over, and was that a reason for the merchant, coveting Chaturika?

Chaturika said, "A few mudras, that I learnt while dancing, would now come handy".

"Your dance? Has the merchant witnessed it?"

Chaturika bent her neck sideways and rejoined, "Yes".

"When did he see"?

"One evening", Chaturika said under her breath.

"What was his take on it?"

"He sent a messenger later on, he would set sail for business and would love me to accompany him".

Devadutta felt relieved as she learnt it, so she was ultimately spared! Again, that old man would never ask her to gratify his sexual desire anymore, given it was true that Chaturika was going to keep him company! She might be his serving-maid even. In a business tour, a retinue of traders would go along with him! It would comprise many men, a number of chariots, cattle-driven carts. Servants and maid-servants would go along with him! Chaturika might be there among those servants and maids! That would happen, for sure. Otherwise, her glow of beauty would turn meaningless, thought Devadutta. That old tycoon would never accept this ugly woman in lieu of her, in any case. Devadutta began to draw a meandering river on the ground, with the piece of chalk. This river was that Oxus, this river and that land were occupying her mind, since quite a few days. Now it occurred to her that Dhruvaputra might have gone to the bank of that river, Oxus. He was awaiting Devadutta by putting up a shack, armed with his books. He knew that Balkh, beside the river, Oxus, was the only place which would be possible for Devadutta to find out. Devadutta knew of that country only! There, in that land, Devadutta's maternal as well as paternal lineage could be traced. Her father, grandfather, great-grandfather—all seemed to inhabit by the river, Oxus, since ages! There, no man would die. Men would keep living eternally, the men who had won death would get back lost youth by having a bath in the river, Oxus, every day. Whatever they would lose each day, would be replaced that day itself!

Chaturika asked, "What are you drawing, my pal?"

"A river".

"Shipra river"?

Devadutta smiled, "Yes dear, whatever you think, it would be so. Do thou know anything of the river, Oxus? Didn't I tell you about it? I think, I did".

Chaturika shook her head. Devadutta might have told Chaturika, but she did not remember. She resumed the topic of the tycoon and said, "Any day the merchant will send a palanquin for me and I have to leave. Shall I be able to come back again, dear?"

"Then you should not go, why should you accompany that old man"?

"My friend, he has taken fancy on me, he is such a man of eminence, he has enormous wealth, all will be mine and your prediction has come true, my luck has undergone a drastic change"!

Keeping the piece of chalk on the floor from her hand, Devadutta went fixing her with a steadfast gaze! Now, it seemed that the words were obviously true! But how would that be true? If the merchant fell for Chaturika, there would be no difference between a beauty and a plain Jane, in this world! She asked, "When will the journey begin"?

The merchant is in the know of it.

"What do you know?"

"I know that I shall have to accompany him, I shall not get to see you anymore, I shall not be able to come to you again, friend. My dear, please help me with a few pieces of advice."

"Which advice"?

"How I shall serve him, how to win the heart of a man, in which manner I shall offer myself so as to make him happy!"

Devadutta said, "Whichever manner you know yourself, you should serve accordingly, that's it".

"But I know next to nothing, my dear friend".

"You are a woman, your youth is what you possess, don't you remember how Uddhav was won over by you?"

Chaturika was shivering visibly. This conversation was a proof in itself that Chaturika had won refuge to the richest tycoon of Ujjwain. The tycoon would send a palanquin for her, loaded with precious ornaments, silk-clothes, sandalwood, flowers and all. She would be nicely dressed to board that carriage to start for the tycoon's.

Beside the palanquin, Mahaparshwa , the pimp, quite like a servant, would come along on foot, who presently sat beyond her door.

Chaturika said, "But my pal, I hadn't won the Sessions-Judge of King's court! He used to oppress me, used to plunder whatever I had, if denied, he used to intimidate me to throw behind the bars, I had borne allegiance to him in fear, and you know that!"

Devadutta advised, "Do whatever would make you win the heart of the merchant, he is an old man, whatever carnal desire he has, it finds manifestation in his expressions, through eyes and face, does he have that bodily strength anymore"?

Chaturika said, "He has... he has heaps of wealth, won't he have that strength in him?"

"Wealth ... so what? Even a beggar can have tremendous power within himself".

"No, dear friend, he who is so rich, on whom Lord Mahakaal's benediction gets showered in such profusion, who has no dearth of anything at all, I am sure, his youth is no less than a young man's! In fact, he is much more successful than them, he is adept in employing sundry tricks of deriving pleasure, numerous formulae, Uddhav is nothing but an oppressor, he, on the contrary, is full of love."

"How do you know all such things?"

"He has paid me a visit already"!

Devadutta was sure that the merchant was really avenging! Let him take revenge, she would be saved! Let the merchant go to the hell, leaving Ujjwain behind, it would mean a blessing in disguise to Ujjwain! She muttered under her breath, "If you do not return, you will be in pain, this drought will not continue forever"!

"If the merchant does not come back, how shall I"?

"If he does not return, it is for the well-being of Ujjwain", Devadutta said.

"What are you saying, dear friend?"

Devadutta skipped the answer. Chaturika grew fidgety. It seemed to her that the Chief Prostitute was going green in envy! She could not even think in her wildest dreams that the merchant would send for Chaturika on her rejection! She said, "Can anyone emulate the merchant in his possession of wealth and riches?"

"How does it matter to the city-dwellers even if he possesses riches?"

"If he leaves, the city will be devoid of its magnificence, its glory, my friend!"

"What does his being rich mean to the city-dwellers?"

"Never say so, my friend, now he is my master"!

Mahaparshwa, the pimp, was feeling irked, sitting outside. He came along with Chaturika to ascertain whether the two men of day before yesterday were 'spies' or not! But Chaturika was lost in the thought of the merchant. Even, Mahaparshwa himself, sitting by the door, was being taken aback while listening to Chaturika, when had the merchant come, when had he again witnessed Chaturika dancing? Why, but he never heard of the merchant visiting Chaturika, at her residence! Hadn't Mahaparshwa known about it, if he had come at all? Clearing his throat, he called out from outside, "Hey Chaturika, why don't you ask Devadutta, about the two men of that day"?

"Which one"? Devadutta asked.

While Chaturika raised the issue, Devadutta laughed Chaturika's fear off.She said, "No spy would ever come to sneak into common man's affairs, who is talking ill of others, etc. They came in search of Dhruvaputra! Yes, Chaturika, to which country are you headed on? To which land will the merchant take you along, as his maidservant?"

"Not as maidservant, the merchant has coveted me, he will honour me properly before accompanying him."

"Where is he going, to which country"?

Chaturika wanted to say, but failed. It had slipped off from her memory. She could not recall, by any means. It came to her memory and again slipped off. Lastly, she rejoined, "But I have forgotten, my dear, it is a long-way-off, across many lands, many rivers, many ravines between mountains".

"Didn't the merchant tell you"?

"Yes, he did, this much I remember, this torturing heat is absent there, here the Sun-God's chariot is getting stuck. There clouds swim in the sky".

"Got it! But which land is this?"

Then Mahaparshwa popped his face in, "Have you forgotten, Chaturika?"

"Why can't I recall, Mahaparshwa?"

Mahaparshwa asked, "Shall I tell?"

"Do you remember?"

Mahaparshwa said, "Let me think and say, silk can be had in that land, yellow silk, that is what I heard, this is an Ionian Greek land!"

"Okay fine, but what is the name of that country?"

Mahaparshwa smiled, "Yes, now it has come up, Chaturika, the Chief Physician told us the name of that land is Balkh, silk of that land is known to be of very high quality!"

"Which country?" Devadutta was all ears, Which country did you say?

Chaturika said, "Balkh, the land of Balkh, the Chief Physician came to say so."

"Which Chief Physician?"

"Nahush Sharman, the messenger of the merchant".

"Which country?" Devadutta asked again.

"Balkh! I heard that country to be far-off!"

"Beside the river Oxus?"

"Who knows? I do not know so much!" Chaturika waved her head.

"Didn't the merchant tell you anything about the river Oxus"?

"His messenger came to tell me, how can I expect him to know so much"?

Devadutta then glanced at the door, called in Mahaparshwa and asked, "Are you that man who came that day"?

"Yes Maa, I am Mahaparshwa, the pimp! I mean to say, this is the whim of the tycoon, they are usually not good, they are cruel, Maa, please make Chaturika understand, she is an ardent fan of yours, will it do her any good if she takes refuge to the merchant?" Saying so, Mahaparshwa came to the threshold to sit, and said, "That is far, far-off, I culled the information in the city".

"Is the merchant setting sail to that land? Are you sure?"

"Yes, he is! Mahaparshwa replied.

"To Balkh, situated on the bank of the river Oxus?"

"Yes, Balkh, to be precise, the Ionian Greeks weave the yellow silk".

Devadutta remarked, "This is that river Oxus, by the side of this river stands that country, there no man dies in that land, there is no senility, no envy, no ailment. There is no discrimination between the Shudras and the Brahmins".

"But I haven't heard of any such thing", Chaturika blabbed out.

"Yes, that land is definitely the land of the Gandharvas". Devadutta whispered, "My fatherland, yellow silk, river Oxus, my father..." Devadutta's eyes glistened with tears, "Is the merchant going to that land?"

"Is it that land, of which you spoke that day?" Mahaparshwa asked. "The land of the Gandharvas?"

"Yes, the name of that country is Balkh indeed"!

"How strange? Am I going to that country?" Chaturika said, "How fortunate I am"!

"Are you telling the truth, Chaturika? Is the merchant going to that country"? Devadutta grew curious to know.

"Yes, exactly! I heard of the yellow silk much before".

"Once reaching there, no one returns from that land. Why will one come back at all? There is no disease, no sense of loss, no sorrow, no death— you are really fortunate, that land is my fatherland!"

Craning his neck from the threshold like a camel, Mahaparshwa quipped in, "Would you like to join, Maa? If you are willing, the merchant will take you along in his chariot, seated beside him."

Devadutta chose to withhold her answer. She sat silent. The chalk in her hand again grew busy in etching the river Oxus on the floor. Devadutta seemed to hear the rippling noise of the stream. She could hear the thunder of the clouds. She could espy the shadow of the mountains. Graceful Gandharvas and Gandharvis were all sauntering around hither and thither,in the green meadows, garbed in yellow silk. A sweet tune was afloat in the air. In the surface of the river, eyeing her own shadow, Devadutta said, "He will take me along, he will take me to that land, whoever he is, my friend or my foe, kind or cruel, young or old, I must go, Chaturika!"

SIXTY-NINE

One morning, a couple of young men came to say, "Nothing doing, as the upper sea has become devoid of water, the nether region has become so too, and who does not know that both are interconnected?"

Parashar could feel that no efforts could detain the residents back in this place. Now, all would set out for the unknown, one after another, leaving Ujjwain. For five days, no water was found even after shovelling the earth at Ratnakar Sagar. Why would people stay back anymore? Rice supply, too, was running low. Later on, alms would fall far short too. What dreadful days were to follow! The Sun-God would not set down anymore semi-lunatic Chief Physician came a few days back, in the evening, to warn them. He said, "Let us see how this day fares".

"It would be of no gain, the labour would turn fruitless, if water is scarce in the upper level, the lower level would suffer the scarcity too".

Parashar said, "Water is there in the river, a few wells are yet to dry up, if it runs out of water during daytime, mother earth supplies it by night".

Lankesh, a youth, said, "Look at that field, the sky is touching the earth, look yonder!"

"Yes, that's true".

Another youth, Prahlad, said, "When the sky-ocean dries up, it sucks water from the seas in the hell. You know that too, don't you? Isn't it true?"

Parashar thought it to be true, but he said nothing at all. Then a youth said, "That has happened exactly. Turning waterless, the sky has drawn up the water from the hell too".

"Then that water would pour down!"

"How will it pour, the heat above has transformed the water into smoke", Lankesh said.

"Where has it gone"?

Prahlad said, "That I cannot say, but when there is no water, there is no point in digging the ocean, let us follow the band of the traders, accompanying the merchant. That evening, the Chief Physician had come to ask us to leave this city, otherwise none would survive. The merchant is setting out for business, the Chief Physician asked us to follow him. At the onset of the forthcoming full-moon fortnight, he would be setting sail to the land of Balkh. How the eccentric Chief Physician also talked of Balkh, inadvertently!"

"Which land"? Parashar asked. Hearing that, the Chief Physician began to shake his head, he was unfamiliar with it. He could not be a soldier to the core, in one life. Chief Physician said, "It was a land of everlasting Spring sans disease, grief, senility, death! Costly yellow silk is everyone's apparel there". Parashar could sense that the youths were getting perplexed, hearing it, since the morning. He said, "Men do not return once they sail to that country. And why will you all go to that land where the merchant is going? That is the land of sorcery, otherwise how can Spring last forever?"

"Is it the truth, you mean?"

"I am asking, if there is everlasting Spring, when does it rain then?"

"Why, during monsoon?"

"Where is the monsoon, there's only everlasting Spring! Then will there be cultivation, crop harvesting during the Spring itself?"

"We have no idea at all".

"Magic is rife there in that land, I know, I am the oldest of all, will you ever know what I shall?"

"No, no, why so, tell me whatever you know," Prahlad insisted.

"None can return from that land, the merchant has grown old, he will not come back, but you all are young chicks".

"Lakes are not providing us with water, we will go wherever our feet take us".

Parashar thought, if one or two started leaving, all would follow at certain intervals. The search for water, digging the lakes, would come to a standstill. The Shudra ghetto would be devoid of souls. And if Ujjwain started being evacuated, desolate, no cloud would ever float in, on its sky. Clouds rush in being attracted to the people, to drench them tender. Even the ruthless man would get soaked in the rains to become kind. Why would the nimbus clouds visit a desolate city, devoid of people? In a vacant city, only sea of fire would roll. Parashar grew anxious, and said, "Now the retinue of traders is yet to set out and that medical bloke is just a madcap".

"Now he has been cured, today only we will queue up to the merchant, we will be his servants, he needs a horde of servants".

Then Parashar said, "Look, go down the pond just for once, for the last time and see what happens".

"What to see, all our efforts prove vain, yesterday we tried our best to remove the stone-slab, we are now devoid of strength, we are at our wit's end".

"Dig by the sides of the stone!"

"Nothing doing, no water's there."

Then Parashar said, "It is there, I saw it in my dreams".

Parashar did not tell the truth. It was just an abrupt fabrication, concocted instantly. In his dreams, he had seen a gold pitcher, down at the bottom of the Ratnakarsagar! What was there in that pitcher? Once the pitcher's sealed mouth was opened, water began to spurt out in torrents. That water filled in the Ratnakarsagar. Spilling over the Lake, the water flew over the meadows. It sprinted on the river. The river had its fill. Seeing water in the meadows and the river, the sky above began to roar. That strange thunder of clouds had woken him up from sleep. Even after waking up, he seemed to hear the rumble of the clouds. Parashar asked, "Did you all hear the thunder of the clouds in the wee hours of dawn? Just as it used to happen long, long ago, during the months of Asad and Sravan!"

"How was it?"

"Have you forgotten that?"

One youth answered, "I have forgotten everything. And after this, I shall forget about monsoon too. Then we will breathe our last, Grandpa, please let go of us, we will go away."

"And what if the water surfaces today"?

"How will that happen, there's no water at all"!

"My dream was at dawn, dreams of that hour are believed to come true!"

A youth swayed his head and joined him, saying, "People say that dreams of dawn must come true".

Then Parashar said, "Again today is Krishna Navami, the dreams of Krishna Navami are even more true, after I woke up, I heard the cry of the peacock and that is also auspicious".

"Then should we go to the Lake?"

"Yes, you must. Lord Mahakaal has stashed away a water-filled gold pitcher in there. Parashar muttered under his breath, Long back, I had seen such a dream of drought and that too at dawn".

"Are you telling the truth"?

"Yes, and after a long interregnum saw this dream!" Parashar took the dream to be true. He did not cook up a story at all. Truly, he seemed to wake up this dawn amidst the thunder of clouds! He seemed to have seen the gold pitcher in his sleep in the waterless Ratnakarsagar. If he hadn't seen, how could he narrate?

Prahlad asked, "How was the dream of drought"?

"Darkness was falling from the sky, darkness like hot ashes as in a tale of olden times, I am about to forget now. In fact, it was a nightmare, I used to see such nightmares frequently then, but failed to construe their significance, as rains and drought happen in two different ways, rains do not continue for long, drought goes on for over a length of time!"

"That's true!" a youth nodded.

Lankesh added, "We, too, used to have nightmares at that time".

"Dreams of drought, fear pivots round drought only".

"Till date, I witness such nightmares".

"Naturally, drought is on, and we are not sure, how long it will continue".

Then all of them had descended into the empty bed of the pond. The old man sat at a distance from the pond, at the base of the neem tree. He could feel that he would be able to detain them only for a day or two at the most, and then, they all would go away, leaving this waterless, empty-bosomed Ratnakarsagar behind. The work came to a stop when the heat of the sun turned sweltering, and then again it began when it cooled down. Just at the approach of the evening, someone came up rejoicing from the bosom of the earth, he was seen crying in delight, shouting in joy, "Yes Grandpa, water is coming up, water is surfacing in the Lake"!

"Are you telling the truth?"

"Yes, yes, see that water is here on my forehead"!

The old man asked, "How did the water surface?"

"That stone-chunk, all day we took to pull it up, now water is here, water has surfaced!"

Breaking the news of the advent of water, he rushed to the ghetto. He seemed to tote the water down to the vacuum of the Shudra ghetto. It seemed that he went off sprinkling the water. Unworldly water-streams began to drench roads, thoroughfares and faces of men. The old man stood up. Then it seemed that from the core of the Ratanakarsagar, a procession emerged. A line of men, including both male and female, began to come up from the hell, daubing water all over. They were coming up from the hell with the tidings of water that surfaced.

Old Parashar looked up at the sky and whispered, "Oh Lord, water is here! Have you sent water down into the hell?"

The young man came to say, "Water is issuing out, it will again fill in the Ratnakarsagar with water, by one night much of it will be filled up."

Old Parashar sat by the side of the water-body, he seemed to hear the noise of water by pricking his ears up, and mused, "So the gold pitcher has offered us water at last?"

"Yes, it has offered but where is the pitcher?"

"Must be somewhere in the hell", someone replied.

Someone said, "How strange! Your dream has come true!"

Parashar could not believe this. How had the word tallied with reality? He had heard a similar tale somewhere, long ago! Today, remembering it suddenly, he made the tale real, mingling it with his dream! If it could be dug continuously, water would surely have spurted out but Parashar had no idea how low the water level had touched. He mused to himself that Lord Mahakaal was really kind, otherwise everyone would have gone away leaving him alone in this ghetto. Where would he go then at this ripe, wizened age? Nowhere, at all. Not even to the city, where there had been water, clouds, yellow silk, crops! Parashar himself did not know about any such place! To him, Ujjwain was the best. Where would he go leaving Ujjwain, river Shipra, Shudra ghetto, Seven Lakes and Mahakaal temple? It was true that he had no right to enter into the temple, yet enjoying the sight of it from a distance had its own charm. There was delight in sitting by the Ratnakarsagar, talking about the Malay mountains, narrating the tale of Udayan, the King of Vatsya and Basavadutta! Parashar knew within, that if again there had been rain during monsoon, chilly weather during winter and return of coo of the cuckoo in the Spring, in this city of Ujjwain, there would not be a trace of disease, grief, senility, death at all! He would be heartbroken to bid adieux to Ujjwain and go elsewhere.

Parashar seemed to doze off. The murmur of water would bring lethargy, and even sleep. He slept off and wanted to hear the water issuing up from the hell, in his sleep. The water contained in the gold pitcher seemed to be endless.

Right at that time, Uddhav drew up on horseback. He was crossing through the border of the Shudra ghetto, but hearing the uproar he entered. A fading light was keeping the earth enveloped like a secret illusion still. He jumped off from the horseback and shouted, "What's up in here?"

A young man bowed his head to rejoin, "Water".

"Water? What do you mean"?

"Water is surfacing in the Lake, Sessions-Judge Sir"!

Being surprised, Uddhav kept looking at the edge of the lake. What do they say, is water coming up? Wherefrom does the water issue? Who has given them water? Nowhere there is a drop of water and it has surfaced in the pond of the Shudras, is it a magical charm or what?

Old Parashar came to stand with folded palms, "Lord, we will be saved now".

"Shudras are never to die,from where do you get water"?

"Mother earth has been kind to us, oh Lord!"

Uddhav noticed that darkness was about to descend on all sides, hereafter. He would have to walk his horse down the way then. He, himself, failed, his pony would fail too to walk down the path in the dark. Nowhere there was the sign of water save one or two pitchers or a well or a river! They were saying that water kept coming up in their pond. There was no need to judge the veracity of their statement. Even, he did not have the inclination to do so. As doubt had surfaced, it should be probed. No water was pouring from the sky, how then would the dry lake get filled with water? All of a sudden, an eerie feeling got the better of him. It might have been an illusion. Explanations might elude the goings-on in the Shudra ghetto! There was no hint of rain yet the pond was full to the brim. He jumped on the horseback. No need was there to stay back. He came to know what he needed to. Now he would have to go to the Chief Priest. They knew black magic, sorcery — the air of conjuring had touched him, this sin needed to be absolved. As Uddhav came abruptly, he went away riding his horse with equal promptness, in the twilight.

Then Parashar said, "Now ensure that none of you would leave Ujjwain, as the nether region has been kind to offer us water, the sky-ocean would surely be kind to us too, call Him, offer your blood from the chest in the meadow, to propitiate Him, young maid and brat keep copulating in the open field, sky will surely bless us with downpour!"

"Will it truly happen?" A youth threw this query.

"That I know, don't you?"

"Yes, we know, we heard that it would cause the harvest to be aplenty".

"Yes, certainly, do so. When I was in my heyday of youth, such had happened."

"Drought?"

"Not a drought like the present one, the month of Asad was going dry, there was rain in Baisakh and Jaisthya, the Grandpa ordered and that worked wonder, downpour began, you obey what I ask you to do, and I think there's nothing to fear anymore, it will surely shower after the act of pure copulation".

Then a youth complained, "But the women do not crave for this".

"What do you mean by 'do not crave for this'?" Parashar was taken aback, how was it that a young maiden did not want to have copulation, surely her mind had veered on to some other man and that was not unlikely even! But copulation must happen, if a young man could have sexual intercourse with a young virgin, that would be even more auspicious, let it be on the sly, but it should happen, let them marry later, but let the virgin bleed on mother earth, as it would crack the sky fetching heavy rainfall.

Some other person said, "This is really strange but whatever he has said is true, the women do not want to have copulation with men, Grandpa!"

Old Parashar kept looking into the darkness. Such a strange thing he had never heard in his life that a young damsel had gone bereft of all desires to unite with a man, sexually. If that was true, then why would the men stay here, what for, exactly? They would venture into the unknown just for the lack of a female company. Yet he thought it to be a personal ordeal of a man. He said, "You all come to me, I shall tell you the ways to entice a woman. Can you recognize Asvagandha leaves?"

Then someone through the darkness spoke out, "We are not willing even."

"No desire? No urge at all to have sexual intercourse with a woman"?

"No, when one day my wife expressed her reluctance, I too began to feel likewise, since then"!

Old Parashar was keen on listening to the sound of water in the darkness. But it was so feeble that it had mingled with silence. These people needed to be detained here in these days of drought. After the rainfall, none of them would go away. But when would be the downpour? There was no such hint in the sky. How could he hold them back presently? A few days had passed by in digging the Ratnakarsagar. Water surfaced. But how much of that water could be raised, how much again would fill the lake up? Within a few days, this illusion of water would vanish and then again someone would be eager to escape. It would be from one to many. Now only women could stop them from going away. Only the affinity to women would hold these men back to this place now. But if the women were averse to sexual intercourse, if a wife refused to have copulation with her husband, why would these men stay behind, in this ghetto?

Parashar said, "If copulation with women is not done, no clouds will appear in the sky".

"But we have lost interest in it". The same answer came from some man.

Another man said the same thing, "No one desires it, irrespective of gender, be it masculine or feminine, Grandpa, it seems that we are getting old, so soon".

"What are you saying?" The old man screamed.

"Yes, I am newly married, my wife is a new bride, but after our wedding, there had been no rainfall. Now we feel no urge for sexual union, Grandpa, though by now my wife would have been in the family way"!

Old Parashar seemed to sit as an omniscient man, having knowledge of the three worlds in the darkness. He said, "That happens, some wives enter the family way a bit late. Ask your wife to see the women who are pregnant in the village frequently. Seeing them, she, too, will feel the desire to be impregnated."

That man heaved a long sigh of despair like the trees in darkness and said, "We are to go elsewhere, leaving this place behind".

"Why, haven't babies been born here, or are they not born now, don't man and woman have sexual intercourse here, if otherwise, then how have all of you been born, or how did I take birth? Let your wife be friends with a pregnant woman, when a woman with a baby in her womb will narrate, stretching her legs forward, how the baby moves and makes its presence known in her womb, even a seventy-year-old woman would love to be a mother again, she will feel desirous of being in the family way."

The man said, "Are you telling the truth"?

"Yes, nothing but the truth, you will get numerous pregnant women by about five to six months, let your wife go and see them".

Then someone else said, "I shall send then".

Another one added, "Me too. After having one child, my wife hasn't conceived anymore".

Piercing the darkness another voice got wafted in, "Then I shall send too, after the demise of the first baby, my wife only weeps and says she can't remember how to bear a child in her womb".

The old man was hearing. Listening to them, he felt that the only way of holding them back to this ghetto was to have their wives impregnated, by any means. None would dare to go to the unknown along with his wife, in the family way. He was really getting surprised to find that they were eager but failed to have copulation. Neither the woman nor the man succeeded.

Then a man asked, "Who among you have a pregnant woman in your house?"

"Certainly, there must be a few," Some other man answered, in the dark.

Then someone threw a query, "In which residence, tell me."

Another one came up to say, "Let me remember first".

"Try to remember, I can't recall though".

Then all went quiet, suddenly. The darkness grew more silent. The bat traversed the dark sky to a darker region, further off. The owl hooted somewhere from some tree! Hairs stood on their end on the old man's body. The old man, too, tried to remember, which house had a pregnant woman! Was any full-bellied, seven-eight-month pregnant woman being seen, lately? Either today, yesterday, day-before-yesterday, last full-moon day, or the new-moon day gone before it, in the month of Baisakh preceding this Jaisthya, in the month of Chaitra preceding that Baisakh, in Phalgun, Spring, winter or autumn? No, they could not remember. Why would they remember even? Really, they did not take note of it. Where had all the slow-moving women in the family way gone, who could be seen on the roads and thoroughfares, previously? The old man seemed to be visibly frightened, without being able to maintain his calm, he said, "Speak up, who have pregnant women in their households!"

None of them replied. At a distance, a vulture-chick cried out on a tree, afar. It made the darkness of the new-moon night even more mysterious. It appeared to the old man that someone was eavesdropping the conversation, staying invisible. How strange! Today, after much effort, water had surfaced! And today again, he was being overcome with fear! Today again the quest for pregnant women was on, and this very day, they could not be traced in the deep recesses of their minds! Perhaps, such a drought would leave things like that! On the happiest day, the shadows of sorrow would thus leap up to engulf all!

SEVENTY

Uddhavnarayan entered the city riding his horse, losing the composure of his mind as well as the sense of direction. Then, coming to a halt, he was taking stock of the whole matter, quite minutely. He had never seen any incident stranger in his life than the dry pond being filled with water. He was a man of suspicious nature. Even after considering sorcery, he did not give up doubts. He had even heard of a gold pitcher there. The water, as they said, had come out of that pitcher. The Shudras were really very mysterious as a race. They used to stay in a separate ghetto, they only knew, what they did secretly. Who knew whether they would have had recourse to the norms of an atheist! Uddhav began to mull over the matter. What was the mystery of water?

Tethering his horse to a tree, Uddhav entered a tavern. There, under the sky, in an ambience dimly lit by the lamp, boozing was on. While drinking, Uddhav disseminated the news among all present there. Fabricating the truth, adding an extra shade to the original. Without making the news widely public, Uddhav would also try to utilize it to his own benefit rather. Why would he let it out as a whole?

Uddhav said, "While returning, I had been stranded at a place, as there was a downpour today".

The drinkers of the tavern were taken aback, "Which year are you talking about"?

"Why today, just today itself".

Hearing this, Uddhav's drinking mates began to laugh boisterously and said, "Have you taken cannabis before coming for a drink, Mr. Sessions-Judge, or what"?

Uddhav began shaking his head, "No, I am telling you just the truth, but the rainfall was a bit strange"!

"How so"?

"It was raining heavily in one locale, but I stood outside its circumference".

"And then"?

"A lake got filled in by the rainwater."

"Then?"

"Many people there began to get drenched by the rains".

"Didn't you get soaked"?

"No, the more I moved towards it, the downpour began to recede further!"

"Where have you seen this?"

"Just on the way of my return, on hearing the noise of men's voices I reined my horse, and then I got to hear the pitter-patter of rains as I walked forward. It was raining heavily, the breeze was soothing, the clouds kept thundering".

"Where are you coming from now"?

Uddhav told a lie, "From the other side of the river, I went to the east."

"Why did you go there?"

"In search of a spy, drought is on, in our country, the enemies will try to make the best use of this opportunity, I am on my frequent rounds these days, keeping vigil on all corners as per the order of the Army Commander. He will perhaps return tomorrow."

None listened to the words he spoke later. All were familiar with Uddhav's verbosity. But if it really so happened in the east, no doubt, it was strange, bizarre rather! Again, Uddhav could not be believed. None in this city would be so adept to emulate Uddhav in lying brazenfacedly. Hence, one from among them cried out, "It happens in dreams… had you fallen asleep on the way"?

"How could I sleep on horseback"?

"I heard the heroes to do thus in the battlefields, they used to sleep on horseback."

Uddhav said, "I can do that too, but today the case was different."

"You might have slept in the shadow of a tree, as in dreams only such things happen".

"No, no, I never fall asleep on my way".

Then someone of the tavern took it for granted that Uddhav was high on having a puff at cannabis. No wonder, he might have lain somewhere, after having a concoction of different inebriating leaves like hemp etc. As they were expressing their doubts in an intoxicated state, Uddhav began to nod, "Really strange, the clouds were rumbling in the sky"!

"In dreams only, such strange things can happen!"

Uddhav slipped into silence. Then one of the companions said that sometimes dreams came to be true and it happened in his life repeatedly.

Uddhav thundered, "This was no dream at all"!

The man accepted it. It was to be accepted rather. Uddhav was a royal servant, he was powerful. But the man did not even forget to narrate his dream. One day, he had seen the second wife of old Durmukh, the owner of the pearl stall. And then it came to be true. She held his hands in the dream. One afternoon, he was walking down the path, all alone, and then he saw the young wife standing by the window.

Uddhav stopped the man saying, "In what way is the rainfall connected to the rainfall"?"

The man nodded, "No link at all! It was Spring at that time, I looked at Durmukh merchant's wife, standing on the road, I gesticulated…"

The man kept narrating a fabricated tale. These words, too, he was imagining, Uddhav was aware of that. But without being able to make out any hint, he roared, "I have come seeing it rain, why are you deviating to some other issue? I know Durmukh's wife to be a chaste, a pure woman devoted to her husband!"

The man recoiled within himself, and then in a low voice said, "Let me come to the point, I have even seen such a dream in which you are afloat in a peacock-boat with the wife of that old man by your side…now are you happy with the truth?"

Uddhav would never be carried away by such words. It was his secret pleasure! Uddhav had also tried once or twice to make a sign at the wife of that old Durmukh, but the old man had an eye on his wife always. Grapevines had it, that the old man never slept at night. It was not possible for her to go out on a romantic rendezvous. Given all probabilities, the matters were just different. Why would this matter meddle with the fact that Uddhav had come seeing it rain?

The man said, "I haven't seen the dream of rains since ages. If it so happened, it would surely come true".

Uddhav said, "No, today's is a fact".

"Then you had been trapped by some sorceress, they can accomplish such things, a magician got me to witness the moon on a pure new-moon night".

Uddhav said, "That is possible for the magicians, but mine is a fact, whatever I have witnessed is real!"

The man of the alehouse said, "Magic appears to be real indeed".

Uddhav got furious in an instant and asked, "Who are you, what is your name"?

The man was slightly frightened, "Why ask my name, what for"?

"Tell me your name, come on, tell me".

"Don't you know me? Don't we meet often in this tavern"?

"Yes, we meet indeed. But I need to know your name".

"Why? Haven't you heard my name before"?

"When did I hear"?

"Very often you hear, don't you ask me"?

"Yes, I do, but do you ever answer"?

"I told you umpteen times, you tend to forget always" … saying so, the man sits lowering his head.

Uddhav said, "I have to remember so many names, one or two can easily be forgotten"!

"Well, then let it be forgotten!"

"No, I have to keep searching the truth, the time is out of joint! These times are optimum for the attack from the alien forces. Certainly, one or two spies are around, they are being tracked, do you get me?"

The man's face went pale. In the dim light, Uddhav saw that the man seemed to be intimidated. It gave a fillip to Uddhav's mental strength. He was so powerful! He was a man of Royal Court, if he said, that, the Sun rises in the west, these men were supposed to believe that. Uddhav asked, "Where is that magician"?

"Which magician"?

"He who had shown you the rise of the moon during a new-moon night"!

The man rejoined, "I do not remember whether it was a new-moon night or not".

"But you just said that it was a new-moon night!"

"Men are prone to errors".

"Why errors, who is that magician"?

The man said, "It dates back long … many years, to be precise".

"How many years? Was then the drought on?"

"Perhaps the month of Baisakh. Naturally,there had been no rain then."

Uddhav was not gratified. He knew that his satisfaction would make the common people take him for granted. Only the dissatisfaction of a royal servant could engender fear among the ordinary citizens. And that was, essentially, the need of the hour. Otherwise, how could they be ruled? Uddhav asked, "Tell me quickly, which country did the sorcerer hail from?"

"He came to the fair in Ujjwain".

"But I know nothing of it"!

"These are from many eons ago"!

"So what? Who says that I shall not know anything of the past"?

The man kept quiet. Uddhav was even more miffed at him. He warned him, "You are not answering all my questions, you stand a chance of being thrown behind the bars"!

He started in fear and screamed, "But for which fault of mine"?

"Answer me, whatever I demand to know of you, where is the magician?"

"I do not know; I haven't seen him anymore".

"How does he look"?

"A man of tall stature, elderly"!

Uddhav asked, "Which country did he hail from"?

Then the man came up with a rejoinder, "No magician or sorcerer is there in reality, it is just a lie, I just said for no reason at all".

"Then who is that 'man of tall stature'?"

"No one", the man said.

Hearing this, Uddhav thundered, "You are confusing me, tell me, who that 'man of tall stature' is, lest you will definitely be imprisoned, now drought is on in the city of Avanti, numerous secret forces become active during drought, they are to be impeded. Later many rules and regulations will be clamped on this city, no easy loitering will be allowed, according to one's will. Are you an atheist?"

The man now got to his feet, "Let me go, the state of inebriation has been intercepted, there is darkness outside, no idea when the moon will come out, or whether it has already arisen. This darkness is simply disgusting, intolerable!"

"But you haven't answered my question!"

The man went silent. He took his seat again. The man thought of going away, disregarding Uddhav! But he was feeling the prick of fear somehow. Uddhav was an out-and-out villainous man. He was unparalleled in this city in causing harm to others, let alone doing good to them. Uddhav was breathing now. He kept quiet too. For sometime, both of them maintained silence and then it was Uddhav who barked like a dog, asking, "Was that man Dhruvaputra"?

The man was taken aback, he asked, "Which man"?

"That magician"?

"May be so".

"Then you are wrong, he is not 'elderly' but young!"

"Yes, exactly so".

"Tell me precisely, which magic had he shown"?

Then the man asked, "Was he tall in stature or short"?

"Of medium height", Uddhav's reply came pat, with a clue.

"Yes, exactly so, of medium height and not old at all".

Such nonsensical bandying of words went on between Uddhav and his drinking-mate. Uddhav seemed to be a bit glad. The man had helped him involve Dhruvaputra, in this matter. Did Dhrvaputra put up a magical show? Did he know that too? He asked, "Could you tell me where could Dhruvaputra be now"?

The man nodded in negative, "He is not here in this tavern".

"Why will he be in this ale-house, I mean to say, had he ever come here often?"

"Yes, of course he used to come, whoever doesn't come... a gentleman and doesn't drink?"

Uddhav was driven to silence. Despair, though little, was pinning him down, inwardly. The lascivious Dhruvaputra seemed to stay back in the city, even after being banished from there! Uddhav's body and limbs stiffened. But again, they became supple, gradually. If the foe could not be encountered face-to-face, how to stand up against him? One way was there... if he could marry Gandhavati according to demonic rules, that is by force! But for that, he would have to muster enough strength, even more...."

The man said, "So, I am taking your leave".

"Where will you go"?

"Where shall I go save my own residence, in this darkness?"

Uddhav stretched his legs, saying, "But I could not finish talking about the rain".

The man said, "You are fortunate to have witnessed rain". Uddhav said, "Strange! If such downpour sets in, no drought would be there anymore"!

"Won't it be there, thank God, all will be saved then"!

Uddhav maintained silence. Tarrying a little while, he said, "For the benefit of the citizens, for the well-being of the city of Ujjwain, for the need of the city of Avanti, it seems that the drought should continue".

"Why, what's the need"?

"You need not know so much, in gamut, I have witnessed a terrible rainfall, which is enough to fill in a big lake and how the clouds thundered, grr...grrr"!

By then, all in the tavern, seemed to take note of the matter with proper attention and then stood up in delight, asking, "Where? When? On which day? Which lake?"

Uddhav began to shake his head and said, "No, everything cannot be disclosed, let the concerned authority be informed first."

Whether Uddhav said or not, his words walked out of the alehouse along with him. Other drinkers brought it in. The words lay strewn beneath the open sky. Being the words of rainfall, it did not take long to get them wings! The words lay hovering like the clouds in the sky of Ujjwain. The words made way to the brothel, the house of the merchant, the palace and the Mahakaal temple. That day, Army-Commander Bikram had come back to the city. His battery of soldiers was on rounds in the thoroughfares of the city. They were looking for prey. They had gone to protect the merchants who had come from far-off lands and the pilgrims, but who would assure security to whom and who again would obey the directives of the King, in verbatim? On hearing about rainfall, when the Chief Priest was planning to look into the matter, the Army-Commander had just returned to the city. It was customary to see Lord Mahakaal on one's return to the city and hence he entered the shrine to listen to a fictitious tale of rainfall!

SEVENTY-ONE

While visiting Lord Mahakaal, the great Army-Commander, Bikram, got to meet up with the Chief Priest, in the inner temple. The heroic Army-Commander, Bikram, was young in age, tall in stature, possessing a wide chest and a bull-like firm shoulder. His voice was grave, solemn, quite manly. Close-cropped, curly hair adorned his head, he had a pair of bright, radiant eyes, and his complexion was fair. He had a healthy well-built physique, both his arms and thighs were brawny, muscular. Bikram sat on the floor, holding his backbone taut, like the pinnacle of the Mahakaal temple. Before him, the Chief Priest looked a mismatch. The Brahmin was old, quite aged in front of this young, virile splendour, was of short-stature, with a bit of stoop even. He was copper-complexioned, with little hair on his head, had a mouth sans teeth, though both his eyes were restive, like a cunning bloke. The door of the base-temple was closed. The Chief Priest had dispensed with the serving-maid of Lord Mahakaal. The devadasi was not swaying the fan for none of the three — Lord Mahakaal, the Priest, the Army Commander.

Chief Priest asked, "Why have you come back so suddenly? Hadn't you set out for the Arabian Sea in the west?"

"Yes", the handsome King's Officer rejoined, "Now I cannot stay leaving Ujjwain behind."

"Then what will happen to the merchants?"

"Why shall I protect the traders and again what responsibility do my battery of soldiers have?"

"Then why did you go there"?

"The King had sent me with a motive of removing me from Ujjwain"!

"Has he come to know about your intention?"

"I don't know, but that is no less impossible, perhaps the rejection by the queen has made the King suspicious!"

Old, Chief Priest stayed quiet for quite some time, and then asked abruptly, "Are you ready"?

"Yes".

"Won't you be scared if the cloud thunders"? The Chief Priest asked.

The young and handsome King's man smiled, "Clouds will not definitely thunder in my fear"!

"Won't you give up desires for the love of clouds"?

"No illusion, no love will engender in my mind, I want the drought to continue".

"Because of drought, the inhabitants of the city are leaving for elsewhere".

"Exit and entrance will continue, even many are pouring in this city from elsewhere, fearing drought."

Old Priest expressed his apprehension, "If rains would make its presence, then?"

"Before that, everything should be settled"!

"Are your troops of soldiers protecting the Ionian Greek business-fellows"?

"No, they are plundering, I have given them the freedom of pillage so that they cannot reach up till this end, I have a hunch that the nimbus clouds of monsoon would invariably come at the heels of the merchants!"

The Chief Priest rested his wizened hand on the head of the royal fellow and said, "If the merchants do not come, if Subhag Dutta sets out on a journey, Ujjwain then is sure to be ruined, giving and receiving will come to an end".

"I shall construct again, I am sure, monsoon will be here".

"How so? The wheel of the Sun-God's chariot is getting stuck"!

"Yes, I heard it on my way of return. This news has spread like wildfire, even far beyond, is it your brainchild"?

The Chief Priest said, "I shared it with the lunatic physician, just by way of joking, but he took it to be true and now everyone in the city is discussing this issue!"

The royal servant stood calm, looking at the stone-image of Lord Mahakaal. He was not speaking anymore. The Chief Priest was observing him, and doing so, he said, "Oh Emperor, I can see the holy mark of royal coronation on your forehead! You will definitely be victorious!"

At the address of the old Priest, the Army-Commander got visibly thrilled. He was waiting to hear such an address since long. The first address made his eyes glow with happiness and then it led on to a sense of contentment. He kept on looking at the idol of Lord Mahakaal only. Only Lord Mahakaal would be able to change his luck, absolutely. To make that address come true! Then, the old Priest whispered, "This is true, that, once you ascend the throne, downpour will be unleashed on this city, and that is for sure!"

"How long will this land be devoid of rainfall!"

"Yes, Lord Mahakaal seems to wait for you, if you shoulder the responsibility of the Kingdom, He would free the clouds, taken captive otherwise, to hover over the sky of Ujjwain, the sky would again have clouds floating in it, you must ascend the throne of Ujjwain!"

The great Army Commander was listening to him. He was being conscious of his own position by the words of the old man. He was even getting doubtless about his future. The merchant, Subhag Dutta, had wanted him. But that merchant himself was going to leave Ujjwain. He had given birth to an ambition for the throne in him! That ambition seemed to be blind like lust, inordinate, beyond right and wrong, as if he would not be calm unless it was fulfilled.

The Army Commander Bikram, said, "The troops of soldiers will be back in a few days, now the ground for occupying the throne was prepared, loud wails reverberate on all sides, men are leaving one place for another in the hope of clouds, every nook is abuzz with the aspersions cast on the King!"

The old man said, "So long the King without masculinity will be there on the throne, man will suffer immensely. Just a few days back, the royal employee, Uddhavnarayan, has uttered a strange thing and it has gone rife in the city. I have called him and he will be here now."

"He is just an ordinary Sessions-Judge"!

"Even an ordinary Sessions-Judge could be of much need, he claims to have witnessed rainfall somewhere, it has to be found out whom he bears allegiance to, for whose benefit he has made the word spread like a wildfire! He is certainly the King's employee, why then he made the lie public, who has asked him to do so? What leads to what else, God knows! Now if it rains, it would surely forebode ill, it would ruin everything!"

The Army-Commander stood up. As he offered his hand, the old Priest also stood up, taking him as a support. Unbolting the door, they came out. At a distance, devadasi Lalita sat, hanging her head low. Even further, sat Subhadra. At the creak of opening the door, both of them stood up. Pointing the forefinger to Lalita, the old man said, "This is the devadasi whom the King had raped".

The Army-Commander was strutting off. He did not stop. The royal demeanours were being more pronounced in him. While walking at his heels, the old Priest said, "Please come to my room, dear Emperor, come thou, maid Subhadra, swing the fan for the King of Ujjwain"!

Coming to the front of the room, both of them found Uddhavnarayan to be present. Looking at the Army-Commander, Uddhav recoiled in fear. His face seemed to shrivel up. Sitting on the floor, he bowed his head down to the feet of the Army-Commander and in a low voice said, "Lord, I am Uddhav, I am innocent".

The Chief Priest had an illusion that Uddhav had bowed to his feet and said, "Where's rain, drought is setting the city ablaze and you have come seeing rainfall somewhere"?

"Yes, my Lord"!

"Tell me the truth, otherwise you would be decapitated".

Uddhav did not raise his head. He kept touching his forehead on the feet of the royal dignitary. The Army Commander found him to be the replica of the Old Priest's past, his prime of youth! And the Old Priest was the distant future of this Sessions-Judge! He had seen the Sessions-Judge, but not thus. Such coward! He touched the back of Uddhav bending low and in a solemn, deep voice he asked, "What have you seen?"

"Water!" Uddhav kept shivering. It seemed to him that a large falchion was hovering over his neck. Only it was to descend, that was all! Oh Lord Mahakaal! What fault was there in visualizing water, talking about the rain?

"Where's water"? The wizened Priest tended to be thunderous!

"At the Shudra ghetto".

Eliciting the rejoinder, the priest turned to the Army-Commander! They exchanged glances. The Priest thought— Why Shudra ghetto again? The Shudra ghetto was the abode of all demons. The habitation of the messenger of Death! Was there any rainfall? When? This could hardly be true. If it would have been true, the Shudra ghetto would have to be demolished. How could there be rain in the Shudra ghetto with no downpour anywhere else? Certainly, some deeper motive must be there behind such spreading of rumour! The Shudras could never be trusted! Now this country was on the verge of a drastic change! Drought would only continue at this point in time.

"How is it that none is here to know about a rainfall"?

"It's not rainfall, it is water, that has surfaced in the Ratnakarsagar!"

"Who told you"? The Priest asked, visibly astonished.

"I have witnessed!"

"How did it surface?"

"I do not know, they are adept in sorcery, charms and incantations".

The Army-Commander then asked Uddhav to leave. Getting to his feet, Uddhav kept looking at the other end with folded palms. He dared not keep looking at the face of the Army-Commander! The Army-Commander ordered, "Go there by dawn tomorrow and tell us how the water surfaced!"

Uddhav answered, "By magic"!

"You must go and investigate who that magician is"!

"Sure, Lord"!

"Come and tell the Priest"!

"Shall do, Lord!"

"No other soul should know about it!"

"None will know, Lord!"

"If anyone knows, you will be beheaded".

"Agreed", my Lord! Uddhav again went down on his knees to touch his head to the ground. He could feel that something was imminent in the city! He could not ascertain what exactly. But he would have to remain alert at this moment of time.

Now Army Commander Bikram told the Priest, "Do you have anything else to ask this man?"

Old Priest asked, "Yes I do, has he really witnessed"?

Uddhav lowered his head to say, "Yes, my Lord"!

"Try to remember whether you have seen with your own eyes or have heard of it!"

Uddhav kept mum. He could not make out what to say. But his conjecture alerted him, neither the Chief Priest nor the Army Commander wanted the rain to pour, hence, this hearsay of downpour would not please them. He thought, why should he be disliked by the royal power, hence, he blatantly said, "Lord, I have heard of it."

"Who told you?"

"A man".

"And then"?

"Just heard of it but how could the rumour spread in my name?"

The old Priest said, "Why didn't you speak the truth so long, go and announce in the city that the news is false and put the man who spread the rumour behind the bars."

Uddhav said, "As you wish, my Lord"!

"And go and search for the real news".

"The Lake is filled with water".

"Have you seen it?"

"Yes, my Lord!"

"Go and spread the word in the city that all is false, the drought is still on".

"Lord, Any magician or someone...?" Uddhav could not finish the sentence in fear. Both the eyes of the Army Commander kept vetting him. He could feel a chill at the nape.

"Go and nab the sorcerer", the Priest ordered.

"He is not there in the city", Uddhav gibbered.

"Go, make sure that no news of rain does any rounds in the city, if anyone says that there's been a downpour, he will be beheaded, got me?"

Uddhav could understand every bit of it. He could comprehend that he would have to be wary of drinking wine. Alehouse, brothel, nowhere he would be free to open his mouth. But he was really fortunate! The Army-Commander had trusted him with a duty. It proved that his significance was being felt. He thought that this opportunity would never be given a miss. Now his progress had started off with elan. In excitement, Uddhav emerged out of the Mahakaal temple, took the horse to the bank of the river, Gandhavati, and stood there. It seemed he was awaiting someone. Someone was to be taken captive. Who will he take captive? The man of that alehouse? But he was not being seen anymore. Uddhav did not even know his name. He kept thinking how to shoulder his responsibility well, which he had been trusted with.

SEVENTY-TWO

For a few days, all the tenements of the Shudra ghetto had been ransacked for pregnant women. How strange! In each house of the habitation, there was no dearth of any woman fit to be pregnant, there was no dearth of any man suitable enough to impregnate a woman, yet no pregnant woman was found anywhere. Old Parashar walked around the Shudra ghetto on foot. He began to feel dejected. He had never come across such an incident in his life. Not just pregnant women, even new-born child was not there in any household.

An old woman said, "The young wife must be a barren one, another one has to be brought in, after waiting for a year. Just in two-three months of marriage, all women get into the family way, but even after so long, she is yet to bear a child in her womb…"

While sauntering around, the old man asked, "Is any baby born in any household here"?

"I don't know".

Since long, no baby had taken birth in any household, and for so long, none had taken note of it. Now it came to draw everyone's attention. That meant, for long, no woman had been pregnant in this locale. Such infertility proved the words spoken by those men that evening, to be true. Both men and women had lost their urge for copulation, beyond everyone's knowledge."

The old man kept sitting all alone, at the base of the distant banyan tree. Water had filled the lake almost to the brim. The old man mused inwardly… The mouth of the gold pitcher went uncorked, and now there was nothing to fear anymore. But fear lay elsewhere. None would stay back even for the attraction of that water. If there would be no desire, no aspiration for something, what would man live for?... The old man looked up to the sky. The kettle of vultures kept circling, far above, in the sky. Old Parashar's eyes narrowed while beholding the spectacle. If rainfall stayed suspended, such things would continue to happen. Then during drought, humans forgot to give birth to children even! Drought would put an end to man's desires and longings. A long, ashen shadow began to stretch, before the eyes of the old man! It seemed to him that, it was useless to live any longer. The lands would be devoid of crops, the sky would harbour no clouds, no house would have a baby, no new wife would be pregnant, the city of Ujjwain was to be barren, sterile! Old Parashar longed to die. Truly, he did. He was trying in sundry ways to stop rendering the city Shudra-less. But it could not be sensed that the Lord of the Skies, Himself, was rendering everything hollow, creating a vacuum from within.

A youth came calling the old man, "Have you fallen asleep, Grandpa?"

Parashar scrambled up to senses, wiped off the astringent saliva and said, "Eyes drooped, heavy with sleep".

"What have you found by going from door to door"?

"That the rumour is really true", the old man replied.

Then he said, "Do you remember Bishaayi, Grandpa"?

"Bishaayi?! Since long he has left us"!

"His wife died during childbirth"!

Parashar could recall. Then a spell of blaze had already begun. Was there any downpour after that? No memory surfaced. Before that? How long ago was it? He failed to remember anything. The old man heaved a long sigh and said, "Now there has to be a heavy shower"!

"Since long, we are getting such hollow assurances. But the clouds are blissfully forgotten of this way"! The man said.

Parashar said, "What shall I do? How powerful am I, Lankesh"?

"You are the one who brought up water from the hell, you are the talk of the town!"

"Who are they talking about me"?

"All are saying, only you will be able to bring down water from the sky!"

"You talked about the gold pitcher, Grandpa, that has come to be true, now you have to tell us how the water will tumble down from the sky, how clouds will hover over"!

Old Parashar threw a vacant stare at Lankesh. Lankesh was muttering under his breath, "Old Grandpa has that power, as he has succeeded in lifting the water from the hell, he must bring the water of the sky down likewise! Otherwise, those who are still in Ujjwain will go away, leaving this city".

"Where will they go? Walk close at the merchant's heels or what"?

"No idea, but we will go to such a place where the women give birth to children every year, pregnant women abound in all households, all houses are replete with human babies. The cries of the children, peals of laughter of the kids are an all-time affair. There, the men and women will be able to taste their youth, if youth is not enjoyed at all, then why is it given to us by God?"

Parashar said, "This place of ours was like that only"!

"It was, now it is not so, nowadays the women do not go in the family way".

Parashar said, "Let us wait and see for a few days more".

"What to see? If water does not pour from the sky, it will not happen too, we will have to take the way that stretches before us— either in the north, south, the east or west!"

Old Parashar said, "That's how you will, but we have no idea how far the stretch of land has been affected by this drought! How far will man go?"

"That far which he needs to remain alive, but Grandpa, if you can bring clouds to the sky then all the women will be pregnant, women generally become pregnant if clouds swim in the sky".

"Who said so?"

"My wife".

"Who, again, enlightened her"?

"She heard that, she said on witnessing the clouds she felt desirous."

The old man said, "We don't have any pregnant woman amongst us, but is the picture the same in the rich men's households in Ujjwain as well?"

"How will we know? Who will tell us?" Lankesh retorted.

"None will help us get it, yet, all the sorrows and woes of life are ours, even the pain of drought has been thrust on us along with the fire, by God!"

Lankesh said, "I heard that the sins are all ours, hence we have the Shudra birth!"

The old man cried out, "Is it then the end of the Shudras? If the women do not get pregnant, Shudras will not take birth in the Shudra families, anymore!"

"If there's no birth, where will we go with our sins, Grandpa? You bring the clouds, have another dream to tell us where the water remains latent in the sky, where there is another gold pitcher!"

The old man kept sitting under the tree. Lankesh went to the lake. Going there, he found that water had risen almost to the brim. Even just a few days back, Ratnakarsagar was thoroughly hard and dry. And after that, it seemed, there had been an invisible rainfall. He threw a gaze at the sky above. He was seemingly enervated by the dry, cloudless sky! He walked towards the ghetto. All were in a fix, they did not know how to make use of the water that had come up. None wanted to touch this magical water anymore. They said, let it be there, they would manage with the river-water, as they were doing for long! His wife, his mother opined thus even. Did all others think in the same vein? They thought, if the hell went dry, ran out of water, then? He would have to ask others.

Old Parashar sat motionless, on the root of the banyan tree. All day long! All day shadows remained there but when it was high noon, the circles of light stayed on the body of the elderly person for quite some time. And later they receded. The sun in the west veered. Looking at the sunlight outside the precincts of the shadows, the old man began to think, what did he exactly know of the clouds? What did he know of the dreams even? He narrated the tale to Lankesh and his mates which he had heard long ago, and how that story of the gold pitcher came to be true! The wizened man thought within, I am just an ordinary human, how can I say when the clouds in the sky will abound? There were a few balls of cloud like deep black shadows and a few again were just like ashen shadows! Dhruvaputra used to say that the birds got impregnated by the clouds only, humans too perhaps toed the same line, it seemed! And he could perceive that lately!

The old man went on thinking likewise, all through the day. Being just a lesser mortal, he had no idea of anything in the least! So many bigwigs were there in Ujjwain! There was the King, his courtiers, Army-Commander, numerous royal employees, how handsome, wise and mighty they were; there were even many pundits, astronomers, the group of traders, rich like the Jews, the line of Priests and amongst them, the Shudras figured nowhere as human beings! The Shudras were never taken as humans by anyone! The Shudras, even themselves knew, that they were not humans. Did any Shudra have the right to usher in clouds in the sky? Were the Shudras entitled to pray for the clouds at all? Was he blessed with the right to dream of the clouds in this birth?

In the evening a few of them had come. Lankesh asked, "Won't you go inside the dwelling, Grandpa?"

The elderly man answered, "No".

"Why not? It is already night, a new-moon fortnight"!

Old Parashar said, "I shall not go to my hut, without ushering in the clouds!"

"Will ever clouds float,if you don't retire to your residence"?

"I shall not have rice, unless I bring in the clouds"!

"Are you sure, Grandpa, that clouds will float if you are in fasting"?

The old man said, "Without bringing clouds, I shall not touch the water even!"

"Will you stay back just in here"?

"Yes, all night, all day long, I shall supplicate to the clouds, even though all leave me here alone, Ujjwain is rendered into a crematorium, I shall sit here to pray for clouds, even if I die asking for clouds, I shall keep asking, keep praying!"

All sat dazed, looking at old Parashar. The man had thrust them into a glaring problem. How would they go away for the unknown, leaving a man who would sit beneath a banyan tree, all alone, without having rice, water or without even dropping by at his residence for a little respite? Once upon a time, this man was an undaunted soldier. He had gone far-off with the battery of armies, crossing numerous meadows and rivers! Listening to those tales, the lads and lasses had attained youth, had come of age. All cried in the dark, looking at the sky, Oh God, give us water, otherwise our old Parashar will die, praying hard to you. For how many days would a man live, without drinking water, without having rice? If the old man dies, we will all go elsewhere, leaving Ujjwain. Not a single Shudra will stay back. They will not stay, will not stay, will not stay back. And will God be able to spend His days in a Shudra-less land? Will the King, the courtiers, the Priest, the Army-Commander be able to reside in an Ujjwain, devoid of Shudras?

That night, none at the Shudra ghetto slept. Not even the children. Even the boys and girls stayed wide awake. The women stayed awake on one end, while the men on the other. Men and women did not retire to bed, did not sit beside one another for amorous exchanges, did not care to touch one another even. They were thinking of Old Parashar! The Village-Chieftain was sitting, all by himself, at the base of the banyan tree, for the clouds! How would they fall asleep?

The darkness of the full-moon fortnight was purblind, only the starlight lent a little visibility. Thousands and thousands of stars bedecked the sky. Casting a glance at the sky, who would say that the sky had gone cloudless since long! While thinking about the clouds, the women kept mulling over sundry other thoughts! Someone had said that if clouds did not surface, no woman would be pregnant. They were praying for clouds on the sly. In the darkness, such a prayer was being lost.

The young wife inquired of an old woman, "How had been your times, Granny?"

"What do you mean by 'How had been your times'? What in particular are you referring to?" The old woman asked.

"Why is it so with us, Granny"?

The old woman said, "I don't know. I had given birth to eleven children, you know, young wife!"

"I, too, want to give birth".

"If you want so, why doesn't it happen"?

"How did you make it possible"?

Hearing so, the old woman giggled, "The way as it happens, the man plants it in our womb, I don't remember everything in detail".

"Ah, how did your husband make love to you?"

"While pregnant, I was given more rice, I used to gobble more".

"No Granny, I mean to say, how did you make love to each other"? The old woman tried to get the drift of the statement. She could understand too, but could not answer so easily. Among her eleven children, five had died untimely, from among the rest of six, four were girls. They were there in that ghetto, they were growing old, along with time. Of the two sons, not a single was there in Ujjwain. Even the old woman had no idea about where they had been to. Her husband had kicked the bucket long ago. Now the old lady was oblivious of everything. Even of her union with her husband! Though that haunted her memory, she could not take it to be the matter of this birth! Her body had bent down, her head had turned hoary, the skin on her body came sagging, the pair of breasts went dry, being shrunk and lost in her chest—how could such a woman engage in sexual intercourse with her husband in the field, in the farm, in the dark courtyard even in the forest lining the river-bank during noon? Was this woman ever beautiful like the woman in front, with well-formed breasts, rotund buttocks and rich tufts of hair? She was no less than her husband in exercising her authority! But all these seemed incredible to her presently. If she had youth, where had it all gone and when? Why didn't she sense that her joyous youth was being stolen by someone, stealthily? The old woman thought all to be a fib. This was only true. This senile existence was the only truth. And, equally true was the birth of her eleven children. The demise of the five of her children was true too. All these were true but neither youth, nor the male, not even their copulation was true! And if not true, then who would have given birth to the babies? The old woman said, "Cloud!"

"Cloud? Is cloud your husband?"

The old woman said, "As birds were made pregnant, I was done similarly by the clouds. It is difficult to be impregnated sans clouds in the sky, had ever been any copulation there in the crop-fields, in the forest or by the riverside, as happened in my previous birth, in my dreams"?

The wife retorted, "That never happens with us!" Such conversations ran through the night. At the approach of dawn, a few of them slept off. Perhaps, they dreamt of the clouds in their sleep, or perhaps they dreamt of sexual intercourse in their dreams, unabashedly. The men dreamt, the women did as well. During their union, they seemed to hear the pitter-patter of the rain. They had dreams of the clouds and the rains too.

Ujjwain was suffering from drought since long! During drought, all dreams used to end in smoke, used to be aborted to failure in the long run. After they woke up, looking at the sky and earth inundated with sunrays, the dreamy mass seemed to have forgotten to nurture dreams even.

Such was common during drought. Though determined to dream, they used to forget to have a dream even. They took this waterless world, red-hot sky, earth and birth-less emptiness to be their destiny. There was no way-out save praying to Lord for the rains. Only the rains would have the possibility of turning into a birth-link!

That dawn vibrated with the noise of the hooves of a pony. Uddhavnarayan, seated on the horse, began to enter the Shudra ghetto, yelling at the top of his voice, "Where, where is that sorcerer, who had ushered water into the Ratnakarsagar"?

The people, who had not even forty winks all night, lined up to the edge of the lake, in slow steps. There only Uddhav kept standing, he had come there at dawn, being well-decked as befitting a royal servant! Uddhav knew full well that sans diadem, silken cloth, so forth, he could not be told apart from the Shudras of the colony! Uddhav shouted, "Who has brought in water,the King orders the news to reach him".

"It is the Village-Chief, Old Parashar!"

"Old Parashar, where is he?"

"Sir, at the base of the banyan tree".

"Go and ask him to come here".

"He is in deep meditation for propitiating the clouds. If the clouds do not pile up...".

Each one of them introduced Old Parashar, one by one. That made both the eyes of Uddhav to distend. But he was a dubious man. He knew the Shudras were not entitled to practise asceticism, hence, where would his meditation lead on to? And was it the right place for practising asceticism? One would have to go to the forests, to the mountains. But it was distinctly seen that water had surfaced. It was clearly seen that the earth had been dug, on the edge of the lake stood earthen heaps. He asked, "The earth had been dug since a few days! Who dug it? By whose order?"

The answer reached Uddhav. Along with it, he also learnt of the gold pitcher. Water was to spurt out of that pitcher and it happened accordingly. Where was that pitcher? The old man knew. Uddhav came down from the edge of the lake. He kept walking. Where was that old man? Gold pitcher! He must go back along with the gold pitcher! But reaching the banyan tree, he found old Parashar, sitting calm at the base of the tree and three women sat touching their head on the ground. To his utter surprise, he found himself look like a hermit, in the truest sense! The old man, who, once upon a time, had been a soldier in the army of Gandharvasen was now engrossed in a serious pursuit of making the rain happen.

Uddhav had come. He ran his horse to cross the Shudra ghetto and stand there. He had not bowed down to the old savant in front of the Shudras. But from here, he paid his respect, from within. Who could tell what remained hidden and in whom? Water had surfaced in Ratnakarsagar! Whether by digging the ground or by uncorking the mouth of the gold pitcher, the water had come to fill the pond, no doubt! When there had been no water anywhere, the old man had raised the water up, and now he would also make it rain. He went to the Mahakaal Temple to bow down his head and say, "Oh Brahmin Lord, the old Shudra is engrossed in meditation for ushering in a downpour".

The old Priest did not react to it, rather he was keen on knowing the niggling details. At the behest of Old Parashar, they had dug the earth of Ratnakarsagar to siphon water to the surface of the pond. Now they were saying that after succeeding in fathoming the hell-sea, the old man would explore the sky-ocean too!

The Chief Priest did not turn deaf ears to a single word. He listened to each word, rather attentively. Uddhav, too, became free of all worries, being able to share everything. He nursed a doubt though there was no way to express it. He was, as though, destined to live with the misgivings.

SEVENTY-THREE

Tamradhvaj had come, all of a sudden, at the close of noonday, when the shadows began to be cast on the courtyard as the sun had gone behind the hut. Gandhavati, Reba, Shivnath, all three of them, saw that this astronomer from Dasharno was gasping for breath, traversing such a long way on foot, under the raging sun! Reba and Gandhavati grew busy to welcome him. The man had come, thirsty. Perhaps, hungry even. Tamradhvaj just slaked his thirst by taking bites at 'tilkut'. Taking a breath, driving off his weariness, he said, "Really, I had gone out of my wits. Since the morning, I am roaming around coming out of home, but the noon is really oppressive these days, all the way not a soul I had come across, even the chirp of the birds could not be heard anywhere, a wake of vultures sat around two-three dead beasts. It seemed to me that many residents of Avanti had left already".

Reba said, "Couldn't you have avoided strolling around, under such a blinding sun, since the morning?"

"I am fed up of living alone, Maa! Acharya is not there, the hermitage is literally a picture of desolation! It seems as if I am awaiting Acharya's return, again it was I, who had burnt his bones, taking them to the bank of the river Shipra!"

Hearing this, Gandhavati screamed in an inaudible voice. Nowadays, fear had crept into her mind. Perhaps, Dhruvaputra had suffered the same fate as Acharya. Shivnath had shared every bit of information with them. On learning so, it occurred to Gandhavati that the same fate might have befallen her father Kartikkumar as had happened to Acharya or Dhruvaputra. She was reminded of this. She could not control herself anymore. She wiped her eyes with the scarf.

Then Tamradhvaj said, "Tidings are here, so many things are transpiring in the city, I am just back from the city. You know, Grandpa, water has surfaced from the underground, in that Ratnakarsagar, located in the Shudra ghetto".

"Strange! Then, water is not yet depleted in the underground!" Reba blabbed.

"No mother, that too is an ocean, so many subterranean rivers are there in the hell, can all of them dry up? Let me narrate the tale of a gold pitcher"!

While listening to the tale, Gandhavati's eyes grew wide. They brightened up. Whether the corked mouth of the pitcher had been opened or not sealed as yet, the water in the Ratnakarsagar will not exhaust.

Gandhavati asked, "Have you seen that gold pitcher"?

"No, that cannot be seen".

Shivnath was thinking, when not a drop of water was anywhere in the city, how could it sneak in the lake of the Shudra locality! What did this incident point to? The Shudras had been blessed with the benediction of Lord Mahakaal! What was up? If rain remained absent for long, would the gods lose their sense of judgment and the power of analysis too? The lowborn Shudras, who were mostly untouchable, who were born just to exculpate themselves from the sins of the previous births, how was it that water surfaced in their locality, in their water-body? And, nowhere else?

Shivnath inquired, "Do they know magical tricks"?

"Why, you had already seen them digging the earth of the pond!"

"Will digging cause the water to surface? Then why aren't the other ponds in the city being excavated? Even the pond in the palace has dried up"!

Then Tamradhvaj talked about another amazing endeavour taken by the people of the Shudra ghetto, old Parashar sat in meditation, if it would not rain, he would fast to death. He was sitting there beneath the banyan tree.

Shivnath said, "The Shudras have no right to asceticism".

"But he has taken his seat there, and again Ratnakar, the hunter, had grown into the sage, Valmiki!"

Shivnath kept quiet. Everything was facing a change. It would really be a matter of wonder, if anyone from among the Shudras, could usher in rain with his ascetic power. Let it happen, let the rains pour down. Shivnath gazed at the indifferent look of the sky. All seemed to have come to a standstill. Shivnath went out. He would go to the bank of the river, Gambhira. Then Tamradhvaj called from behind to say, "Grandpa, there's another piece of news for you!"

Shivnath paced forward, "Yes, what do you have to say"?

"I have met that man named Mahaparshwa."

Shivnath withdrew a little. He had not disclosed anything of that day to either Reba or Gandhavati. Not about the brothel, for sure. Now how would it be, if Tamradhvaj kept talking of that enchanting whore in front of all? Lifting his hand up, Shivnath said, "Let it be left at that. We will talk later".

Tamradhvaj got the hint. Yet he had not given up. He came out of the courtyard following Shivnath and said, "Devadutta, the whore, will be leaving this city with Subhag Dutta, the merchant".

"What do you say"? Shivnath turned around, astonished.

"Yes, a barrage of astounding events happens everywhere and the drought is the chief cause behind it".

"Dhruvaputra had been beaten just for a whore and the merchant had become ferocious in wrath following the whore's refusal, I came to know that day".

"Yes, that day we heard Devadutta saying that, 'the tycoons are usually ruthless'!"

"Then how could she be mesmerized by the tycoon again?"

"Mahaparshwa is overjoyed presently", Tamradhvaj said.

They were on the street now. The way had coursed down towards the river. At the close of the daytime, a breeze was blowing from the south-western direction. The earth was feeling soothed.

Shivnath asked, "Isn't he the pimp, the keeper of the whores' doors?"

"Yes, reaching the overture of Devadutta to the merchant, he had got a pearl necklace. He was moving about wearing it on his neck. Seeing me, he treated me quite cordially."

"What is the reason of Devadutta's change of opinion"?

The pimp said, The merchant will go to the land of the Gandharvas, that land happens to be the fatherland of Devadutta. learning it her mind has undergone a change. Mahaparshwa is beside himself with joy, he says he will also follow the band of traders, even that being the land of his previous birth , he is in fact, an accursed Gandharva - a lunatic!"

Hearing this Shivnath said, "The count of insane folks is on the rise!"

Tamradhvaj smiled, "That can obviously be said, but he was invariably a Gandharva in his previous birth — many such matters were discussed. But as Devadutta is going to leave this city for good, you have reason for feeling relieved for Dhruvaputra"!

"Does it matter to be concerned about the man who is not there in the city, at all?"

"He will be back, I suppose!"

"Will he, are you sure?"

"Can anyone go away by leaving Ujjwain for good? Is there any city like this? May it be Balkh or the land of the angels"!

"When will he come back?"

"When he will feel like returning!"

Shivnath said, "Reba, Gandhavati all are avid to listen to such news from you, please go and see them".

Tamradhvaj came back to the courtyard. He found a wooden stool kept in the middle of it. Now, the sun had receded. Beneath the open sky, while taking his seat on the wooden stool, he found Gandhavati nowhere nearby. Reba Maa sat at a little distance. Reba seemed to await Tamradhvaj! Without getting to see Gandhavati, Tamradhvaj was overcome by an anxiety, finding only Reba, waiting. As he sat down, Reba said, "I have something to tell you".

"I know", Tamradhvaj smiled, just to conceal his anxiety.

Reba said, "What do you know"?

Tamradhvaj shook his head, and said, "That whore, who was at the centre of a rumour, who was the cause of Dhruvaputra's quitting the city, is about to leave the city herself".

Tamradhvaj could not find any response from Reba to such news! He was not even surprised failing to detect it. Yet he said, "Dhruvaputra may return now, he won't be able to resist the temptation of coming back".

"Who says so, when all are escaping, why will he return, that cruel man?"

"Nothing runs in the same manner, forever".

Reba said, "Dhruvaputra is dead to me. Let his matter be not raised".

"What are you saying, Maa"?

"To speak the truth, he might even die like your Acharya"!

"Are you praying for his demise"?

"He should not return to us! I want to tell you something".

Tamradhvaj had lowered his head. He seemed to hear the noise of Gandhavati's breathing. Reba again said, "Shall I say this or will you hear from Gandhavati?"

"Does it relate to you or Gandhavati"?

"Both of us, look, my husband is yet to be back, I cannot leave Ujjwain at all, I shall stay back in this hut itself."

"Who asks you to leave"?

"One has to leave, those who would want to live, must think of leaving Avanti, Ujjwain. How long will you be here, won't you start for Dasharno? I am hearing that the city is being evacuated, with no souls to be around!"

"Rightly learnt! But where shall I go leaving all of you, if I leave for Dasharno, you, Gandhavati, Grandpa, all will have to come along with me".

Reba shook her head to desist, "No, I shall not go, who knows if my husband returns"!

Tamradhvaj said, "Then no one will leave".

"No, they will, but I have no way to escape. Look, you are like my son just as Dhruvaputra was. I shall be waiting for my husband, all my life, I shall even accept widowhood in the hope of his return, if the period of his banishment ends at all!"

Tamradhvaj whispered, "I have heard that song of yours, Maa!"

"Which song?"

"That song, that number!"

"Which song, where did you get to hear it"?

Tamradhvaj said, "In the city, Maa! Heard in the forest, in the middle of large tracts of grassland, in the darkness, in moonbeams, amid oppressive sunlight even".

"My song? Which song of mine…?" Abruptly Reba grew anxious to know.

Tamradhvaj hummed the tune, learnt from Devadutta, in exact perfection and made it float in the air. He went crooning,

"On my husband's chest lean my pals, all the neighbour women…

My own husband was in alien land, like a lost cloud, by then…"

"Sing this song once again, come on", Tamradhvaj reiterated.

Listening to it, Reba was eager to hear this again. Tamradhvaj crooned again,

"Blossoms sprout on mango tree… Ashok flowers are being shed … My consort's off to another land … I remember him, instead."

Her face seemed to redden. Hanging her face low, Reba said, "From whom have you heard it? Who, in the city, shared this with you? But no one is expected to know of it, I have never sung this song, yet the words encase my feelings in the self-same tune and words".

"Haven't you ever crooned the numbers in your mind, Maa?"

Reba's tears coursed down her cheeks, she said, "Now I think it to be my song, my son, who has told you of this song of mine"?

"No one has told me, I just surmise".

"Tell me again, let my heart be soothed, my son, who has composed this song?"

"Don't you know the composer, Reba Maa?"

"No, but I think I heard this in the stupor of sleep, in a lackadaisical afternoon, in the dense night of monsoon, during the months of Phalgun and Baisakh, in biting chill of winter, in the month of Aghran".

Tamradhvaj said, "I know this song to be composed by you".

"How do you know, who says, I hadn't gone to make anyone listen to this song, none knows about it, my son! What a shame!"

"Is this song true?"

"It seems to be true, it seems to be composed by me, but how come you know about it?" Reba threw both her hands to the sky, whispered, "Since long he is not there, since so long! As if I am awaiting him since the last birth. You are like my son, how could you find out all the darkness and light of your mother's mind, oh you young soul, so many Springs and Winters have passed by before my eyes! My husband is yet to see his banishment come to an end"!

Tamradhvaj said, "Maa, would you like to hear some more"?

"What should I listen to … more songs"?

"Yes…

My husband went missing, to become Shiva, the Lord,

Smearing ash and dust all over his body,

By the path I sit and think Time is naughty,

Won't he be back, isn't it time yet, Oh God?"

Lifting her face with tears in her eyes, Reba said, "Is this your composition?"

"No."

"You heard in the stretches of grasslands, in moonshine, in the forests, during noontide, so is this your composition?"

"No, Maa, I am a non-poet, how can it be my composition, I knew it to be yours, you had composed it in your mind, you had made him listen to it."

"Are you speaking of Dhruvaputra?"

"Yes."

"He is just like my son,how can I make him listen to these lines?"

"But he ascribed it to you, as the author of these lines, you, yourself had sung out to him, he said!"

Being surprised, Reba stared at Tamradhvaj, befuddled. She failed to utter a word. Tamradhvaj was talking about Dhruvaputra. Dhruvaputra, himself, had ascribed this song to Reba Maa, before leaving. It was her composition. Hearing this, Reba said, "The song that talks about my heart seems to be my own composition, no doubt! My son, it was Dhruvaputra who had himself composed it!"

"Perhaps it is so, he said that you had sung this song in your mind".

"That's true, but the composition is not mine, I am an ordinary wife of a soldier, do I have that expertise? But while I feel sad remembering my husband, I look down the deserted street, such happens with me, my son, it seems to me as if, someone has banished my husband and hence he is not coming back. As though, someone has gone far-off to the summit of the Ramgiri hills, sky, only the sky runs above the head. In the monsoon that sky gets overcast with dense clouds, those clouds sail afar, perhaps through the land of Dasharno, traversing Betrabati to Ujjwain, they keep heading towards Ujjwain, with a message from my husband, it seems."

A shiver electrified the body of Tamradhvaj. He began to listen to the woman whose husband was off to an alien land. He seemed to have opened the doors, had unbolted the mind of this woman. All the words which remained locked within, in the dark, began to gush forth like a free-flowing stream. Reba kept saying, she could not tell anyone the words of her mind, her imagination and dreams of the morbid days and nights! Today Tamradhvaj had kindled the flame. The song which the astronomer from Dasharno had sung to her seemed to be her own song, the song of her own mind. Reba kept weeping and telling him all in detail. She kept talking about her dearly-loved man, like a nubile young girl! Her bashfulness was no more. She hardly was aware of what she was saying and to whom.

As Reba stopped, Tamradhvaj said, "Maa, so Dhruvaputra himself had composed the lines of these songs!"

"Exactly so, who else than himself would be able to do that?"

"Maa, if the clouds do not surface, who will narrate your husband's stories to you?"

"I am sitting here also for the clouds".

Then Tamradhavaj went to his knees in a posture of supplication. She said, "Maa, you better think of your husband, clouds will hover over, he will be back in the form of clouds. Maa, I have a prayer".

Reba, the mother, replied, "Even I have a prayer to say, my son"!

Tamradhvaj said, "Maa, I am praying for Gandhavati, to you"!

Maa Reba rejoined, "I am praying to you for my child, my son, please accept Gandhavati! She covets you,she has taken this for sure that Dhruvaputra will not be back anymore. If love goes unrequited, everyone turns furious, both male and female. Dhruvaputra is no more there in her mind, she is enchanted by your love. Better start for Dasharno taking her along, leaving this burnt-out country for good. I shall be here, after the passage of dozen years, I must accept widowhood, yet I shall keep waiting. Gandhavati's grandfather must be there, I am like her daughter, he will not be able to leave me in the lurch, he will never go away, we will keep awaiting the clouds and Gandhavati's father! Tamradhvaj, my son, are you listening?"

Tamradhvaj marked, Gandhavati had come to stand there, yonder, in the twilight, in front of the hut!

SEVENTY-FOUR

That day, Tamradhvaj and Gandhavati got married, as per the Gandharva system. Almost at that moment, during twilight. Gandhavati had woven garlands of jasmine. She put that garland on the neck of Tamradhvaj. The garlands got exchanged. Reba got thrilled by witnessing it, secretly. She could not be sure whether the tears were of joy or of sorrow. Reba came near. Both of them bowed down to mother. In an emotion-laden voice, Reba said in a sorrowful voice, "My son, you have accepted her in your life, now please leave this city along with her, you are young in age, you will not be able to stay here in happiness".

Tamradhvaj said, "You do not have to fear anymore, Maa"!

"I am overcome with fear, eyes of wolves and vultures are ogling, all around. I ask you to leave by the dawn tomorrow, if not tonight".

Tamradhvaj said, "How can that be, I am now in love with Ujjwain, the old man of Shudra ghetto has gone down to meditate, the merchant is setting out for distant lands, I want to be witness to the goings-on of Ujjwain".

"Even Bidisha is your city".

"I must go, as and when clouds float adrift to Ujjwain, I shall start for Bidisha".

Yet, the shadow of fear did not leave Reba's face, she said, "There's an old woman here, all the time she is paying visit to us, please protect my daughter from her. Old Parvati is the messenger, the representative of pervert royal servants, merchants, businessmen, shop-owners. She is dreadful, whichever task she takes up, she must succeed in it".

Tamradhvaj smiled, "Nothing to worry about anymore, Maa"!

"My son, that old crony has caused ruin to many a household, she is adept in hypnotism".

Tamradhvaj nodded, saying, "Have faith in me".

"Can ever be a wedding successful in a new moon or intense darkness?" Gandhavati expressed her fear, being alone.

Hearing this Tamradhvaj said, "Rules are bent during the times of drought. While the earth stays thirsty for long, she even takes the downpour in winter, joyously. Look Gandhavati, are you keen on leaving Ujjwain"?

Gandhavati asked, "Shall I light the lamp"?

"There's no need of it, the glow of the stars is no less, I can see down to the bottom of your mind, are you eager to leave for Bidisha right now?"

"If clouds are already there, in your city!"

"That is even possible".

"How is the rainfall there"?

"Amazing! The clouds swim in to cast their shadows on the river, Betrabati! How enchanting is the charm thus created!"

Gandhavati said, "The days of cloud are already here, when will the month of Asad begin? How many days are left"?

Tamradhvaj counted to say, "Six days".

Gandhavati asked, "When will we set out for the city of Bidisha"?

Tamradhvaj rejoined, "We will, let us wait for a few days".

Gandhavati said, "Who will we wait for in this accursed country, I do not want to stay here, let us start by the wee hours of dawn, today, if possible".

Tamradhvaj was not surprised. But, won't Gandhavati feel sad for leaving her mother, grandfather, behind? Gandhavati said, "They have given their consent".

"They will definitely permit us to start, but will you be able to leave?"

"Yes, I will, I am not eager to stay back here for another moment!"

Tamradhvaj asked, "But if your father comes back, Gandhavati"?

"Maa will take him along to see us there, in Bidisha"!

Tamradhvaj kept quiet. It seemed to him, that Gandhavati was ruthless. Again, it occurred to him, that this was just natural. As Gandhavati had depended on him, she was keen on forgetting the memories of her former love! To erase Dhruvaputra, she had to leave this Gambhira, this city of Avanti! But what would he do? Would he leave this city, being burnt incessantly? How to leave, was beyond the comprehension of Tamradhvaj. It occurred to him, that something would transpire in this city! That too very soon. Various incidents foreboded it. Surfacing of water in Ratnakarsagar; old Parashar, the village-chief's, passing into meditation; Devadutta's promise being reneged on, her self-surrender to the merchant and his union with Gandhavati— all these events had transpired, some more would certainly follow, and that slept in the womb of future. Tamradhvaj wished to wait for that future. He was eager to see on his own whether this city, continually burnt by the sun would come back to a stable state at all! Whether clouds would float in, in this country of Lord Mahakaal, once more!

Gandhavati said, "Through the hours of tonight I shall listen to you about the city of Bidisha and then in the small hours of dawn I shall set out for my husband's place".

Tamradhvaj said, "But Gandhavati, I am now enamoured of this city, this village, this country, above all".

Gandhavati said, "This country is awaiting something even more heart-rending, why will we stay back to witness that day?"

Tamradhvaj thought that Gandhavati's words might have been true. Even harder truth was fast asleep in the womb of future. Would they be able to put up with this, if that sprang up to life? But there was a difference in nature between that which kept happening in the city since many years and the events which were coming up in sequence since the last few days! The incidents which were happening presently seemed to arouse hope in the mind of the people, water surfacing at Ratnakarsagar, Devadutta's journey to her father's place, Gandhavati's wedding — all were simple truths, nothing causing mental affliction or the ilk. Then, it was worth waiting.

Gandhavati said, "All these are trivial happenings, such insignificant welfare would never pervade as a stupendous one in the sky of Ujjwain, and there seems to be no connection between these pleasant happenings and the natural disaster! Please talk about Bidisha, how is that river, Betrabati?"

Tamradhvaj said, "Its water is blue, crystalline, so transparent that the pebbles at the bottom can be seen clearly, during monsoon that river turns turgid, a column of water falls from the North, on both banks of the river, Betrabati, run the bushes, comprising wild jasmine, screw-pine and ketaki flowers".

"I know!" Gandhavati whispered, "How do the houses look there"?

"The houses are surrounded by the fences of Ketaki blossoms, even dry leaves are not allowed to remain strewn inside the courtyard. The wives, whose husbands have been abroad on work, remember them by looking at the clouds, their consorts go abroad to earn ahead of monsoon, agricultural opportunities being aplenty, abroad".

"Will you go too?"

Tamradhvaj smiled and said, "I must if I have to, listen Gandhavati, there is the temple of Lord Vasudeva, in Bidisha, in front of which stands a Garuda-tower, erected by an Ionian Greek named Heleodorus, who was the messenger of the Ionian Greek King of Purushpur. The fragrance of joss-sticks, incense and resin pervade the premises of the Lord Vasudeva temple, in the mornings and evenings, and there is Nichoih massif…"

Gandhavati was familiar with the Nichoih massif and its caves, she heard of them. Yet, she wanted to hear again. In the small hours of night, Gandhavati stood up with Tamradhvaj and said, "Let us go out now, Maa knows, Grandpa too, tell me, will it be right to delay any further?"

Gandhavati herself dragged her husband along, it seemed. The night was so cool, so pleasant! In such soothing coolness, they would reach the hermitage. Then, from there she would start for her husband's place. Tamradhvaj called in darkness, "Grandpa, Maa, we are leaving then".

Unbolting the door, Reba emerged from a room, and, Shivnath came out from another. They descended into the courtyard. Both of them saw the two faces in the light latent in the darkness and Reba said, "See that my daughter does not suffer from dearth of rice".

"No, that won't happen".

"Make sure, she wins your love".

Tamradhvaj said, "Rest assured, your words will be honoured, Maa!"

"Let her not be estranged from you ever, let her not be a woman, whose husband stays abroad".

Tamradhvaj replied, "This will also be truly honoured, Maa!"

A little tilkut, barley, wheat, rice, a pair of ornaments and a few knick-knacks— Tamradhvaj took folding them in a small baggage, tucked at the tip of a stick. He placed the stick on his shoulder. Shivnath came to tie a pink headgear to his head. They started off. Coming out of the hut, the youth from far-off Dasharno held Gandhavati's hand. The boundless sky stretched far above their head, stood the planets and stars, the Milky Way, the nebulae, in the huge universe they became more dependent on one another, it seemed. Gandhavati was weeping. Stepping down into the road, her eyes seemed to be overcast with clouds. Tamradhvaj assured her, "You have nothing to be afraid of, Gandhavati"!

"If I go back…"Gandhavati stopped short.

"There's no point of return, they bade adieux to us to make us set out on our journey"!

Gandhavati resumed walking. Walking towards the east through a stretch, fit for journeying on foot, they could see the darkness to melt, gradually. Sometimes meadows on both the sides, sometimes wild hedgerows and copses, sometimes again old trees of yore, the black soil, the nature — bereft of all, indigent. Gandhavati's footprints were being etched on the dust of the road. She was leaving Gambhira, bidding adieux to it and the footprints remained witness to this fact!

"We are heading to the hermitage, right?"

"No, we are going to the Shudra ghetto, straight from the shrine of Lord Mahakaal".

Gandhavati stopped, "But why"?

"You and I, will never be able to come out of his shadow", Gandhavati!

Gandhavati said, "I know about that Shudra colony".

"Did Dhruvaputra tell you"?

"Yes, but why will we go there"?

"Let us go, Gandhavati, if we set out on our journey on seeing water, that journey will be an auspicious one. Ratnakarsagar is full to the brim with water and there is a hermit, we will seek his blessings before we set off".

Gandhavati wondered whether Dhruvaputra had come back to her, in another incarnation! Only Dhruvaputra could utter such words! Alas! She failed to rein her mind, keep it under control. He, for whom she wished to leave Ujjwain, Gambhira, was walking by her side, in another form, holding her hand. She thought that Dhruvaputra was no more, and presently she wished Dhruvaputra to return alive. Tears welled up to her eyes again. For the harsh rejection of whom, she was leaving Ujjwain, Gambhira, river Shipra, the Mahakaal temple, fearing whose return she was leaving her mother alone, that man himself seemed to walk by her side, close at her heels! Tamradhvaj drew up, wiped off Gandhavati's tears with his scarf and holding her face between his hands lightly, he said, "It were as if I came to Gambhira today, seeking your hands in marriage, and how strangely my prayer has been answered! You are now journeying to Bidisha with me! All seem just a miracle, you know!"

Gandhavati drooped her eyelids and said, "I have never seen such a dawn"!

The morning birds were waking up. Their chirps and trills kept filling up all nooks and corners. They were yet to fly off to the unknown from Ujjwain. It appeared to Gandhavati that all was not ruined, not destroyed. Perching on the branch of a tree, an unknown bird kept singing in dulcet voice, the paean of the morning light and Gandhavati walked on, listening to it. She kept walking forward, leaving behind the bushes and woods, flanking the road on both sides. While traversing, she said, "Sometimes Grandpa, sometimes someone else had described this way, leading from Gambhira to Ujjwain, they painted the path in front of my eyes, now all seem to be so true! At the bend of this way, to the front, we will be greeted by the river, Shipra, there a Peepul tree stands, and all take respite in the shadows of that tree".

Tamradhvaj added, "True! Even Dhruvaputra sat at the base of that Peepul tree, many a time"!

Gandhavati came to a standstill. She could not even guess that Dhruvaputra's name would still be uttered by Tamradhvaj! How daring this man could be! How self-confident he was, that he did not hesitate to name the ex-lover of his newly-wed wife,in her presence, knowing full well of her amorous affair with him in the past! Gandhavati kept on looking at the courageous man! Wide chest, straight physique, and as he had taken off the headgear, the man from Dasharno looked like a valiant hunter, with his close-cropped, curly hair! Copper-complexioned body, flippant eyes, a pair of pitch-black eyebrows, a hint of thin beard on his cheeks! Suddenly, Gandhavati felt desirous of Tamradhvaj! Right at that moment, Tamradhvaj had driven her utterly horny! It seemed, as if her body quivered in desire, her chest grew heavy, both her breasts became taut and stood firm. Strangely enough, Tamradhvaj did not take note of all such things, he spoke up, "Look Gandhavati, when I came to Ujjwain, at that time, a man had narrated a bizarre tale to me, would you like to listen to it?"

Slowly, Gandhavati placed her two palms on the chest of Tamradhvaj, she said, "That can be given a patient hearing when we sit on the bank of the river!"

Tamradhvaj said, "Let that be so. I am thinking, how colourful life is, and as we are colour-blind, we cannot recognize any shade at all, all appear to be grey to us!"

Gandhavati said, "Neither of us is colour-blind, not you, not even me".

"Who can tell"! Tamradhvaj was lost somewhere. Gandhavati was breathing on the nape of the neck of Tamradhvaj. That breath was hot, but it failed to elicit any reaction from Tamradhvaj. In him, the yarn began to expand in colours, fold by fold, thread by thread. Reaching near the peepul tree by the river, Tamradhvaj said, "Listen Gandhavati, when I had come to Ujjwain for the first time, a trader, named Manibhadra told me about a village on the outskirts of the city, the hamlet, the river, Gambhira, the cane-forest...I was totally oblivious of Manibhadra, you know. While coming to Ujjwain from Bidisha, many a man had imparted many an advice, shared many a view, I had asked each and every one about Ujjwain, it was a new, unknown city to me, and I had come there to learn astronomy. Manibhadra, like others, had talked much about Ujjwain and the river, Gambhira, along with it".

Gandhavati asked, "Did he come to our Gambhira"?

"No, but the way he described tallied with whatever I had come across, right from the hut, the compound, the kadam tree to the well on the roadside along with the fragrance of the champak flowers!"

Gandhavati now curved her neck like a wary doe. She was listening to thewords of the man, looking at the waterless river. But she failed to keep looking on for long. She saw the nonchalant eyes of the man, instead. How undaunted! Who was he talking about? Who was that Manibhadra who happened to know everything about Gambhira, from the clumps of cane to the well, the compound in their hut, champak flower, the blue water of Gambhira and all in such detail? Only one man used to know all of it! Was Tamradhvaj concealing anything from her? Did Gandhavati's husband harbour any suspicion at the back of his mind? Gandhavati was overcome with fear. And how would she make him understand that Dhruvaputra never surfaced in her memory, only this man won all her attention lately, day in, day out, pervading the wakeful hours and those of sleep?

Tamradhvaj asked, "Aren't you curious to know, how Manibhadra had come to recognize all such things"?

Gandhavati nodded and then asked, "Who is Manibhadra"?

Tamradhvaj answered, "I had forgotten Manibhadra, in fact, I did not remember him. It is customary to seek information of an unknown place, before setting out for it. And, it was my maiden journey to a place, leaving Bidisha for the first time. I was really ignorant as to how Ujjwain as a city would be, or how the people of Ujjwain would accept me! O meeting your grandpa my memory was jogged faintly, and coming to Gambhira, I found that things were falling in place, all exactly tallying with what I had been told in verbatim, even the dust on the road proved no exception! So strange!

Gandhavati sat down on the ground, on the bed of grass. Placing both her palms on the ground, she seemed to seek support from the earth and said, "How did he come to know about Gambhira?Please tell me. Did he have the magical mirror?"

Tamradhvaj said, "I did not have any chance to meet that person who had passed all such information to Manibhadra!"

"Who could narrate in such a manner that, a trader from Pataliputra would remember each information in verbatim and would commit no error in describing the same?"

Tamradhvaj sat in front of Gandhavati bending his knees and said, "My tale is yet to be finished, Gandhavati, I thought, these words will remain hidden forever, I shall never let you know, but now, after the marriage it seems that you, too, should know all of it".

Gandhavati was running short of breath. She sat, hanging her head low. A fear kept pricking his mind now! She was the beloved of a man and that was known to this man, presently her husband. How generous could a man be, how far could he be free of suspicion? He was perhaps trying to take a peek into Gandhavati's mind, by ruse. Where would she go then? Would she then go back to that water-body at Gambhira, where one day, Dhruvaputra…

Tamradhvaj said, "Listen Gandhavati, Manibhadra had told me that someone had attempted suicide in the water of Gambhira. It was the full-moon night of Chaitra. All of a sudden, Goddess Saraswati appeared before his eyes, the Goddess was standing on the sand-bed, and, desisted him from taking his own life!"

Gandhavati took the vast world for support. When had her veil slipped off from her head unawares, and her dry, unkempt hair was quivering in the morning breeze? Tamradhvaj kept witnessing the beauty of the earth in Gandhavati, whose eyes were pools of tears! It was the same woman standing in sundry, varying beautiful forms! Sticking out his hand, Tamradhvaj touched Gandhavati's thighs and asked, "Do you remember, Gandhavati"?

"Yes, I do, quite vividly, it was I who had narrated the tale of exit".

"I have not seen the handsome man of whom Manibhadra had said, who had talked about Ujjwain and Gambhira to him in turn and Manibhadra also said that he met him just for once! If I had not gone to Gambhira with your Grandpa, I would never have another opportunity to go there. True, I had come to learn astronomy, but I was in the dark about the growing feeble-sightedness of the Acharya himself! I had even forgotten of Manibhadra. Stepping into Gambhira, I seemed to find my way, gradually".

Hearing him, Gandhavati expressed her feelings, "Can it be so? Really?"

Tamradhvaj could not get the drift of Gandhavati's query. Without answering her directly, he said, "That handsome man had said that, Goddess Saraswati had her abode in the cane-woods by the bank of the river, Gambhira, and the Goddess herself had opened his eyes of enlightenment".

Gandhavati lowered her head, and mused in a whisper, "Then couldn't he recognize me that night? I had called out to him a number of times".

Tamradhvaj said, "He had seen the Goddess and then he had walked down to the south-east, where the river, Reba, flew, stood the Vindhya range, the land of Dasharno, from which end the first light of wisdom descended on the bank of the river, Saraswati. Listen Gandhavati, how could he come back to the woman in another form, in whom he had witnessed Goddess Saraswati? So long, I had groped in the dark for the right path, I thought, a man would temporarily be distracted by the beauty of a prostitute. But why wouldn't he come back, even that delusion being over"?

"Why did he have such distraction"?

"Perhaps, Dhruvaputra was looking for a refuge somewhere, either in the unending darkness of death or in the light of knowledge. Lastly, knowledge emerged triumphant as Truth, coming back from death was like returning to the light of knowledge. Gandhavati, do you know anything about Goddess Saraswati?"

"He used to speak of some river named Saraswati".

"That river is not there anymore, it has been moribund, depleted".

"It has become subterranean now, once upon a time, both its banks exhibited abundance of crops, the people were well-to-do, the harvest on both banks of the river owed to the river-water, a huge river whose ends stood blurred to a man's vision. And that river only stays before my eyes, till date!"

"Long back, in the distant past, that river lost its significance. The river can only be heard of now, it can't be seen by anyone, but how is it that its splendid form pops before your eyes?"

Gandhavati answered, "Well, as he left Ujjwain, did Goddess Saraswati too follow suit as per his own narration? Goddess Saraswati is the deity of harvest, the Goddess of creation. Is that why, the earth has gone cloudless and the road to all creations stands blocked?"

Tamradhvaj was being mesmerized by the words of his young wife! After so long, he was feeling relieved! Dhruvaputra seemed to stand in between them since last evening, after they tied their nuptial knot! Now, he was receding. Gandhavati was looking free of all worries now! Taking one hand of Tamradhvaj and placing it on her breast, she said, "I am just an ordinary being, please behold just me within myself, my husband"!

Tamradhvaj came much closer to his young wife! Placing one hand on her breast, lifting her face with another, he planted kisses on both her eyes and said,

"Gandhavati, I know, you are just a small river, not like the Saraswati, inundating both its banks. I am just an ordinary fellow, not afraid of a little river though a huge, long river leaves me jittery."

SEVENTY-FIVE

Army-Commander Bikram had returned. The troops of soldiers were returning from that expedition, in droves. Varied information flew into the city regarding the soldiers, protecting or plundering the merchants! If they were protected, they would have reached Ujjwain by now. If the traders would come, the nimbus clouds would have hovered over their heads. The advent of the clouds would have put an end to the period of drought! The people of the Shudra ghetto used to talk about the return of the soldiers, sitting by the Ratnakarsagar, in the evening.

The youngest man of the locality, Lankesh, was saying, "If the battery of armies does not intervene, water from the sky would surely tumble down on the ground of Ujjwain, this time!"

A middle-aged man said, "Does the retinue of armies have that power?"

Lankesh said, "We have not seen the gods of heaven, but we have seen the armies, that day the King's courtier, Uddhavnarayan, had come to take a look at the water of the pond, why did he come here, at all?"

"Why did he come? Just for the sake of coming over, that's it"!

"He doesn't go anywhere without a reason,I know him well."

"Then what to do?"

"There's no relief for us if water does not pour from the sky now!"

Such discussions were on, in the Shudra ghetto. In the darkness after evening, in the light of the stars, till late into the night, all through the night. At that time, the rich, the revered, the courtiers, the King's men, all kept wondering, as the pond of the socially-inferior Shudras got filled in with water, how long would theirs go hard and dry?

A platoon of soldiers had reached the city last evening. Just reaching here, they received the order of a new expedition. They did not get even proper respite at night. They went out at dawn, at the behest of their new Chieftain. Hence, before the break of dawn, the infantry had marched into the Shudra ghetto. How far was the Shudra colony from the palace? The time taken by the infantry to cover such a distance was not more than usual, rather less. The weariness of long and aimless expedition seemed to have drawn an ashen shadow in front of this infantry, but in the hope of getting respite on completion of this venture and in fear of the new leader of the army-platoons, they hurriedly reached the Shudra ghetto. They came in an array, led by the kettledrum-player and the trumpet-blower, even ahead of them, having the Chief of the Platoon on the back of the white Tibetan pony, with a black turban on his head, to which a peacock-feather was tucked. The dark shade of the turban mingled with the peacock-blue of the feather reflected a new colour, peacock-bluish. The new chieftain had stayed back in this city only, he had not gone on any expedition, no sunbeams scorched him, hence he was not touched by any fatigue at all. He was clad in an olive-green suit and on his chest was a grey armour. From his waist dangled a small scimitar. The chieftain was known to many from among the infantry. He had been rejected while coming to join this infantry. How could that youth become a sessions-judge of the royal court, and then on promotion to a Chieftain of a wing of the army comprising fifty infantry, the leader of this particular expedition? A retinue of infantry it was, but he was known for not travelling anywhere without his horse!

The boys and old men of Shudra ghetto were rubbing their eyes in the light of dawn. The nights were very short. Again, one man had gone into ascetic austerities and hence they hardly had their sleep. When the soldiers had been far-off, inside the meadows, Lankesh could hear the noise of their kettledrums and trumpets! Lankesh's auditory sense was quite sharp. Grapevine had it, that, he could even hear the sound of falling leaves. He was heard to say that, if ever clouds hovered over the sky of Ujjwain behind all eyes, he would definitely sense it before all. The clouds have a rumbling sound which cannot reach the ground of the earth, but it would not fail to be wafted to his ears. It was Lankesh who said, "The armies are coming in our direction".

"Are they coming or passing by"? An elderly man put his query.

"No, no, they are coming, coming in this direction, but why here?"

Then another elderly man said, "The soldiers are on the way, they will return from there to the palace, they had gone to the west."

"N-no, the platoons of army are at this end only, look yonder, they can be seen".

All could see them. It seemed as though nearly fifty soldiers came running through the meadows. Who were preceding them? Were these the alien soldiers then?

Had Ujjwain again fallen into the clutch of the Huns? With such drought on, anything might happen now. Everything seemed to be possible during the drought.

Lankesh asked, "In case they are alien soldiers, what will we do?"

Old Parashar knew but he was engrossed in meditation! Would they disrupt his meditation then?

Lankesh rejoined, "Let us confirm first, it could be the King's army as well."

"Why will the King's soldiers approach this nook? We can go to the palace, if the King calls for us."

Lankesh moved forward. A few more filed in, at his heels. A few more too. Lankesh stopped short, walking to the fore towards the meadows, taking along an ammunition-free infantry with him. He looked closely and found it to be the King's army. And this man on horseback was known to him! That Uddhav, the Sessions Judge! When had that Sessions-bloke become the Chief of the army-troops? Even just a few days back, he had dropped in.

The infantry came to a halt, near the Shudra ghetto. Uddhav, on horseback, found almost thirty people in front of him. All were men. All of them seemed to raise a barricade in a war-mongering posture! Uddhav, just a day before, had become the Chieftain of this infantry, comprising fifty soldiers. Leader of fifty soldiers, the Chief of soldiers! How would Uddhav know that the information of this Shudra ghetto with which he had gone to the Priest and then to the Army-Commander, to be so precious? His promotion fell on his lap! At the behest of the Army-Commander, he was at the helm of this adventurous exploration! Not even in his wildest dream, Uddhav had thought this to happen! How strange incidents would occur in a man's life, he would not be surprised if Devadutta, the whore, would be eager to serve him now! He was none other than the leader of the infantry, in fact, he had come to the palace once, looking for a job along with these men who were his subordinates presently — that bugle-player, that man with the kettledrum! He waited along with the peasants of the village, the Shudras, the tanners, the hunters, all night, just for an appointment as a soldier. But Uddhav was denied an opportunity, he was kicked aside by the Chief of the platoon instead. Those coming a cropper, were being spurned and removed! Even that man was not alive, that leader! This time only he died of stomach disorder. The battery of army had thrown him into a field, before marching down, with no leader to lead them on. His death catapulted Uddhav to this promotion! Without his death, it would not be possible. He was a peasant of the village, a shepherd-King almost without any land, he used to spend his days on meagre livelihood, and lately he was the 'lord' to fifty men! Wherever he would stop with his fifty soldiers, he would lord over the non-soldiers too, at that place. Fifty subordinates, sickly, half-ill infantry soldiers were always ready to carry out his orders at the point of his weapons. If he ordered them for pillage, they would go plundering. If he asked them to fetch a woman for enjoyment, they would do that for their new lord. Uddhav was now the Lord! Such a prolonged drought had wrought such a big change in his life! Let this rainless period continue, let not the Sun-God set down, let the wheel of His chariot truly get stuck in the skyways. Let flames pour down from the sky, at dawn as well as at dusk. It would surely elevate him to a better position. The events which appeared impossible would be made possible! That was even happening in numbers. Otherwise, how could the most beautiful whore of the city, Devadutta, surrender herself to the merchant? If more fire would be disgorged by the sky for a much longer period, the paragon of beauty of Gambhira village would walk up to Uddhav, on her own. There would be no need to send a messenger for her or to force her. Inside the earth of fire, there would be no other pleasure better than outraging the modesty of a pure virgin! Now after this successful expedition, everything would be made possible.

Uddhav jumped off from the horse's back. Placing his hand on the scimitar on his waist, he ordered a soldier to tether the horse to the Ashok tree. Blood in Uddhav's veins went racing. He thundered, "Where is that old Parashar? I heard that the man was with the army once upon a time."

Lankesh moved forward by a step and asked, "Why is this platoon of soldiers here?"

Uddhav roared, "Am I to give that explanation to anyone? I am Uddhvanarayan, the Chief of this battery of army, the Leader of this troop of soldiers! How many men are here?"

Lankesh said, "Many men have left already, the present count is not known".

"A troop of soldiers will be sent to fetch those who have left, thou haven't left yet, what's thy name?"

Uddhav knew him. He knew him since he was a Sessions Judge. Now he could not recognize him after winning the post of the Chief of the infantry troop. Lankesh tried to guess something, but failed. He surmised, something evil would befall them, lest why would Uddhav, the Sessions-bloke would appear during these early hours of morning with infantry soldiers? The new attire of the Sessions-Judge was a pointer to his new position. Did Uddhavnarayan, winning a new position, as a chief of fifty soldiers come to plunder, for just no reason at all? It was nothing unusual with Uddhav, he used to do such things. As hearsay affirmed. And it could be accomplished by the retinue of armies even. Lankesh thought, if the armies had come with any such intention, they would resist it. Then they would march to the King. From the King to the Army Commander. Though Uddhavnarayan was with the infantry soldiers, he was just Uddhav, his oppression would not be tolerated without putting up any protest.

"What's wrong? Why aren't thou telling me thy name?" Uddhav thundered.

As Lankesh uttered his name, Uddhav laughed out boisterously. "Today Ravana would be slain, it is because, these bloody Shudras are enjoying much importance, as a consequence, rains cease, menstruation of women gets suspended, hey thou, son of Satan, have thou made everyone come in here, how many are left out?"

Lankesh's face grew darker. Receding a step further, he said, "Why, what for?"

Uddhav noticed that, the youth had never addressed him as 'Lord'! Uddhav, on winning lordship lately, grew keen on hearing that address. He burst out in anger, "I am thy Lord, thou vulture, go down on thy knees, ask old Parashar to come here".

The middle-aged folks could understand that the appearance of the infantry troop had some serious reason behind it. The reason was incomprehensible. They had done no such harm that the platoon of soldiers would be there. Lankesh noticed that the troops of armies were growing restive. They were waiting eagerly for Uddhav's command. Would he go down on his knees and address Uddhav as 'Lord' and thus pacify him? But what was his crime? It was heard that, of yore, each male of the Shudras had to keep a bell, tied around his neck. If they entered the city, the tinkle of the bell would make the people of higher castes protect themselves from the shadows of the Shudras. That law was no more binding. They, on their own accord, used to follow their own laws and ways of living, during the rule of King Gandharvasen and King Bhartrihari. Neither a soldier nor a sentry had ever entered this ghetto with their swords, unsheathed! Till date, King Bhartrihari was there on the throne. Then, why did the platoons of army come here? Then would Uddhavnarayan again suspend the bell from their neck or shackle their feet? Lankesh sat down gingerly. He folded his knees. He wanted to know why they had come to their ghetto. He was feeling anxious, he was on tenterhooks.

Uddhav roared, "Sit down with lowered heads, fold your palms, you vulture-chicks. By whose order have you dug this lake, Ratnakarsagar?"

Lankesh got the wind of the matter, he sprang up on his feet and said, "For long we are not having rainfall, we have dug the pond and lifted water from the bosom of the hell!"

"Why do thou stand up, sit down as thou did!"

Feigning not to hear his words, Lankesh spoke out, "Since seven days we have dug the earth, and then the mouth of the gold pitcher was unplugged".

Learning about the gold pitcher, Uddhav was all ears… "Gold pitcher? Where is it? Pull out the gold pitcher, was there a gold pitcher in the depth of this lake? Did thou go to the King to seek his permission? Did thou return the gold pitcher to the King?"

Lankesh rejoined, "The gold pitcher is down there, in the hell"!

"Wolf-cub thou, telling a lie? Nab him, he has hidden the gold pitcher, lifting it from Ratnakarsagar"!

Springing up, four soldiers flung off to hem in Lankesh and throw him flat on the ground. And while witnessing that, all others were about to escape, Uddhav thundered, "I am thy Lord, none will be spared, none will be allowed to leave till the gold pitcher is retrieved and none should go near the water of Ratnakar sagar, no vulture-chick of Shudra community dare touch that water to desecrate it, that water is now the property of the palace"!

The troop of soldiers hemmed in the people, though one or two were able to escape the clutch. A soldier began to chase the truant man. Pulling out the scimitar from his waist, Uddhav seemed to rejoice by cutting the air with it!

He ordered the drum-player to beat his drums, the man with the horn to blow his horn and roared, "Victory be to the army troops of the Great Army-Commander Bikram! The opponents have surrendered themselves, go, stand on the four corners of Ratnakarsagar, take care not to let the shadows of the Shudras fall on the water-surface, it will be defiled then, it will again dry up".

Dragging the emaciated, worn-out men, the soldiers forced them to stand under the sun! It was beyond their comprehension, for which fault of theirs, all of them had been captivated in the hands of the line of soldiers or Uddhavnarayan had come to possess Ratnakarsagar! There had been no water in any other water-body, hence the army was entitled to possess the lake! They did not resist their action. No means had been there to put up their protest! They did not obstruct them, what were they accused of then?

Uddhav demanded, "Where has the gold pitcher been stashed away"?

All of them shouted in unison, "We have not seen any gold pitcher, Lord"!

"We have only heard about the gold pitcher, that's it", an old man reasoned.

As the address 'Lord' made Uddhav happy, his wrath shot up too. He was the Lord of so many men! These men would call the merchant their Lord, the Great Army Commander their Lord, if they would get to see the King, they would address Him as Lord only, if that fortunate, they would be compelled to honour the Priest of Lord Mahakaal with the address 'Lord' too. They almost lay down in supplication before him, addressing him as 'Lord'! Only Lankesh lay supine on the ground and an unsheathed sword was held vertically on his chest by a soldier. Uddhav announced, "There's no room for a lie in Ujjwain. Come, fetch me thou the gold pitcher, otherwise because of the crime of stealing it, all would be beheaded, would be burnt alive like Utanka, tell me, where is the pitcher?"

None spoke out a word. Failing to elicit a rejoinder Uddhav grew more furious, he said, "Thy punishment may be lessened if the gold pitcher is retrieved, thou Shudras have no right to touch the gold pitcher, come on, where is the pitcher?"

Abruptly, Lankesh sprang up to say, "In the hell".

"Catch him, go catch him", Uddhav shouted.

Four soldiers had caught him tightly. Again, Lankesh was taken as a captive. But did Uddhav know that he was not keen to escape? Lankesh was sure that if he tried to escape, he would be nabbed. If the soldiers so wished, they could catch him from any distance he would escape to. As he could not face Uddhav lying supine on the ground, he had to jump up to his feet, pushing away all the soldiers who kept him cordoned.

Uddhav declared, "Thou must be decapitated by the great Army-Commander today"!

Hearing this, Lankesh stood, fixing his eyes still on Uddhav's. He knew that the great Army-Commander and Uddhav were different individuals. The Great Army Commander might free him without beheading him, powerless as he was! Many such precedents were there to refer to! But Uddhav would not be able to do so. Uddhav had only one place to show his might…to him, just to h-i-m! The Great Army-Commander could easily claim the water of Shudra ghetto without decapitating him! As this troop of soldiers kept doing, at the insistence of the great Army Commander! Uddhav, himself, could never dream of taking the possession of the water with his fifty soldiers! He did not have such grey matter! On Uddhav's appeal, no one save the Great Army Commander himself knew whether he would decapitate Lankesh or not. The Shudras had dug the pond and extracted water from it, while the platoon of soldiers had come to snatch it off. Look, failing to match Lankesh's stare, Uddhav was saying, "This city has seven lakes, it can hardly happen that only Ratnakarsagar would have water while others would not. According to the directives of the Great Army Commander, water has to surface in the other lakes as well, namely, Govardhansagar, Kshirsagar, Vishnusagar, Pushkarsagar, Purushottamsagar, Shivsagar—the Shudras have to dug in these lakes also. If all the lakes would have water to the brim, it would be to our utter relief, lest the city would not survive, and hence the order came from the Chief of the Armies."

Lankesh said, "We have dug our lake, we have prayed to the God of the Oceans and then the water has surfaced!"

On hearing Lankesh speak, Uddhav ran towards him with his unsheathed sword. Why was this man speaking? This man was a penalized criminal, waiting to be decapitated! This man was demeaning the power of Uddhav with his words! Uddhav kept touching his sword on his chest in such a manner that it would pierce the core of his heart! But for how long would he hold the sword in this manner on the chest of Lankesh? He was not accustomed to it. And, it would demand all his attention to Lankesh, naturally, mighty Uddhav would not be able to brag his power to the innocent residents of the Shudra ghetto, devolved on him by the Great Army Commander. Lowering the sword, he moved away from Lankesh. He boomed in anger, "Vulture-chick, thou would have to face the music! I shall behead thee by the order of the Great Army Commander! All of this Shudra ghetto are being taken captive as of now, all will accompany me to the city. Going there, they would have to dig all the six water-bodies to make the water surface, but before that I need the gold pitcher! Tell me, where have thou stashed away that gold pitcher, if it can't be had, the troop of soldiers will enter each hut, if it can't be retrieved, they will set all the huts on fire and the armies are empowered to do it. They can do anything! Where is that old man, Parashar? Call him, he won't be spared too, for being an elderly person, I heard that siphoning the water up by digging the earth is his brainchild. Who asked thee to dig Ratnakarsagar? Nowhere is there any hint of water but thou all need it! At whose insistence have thou dug the earth to extract water? Is this earth thy own? The courtiers, the rich men and powers-that-be are not getting water and it is thou who are extracting water from the womb of the hell! Does the hell belong to thee? Hundred years of sin cause a Shudra-birth and how do the Shudras dare dig the earth of the dry lake...?"

Uddhavnarayan kept roaring! Uddhav's voice took after the wild dog which kept barking, without cessation. Hearing that, one from among them lost his consciousness and collapsed on the earth!

Thus, some of them fainted, a few recoiled in fear and a few again thought, was it so necessary to see the face of water by digging it, day after day? The water had now passed on to the custody of armies. Yonder stood Ratnakarsagar —four soldiers had been deployed on all four corners of the water-body, with unsheathed swords in their hands. The women were returning with empty pitchers. The youngest of all youths of the locality, Lankesh, had been pinioned by the soldiers. Uddhav, the leader, kept yelling, "Who has emerged triumphant, who?"

The people of the Shudra ghetto said together, "The Great Army-Commander of the King!"

"Whose water is this, whose?"

"Of the Great Army-Commander, of the King"!

"Whose is then the Ocean of Hell now?"

"Of the Great Army-Commander and of the King!"

"Whose is the Ocean of the Sky?"

"Of the Great Army-Commander..."

Brandishing the sword against the sky, Uddhav thundered again, "Gold pitcher, whose will that gold pitcher be"?

The voice of the populace withered away,however they could utter, "Of the King, of the Great Army-Commander"!

An intelligent man spoke out, "The gold pitcher belongs to Lord, Lord Uddhav, the leader of the troop of soldiers!"

Uddhav then ordered, "Then fetch me the gold pitcher, go thou"!

All fell silent. The silence began to intensify. Night seemed to wear on, during the daytime itself!

Where was the gold pitcher? No one had ever seen it at all. The gold pitcher kept floating on the surface of the Ocean of the Hell with a reserve of unending water! All kept thinking, if they could hand the gold pitcher to cruel Uddhav, this period of drought would perhaps come to an end, the city of Ujjwain and Avanti, the two rivers, Shipra and Gandhavati, would be surging with water! The clouds would come to hover over the pinnacle of the shrine of Lord Mahakaal, with the tidings of the husband from an alien land for his estranged wife!

SEVENTY-SIX

Gandhavati and Tamradhvaj had entered the city at the crack of dawn. Pindrop silence enveloped the city at dawn. The morning breeze was soft, soothing, cool. While walking towards the Mahakaal shrine, they had heard the sound of the bugle, the beating of the drums. To their utter surprise, they saw the troops of soldiers, marching eastward. At the sound of the horn and drums, Gandhavati halted to ask in a whispering tone, "Are they headed to a war?"

Tamradhvaj was taken aback, Now, where will they go for war again? He was roaming around the city even yesterday, but no information of war reached his ears and how would this small platoon dare go for war? The weary soldiers seemed to walk, gasping. Failing to elicit an answer from Tamradhvaj, Gandhavati endorsed her own conjecture herself, saying, "Yes, they are definitely going for war! Such bugles are blown, such drums are beaten, I remember quite vividly."

Tamradhvaj then chanced to see Uddhav, on horseback. He was leading the troop as its Chief. He pulled Gandhavati away to hide behind the rain-tree. This was the first time, he was feeling fear, on his visit to the city of Ujjwain. So long, he used to roam around alone, without any fear in his mind. Acharya was no more, the hermitage was nearly closed, but the royal support had not stopped yet as none, anywhere, was aware of Acharya's demise, rather it did not reach them. And as he was the disciple of Acharya, none would dare disturb him in this city, he was sure. But as he heard of Uddhav from Gandhavati and later as he came to know him by his aimless circumambulations in the city, Tamradhvaj was struck with fear. In the capacity of a leader of a small battery of army, Uddhav was heading towards the east. Where was he going? Uddhav was a Sessions-Judge, when again was he appointed as the leader of the platoon of soldiers? Wasn't this a dreadful selection? With Uddhav as the Chief of the army platoons, it would have been difficult for Gandhavati to live here. As the armies marched past, frightened Gandhavati said, "Hope they're not heading on to our village!"

"Who knows? That is not even impossible but then they would have to change direction"!

Gandhavati rejoined, "Yes, our village is not in that direction"!

Tamradhvaj said, "Yes, they are following another way".

"What's there in that direction?"

Tamradhvaj said, "Come Gandhavati, let's pray to Lord Mahakaaleswar before we set out for Bidisha, Ujjwain will not remain fit for human habitation anymore, that rogue has been promoted to the Chief of Platoons of soldiers! Men here would have an insufferable existence, such prolonged drought has caused the King, the Army-Commander, and all others to lose their intelligence and analytical acumen, all decisions taken prove to be wrong."

Gandhavati asked, "What's there in that direction"?

Tamradhvaj assured her, "You have nothing to be afraid of, Gandhavati!"

Gandhavati spoke up, "I am afraid, Uddhav might oppress my mother without finding me there! I heard that the soldiers can do anything, and their crime is not considered as a crime at all".

Tamradhvaj said, "That's true, but that is in case of a defeated nation. In one's own country, the armies usually commit no wrong and if they do, the King does not take it well".

Gandhavati said, "Does that crime reach the King's ear at all"?

Tamradhvaj said, "One day it will reach, for sure"!

Gandhavati kept quiet. She was walking slowly. Her hand was held by Tamradhvaj, with a turban in his head, a small baggage on a wooden-stick across his neck. They seemed to be new visitors from another land who had come to pay their respect to Lord Mahakaal, just as people used to come and leave even a few days back. It was quite natural in this city, at that time!

Walking a few steps forward, Gandhavati seemed to thunder, she turned around in a suppressed anger and gave vent to it aloud, "Why won't the army of a nation commit crime as led by a man like Uddhav? It definitely will--we are undone! Does he have any worth to be the chief of a battery of soldiers?"

"Let go of it, Gandhavati, we are not going to stay back in this country anymore".

"Was it not you who said that the times are changing, we will be blessed with health and well-being, the monsoon clouds will surely float in?"

"Yes, if not so, then why did Ratnakarsagar stand full to the brim with water"?

All of a sudden, Gandhavati said, "Water hasn't surfaced!"

"What do you mean by 'hasn't surfaced'? I am talking about Ratnakarsagar of the Shudra ghetto".

Gandhavati reiterated, "Nowhere water has welled up".

Tamradhvaj said, "I have seen the water with my own eyes. We are yet to go to Shudra ghetto. After seeing Lord Mahakaal, we will go to the Shudra ghetto. Having a look at the water of Ratnakarsagar, we must set out on our way to Bidisha!"

Gandhavati said, "Whatever you have seen is false, in this city, there is no water anywhere. Uddav is now the captain of the retinue of soldiers. Go and see, everything has undergone change, that water is there no more! Oh Lord Mahakaal, does Uddhav stand beyond your range of vision?"

Tamradhvaj held Gandhavati firmly, assured her, "No agitation, please! We have to travel a long way. Both good and evil co-exist in this world like day and night, Uddhav might have got a promotion, but our lives got intertwined with each other at the same time as well, can it be denied? Is it untrue?"

Gandhavati got clung to Tamradhvaj, shadows of fear seemed to be cast on her being, she mused under her breath, "If it becomes false! I am so panic-stricken, it appears that whatever is auspicious is untrue, only Uddhavnarayan is true, he will tear our lives asunder, with the aid of his platoon of soldiers. I shall have no chance to come to Ujjwain ever, I shall have to leave Ujjwain for good!"

Tamradhvaj thought it to be just the truth! When would Gandhavati again come here from Dasharno? The distance was not less too. He kept planning in his mind, how he to take Gandhavati through that far-flung way! Where and in which inn would they take refuge? Again were the roadside inns still there, given such oppressive drought? Were there colonnades of trees dotting the edges of the road to offer cool shadows to the wayfarers? Or even the well-to-do villagers flanking the way? Green forests, murmuring cascades, rivers … and all? Were they still there? The wives from the villages in vicinity would rush in to have a look at Gandhavati, thus brightening the shades of the tall trees of the forest, ruffling the stillness around the banks of the river! They would giggle and fall on each other and would lift Gandhavati's face in their hands, to look into her eyes, to know her well! To which village do you belong, to whom are you married, to which country are you heading on? Hearing that, Gandhavati would fall silent, losing all words, fixing a gaze on the ground, lowering her face. Then some old woman would approach Tamradhvaj, read his face in all details, keep laughing to say, 'The wife does not raise her face because of the pride of her husband! If such a man would appear in life, any woman would love to get married again, he is none but Lord Mahadeva, from where do you hail, my son, would you like to accept a co-wife of that bride'?

Hearing so, Gandhavati raised her face.

Seeing Gandhavati, that ancient woman pirouetted for once, lifting the border of her sari, and then kept crooning a few lines of a song! Stopping her humming in the midway, she said jovially, "Hey you bride, make me your co-wife please! You would cook and serve and I shall keep rocking with our husband, I shall feed him milk, sweetmeats, payasam, and then, I shall lull him to sleep,- sleep, my son, sleep, yonder Uddhav is coming on a donkey-back, Uddhav has large, protruding teeth, bloodshot eyes, reddish tongue, long nails on both the hands and feet and hairs all over the body…!"

Tamradhvaj got startled, before his eyes stood Mahaparshwa. He rubbed his eyes, it seemed he was in a stupor so long, over all the hours, he seemed to drift from happiness to fear! Gandhavati sat close by him, covering her face with her scarf and looking at the ground. And Mahaparshwa was hesitating on seeing a woman beside a man he was familiar with. He could sense that the woman might be the man's wife. That possibility was the supreme one. The way he came to know this person from Dasharno, in a day, it would be difficult to think of him otherwise. Yet, a proper investigation would be better. The other day, as they had a conversation while going to Devadutta's residence, he was given to understand that this man was a bachelor, was staying in a far-off land just to master the art of astronomy. How could he win a wife in the meantime? Of course, he got associated with her lately, he had not come from Dasharno to this distant land with his wife for his studies, for sure! Or something else? Mahaparshwa could not see the face of the lady! If he could study her face, her features, he could easily read her intention! Who would she be to this man, to be precise? Was she his wife or a woman, he was having an affair with? Certainly, Tamradhvaj was not enticing a wife of any household, away! In the conversation with Devadutta, a name of a woman floated … what was her name? She was the daughter-in-law of that old man. That son again had not returned from war! Not returned but not dead even! He might have stayed back in such lands, who could tell? Such was not unusual in case of the soldiers, they would stay back in other lands of their choice, if so desired! Then they would appropriate themselves to the ways and manners of the men of that nation! Didn't the Ionian Greeks settle elsewhere? Were they not seen in Saurashtra or Malavya? While managing clients for the brothel, Mahaparshwa had come to know all these home truths of men of various nationalities. Those were the men who told him which ancestors had come here on war…thus the Ionian Greeks had settled at sundry different places! The country to which tycoon Subhag Dutta felt tempted to travel and even Devadutta felt enticed as well was Balkh. It was learnt that even the Gandharvas were associated with the army in their land at some point in time! While coming for war, they had stayed back there on the bank of a river, in which repeated dives would make one even more beautiful! Many more dives would assure deliverance of one's body and soul from filth and dirt! The more one would dive, the more he would be free of his sins of this life. Devadutta shared all such information. Devadutta had told Mahaparshwa about the river, Oxus. She said, only the lure of going to the bank of Oxus compelled her to make a truce with the tycoon! There, a massif of mountains ran till the horizon, and, the shadow of that range used to fall on the surface of the water of the river, Oxus. Lure of that river was dragging along Mahaparshwa, who was also going there as a part of the tycoon's trader-team! Chaturika would come along with Mahaparshwa! Though not fully agreed, Mahaparshwa was sure that she would come, finally. She would not go for her love of the river or the shadows of the mountains on it, but in the hope of winning the old tycoon's heart! Alack, what a pity, oh woman! She, herself, would never be able to read her own mind!

Mahaparshwa inquired, "Hope everything's well?"

Tamradhvaj, with folded palms reciprocating the respect said, "Yes, how about you? All is well, I believe! That day you really helped us immensely! Has the merchant set out on his journey?"

Mahaparshwa turned a deaf ear to Tamradhvaj's query. Till his curiosity was satisfied, he would not give up. This was his nature. He was always suspicious, was in the habit of finding evil even in good. It was not even unusual that, a wife of a family was hiding her face behind her scarf, coming on a rendezvous at such an early hour of the morning, in broad daylight! In a city which had not seen monsoon since long, whose rivers and ponds lay stark dry, whose sky began to bend, little by little, being severely burnt, it was not at all impossible for such strange things to happen! Such would be, perhaps, natural if there had been no downpour since ages, men would naturally lose the sense of telling apart good and bad. During daytime too, in bright light of the day, the daughters and wives of ordinary households would go out on a love tryst. Well, was there a night, yesterday? And evening? And then, night, the call of the jackal spelling out clear division of hours of that night, and then an intense night? Yes, it had been so, as it seemed to Mahaparshwa. He sat outside Chaturika's room since the evening. Chaturika was terribly angry! Dreadfully! If possible, she would have killed Mahaparshwa or impaled him on pike or burnt him alive! But was it the matter of yesterday or the day before? Might be the day before yesterday! Mahaparshwa asked abruptly, "Well Sir, was it last evening or the day before yesterday? Could you please tell me the exact day?"

Tamradhvaj started up, "Has the merchant left the day before yesterday?"

Mahaparshwa stuck out his tongue, being ashamed, and said, "No, no, he will start day after tomorrow, but day before yesterday, there was an evening, wasn't it"?

Gandhavati was taken aback, let alone Tamradhvaj. She stole a glance at Mahaparshwa from behind her scarf. Had he gone insane? If it did not rain, man would turn insane, gradually, her mother as well as her grandfather had said so. Were the symptoms of lunacy growing pronounced in him? Then why would he say whether there had been an evening, the day before yesterday? Didn't he know whether it had been so or not?

Listening to Tamradhvaj's rejoinder, it seemed to Mahaparshwa that, there had been no evening yesterday. That would be correct. It was not yesterday, rather the day preceding it, when he kept sitting in the courtyard in front of Chaturika's room. And Chaturika was disgorging obscenities on him, incessantly! She was pinning him down with uncouth remarks, like smarting arrows! After that, there had been no evening at all. As there had been no evening, day could not be told apart from night! Stepping out of the house, a wife of a respectable family had covered her face with a scarf. Hence the prediction of the Chief Physician, Nahush Sharman, came to be true! Mahaparshwa glanced at the firmament! Really, the wheel of the chariot of Sun God got stuck in the celestial sphere!

Tamradhvaj grew curious, he asked, "Why? Why wouldn't be there any evening?"

Mahaparshwa began pulling his own hair, kept muttering under his breath, "After that there had been no evening, Sir, only day persists, yes, I am sure".

"Since the morning, day continued".

"Yes, neither morning, nor daytime seems to know any end. At this time, the beloveds are in real trouble, you can say, the times of rendezvous are now a thing of the past, extramarital relationships are in jeopardy, I have to escape from this city with the merchant. Will you go Sir, to the land of the river Oxus, a bath in that river would make one absolved of all sins of one's life?"

"We are going to Bidisha, returning to the land of Dasharno".

"Escape, go off soon, daytime in Ujjwain is not coming to a close".

"What are you saying"? Tamradhvaj was taken aback presently. By then, it was clear to him what this tall and lanky man, similar to a palmyra tree in looks, intended to say.

"Well, what I am saying is all true, not a whit of it is a lie. Since yesterday, the daytime knows no termination, Ujjwain will burn by sunshine, till it faces utter ruin".

Gandhavati took a look at Mahaparshwa through the cover of her scarf. She had not seen a madman before. This was the first time. The man was emphasizing each view he maintained. Since yesterday, according to him, only daytime kept continuing. Gandhavati giggled, the vibration of her laughter sent ripples across her body. She seemed to flow like a stream. So long, as she was feeling fear, sense of peril, all seemed to fly off in a jiffy. Holding Tamradhvaj's hand in a trice, she demanded to know, "Who is he?"

"A man of this city, he had done me a favour once".

Gandhavati laughed again, "Is he mad"?

"No, no, not at all, the sunshine has left his head, heated up."

Gandhavati said, "Can such a thing happen at all? We spent all the night in the darkness of the path, we walked under the starlight, and this man is saying that there had been no night, only the day prolonged! Who will utter such nonsense save a madcap?"

"Yes, that's it", folding his palms, Mahaparshwa greeted Gandhavati. By then, he had stolen a glance at her face. Oh, so beautiful! Who said that Devadutta was a paragon of beauty? No other woman of the world seemed to be so beautiful like this lady. Who was she? Such a woman could easily be made the Chief Prostitute; that could definitely be done. Devadutta would leave for the land by the river Oxus, this angel could be taken there, to stay at her residence. If this woman would become the Chief Prostitute, Mahaparshwa would give up the idea of going to the land by the river, Oxus. He would stay beneath her feet as her servant. After such thoughts, Mahaparshwa asked, "Sir, where are you going with this paragon of beauty"?

After getting a reply, Mahaparshwa said, "Who is she, daughter of which family, wife of which household, is she anyone's wife, how have you got her, what's her identity?"

Tamradhvaj got visibly perturbed. Gandhavati recoiled in fear. Her smile had disappeared. He tugged Gandhavati by her arms, saying, "Come, the heat is being oppressive".

"Sir, if you ask me, I can inform the brothel, the Superintendent of the brothel is there in the King's court, I can take this woman to him. Everyone will be happy to get such a heavenly beauty, even the King! Chief Prostitute is going away, leaving this city… I know the Sessions-bloke, Uddhav, I can go and call him!"

Screaming in fear, Gandhavati took Tamradhvaj in a firm clasp. Then, Tamradhvaj turned stern, he spoke out harshly, "You are nothing more than a worm of the Hell! Dealing with the dirt,your mind rests on that only! We are man and wife, how dare you insult us thus, without being properly aware? Will we move the King's court for justice?"

Hearing so, Mahaparshwa left them soon, in utter haste. Oh God! Why did he fail to comprehend such a simple truth? Alas! Oh alas! It would be an utter relief to him now to follow the tycoon who would leave this city soon.

SEVENTY-SEVEN

Gandhavati had never seen the Mahakaal temple before. Even she had not seen the river, Gandhavati. This was her first visit to the city of Ujjwain. Joy was much less in the wonder of exploring the city for the first time, though since last night they were man and wife—she and Tamradhvaj! Life's pace and movement had changed altogether. Both of them were truly carrying along the thrill of the mind as well as the body.

The peak of the Mahakaal shrine had touched the sky. That pinnacle was gold-tipped. The river, Gandhavati, which was flowing by the Mahakaal shrine was nearly devoid of water. Dry sand was blowing in the wind. Gandhavati seemed never to have seen the river becoming such destitute! Their own Gambhira had dried up too, it was just a semblance of a slim water-line, flowing in the middle, like a strand of hair. Yet, she seemed not so indigent. Though each year during Baisakh, the river, Gambhira went devoid of water, this year it was even more moribund. Nature herself being bare, how could the river look less void? The Mahakaal temple, standing by the river, Gandhavati, seemed to exhibit its enormity underneath the sky, even more, during these days of drought. That temple had no vacuity, rather under the oppressive sun, the sunburnt stones on its body were growing even harder. Sunshine was too oppressive on the stones! It was really painful to plant a bare foot on the open space inside the temple. This temple seemed to have disowned Gandhavati and her husband like an insolent general of the King's Court!

Gandhavati suggested, "Come, let us go back".

"Won't you pay your respect to Lord Mahakaal"?

Gandhavati bowed down with folded palms and then muttered, "Oh Lord Mahakaal, protect us, save Ujjwain"! Tamradhvaj said, "I do not know whether we will be able to come here once again!"

Gandhavati kept quiet. Lord Mahakaal, she was praying to, seemed to be some other God! Alas, oh mind! Why was she being overcome by the memories of Dhruvaputra as she stepped to the front of the temple? She was now the better half of Tamradhvaj. She stood touching Tamradhvaj. Why did Dhruvaputra loom large over the inner desolation of her mind now? Dhruvaputra used to describe this temple of Lord Mahakaal. This temple of Lord Mahakaal had famed Ujjwain as a Golden City on all ten directions, all around! She was standing on the terrace of that temple! Fire kept raging above her head. Fire singed her feet from below. The temple was such blessed with riches that the river which flew by its side, held its head low. Compared to the treasures of Mahakaal, the river was utterly poor, visibly destitute. Tamradhvaj took Gandhavati's hands to say, "Then let us go back".

"Yes, let's return, I am feeling scared.

"Why? Why scared, coming to God's abode?"

"I do not know but why is the temple so desolate"?

"They are there, all of them are inside the temple. At the advent of the evening, people from this place or far come here in droves, but now the heat-wave is on. People in the city itself are very few in number".

Gandhavati closed both her eyes. She tried to concentrate on Lord Mahakaaleswar, the blue-necked Lord Mahadeva! In the secluded darkness, Dhruvaputra's face bobbed up. As she was leaving Ujjwain for good, she would never ever be able to come here again, it seemed. Would she ever get to see Dhruvaputra? Let Dhruvaputra be blessed, let him be back, let him return! The pigeons, which had nested in the holes in a row, cooed. It seemed to Gandhavati that even the pigeons were saying the same. The stones under her feet were not so heated, anymore.The heat of the sun lessened too,she could feel. Gandhavati suggested, "Let us set out on our journey".

While walking, it happened to Gandhavati that the shadows aslant on the temple kept impinging Dhruvaputra's form in silhouette into her mind. Quite soothing, cool was that shadow. She was on her way to Dasharno on foot. Remembering Dhruvaputra, the sunshine seemed to be soft, benign, all seemed to be still, calm. She held Tanradhvaj's hand firm, she gibbered, "How had all this happened?"

"Yes, I had come here to master astronomy and then how all this had transpired, I wonder, how?"

Gandhavati asked, "You had come to calculate and then what had happened?"

"I had thought of going out in search of Dhruvaputra, but how all this had taken place!"

Gandhavati reasoned, "Things would never come to such a pass, if Dhruvaputra had not left Ujjwain!"

"What would happen then?"

"We are ignorant of that too".

"Perhaps the same would have happened, in some other manner, in some other way! You mean, I would have never met you by any means at all?"

Gandhavati had gone silent. She was wondering why would Dhruvaputra return to this wretched, impoverished city at all? On his return, he would journey to Gambhira to find that Gandhavati was not there. He would again come back to the city to see to his utter dismay that even the whore had left. He would turn back to the lakes to find not even a hint of water in them. He would walk up to the river, Gandhavati, and would find it emaciated to a skeletal form, thus demeaning the beauty of the temple of Mahakaal to a great extent. That river was a part of the temple's glory too. Now Gandhavati could feel why the temple failed to draw her in. Why had the idol failed to welcome her inside the temple? The temple stood like Uddhav, the despot, and grandeur of the temple seemed to be a thing of the past. How could the deity of a temple stay in glory, in pride of opulence, if the people ran in search of water like the ever-thirsty swallow, if the meadows turned desiccated, dry, drooping to an imminent demise? She asked Tamradhvaj, "Are you really keen on visiting the Shudra ghetto"?

"Yes, I will… you will get to see the abundance of water there"!

Gandhavati stood in the sun, the scarf had slipped off from her head as she exclaimed, "Has then Lord Mahakaal walked down to the Shudra locality, dear?"

Tamradhvaj shivered, "What do you say, if it reaches the ear of the Chief Priest, you will be burnt alive, such utterances are prohibited!"

Gandhavati tugged at the scarf to cover her head and said, "Then Lord Mahakaal is water Himself, you mean?"

"Right, Lord Mahakaal is water Himself".

"Is Lord Mahakaal the rain then?"

"Yes,Lord Mahakaal is the rain".

"Is Lord Mahakaal the cloud?"

"No doubt, He is".

"All the things on earth sum up to Lord Mahakaal then"?

"Yes, Lord Mahakaal is everything and all. Beyond Him, there is nothing in this world!" Tamradhvaj said.

"Then has Lord Mahakaal truly retired to the Shudra colony"?

Tamradhvaj said, "Water has truly surfaced in Ratnakarsagar, and if Lord Mahakaal is water, then He remains intermingled with the water of that lake. Water itself is Life!"

"Mahakaal Himself is Life"! Gandhavati whispered.

"Let's go, Gandhavati, let us see Lord Mahakaal in the Ratnakar sagar and the savant, Parashar, sitting there! And then let us leave Ujjwain!"

While reaching there, they came to an abrupt halt. Again, the sound of kettledrums and the bugles was being wafted in. The sound began to reach closer, gradually. Being ponderous, it kept pervading the sky, the sunshine. Was then the retinue of soldiers returning? Which platoon of soldiers? Those who had gone out to war in the morning? How was it that the war got concluded so soon? Where did the battle happen, which even ended so soon? Or was it a different platoon, which had gone to protect the merchants from the dacoits and returning presently? Gandhavati pulled Tamradhvaj, taking shelter behind the Peepul tree, tucked far off the way.

The soldiers were returning, victorious. Uddhav's platoon was coming back, rejoicing. Uddhav was leading them, at the helm of all. Maiden battle, maiden victory! In utter joy, he was lifting the unsheathed sword up and again he was slashing it down. His thin arms could not bear the weight of the sword, yet the sword was the symbol of power, hence, he had to exhibit his valour, once being able to display it, Uddhav's body would grow stronger, handsomer. As Uddhav held the sword up against the sky, it seemed, he would pierce the sky with the tip of the weapon! As the sun reflected on the open sword, the weapon dazzled. Gandhavati remembered the gold-tipped pinnacle of the shrine of Lord Mahakaal. What for did she remember it? Being scared, she shut her eyes. The noise of the bugle and the horn reached crescendo, growing poignant, sombre. There the retinue of Uddhav's soldiers showed up. The front end of the rope was held in the hands of the infantry troop. At the other end of the rope, both hands of the men stood captive, being tied firmly. The soldiers rejoiced uproariously, the prisoners were walking with their heads, hung low. They were bending like bows, as they walked on. While witnessing such sight, Tamradhvaj screamed in pain, in a muffled tone, "Oh God! What's wrong? Who are being taken along... why so... where had the armies been to?"

At the scream of Tamradhvaj, Gandhavati opened her eyes, and while doing so, she thought that this was not the way to Gambhira. Then, how would the armies return from Gambhira? Thus, being relieved, she found that the soldiers were dragging quite a few dark-skinned, hunter-like men! Who were they? Were they the residents of the forest? Was Tamradhvaj familiar with them?

Tamradhvaj said, "The platoons are returning from the Shudra ghetto."

"Why, what's wrong?"

"I don't know, they are taking the Shudras captive".

"Are they thieves or robbers?"

Tamradhvaj replied, "They are innocent! Almost for a fortnight, they dug Ratnakarsagar to make the water surface from the core of the hell. How are they taken guilty? What for?"

Gandhavati said in a low voice, "If Uddhav is at the helm of these soldiers, he will ruin everything, I had already predicted".

Both of them sat behind the peepul tree, under its shade, huddling together. Uddhav, the Army-Chief, was mad in joy, on winning the battle. He was taking so many men as prisoners to the capital, what more success would he dream of? Uddhav went forward, roaring. The infantry followed behind. A little later, the road stood desolate, calm. The sun-baked meadows, on the other end of the road, stood in dreadful silence.

Gandhavati was reluctant to leave the shade, she said, "Why have they been taken away?"

"No idea. So the platoon of soldiers had gone to the Shudra ghetto, I see!"

"They are the ones who have made the water surface in that lake!""Yes, all of them are Shudras!"

Gandhavati said, "But that water is Lord Mahakaal!"

"Yes, just like this shade!"

Gandhavati said, "Perhaps Lord Mahakaal had emerged from the shrine that day, I mean the day when water surfaced in that lake"!

Tamradhvaj was highly impressed, he asked, "Who has taught you to think thus?"

Gandhavati replied, "You! Just you! Did the army troop go there as Lord Mahakaal was stationed with them, at the Shudra Ghetto? Do you know anything?"

Then, Tamradhvaj was thinking how a battery of armies had marched towards the distant Shurparak port to offer protection to the Ionian Greek merchants. A few days back, he had a conversation on this matter with Gandhavati's grandfather. He said that the armies had gone there to arrest the movement of the clouds. The armies wished the period of drought to prolong. Let the scarcity of water be there, the advantageous conditions for their dare-devilry would then continue unabated. Their wish had come true. The armies had marched on to a point, where the lake got filled with water. Did the soldiers rush there to destroy that water? How terrifying it sounded! How terrible a truth it was! The reason for which the armies had gone to Shurparak port got gratified truly in their expedition to the Shudra locality. He helped Gandhavati to get to her feet and asked, "Come, let's go".

Shudra ghetto wore a grim look. Many of the men had gone away with the platoon of Uddhavnarayan. Uddhav had left deploying four sentries on the four corners of the water-body. The Shudras were directed not to touch the water of the pond. By order of the King of Ujjwain, and the Army-Commander - water, land, shades, light, sunlight, rains - all stood controlled by the King. Uddhav had announced it. It had been a cardinal sin to extract water from the hell, without any permission of the King! This offence would even be more culpable, if the downtrodden Shudras touched it! The Chief Priest of Mahakaal temple, the Lord Brahmin, would pass directives on how to utilize this water, he would come to consecrate the water and then it would be borne to the city.

Hearing this, tears streamed down both the eyes of Gandhavati. The Shudra-women had surrounded them. They sat with empty pitchers, at a little distance from Parashar, the savant. Uddhav was not so daring to ruin the meditation of Parashar, the hermit. He had taken the youth as captive. He would make them dig the other six ponds, lying across the city, devoid of water.

The four soldiers sat together by the edge of the lake, beneath a neem tree, with faces like deadpan. Gandhavati said, "May I have a pitcher, please?"

"What for? Culling water from it has been prohibited, as per the directives of Uddhav".

Hearing so, the veil dropped off from the head of Gandhavati. She was boiling in fury. She was reminded of the day, long back, how Uddhav had appeared on horseback, beside the well. She could feel that Uddhav would grow more ferocious, more tyrannical, on winning the responsibility of the army troops. Being armed with the power of controlling the battery of soldiers, Uddhav would turn more depraved. Gandhavati thought of opposing Uddhav, before leaving. As far as she knew Uddhav, once resisted, he would not take long to react. She told them to tell Uddhav that the daughter of Kartikkumar of Gambhira village, the beloved of Dhruvaputra, the ladylove and wife of the astronomer of Dasharno, Tamradhvaj, had flouted Uddhav's order. It was Gandhavati who had touched the water, it was she who had distributed water among the residents here.

Tamradhvaj said, "Would they have to accept the charity of the same water which actually belonged to them?"

"Such is charity, since times immemorial"! Muttered an elderly Shudra lady.

A young maid cautioned, "If the Army-Commander's order is flouted, immense loss is what we would have to incur"!

"I am going to disobey the order,you will draw water! Lord Mahakaal is there above all and the Sun and the Moon have not vanished yet."

The old Shudra woman began to shake her head in desperation, "How much water can you lift, Maa, even though you draw water, it is us who would have to suffer, such goes the directive of the Army Commander. In the evening, he will send a soldier, a young maid has to be sent with him, he will have pleasure at her cost otherwise, he will incite the soldiers to pounce upon the wives and daughters of our households. Oh God, that will be real terror! All of us have to escape leaving all our dwellings behind!"

Gandhavati still insisted, "Yet give me your pitcher, a water-filled pitcher is auspicious for undertaking journeys, let me at least bend the order of Uddhav, before I leave."

"Your touch will not mean flouting his order, you are not a Shudra-woman, Maa!"

Gandhavati was driven to silence. The women all sat hither and thither with their empty pitchers under the huge shade of the banyan tree. At the base of the banyan tree, old Parashar sat still like Lord Buddha, who had taken birth eons ago. The Village-Head had promised to open his eyes if only he heard the thunderclap of clouds. He was earnestly praying for the clouds, as all said.

Gandhavati said, "If I do not touch water, I shall not even cast a glance at it."

Tamradhvaj said, "Water is Lord Mahakaal Himself, can't we look at the lake filled with water to its brim, Gandhavati?"

"The water to which they have no claim, I haven't too".

Hearing so, the elderly women, young maids, the middle-aged Shudra women, all showed immediate concern, "How will that be Maa, you are not born in a Shudra family! We are very fortunate as you have come here with your husband, now perhaps in each household, our daughters will be pregnant, now in all our houses little kids will cry and scream, now our households will be happy nooks comprising our husbands and children… But where are our husbands? They are imprisoned by Uddhav, he says, he will not free them unless the clouds pile up in the sky. He has also added that, the Chief Priest has taken all measures to ensure the clouds not to appear. If our husbands do not come back, how will we have babies in our womb, our husbands are like clouds— at the advent of clouds in the sky, they turn to us, on the appearance of clouds, we are impregnated, such is the way of life with us since long, without clouds, we stay unhappy, dry, ungratified, Maa…"

The Shudra women were humming around Gandhavati. Encircling her, they were reiterating about the clouds, about the downpour. Each one of them had different manner of expression. How at hovering of the clouds, the peacock used to address his peahen, expanding his tail, someone said, someone else again described how a deer approached his doe, beneath the shadow of the clouds! Someone was narrating how she had gone to a man during a rainy night and then she kept wondering where he had gone away, beyond her knowledge! She kept awaiting him, till date. If clouds would hover over, that man would surely come back to her. A young Shudra maiden brought her mouth near Gandhavati's ear to ask, "What's wrong with you, my friend, what's up?"

What exactly would happen to me? Gandhavati was trembling. She was seeing Tamradhvaj who stood at the edge of the shade of the banyan tree. There was a chiaroscuro of shade and sun on his body. Both the eyes of her husband were a-dazzle. Tamradhvaj beckoned at her, "Come here"!

The young Shudra maiden intimately brought her lips to her ear and asked, "Exactly where has this man accepted you, by the river, beside the forest or inside the meadows? As both of you have spent the day on the road, where and when did you become one, did you wake him up or did he call you"?

Gandhavati kept quiet, she lowered her head.

The young woman touched her breasts and said, "Tell me, my husband has been taken away by Uddhav, when he will be back, I shall tell about this couple to him, both of you will be my clouds, will be the water of the sky, tell me, oh damsel, what had happened and how, see how the very look at you has made my breasts go firm, my body, a-shiver. Touch my breasts and see yourself, hey girl…"

Gandhavati covered her face with both her hands. And seeing that, the young woman whispered in her ears, demanded to know the nitty-gritty of lovemaking, asked what her husband had said while showering kisses on her, what he had said while holding her breasts!

Gandhavati could comprehend that these women, though they had lived with their men, were not at all gratified. It seemed, they did not enjoy the company of their husbands or men since ages. They had been oblivious of the art of lovemaking. Being newly-wed, the desire consumed them, bit by bit. The young wife was not alone, all the Shudra women kept giggling surrounding her, they repeatedly wanted to know the same fact, where, when and how her husband had made love to her for the first time and how was the thrill of that union?

Gandhavati moved to Tamradhvaj, slowly. She held his hand. It seemed to her that as all the youths had been held captive and had been taken to the city, the women of the Shudra ghetto grew extremely fervent. Desire was getting the better of them, by degrees. She got startled. Weren't these women saying that they could not conceive as the clouds disappeared from the sky? Without the appearance of the clouds, they would not be desirous, without clouds they would keep drying up from within. Now, she was thinking of something else. Gandhavati took Tamradhvaj to stand in the sun for stealing a glance at the sky. Did the clouds appear? The monsoon clouds of Asad, of Sravana — did the rainclouds make their presence felt in the sky of Ujjwain? Were the women growing amorous for that reason?

The ashen sky dazzled both her eyes. Yonder, the Shudra women sat down on the ground. They were depressed at present, the avidity that was there in them even a few moments back, had subsided. Being fatigued, they were drawing long breaths now. There, even beyond, the Village-Chief, who turned ascetic, was sitting calm, still. All around him, the endless silence hovered, quite intense. Gandhavati looked up to the face of Tamradhvaj and asked, "Did the cloud float in?"

"I do not know! Where are the clouds? Only the sky stretches high above!"

"Then why did the women, the wives grow desirous, just a few moments back?" Gandhavati kept shaking her head. She was lost in an inscrutable search, looking up above, it seemed.

SEVENTY-EIGHT

After a long interregnum, the King had come to the house of Devadutta, the Chief Courtesan. Alone, on the sly. Next morning, Subhag Dutta would set out on his journey. In that tour, Devadutta was to accompany him. The King came to know lately that the merchant, even at this ripe old age was madly in love with Devadutta, the whore. Only Devadutta could put a stop to Subhag Dutta's setting out on the journey and none else. The King could make Subhag Dutta cancel his plans of leaving the country by coercion with the aid of his army but that would be highly unethical. Another problem might crop up as its consequence. The merchant was handsomely rich and his command on the minds of all the people of Ujjwain could not be gainsaid. Who wasn't impressed by the merchant? Everyone right from the Chief Priest to the Army Commander. Devadutta was aware of everything. The King wanted the merchant to stay back in Ujjwain during these times of peril.

Throughout the day, Devadutta had distributed all her belongings among the whores. Chaturika had not come, however. Though she called for her, Chaturika chose not to respond. In the evening, in an almost desolate room, with a vacant heart, lighting a lamp, Devadutta sat all alone. Just then, the King had come. The King was announced by that tall, lanky Mahaparshwa, the pimp. He could not understand himself where he was or what time it was! Incessantly he was carrying all sorts of wrong information, from one end of the city to the other, he was dropping by at Chaturika's residence and being chucked out, was rushing to Devadutta's door. Gasping, he came into the room to announce, "Here's the King!"

Devadutta was taken aback, "What do you mean by 'The King'"?

"The King of Ujjwain, Maa! He is waiting for you in the courtyard, he asks me to reach you the news of his visit. I could not recognize Him in the darkness, at first"!

"Then how could you spot Him?"

"How to recognize him? His face is covered. He has come here behind all eyes!"

"He is the King after all, if he has to go anywhere, it is natural for him to conceal his own identity!"

"The King asks me to deliver the information to you, King Bhartrihari is here at your door, you will set out tomorrow, perhaps the King has come to bid you farewell, Maa! Let me go downstairs to welcome the King!"

"Who else is there?"

"No one else! He has come alone, if he doesn't introduce himself, who will take him to be the King? But you know the King well Maa, so please go and identify him!"

Devadutta thought— Who knows if it had been someone else? Then she laughed within. Who else will it be? Who else is there in this city, so blind in love for her? And who again will approach her with a false identity? Again, why so? The King had come to stand in the courtyard, all alone - Devadutta was deeply moved. After such a long hiatus, the King had come to see her! Devadutta seemed to have everything she had dreamt of in her life and this was the end of all. Another life would begin beside the river Oxus in her fatherland, in the country of Balkh! That life would make her forget her days in Ujjwain. Tears welled up in Devadutta's eyes. She said, "Come Mahaparshwa, let me usher in the King, I fail to understand till date whom I had fallen for, this King or that blue-eyed youth, Dhruvaputra! Sometimes it strikes me that Dhruvaputra means everything to me and later I think, the sad King of Ujjwain is the world to me. Come Mahaparshwa, let us go and welcome King Bhartrihari in."

Mahaparshwa could not make the head or tail of Devadutta's words. But it seemed to him, her assumption was baseless, it was not Dhruvaputra, it was the King who had come instead. Dhruvaputra had gone somewhere, God knew where, a vagabond after all! How would he come here? It was really next to impossible to comprehend the inner recesses of a prostitute's mind. Coming in contact with sundry men, they would not be won over even by the best man, any woman could dream of! Mahaparshwa walked at the heels of Devadutta. With the lamp in her hand, Devadutta began to move forward along the perfectly silent corridor in darkness. The house was calm and quiet. Neither any restlessness nor any noise was there anywhere. No stealthy whispers even. Only the bells on Devadutta's anklet began to sound faintly in the dark, at this hour. Devadutta had freed her domesticated birds in the morning: the male and the female popinjay. If they had been there, they could have screeched on waking up, abruptly. In the holes of this house, many pigeons took refuge. They kept cooing in their sleep. This evening, they were not making any noise. Devadutta knew not, whether the flight of pigeons had left her house or not. The beasts and birds could sense everything, well ahead. Any house without any human would never be a suitable home for the kit of pigeons. And Devadutta was going away, leaving the city. Who would come to stay in this house, once she left? None at all. Would the new whore, who would replace her as the Chief Prostitute, be willing to stay in this shady nook of Devadutta? Some day this house would collapse. It would be the snake's pit; the black owl, the bat, all would find a safe haven in this house.

Devadutta came to stand in the courtyard. The Navami moon of the new moon fortnight was yet to make its presence in the sky. But it was crystal clear who had come there in the courtyard. The King stood still, looking at the sky. His face was covered with a scarf, but the royal attire would be enough to help one recognize him. From where would Dhruvaputra manage the royal robe? Resting the lamp on the floor, Devadutta bowed there on the ground itself and said, "Lord, you are welcome"!

As Devadutta got up, the King lowered his face. The lamp was again taken up by Devadutta in her palm, the flame was flickering in the soft breeze. It snuffed out. The darkness outside would cause no problem. But the darkness inside would seem to be suffocating. It would be quite a trouble to breathe in there. Why had the lamp got extinguished despite the absence of light? The King said, "May you be blessed", in a feeble tone, almost inaudible.

It was the maid's good fortune that the King had stepped into her house!

The King did not utter anything more. He followed Devadutta. Through the darkness of the extinguished lamp, Devadutta was leading him inside. The tinkling of her anklet-bells led the King through the long verandah. Mahaparshwa kept standing outside. He could not understand what he would do at that moment. Would he keep waiting at the door or move on to another place? Tomorrow the journey would begin, he had not decided yet, whether he would leave with them or not. Chaturika had said neither 'yes' nor 'no'even. Again, Mahaparshwa could not also decide whether to leave or not. Now it was monsoon but since quite a few years, there had been no rainfall. This period would pass by, the monsoon would come to an end, then after a long interregnum, the month of Kartik would arrive, the full-moon would then hang close to the Krittika star. He would then reach the land of the Gandharvas. An 'if' loomed large behind. When the monsoon would end, they would be in a land named Gandhaar. Well, if there would be no monsoon at all, how would it come to a close? If the monsoon would not end, they would never be able to reach Gandhaar. Where would they go then? Mahaparshwa kept walking. He would not have to think about all these details, if Ujjwain stood blessed with monsoon.

The King had come to pay a visit to Devadutta's residence. Devadutta was leaving— would then this be the last chance of merrymaking together?! Mahaparshwa laughed out noisily. How would it be then? How weary was the King's voice, how poor was the manner of his coming over! The King would announce his visit aloud, driving all nooks astir, would send his messenger, would ask for Devadutta to see him in the palace, but nothing took place, he chose to come stealthily, instead. Why did he come, on the sly? Wasn't it the King who had come? Or was it someone else? In the darkness, nothing could be made out. Did anyone else come in the guise of the King? What was going on in this city? The King was visiting the bawdyhouse, in the dark, stealthily! During drought, nothing could be perceived. Mahaparshwa kept walking. The merchant would set out on his journey, just the following day. All day long, the preparations were on, in front of the merchant's house. The horde of traders who would accompany him were busy in preparing themselves. Stout and strong bulls would be drawing the cattle-cart. Strong and well-built oxen, with horns curved as spear-like missiles, would also draw the carriage. Donkeys were more than fifty in number. Mahaparshwa had not taken any count of them. He did not stop there at all. Just had gone there for a round of visit. But he had circled umpteen times, and it left him with an idea that the number of donkeys would be even more. They would act as beasts of burden, carrying maximum weight, and there would be man-borne palanquins. Of them, one would be for the merchant and the other for Devadutta. The other merchants would take palanquins as well, they had chariots too, brawny and muscular men were flexing their muscles, standing before the merchant's house. They would accompany them. Mahaparshwa was trying to make out, how Chaturika and him would join this bandwagon! If they would come along, at all. Where was the palanquin or a chariot or even a cattle-drawn carriage? Would they join them on foot?

In the dark, Mahaparshwa drew up to Chaturika's courtyard. Now, he would have to send the news of his arrival like the King. Who had entered the house of Devadutta in the guise of the King? Mahaparshwa had been there, and hence the news of his arrival had reached Devadutta's inner court, accordingly. But here, who would reach the news? Mahaparshwa stood in the dark and got lost in contemplation. If someone like him had been posted, he could be announced as the King who had come to Chaturika's residence to seek her company. Let the whore come to welcome the King. Mahaparshwa began to ponder, the King might easily come to Chaturika's place. Devadutta was now the ladylove of the merchant. Who shall the King approach, on his rejection by the whore, Devadutta? Chaturika! In the city, a hearsay was even rife that the queen was not kind to the King. The King had gone to the temple of Lord Mahakaal to outrage the modesty of a devadasi, stealthily, all alone, in the dark of the night. Alas! What was going on in the city? The King of Ujjwain was to rape a devadasi, but why was there any dearth of women in the city? Was devadasi Lalita more beautiful than Devadutta, was her youth so alluring to the King that he had to see her in the dark of the midnight, all alone … All this was known to each soul, in the city.

It seemed to Mahaparshwa, that, if the King could go to enjoy the company of Devadutta, secretly, he could easily come here to Chaturika, as well. And as the King was known to indulge in such wrongdoings, anyone could enter Devadutta's house in the King's guise. And that exactly had happened. The King had come to Chaturika. The King was a lustful, lascivious man! He coveted the company of women of various sorts, of various shades of beauty. Hence, as he had gone to the devadasi, he had been here to the serving-maid, Chaturika, as well. Again, the queen Bhanumati used to stay with the Army-Commander. Someone else had come to Devadutta in the guise of the King. All such facts were known to everyone in the city. Mahaparshwa pulled his own hair, he wanted to understand properly, which woman had been approached by whom:

1] The Army- Commander had gone to the queen Bhanumati -this was a fact, known to all.

2] The King had come to see Chaturika, the serving-maid.

3] Devadasi had gone to the Priest's room,

4] Who, then, had come to Devadutta, in the guise of the King?

No wonder, it could have been the merchant. But the merchant was setting out on a journey to the land of the Gandharvas with Devadutta, then why would he have to come stealthily to her, covering up his own identity? It might be possible that Uddhav had sneaked in. No … he would not dare do so. Some thief might have come to Devadutta's place, in the King's guise. Uddhav might come in here! If so, he would withdraw in fear, like a frightened dog, folding his tail. He had no courage to stand before the King. Mahaparshwa pounded on the closed door, "Chaturika, hey Chaturika"!

"Who? Are you Mahaparshwa, my brother"? How calm was the voice of Chaturika!

In a calmer, more solemn voice, Mahaparshwa answered, "Good be with you, the King desires you, Chaturika!"

The King! In a few seconds, the door opened. Chaturika came outside with a lamp in her hand. Mahaparshwa had moved away, quite further. He had covered his face with the scarf, stood still, without uttering anything. Chaturika was visibly startled. Who was there? It was just desolate, out in the open. She moved forward with the lamp in her hand. She felt scared, uncanny.

Mahaparshwa had retreated to the darkness. Now, it seemed to him that he was the real King of this Ujjwain. Chaturika was out in search of the King, with a lamp in her hand. If any soul would be there, it was just him. He was invariably the King then. The King of Ujjwain. His voice had made Chaturika to unbolt the door!

In the glow of the lamp, Chaturika could see that tall, lanky man. Though the face was covered, but who else could that extremely tall man be, in this city? Lowering the lamp on the ground, behind a cover, she called out to Mahaparshwa, "Hey, who are you?"

"The King desires you, Chaturika!"

"Hey thou scoundrel, come forward, why have thou covered thy face?"

"The King is in front of you, Chaturika!"

Chaturika was again perplexed. Where was the King? Had he really been there? Where had he gone then? Nothing could be recognized in such strange darkness. She folded her palms and said, "Oh King, if you are here, this maid wants to offer herself in devotion to your feet, accept my regards, oh King!"

Mahaparshwa got excited. So, he was the King, the real King! If he would be the King, and reach Chaturika's door in that capacity and Chaturika failed to recognize him in disguise … then who might have gone into Devadutta's room? How pitch dark it had been at that time! In such darkness, it was really difficult to perceive who was seeing whom and in which guise!

Chaturika entreated, "Oh Lord, please reveal yourself to this maid of yours! This maid will serve you, this maid is truly wretched, I am really blessed to know that Lord covets me!"

Mahaparshwa was thinking at the back of his mind, who had really gone into the room of Devadutta! The whore could not make out anything in the darkness, but he could, he had a 'but' at the back of his mind. That was not the King, but someone else. None had been to Chaturika's room, let alone the King, it was he who dropped in, yet, Chaturika had taken him as the King only, in the dark.

Mahaparshwa stepped forward and called out, "Chaturika"!

"Where is he? I mean, the King!"

"I am the King, Chaturika! Listen to me! Someone had entered the house of Devadutta , in disguise of the King, but she would start by now for the land by the river, Oxus, leaving all her possessions behind! Who had been there to see her, Chaturika"?

Chaturika was taken aback, she could not get anything, yet said, "The old merchant"?!

"No, he will take her along, tomorrow"!

"Then who could it be? Perhaps the King!"

"No, it was not the King though Devadutta had taken him to be so and welcomed him to her inner court. Just as she stepped into the courtyard, the lamp she had in her hand got snuffed out! I wonder why it had extinguished even though there was no wind! She had her hand covered as well but as she drew up to the King...!"

Chaturika placed her hand on her cheek, asking in astonishment, "Are you speaking the truth, Mahaparshwa brother?"

"Shall I come this far just to tell a lie"?

"Couldn't thou discern who it had been?"

"It was dark, again he stood in the darknes., I thought, the King had come on a secret tryst, hence he needed to conceal himself. Now it seems that it was not the King but someone else"!

Chaturika said, "Don't thou know the King, thou rogue"?

I have seen him from a distance. But how to recognize him as his face and head were all covered? I dozed, sitting on the threshold, I was thinking, which palanquin would we be in, I would rather go on foot, but how would thou go? Right then he came, how discordant his voice sounded, it was more of striking a bell-metal plate than a human voice, and that King ordered me, "Go and tell the woman that the King has come"!

"Did he say so, in that manner"?

"Yes! May be, he was drunk"!

"Would the King come being drunk, do you think so"?

Mahaparshwa shook his head to say, "How can I say, if the wine is easily available to the King, why won't he drink it? "And if the King has the right to see Devadutta at her house, why won't he go then?"

"What did he say ... think and tell me"!

"The whore will be leaving tomorrow, go and announce, the King has come!"

Chaturika slapped her forehead, Alas! Oh alack! Couldn't you understand, Mahaparshwa brother, it was some other man, who made way into my friend's room in guise of the King, oh what an utter ruin! Will the diction of the King be like that, will he address anyone in such an uncouth manner? He is the King of Ujjwain after all! He is a poet, he is a suave and cultured gentleman to the core!"

"Then who was he"?

"A man we are familiar with, certainly! He had taken the advantage of darkness-- a robber, a depraved thief, no doubt, but a person known to us! Tell thou, whose diction could be so obnoxious?"

Mahaparshwa kept rocking, to and fro. He could recognize and find his name at the back of his mind but failed to mouth it! Again, if it sprang up to his lips, would he be able to utter it yet? He seemed to recognize him now. His affected bell-metal-like voice could not however muffle his real tone, it seemed. As he was confused, he came to startle Chaturika with this guise of the King! As the King had come here, the King had not been to Devadutta's house. The King had not been there. Who had then gone? The man who had gone there turned to be frightful over the last few days! He was throwing this man or that, into the prison, indiscriminately. He kept intimidating them! Plunder had begun in the very precincts of the city! This drought had really ruined everything, absolutely!

Chaturika said, "So you could not recall, you nincompoop"!

Mahaparshwa kept swinging his head and said, "What if I can remember even, he hasn't entered your room!"

"I know my friend has marred my chance, if she would not have agreed, the merchant must have taken me with him, but the man is an old, wizened man, an arrant knave. I think, my friend has meant good to me, what could I do by sailing up to the land by the river, Oxus? It is her paternal residence, she should go. But who had entered her room, oh Mahaparshwa, couldn't thou spot him? No, it can't be the King but someone else, as my mind says"!

In a muffled voice, Mahaparshwa said, "Yes, I know".

"You know, yet didn't caution my friend!"

"Much later, I could recognize him but then I was overcome with fear, if he would take me a captive! Uddhav is now the chief of the soldiers and he does not take me as a human!He is the man who had come there in the disguise of the King, kicked me out from the door! What will now happen, Chaturika?"

Chaturika suggested, "Come, let us go and save my friend! But why had he come assuming the identity of the King? What for?"

SEVENTY-NINE

Mahaparshwa and Chaturika were struck with fear. Both of them kept trembling in worst apprehension. Shuddering in fright, they came out of the house of Devadutta. Pitch-black darkness enveloped both the inner house as well as the outer. Yet in Devadutta's room a lamp was lit. In the light of that lamp, both of them had seen the paragon of beauty of the city, lying supine, nowhere on her body stood a piece of cloth! Mahaparshwa had covered his face with both hands! He sprang out of the room! Chaturika was there. She had covered Devadutta's body with torn and tattered pieces of cloth. Touching her, she found no vibration of life anywhere. Blood oozed from the corner of her lips, both her eyes were distended, the eyes seemed to struggle to pop out of the socket! It was a bloodcurdling scene. They were horrified.

Chaturika called out, "Mahaparshwa brother"!

Mahaparshwa responded from the darkness outside, "I am here"!

"What shall I do now? What has happened to my friend"? Chaturika sobbed.

"Come out Chaturika, a serious crime has taken place, come, let us escape!"

"And will my friend lie thus"?

"Let her be so, if hint of life had been there, we would have gone to call a physician, we could also be able to trace the cause behind it, we would try to know about that man who had come, hiding his face behind a black scarf!"

"King"!

Entering the room, Mahaparshwa had tugged at Chaturika's hand, "Your friend could not go to the land by the river, Oxus, could not set sail to the land of the Gandharvas! Alas! If I could have sensed it at all, at that time! Come away, Chaturika, a terrible incident has ensued, if someone comes in here by any chance, they will put the blame on us!"

Emerging outside, standing under the dark sky, they were trembling in fear. Would they leave Devadutta, the friend of Chaturika, such uncared-for, or would they run to the tycoon's place? Would they inform him? Or, would they go straight to the palace? But they would not be able to get the door opened, or, wake the sentries up! Then where would they go? Then Mahaparshwa remembered the two men who had come once, an elderly and a young one, a young astronomer, Tamradhvaj being his name! Where had he gone away with his new bride? If he could apprise him of this fact, he could have been free of all worries. What would they do now? Would they tell Uddhavnarayan? The hairs on Mahaparshwa's body stood straight on their ends, he felt chill in the air. No, it would not be shared with Uddhav. Though Mahaparshwa could not reason for his hesitation! Brandishing the Army-Commander's sword in his hand, Uddhav seemed to brag and walk tall in pride across the city like a giant! Chaturika dragged him to the main thoroughfare of the city. It was late into the night, though the road was not absolutely desolate, at some corners a few souls could be seen sitting, here and there, or standing to soothe their body with the coolness of the earth! Chaturika, half-concealing her face behind a veil, hid herself along with Mahaparshwa, in the darkness beneath the Kadam tree, on the edge of the road. In a suppressed tone, she asked, "Who had come?"

Mahaparshwa cautioned her, "Forget Chaturika, forget, all corners of the city are rampant with sins. Had it ever happened here that a whore had been slain thus?"

"Who had come, tell me, who!"

"I don't know, the face was hidden behind a black scarf in the darkness".

"What had he said"? Literally kicking me to my consciousness, he announced, "King"!

"But you aren't taking him to be the King, right"?

"I know next to nothing, Chaturika"!

"Why did you go to my place to announce yourself as King, who had come to see me actually?"

"I do not know".

"The King had not come,the King's diction could never be so uncouth".

"I do not know".

"Tell me, oh Mahaparshwa, who had come here! My friend is no more, she died of severe pain, the slayer has robbed my friend of whatever she possessed. I demand to know, who the slayer is."

Mahaparshwa comforted her, "Come Chaturika, let me reach you home".

"I shall not go back home, you rogue, tell me why have you come to me at such late hours of the night, why again have you taken me to my friend, were you overcome with fear, did you sense that things could take such a ghastly turn?"

"I do not know".

"Why have we gone to see my friend"?

"I know nothing, Chaturika".

"When you had come here, my friend was still alive".

"Yes, she was alive. He had come to her".

"Tell me who had come"!

"It was stygian dark, no moon was there in the sky, even the lamp snuffed out or she extinguished it herself, it was next to impossible to recognize him"!

"My friend used to know the King"!

"In the darkness, she could not spot him, the lamp got extinguished and the King began to follow her"!

"Was he King at all"? Chaturika said, "Think hard and tell me who had come there in lieu of the King"!

"The King had gone to your door!"

"That was not the King but you"!

"I know nothing, Chaturika, come let me reach you home, let me relax on your threshold, my hands and feet have gone into a tizzy"!

They started for home in gingerly steps. Coming out of Devadutta's residence, they had come to the other end of the city. Now they had to go a long way! While walking, Mahaparshwa said, "At the break of dawn, the tycoon's palanquin will come to take Devadutta in, they will find the whore, lying dead, who had struggled hard to live, till her last".

"She would go to the land by the Oxus river, an ablution in that water would make one get back one's youth, the ugly-looking woman would turn beautiful, her father and mother were known to walk by the bank of the river, the Gandharvas used to sing"! Chaturika went on in a singsong voice.

"The King had come, but he had gone to your door".

"Why will he draw up to my door, you had come assuming a false identity of the King"!

"If the King comes to your door, can't he go to Devadutta's as well?"

"You were there at my door, what do you want to say, the King had not gone to my friend's door, just as you had called upon me in the King's name?"

"No idea".

"You know everything, come on tell me".

"If the King goes to your door, can't he go to hers"?

"Even then the matters remain the same — it was not the King! Then who had come to put an end to my friend's life, who could be such daring to drop by at the Chief Prostitute's house with a false identity of the King? My friend was a secret admirer of the King, I had reached the King numerous billets from her"!

The two were walking together to the dwelling of Chaturika, towards the red-light district. They were conversing in a low whisper. Just then, the stomp of the horse's hooves reached their ears. Mahaparshwa did not get any nook to hide, with Chaturika's hands in him! Without having any tree at that place, they could not conceal themselves anywhere! Just as frightened Mahaparshwa was thinking of taking an action, his conjecture came to be true when Uddhav's horse ambled up with the scoundrel, on its back. On seeing them, Uddhav jumped off from the back of the horse. Scrutinizing their faces with the help of the burning flambeau, held in his hand, he reined the horse to obstruct their path and asked, "How is it that both of you are out on the street at such late hours of the night"?

Chaturika did not answer. Mahaparshwa stood lowering his head. Uddhav thundered, "Where had you been to, wherefrom are you coming?"

"We are not coming, rather we are on our way back home," Chaturika replied.

"Hey you slut, didn't you say that you would accompany the merchant, aren't you going?"

Chaturika cocked up her face to say, "Devadutta will go".

"Who will go"? Uddhav seemed to shudder a bit.

"Devadutta will go and I shall go too, by tomorrow dawn"!

"Where will you go, stay back here at home, I, myself, shall see you there! Hey you dolt, where did you go with this woman?"

Mahaparshwa maintained a studied silence. Uddhav threatened, "I can imprison you both, right at this moment, tomorrow morning, I can impale you on a spike, I can even burn you alive, do you know who now I am, tell me where you had been to"!

"Nowhere at all, we are taking a stroll on the road, because of the maddening heat!"

"Why are you moving along with this damsel"?

"She asks me, that's why, she says, she is scared of moving alone".

"Didn't she plan to go with the merchant to Balkh"?

"Devadutta will go", Mahaparshwa said.

Uddhav thought of something inwardly and said, "Had the King gone to Devadutta's place"?

I have no idea, oh Lord! Folding his palms, Mahaparshwa bowed down to Uddhavnarayan, addressed him as 'Lord', and hung his head low. That fear was again hemming him in. Devadutta's corpse popped up before his vision. She tried her best to live, before dying. Devadutta did not want to die before going to the land by the river, Oxus. That slayer had a feast on her flesh by coercion. His face was covered with a black scarf. His voice had a metallic edge to it. He was a person, who they were familiar with. Though he tried to hide himself, he failed in doing so.

"Don't you know whether the King had gone there or not"?

"No, my Lord!"

"The King was not there in the palace for a long time, I suppose".

"I can't say, I am an ordinary pimp, I keep reaching the client to the whore's chamber".

"Didn't you go to Devadutta's place in the evening"?

"No, my Lord, why shall I go to that house, I am a run-of-the-mill pimp".

Uddhav roared, "Now I am the Army-Chief! The Army-Commander himself has offered me this position, I have been victorious in the first battle, I have bundled up and dragged the men of the Shudra ghetto straight to the city, do you know"?

"Yes, I know, my Lord".

"If you lie, you would be beheaded, tell me whether the King had gone to that prostitute's house in the evening or not! I have all information about it".

"Lord"?

"Didn't the King kick you out of your slumber? Tell me the truth, come on"!

"No, my Lord".

"Didn't you welcome the King to the whore's chamber"?

"No, my Lord".

"Tell me the truth, I am a man of the palace, nothing can happen beyond my knowledge, if you do not speak the truth, I shall decapitate you, here and now," saying so, throwing the flambeau away, he unsheathed the scimitar. Holding the weapon on his chest, he boomed, "Are thou returning from Devadutta's residence, both of you, I mean? Why this way then"?

"No, my Lord", Mahaparshwa was recoiling in fear.

"I knew that you would go there, coming here I did not find this harlot at home. On whose permission do you go out on the way with this dolt? I shall hound you out of this city, you floozy, I shall make five soldiers stalk you, they will lift you from home and will outrage your modesty, all five at one go, now tell me, where had you been to?"

Mahaparshwa could sense that he was nabbed. Chaturika too understood what Mahaparshwa could not make her understand anything that was being made crystal clear by Uddhav. She felt a cold shudder snaking down his body as she could guess who had entered Devadutta's chamber in the darkness, with fake identity of the King! She hung her head in fear and stood stock-still. Mahaparshwa had not said a word to her though he talked almost in entirety. And the little that was left, was being added by Uddhav, his unsheathed scimitar was glittering in the dark. There, far-off, in the eastern end, the sliver of moon could be seen. Chaturika was nearly suffocating. Mahaparshwa's excessively tall frame had slouched to such small a stature! She withdrew herself into the slough of the snail and seemed to be out of fear! Uddhav was saying that he had the information that Mahaparshwa was at the entrance of the house. Then, the King appeared and the news of King's presence had been carried inside by Mahaparshwa himself ... Uddhav kept telling all in exact sequence as had happened. But then ... what was the news? When did the King come out of that paragon of beauty's house? The King seemed to have been metamorphosed into a dog of the months of Bhadra or Ashwin. The honour of the throne was defiled. For once, he had gone to enjoy the devadasi and later on, the Chief Prostitute. And how many similar instances had been there in between? Who could tell where the King was going at the advent of the dark? Why would the King be out on love-tryst? If he so desired, would there be any dearth of women?

Chaturika implored, "Please let us go, we are hungry".

"You won't get rice to appease your hunger anymore. Don't you know what had transpired there? But you had been to that place, hadn't you?"

"Yes".

"If not you two, then who would dare cover her body with clothes? Look Mahaparshwa, I might ask you to be a witness, as and when necessary, the crime the King has perpetrated is just heinous, dreadful. You can fathom its dreadful intensity, I suppose, though you have to talk in favour of the King now, speaking against him can't be allowed".

Being nonplussed, Chaturika kept staring. Uddhav again leaped up on the horseback and said, "Tomorrow at dawn, come in front of the temple of Lord Mahakaal. I am now going to the merchant's place.

N-no, better you go to reach the merchant this news, Chaturika can go alone. Look there, the moon is rising".

The moon was quite emaciated, the moon was very dry, it had neither illusion in it nor could it create any illusion. Mahaparshwa moved forward. Uddhav raised the flambeau, unbridled the horse to gallop fast and vanished in the dark. As Uddhav left, Mahaparshwa came back. He kept moving along that road in darkness. This thoroughfare, as a whole, was known to him like the back of his palm. On the way itself he stayed, day in, day out. In this darkness, which message would he have to deliver to the merchant? He was calling Chaturika in the dark, in a subdued tone. He got a response from her. And really, he felt relieved.

Chaturika asked, "Haven't you gone"?

"No, I felt scared, you were yet to move on".

"I am feeling scared too, Mahaparshwa brother, I cannot move ahead in the dark, if my friend dies in that manner, what will happen to me, oh Lord Mahakaal?"

Mahaparshwa held the hand of Chaturika, "We have to escape from Ujjwain."

"Why, what's up?"

"Can't thou get, Chaturika, what's up? How could Uddhav know everything? Who had kicked me to senses and when, after the evening, how does he know every detail of it!"

Chaturika said, "Do not talk. He might remain in hiding somewhere nearby, Mahaparshwa brother, let us flee, Uddhav will ask you to be his witness!"

"I have to tell a lie against the King, how shall I say? If otherwise, Uddhav will put an end to my life, Chaturika! Enough is enough, let us escape or both of us will have to die, for sure!"

But by night, they could not escape. They got to see two soldiers were deployed in front of the door. They said that they had come at the behest of Army-Chief Uddhav, they would have to go to the Mahakaal temple at the crack of dawn. There, the Army-Commander would be present. Army-Chief Uddhav had forbidden them to go anywhere. Mahaparshwa sat, cowered. The two soldiers were conversing between themselves. Their exchange of dialogues began to reach his ears. Both the soldiers had unsheathed swords in their hands. Mahaparshwa had never got the feel of a sword! A very glance would say that it was baying for blood. Bolting the door from inside, Chaturika fell crying. She could cry, at least, behind closed doors.

One of the soldiers said, "The King raped, killed even".

Another soldier said, "The King had gone there, covering his face with a black cloth".

The first one said, "He had even blown off the lamp of Devadutta".

"Oh! What will happen tomorrow, should we speak in favour of the King or against him?"

"I have no idea of what would be to our advantage, the King can rape, but I can't believe that he can kill."

"He had outraged the modesty of the devadasi in the darkness, no doubt, and if Lord Mahakaal had not saved, Lalitadasi would have to die that day".

The first one said, "The King has perpetrated such a heinous deed that it will reach the city-dwellers by tonight! That stupid pimp had seen the King, why was he there at that time? What took place could even transpire behind all eyes, none would then have any wild guess as to who had slain her!"

The second one said, "He was there in fear of the King, hey scoundrel, tell us what the King did, how the crime ensued, and how again was she raped?"

Mahaparshwa began to shudder again. Burying his head between his knees, he began to cover himself. The two soldiers grew weary, gradually, conversing. They started dozing. In course of time, they dropped off. Mahaparshwa found the moon in the mid-sky which indicated that the night was nearing almost to a close. He got up. He nudged Chaturika's door open. The lamp was burning inside. The whore sat silent. Mahaparshwa motioned at her to come out. Just as Chaturika tiptoed out of the room, one of the soldiers spoke out something. Both of them cowered in panic. Then they could make out that the soldier was mumbling in his sleep. His sleep was not so deep then. He might wake up at any moment. Coming out, the two began to run, losing all sense of direction!

EIGHTY

Where was Mahaparshwa, where was Chaturika even? They had fled from the city. In search of them, Uddhav's platoon of soldiers kept rushing from one corner to the other and Uddhav kept running his horse helter-skelter, at every possible direction, he took to be proper. Where had they gone in hiding: Mahaparshwa, Chaturika? They were the chief witnesses to the murder of Devadutta. It was only Mahaparshwa, who had seen the King. It was Mahaparshwa, who had entered the vacant bawdy-house to announce the presence of the King. The whore had come out to welcome the King. Then the King had gone inside. Thereafter, the whore was found slain in her chamber, raped and without a piece of raiment on her entire body. After oppressing her sexually, the whore had been stifled to death. Alack! Oh alas! Such had never taken place in Ujjwain! The throne of Ujjwain was to be claimed by a holy, pure, immaculate soul! King Gandharvasen had been a man without any blemish! Kings were supposed to be like that only. Which idol were the inhabitants of the city of Ujjwain looking up to?

The news reached the residents of Ujjwain! Just in a day, the death news of the whore had been fabricated in such a dreadful manner that it was blown out of proportions! That very night, the news of her demise had made way to the tycoon. It was Uddhavnarayan who had come with the news. He had a letter from the Priest in his hand. That letter had again been penned by the Army Commander himself. The tycoon did not postpone his journey. He had left the city with his retinue of traders. He aimed at reaching the land of Balkh before the advent of winter. The winter would be gradually oppressive as he would move towards the north, leaving Purushpur, Taxila, Gandhaar behind. Before the winter set in firm, they would love to start for the south again. The merchant had left the city with a deep void within. He had been left drooping in just one night by Utanka's demise and the same happened with Devadutta's, as well. Those who had met him up said, the merchant would perhaps not be able to reach the land of the Gandharvas, finally. The line of traders would come back.

A part of the city-dwellers was left panic-stricken by the news of Devadutta's murder. What was wrong? Could King Bhartrihari really do such an abominable deed ever? Was it possible even? Being the King of Avanti, did he have any dearth of woman at all? Was he so sordid a man, deep down? Would he kill a woman? Women are generally weak, powerless. And again, she was the Chief Prostitute, to be enjoyed especially by the King. By order of the King her journey to Balkh could have been cancelled even though she dreamt of going there! Who, in this city, had not known about her journey to Balkh?

Devadutta was a beauty, nonpareil. No other beautiful prostitute of this city would ever match her in charms and beauty! Never ever was such a beauty around! Devadutta was even a woman of higher virtues than her mother, Rasamanjari! The way she had died had created a stir in the city. The stir did not subside even in a couple of days that followed, it was on gradual increase rather. The citizen who was in the dark, came to know about the prostitute being slain by the King! Had the King turned insane? The city-dwellers had no such experience of prolonged drought ever before! Was it because of drought that the King was turning insane, gradually? Otherwise, how would the King enter the Mahakaal shrine on the sly, to rape an ordinary devadasi inside the holy precincts of the temple and come back nonchalant? Who had ever heard that a King covered his face in the dark and went out, going mad in lust? Who had ever heard that a King would go on a love-tryst? All the beautiful, rich belles of the city of Avanti would approach the King, on their own! The King would be none other than God! Why would he be such that the common city-dwellers would feel ashamed?

During afternoon, the senior citizen, Durmukh, had been out to have a whiff of cool air. Let alone him, the city thoroughfares were now getting filled with the commotion of the ordinary dwellers, gradually. As though, a fare had just begun, at the close of the day. The city was almost sans a soul, all over the noon, all the daytime! The roads lay deserted, under the terrible sun! That desolate thoroughfare looked like a dead python! That silence had occasionally been interrupted by the onward and receding movements of the chariot-wheels and the stomping of horses' hooves of the cavalry. Unsheathed swords seemed to have a frightening swish in the streets of the city. If any citizen would dare come to the front, he would be decapitated. Elderly Durmukh had seen middle-aged Basudev, who had just crossed his youth, walking towards the shrine! He was calling out to him, "Hey you Basudev, Listen, wait, come and hear me, the King is now keen on decimating women. He has taken the sceptre in his hand, stop a while, tell me what have you heard?"

Basudev halted and said, "What can I comment on this? The matter is really heartrending!"

"Yes, the whore has been stifled to death, such deaths are really painful! But dying by fire is even more pathetic, what do you say?"

"I do not know. The manner Devadutta has died is really ghastly, the murderer needs to be tracked down, she was a woman of commendable qualities!"

The elderly Durmukh smiled, "Did you frequent her place"?

"She was the Chief Prostitute, protected by the King, enamoured of the King, I am just an ordinary man. But yes, once I had seen her dancing in the courtyard of the Mahakaal temple, how exceedingly beautiful she looked in her dance postures! She seemed to be effulgent like a flame, aglow, as she went dancing".

The elderly man was irked, he said, "Come on Basudev, such women face this destiny only! Her mother was Rasamanjari, the whore, she had again fallen in love with an Ionian Greek, what a ruinous woman, no man of this country would have been her choice, she needed a man from a foreign land and she too had a sad demise!"

"Who, who are you talking of?"

"An Ionian Greek! She had been killed in Saurashtra, I am aware of this fact. Rasamanjari was even more beautiful… right?"

"I haven't seen her, but as people used to say, her beauty was matchless, Devadutta fails to emulate her in beauty!"

"Why will it not be so, she has Ionian Greek blood in her. Look Basudev, if a woman craves the company of numerous men, she must have to die thus, at last"!

Basudev replied, "The only duty of a whore is to entertain innumerable men!"

"The unfaithful women would have to suffer such an end, whatever has happened is just the right, now women must be wary, the women of common household must not go on love-trysts. Let the whores now leave for the land of Balkh!"

Basudev remarked, "The incident is quite a sad one, perilous too! how can a whore be unfaithful, I don't get you, all used to know that she was accompanying the merchant to Balkh!"

"Perhaps, the King had no consent to it".

"If so, then the King would have ordered her not to go! Is then the King, the murderer?"

"He who had taken the King to the whore has divulged the matter. Do you know Mahaparshwa, the pimp, Chaturika, the slut?"

"But they are not here in the city!"

"They would have been murdered, if they had stayed back in the city! Who would like to be in the wrath of the lustful King? That whore, Chaturika, might have been raped after this, or slain".

"Did they narrate this fact themselves?"

"They had shared this with the Army-Chief, Uddhav, Uddhav had nabbed them in the dark, don't you know all such facts? Where do you stay, Basudev?"

"If I do not get to hear from them on my own, I can't believe all this stuff."

"Why, the words of Uddhav, the Army-Chief?"

"That Sessions-man! His words cannot be believed".

"What are you saying, Basudev, can then the pimp's words be trusted? He's a great sinner, he is an illegitimate child of a whore-woman and Chaturika is no less too. On the termination of youth, a woman becomes even less in importance than a bitch, none will look at her, don't you agree with me on these views? I hope you do."

Basudev was astonished. The old Durmukh kept gliding from one topic to another! He wanted to leave. In this quiet afternoon, he was even least interested to talk to Durmukh, the old man! He did not like the man. But his own likes and dislikes hardly mattered in this case, the old man had held him in a firm grip and went asking, "How is your wife?"

"This is not fair to discuss such a matter."

"Look, I cannot accuse all women of being unfaithful, my first wife, who had died of illness, was quite sweet-tongued, very faithful and devoted to her husband, I am sure, your wife is just like her, but my young wife is drawn towards another man, and my doubt is proven true! I plan to marry again, do you know of any good, nubile woman"?

By now, Basudev could guess the old man's motive! He wanted to wring his hand off his grasp and leave. But he failed to do so. Even at this age, the man had immense strength. Again, Durmukh had come back to the old topic, he kept saying, "Women are difficult to understand, their minds are always filled with sinful thoughts to the brim, and the whore has been slain for just this reason! Whatever the King has done, that is for the welfare of the people of Ujjwain, for the good of the city! Young maidens are extremely dreadful!"

Basudev grew stern, he said, "Let go of my hand, the King is not of such cruel nature, he cannot perpetrate such a heinous deed"!

"What are you saying, Basudev, this is Uddhav who has gleaned all information, in fact he was a spy, and is now an Army-Chief, he has learnt all about the diabolic incident himself!"

"Has he seen with his own eyes?"

Durmukh began to jerk his head and in a subdued tone he cautioned him, "Be very cautious, Basudev, you know just the contrary to what the city-dwellers know. Such should not happen, you must know the same as others do. Whoever doesn't know that the King has gone mad in lust?"

"I do not believe this".

"Everyone in the city has come to know about it".

Basudev said, "The King is of a different nature altogether… these rumours are doing rounds, I think it's because of drought! Once it starts raining, people will not subscribe to such belief anymore".

Durmukh smiled, "Will that whore spring up to life, once it starts raining? She has already been cremated! In my opinion, that stigmatized body of the whore would better be thrown into the Mahakaal forests. Let the jackals and vultures have a grand feast on her decomposed flesh!"

"Jackals and vultures have devoured her, to be precise"! Basudev quipped in.

"What do you mean, she has been cremated on the bank of the river, Gandhavati!"

"Otherwise, how could she die in that manner"?

"The King has slain him!"

"I can't believe this. He is a man with a tender heart. That cannot be his handiwork and why again will he kill an innocent, powerless prostitute?"

"What can't an insane do and again if he is overcome with lust"?

Basudev shook his head to say, "Talking ill of the King is a cardinal sin, Sir! I am leaving!"

Hearing this, old Durmukh held him back even more firmly and said, "We are talking between ourselves, who will know, yet listen to me, have you looked up at the night-sky of Ujjwain?"

"No, Sir!"

"It is being heard, that a new star…"

"I am poor at recognizing stars!"

"I too am, though my wife can locate them, my eyes cannot trace the distant stars, but my wife's can!"

"What is she saying?"

"That woman is not uttering a single word, she does not like me. Please be on the look-out for a calm and gentle bride, yes as I was saying, there has appeared a new star in the sky!"

"Who told you?"

"Why, Uddhav? Appearance of a new star in the sky means the transpiration of a slew of incidents and that exactly is happening. Otherwise, why will the King be keen on raping a devadasi, why will he kill the Chief Prostitute even? Look Basudev, it is the worst of the times, do you know the reason behind such a prolonged drought?"

Fanning himself with the scarf, Basudev said, "Man's reasoning ability is marred by long droughts, otherwise everyone knows that the King will never do such a deed!"

"Of which deed are you talking?"

"The murder of the Chief Prostitute! Do you believe this?"

"I have to, this is the indication of the appearance of a new star in the sky. One has to understand that … otherwise why will an incident ensue, quite unexpectedly? Can a King ever turn insane on his ascension of the throne?"

"Who has told you so?"

"Which fact?"

Basudev was visibly irked, he said, "You can never follow a question if asked once! I hate to prolong our discussion any further!"

The old man replied, "Yes, it is the fact, Uddhav is primarily a spy, he hails from the lineage of spies, he is the source of all information. The King has gone insane now, let the young maidens of the city be wary. When a new stellar body takes birth in the sky, such cataclysm is not unusual".

Basudev then disengaged his hand with a jerk and said, "You can even assume the truth yourself, whoever doesn't know the King Bhartrihari? Why are you telling such string of lies, don't you know Uddhav?"

"Uddhav is very gentle and good-natured!"

Basudev left on foot. He could sense some untoward incident might be in the offing. And that was being foreshadowed by all these happenings. He had no idea at all of what could have transpired! But he could sense that much power had been devolved on the knave, Uddhav, than he deserved. He was making it public that the King was the slayer; the King, being insane, was still occupying the throne … was it his own version or somebody else's? While walking, Basudev got to hear those words once again, from both ends of the road. The same words! He cast a glance at the sky. If monsoon clouds would have hovered over the sky of Ujjwain, people's heart would have been softer once again. In the darkness, Basudev walked down to the river, Gandhavati. He stood alone. He was just an ordinary individual. A petty man must keep his lips always shut! But Basudev failed to do so. His body shuddered at the noise of the horse-hooves. Turning back, he saw a man with a flambeau, aflame, in his hand. He was running towards him on horseback. From the seat on horseback, he cried out, "Who is Basudev?"

Basudev spun back, "It's me"!

Jumping off from horseback, reading the face of Basudev in the light of the flambeau, Uddhavnarayan thundered, "Son of bitch, you Basudev, I am rightly informed by old Durmukh, I could nab you just at this end! What have you talked about the King…come on, tell me!" The unsheathed sword seemed to snake up and flash against the dark sky. In sheer fury, it came down straight on the neck of Basudev!

EIGHTY-ONE

Queen Bhanumati said, "A smell is being wafted to the nostrils, hey Nipunika, can you sniff it?"

The old maid waved her head, saying, "But where, in the room or outside?"

Queen Bhanumati said, "Perhaps it is being wafted in from outside. Oh gosh! Something is lying dead, getting decomposed! Hey you old maid, is it that whore whose corpse is going stale? Do you know, can you sense anything, Nipunika?"

The maid kept quiet. Then she could sense a faint smell in the air. Issuing from somewhere. It might be here in this room or in the long verandah. In some corners of the palace. If conscious, the smell would hit the nostrils, if not, nothing would be there at all. Even at such a ripe age, Nipunika's olfactory organ was functioning properly, her ability of smelling was sharp. Pacing up and down noiselessly in the inner house of this palace, one room after another, along the long stretch of the verandah, she had acquired a rare virtue of sensing everything. She was familiar with myriads of smell, various smells of a man, different smells of animals lesser in status than human. Sitting at any corner of this palace, she could get a feel of any man coming in or taking an exit. Nipunika could scrounge the information of the entrance of the King from air, the place to which his stepbrother Bikram was going, whether the merchant had come in or it was the Chief Priest of Mahakaal temple or a petty soldier! She could sense the odour. Long back, one day, Chaturika, the whore, had come to her with a missive from the Chief Prostitute to be handed to the King — now, if Chaturika again would come to this palace, behind all eyes, Nipunika would be able to identify her, sniffing the smell in the air. At this moment, there was a smell in this room. It smelt fetid, like a dead rat. Nipunika took the smell. She was accustomed to all sorts of smell, no odour stirred in her the will to throw up. Nipunika saw the queen seated on the bed, being fatigued. The bed was a bit ruffled. Through the smell, she could sense that the it seemed to be issuing from the bed itself. She muttered, "Are you still getting the smell, Maa"?

"Yes, I do, Nipunika! What's wrong? Has a prostitute been killed in this city?"

"Man is to commit crimes".

"But this is a deadly crime"!

"Let the criminal be nabbed!"

"My head hangs in shame, Nipunika, what shall I do on hearing this? Shall I die? Or, where shall I go if I don't die?"

The maidservant assured her, "Let it be left at that, Maa, you were born to be a queen, you will remain just a queen!"

"Do you know all news about the King, Nipunika?"

The maid rejoined, "No, I don't".

"Why don't you know this if you know all? Do you take the King to be a lunatic at a glance? What are the symptoms of insanity, Nipunika?"

Nipunika said, "I do not know, my father was a lunatic, all day long, he used to say that he would be a King! I don't know, Maa, father breathed his last by thinking that he would be a King!"

"Do you hear anything? What's going on in this city?"

Nipunika shook her head, "I am getting the smell, Maa, aren't you the Goddess Lakshmi of the city of Avanti?"

"No idea about what I am".

"How will that ignorance do, Maa, you are none other than the queen of Avanti!"

Bhanumati said, "The King has slain the whore with his own hands, and before driving her to death, he had compelled her... Oh Nipunika, is it the King's doing?"

Nipunika said, "No, it can never be the King's deed".

"Then whose queen am I? Who is there on the throne, Nipunika"?

The old woman said, "The King is there, King Bhartrihari, such a King had never ascended the throne of Avanti, to me the King seems to look soft like a ball of rain-cloud, Maa!"

"Phew!" The queen laughed, wringing her hands back, she loosened the bra, dishevelling her hair she began to annul her dressing-up and said, "Well said, my maid! Otherwise, why would you be my maidservant and why am I the queen? He, who seems to be 'soft like a ball of rain-cloud' to you, why, in his tenure, is there no rain for over two terms of monsoon? Why does only drought continue for over the last two-and-a half years? Did you witness such a drought ever, you old crone?"

The old maid replied, "Yes, I did."

"Where, when did you experience?"

"Long, long ago, my mother used to say that her mother had come to this country along with her grandmother from the desert-land, during a terrible drought, when for seven years there had been no rainfall, all the roads and thoroughfares were fraught with human skeletons, bones and ribs, strewn all over!"

Bhanumati said, "In desert lands that is natural to happen".

"No, it was not so, it happened in that year only. May be rains are scarce, yet downpour does happen, that drought had brought my grandmother and mother to this country".

Bhanumati was concerned, "Then will it go on for seven years here? It is almost three years now".

"Why so, Maa, it will rain, only for the deeds of Ujjwain's King, there will be downpour."

"But his deeds are terrible"!

The maid said, "I do not believe this, Maa"!

"How is it that you do not believe? How about that devadasi?"

"He had no fault, Maa, even the devadasi did not know that the King had been there, and it is also true that she welcomed him, to err is man, Maa, there had been no oppression on that devadasi, the King had not compelled her!"

"How do you know whether he forced her or not?"

"Didn't you ask him?"

"I did not feel like asking. Why would the King's eyes droop so low? Instead of looking up and beyond, which creature does look at such nadir, tell me, thou crone!"

Nipunika said, "Our King is not like that!"

"And the murder of a prostitute was perpetrated?"

"I am getting that stench, rightly said, Maa, the flesh of the whore is still getting decomposed, though she had been cremated just the following day!"

"I am getting too, if not insane, who can perpetrate such a deed?"

"Only a ruthless person, a greedy one, and a brute can do such a deed", the maid uttered each word, distinctly.

"Then how can your King be soft as a ball of cloud"?

The old maid asked, "Did you believe this?"

"Yes, I did, how can I help that, all residents of the city have come to know of it!"

"Have the city-dwellers believed this, Maa?"

"Definitely they have done, no one has forgotten about the rape of that devadasi at all!"

"Devadasis are always to be enjoyed by the King only", the maid reasoned.

"On the sly, in the shrine, under the veil of darkness, you mean?"

Nipunika said, "The stench is on the rise now, Maa, the gusts of wind are wafting in through the window, can you smell it, Maa"?

Queen Bhanumati nodded. Then stopping all enigmatic utterances, the maid, Nipunika said, "Why don't you think, Maa, that all you have heard is wrong. Don't you know your husband, is he such a man?"

"I do not know him"!

"Don't you know your husband, think before you speak, Maa"!

"I do not know him, Nipunika, I do not!"

"Can't you recognize him even if you look at his face?"

"No, dear Nipunika, no", Bhanumati said.

The old maidservant, Nipunika, heaved a long sigh and said slowly, "God knows, if Avanti's Lakshmi fails to recognize the Lord of Avanti, then how can this city dream of its welfare, how will clouds float in, how will there be rain, listen to me, Maa, whatever you have heard are all lies, nothing can be more blatant than such lies!"

"Are you speaking of the King?"

"Yes Maa, our King cannot do it, none believes in such a rumour"!

"There are witnesses!"

"No, they are not here in this city, these are all lies!"

"The people of the city have come to know that the King is an insane".

"All are lies, you know well that this is far from the truth. What did the Army-Commander tell you, Maa, did he come into the inner house, to talk ill of the King?"

"He has just stated whatever the people of the city are saying." The city-dwellers are not uttering anything, if they do, they will not live anymore".

"Why won't they live anymore?"

"The authority of this city rests with the battery of armies now, the soldiers are on the rounds across the city, the spies abound in streets and lanes, whatever the retinue of armies are saying, the common citizens have to speak in unison, the King can never perpetrate such a crime, even though the drought continues and men sail through rough waters, not a single soul does believe this!"

Bhanumati said, "What shall I do now? But I have already believed this"!

Old maidservant said, "So you believe that the Sun-God rises in the West?"

Dodging a straight answer Bhanumati said, "The merchant is taking the whore along with him to Balkh, the whore would never return once she lands in that country! If the King had any objection to it, why didn't he forbid her, the armies could have blocked the harlot's way at the behest of the King! But has this deed been committed like a real man?"

"No, it hasn't been so".

"The clan of traders will pass through the Kingdom of the Huns. If the King's consent would be to the contrary, who would dare transgress the order of the King, tell me?"

"None at all".

"I have to keep my face veiled in shame, in disgust! He is none but my husband and he can even go for such a heinous deed like slaying a prostitute, the murder of an innocent, weak woman!"

The old maidservant said, "Do you believe, Maa, that the Sun-God sets in the east and the glimpse of the moon, the planets and the stars cannot be had again?"

"No wonder that may happen, since ages this city has not witnessed any downpour!"

"Do you believe, Maa, that stones can float on the surface of water?"

Bhanumati was driven to silence. After so long, everything began to appear clear to her. Whatever she was saying, this maidservant was speaking just the opposite.

How dares she? Being a maidservant, she even speaks in symbols, in signs and innuendoes! The queen howled, "Are you speaking in favour of the King, Nipunika? But no one is doing so".

"I live on the rice that He kindly provides".

"Go Nipunika, there's no certainty of any happening, whatever you have told me, do not share it with others, if you do you would be decapitated, you would suffer the same fate as Devadutta's, you would have to die like her! She has breathed her last and I have been saved! As long as she had been alive, even the queen of Avanti could not say that she was unparalleled as a beauty under the sun… such a dreadful woman would have such sad demise only!"

Nipunika, the old maid said, "But she was going away for good, never to return."

"Could have returned even and I did not know that she was leaving, rather came to know about it all, after her death!"

Old Nipunika shivered, "Oh! Didn't you know? Really?"

"I was not in the know of it, I had no idea that the harlot was leaving stealthily, perhaps she could sense something else!"

The old maid's heart missed a beat. She sat lowering her head. She lost all courage to raise her face and look at queen Bhanumati now. Bhanumati was saying, "All's well that has occurred, but why has the King committed such a heinous deed himself? I think, preceding that, the whore had some heated exchange with the King, and failing to control himself, the King had put an end to her life"!

The old maid waved her head, "No, the King hasn't killed her"!

"If you keep saying so, Nipunika, you would not be living hereafter!"

Nipunika kept silent. Queen Bhanumati motioned at her to leave.

The old maid did not leave. She kept standing still. Seeing that, the queen cautioned her, "Whatever you have said, erase that off from your memory and never repeat it!"

The old hag said, "I haven't said anything at all".

"You said, but whatever you said is false, don't utter a lie any further!"

"I have not told a lie, Maa, how can I tell a fib standing in this palace? This is Lord Mahakaal's abode, He will watch everything.".

Bhanumati said, "He is taking stock of the King's sins".

"The Sun and the Moon are still there!"

Bhanumati said, "Don't ever speak so, you maid! You are my maid, whatever I shall say you should speak in unison, now say that, The crime of slaying the prostitute is the King's sin!"

The old maidservant did not say. Why would she? She was old enough to understand things. Wasn't she? Youth had bidden her farewell, her body arched forward, death tiptoed closer, what would she fear now? How could she deny the debt to the King who had fed her since so many years? She could feel everything in the inner recesses of her mind. How and what had happened was not unknown to her at all! How would she utter such words, as being taught?

Queen Bhanumati insisted, "The nasty whore has been killed by the King, why do you cower to utter these words?"

"Maa, you are the Goddess Lakshmi of this city of Avanti, please stand by the King!"

"Nipunika, I wish I could die in disgust!"

The old maid said, "Oh no! Why will you die, you won't"!

Bhanumati stopped short to look at the face of the old hag. It was just a deadpan! She kept standing, yet was not lending her ears to anything! How was it possible? How could the old maid keep her eyes open? It did not seem to her that the crone had any fear at all. The queen was really in fear, having such an intrepid, old crone! It was even beyond her knowledge what this old maid would tell the King and when! Bhanumati was even utterly suspicious of her nature for sharing the facts with the King! In fact, Bhanumati failed to know this old maid of hers to the core, even after such length of time. Bhanumati grew restive to find the old crone expressing suspicion on her words, while all were tight-lipped. What for was this old crone speaking in favour of the King?!While any word in the King's favour was being nipped in the bud, why wouldn't she believe that the King was the man behind the prostitute's assassination! Bhanumati came charging, "What do you want to say, Nipunika?"

"Do you want to hear it once again, Maa?"

"You had said but when?"

The old maidservant kept shaking her head and came out into the verandah. And stepping into the verandah, she found the sad, morose King, standing at the other end, looked at the sky throwing his head up. Tears welled up to the old maid's eyes. The King seemed like an innocent lad to her!

EIGHTY-TWO

The Royal Court was vacant. The King was in the inner house. The queen had been there too. The sky stood vacuous. The frightened maid went past the King, silently. The King failed to take notice of it. His dull eyes were fixed on the cloudless sky. It seemed to the King that without any miraculous incident, clouds would not appear in the sky. The belief that the clouds would hover was getting belied, bit by bit. No such man was there who could usher in clouds in the sky. Was there any magician of any sort? Let clouds amass in the sky, with the aid of sorcery. At the advent of the clouds, people would start talking against the fibs which were doing rounds in the city. King Bhartrihari surmised thus.

Nipunika, the maid, engrossed in herself, came out to stand in the wide courtyard, in front of the palace. How intense was the turbid sunshine! Even the grass on the courtyard had dried up.

The old maidservant threw a look at the sky. Placing a hand on her forehead, going towards the main entrance, she saw one of the doorkeepers, walking in.

The old maid stopped to ask, "Any news?"

"A madcap has come!"

"This city is being fraught with madmen, if rains do not pour such things will increase, go, drive him away!"

"He will not budge an inch. He says, he is here with the information on clouds!"

"What does he mean to say?" Old Nipunika was surprised. "Which information?"

"Of clouds, he says that he can make the downpour happen".

"An insane, no doubt!"

"He has such tall claims!"

"Shoo him away!"

"He won't leave, he is stubborn, he wants to talk to the King, he is coming from a far-off land".

"Can all the common men talk to the King"?

The sentry said, "After all this, I feel like pricking him with the tip of the spear. But the appearance of the man wins my sympathy. He is again saying that he can make the downpour happen".

Now old Nipunika shuddered in fear. Was this any collusion? Alluring the King with rains, shoving him into another peril...! He will make the shower happen! The old maid thought, he might either be a lunatic or a mean plotter. None save Lord Mahakaal could only make the rains pour in torrents! Old maid said, "Come, let's go and see how expert he is in bringing the rains down, let there be an initial demonstration then!"

First, he would talk to the King! The sentry began to walk and Nipunika went at his heels. She was really overcome with fear. Whatever was not to happen, kept happening in this city. What was the motive of this man who had come during this period of drought with a promise of making rainfall happen! The old maidservant threw a glance at the sky. Then she turned to look at the inner house. Nothing could be seen at all, but the King's glance at the sky was making him heave long sighs, as he stood by the window. Queen Bhanumati was thinking of the Army-Commander, Bikram. In the King's chamber the inkpot, the duck-quill - all lay intact, though he hardly picked them up these days.

Thinking thus, the old maid stopped and said, "It would be better if you ask that man to leave, don't you see that all untoward happenings are going on in this city? If any other ensues! Can anyone bring down shower?"

The sentry said, "Sometimes men are found, who can perform such unusual things! During daytime they can bring in night, everything is possible through magic. Don't you know that man can be made invisible too?"

The bell had gone. The guard grew restive and said, "There the man swings the bell again, better you arrange a meeting with the King!"

The old maidservant said, "Let me have a look at the man first, the times are not proper, the way the miscreant had taken off the life of Devadutta, can't I understand anything or what, or the inhabitants of this city? No doubt, all of them are going mad because of lack of rain, otherwise, how could they spew such slander against the King, why don't men snatch off the tongue of that rogue?"

"Keep quiet! Be calm! The wind has ears too! The sentry put a finger on his lips!"

"That's why I utter these words! I am already into my senile years, what can happen to me, will they kill me? Let them do it, who will again kill me, let him come!"

The sentry understood that the old maid was also speaking as if she had gone out of her mind. He thought, to remain silent would be more of intelligence. The old crone too trailed off to silence, gradually. They came out of the main entrance, walking. The old woman saw a man, standing there, leaning against the wall. His cheeks were thickly covered with beard, his attires were soiled, hairs were unkempt, kinky, rough, his complexion was coppery dark, being burnt under the sun of drought, his body was slightly bent. He had a satchel dangling from his shoulder, looking almost like a portmanteau. At a glance, the man seemed to be a vagabond, probably hailing from some alien land. Such men are making an entrance into Ujjwain and taking an exit subsequently, quite often. They used to come from far-off villages, distant lands, with a thought of being a King in future, stepping once into Ujjwain. As if riches, gems and treasures lay strewn in the paths of Ujjwain. They just waited to be picked and treasured. Later on, making a foray into this city, coming a cropper, they moved on hither and thither, as a vagabond. This man of a foreign land was no less cunning. Entering this city, he had come straight to the King. Could he usher the monsoon at all? In fact, getting to know the weak spot of the King's mind, he had come in the hope of earning a few farthings. Old Nipunika asked, "What are you looking for?"

"To see the King!"

"Why will the King see you: a vagabond, an insane!"

The man did not raise his face, in a subdued tone only said, "I have some information about rainfall".

"You are lying, look, since the last two- and- a-half years or even more, there had not been even a drop of rain, no downpour from the sky and now please do not come with a false solace!"

"Just the truth, the King is in utter jeopardy!"

"Which peril?"

The man said, "There's no water, I shall make it pour".

Nipunika was drawn into deep thinking. Was he speaking the truth or just a lie? Nipunika, however, knew that it was possible to cause downpour, with the help of sorcery. She had only heard of it, but had never been a witness to it.

The sorcerers could do anything, making downpour was a just a child's play to them. Could that man be a magician? Hadn't Nipunika seen any magician before? Were they like him? She heard that they were adept in transforming an old woman into a young maiden and vice-versa. She moved forward to ask, "Are you a magician"?

"Why, what's the need"?

"You are saying that you will make rains happen, but that will be accomplished by magic!"

The man rejoined, "Yes, I am a magician".

"Do you know hypnotism"?

"I know", the man was smiling, lowering his head.

"With your charms, can you transform a donkey into a man and vice-versa"?

The man replied, "That can be done".

"Can you metamorphose a young maiden into an old crone"?

"I can do it".

Then, the old maid's heart kept palpitating. Yes, the man was speaking the truth! From which land had he come? Being asked, he said, "That's far-off, I am now coming from Uttarpur"!

"Is there any rain there"?

"No, there's no rain, I am here to meet the King".

"You will get to see him, but listen you magician, you have to transform one young maiden into an old, decrepit woman and a crone into a beautiful maiden!"

Hearing this, he laughed and asked, "Who is the crone anyway, is it you?"

Old serving-maid, Nipunika, maintained silence. She did not reply. Not coming up with a rejoinder was enough to prove that whatever he had said was true! Then the old woman said, "The young maiden is queen Bhanumati. Unfaithful, the other man in her life, the step-brother of the King, Army-Commander's love has driven her mad…can you do it, oh Magician?"

"Lead me to the King"!

"Before that tell me whether you will be able to do as I ask". The sentry had come forward to say, "Is it possible for making an old woman a young one, in reality, or is the crone out of her wits?"

Without uttering a word, the man entered the main premises of the palace, through the unguarded door. Following him, the old serving-maid began to walk, stooping low. The old woman thought, Yes, the man will surely be able to do it. If he succeeds, the queen will turn into a serving-maid! Will the Army-Commander pay any heed to the old queen then? The maidservant thought— I shall definitely turn into young maiden but who will be my mate? I had reared up the King so affectionately… then? The King is just like my own child! While walking, the maid thought that there was no need of it! Rather, queen Bhanumati should get transformed into an old woman! Then only she would understand. But before all, the rain must pour on earth. The maid called out to the man, "Please wait, the court is lying vacant, the King will go there, go, sit there by the door".

The man smiled. How beautiful was that smile! The serving-maid was amazed. Then, she was reminded that, he was a magician! The way he would love to display his smile, she would be seeing just the same. And if that was true, the man could inundate the meadows, rivers, streams, and the seven lakes of Ujjwain with water, by making the clouds float in the sky! Alas! The plight of the King was so pathetic, just because of lack of rains! Inwardly, she used to take the King as her son. The old hag stepped forward and said, "Nothing more is needed, do whatever you have come for"!

"What's not needed?"

"Let me be as I am, rather you usher in water, let the queen be as she is, better you bring in clouds, if there is cloud, if there is rain, the queen's mind too, would undergo a change. Just amid all these things, the courtesan had to die, it's learnt that she was eager to go to her father's place, which lay far, far-off."

The man said, "Let the King be informed. I shall keep waiting."

The old maid came running to the inner house. Let it rain indeed! Only because of absence of the rain, she was occupied by evil thoughts! Entering inside, the old woman found the King standing at the same spot, his gaze, stuck to the sky. She stood behind Him for quite some time. If the King would care to look back at her! King Bhartrihari seemed to have no stir of life. Lastly, the old woman bowed down on the ground, in a low, sad tone, drew the attention of the King, "Let me pray, oh King, a sorcerer has come from a foreign land, he is keen on seeing you, would Your Highness like to come to the Court"?

The King spun around. On seeing the old maidservant, instead of being vexed he said, "No one is there in the court today!"

"No, none is there,it stands vacant, empty, desolate".

"What about my Army-Commander, Bikram"?

"No, he is not there, perhaps he is there in the temple"!

"My Officers-in-Charge"?

"None is there save a magician, who keeps waiting for you".

Being taken by surprise, Bhartrihari asked, "Who is he? What's his identity?"

"I do not know, he seems to be a man from an alien land, he promises to usher in water"!

"Water, I mean, will he make it rain?"

"Yes, my King, only the sorcerers can do it".

"Does he claim so"?

"He has said so, he looks like a magician. How sweet his smile is!"

Bhartrihari said, "Must be a lunatic! Owing to lack of rainfall, the number of lunatics is on the rise, all around! Ask him to leave".

The old maidservant said, "See him for just once, my King, he will usher in clouds in the sky with his sorcery, he will inundate the city with rain, he can make everything possible"!

The King smiled. "Rainfall by magic, you mean? Once the magical charms are over, the clouds will vanish too". Was there anyone in this city who had mastered sorcery? Someone might be there, but he was not aware of anyone! So what? Even if a magician wasn't there? This man was a foreigner! So, will a magician from another land put an end to drought? He kept walking. In fact, he was feeling fed up with all the bizarre happenings around!

He was trying to live by holding on to a piece of straw, like a drowning man! Nipunika followed the King!

The King emerged from the inner house. While walking at the heels of the King, the corners of the old serving-maid's eyes grew moist. Was this the son of the King of Ujjwain, Gandharvasen? A quasi-insane vagabond had come to meet him, and he was going to the deserted court to see him! Magic would really not hold good to be true till the last! As it would exhaust, all things again would catapult to its previous state. The old woman felt that she, herself, was going insane too. Otherwise, why would she come to the King, being carried away by the words of the magician? If now on reaching there she found the man to have vanished, then?

On the threshold of the Royal Court, the man sat waiting. The old woman drew up to him. She was panting for breath, she said, "The King has come to the court, tell me the truth, can you really bring down water?"

The man smiled. That sweet, winsome smile! The smile had won over the old woman. She was overcome with affection for a child! It seemed to her that, this man had not come to tell a lie! The old woman said, "Never utter such a word, my dear, which frightens the King, never tell a fib to the King, it is a sin, mind you, if it really rains, the city-dwellers will respect you like a messiah. Lord Mahakaal will be with you, now be off!"

The man got to his feet. He entered the courtroom in slow steps. Could ever a courtroom be such deserted? To his utter surprise, he found the King, standing at a distance, with a long, pulled face! He did not sit down. He would not be at peace with himself, if he took a seat. Who would he have to face?

The desolate court gave him an impression that the court had got dissolved lately. Just now the courtiers had left, perhaps. Just only one visitor was left to see him. No, he was not standing like a beggar. He was coming to meet him, with his head held high.

Lowering his head, he said, "Hail to thee, oh King, hail to the city of Ujjwain! Let this land be blessed with rainfall again, let crops be green again, let the rivers be filled with water, let the seven lakes have blue-, red-, white- lotuses to deck their surfaces".

With his voice choked with emotions, the King said, "Such words were not spoken so long by anyone, none had ever expressed such desire since long! Who are you?"

"I hail from an alien land. Presently, I am coming from the land in the North-east".

"To which land do you belong?"

"All the countries, right from the Ramgiri hills to Alkapuri in the Himalayas happen to be my native land. Oh King, may I speak the truth?"

"Please tell me, fearlessly".

"In olden times, whenever I had traversed any land in any direction, the peals of ovation hailing the King were what I used to hear, the subjects were in true happiness, glory was writ large everywhere. Again, while returning by the same way, I heard something else, the people were suffering deep misfortune, rain had been nowhere, green crops got withered away, the rivers lay bare, slanders against the King were rife in the air. All kept complaining that, it was the King for whom the clouds had drifted elsewhere. Believe me, oh King, I am speaking nothing but the truth!"

King Bhartrihari's eyes glistened with tears, the words were so true! His subjects had fallen in abject misfortune, and he, himself, was drowning deep down into the abyss of sorrow, inch by inch.

EIGHTY-THREE

The King said, "I am aware of all this. Can you make it rain"?

The man said, "Oh King, the rains will definitely pour, if it fails this year, next year it will surely happen, the Nature will undergo change, she will not remain like this, but have you heard of the appearance of a new star in the skies of Ujjwain, did ever Acharya Brishvanu tell you about it"?

"He hadn't believed it".

"Oh King, I have heard of a new star, on my way to Ujjwain"!

"Man's thoughts are varied, and just because of that, he can stay alive".

"Oh King, I have even heard that, far towards the North East, crossing beyond a village, Acharya Brishavanu had breathed his last in a never-ending stretch of grassland...!"

"Isn't Acharya alive?" King Bhartrihari screamed in grief.

"No, the blind astronomer had set out on his journey, towards the Himalayas"!

"That I am aware of".

"He wanted to proceed along that way, through which Yudhisthira had ascended the Heaven".

"Might be so".

"On his way, he breathed his last, as was the fate of all four Pandavas"!

"It might be so, though I know next to nothing about it".

"He had died in the limits of your country only"!

"I have no idea, I wonder why I don't know, why hasn't anyone informed me about this"?

"You, too, were not keen on knowing about his whereabouts".

King Bhartrihari lowered his head. True. He had no such keen attention at anything at all. Drought had robbed him of his sharp intelligence, it seemed. Alas! Why didn't he bring the Acharya back? He asked, "How did the Acharya die? Where was his body cremated?"

"By this river, Shipra... not his body, but just a handful of his bones".

"How did you come to know"?

"I have come to know, my King, none can accomplish anything in this world alone, be it a destructive deed or creative. Taking the bones to the river, Shipra, his own disciple had cremated them by this river. Okay, let bygones be bygones! What I am trying to say is that, the village in which Acharya had taken refuge for a night is known as Kalamukhi. Kalamukhi is a village-Goddess"!

King Bhartrihari was in for a surprise. There had been a village in his Kingdom named Kalamukhi, there was the habitation of hunters who were basically Chandaals. Acharya had been to this village .... this man was coming straight from there.

"What next"? The King had now taken his seat. He motioned at the guest from the foreign land to be seated. He sat down and said, "My King, let us not sit here, you have to go elsewhere to listen to the news with which I've come. Someone might come here, right now, the thing I have come to share with you demands silence, a river bank and darkness"!

The King was lost in sundry trains of thought, in silence. This man from an alien land was imploring his lone presence. This stranger was asking for his presence in the desolation of riverside! His body shuddered. Who was this man in reality? A spy? A secret assassin? The criminal who had slain Devadutta, so ruthlessly? Could he be this man or any protege of him? He could feel that he had become terribly lonely. In his own city, a whore had been murdered, but he failed to come up with any clue leading to solution of the mystery! Whatever he had heard, he could not believe.

How were all such rumours spreading like wildfire in the city? He kept watching this stranger minutely.

Then the foreigner said, "You need not be afraid of me, dear King! Do I look like someone with an ulterior motive"?

"I do not know, appearance is very often deceptive! Man's face does not always correspond with the truth".

"I am not telling a lie, in the name of Lord Mahakaal, I swear, please come, the

King of Ujjwain used to win the respect as the King of the Universe and I am just a lesser mortal, a vagabond. Since long, I am wandering in countries beyond my own. On the thoroughfares, I heard a lot of people praising you in high-flown words and now all are talking ill of you with the same fervour. I feel undone, I feel sad within. I know, the King has got to play no role in here, everything is happening according to the caprices of Nature. But people do not want to perceive it, they want to know about the new star in the sky, they believe that as impact of Venus had caused drought, the new star will surely cause rainfall to happen. Oh King, please come, Acharya's hermitage has closed down, we can talk there by the riverside in the evening, in front of the temple of Lord Mangalnath".

King Bhartrihari made up his mind. The man from the distant land went out of sight, gradually. The King was feeling excited within. Who was this man? Why had he come, what did he want to say? He could make out nothing at all. But it was crystal clear that the foreigner knew everything. He knew what he himself even did not know. Strange! He began to walk back to the inner house.

The old maidservant had dozed off. When the conjuror was passing by the door, the old woman opened her eyes and saw him. She called out to him. But he did not turn back. When would the rain pour? If she would know beforehand, whether in the afternoon or during noon, she would come to stand in the courtyard. But why was the man leaving? The old woman scrambled to come into the open. Where was the sentry? There, he was taking a nap, in broad daylight. The old woman looked at the magician, who was speeding away to disappear at a distance. She kept looking at the way. Now it seemed to her that sorcery was just a fib, a myth! Rain would never pour down on this city. The man had conned and left. But the King? Where was he? Was he safe and sound? Was this foreigner a secret assassin? The old woman began to walk towards the palace again. In brisk steps, praying to Lord Mahakaal! Oh Lord Mahakaal! Let King Bhartrihari live long, let Ujjwain prosper, let rain be here, let all stigmata of the King be washed away!

That evening, the King started off along the road leading to the temple, to walk towards the river bank of Shipra, with a flambeau in his hand. He had covered his face with a piece of cloth. He would have to go, stealthily. The man had asked him to go thus. Not even a soul should know about his movements. None would divine anything in the least. Leaving the burning flambeau on the God's way, the King began to walk along the bank of the river, Shipra, in darkness. Today was the eighth day of the new-moon fortnight! The moon was not there in the firmament. The King did not have any trouble to walk along the way in darkness, lit faintly by starlight! He had gone by this way, umpteen times, to the temple of Mangalnath, to the hermitage of Acharya Brishavanu. King Bhartrihari knew the way like the back of his palm, where it had taken a turn, where it grew narrow, where the way had become undulated, at which point again it had sloped down abruptly, and got steep immediately after! He stole a glance at the sky. Monsoon sky would never wear such a look. The King could espy the Ursa Major, in the Western sky, drooping slightly to the North. He halted. Turning towards the South, he saw the Pole Star [Dhruva], shining bright. Going down to the West from the last of the Seven sages, Marichi, one would find Purbaphalguni, straight below which stood the star, Uttarphalguni. The King knew well that the star, Swati, stood just above his head. Just behind that, the galaxy had descended straight from the North to the South, with its flow of starlight. Just to the front, the King could locate the planet, Venus, setting straight down in the Western horizon. It seemed as if he was walking forward with an eye on the planet, setting down.

On reaching the Mangalnath temple, he got to see the man from an alien land. The temple dated back numerous years. Staying all day long, after the worship of lord with lights, in the evening, the Priest used to go towards the city. The temple of Acharya which stood there at a little distance, stood without a soul presently. The bank of the river Shipra was looking more impregnable under the dark maze of all the trees. The King got to see the light of the lamp, in the courtyard of the shrine. No wind blew. The trees seemed to get lost in deep sleep. The King stopped awhile. His heart missed a beat or two. Where was the youth from Dasharno, who had been there at Acharya Brishavanu's hermitage? The King was reminded of the day when Acharya had gone away. He began to be amazed at the crescent-shaped beauty of the river, Shipra. He looked on at the water in the river. Darkness was thick and intense there. He was reminded of another monsoon. The murmur of the river could be heard, through all the seasons. Then did the river too had gone away, leaving the bank of Shipra? The Acharya had left, his disciples followed suit, the clouds on the sky too did — he, all alone, had been left on this desolate bank of the river! He heard a call from behind, "Welcome, oh King!"

"Where shall I have to go?"

"Let us sit there in the courtyard of the shrine. If desired, the lamp will stay lit, if opposed, only starlight will be there".

The King had come to the courtyard of the temple in measured steps. He found the lamp aglow in front of the deity. In the dark courtyard, a seat had been laid for him. He sat down. The stranger sat just facing him. Now he could be seen quite clearly. The King could not recognize him in daylight, but now it seemed he was no stranger at all. The King demanded, "Let me first be allowed to know of your identity."

"I am just an ordinary man, just a vagabond".

"How dare a vagabond welcome the King of this city to this deserted riverside, you run the risk of being held a captive, you know!"

The man from the alien land smiled softly, "Whoever doesn't know King Bhartrihari, as citizens, the inhabitants of this Kingdom have the advantage of knowing their King in and out! But this is a misfortune of the King that he does not know even a single subject, rather there is no way at all to recognize them".

Bhartrihari asked, "Why have I come here"?

"To learn about the new star which has appeared in the sky lately!"

"Since long, I am hearing about it! Acharya Brishavanu had gone away saying that, all these are simply false notions, nothing as such does exist, cannot happen even".

The man from the other land said, "But it has happened! The way through which I had come, there I heard the praise of this new star and the King, vilified!"

Bhartrihari started... Speaking ill of the King is not unknown to him. Even the tale of the stigma! But of which star is this stranger speaking? Who is this man? From where has he come?

The young man from another land said, "You will get to hear about me later, now listen to the tale of the star".

"I have no faith in it".

The stranger fished out a small mirror from his portmanteau. He held it before the face of the King and asked, "Can you recognize yourself, Your Highness?"

The King watched the darkness in the mirror. A faint corporeal image could be seen in the mirror but that could not make him recognize himself, he knew it quite well that the face that looked strange in the pervasive darkness was of none but his own! Hence he spoke out, "Yes I can recognize myself"!

"Can you still recognize yourself"?

Engrossed in himself, the King did not notice that the mirror had slipped away from the darkness, he answered, "Yes"!

The youth of the other land laughed, "The mirror is not there at all, what will you see in it, oh King? In fact, what man thinks at the back of his mind, that only he sees being reflected in the mirror, whatever the mirror be, calm surface of water or a bright metallic sheet or pitch-black, deep darkness, whatever you are citing from your own belief will not remain as the truth till end, my King, do you know the reason behind this protracted drought"?

"No, I do not know, can you really bring down rain, you sorcerer?"

The man from the other land said, "Nature has turned ruthless, and again She would turn kind, many places of this country are being devoid of rain, while going away I had seen green forest, green universe, fertile soil with green, plentiful harvest, but while returning, to my utter dismay, I found all had undergone change, all kept burning, Oh King, you are in the teeth of peril"!

King Bhartrihari kept looking into the darkness. The last words which made way to his ears had been there in his mind as a premonition, but he was ever firm in his faith that, what had never happened in Ujjwain, would never take place. Why would the King be in jeopardy? The duty of the King was to protect his subjects in danger. Unless attacked by the alien forces, Ujjwain would never be jeopardized!

"Attack by alien forces"? The King threw his doubt in the air, "Is any barbaric force trying make a foray into this country"?

"No, your step-brother, he is the new star in the sky of Ujjwain"!

The King came to learn about an already-known fact once again and blabbed out, "But the astronomers had not predicted it".

"They haven't, but the fact is that, Honourable King, this natural disaster has assumed a huge proportion, famine has broken out, a few days later you will get to see that hungry people are making a beeline into the city. Since long, scarcity of crops and harvests is on. This country has to be saved from such a disaster!"

"Let there be a downpour! If Nature is unkind, what shall I do"?

"Honorable King, doesn't anyone know that? Yet men will only have faith in the King, who, they think, can make everything possible! Your step-brother will usurp the throne with a vow of protecting the nation, today, tomorrow, any day, any moment"!

King Bhartrihari went quiet, for quite some time he kept mumbling, "Has the prostitute been murdered just for that reason"?

"Yes, you are aware of everything! Who will stand in favour of a stigmatized King"?

"I know but the city is ablaze, I cannot turn harsh, you have rightly said, I think my inability to protect the country from this drought is my failure, if so, then why shouldn't the city-dwellers hold me responsible for this protracted drought"?

"Revered King, the armies are against you, the city-residents want rain, but they do not know how it can happen, they think that once you are dislodged from power, it might help in some way or other. Hence, the city-dwellers will not speak at all, those who will, they will be beheaded. During the times of peril, men catch at a straw even. The common residents of this city think that the dethronement of the King may cause this peril to be warded off and it may rain again!"

The eyes of the King moistened. In the darkness, as silent downpour, tears began to course down the eyes of the King. Then the man from a far-off land said, "The people of this city think in one way and the people from a distant village think in a different vein. Oh King, the inhabitants of Kalamukhi village had no idea that they had a King, though that hamlet falls in the precincts of your Kingdom, they are burning in drought too, but their belief is that, the King suffers because of their sins! They are hunters, they are lowborn Chandaals but they keep waiting with a virgin-maid for the King, with a healthy, disease-free calf and perfect soil since they have heard about their King from Acharya Brishavanu!"

"Then?"

"They are coming"!

"When are they coming"?

"They are about to reach this city to greet their King. According to them, if the King leaves the city-capital for the village Kalamukhi and if he seeks the hands of the virgin maid of Kalamukhi being there and accepts her virginity then this period of drought will definitely come to a close, the calf will fortify the virility of the King, a chaste virgin is there among the race of the hunters only"!

The King could feel that he had stayed in sheer darkness for so long!

EIGHTY-FOUR

King Bhartrihari said, "The first time in my life, I can comprehend that it is the King who bears ignorance in him the most."

"May not be true, yet it is the King who retires in the most intense darkness"!

"Why?"

"Perhaps it is the law of ruling a Kingdom, that more the power much more ignorance is bred. Power itself gives birth to ignorance"!

"How can it be so"?

The stranger from another land said, "He wants to be free of all worries by retiring into darkness, lest how could the King remain in the dark about the obsequies of Acharya being performed on the bank of the river, Shipra? The Acharya, being hapless, had to accept death all alone, in the middle of a vast meadow, with the jackals and the vultures having a feast on his corpse and the King knowing next to nothing of it! The woman with amazing qualities, who had only longed for going to her father's land, Balkh, got slain, for no reason whatsoever, by a lecher blind in lust. The King stayed blissfully ignorant of it. He even did not know why he would have to shoulder the responsibility of the crime himself! The King remained ignorant of how his soldier's daughter-in-law got humiliated by his own employee and how the men of the Shudra ghetto went behind the bars for standing against the drought! Strangely enough, all these facts are known to the city-dwellers"!

King Bhartrihari hung his head in shame!

The man from a far-off land said, "The merchant's servant was an innocent hill-boy, why he had been grown into a ruthless youth, the King is ignorant about it. Why he had set the Shudra ghetto on fire, why again he himself had to die in the deplorably cruel manner, the King's Army-Commander knows the reason but the King doesn't".

King Bhartrihari said, "This drought has rendered me into such a being"!

The stranger from the far-off land said, "But the King had never thought of combatting drought at all"!

"I had no idea of how to stand against it"!

The King doesn't know, but the commonest of the common man of Shudra ghetto is aware of it.

The King asked, "How do they know? But the King will not go to dig the lake, do you mean to say so"?

"No, in this city when the merchant left a young man in a pool of blood, by the edge of the road, none had gone to save him in fear of Utanka, he had been sheltered by the people of the Shudra ghetto, who nursed him back to his health".

The King looked into the darkness, being dazed. Who was this youth anyway? Who could be this man from an alien land? Was it that young man from Dasharno, whom he saw at the hermitage of Acharya as a learner, whom he had met here on the bank of the river, Shipra, quite a number of times? In the darkness, he was being reminded of him. He said in whispers, "I have no idea of that incident! Anyway, who are you?"

"I am a vagabond, spanning from the South Sea to the Himalayas is my native land, from Purbachal to the far-off Gandhaar, Purushpur, Balkh, the river, Oxus, and Ural lake in the further North."

King Bhartrihari, in utter amazement, was listening to the tramp, the stranger. Now, it occurred to him that, the man might be a magician. A hypnotizer. He wanted to be responsive and while being conscious, he inquired, "How can a King stand against drought?"

"He will protect the soldier's daughter-in-law, if she is jeopardized, he will stand beside the prostitutes, beside the innocent citizens in times of peril. He should keep the Shudras alive, and to stand beside the endangered is putting up resistance to drought, to the lack of rainfall".

King Bhartrihari dropped his head down and said haltingly, "The King could not concentrate upon ruling the Kingdom because of this prolonged drought. He kept holding himself responsible for this pervasive sterility, for such famine."

The man from the other land said, "If the King would have been conscious, if all the incidents which have already transpired in this city could have been averted, that menace of drought might not be such dreadfully all-pervasive!"

King Bhartrihari stayed silent. He looked at the sky. It seemed that moon would rise even much late. He would have to return to the palace, long before that. He was overcome with fear. It occurred to him, that he was standing against himself in the darkness. As if he were talking, standing before the magic mirror! He was trying to recognize at least one star in the sky! But he was failing to do so. Everything turned topsy-turvy to him. It seemed as though, the stars in the sky had changed their respective places to drift elsewhere at their own convenience. Perhaps, the seven stars of the Ursa Major had moved off to seven varying directions in the sky! Prolonged drought might even give rise to such occasions, it appeared. The King said, "I have to go back".

"Oh King, where will you return? Perhaps, your brother, Army-Commander, Bikram, has taken possession of the palace by now, the queen is with him, dear King! I am here to bring you to safe haven, just think that you have come here, forgoing your claims to the throne, the palace, so on, so forth".

The blood seemed to catch fire. The King grew restive. He stood taut like an enraged lion and roared, "How dare you? How audacious of you to think of saving the King of Ujjwain! I shall go back to my palace on my own."

The man from the other land said, "You will be slain"!

"I am not afraid of dying"!

The stranger from a distant land went on, "The hunters, the rustic men from Kalamukhi village are about to make their presence felt here in this city, they will honour and welcome their King to their hamlet: disease-free, healthy calf has been kept for you, a virgin is there for sexual union, arable land with fertile soil is there, again they are sure that if the King does not go there, it will not rain in their village! Where will you return, King of Kings, Lord Bhartrihari? If you go back, the inhabitants of Kalamukhi hamlet will be rendered destitute, and one word more, if the King loses his life in the precincts of the palace, a new King will come to ascend the throne, but King Bhartrihari's life is quite dear to me, my Lord! The hunters never knew that they had a King, they are keen on making their King know their country - the clouds, the soil, the forests, the rivers, the sorrows of men, the weal of mankind, the way they live, their love, lack of love, their successes, their failures…!"

King Bhartrihari had been carried away, he said slowly, "I can get off to the hamlet of the hunters along with them, leaving my throne behind, but will it save my golden city of Avanti, my golden Ujjwain?"

The stranger went speechless now. All fronts had gone eerily silent. Then the King asked, "Tell me who you really are"!

The man from a far-off land, did not come up with a rejoinder any more. It seemed to the King that this man was not any stranger at all. He was almost like that youth of Dasharno, though it was not him! Who could this man then be? Only he had mesmerized him thus, here, one day!

The King demanded again, "Tell me truly, who you are"!

"I am a vagabond"!

"I don't believe you, don't you really know how to bring down rain, aren't you really a magician? If you know sorcery then do apply that knowledge to soothe the city-dwellers with the raindrops! Perhaps the city-inhabitants are in the spell of slumber, let them be all ears to the thunderclap in their sleep, the pitter-patter of rainfall, the swoosh of the cool, monsoon breeze, let all nooks and corners be inundated with the rainwater. Please do construct such a truth, oh Sorcerer!"

The foreigner said, "Oh King, but when the truth of magical charm will reach its end, the people will come to know that the King had taken them for a ride, it was nothing but a fake dream"!

King Bhartrihari again lowered his face and in a feeble, inaudible voice said, "The King keeps the audience charmed by the spell of magic, the residents of the other parts of the Kingdom do not know their King even, when the magical charm trails off to nullity, the lifespan of the King draws to its close too, or otherwise he is dethroned. But I am so unfortunate that I could not even spread a magical charm around! I failed miserably! Disclose your identity, you do not seem like a stranger to me"!

The stranger seemed to withdraw a bit and said, "I am, of course, a stranger"!

"No, I know you, the drought is causing to lose my memory all the time, it is leaving me with a blunt sense of justice at every moment! But who are you?"

The stranger kept silent for a while and said, "I am a man without any identity!"

"A man without any identity! But how can that be?"

The man from some other country replied, "This drought has lent me a new lease of life, you can even take this drought as the moment of my birth, you can consider my birth during this period of sterility, it appears to me that I, myself, am the representative of another man, who had witnessed the monsoon clouds, the rain, the crops..."

"I can't get you, please speak lucid, comprehensible"!

The stranger said, "In what way will it help you, getting to know my identity, dear King? I am just an ordinary human, in my earlier birth, I was born here in this city, my father was into trade and business, I had been orphaned at a tender age, if I am ever reminded of my earlier birth, my heart shudders even at this moment! I want to get rid of this memory, but it follows me like an intimidating shadow of lost time!"

"Then?"

"I am a tortured soul, I had even rejected the lady, enamoured of me, quite silently! All such things seem to be like remembrances of my previous birth! After such insult, I left this city, and while I was about to drown myself in the deep waters of the river, Gambhira, in a bid to commit suicide, Goddess Saraswati appeared before me...!"

Dhruvaputra was narrating and the King was listening to him in rapt attention.

At that moment, far, far-off, Tamradhvaj and Gandhavati had taken refuge under an ancient banyan tree, along with a band of travellers who were heading on to Dasharno! A few of the travellers were conversing among themselves, a few of them were busy in making arrangements for cooking, while Tamradhvaj sat with Gandhavati, taking her hand in his, facing a narrow river at a little distance. During night, nothing could be perceived, but during daytime, all these tracts of land looked so different! All seemed to be devastated, burnt up by the raging, scorching sun — the soil, the sky, everything all around!

After a long time, they had been free from fear! They were struck with panic, if Uddhav, who had lately got the dominance over a section of the army, would come chasing them from behind! Abducting a woman was just a natural affair to the retinue of soldiers, under the rogue's command!

After such a long time, Tamradhvaj leaned towards Gandhavati, free of all worries and panic, and said, "Can you get to see the star, Arundhati?" Gandhavati was thrilled! Tamradhvaj had touched the thighs of Gandhavati. Gandhavati grew restless. Tamradhvaj touched her breasts. Gandhavati grew desirous. Turning around, she took hold of Tamradhvaj with both her hands. Bringing her mouth to his ear she welcomed, "Do come"!

The universe and the heavens began to sway in front of Tamradhvaj's eyes! Gandhavati seemed to be all-pervasive! In the darkness, Gandhavati had made him lie prostrate, on the untilled soil. Tamradhvaj felt like being more drawn towards her! Taking Tamradhvaj in with the whole of her being, Gandhavati began to whisper, "Yonder I can see the Ursa Major, Arundhati, the Pole Star, there...look yonder..."

Then, Dhruvaputra began to reveal himself to King Bhartrihari. The King said, "I could do nothing against this lack of rain, though you are speaking of so many things even you do not have any idea of how to usher in the rain!"

Dhruvaputra said, "I am an ordinary mortal, Goddess Saraswati has kindly blessed me with a new birth by being present before me in the deep waters of the river, Gambhira! Oh King, after that, I kept roaming around, being witness to a golden city being burnt, how the green leaves of the tree turned auburn, how they took the tinge of black afterwards, how the soft earth turned into hard stone, how the rivers and lakes dried up, how the people turned to be ruthless, how love-affection-compassion all began to fade away! And amidst such dreary realities, the inhabitants of the Shudra ghetto began to work hard in quest of water, the elderly Chief-of-the-Village had given up having food, and I cannot narrate, my King, how I was getting changed into a better leaf in my deeper self, how I was trying for a way-out of the strange darkness which was engulfing me from all the ten directions! I had a premonition of having terrible times with lack of crops and harvest ahead, even babies will stop being born, man will forget to bring another soul in this world, the woman will never know how to conceive! I, then, kept contemplating on human birth, I began to be reminded of Lord Mahadeva, the God of all Gods, of Uma, the ascetic, the nights of their union, the tale of the birth of Kartikeya…"

King Bhartrihari was feeling mesmerised. He could not veer his eyes from the darkness. It seemed, as though, the darkness was becoming voluble. Now the darkness was nothing but this universe, the charm of magic, which kept pervading the sleep, by degrees, bit by bit.

Dhruvaputra said, "Oh King, I am an ordinary being! With which sceptre of the King can I stand in protest against this unkind face of Nature, what a common man of my standing can do more save just expressing his inner desires! I wish there would be downpour, good harvest, union of man and woman, I wish babies to be born, but this drought has left women to live away from their men who are abroad, all the men have been banished, some to the battlefield, some have been thrown behind the bars, a few of them have been thrown out from the cities, banished far-off to desolate stretches of meadows, perhaps one poet could feel that only the rainclouds might put an end to this period of banishment!"

"Who is he?"

"The poet who had written about the night of the union of Parvati and Lord Mahadeva! He, himself, began to compose 'shlokas' on the memories of clouds, oh King, that poet has just come to feel that his shlokas, his poetry can stand against this unkind Nature! This is not the duty of a poet to sit on the throne, his duty is to reveal the truth that he feels in his own heart, while living in the world of mankind! The poet, who has witnessed the cloud of Asad since his birth, to him the memory of clouds will surface again and again, during the times of drought!"

"Are you that poet?"

Darkness stood intense and silent and then he spoke out, "Perhaps that poet is on his way to Dasharno now! That poet may be lost in the sweetness of union either in a hut of a hunter in the village of Kalamukhi or Magadh, or in Kosala, Pataliputra, or on the bank of the river Ganga, or the riverbank of Reba, or on the bank of river Betrabati, in the caves of the Nichoih hills, on the way to Alkapuri, on the foothills of Ramgiri, or on any bank of an unknown river…!"

King Bhartrihari asked, "How to trace that poem"?

The poet, however, does not know whether it has become a poem but the poet has composed the incantations of the rain, the mantra, which can make the downpour possible!"

The man from another land got to his feet, kept whispering, "As he is a poet, he can strive at least, to compose the mantra for ushering in the rain, in these terrible times of drought"!

The man fetched a lamp from inside. He placed the lamp in front of the King. From his satchel, he began to fish out a salver for placing an offering to God. Before beginning to read, he uttered in the light of the lamp, Oh King, let this incantation be true, let it prove itself to be true! The poet had not just stayed here, he stood up in arms against this drought!

Chanting of mantra began, a man from a foreign land or of this Ujjwain - the King could not perceive who exactly kept reciting the lines! It seemed to him, as if his voice was emerging from the dark soil, it appeared to him that the sounds reverberated from the dark sky, even the foliage on the trees were reciting the amazing, mesmerizing mantra:

Kaschit Kanta Birahaguruna Swadhikaar pramattah

Shapenastanga Mitamahima Barshabhogyena Bhartuh!

[Once a demigod, being imprecated by his master, Kuvera, had been banished for a long period of monsoon, for missing his ladylove and thus committing errors in his work. The demi-god was being oblivious of the treasures he was in charge of!]

The mantra was being chanted! The mesmerized King kept losing his speech. He cast a glance at the sky. How strange! He seemed to hear the roar of the clouds, the thunderclaps! The air seemed to cool down. The King could hear the footfalls of innumerable men! Perhaps the hunters were rushing from the Kalamukhi village, beating their drums! Or, he was perhaps confusing the roar of thunderclaps with the footfalls of men or the sound of beating the drums! The King could feel that Nature, the city of Ujjwain, Lord Mahakaal— all awaited the chanting of this mantra, this incantation! The fragrance of the rain-drenched earth was being wafted to his nostrils. He wondered - the magical spell had never proved to be so true! This seemed like an Everlasting Truth!

Then far-off, while accepting Tamradhvaj in her being, under the wide sky, on the bank of a river, Gandhavati could see the Ursa Major,Arundhati, all vanishing from her range of vision! All the stars in the sky were being enveloped by the balls of cloud! CLOUD! Was it really cloud or had she gone blind in the joy of union, not just of two bodies but of souls? Gandhavati cried out aloud, "Hey, can you see?"

"I am being lost into your eyes!

Growing darkness keeps engulfing the skies!

CLOUDS ARE HERE, GANDHAVATI!"

Tamradhvaj whispered, "A downpour is in the offing!

Oh! how strange!

So, the rain is here!"

Finally!!

THE END

Glossary

Abhra:	Mica
Acharya:	A Spiritual Teacher
Agastya:	Canopus
Aghran:	Eighth month of the Bengali Calendar
Aguru:	Purely Indian essence
Airavat:	White or Black Mythological Elephant
Aksu:	River Oxus
Alakshmi:	Foil to Lakshmi, the Goddess of abundance and prosperity
Alakta:	Hindu girls in those times used to beautify their feet with red lac-dye on their borders
Alpana:	An auspicious painting done on walls, floors and seats during festivals or just for beautification, with rice—pulverized and dipped in water
Anna:	Certain denomination of a rupee
Aparajita:	Flower of Clitoria genus
Arati:	Propitiating God's image with artistic display of lights
Asad:	Third month of the Bengali Calendar
Ashokkali:	The buds of Ashok flowers
Ashram:	Abode of spiritual activities, usually owned by a Spiritual Guru
Ashwin:	Sixth month of the Bengali calendar
Atashi:	Golden-coloured flowers
Ayan:	Interval between two solstices
Ayurveda:	Indian method of treatment with herbs and plants
Bai/Dasi:	Maid-servant
Baisakh:	First month of the Bengali Calendar
Bakul:	Small white flowers with beautiful fragrance
Bel, Tagar:	White flowers, which widely bloom in India

Bhadra:	Fifth month of the Bengali Calendar
Bhrasta:	Gone astray Deepavali: Festival of Lights
Bon Juthika:	Wild Jasmine
Brahmahriday:	A star symbolizing the heart of Lord Brahma
Brihidhanya:	A certain variety of paddy
Chaiti Purnima:	Full moon day in the month of Chaitra
Chaitra:	Twelfth month of the Bengali calendar
Champak:	Certain flower belonging to Magnolia family
Chandaal:	Popular, indigenous race, lower in caste, even untouchable once upon a time
Chandana:	A kind of parrot with red-streaks around its throat
Chandrahaar:	Moon-necklace
Chhatim:	Tall tree with digitate leaves
Deepavali:	Festival of Lights
Dhanteras:	Thirteenth day of a lunar fortnight, considered as auspicious for buying riches and jewels
Dhruvanakshatra:	Pole Star
Ekadashi:	A holy day for the Hindu widows and others for fasting and observing important rituals
Gandharva:	Demi-god, proficient in music and war [female: Gandharvi]
Garuda:	A Mythological bird, which Lord Vishnu used to ride
Ghagra:	Indian long skirt for women
Ghee:	Clarified butter
God's Way[Debapath]:	The secret way that leads from the palace of King Bhartrihari to the temple of Lord Mahakaal
Guvak:	A kind of betel-nut
Kajal:	Collyrium, black semi-fluid, applied to the rims of the eyes
Kala:	Nearly 8 seconds in the scale of time
Kalamukhi:	Black-faced Goddess
Kalpa:	Almost 864 million years, which is the span of one epoch, also known as one day and one night of Brahma, the Lord of Creation
Kalyug:	The last part of the four epochs
Kamadeva:	God of Lust

Kandarpa:	The handsomest God of Love and Passion, according to Hindu mythology
Kartik:	Seventh month of the Bengali Calendar
Kartik Purnima:	Full-moon night in the month of Kartik
Kashtha:	Small measurement of time
Ketaki:	Screwpine flower
Krishna Chaturdashi:	Fourteenth day of a new-moon cycle
Krishna Saptami:	Krishna Saptami: Seventh day of a new moon fortnight
Ksheer biscuit:	A biscuit made of milk, thick and condensed by hard boiling
Kumkum:	Red coloured paste or dot as applied on forehead or fragrant water sprinkled on an august occasion
Kunda:	Variety of multi-petal jasmine flower
Kurubok:	Red Amaranth
Kushandika:	A certain ritual performed during Hindu marriage
Lav, Tut:	Measures of Time
Madanotsav:	Festival on the occasion of worship of the God of Love
Maagh:	Tenth month of the Bengali Calendar
Mahakaal/ Mahakaaleshwar:	Another name of Lord Shiva
Mahalata:	Long, creeper-like mob-chain worth a fortune
Makar:	Capricorn
Malati:	A flower belonging to Indian Jasmine family
Malaviya:	Local dialect of Ujjwain
Mandar:	Coral flowers
Mangalsutra:	A string worn around the neck by a Hindu, married woman
Mantra:	Incantation
Mausam:	Wind causing rainfall, mostly during monsoon
Mekhala:	A typical kind of sari from the North-East
Mohur:	An obsolete Indian gold-currency
Mridanga:	Variation of Indian drums
Mudra:	Different postures made with the palm and fingers of a danseuse
Naalika:	Small measurement of time

Neelkantha:	When during sea-churning gall surfaced, it was Lord Shiva who drank it, without any second thought. Hence his throat went blue and he was popularly revered as Neelkantha Shiva.
Neem:	Tree of Margosa group
Panchapradip:	Five lamps fitted on a Bell-metal stand
Payasam/Paramanna:	Sweetened milk-rice
Phalgun:	Eleventh month of the Bengali Calendar
Phalguni Purnima:	Full-moon day in the month of Phalgun
Prahar:	Count of three hours be it day or night
Pratipad:	Day following the new moon
Pulao:	Fried Rice made tasty with condiments
Pushkarbartha:	Cluster of rain-causing clouds
Rambha, Menaka:	Beautiful nymph-dancers of the Royal Court of Heaven
Rasasatra:	Scripture that deals with the art of lovemaking
Ratidevi:	Goddess of love
Sankranti:	Last day of a Bengali month
Saptalahari Haar:	Seven-stringed necklace
Saptami:	Seventh day of the new moon fortnight
Sapta Sarovar:	Cluster of Seven Lakes
Satavisha:	24th of the 27 stars
Seuli:	White flowers with orange stalks which bloom in Autumn
Shlokas:	Poetic lines in Sanskrit
Shudra:	Last order of the Caste-Division
Shukla Ashtami:	Eighth day of full-moon
Shukla Chaturdashi:	Fourteenth day of the full-moon cycle
Sraddh:	Offering obsequies to the dead by one's near ones
Sravan:	Fourth month of the Bengali calendar
Sringara Rasa:	Art of the union of man and woman in love
Tamal:	Dark-stemmed sacred tree which Lord Krishna was fond of
Tantra:	Spiritual practice of esoteric charms
Tantrik:	A spiritual person who worships God through Tantra
Takshak:	Venomous snake
Thou:	An informal address of endearment

Til:	Oil-producing seed
Tilkut:	Kind of sweetmeat made of sesame
Tithi:	Momentous days according to lunar and solar movements
Tonga:	Horse-drawn carriage
Trayodashi:	Thirteenth day of a lunar cycle
Tripurasura:	A formidable demon
Uttariya:	Scarf
Vaishya:	The third order of the classification of caste
Vajrayni:	Tantrik of a Buddhist order
Vallaki:	Variation of violin
Varna:	Castes in ancient Indian Society according to the jobs men used to do
Varundeva:	Lord of the rain
Veena:	A stringed instrument like Sitar
Yamah:	Hindu God of Death
Yajna:	Propitiating the Gods with sacrificial offerings[in fire]
Yoga:	An ancient Indian art of different postures for keeping oneself healthy and agile and connected with the Divine Entity
Yojana:	Five miles
You:	A formal address

Black Eagle Books

www.blackeaglebooks.org
info@blackeaglebooks.org

Black Eagle Books, an independent publisher, was founded
as a nonprofit organization in April, 2019. It is our mission
to connect and engage the Indian diaspora and the world at
large with the best of works of world literature published
on a collaborative platform, with special emphasis on
foregrounding Contemporary Classics and New Writing.

PRAISE FOR

CODA

"This is an 'I can't put it down' thriller. Its plot is intricate, its characters fully developed, and its descriptive passages rich in detail. This is a highly recommended work."

—Dan Clancy, Playwright

"*Coda* is a thriller that forever changed my view of Tchaikovsky's life and times. As it reminds us of the corrupting price of power, it is especially meaningful today."

—George R. Zuber, Filmmaker/Director

"Arthur Levy scripts a compelling narrative that kept me glued to the page. Tchaikovsky's doom in the extreme prejudice of Czarist Russia parallels the status of today's Russian gay community. Levy proves a plausible and unique conclusion for the Pathetique Symphony in place of the traditional music history legend."

—Dr. R. Paul Urbanick, Professor Humanities/Music

"*Coda* is fascinating reading that makes history and the story of Tchaikovsky come alive. What makes *Coda* an exceptional novel is the quality research behind this book, which animates the action in the reader's imagination. Arthur Levy gives life and insights to life by writing about one of the most interesting musicians in history, Pyotr Ilyich Tchaikovsky. I listened to his sixth symphony as I read this intriguing book. Don't miss the opportunity to be drawn into a mystery that you won't want to put down."

—Dr. Tim White, Author, *Ulysses Dream*,
Adjunct Professor, Northwest University

CODA:
A Tale of Tchaikovsky's Secret Love

by Arthur J. Levy

Published by

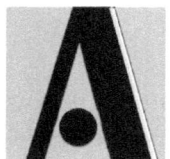

KNIFEDGE MEDIA

www.KnifedgeMedia.com
Info@KnifedgeMedia.com
Fort Lauderdale, FL